MW00789504

ALLISON • SARIN • FLEMING • COGAR

GIANT DAYS™

VOLUME FOUR

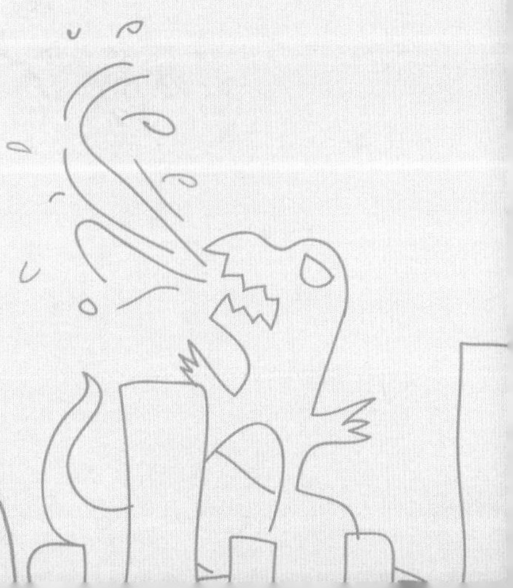

Published by
BOOM! BOX™

COLLECTION DESIGNER
MARIE KRUPINA

COLLECTION EDITORS
SOPHIE PHILIPS-ROBERTS
DAFNA PLEBAN

ROSS RICHIE Chairman & Founder
JEN HARNED CFO
MATT GAGNON Editor-in-Chief
FILIP SABLIK President, Publishing & Marketing
STEPHEN CHRISTY President, Development
ADAM YOELIN Senior Vice President, Film
LANCE KREITER Vice President, Licensing & Merchandising
BRYCE CARLSON Vice President, Editorial & Creative Strategy
JOSH HAYES Vice President, Sales

SIERRA HAHN Executive Editor
ERIC HARBURN Executive Editor
RYAN MATSUNAGA Director, Marketing
STEPHANIE LAZARSKI Director, Operations
METTE NORKJAER Director, Development
ELYSE STRANDBERG Manager, Finance
MICHELLE ANKLEY Manager, Production Design
CHERYL PARKER Manager, Human Resources
ROSALIND MOREHEAD Manager, Retail Sales

BOOM! BOX™

This book belongs to:

Name: _____

SHEFFIELD UNIVERSITY

FALL SEMESTER, SECOND YEAR

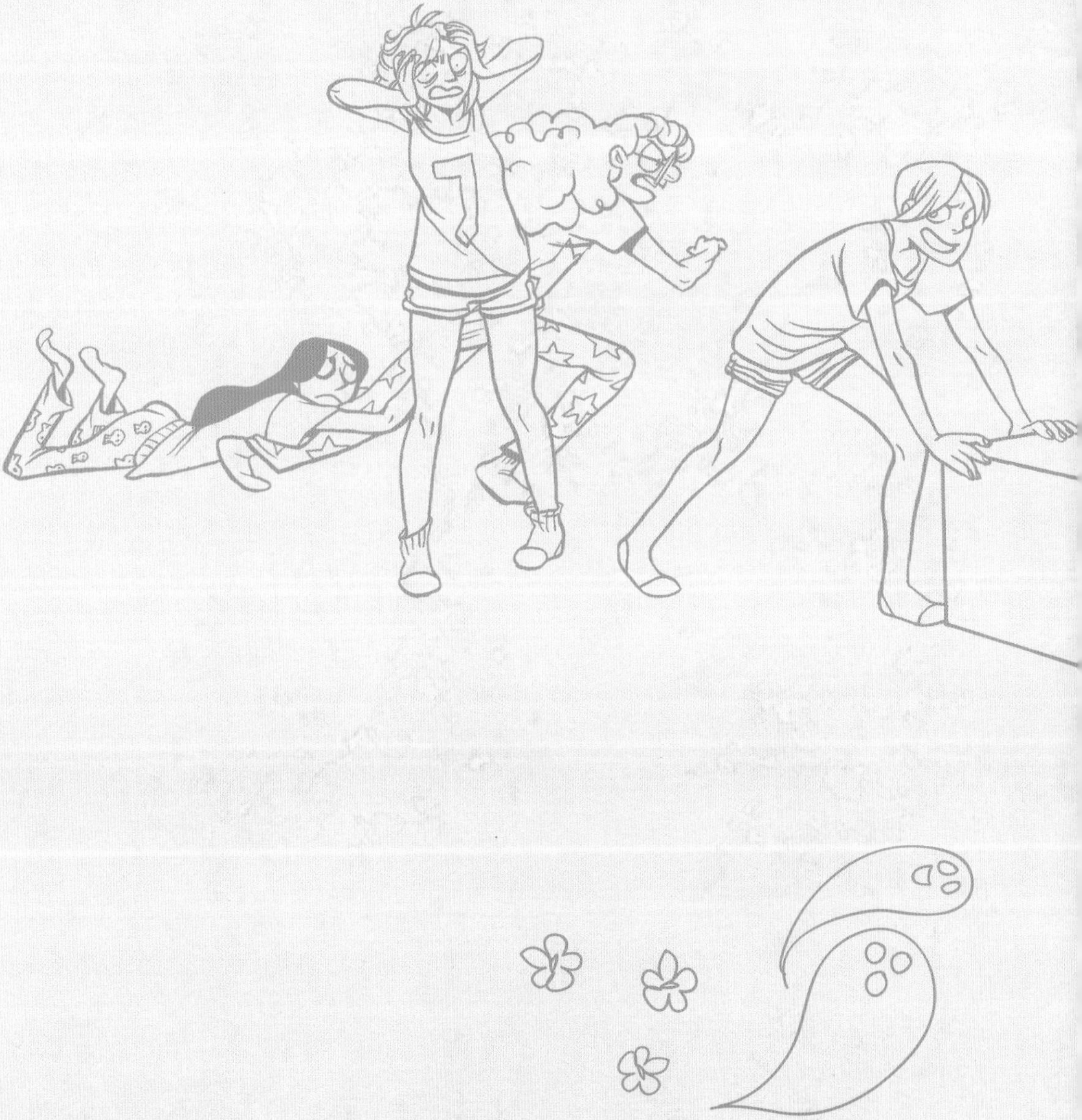

GIANT DAYS™

VOLUME FOUR

CREATED & WRITTEN BY
JOHN ALLISON

ILLUSTRATED BY
MAX SARIN

INKS BY
LIZ FLEMING
WITH IRENE FLORES (CHAPTER 31)

COLORS BY
WHITNEY COGAR
WITH KIERAN QUIGLEY (CHAPTER 31)

LETTERS BY
JIM CAMPBELL

LIBRARY, BOOM! ELITE, AND NOT ON THE TEST
EDITIONS COVER ART BY
MAX SARIN

SERIES DESIGNER
MICHELLE ANKLEY

SERIES ASSISTANT EDITOR
SOPHIE PHILIPS-ROBERTS

SERIES EDITORS
JASMINE AMIRI
SHANNON WATTERS

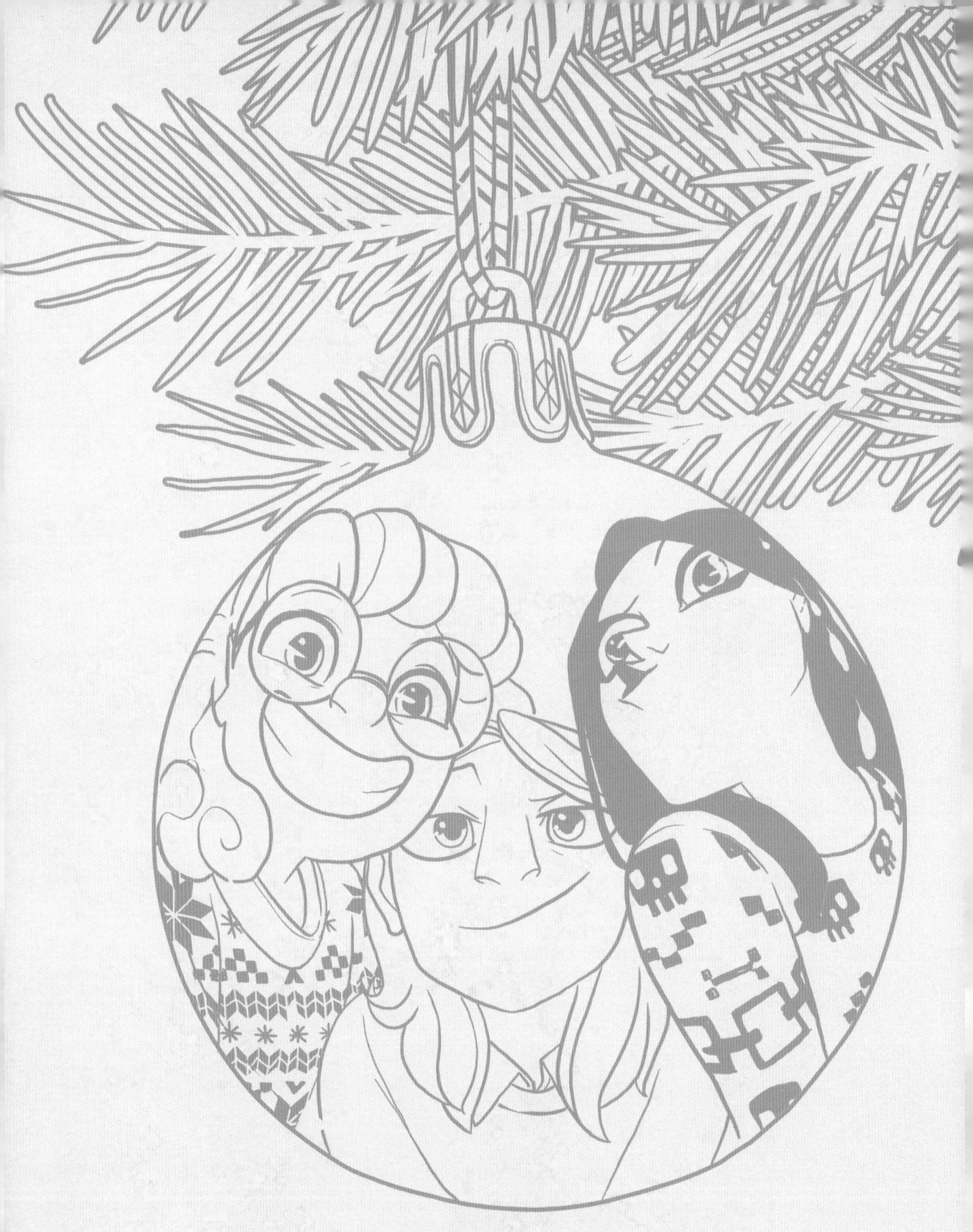

CHAPTER TWENTY-FIVE

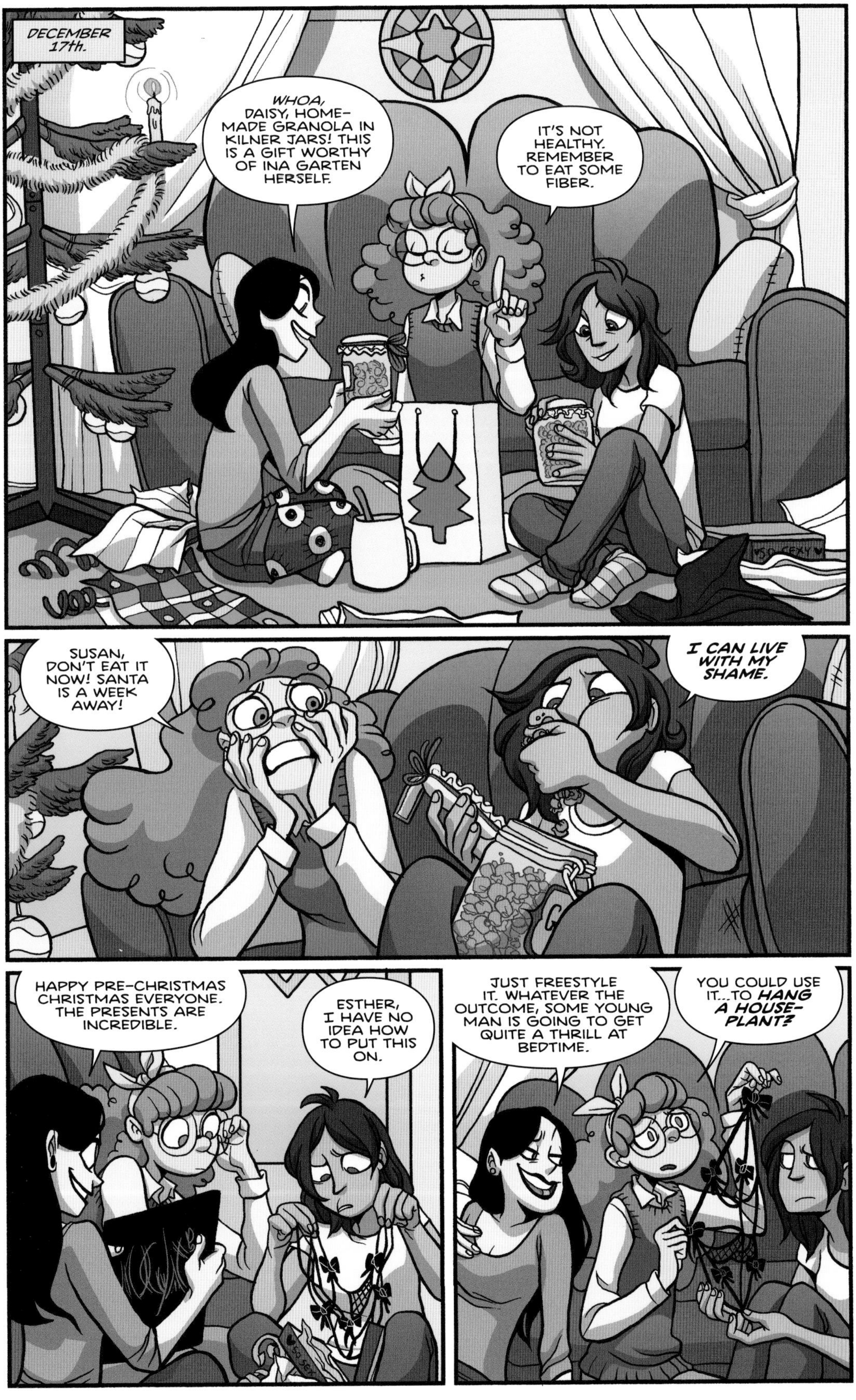
DECEMBER 17th.
WHOA, DAISY, HOME-MADE GRANOLA IN KILNER JARS! THIS IS A GIFT WORTHY OF INA GARTEN HERSELF.
IT'S NOT HEALTHY. REMEMBER TO EAT SOME FIBER.
♥SO SEXY♥
SUSAN, DON'T EAT IT NOW! SANTA IS A WEEK AWAY!
I CAN LIVE WITH MY SHAME.
HAPPY PRE-CHRISTMAS CHRISTMAS EVERYONE. THE PRESENTS ARE INCREDIBLE.
ESTHER, I HAVE NO IDEA HOW TO PUT THIS ON.
JUST FREESTYLE IT. WHATEVER THE OUTCOME, SOME YOUNG MAN IS GOING TO GET QUITE A THRILL AT BEDTIME.
YOU COULD USE IT...TO HANG A HOUSE-PLANT?

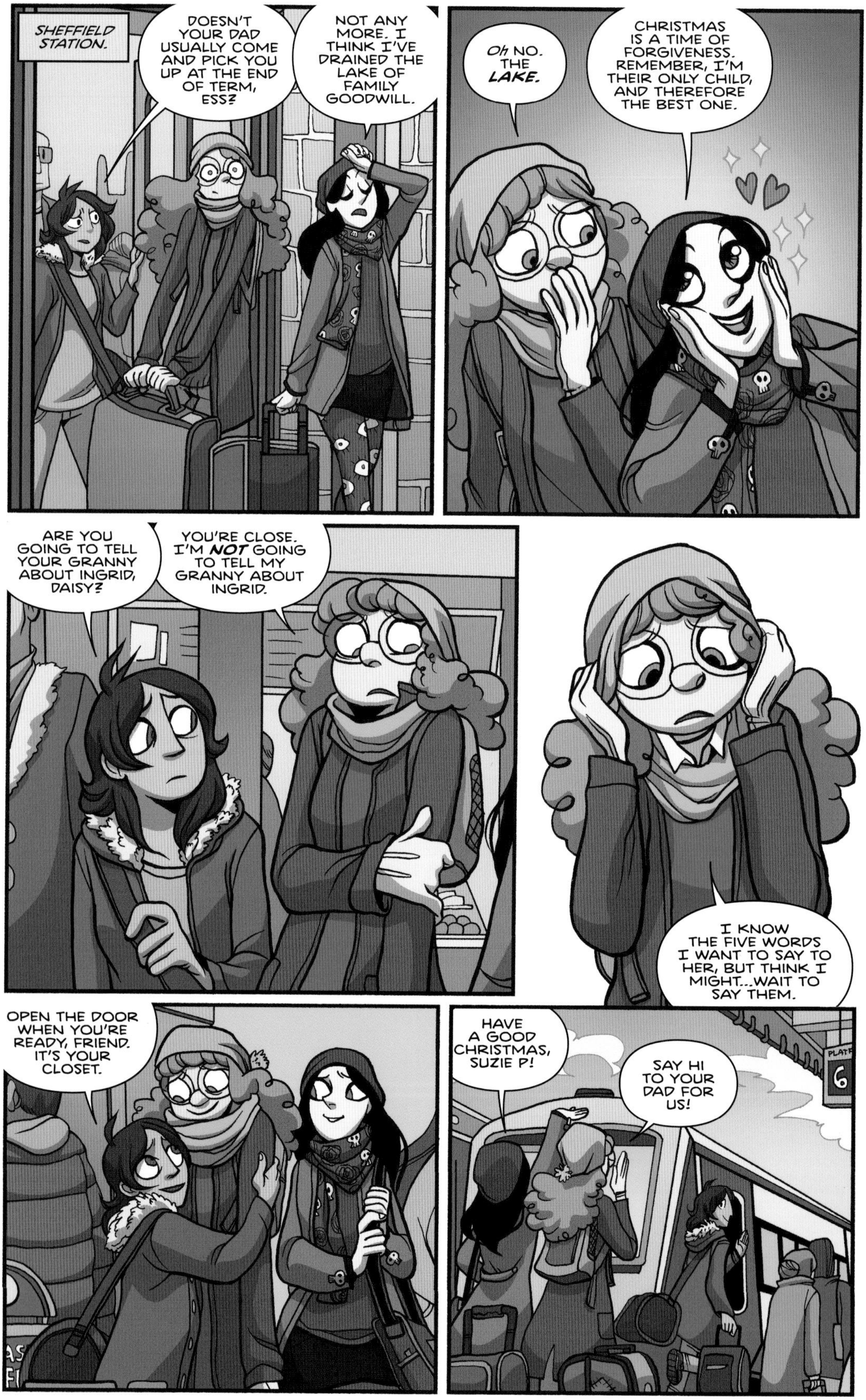
SHEFFIELD STATION.
DOESN'T YOUR DAD USUALLY COME AND PICK YOU UP AT THE END OF TERM, ESS?
NOT ANY MORE. I THINK I'VE DRAINED THE LAKE OF FAMILY GOODWILL.
Oh NO. THE LAKE.
CHRISTMAS IS A TIME OF FORGIVENESS. REMEMBER, I'M THEIR ONLY CHILD, AND THEREFORE THE BEST ONE.
ARE YOU GOING TO TELL YOUR GRANNY ABOUT INGRID, DAISY?
YOU'RE CLOSE. I'M NOT GOING TO TELL MY GRANNY ABOUT INGRID.
I KNOW THE FIVE WORDS I WANT TO SAY TO HER, BUT THINK I MIGHT...WAIT TO SAY THEM.
OPEN THE DOOR WHEN YOU'RE READY, FRIEND. IT'S YOUR CLOSET.
HAVE A GOOD CHRISTMAS, SUZIE P!
SAY HI TO YOUR DAD FOR US!
6

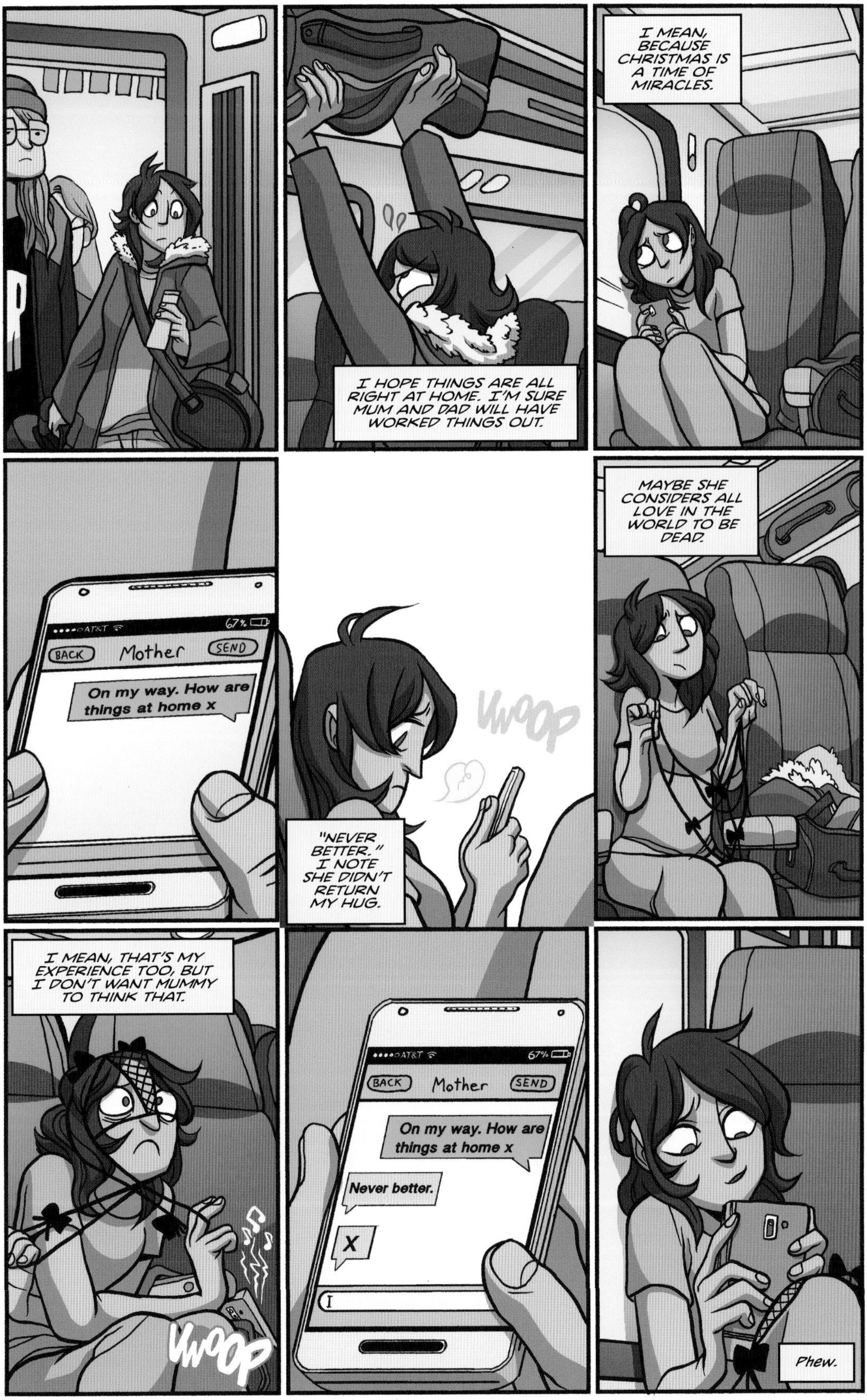
I HOPE THINGS ARE ALL RIGHT AT HOME. I'M SURE MUM AND DAD WILL HAVE WORKED THINGS OUT.
I MEAN, BECAUSE CHRISTMAS IS A TIME OF MIRACLES.
●●●●○AT&T 67%
BACK
Mother
SEND
On my way. How are things at home x
"NEVER BETTER." I NOTE SHE DIDN'T RETURN MY HUG.
VWOOP
MAYBE SHE CONSIDERS ALL LOVE IN THE WORLD TO BE DEAD.
I MEAN, THAT'S MY EXPERIENCE TOO, BUT I DON'T WANT MUMMY TO THINK THAT.
VWOOP
●●●●○AT&T 67%
BACK
Mother
SEND
On my way. How are things at home x
Never better.
X
Phew.

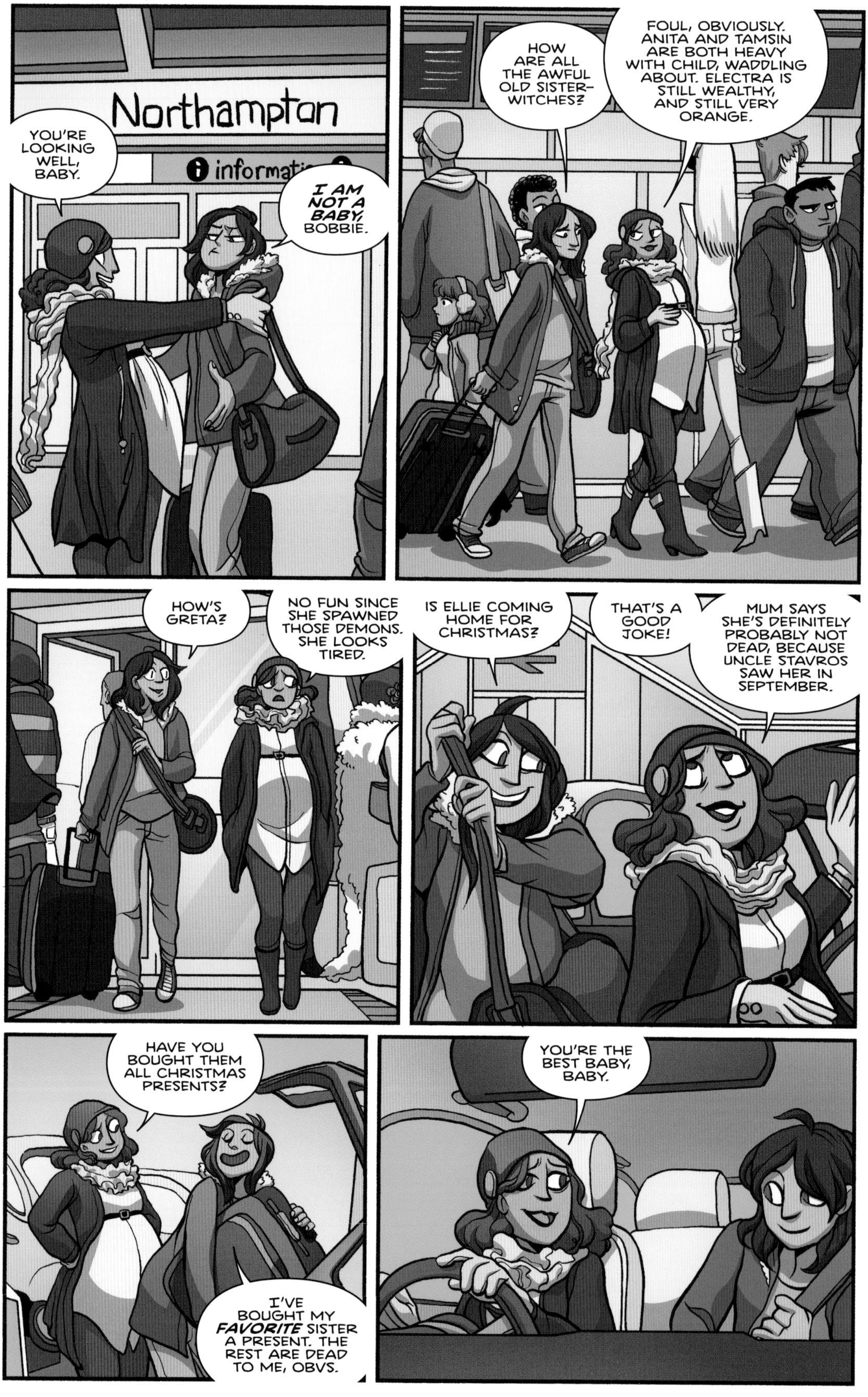
Northampton
information
YOU'RE LOOKING WELL, BABY.
I AM NOT A BABY, BOBBIE.
HOW ARE ALL THE AWFUL OLD SISTER-WITCHES?
FOUL, OBVIOUSLY. ANITA AND TAMSIN ARE BOTH HEAVY WITH CHILD, WADDLING ABOUT. ELECTRA IS STILL WEALTHY, AND STILL VERY ORANGE.
HOW'S GRETA?
NO FUN SINCE SHE SPAWNED THOSE DEMONS. SHE LOOKS TIRED.
IS ELLIE COMING HOME FOR CHRISTMAS?
THAT'S A GOOD JOKE!
MUM SAYS SHE'S DEFINITELY PROBABLY NOT DEAD, BECAUSE UNCLE STAVROS SAW HER IN SEPTEMBER.
HAVE YOU BOUGHT THEM ALL CHRISTMAS PRESENTS?
I'VE BOUGHT MY FAVORITE SISTER A PRESENT. THE REST ARE DEAD TO ME, OBVS.
YOU'RE THE BEST BABY, BABY.

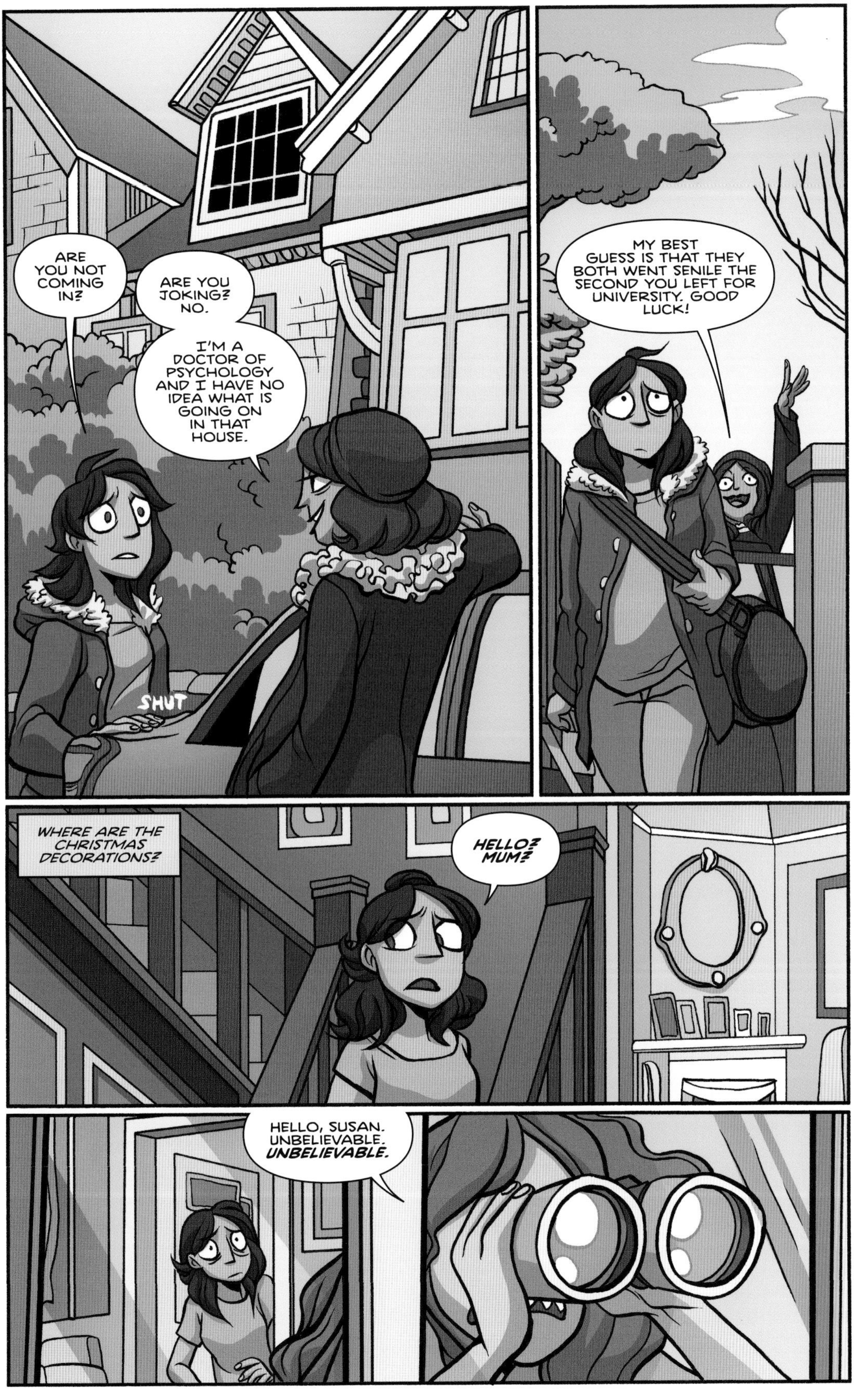
ARE YOU NOT COMING IN?
ARE YOU JOKING? NO.
I'M A DOCTOR OF PSYCHOLOGY AND I HAVE NO IDEA WHAT IS GOING ON IN THAT HOUSE.
SHUT
MY BEST GUESS IS THAT THEY BOTH WENT SENILE THE SECOND YOU LEFT FOR UNIVERSITY. GOOD LUCK!
WHERE ARE THE CHRISTMAS DECORATIONS?
HELLO? MUM?
HELLO, SUSAN. UNBELIEVABLE. ***UNBELIEVABLE.***

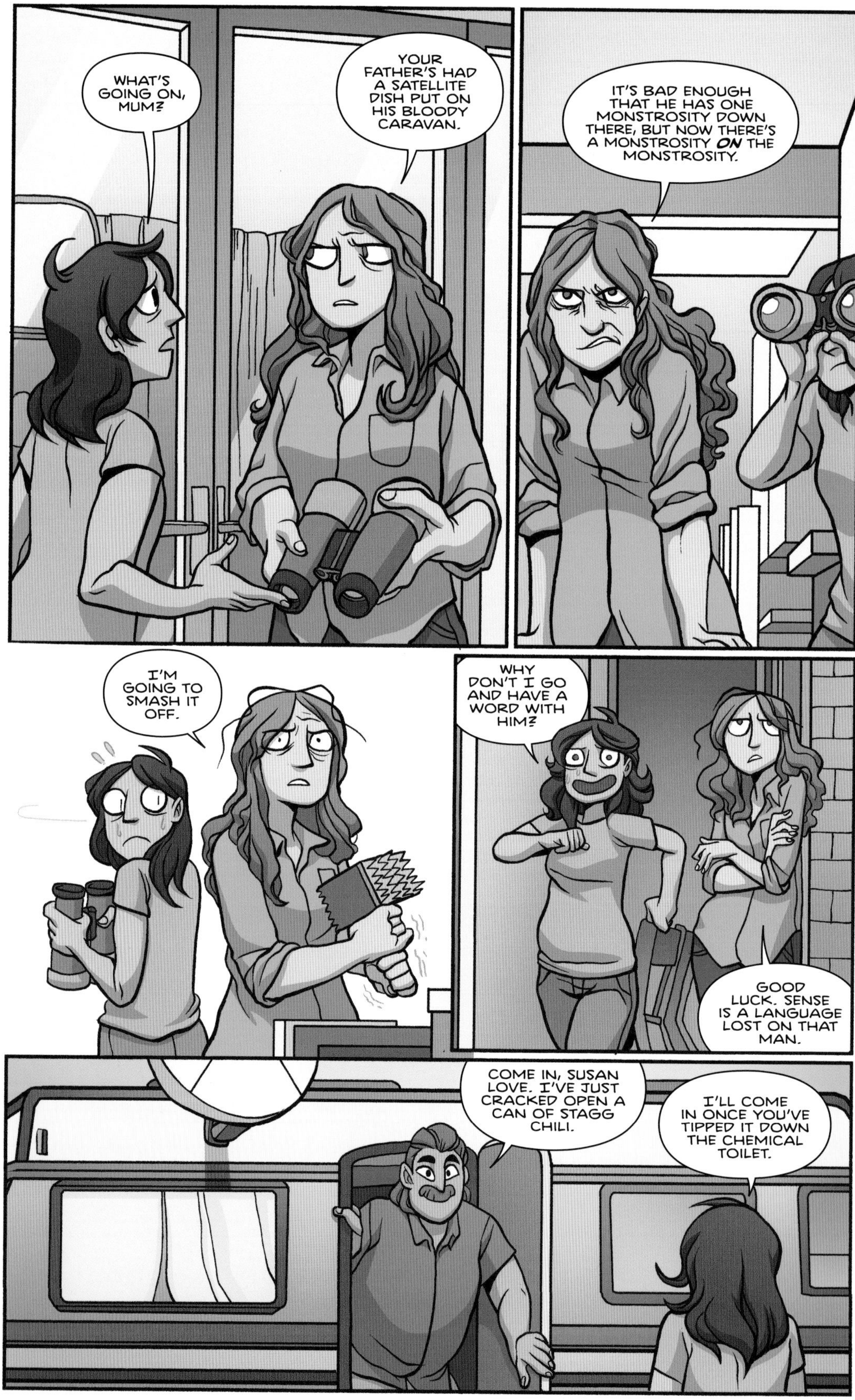
WHAT'S GOING ON, MUM?
YOUR FATHER'S HAD A SATELLITE DISH PUT ON HIS BLOODY CARAVAN.
IT'S BAD ENOUGH THAT HE HAS ONE MONSTROSITY DOWN THERE, BUT NOW THERE'S A MONSTROSITY ON THE MONSTROSITY.
I'M GOING TO SMASH IT OFF.
WHY DON'T I GO AND HAVE A WORD WITH HIM?
GOOD LUCK. SENSE IS A LANGUAGE LOST ON THAT MAN.
COME IN, SUSAN LOVE. I'VE JUST CRACKED OPEN A CAN OF STAGG CHILI.
I'LL COME IN ONCE YOU'VE TIPPED IT DOWN THE CHEMICAL TOILET.

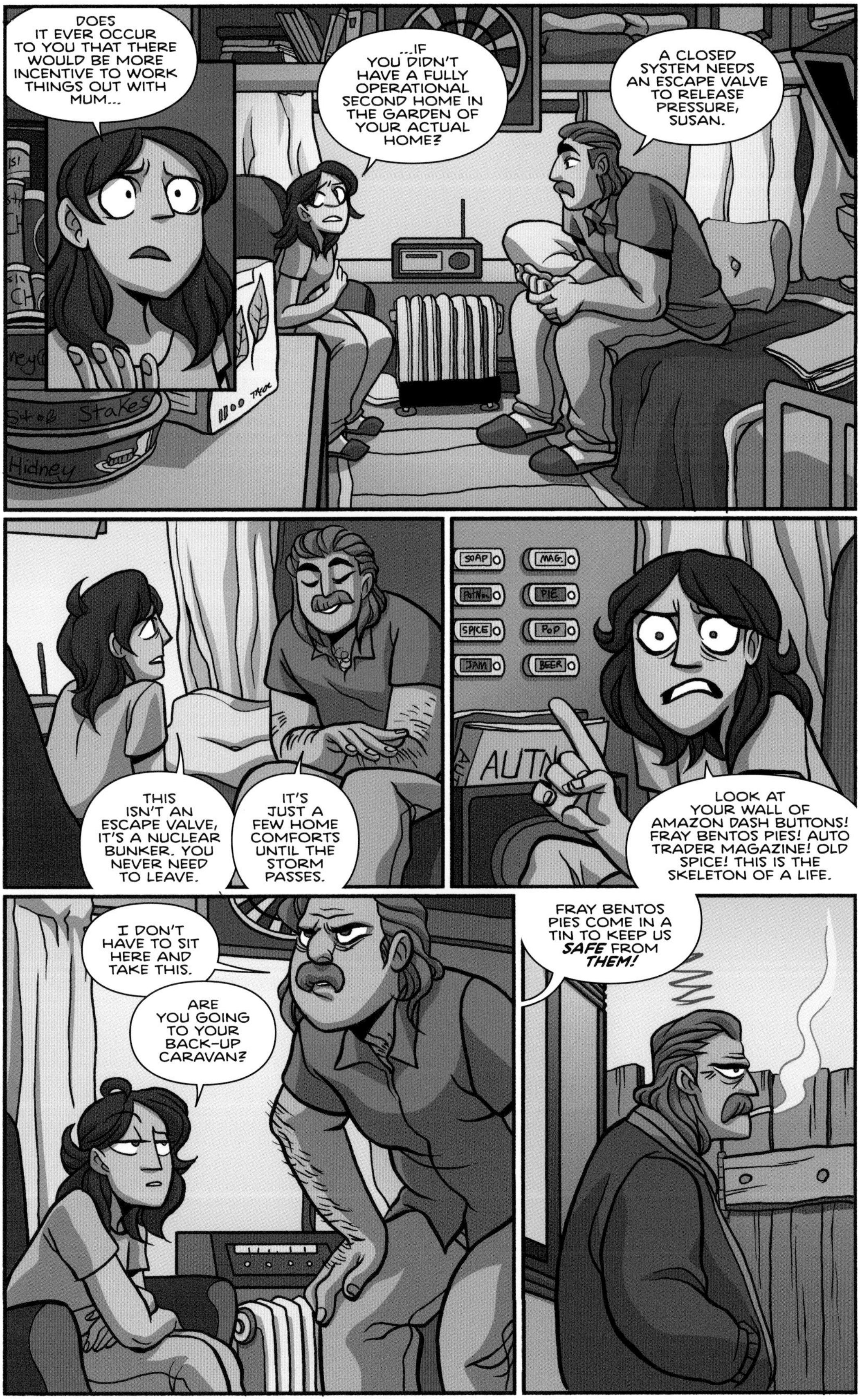

DOES IT EVER OCCUR TO YOU THAT THERE WOULD BE MORE INCENTIVE TO WORK THINGS OUT WITH MUM...
...IF YOU DIDN'T HAVE A FULLY OPERATIONAL SECOND HOME IN THE GARDEN OF YOUR ACTUAL HOME?
A CLOSED SYSTEM NEEDS AN ESCAPE VALVE TO RELEASE PRESSURE, SUSAN.
THIS ISN'T AN ESCAPE VALVE, IT'S A NUCLEAR BUNKER. YOU NEVER NEED TO LEAVE.
IT'S JUST A FEW HOME COMFORTS UNTIL THE STORM PASSES.
SOAP
MAG.
PIE
SPICE
POP
JAM
BEER
LOOK AT YOUR WALL OF AMAZON DASH BUTTONS! FRAY BENTOS PIES! AUTO TRADER MAGAZINE! OLD SPICE! THIS IS THE SKELETON OF A LIFE.
FRAY BENTOS PIES COME IN A TIN TO KEEP US SAFE FROM THEM!
I DON'T HAVE TO SIT HERE AND TAKE THIS.
ARE YOU GOING TO YOUR BACK-UP CARAVAN?

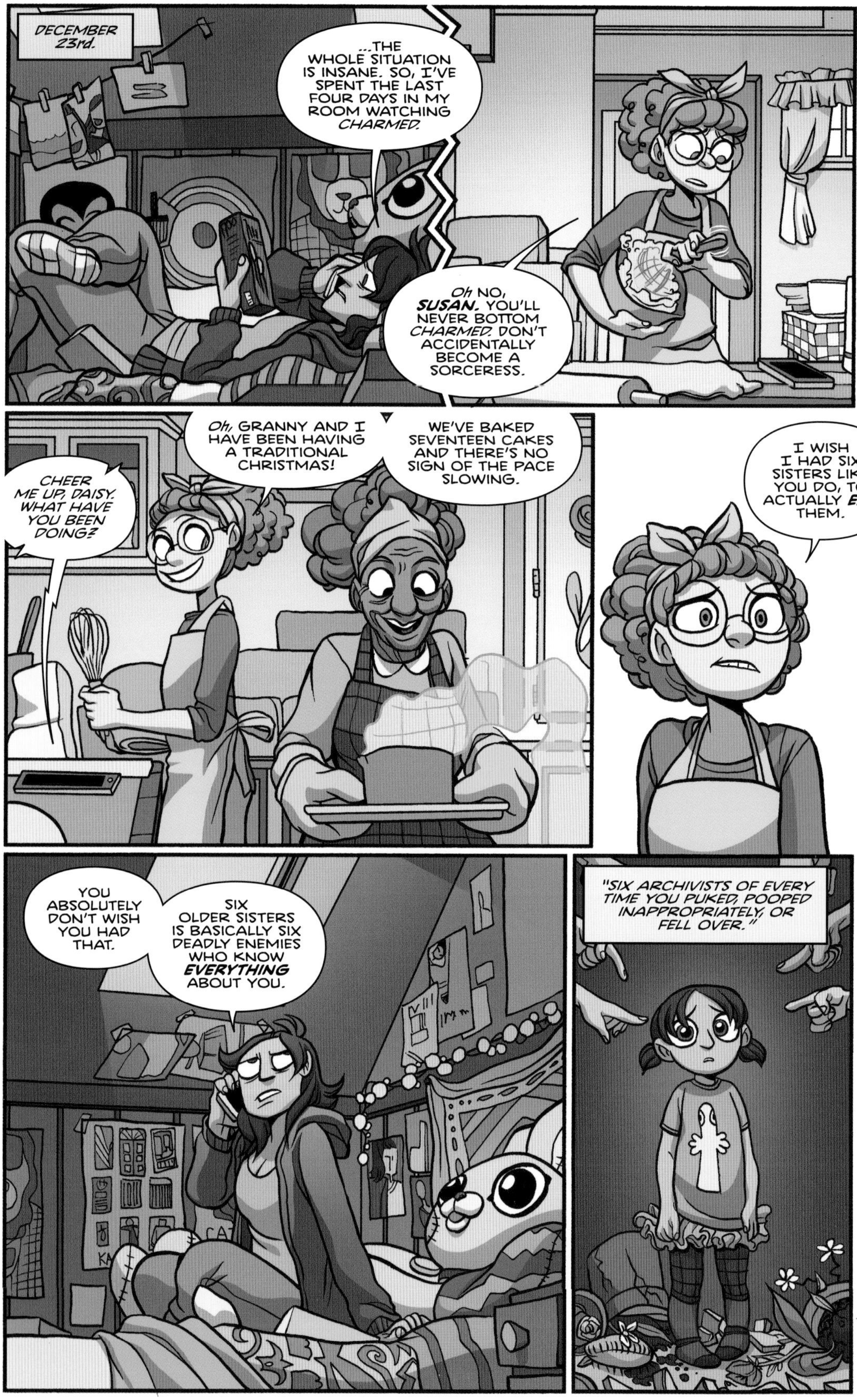
DECEMBER 23rd.
...THE WHOLE SITUATION IS INSANE. SO, I'VE SPENT THE LAST FOUR DAYS IN MY ROOM WATCHING CHARMED.
Oh NO, SUSAN. YOU'LL NEVER BOTTOM CHARMED. DON'T ACCIDENTALLY BECOME A SORCERESS.
CHEER ME UP, DAISY. WHAT HAVE YOU BEEN DOING?
Oh, GRANNY AND I HAVE BEEN HAVING A TRADITIONAL CHRISTMAS!
WE'VE BAKED SEVENTEEN CAKES AND THERE'S NO SIGN OF THE PACE SLOWING.
I WISH I HAD SIX SISTERS LIKE YOU DO, TO ACTUALLY EAT THEM.
YOU ABSOLUTELY DON'T WISH YOU HAD THAT.
SIX OLDER SISTERS IS BASICALLY SIX DEADLY ENEMIES WHO KNOW EVERYTHING ABOUT YOU.
"SIX ARCHIVISTS OF EVERY TIME YOU PUKED, POOPED INAPPROPRIATELY, OR FELL OVER."

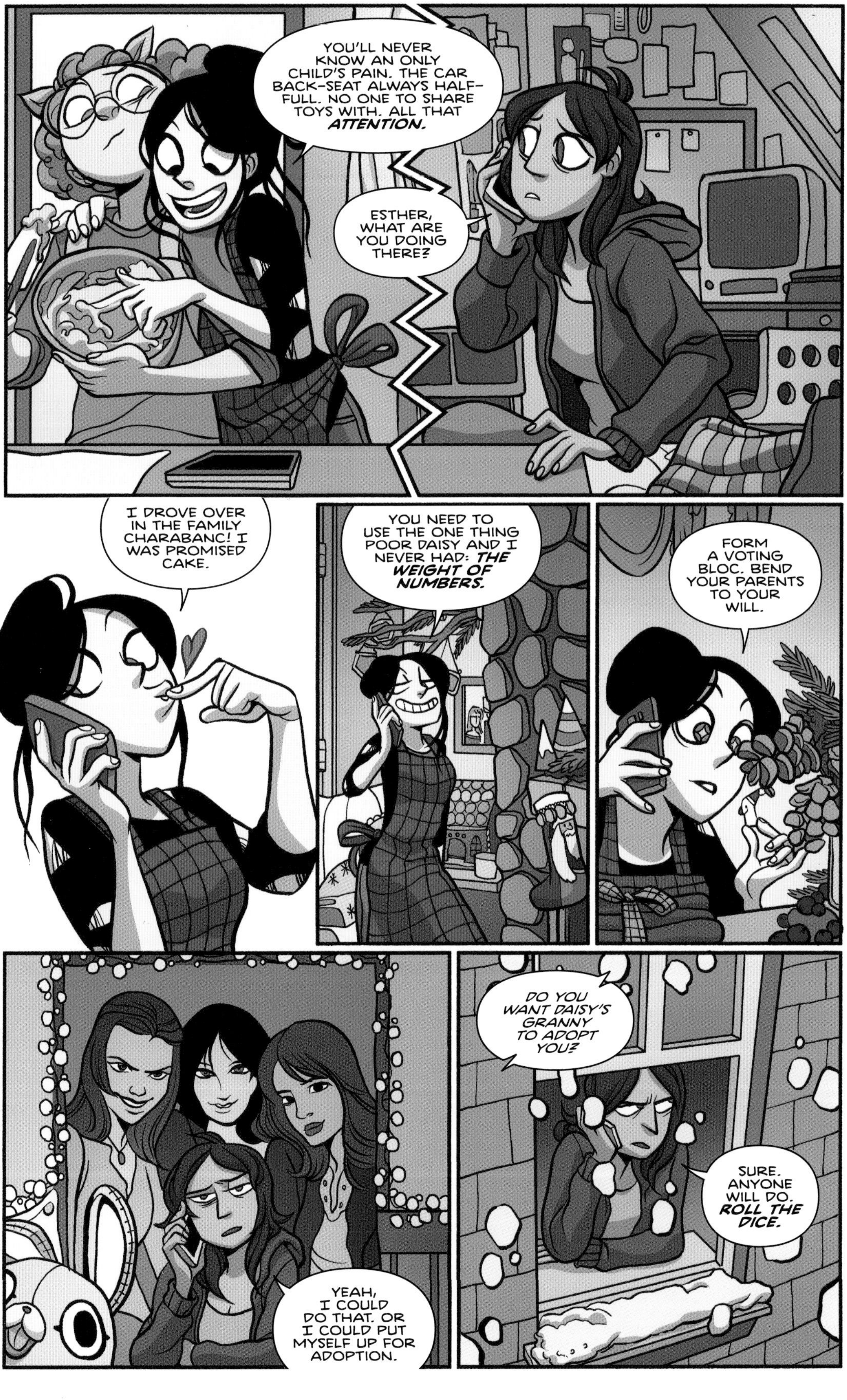
YOU'LL NEVER KNOW AN ONLY CHILD'S PAIN. THE CAR BACK-SEAT ALWAYS HALF-FULL. NO ONE TO SHARE TOYS WITH. ALL THAT *ATTENTION.*
ESTHER, WHAT ARE YOU DOING THERE?
I DROVE OVER IN THE FAMILY CHARABANC! I WAS PROMISED CAKE.
YOU NEED TO USE THE ONE THING POOR DAISY AND I NEVER HAD: ***THE WEIGHT OF NUMBERS.***
FORM A VOTING BLOC. BEND YOUR PARENTS TO YOUR WILL.
YEAH, I COULD DO THAT. OR I COULD PUT MYSELF UP FOR ADOPTION.
DO YOU WANT DAISY'S GRANNY TO ADOPT YOU?
SURE. ANYONE WILL DO. ***ROLL THE DICE.***

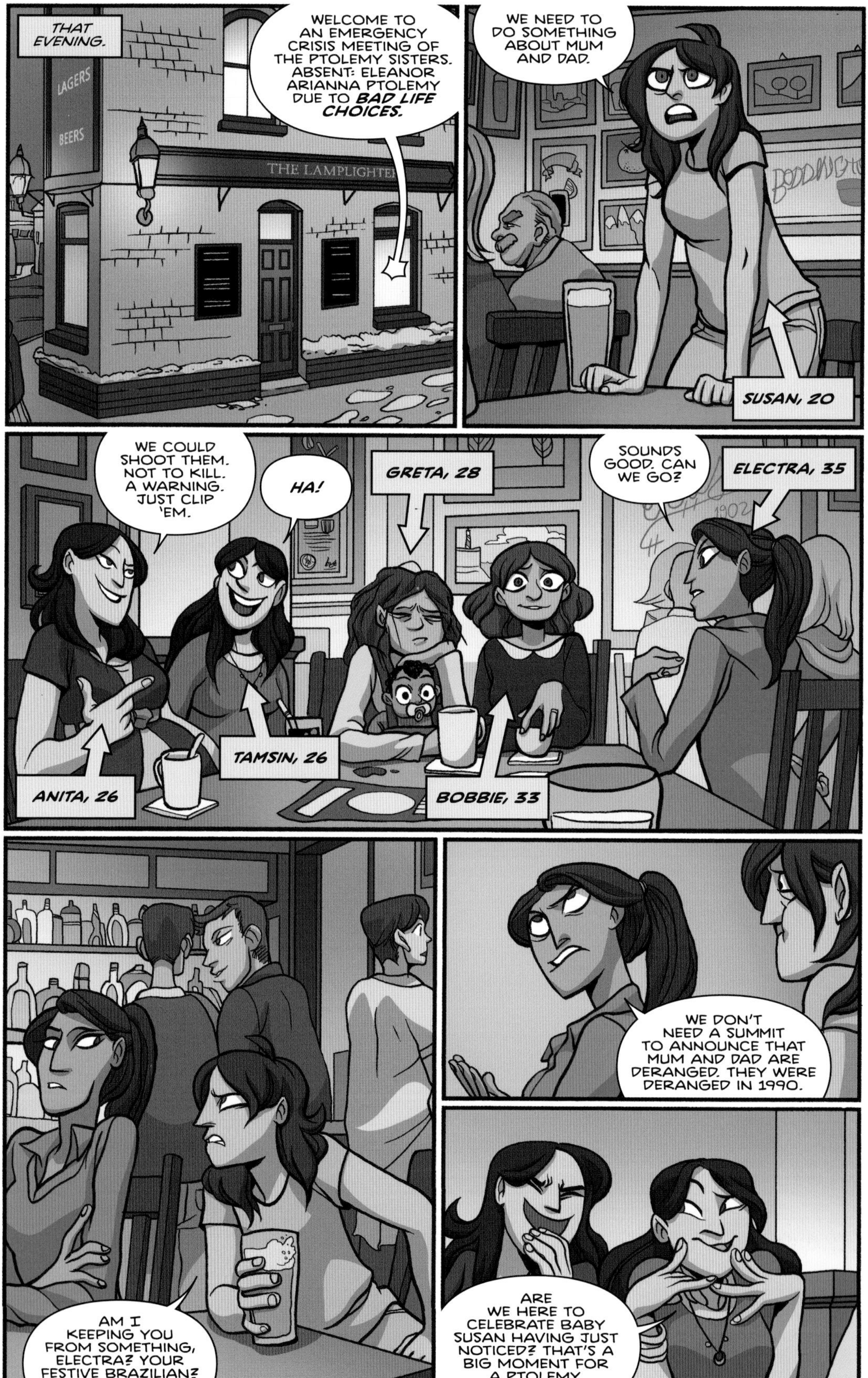
THAT EVENING.
LAGERS
BEERS
THE LAMPLIGHTER
WELCOME TO AN EMERGENCY CRISIS MEETING OF THE PTOLEMY SISTERS. ABSENT: ELEANOR ARIANNA PTOLEMY DUE TO BAD LIFE CHOICES.
WE NEED TO DO SOMETHING ABOUT MUM AND DAD.
SUSAN, 20
WE COULD SHOOT THEM. NOT TO KILL. A WARNING. JUST CLIP 'EM.
HA!
GRETA, 28
SOUNDS GOOD. CAN WE GO?
ELECTRA, 35
ANITA, 26
TAMSIN, 26
BOBBIE, 33
WE DON'T NEED A SUMMIT TO ANNOUNCE THAT MUM AND DAD ARE DERANGED. THEY WERE DERANGED IN 1990.
AM I KEEPING YOU FROM SOMETHING, ELECTRA? YOUR FESTIVE BRAZILIAN?
ARE WE HERE TO CELEBRATE BABY SUSAN HAVING JUST NOTICED? THAT'S A BIG MOMENT FOR A PTOLEMY.

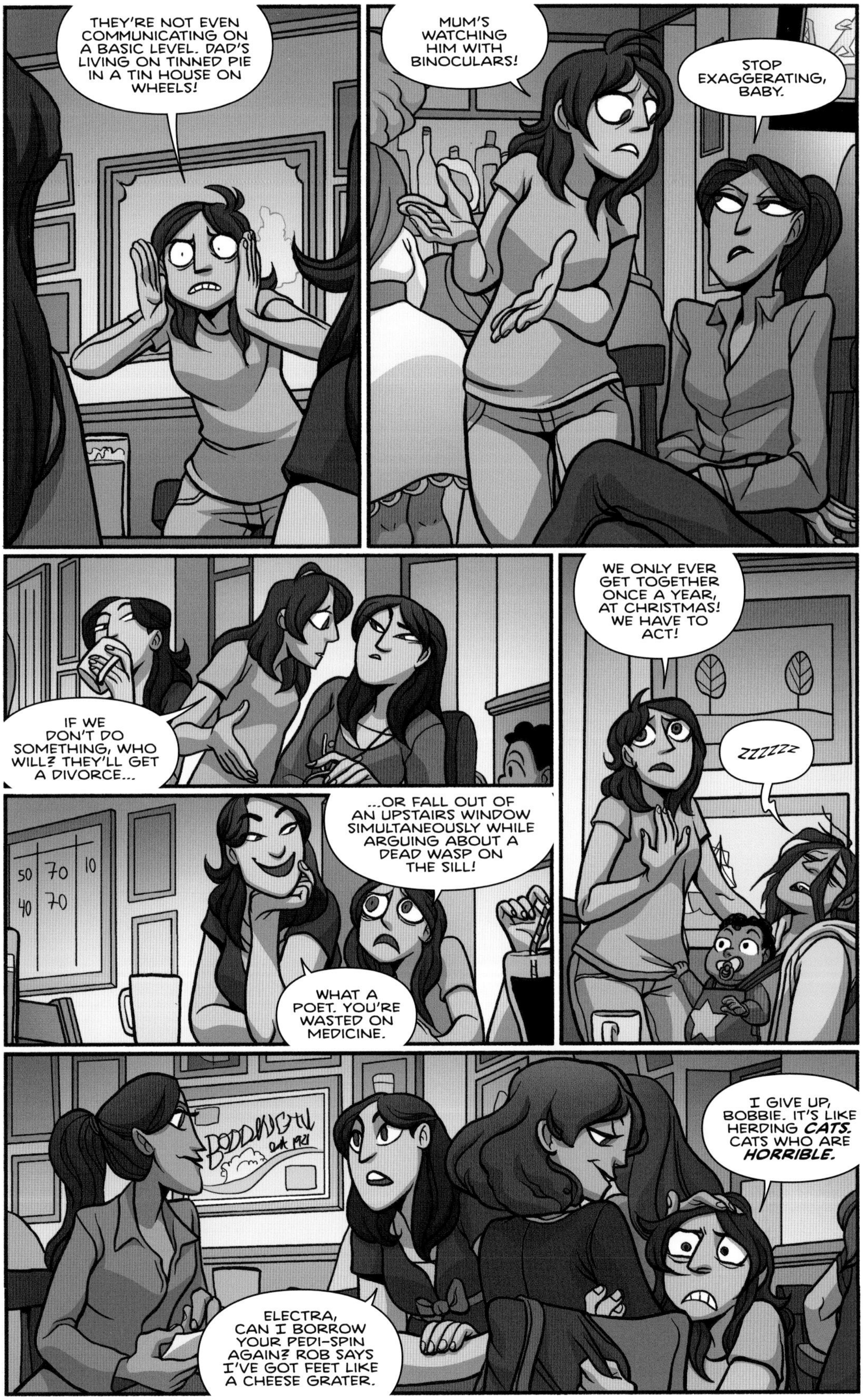
THEY'RE NOT EVEN COMMUNICATING ON A BASIC LEVEL. DAD'S LIVING ON TINNED PIE IN A TIN HOUSE ON WHEELS!
MUM'S WATCHING HIM WITH BINOCULARS!
STOP EXAGGERATING, BABY.
IF WE DON'T DO SOMETHING, WHO WILL? THEY'LL GET A DIVORCE...
WE ONLY EVER GET TOGETHER ONCE A YEAR, AT CHRISTMAS! WE HAVE TO ACT!
...OR FALL OUT OF AN UPSTAIRS WINDOW SIMULTANEOUSLY WHILE ARGUING ABOUT A DEAD WASP ON THE SILL!
50 70 10
40 70
WHAT A POET. YOU'RE WASTED ON MEDICINE.
ZZZZZZ
I GIVE UP, BOBBIE. IT'S LIKE HERDING **CATS.** CATS WHO ARE ***HORRIBLE.***
ELECTRA, CAN I BORROW YOUR PEDI-SPIN AGAIN? ROB SAYS I'VE GOT FEET LIKE A CHEESE GRATER.

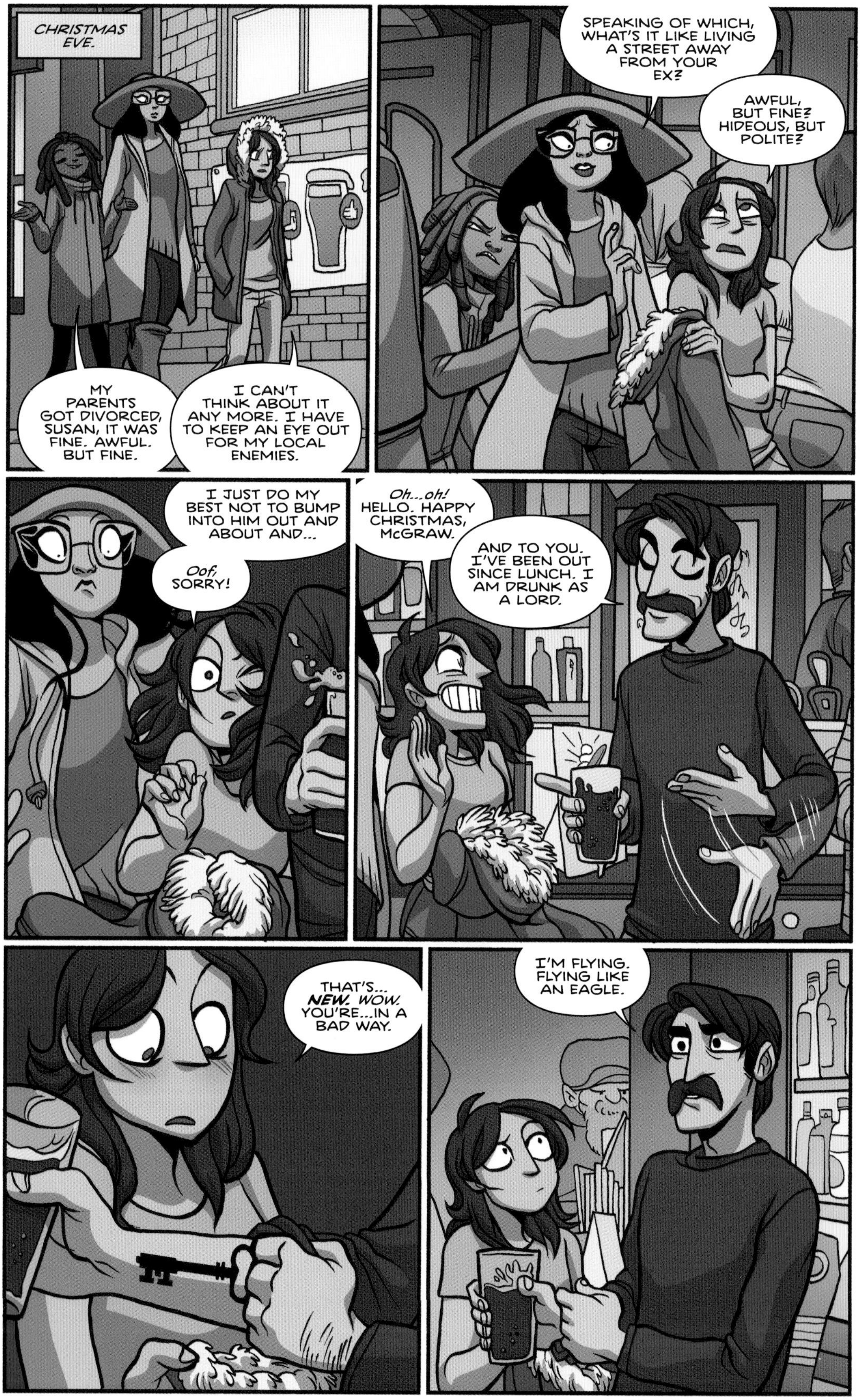
CHRISTMAS EVE.
MY PARENTS GOT DIVORCED, SUSAN, IT WAS FINE. AWFUL. BUT FINE.
I CAN'T THINK ABOUT IT ANY MORE. I HAVE TO KEEP AN EYE OUT FOR MY LOCAL ENEMIES.
SPEAKING OF WHICH, WHAT'S IT LIKE LIVING A STREET AWAY FROM YOUR EX?
AWFUL, BUT FINE? HIDEOUS, BUT POLITE?
I JUST DO MY BEST NOT TO BUMP INTO HIM OUT AND ABOUT AND...
Oof, SORRY!
Oh...oh! HELLO. HAPPY CHRISTMAS, McGRAW.
AND TO YOU. I'VE BEEN OUT SINCE LUNCH. I AM DRUNK AS A LORD.
THAT'S... ***NEW.*** *WOW.* YOU'RE...IN A BAD WAY.
I'M FLYING. FLYING LIKE AN EAGLE.

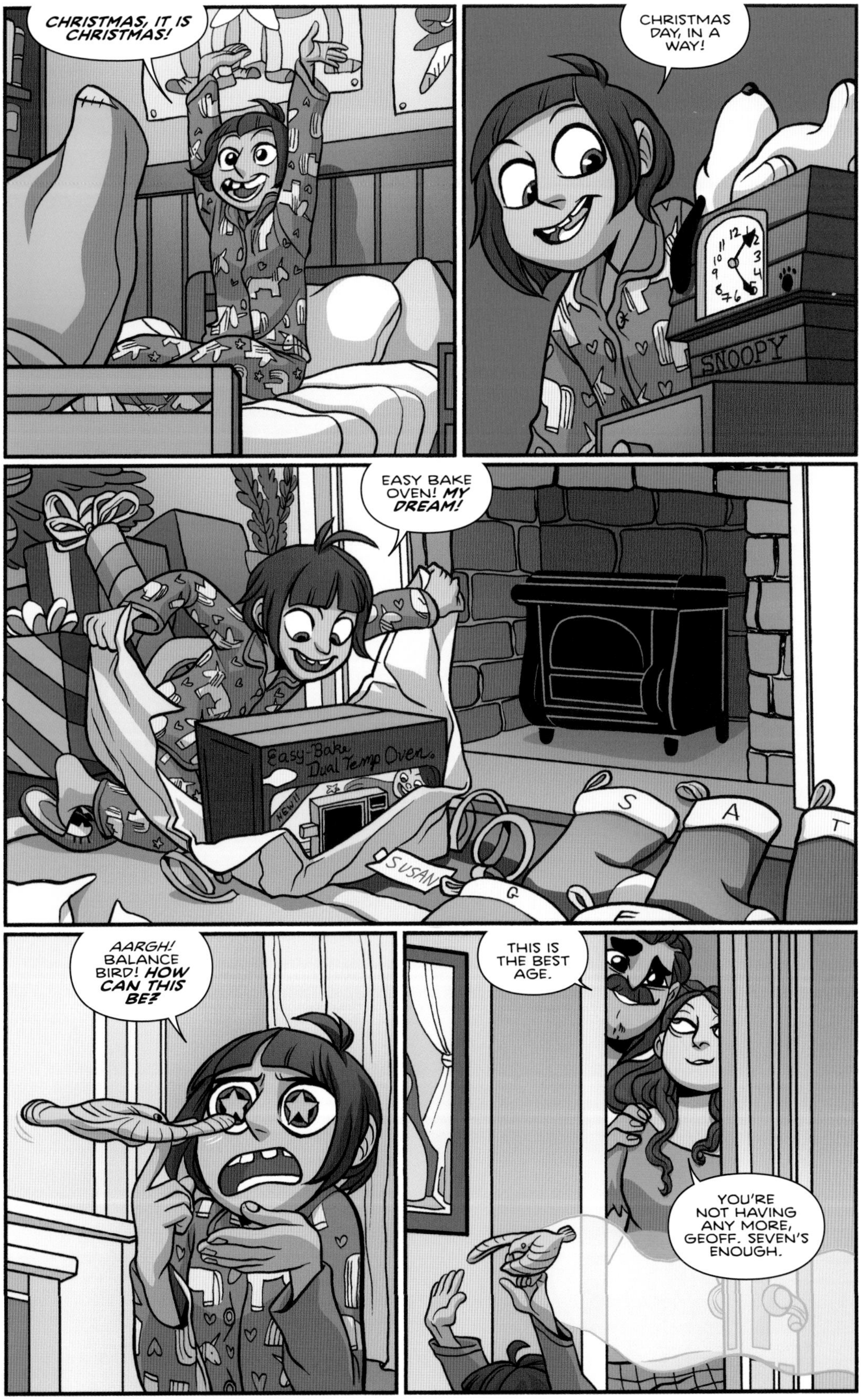
CHRISTMAS, IT IS CHRISTMAS!
CHRISTMAS DAY, IN A WAY!
SNOOPY
EASY BAKE OVEN! MY DREAM!
Easy-Bake Dual Temp Oven.
NEW!!
SUSAN
S
A
T
AARGH! BALANCE BIRD! HOW CAN THIS BE?
THIS IS THE BEST AGE.
YOU'RE NOT HAVING ANY MORE, GEOFF. SEVEN'S ENOUGH.

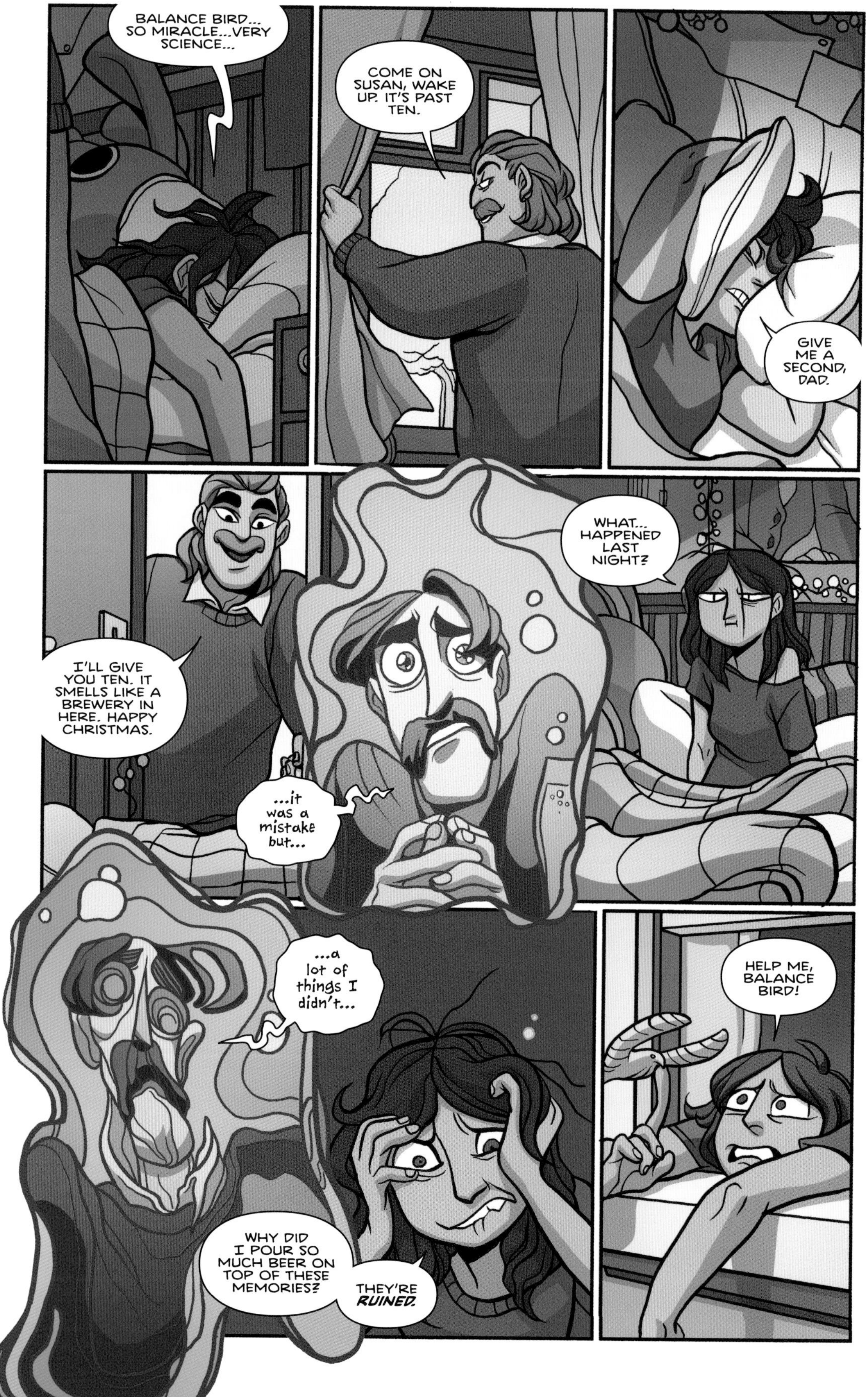
BALANCE BIRD... SO MIRACLE...VERY SCIENCE...
COME ON SUSAN, WAKE UP. IT'S PAST TEN.
GIVE ME A SECOND, DAD.
I'LL GIVE YOU TEN. IT SMELLS LIKE A BREWERY IN HERE. HAPPY CHRISTMAS.
WHAT... HAPPENED LAST NIGHT?
...it was a mistake but...
...a lot of things I didn't...
WHY DID I POUR SO MUCH BEER ON TOP OF THESE MEMORIES?
THEY'RE *RUINED.*
HELP ME, BALANCE BIRD!

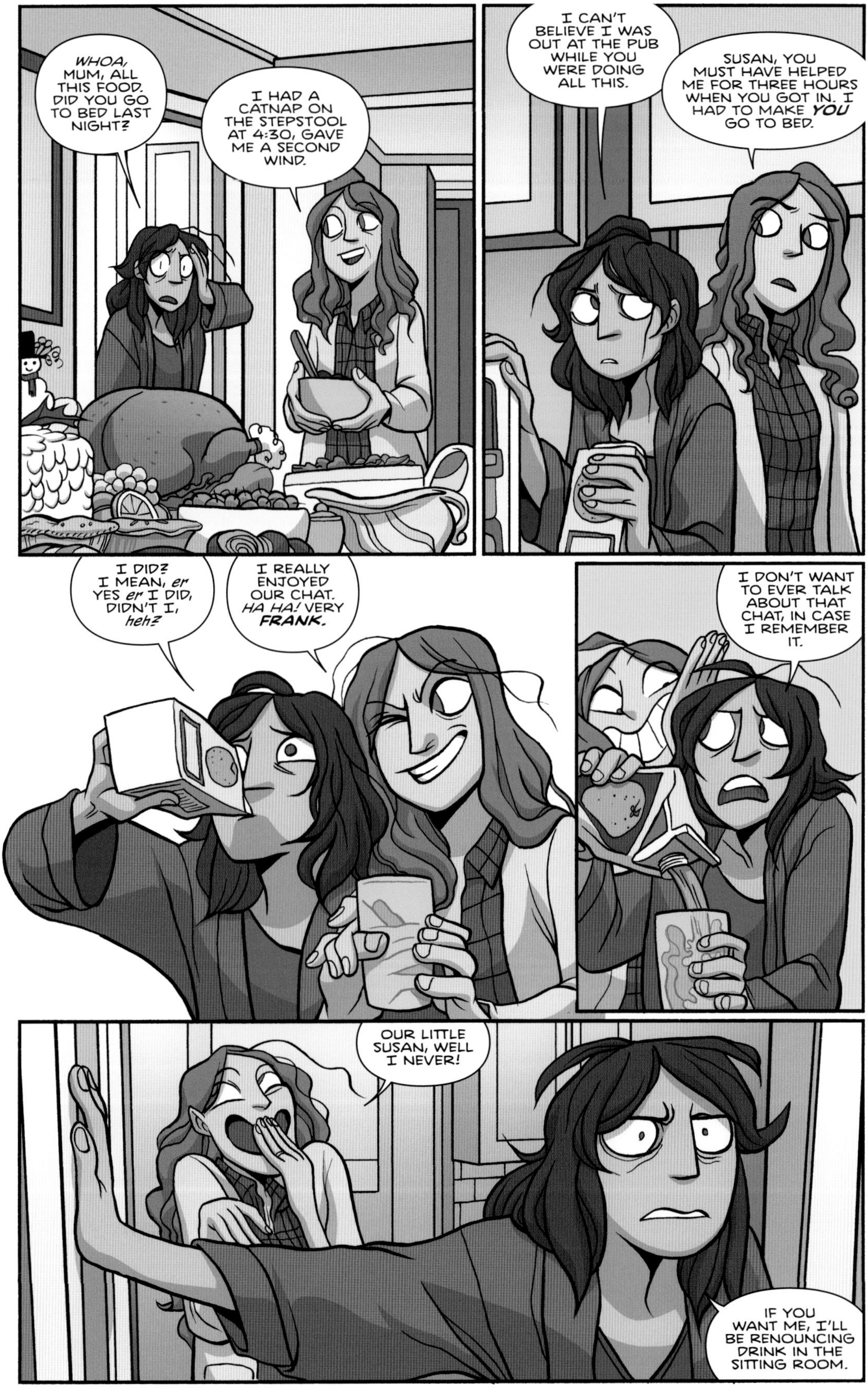
WHOA, MUM, ALL THIS FOOD. DID YOU GO TO BED LAST NIGHT?
I HAD A CATNAP ON THE STEPSTOOL AT 4:30, GAVE ME A SECOND WIND.
I CAN'T BELIEVE I WAS OUT AT THE PUB WHILE YOU WERE DOING ALL THIS.
SUSAN, YOU MUST HAVE HELPED ME FOR THREE HOURS WHEN YOU GOT IN. I HAD TO MAKE ***YOU*** GO TO BED.
I DID? I MEAN, *er* YES *er* I DID, DIDN'T I, *heh?*
I REALLY ENJOYED OUR CHAT. *HA HA!* VERY ***FRANK.***
I DON'T WANT TO EVER TALK ABOUT THAT CHAT, IN CASE I REMEMBER IT.
OUR LITTLE SUSAN, WELL I NEVER!
IF YOU WANT ME, I'LL BE RENOUNCING DRINK IN THE SITTING ROOM.

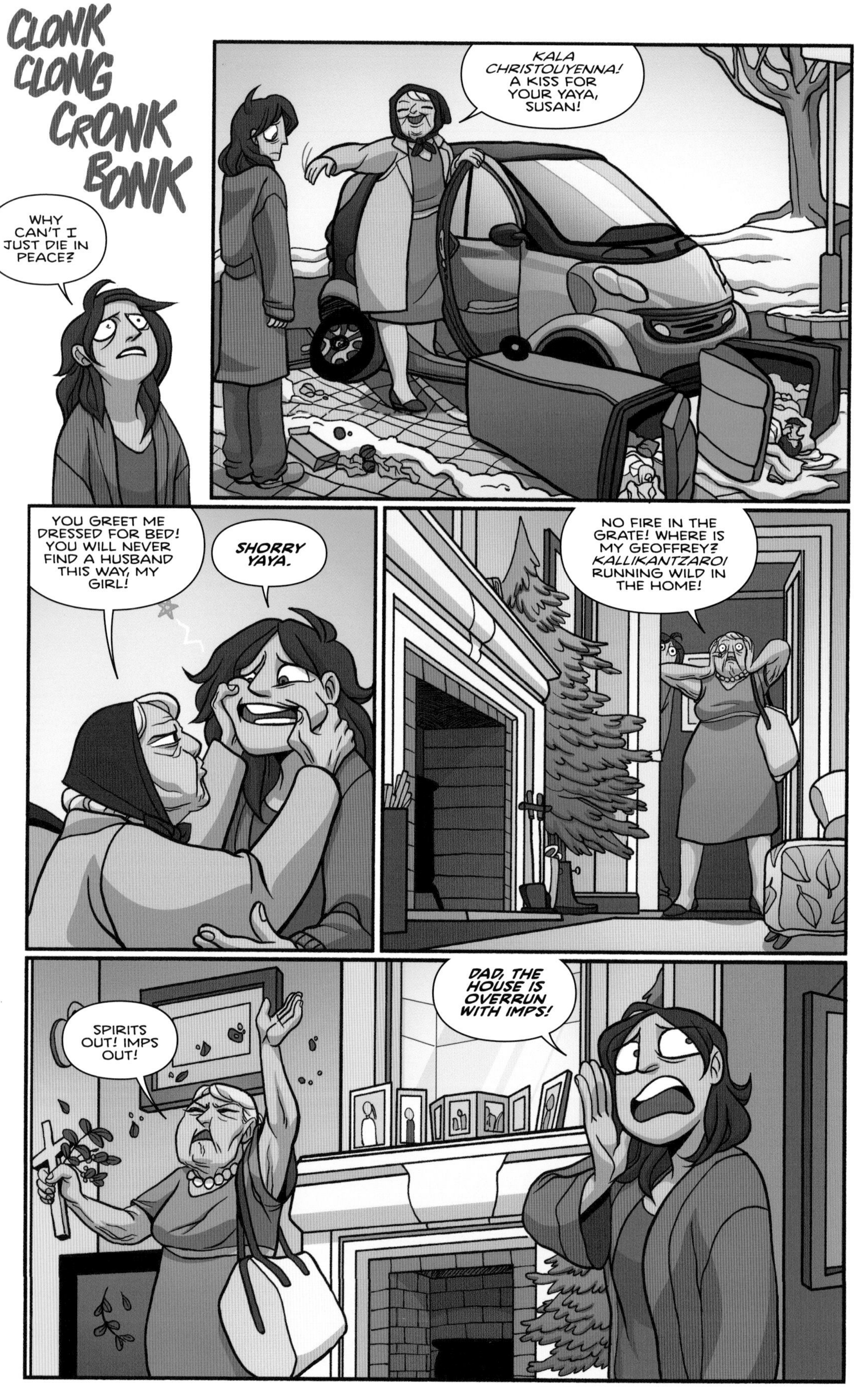

CLONK CLONG CRONK BONK
WHY CAN'T I JUST DIE IN PEACE?
KALA CHRISTOUYENNA! A KISS FOR YOUR YAYA, SUSAN!
YOU GREET ME DRESSED FOR BED! YOU WILL NEVER FIND A HUSBAND THIS WAY, MY GIRL!
SHORRY YAYA.
NO FIRE IN THE GRATE! WHERE IS MY GEOFFREY? KALLIKANTZARO! RUNNING WILD IN THE HOME!
SPIRITS OUT! IMPS OUT!
DAD, THE HOUSE IS OVERRUN WITH IMPS!

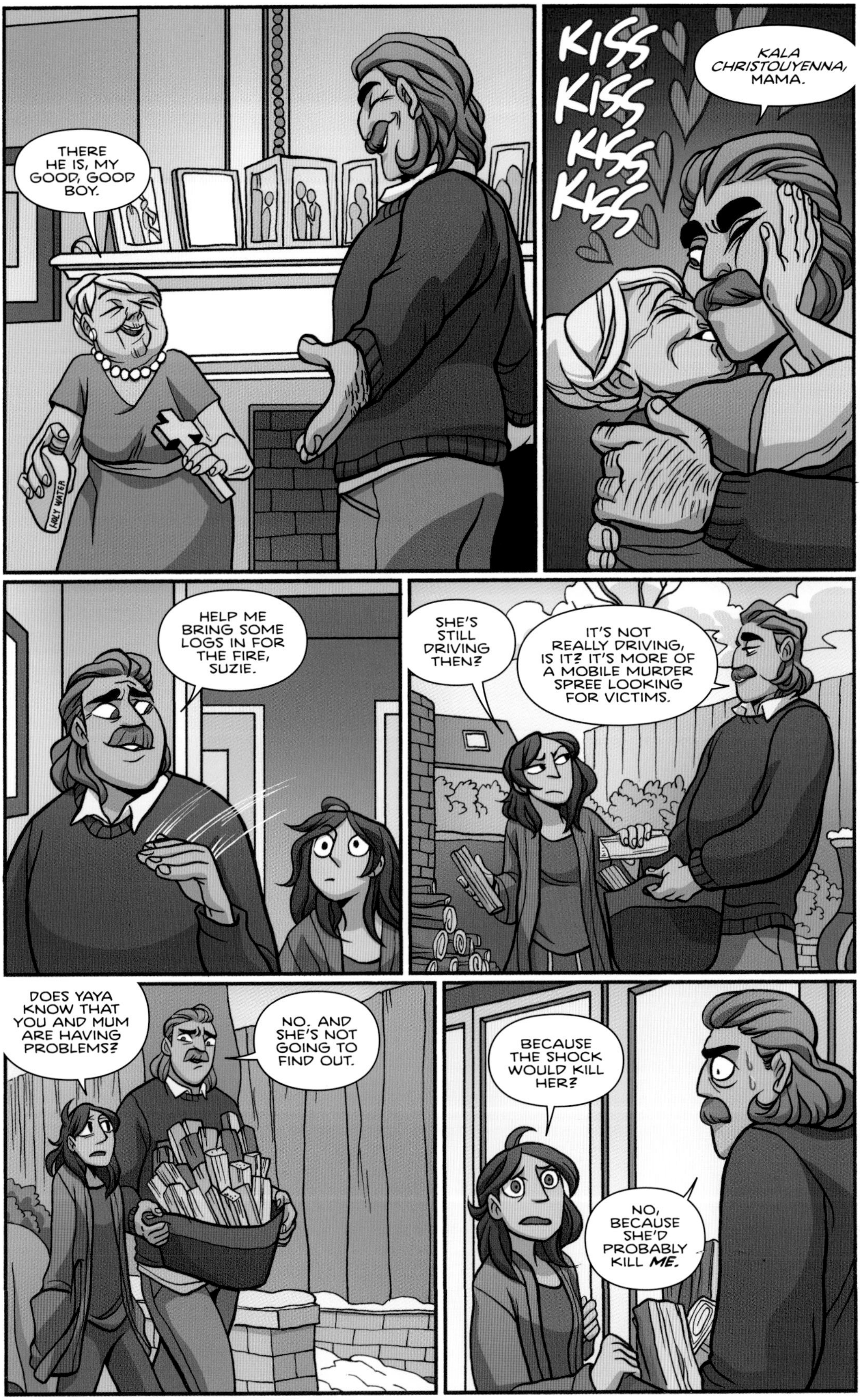
THERE HE IS, MY GOOD, GOOD BOY.
HOLY WATER
KISS KISS KISS KISS
KALA CHRISTOUYENNA, MAMA.
HELP ME BRING SOME LOGS IN FOR THE FIRE, SUZIE.
SHE'S STILL DRIVING THEN?
IT'S NOT REALLY DRIVING, IS IT? IT'S MORE OF A MOBILE MURDER SPREE LOOKING FOR VICTIMS.
DOES YAYA KNOW THAT YOU AND MUM ARE HAVING PROBLEMS?
NO. AND SHE'S NOT GOING TO FIND OUT.
BECAUSE THE SHOCK WOULD KILL HER?
NO, BECAUSE SHE'D PROBABLY KILL ME.

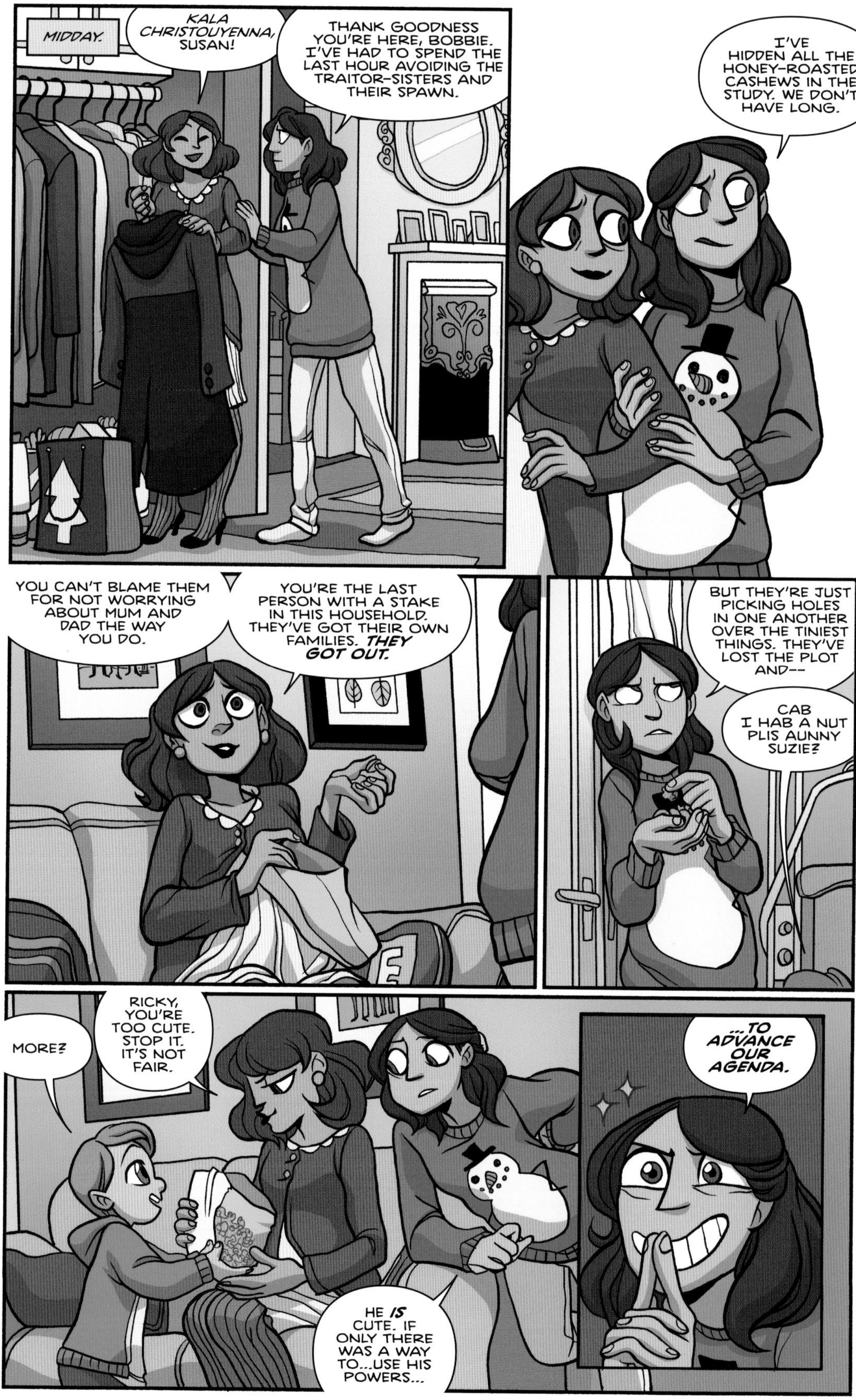
MIDDAY.
KALA CHRISTOUYENNA, SUSAN!
THANK GOODNESS YOU'RE HERE, BOBBIE. I'VE HAD TO SPEND THE LAST HOUR AVOIDING THE TRAITOR-SISTERS AND THEIR SPAWN.
I'VE HIDDEN ALL THE HONEY-ROASTED CASHEWS IN THE STUDY. WE DON'T HAVE LONG.
YOU CAN'T BLAME THEM FOR NOT WORRYING ABOUT MUM AND DAD THE WAY YOU DO.
YOU'RE THE LAST PERSON WITH A STAKE IN THIS HOUSEHOLD. THEY'VE GOT THEIR OWN FAMILIES. *THEY GOT OUT.*
BUT THEY'RE JUST PICKING HOLES IN ONE ANOTHER OVER THE TINIEST THINGS. THEY'VE LOST THE PLOT AND--
CAB I HAB A NUT PLIS AUNNY SUZIE?
MORE?
RICKY, YOU'RE TOO CUTE. STOP IT. IT'S NOT FAIR.
HE *IS* CUTE. IF ONLY THERE WAS A WAY TO...USE HIS POWERS...
...TO ADVANCE OUR AGENDA.

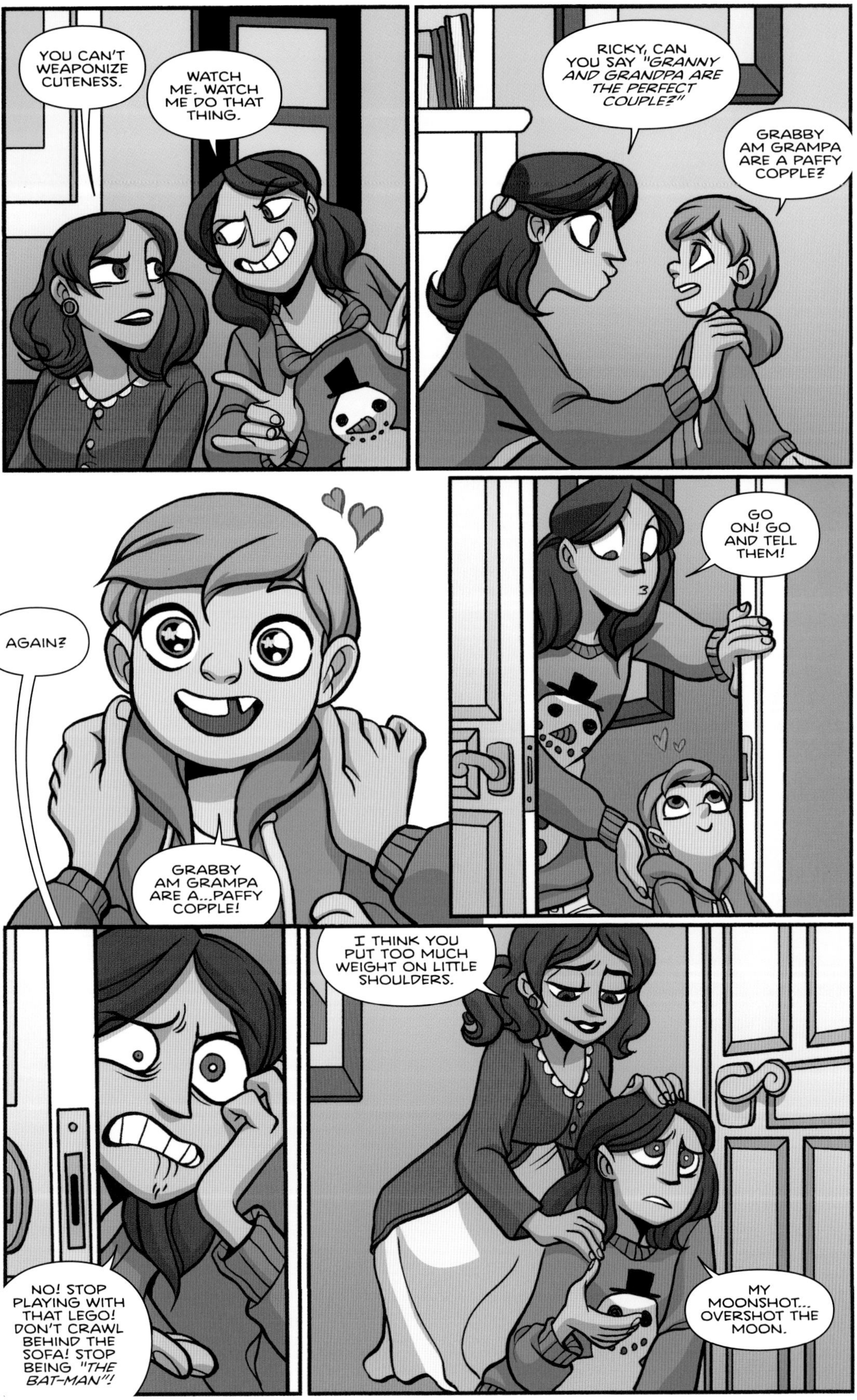
YOU CAN'T WEAPONIZE CUTENESS.
WATCH ME. WATCH ME DO THAT THING.
RICKY, CAN YOU SAY "GRANNY AND GRANDPA ARE THE PERFECT COUPLE?"
GRABBY AM GRAMPA ARE A PAFFY COPPLE?
AGAIN?
GRABBY AM GRAMPA ARE A...PAFFY COPPLE!
GO ON! GO AND TELL THEM!
NO! STOP PLAYING WITH THAT LEGO! DON'T CRAWL BEHIND THE SOFA! STOP BEING "THE BAT-MAN"!
I THINK YOU PUT TOO MUCH WEIGHT ON LITTLE SHOULDERS.
MY MOONSHOT... OVERSHOT THE MOON.

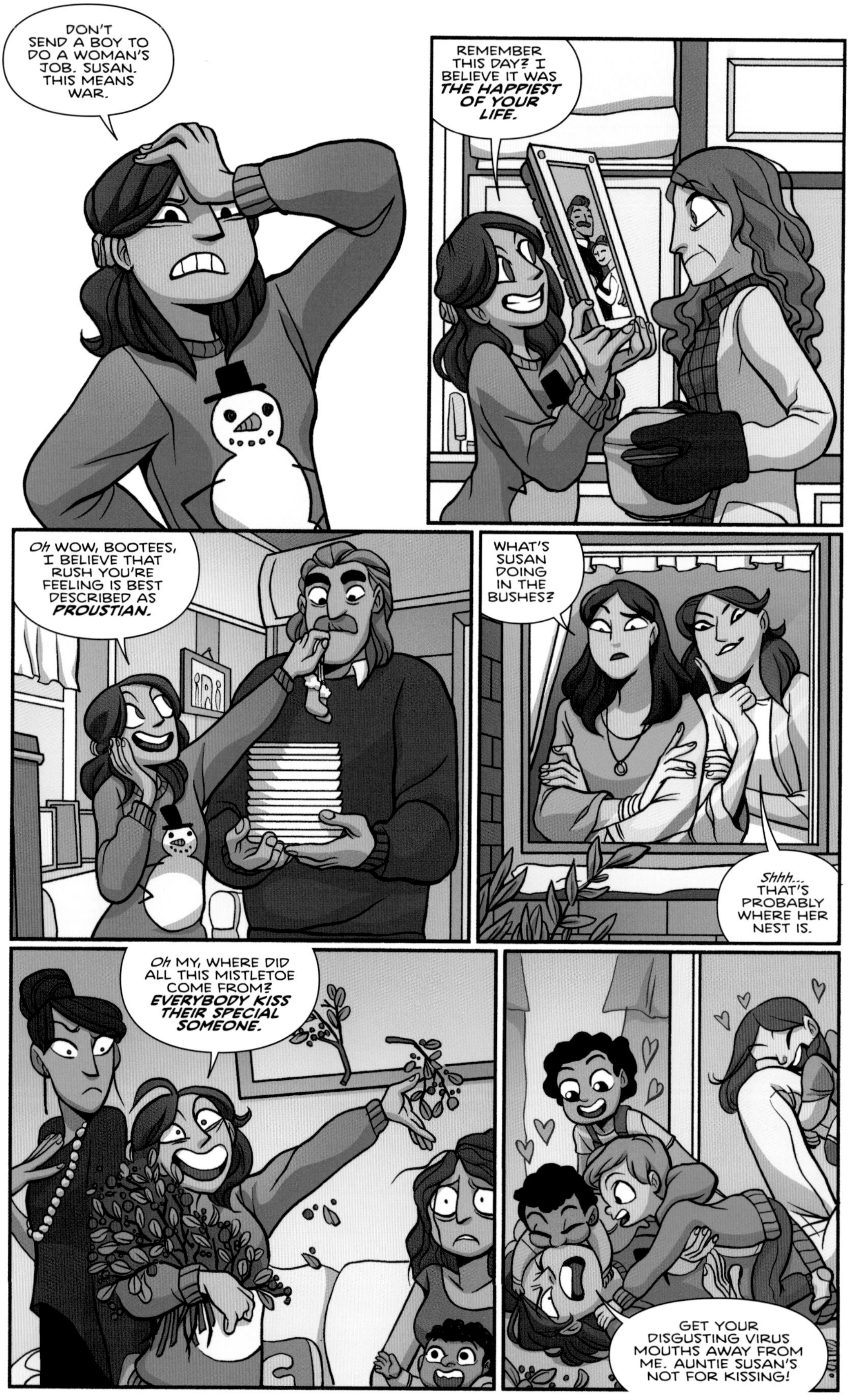
DON'T SEND A BOY TO DO A WOMAN'S JOB. SUSAN. THIS MEANS WAR.
REMEMBER THIS DAY? I BELIEVE IT WAS ***THE HAPPIEST OF YOUR LIFE.***
Oh WOW, BOOTEES, I BELIEVE THAT RUSH YOU'RE FEELING IS BEST DESCRIBED AS ***PROUSTIAN.***
WHAT'S SUSAN DOING IN THE BUSHES?
Shhh... THAT'S PROBABLY WHERE HER NEST IS.
Oh MY, WHERE DID ALL THIS MISTLETOE COME FROM? ***EVERYBODY KISS THEIR SPECIAL SOMEONE.***
GET YOUR DISGUSTING VIRUS MOUTHS AWAY FROM ME. AUNTIE SUSAN'S NOT FOR KISSING!

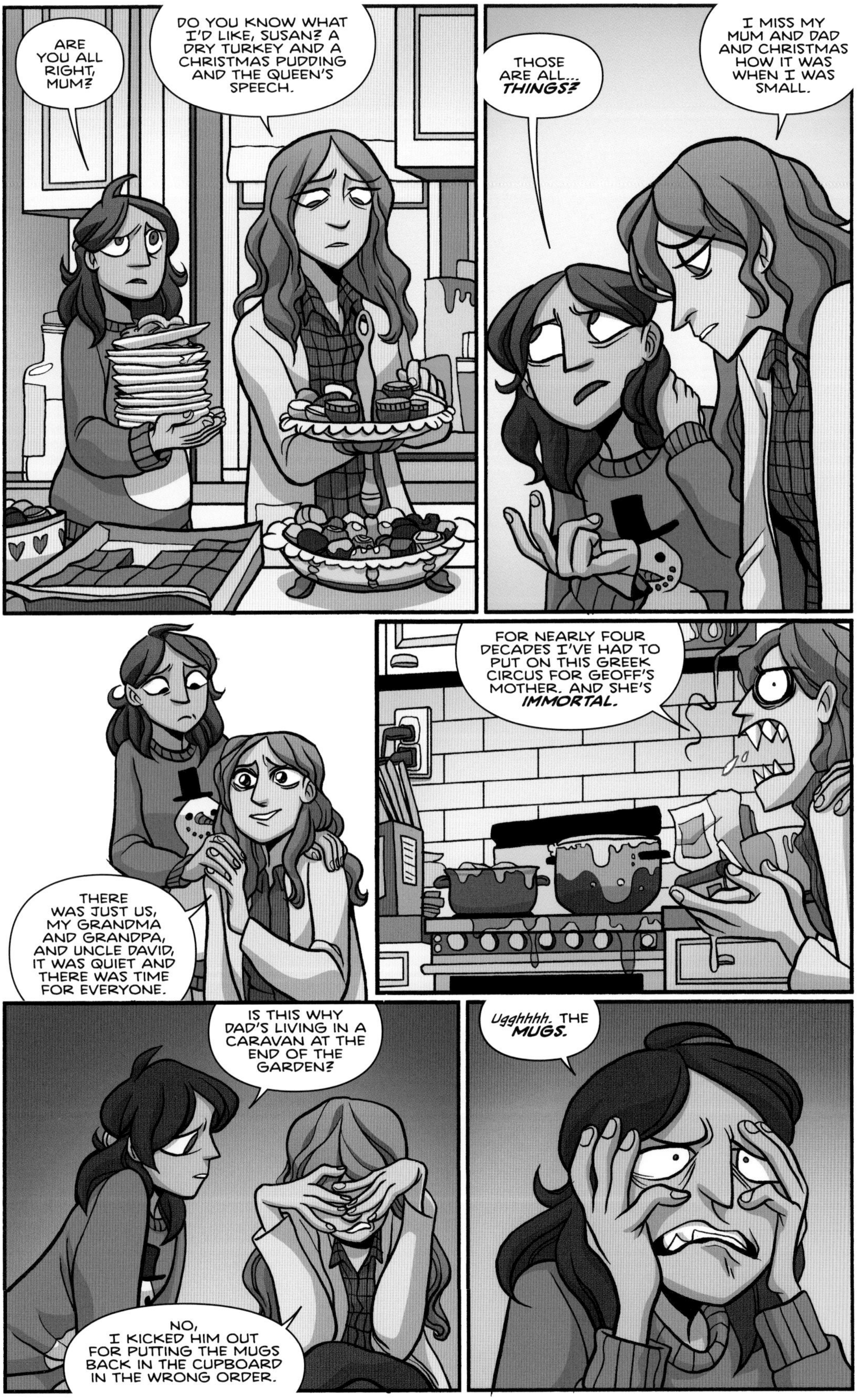
ARE YOU ALL RIGHT, MUM?
DO YOU KNOW WHAT I'D LIKE, SUSAN? A DRY TURKEY AND A CHRISTMAS PUDDING AND THE QUEEN'S SPEECH.
THOSE ARE ALL... THINGS?
I MISS MY MUM AND DAD AND CHRISTMAS HOW IT WAS WHEN I WAS SMALL.
THERE WAS JUST US, MY GRANDMA AND GRANDPA, AND UNCLE DAVID, IT WAS QUIET AND THERE WAS TIME FOR EVERYONE.
FOR NEARLY FOUR DECADES I'VE HAD TO PUT ON THIS GREEK CIRCUS FOR GEOFF'S MOTHER. AND SHE'S IMMORTAL.
IS THIS WHY DAD'S LIVING IN A CARAVAN AT THE END OF THE GARDEN?
NO, I KICKED HIM OUT FOR PUTTING THE MUGS BACK IN THE CUPBOARD IN THE WRONG ORDER.
Ugghhhh. THE MUGS.

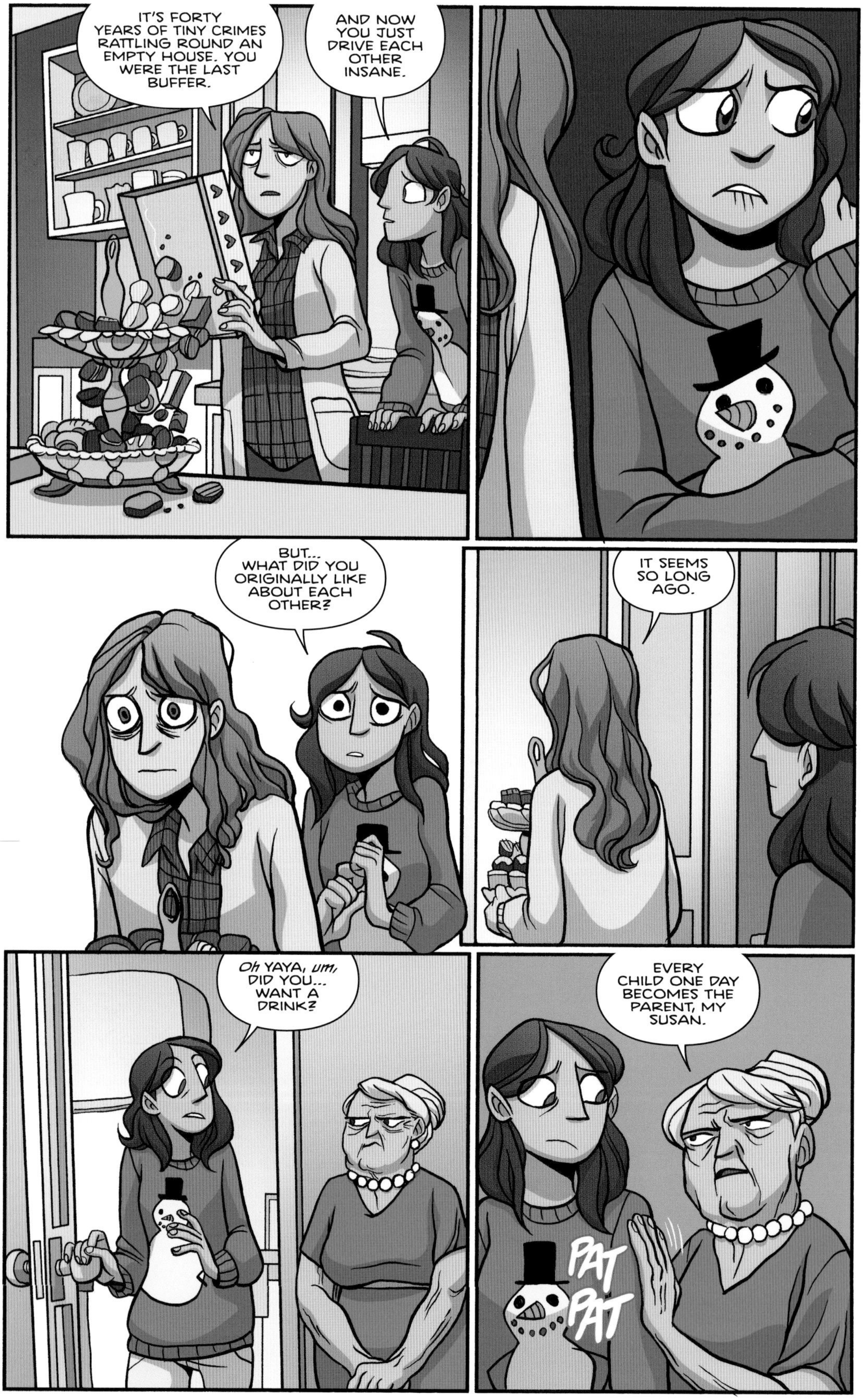
IT'S FORTY YEARS OF TINY CRIMES RATTLING ROUND AN EMPTY HOUSE. YOU WERE THE LAST BUFFER.
AND NOW YOU JUST DRIVE EACH OTHER INSANE.
BUT... WHAT DID YOU ORIGINALLY LIKE ABOUT EACH OTHER?
IT SEEMS SO LONG AGO.
Oh YAYA, um, DID YOU... WANT A DRINK?
EVERY CHILD ONE DAY BECOMES THE PARENT, MY SUSAN.
PAT
PAT

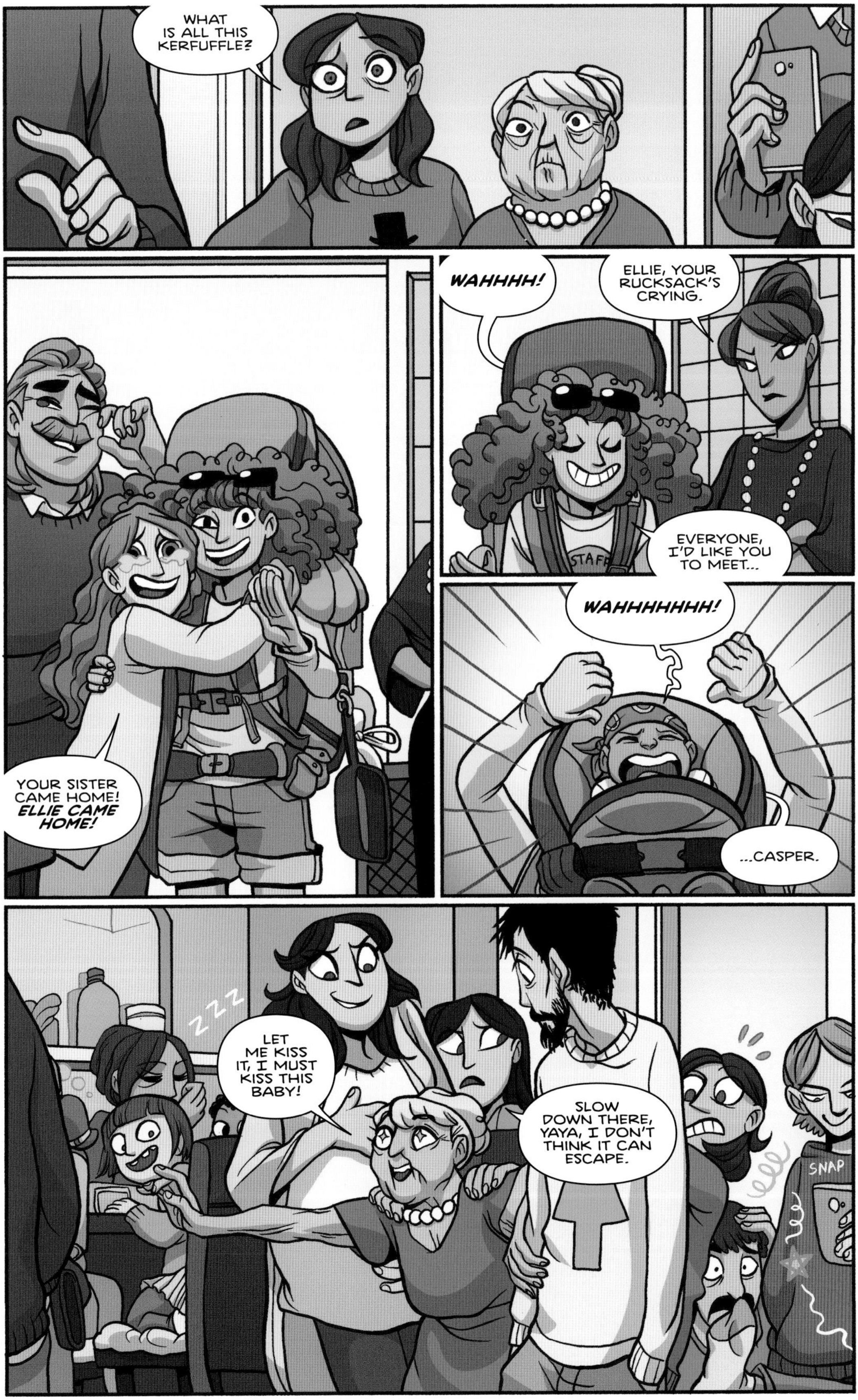
WHAT IS ALL THIS KERFUFFLE?
YOUR SISTER CAME HOME! ELLIE CAME HOME!
WAHHHH!
ELLIE, YOUR RUCKSACK'S CRYING.
STAFF
EVERYONE, I'D LIKE YOU TO MEET...
WAHHHHHHH!
...CASPER.
Z Z Z
LET ME KISS IT, I MUST KISS THIS BABY!
SLOW DOWN THERE, YAYA, I DON'T THINK IT CAN ESCAPE.
SNAP

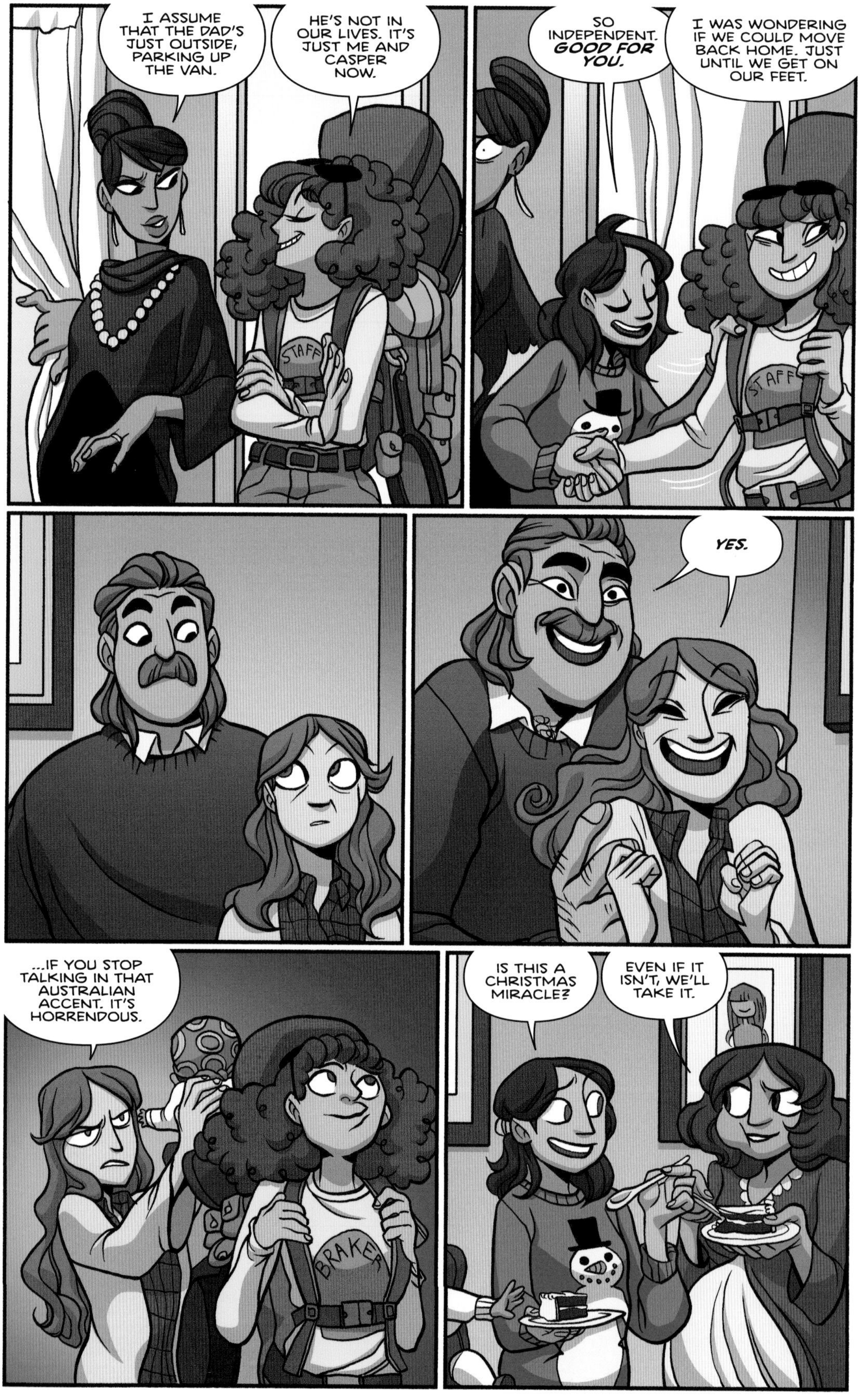
I ASSUME THAT THE DAD'S JUST OUTSIDE, PARKING UP THE VAN.
HE'S NOT IN OUR LIVES. IT'S JUST ME AND CASPER NOW.
SO INDEPENDENT. GOOD FOR YOU.
I WAS WONDERING IF WE COULD MOVE BACK HOME. JUST UNTIL WE GET ON OUR FEET.
STAFF
STAFF
YES.
...IF YOU STOP TALKING IN THAT AUSTRALIAN ACCENT. IT'S HORRENDOUS.
BRAKER
IS THIS A CHRISTMAS MIRACLE?
EVEN IF IT ISN'T, WE'LL TAKE IT.

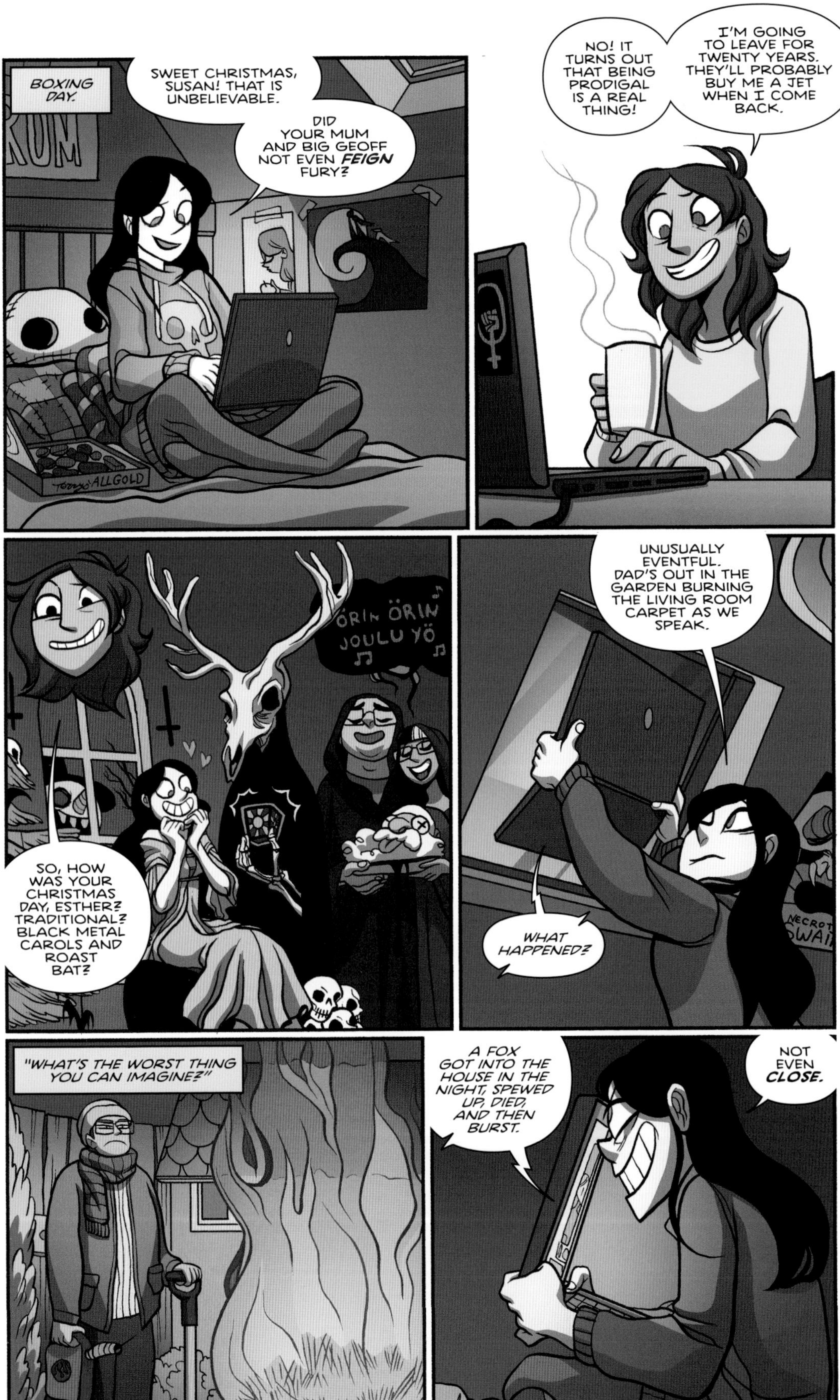
BOXING DAY.
SWEET CHRISTMAS, SUSAN! THAT IS UNBELIEVABLE.
DID YOUR MUM AND BIG GEOFF NOT EVEN FEIGN FURY?
NO! IT TURNS OUT THAT BEING PRODIGAL IS A REAL THING!
I'M GOING TO LEAVE FOR TWENTY YEARS. THEY'LL PROBABLY BUY ME A JET WHEN I COME BACK.
ÖRIN ÖRIN JOULU YÖ
SO, HOW WAS YOUR CHRISTMAS DAY, ESTHER? TRADITIONAL? BLACK METAL CAROLS AND ROAST BAT?
UNUSUALLY EVENTFUL. DAD'S OUT IN THE GARDEN BURNING THE LIVING ROOM CARPET AS WE SPEAK.
WHAT HAPPENED?
"WHAT'S THE WORST THING YOU CAN IMAGINE?"
A FOX GOT INTO THE HOUSE IN THE NIGHT, SPEWED UP, DIED, AND THEN BURST.
NOT EVEN CLOSE.

IS YOUR DAD GOING TO MOVE BACK INTO THE HOUSE?

YES. AFTER TWO SHERRIES, MUM CONCEDED THAT "A CARAVAN IS NO PLACE FOR A MAN TO LIVE HIS LIFE".

DAD ACTUALLY STOOD UP FOR THE CARAVAN. IT WAS QUITE TOUCHING.

ANY OTHER NEWS OF NOTE?

"NOT REALLY. I MIGHT HAVE SEEN McGRAW ON CHRISTMAS EVE.

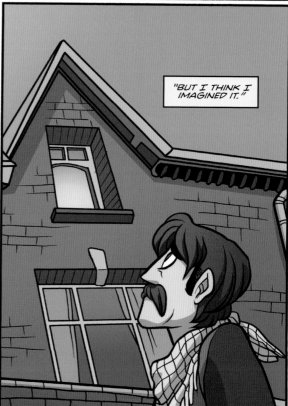

"BUT I THINK I IMAGINED IT."

CHAPTER
TWENTY-SIX

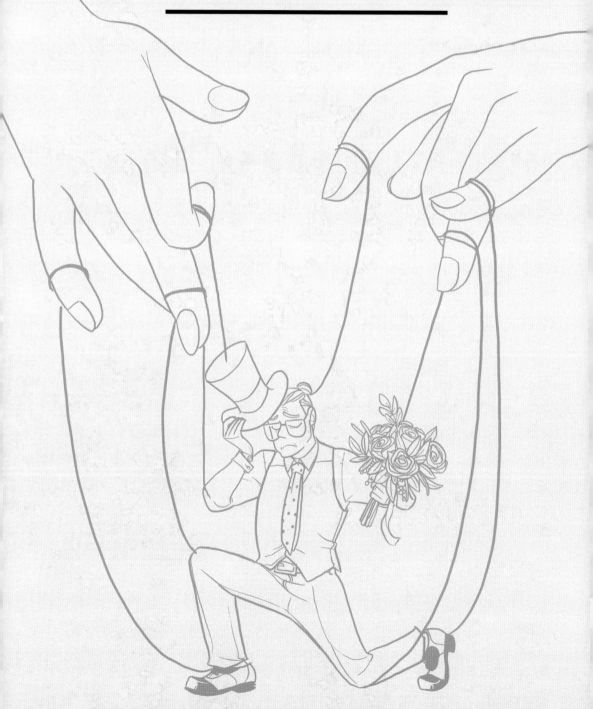

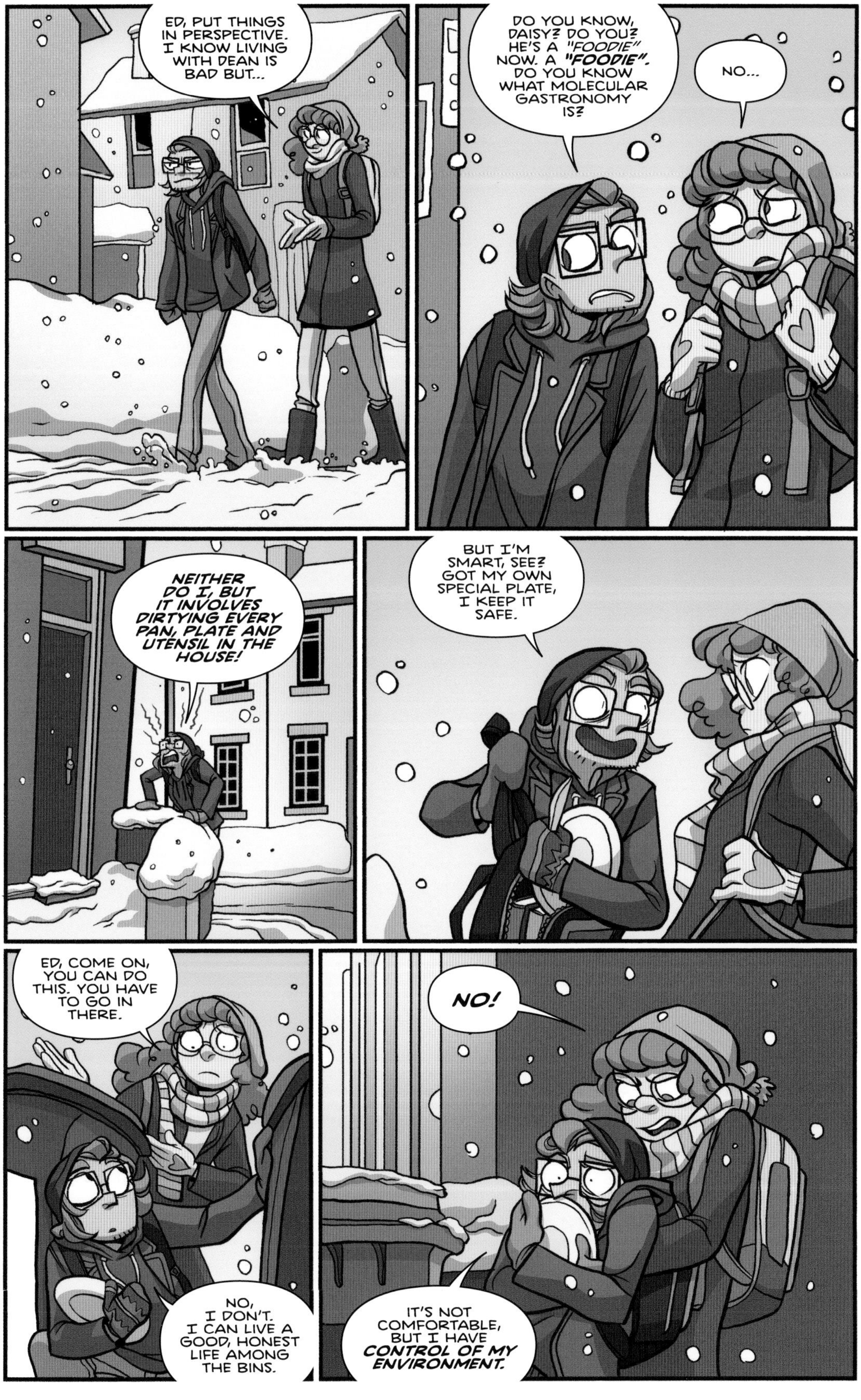
ED, PUT THINGS IN PERSPECTIVE. I KNOW LIVING WITH DEAN IS BAD BUT...
DO YOU KNOW, DAISY? DO YOU? HE'S A "FOODIE" NOW. A "FOODIE". DO YOU KNOW WHAT MOLECULAR GASTRONOMY IS?
NO...
NEITHER DO I, BUT IT INVOLVES DIRTYING EVERY PAN, PLATE AND UTENSIL IN THE HOUSE!
BUT I'M SMART, SEE? GOT MY OWN SPECIAL PLATE, I KEEP IT SAFE.
ED, COME ON, YOU CAN DO THIS. YOU HAVE TO GO IN THERE.
NO, I DON'T. I CAN LIVE A GOOD, HONEST LIFE AMONG THE BINS.
NO!
IT'S NOT COMFORTABLE, BUT I HAVE CONTROL OF MY ENVIRONMENT.

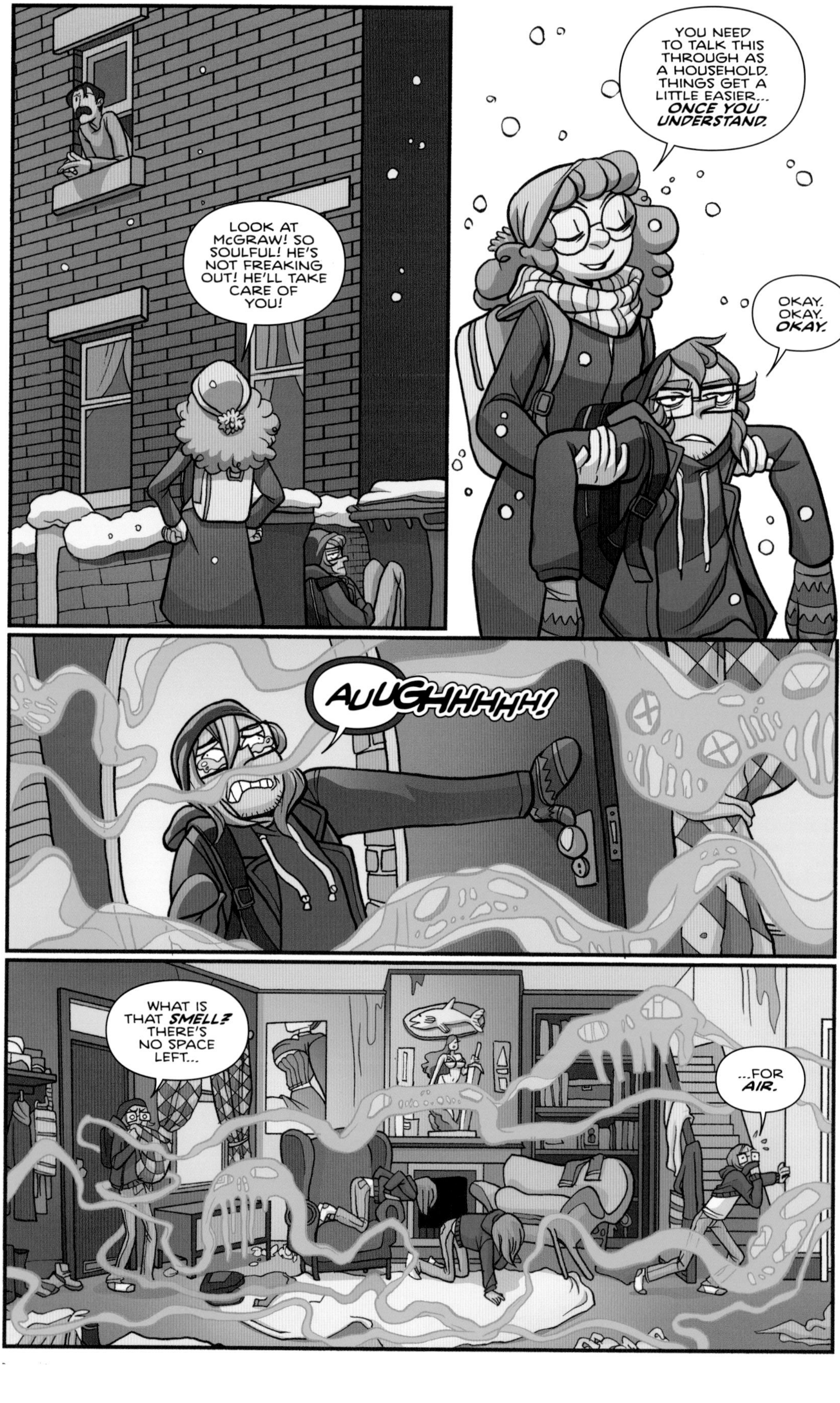
LOOK AT McGRAW! SO SOULFUL! HE'S NOT FREAKING OUT! HE'LL TAKE CARE OF YOU!
YOU NEED TO TALK THIS THROUGH AS A HOUSEHOLD. THINGS GET A LITTLE EASIER... ONCE YOU UNDERSTAND.
OKAY. OKAY. OKAY.
AUUGHHHHH!
WHAT IS THAT SMELL? THERE'S NO SPACE LEFT...
...FOR AIR.

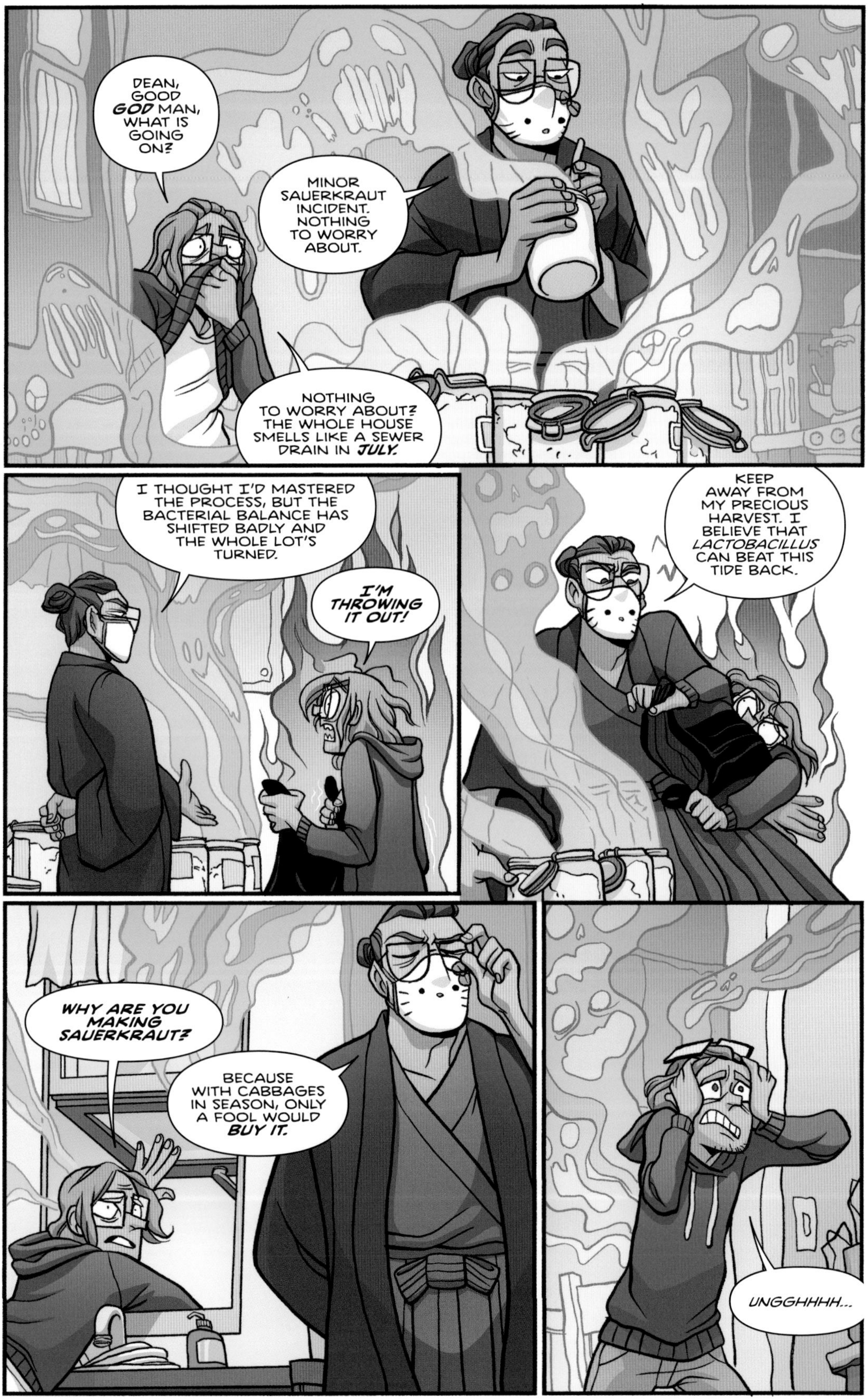
DEAN, GOOD GOD MAN, WHAT IS GOING ON?
MINOR SAUERKRAUT INCIDENT. NOTHING TO WORRY ABOUT.
NOTHING TO WORRY ABOUT? THE WHOLE HOUSE SMELLS LIKE A SEWER DRAIN IN JULY.
I THOUGHT I'D MASTERED THE PROCESS, BUT THE BACTERIAL BALANCE HAS SHIFTED BADLY AND THE WHOLE LOT'S TURNED.
I'M THROWING IT OUT!
KEEP AWAY FROM MY PRECIOUS HARVEST. I BELIEVE THAT LACTOBACILLUS CAN BEAT THIS TIDE BACK.
WHY ARE YOU MAKING SAUERKRAUT?
BECAUSE WITH CABBAGES IN SEASON, ONLY A FOOL WOULD BUY IT.
UNGGHHHH...

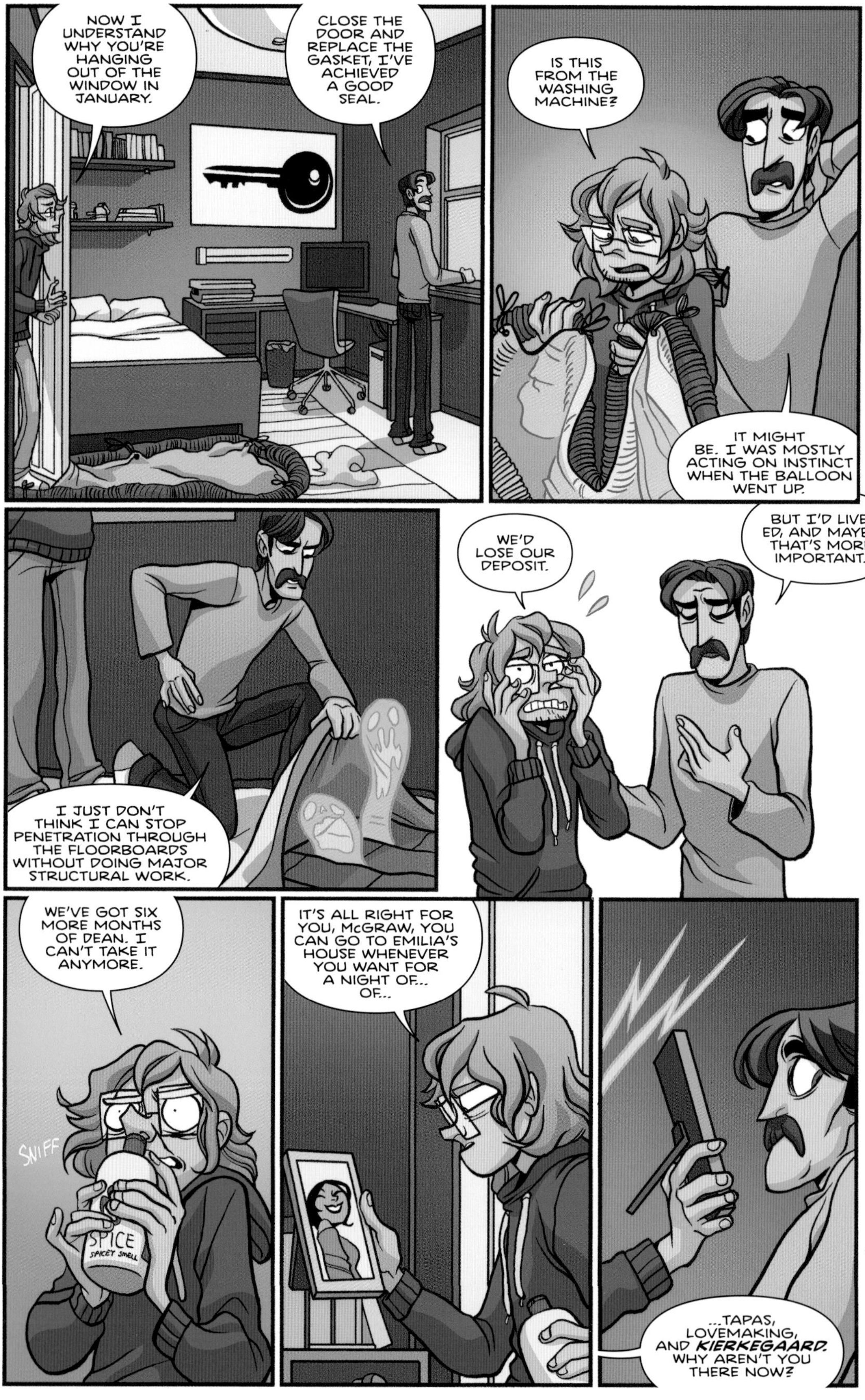
NOW I UNDERSTAND WHY YOU'RE HANGING OUT OF THE WINDOW IN JANUARY.
CLOSE THE DOOR AND REPLACE THE GASKET, I'VE ACHIEVED A GOOD SEAL.
IS THIS FROM THE WASHING MACHINE?
IT MIGHT BE. I WAS MOSTLY ACTING ON INSTINCT WHEN THE BALLOON WENT UP.
I JUST DON'T THINK I CAN STOP PENETRATION THROUGH THE FLOORBOARDS WITHOUT DOING MAJOR STRUCTURAL WORK.
WE'D LOSE OUR DEPOSIT.
BUT I'D LIVE, ED, AND MAYBE THAT'S MORE IMPORTANT.
WE'VE GOT SIX MORE MONTHS OF DEAN. I CAN'T TAKE IT ANYMORE.
SNIFF
SPICE
SPICEY SMELL
IT'S ALL RIGHT FOR YOU, McGRAW, YOU CAN GO TO EMILIA'S HOUSE WHENEVER YOU WANT FOR A NIGHT OF... OF...
...TAPAS, LOVEMAKING, AND KIERKEGAARD. WHY AREN'T YOU THERE NOW?

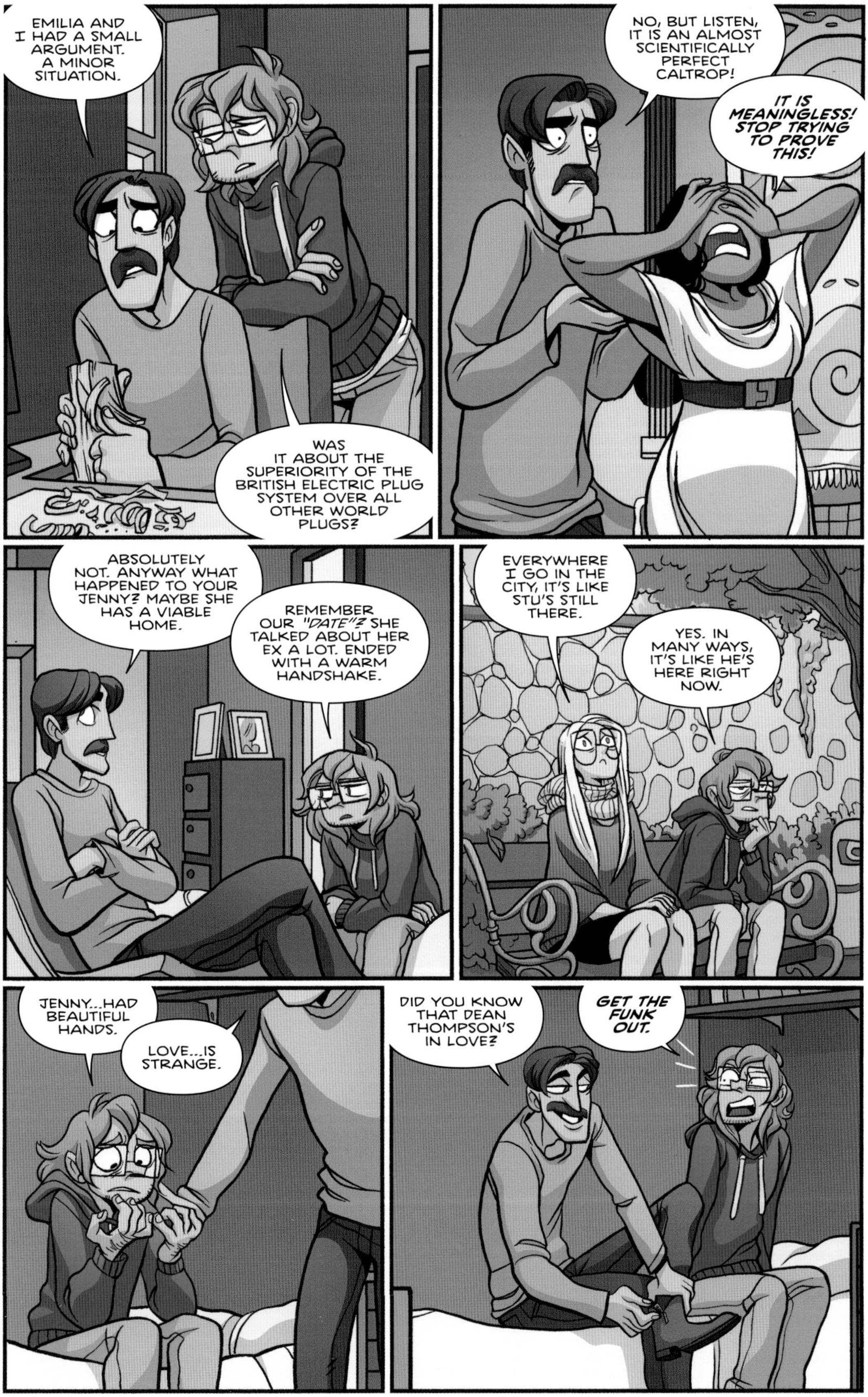
EMILIA AND I HAD A SMALL ARGUMENT. A MINOR SITUATION.
WAS IT ABOUT THE SUPERIORITY OF THE BRITISH ELECTRIC PLUG SYSTEM OVER ALL OTHER WORLD PLUGS?
NO, BUT LISTEN, IT IS AN ALMOST SCIENTIFICALLY PERFECT CALTROP!
IT IS MEANINGLESS! STOP TRYING TO PROVE THIS!
ABSOLUTELY NOT. ANYWAY WHAT HAPPENED TO YOUR JENNY? MAYBE SHE HAS A VIABLE HOME.
REMEMBER OUR "DATE"? SHE TALKED ABOUT HER EX A LOT. ENDED WITH A WARM HANDSHAKE.
EVERYWHERE I GO IN THE CITY, IT'S LIKE STU'S STILL THERE.
YES. IN MANY WAYS, IT'S LIKE HE'S HERE RIGHT NOW.
JENNY...HAD BEAUTIFUL HANDS.
LOVE...IS STRANGE.
DID YOU KNOW THAT DEAN THOMPSON'S IN LOVE?
GET THE FUNK OUT.

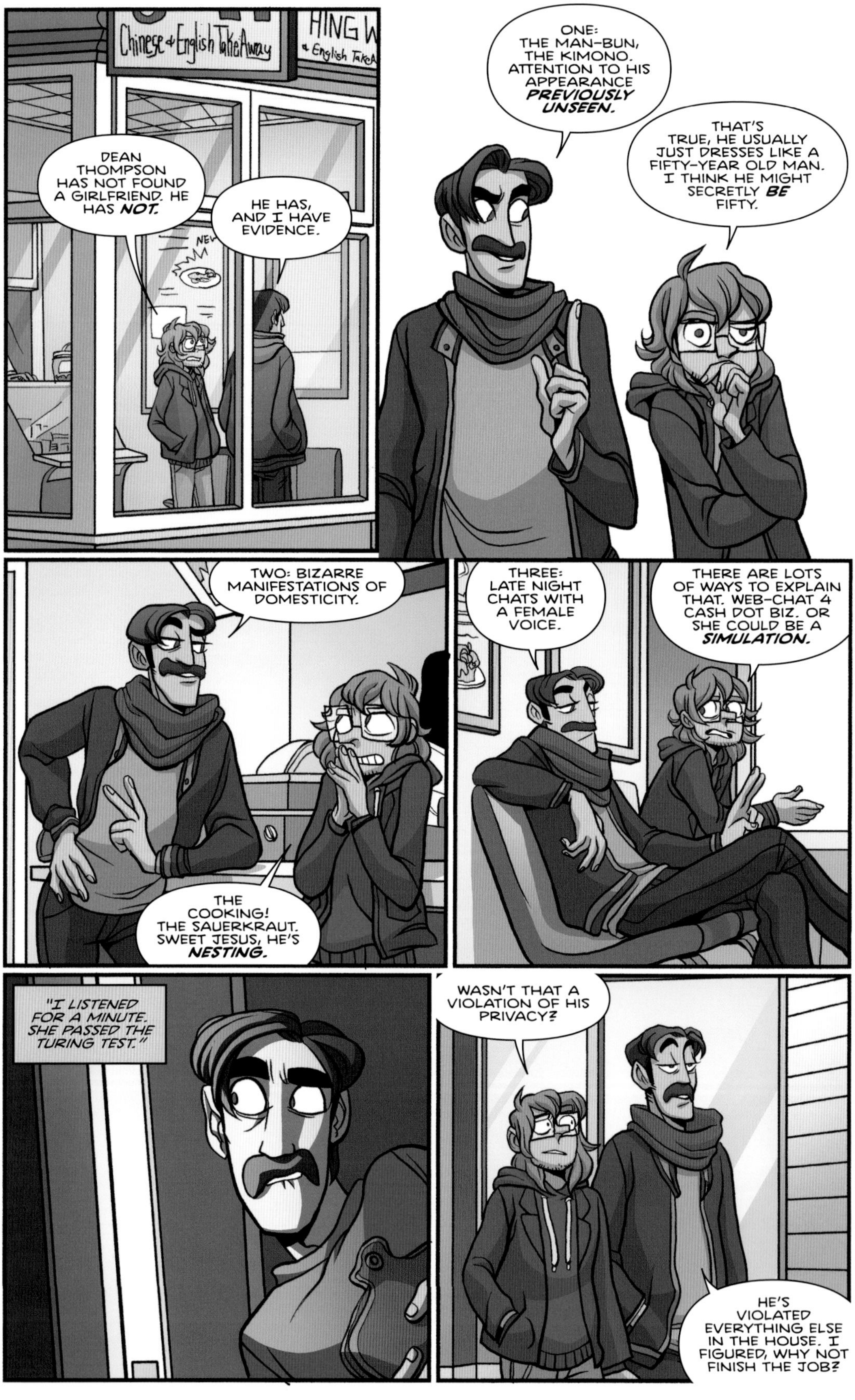
Chinese & English Take Away
HING W
& English Take
DEAN THOMPSON HAS NOT FOUND A GIRLFRIEND. HE HAS NOT.
HE HAS, AND I HAVE EVIDENCE.
ONE: THE MAN-BUN, THE KIMONO. ATTENTION TO HIS APPEARANCE PREVIOUSLY UNSEEN.
THAT'S TRUE, HE USUALLY JUST DRESSES LIKE A FIFTY-YEAR OLD MAN. I THINK HE MIGHT SECRETLY BE FIFTY.
TWO: BIZARRE MANIFESTATIONS OF DOMESTICITY.
THE COOKING! THE SAUERKRAUT. SWEET JESUS, HE'S NESTING.
THREE: LATE NIGHT CHATS WITH A FEMALE VOICE.
THERE ARE LOTS OF WAYS TO EXPLAIN THAT. WEB-CHAT 4 CASH DOT BIZ. OR SHE COULD BE A SIMULATION.
"I LISTENED FOR A MINUTE. SHE PASSED THE TURING TEST."
WASN'T THAT A VIOLATION OF HIS PRIVACY?
HE'S VIOLATED EVERYTHING ELSE IN THE HOUSE. I FIGURED, WHY NOT FINISH THE JOB?

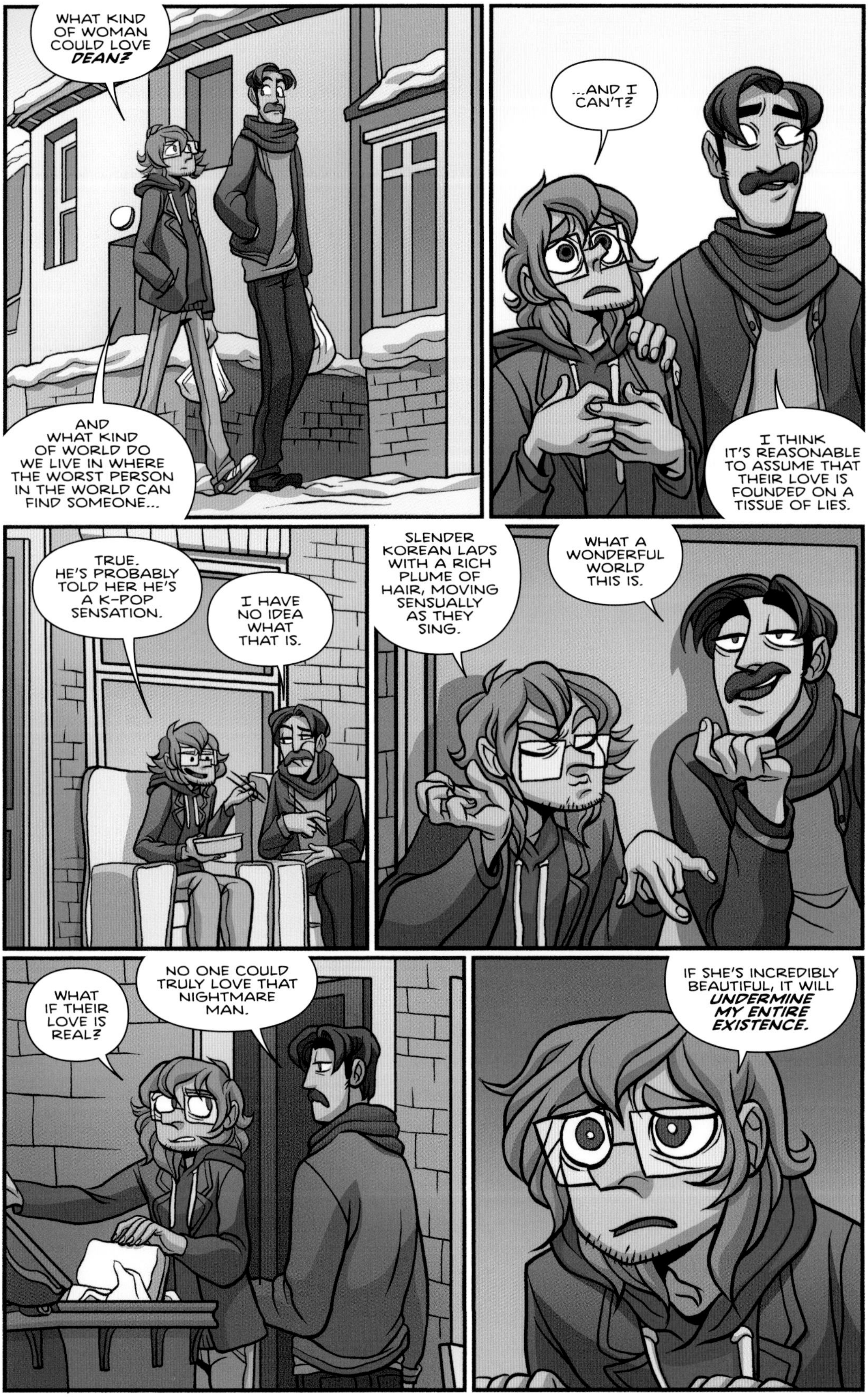
WHAT KIND OF WOMAN COULD LOVE *DEAN?*
AND WHAT KIND OF WORLD DO WE LIVE IN WHERE THE WORST PERSON IN THE WORLD CAN FIND SOMEONE...
...AND I CAN'T?
I THINK IT'S REASONABLE TO ASSUME THAT THEIR LOVE IS FOUNDED ON A TISSUE OF LIES.
TRUE. HE'S PROBABLY TOLD HER HE'S A K-POP SENSATION.
I HAVE NO IDEA WHAT THAT IS.
SLENDER KOREAN LADS WITH A RICH PLUME OF HAIR, MOVING SENSUALLY AS THEY SING.
WHAT A WONDERFUL WORLD THIS IS.
WHAT IF THEIR LOVE IS REAL?
NO ONE COULD TRULY LOVE THAT NIGHTMARE MAN.
IF SHE'S INCREDIBLY BEAUTIFUL, IT WILL *UNDERMINE MY ENTIRE EXISTENCE.*

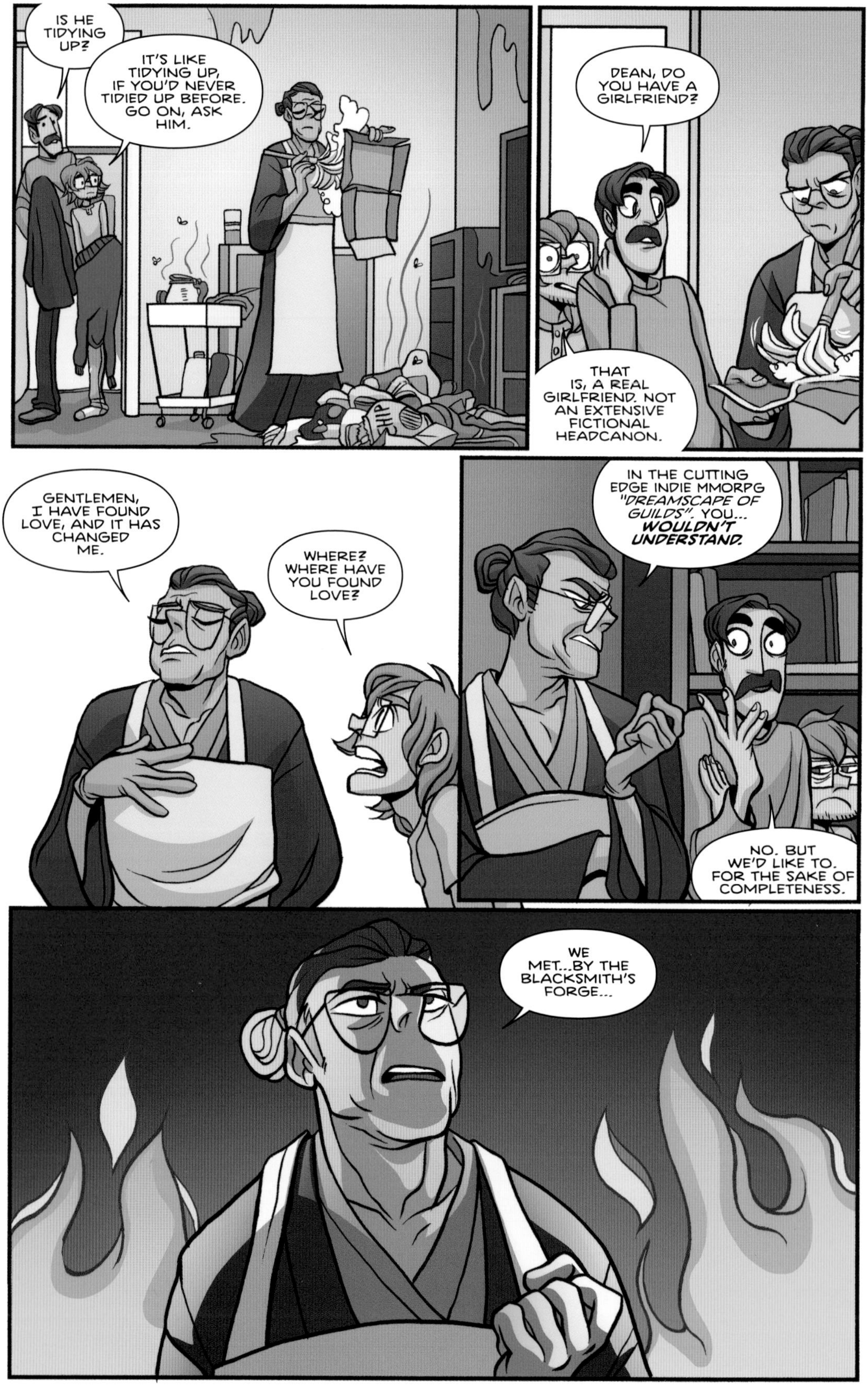
IS HE TIDYING UP?
IT'S LIKE TIDYING UP, IF YOU'D NEVER TIDIED UP BEFORE. GO ON, ASK HIM.
DEAN, DO YOU HAVE A GIRLFRIEND?
THAT IS, A REAL GIRLFRIEND. NOT AN EXTENSIVE FICTIONAL HEADCANON.
GENTLEMEN, I HAVE FOUND LOVE, AND IT HAS CHANGED ME.
WHERE? WHERE HAVE YOU FOUND LOVE?
IN THE CUTTING EDGE INDIE MMORPG *"DREAMSCAPE OF GUILDS"*. YOU... ***WOULDN'T UNDERSTAND.***
NO. BUT WE'D LIKE TO. FOR THE SAKE OF COMPLETENESS.
WE MET...BY THE BLACKSMITH'S FORGE...

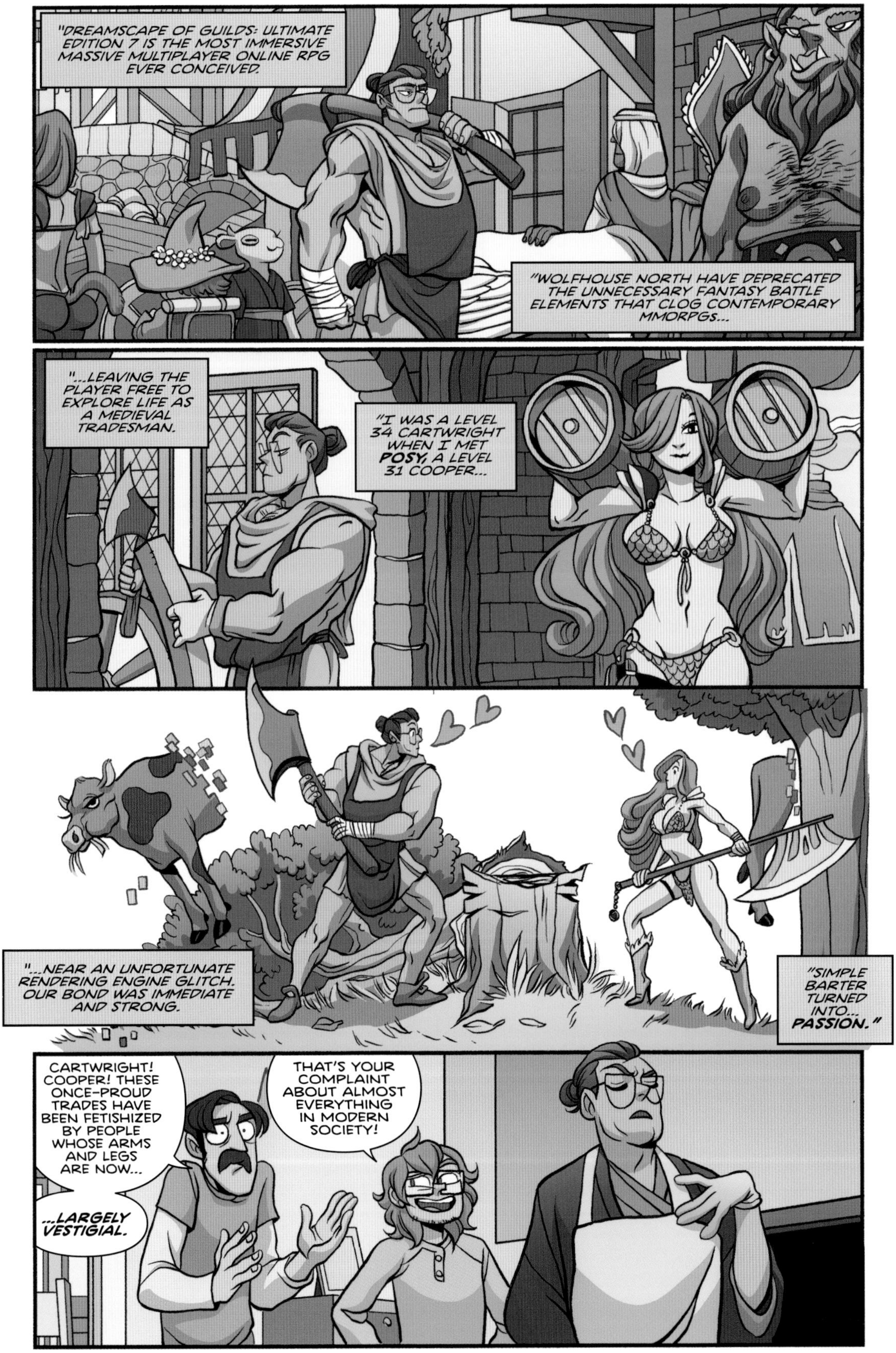
"DREAMSCAPE OF GUILDS: ULTIMATE EDITION 7 IS THE MOST IMMERSIVE MASSIVE MULTIPLAYER ONLINE RPG EVER CONCEIVED.
"WOLFHOUSE NORTH HAVE DEPRECATED THE UNNECESSARY FANTASY BATTLE ELEMENTS THAT CLOG CONTEMPORARY MMORPGS...
"...LEAVING THE PLAYER FREE TO EXPLORE LIFE AS A MEDIEVAL TRADESMAN.
"I WAS A LEVEL 34 CARTWRIGHT WHEN I MET POSY, A LEVEL 31 COOPER...
"...NEAR AN UNFORTUNATE RENDERING ENGINE GLITCH. OUR BOND WAS IMMEDIATE AND STRONG.
"SIMPLE BARTER TURNED INTO... PASSION."
CARTWRIGHT! COOPER! THESE ONCE-PROUD TRADES HAVE BEEN FETISHIZED BY PEOPLE WHOSE ARMS AND LEGS ARE NOW...
...LARGELY VESTIGIAL.
THAT'S YOUR COMPLAINT ABOUT ALMOST EVERYTHING IN MODERN SOCIETY!

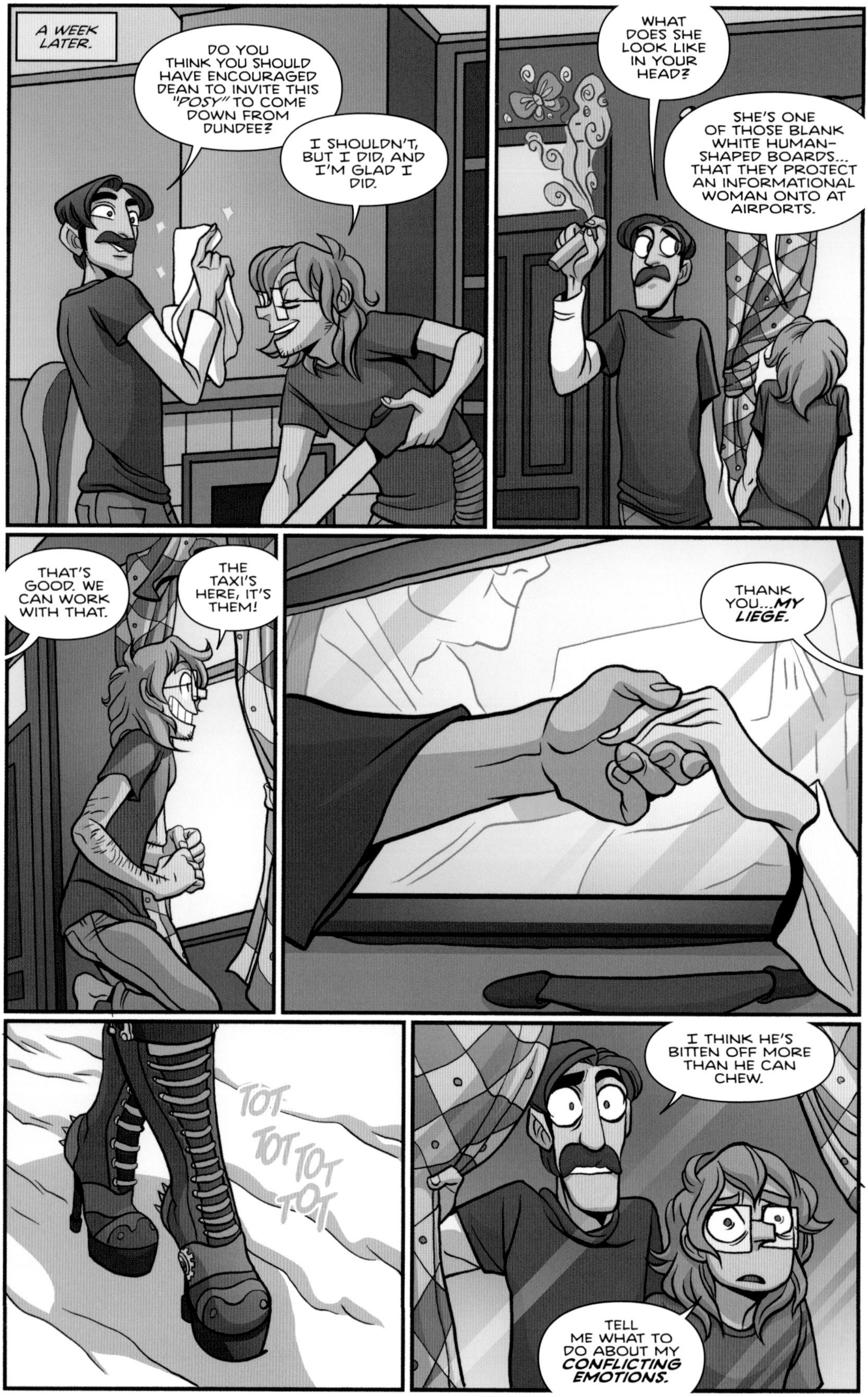
A WEEK LATER.
DO YOU THINK YOU SHOULD HAVE ENCOURAGED DEAN TO INVITE THIS "POSY" TO COME DOWN FROM DUNDEE?
I SHOULDN'T, BUT I DID, AND I'M GLAD I DID.
WHAT DOES SHE LOOK LIKE IN YOUR HEAD?
SHE'S ONE OF THOSE BLANK WHITE HUMAN-SHAPED BOARDS... THAT THEY PROJECT AN INFORMATIONAL WOMAN ONTO AT AIRPORTS.
THAT'S GOOD. WE CAN WORK WITH THAT.
THE TAXI'S HERE, IT'S THEM!
THANK YOU... MY LIEGE.
TOT TOT TOT TOT
I THINK HE'S BITTEN OFF MORE THAN HE CAN CHEW.
TELL ME WHAT TO DO ABOUT MY CONFLICTING EMOTIONS.

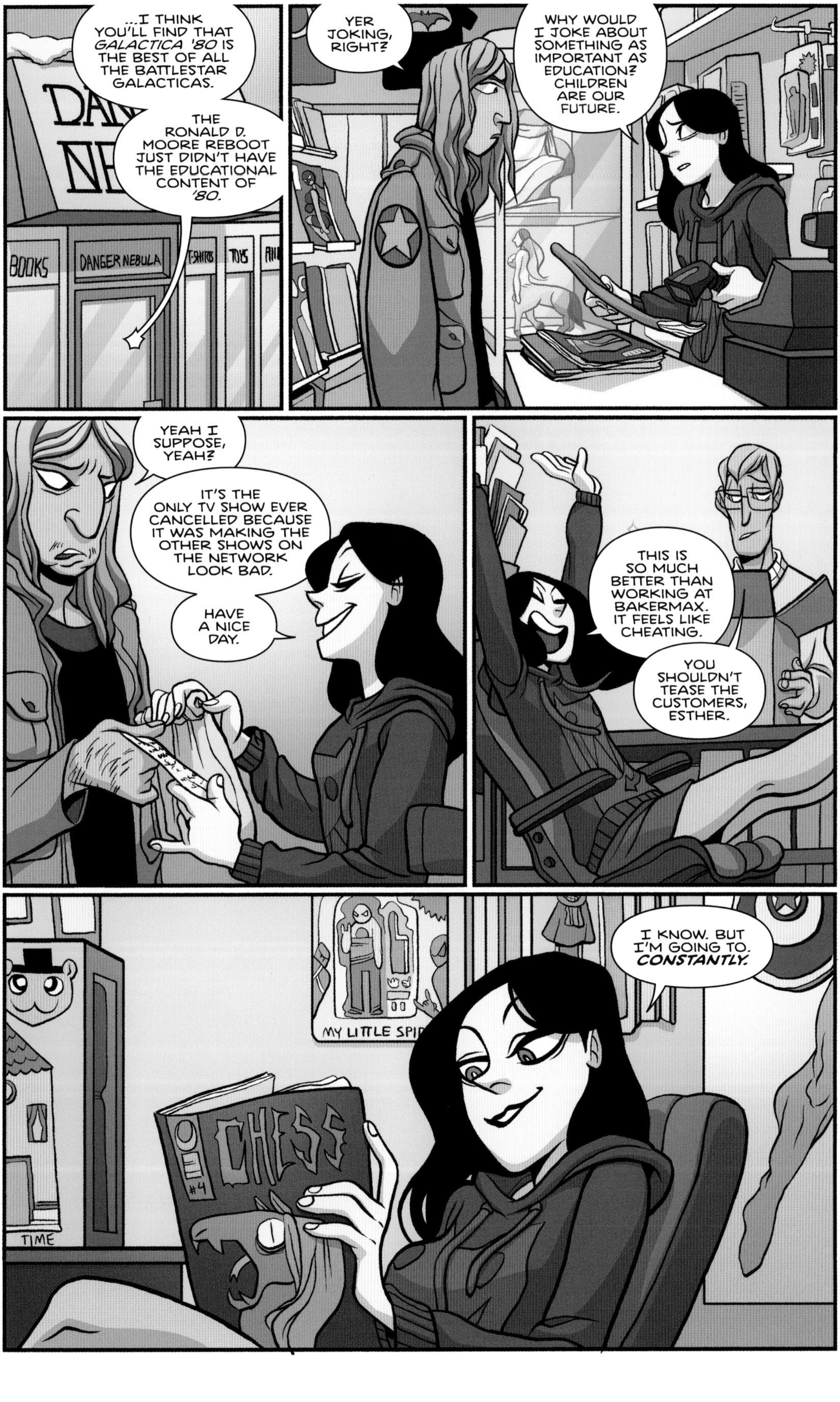

...I THINK YOU'LL FIND THAT *GALACTICA '80* IS THE BEST OF ALL THE BATTLESTAR GALACTICAS.
THE RONALD D. MOORE REBOOT JUST DIDN'T HAVE THE EDUCATIONAL CONTENT OF *'80.*
BOOKS
DANGER NEBULA
T-SHIRTS
TOYS
YER JOKING, RIGHT?
WHY WOULD I JOKE ABOUT SOMETHING AS IMPORTANT AS EDUCATION? CHILDREN ARE OUR FUTURE.
YEAH I SUPPOSE, YEAH?
IT'S THE ONLY TV SHOW EVER CANCELLED BECAUSE IT WAS MAKING THE OTHER SHOWS ON THE NETWORK LOOK BAD.
HAVE A NICE DAY.
THIS IS SO MUCH BETTER THAN WORKING AT BAKERMAX. IT FEELS LIKE CHEATING.
YOU SHOULDN'T TEASE THE CUSTOMERS, ESTHER.
I KNOW. BUT I'M GOING TO. ***CONSTANTLY.***
MY LITTLE SPID
CHESS
#4
TIME

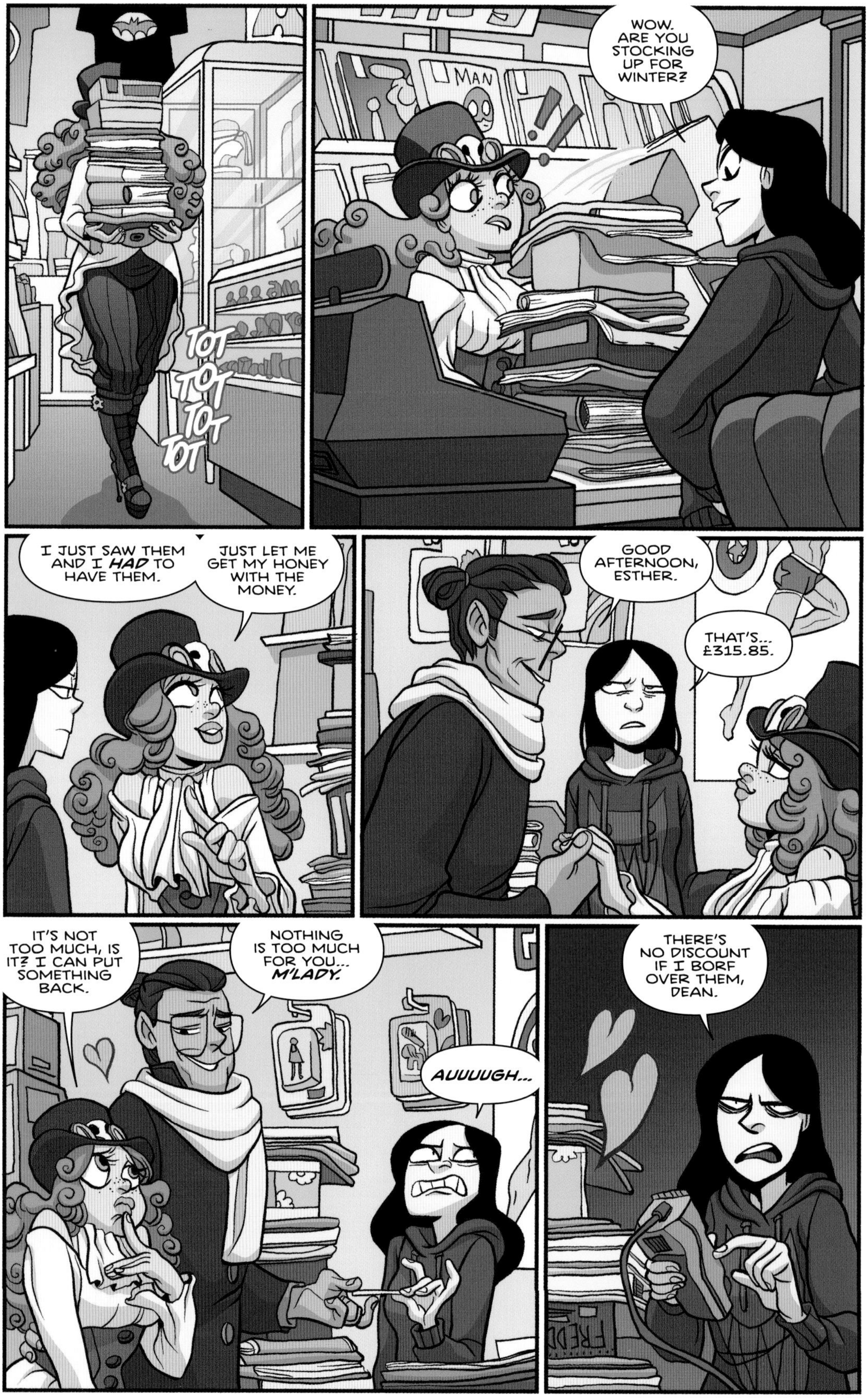
TOT
TOT
TOT
TOT
MAN
WOW. ARE YOU STOCKING UP FOR WINTER?
I JUST SAW THEM AND I *HAD* TO HAVE THEM.
JUST LET ME GET MY HONEY WITH THE MONEY.
GOOD AFTERNOON, ESTHER.
THAT'S... £315.85.
IT'S NOT TOO MUCH, IS IT? I CAN PUT SOMETHING BACK.
NOTHING IS TOO MUCH FOR YOU... *M'LADY.*
AUUUUGH...
THERE'S NO DISCOUNT IF I BORF OVER THEM, DEAN.

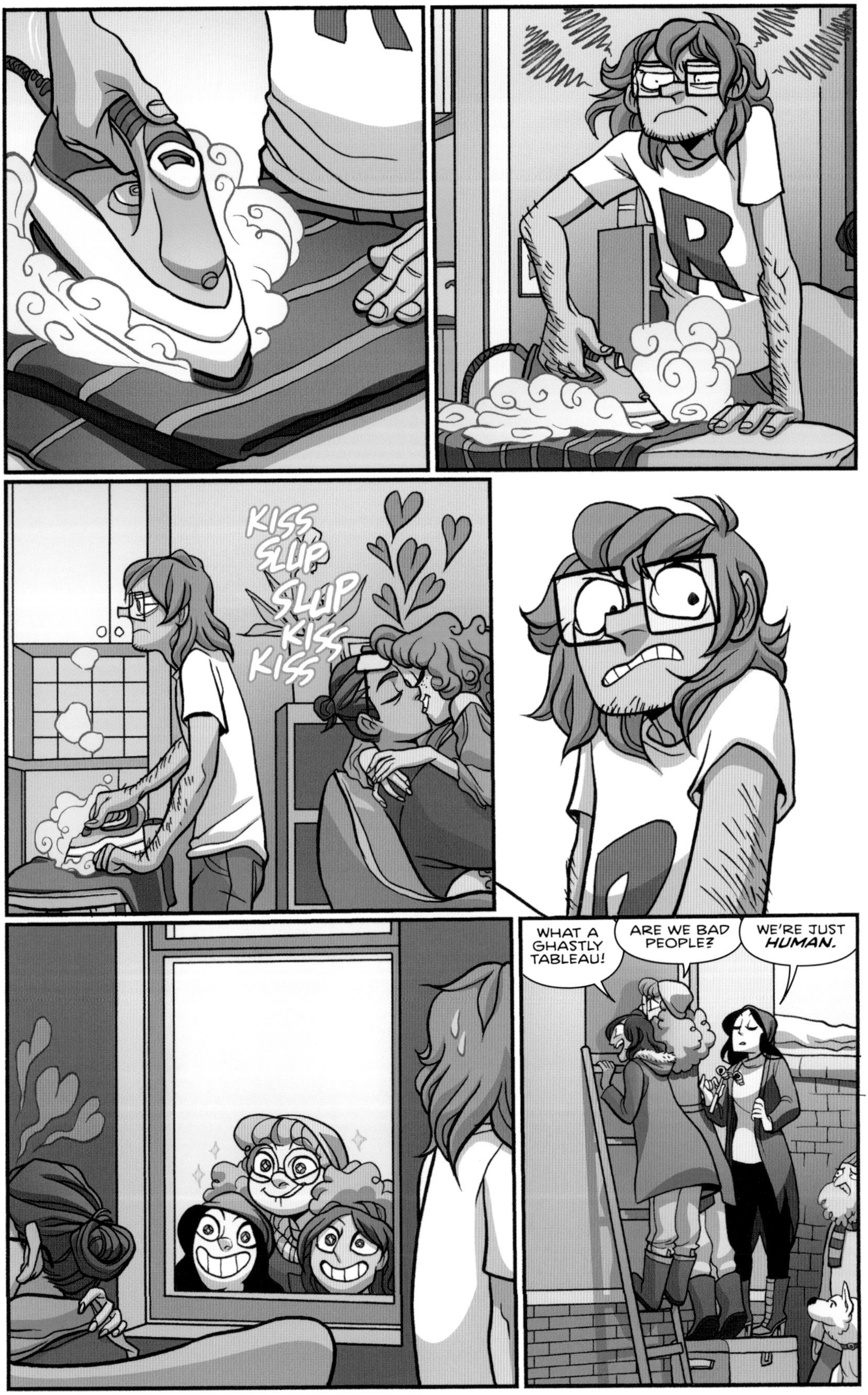
KISS
SLUP
SLUP
KISS
KISS
WHAT A GHASTLY TABLEAU!
ARE WE BAD PEOPLE?
WE'RE JUST *HUMAN.*

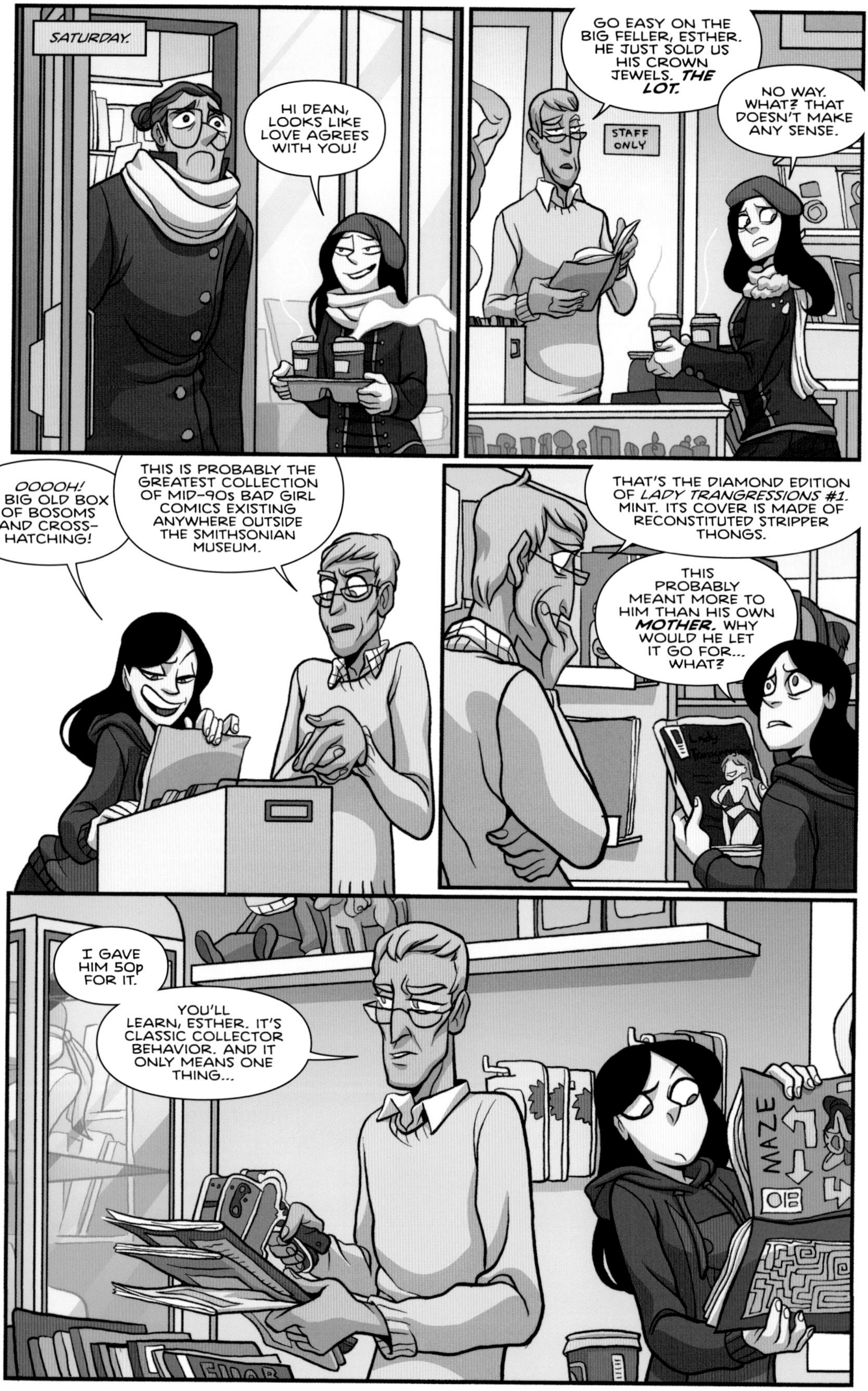
SATURDAY.
HI DEAN, LOOKS LIKE LOVE AGREES WITH YOU!
GO EASY ON THE BIG FELLER, ESTHER. HE JUST SOLD US HIS CROWN JEWELS. ***THE LOT.***
STAFF ONLY
NO WAY. WHAT? THAT DOESN'T MAKE ANY SENSE.
OOOOH! A BIG OLD BOX OF BOSOMS AND CROSS-HATCHING!
THIS IS PROBABLY THE GREATEST COLLECTION OF MID-90s BAD GIRL COMICS EXISTING ANYWHERE OUTSIDE THE SMITHSONIAN MUSEUM.
THAT'S THE DIAMOND EDITION OF *LADY TRANGRESSIONS #1.* MINT. ITS COVER IS MADE OF RECONSTITUTED STRIPPER THONGS.
THIS PROBABLY MEANT MORE TO HIM THAN HIS OWN ***MOTHER.*** WHY WOULD HE LET IT GO FOR... WHAT?
I GAVE HIM 50p FOR IT.
YOU'LL LEARN, ESTHER. IT'S CLASSIC COLLECTOR BEHAVIOR. AND IT ONLY MEANS ONE THING...
MAZE

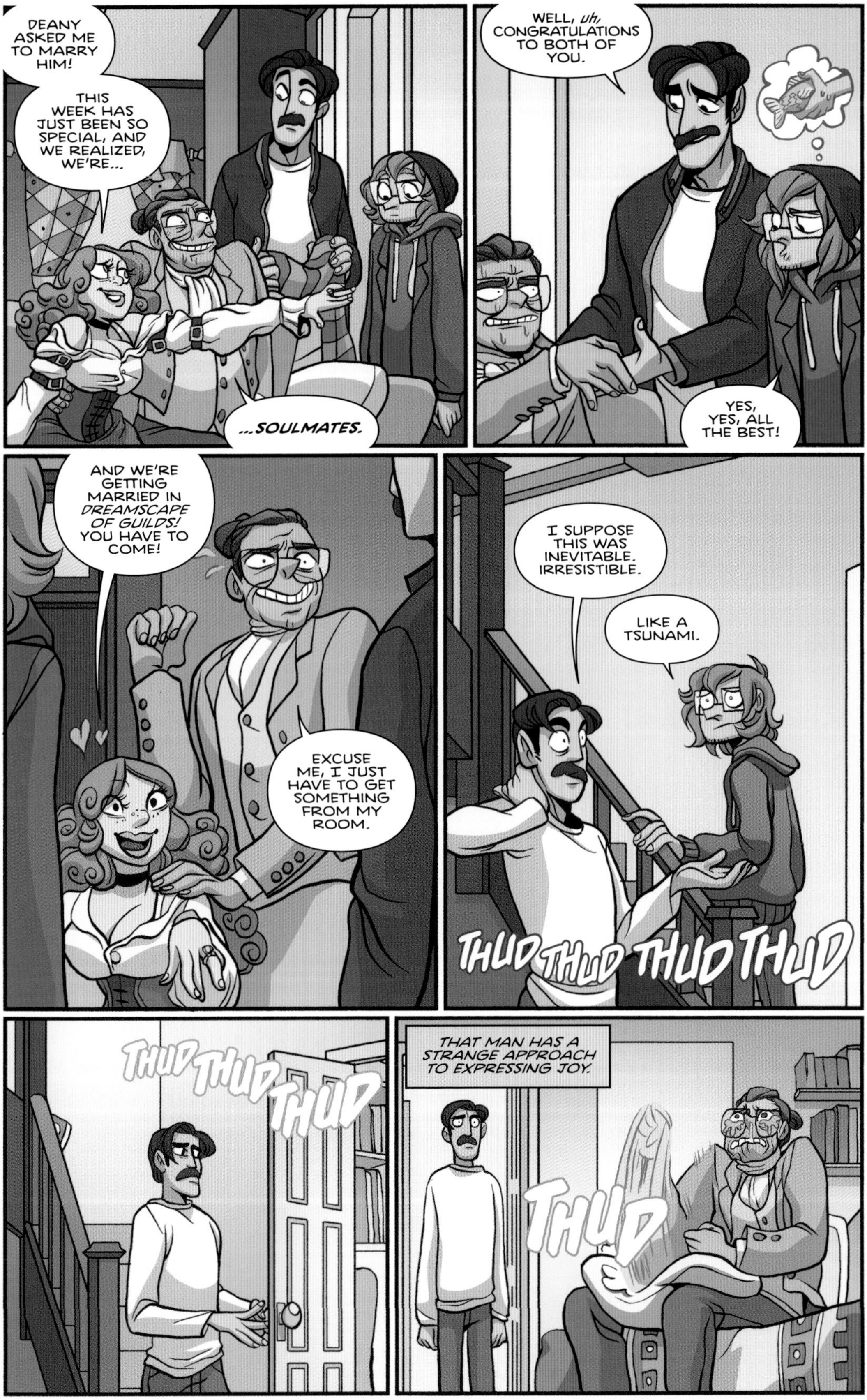
DEANY ASKED ME TO MARRY HIM!
THIS WEEK HAS JUST BEEN SO SPECIAL, AND WE REALIZED, WE'RE...
...SOULMATES.
WELL, *uh,* CONGRATULATIONS TO BOTH OF YOU.
YES, YES, ALL THE BEST!
AND WE'RE GETTING MARRIED IN *DREAMSCAPE OF GUILDS!* YOU HAVE TO COME!
EXCUSE ME, I JUST HAVE TO GET SOMETHING FROM MY ROOM.
I SUPPOSE THIS WAS INEVITABLE. IRRESISTIBLE.
LIKE A TSUNAMI.
THUD THUD THUD THUD
THUD THUD THUD
THAT MAN HAS A STRANGE APPROACH TO EXPRESSING JOY.
THUD

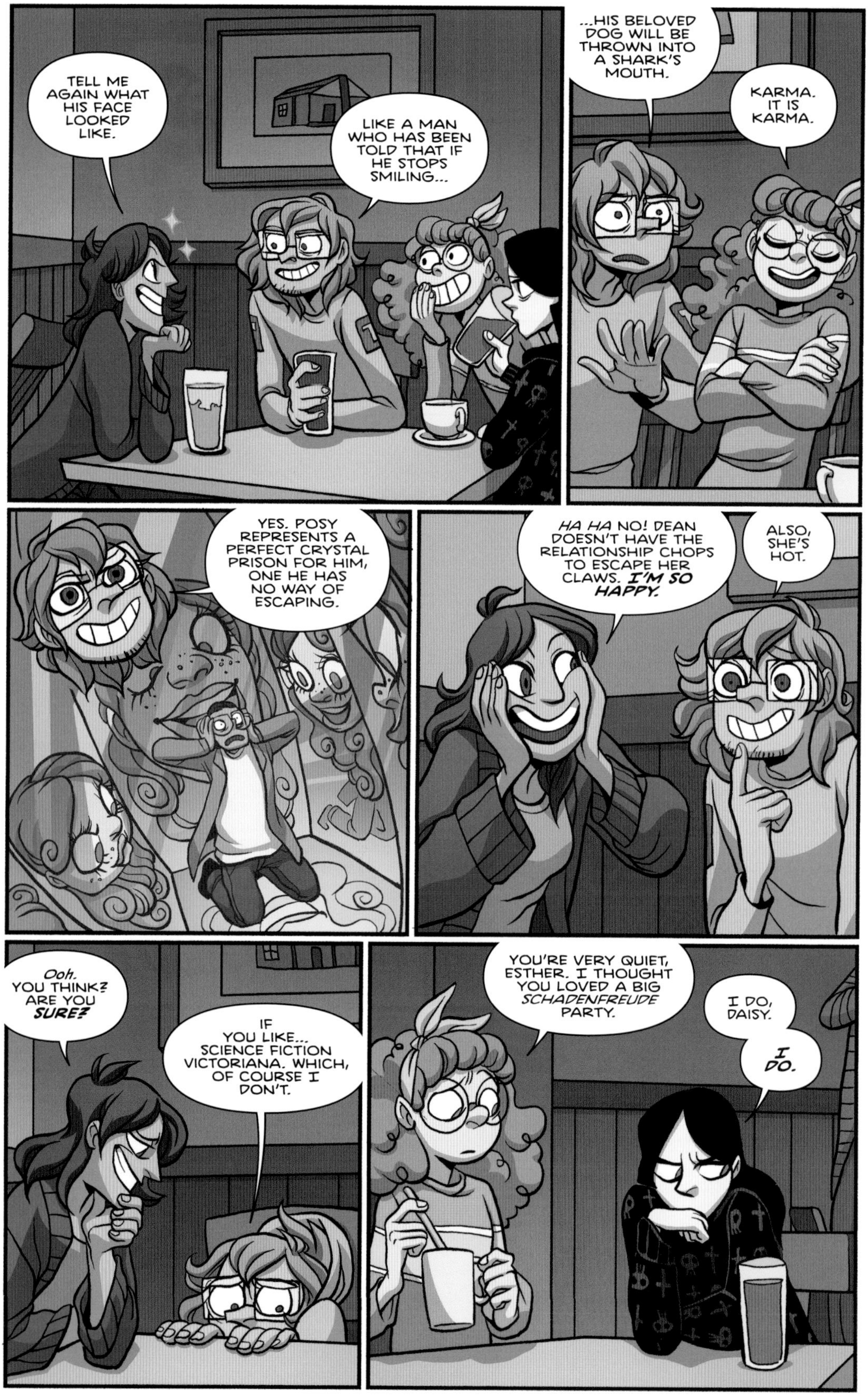
TELL ME AGAIN WHAT HIS FACE LOOKED LIKE.
LIKE A MAN WHO HAS BEEN TOLD THAT IF HE STOPS SMILING...
...HIS BELOVED DOG WILL BE THROWN INTO A SHARK'S MOUTH.
KARMA. IT IS KARMA.
YES. POSY REPRESENTS A PERFECT CRYSTAL PRISON FOR HIM, ONE HE HAS NO WAY OF ESCAPING.
HA HA NO! DEAN DOESN'T HAVE THE RELATIONSHIP CHOPS TO ESCAPE HER CLAWS. I'M SO HAPPY.
ALSO, SHE'S HOT.
Ooh. YOU THINK? ARE YOU SURE?
IF YOU LIKE... SCIENCE FICTION VICTORIANA. WHICH, OF COURSE I DON'T.
YOU'RE VERY QUIET, ESTHER. I THOUGHT YOU LOVED A BIG SCHADENFREUDE PARTY.
I DO, DAISY.
I DO.

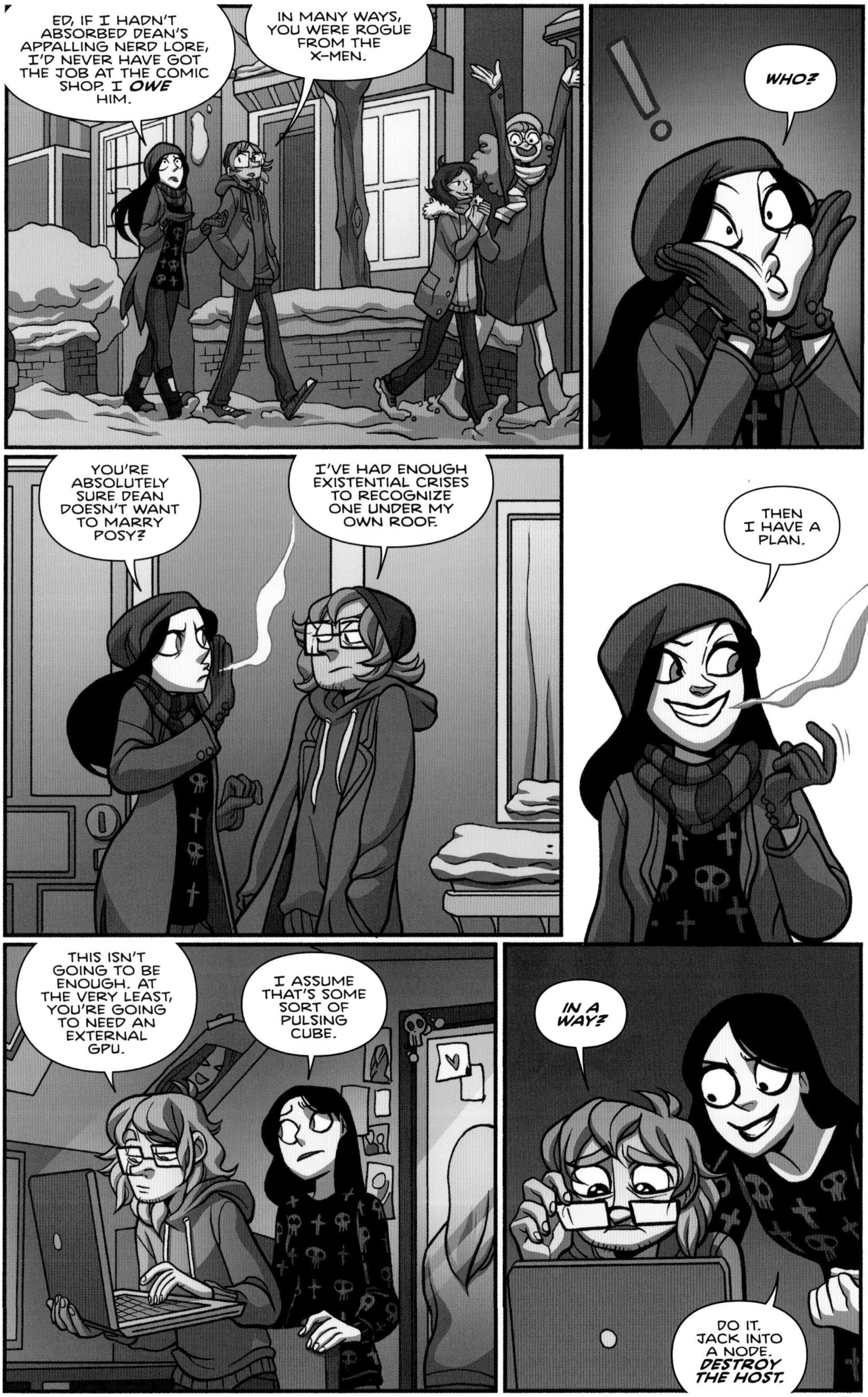
ED, IF I HADN'T ABSORBED DEAN'S APPALLING NERD LORE, I'D NEVER HAVE GOT THE JOB AT THE COMIC SHOP. I *OWE* HIM.
IN MANY WAYS, YOU WERE ROGUE FROM THE X-MEN.
!
WHO?
YOU'RE ABSOLUTELY SURE DEAN DOESN'T WANT TO MARRY POSY?
I'VE HAD ENOUGH EXISTENTIAL CRISES TO RECOGNIZE ONE UNDER MY OWN ROOF.
THEN I HAVE A PLAN.
THIS ISN'T GOING TO BE ENOUGH. AT THE VERY LEAST, YOU'RE GOING TO NEED AN EXTERNAL GPU.
I ASSUME THAT'S SOME SORT OF PULSING CUBE.
IN A WAY?
DO IT. JACK INTO A NODE. ***DESTROY THE HOST.***

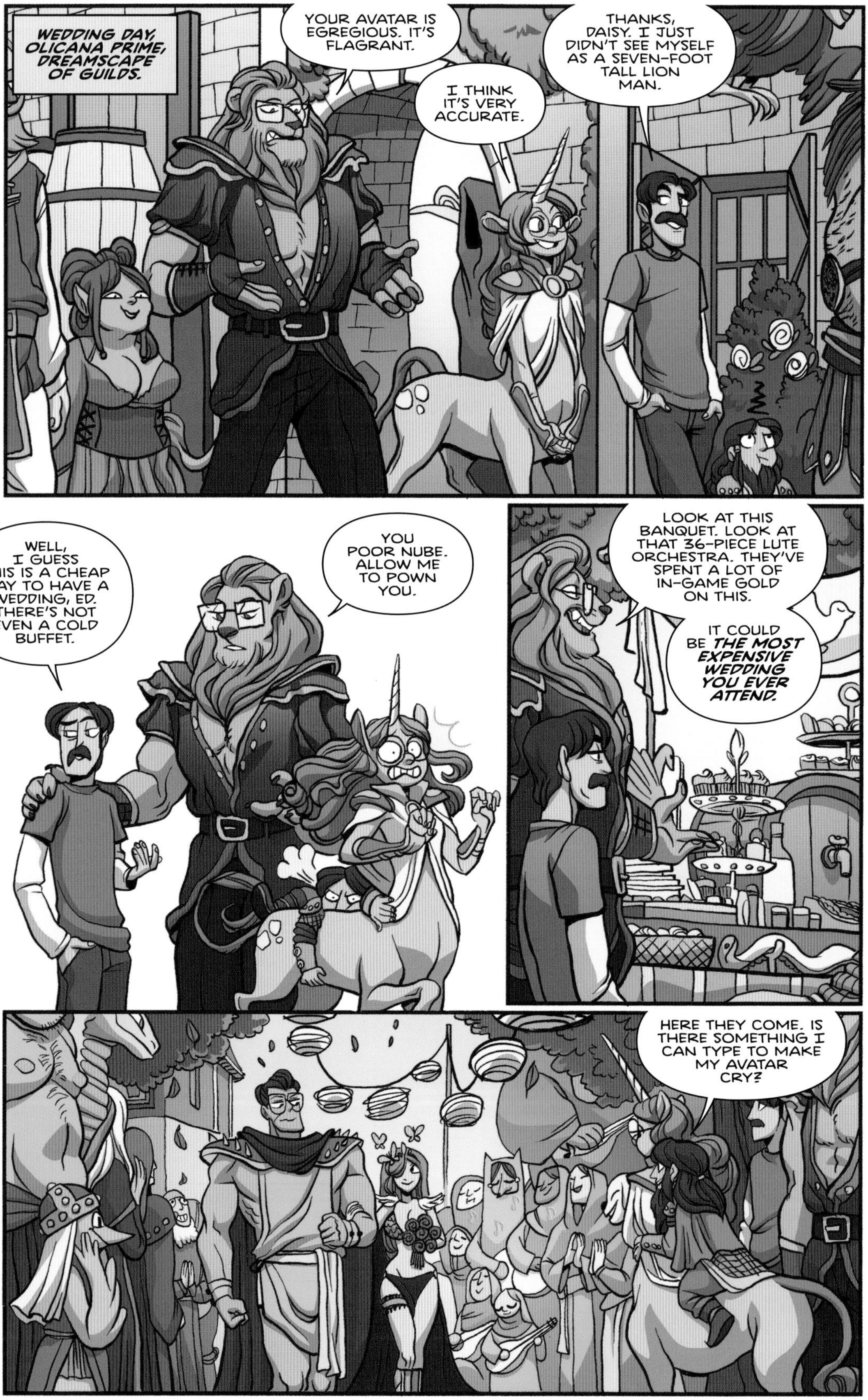
WEDDING DAY, OLICANA PRIME, DREAMSCAPE OF GUILDS.
YOUR AVATAR IS EGREGIOUS. IT'S FLAGRANT.
I THINK IT'S VERY ACCURATE.
THANKS, DAISY. I JUST DIDN'T SEE MYSELF AS A SEVEN-FOOT TALL LION MAN.
WELL, I GUESS THIS IS A CHEAP WAY TO HAVE A WEDDING, ED. THERE'S NOT EVEN A COLD BUFFET.
YOU POOR NUBE. ALLOW ME TO POWN YOU.
LOOK AT THIS BANQUET. LOOK AT THAT 36-PIECE LUTE ORCHESTRA. THEY'VE SPENT A LOT OF IN-GAME GOLD ON THIS.
IT COULD BE THE MOST EXPENSIVE WEDDING YOU EVER ATTEND.
HERE THEY COME. IS THERE SOMETHING I CAN TYPE TO MAKE MY AVATAR CRY?

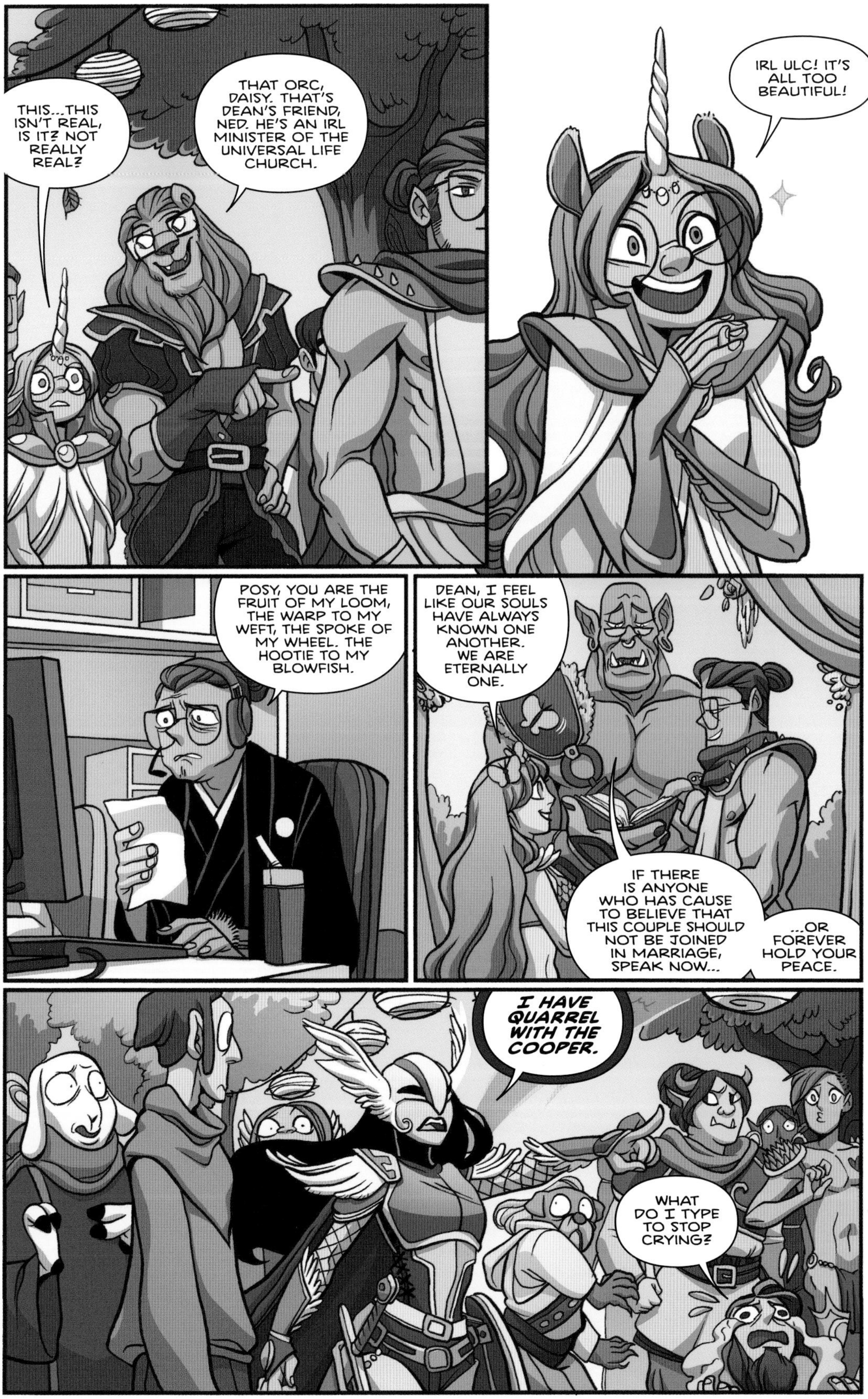
THIS...THIS ISN'T REAL, IS IT? NOT REALLY REAL?
THAT ORC, DAISY. THAT'S DEAN'S FRIEND, NED. HE'S AN IRL MINISTER OF THE UNIVERSAL LIFE CHURCH.
IRL ULC! IT'S ALL TOO BEAUTIFUL!
POSY, YOU ARE THE FRUIT OF MY LOOM, THE WARP TO MY WEFT, THE SPOKE OF MY WHEEL. THE HOOTIE TO MY BLOWFISH.
DEAN, I FEEL LIKE OUR SOULS HAVE ALWAYS KNOWN ONE ANOTHER. WE ARE ETERNALLY ONE.
IF THERE IS ANYONE WHO HAS CAUSE TO BELIEVE THAT THIS COUPLE SHOULD NOT BE JOINED IN MARRIAGE, SPEAK NOW...
...OR FOREVER HOLD YOUR PEACE.
I HAVE QUARREL WITH THE COOPER.
WHAT DO I TYPE TO STOP CRYING?

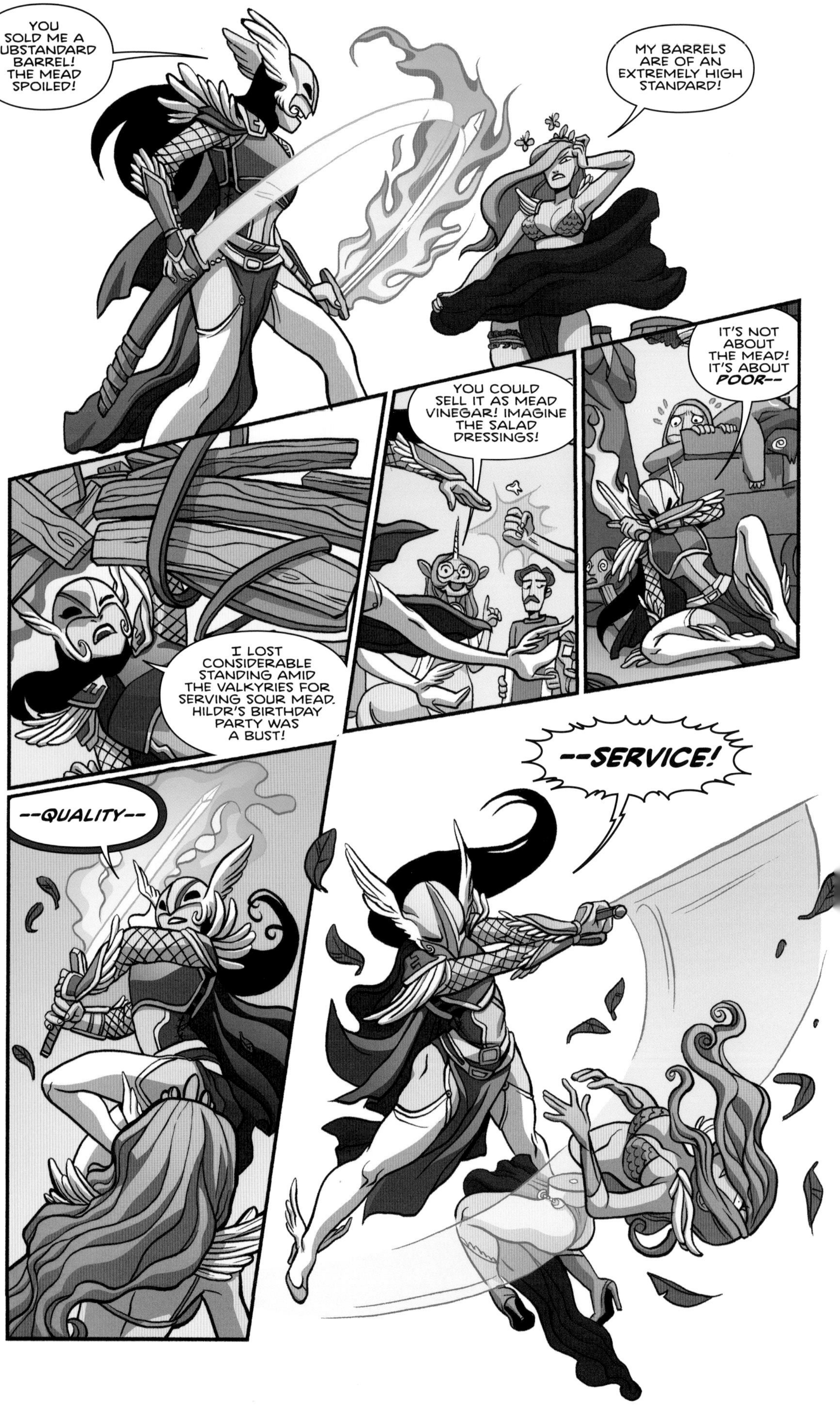
YOU SOLD ME A SUBSTANDARD BARREL! THE MEAD SPOILED!
MY BARRELS ARE OF AN EXTREMELY HIGH STANDARD!
I LOST CONSIDERABLE STANDING AMID THE VALKYRIES FOR SERVING SOUR MEAD. HILDR'S BIRTHDAY PARTY WAS A BUST!
YOU COULD SELL IT AS MEAD VINEGAR! IMAGINE THE SALAD DRESSINGS!
IT'S NOT ABOUT THE MEAD! IT'S ABOUT *POOR--*
--QUALITY--
--SERVICE!

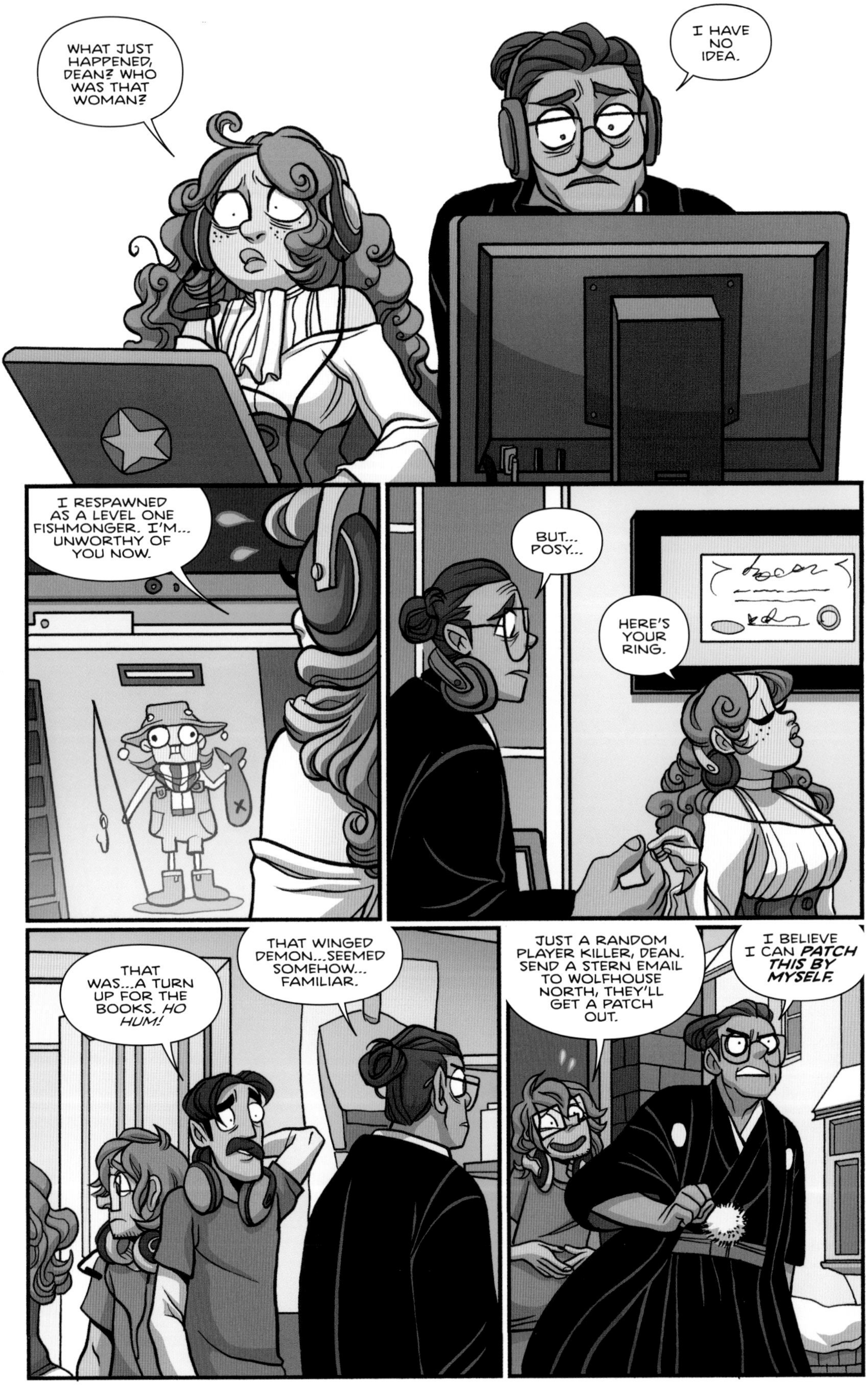
WHAT JUST HAPPENED, DEAN? WHO WAS THAT WOMAN?
I HAVE NO IDEA.
I RESPAWNED AS A LEVEL ONE FISHMONGER. I'M... UNWORTHY OF YOU NOW.
BUT... POSY...
HERE'S YOUR RING.
THAT WAS...A TURN UP FOR THE BOOKS. *HO HUM!*
THAT WINGED DEMON...SEEMED SOMEHOW... FAMILIAR.
JUST A RANDOM PLAYER KILLER, DEAN. SEND A STERN EMAIL TO WOLFHOUSE NORTH, THEY'LL GET A PATCH OUT.
I BELIEVE I CAN ***PATCH THIS BY MYSELF.***

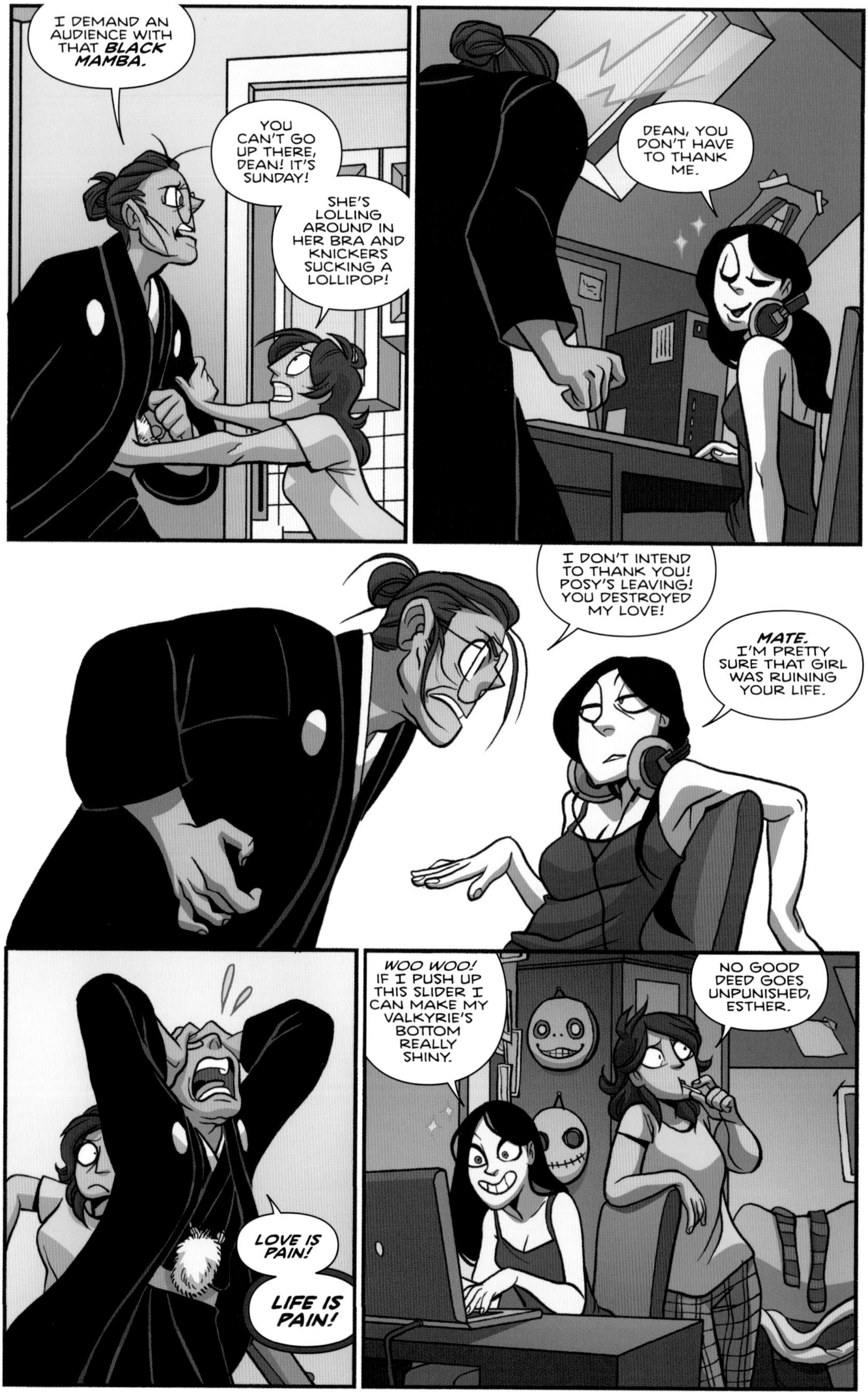
I DEMAND AN AUDIENCE WITH THAT BLACK MAMBA.
YOU CAN'T GO UP THERE, DEAN! IT'S SUNDAY!
SHE'S LOLLING AROUND IN HER BRA AND KNICKERS SUCKING A LOLLIPOP!
DEAN, YOU DON'T HAVE TO THANK ME.
I DON'T INTEND TO THANK YOU! POSY'S LEAVING! YOU DESTROYED MY LOVE!
MATE. I'M PRETTY SURE THAT GIRL WAS RUINING YOUR LIFE.
LOVE IS PAIN!
LIFE IS PAIN!
WOO WOO! IF I PUSH UP THIS SLIDER I CAN MAKE MY VALKYRIE'S BOTTOM REALLY SHINY.
NO GOOD DEED GOES UNPUNISHED, ESTHER.

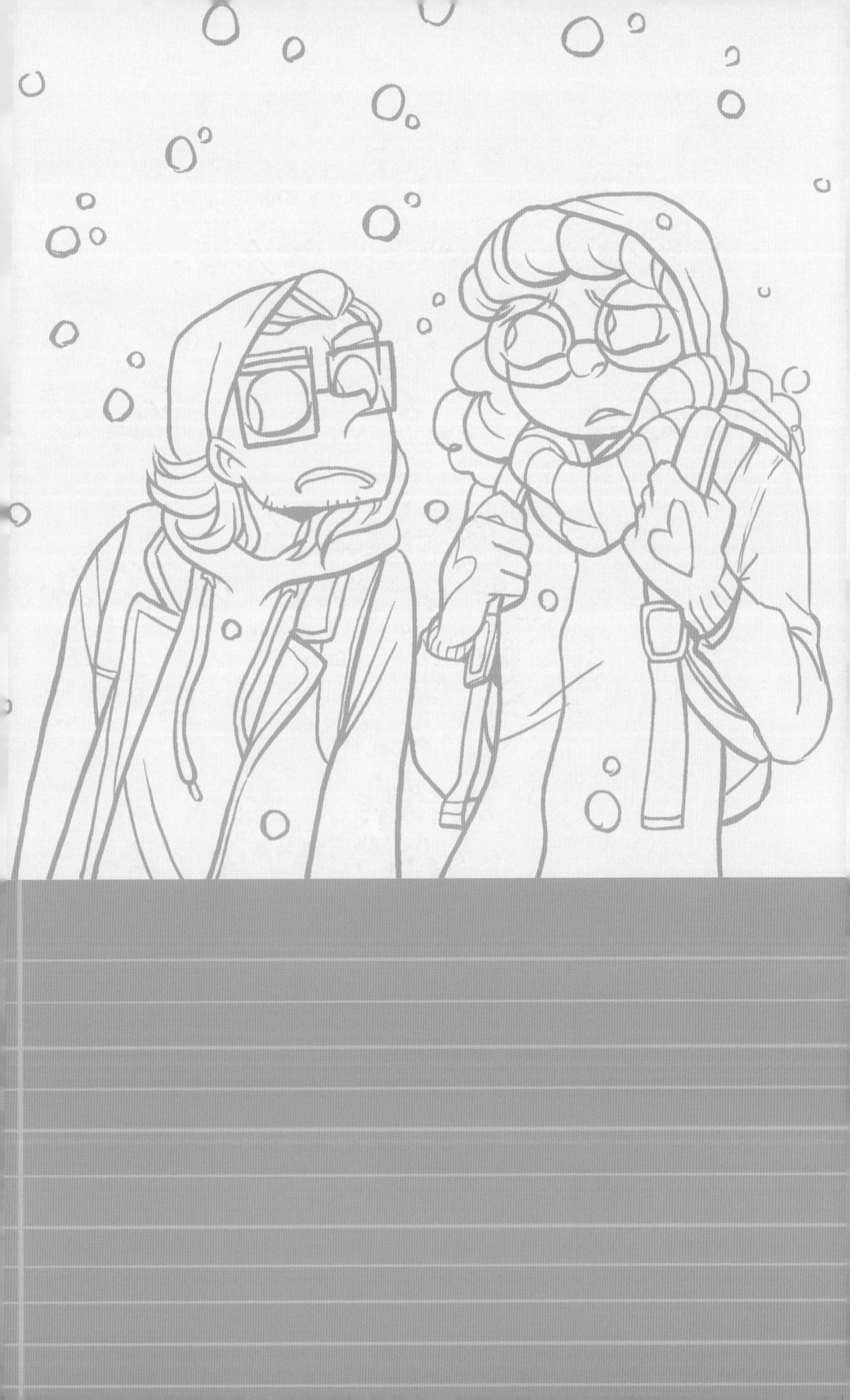

CHAPTER TWENTY-SEVEN

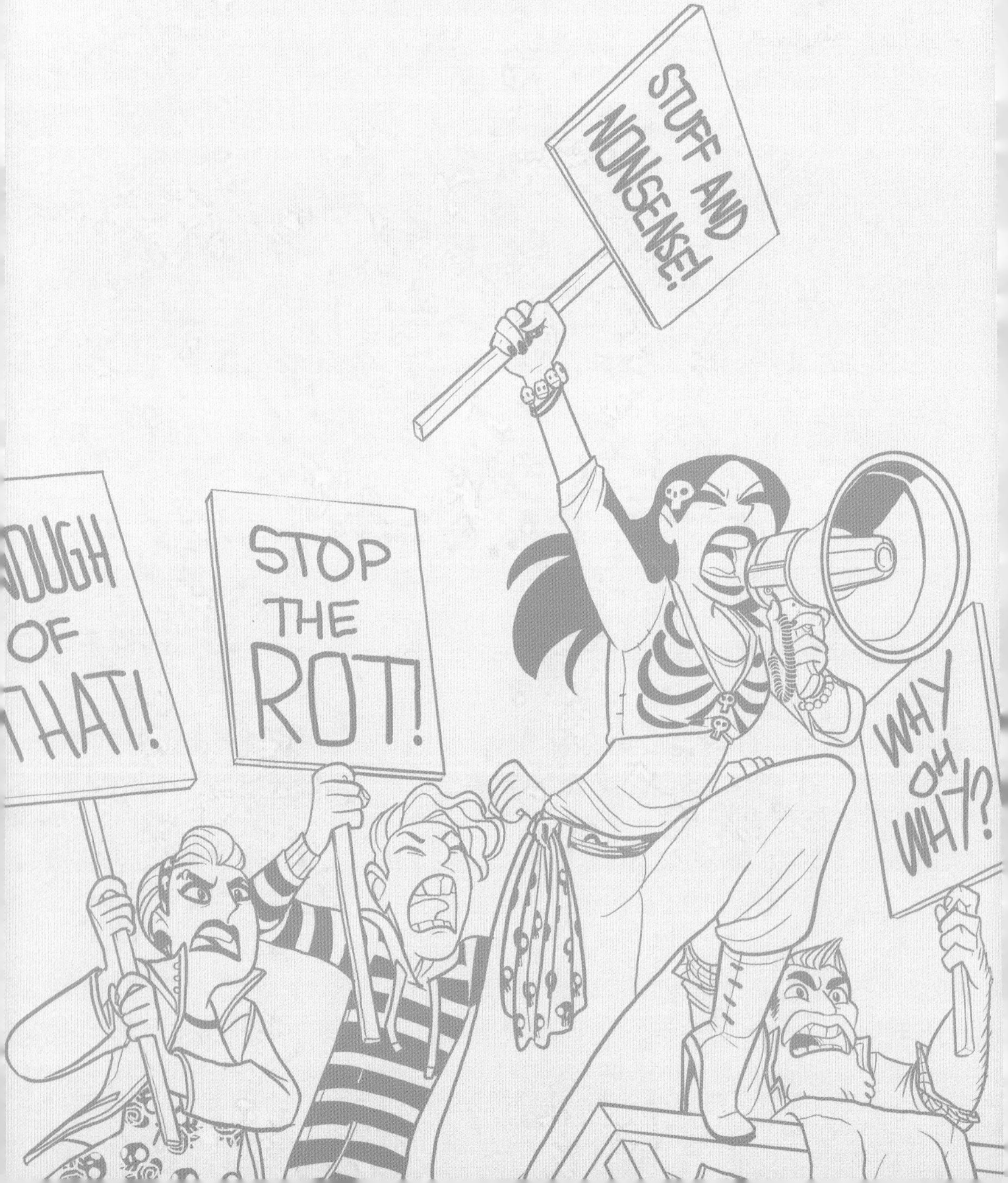
STUFF AND NONSENSE!
STOP THE ROT!
WHY OH WHY?!

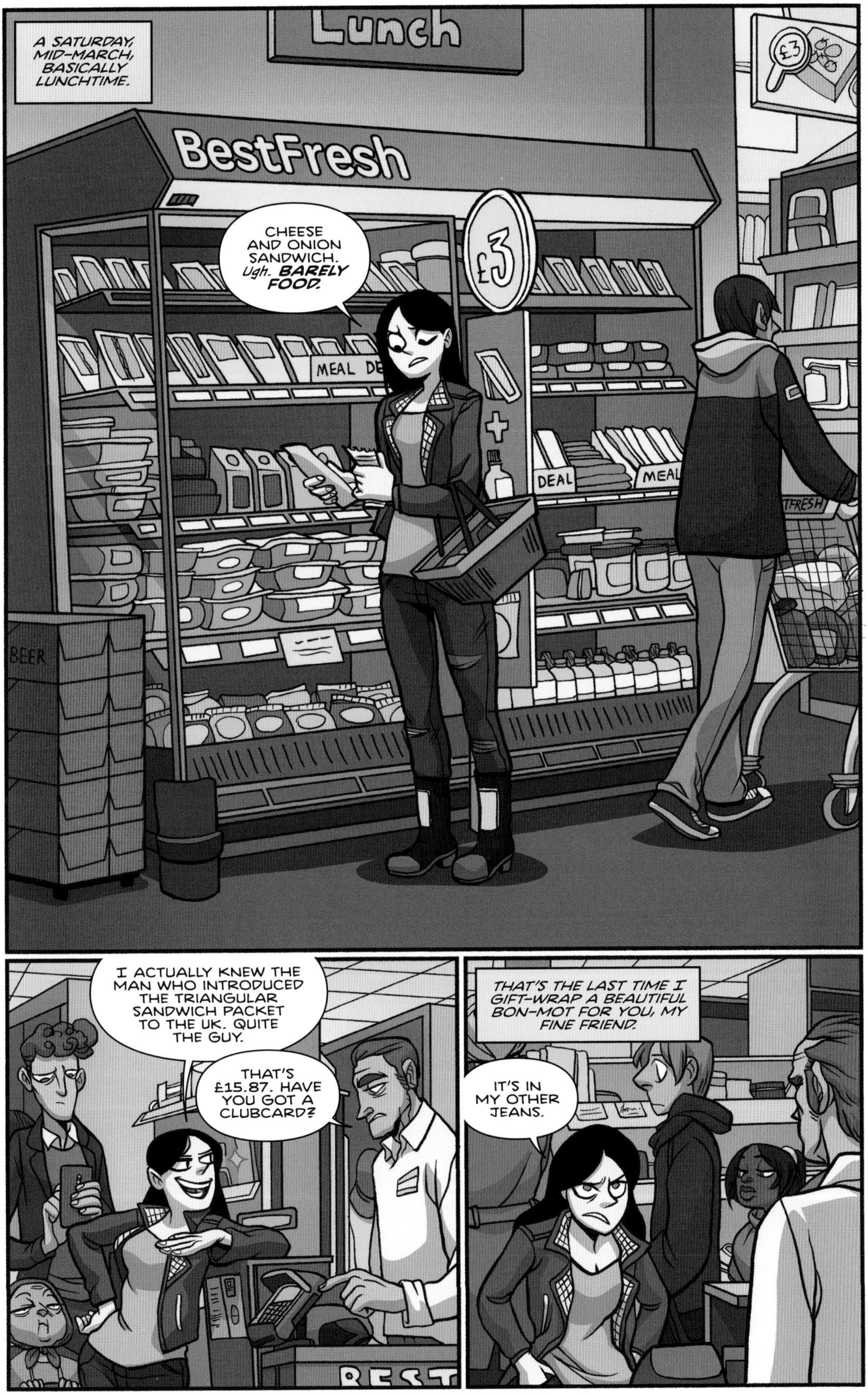
Lunch
A SATURDAY, MID-MARCH, BASICALLY LUNCHTIME.
BestFresh
£3
CHEESE AND ONION SANDWICH. *Ugh.* ***BARELY FOOD.***
MEAL DE
DEAL
MEAL
BEER
TFRESH
I ACTUALLY KNEW THE MAN WHO INTRODUCED THE TRIANGULAR SANDWICH PACKET TO THE UK. QUITE THE GUY.
THAT'S £15.87. HAVE YOU GOT A CLUBCARD?
BEST
THAT'S THE LAST TIME I GIFT-WRAP A BEAUTIFUL BON-MOT FOR YOU, MY FINE FRIEND.
IT'S IN MY OTHER JEANS.

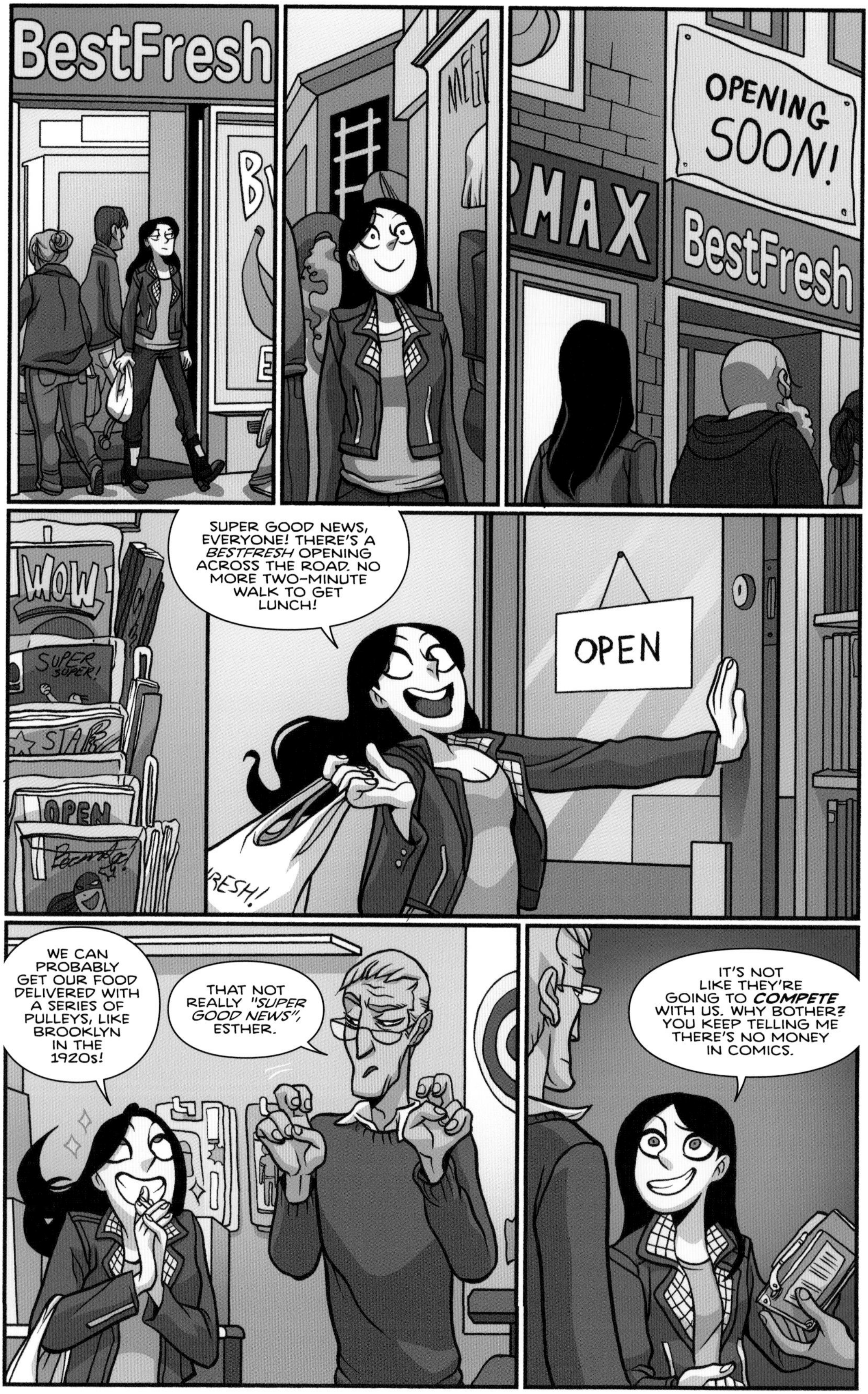
BestFresh
OPENING SOON!
BestFresh
SUPER GOOD NEWS, EVERYONE! THERE'S A *BESTFRESH* OPENING ACROSS THE ROAD. NO MORE TWO-MINUTE WALK TO GET LUNCH!
OPEN
WE CAN PROBABLY GET OUR FOOD DELIVERED WITH A SERIES OF PULLEYS, LIKE BROOKLYN IN THE 1920s!
THAT NOT REALLY *"SUPER GOOD NEWS"*, ESTHER.
IT'S NOT LIKE THEY'RE GOING TO ***COMPETE*** WITH US. WHY BOTHER? YOU KEEP TELLING ME THERE'S NO MONEY IN COMICS.

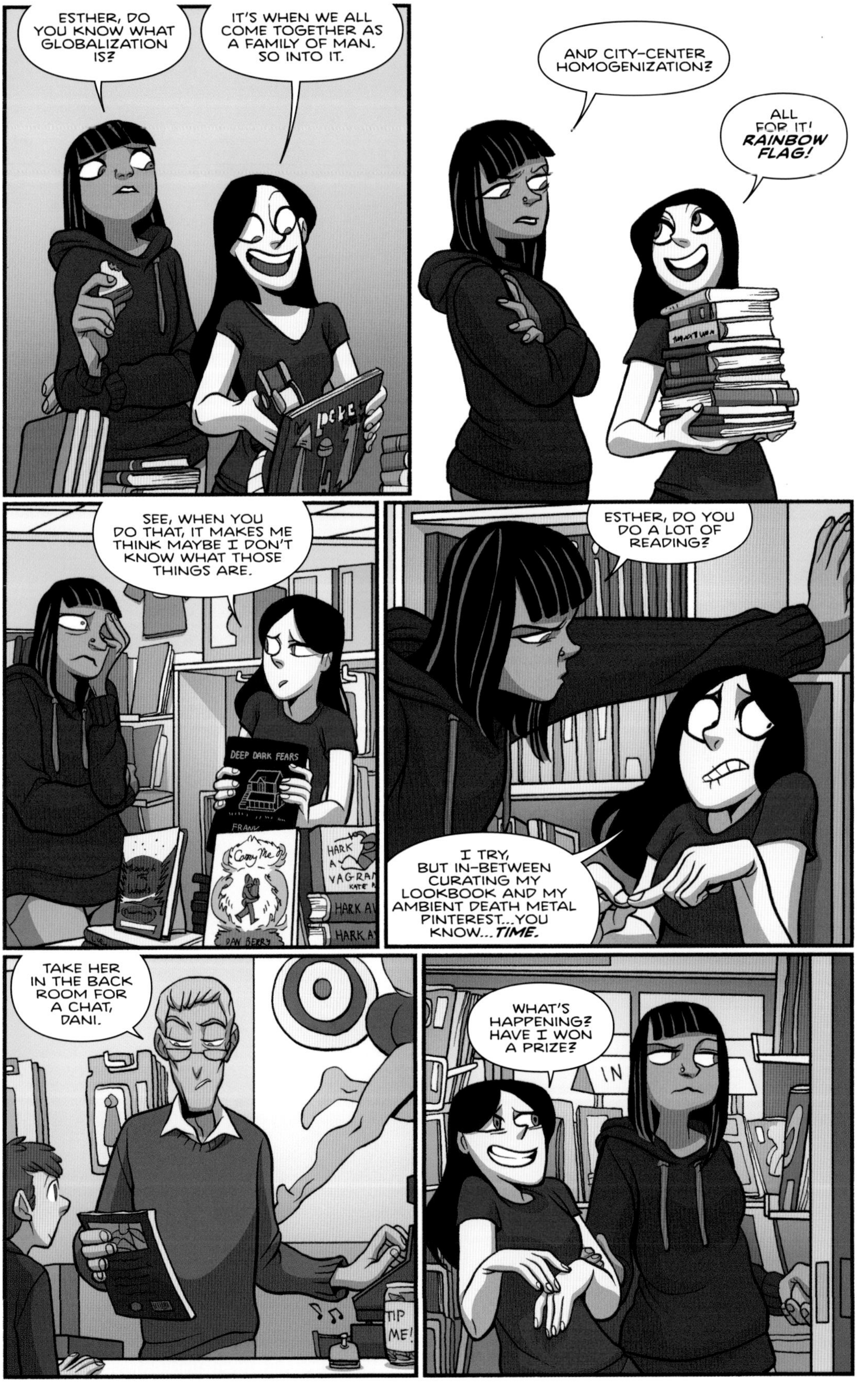
ESTHER, DO YOU KNOW WHAT GLOBALIZATION IS?
IT'S WHEN WE ALL COME TOGETHER AS A FAMILY OF MAN. SO INTO IT.
AND CITY-CENTER HOMOGENIZATION?
ALL FOR IT! ***RAINBOW FLAG!***
SEE, WHEN YOU DO THAT, IT MAKES ME THINK MAYBE I DON'T KNOW WHAT THOSE THINGS ARE.
DEEP DARK FEARS
HARK A VAGRANT
DAN BERRY
ESTHER, DO YOU DO A LOT OF READING?
I TRY, BUT IN-BETWEEN CURATING MY LOOKBOOK AND MY AMBIENT DEATH METAL PINTEREST... YOU KNOW... ***TIME.***
TAKE HER IN THE BACK ROOM FOR A CHAT, DANI.
TIP ME!
WHAT'S HAPPENING? HAVE I WON A PRIZE?
IN

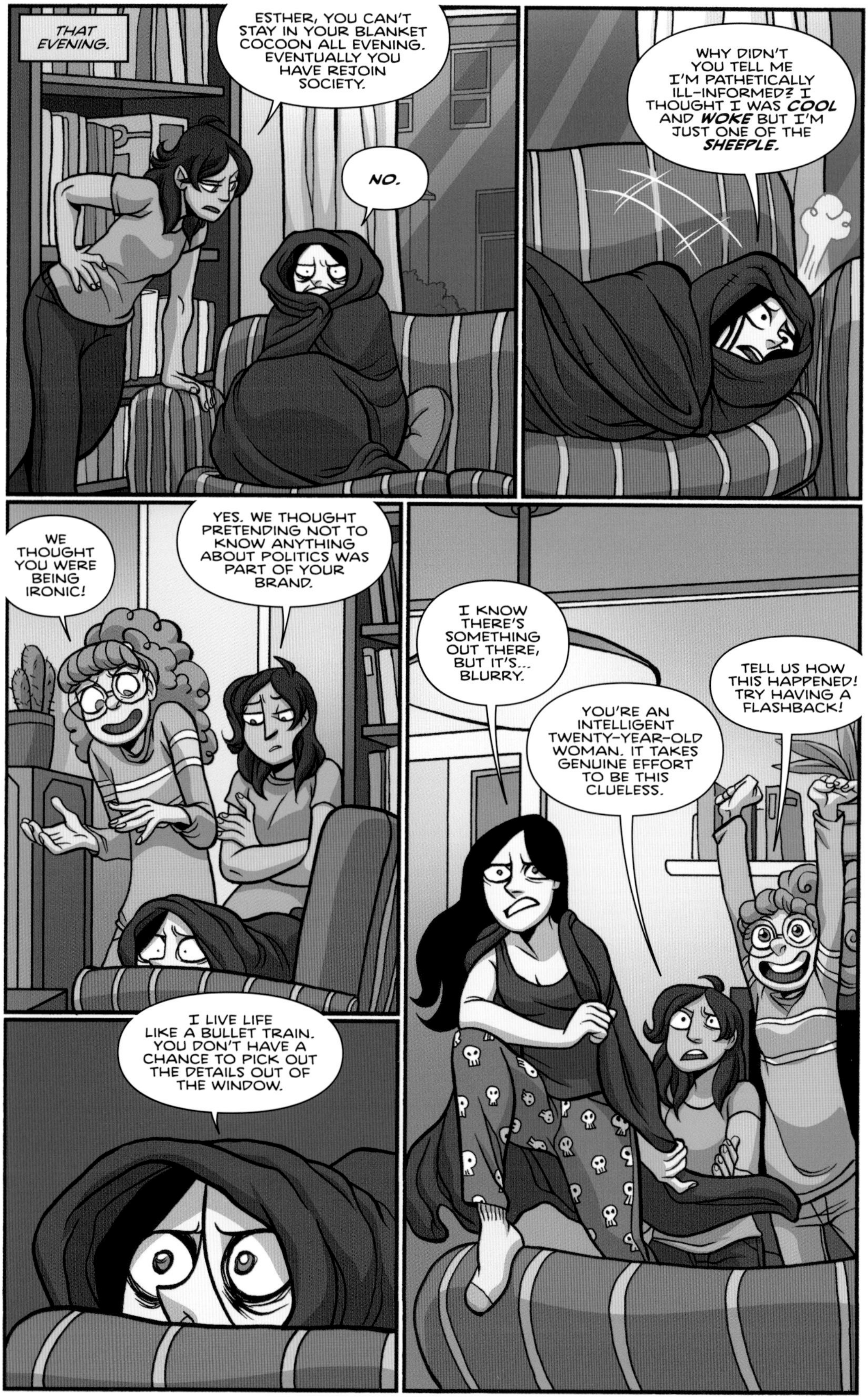
THAT EVENING.
ESTHER, YOU CAN'T STAY IN YOUR BLANKET COCOON ALL EVENING. EVENTUALLY YOU HAVE REJOIN SOCIETY.
NO.
WHY DIDN'T YOU TELL ME I'M PATHETICALLY ILL-INFORMED? I THOUGHT I WAS COOL AND WOKE BUT I'M JUST ONE OF THE SHEEPLE.
WE THOUGHT YOU WERE BEING IRONIC!
YES. WE THOUGHT PRETENDING NOT TO KNOW ANYTHING ABOUT POLITICS WAS PART OF YOUR BRAND.
I LIVE LIFE LIKE A BULLET TRAIN. YOU DON'T HAVE A CHANCE TO PICK OUT THE DETAILS OUT OF THE WINDOW.
I KNOW THERE'S SOMETHING OUT THERE, BUT IT'S... BLURRY.
YOU'RE AN INTELLIGENT TWENTY-YEAR-OLD WOMAN. IT TAKES GENUINE EFFORT TO BE THIS CLUELESS.
TELL US HOW THIS HAPPENED! TRY HAVING A FLASHBACK!

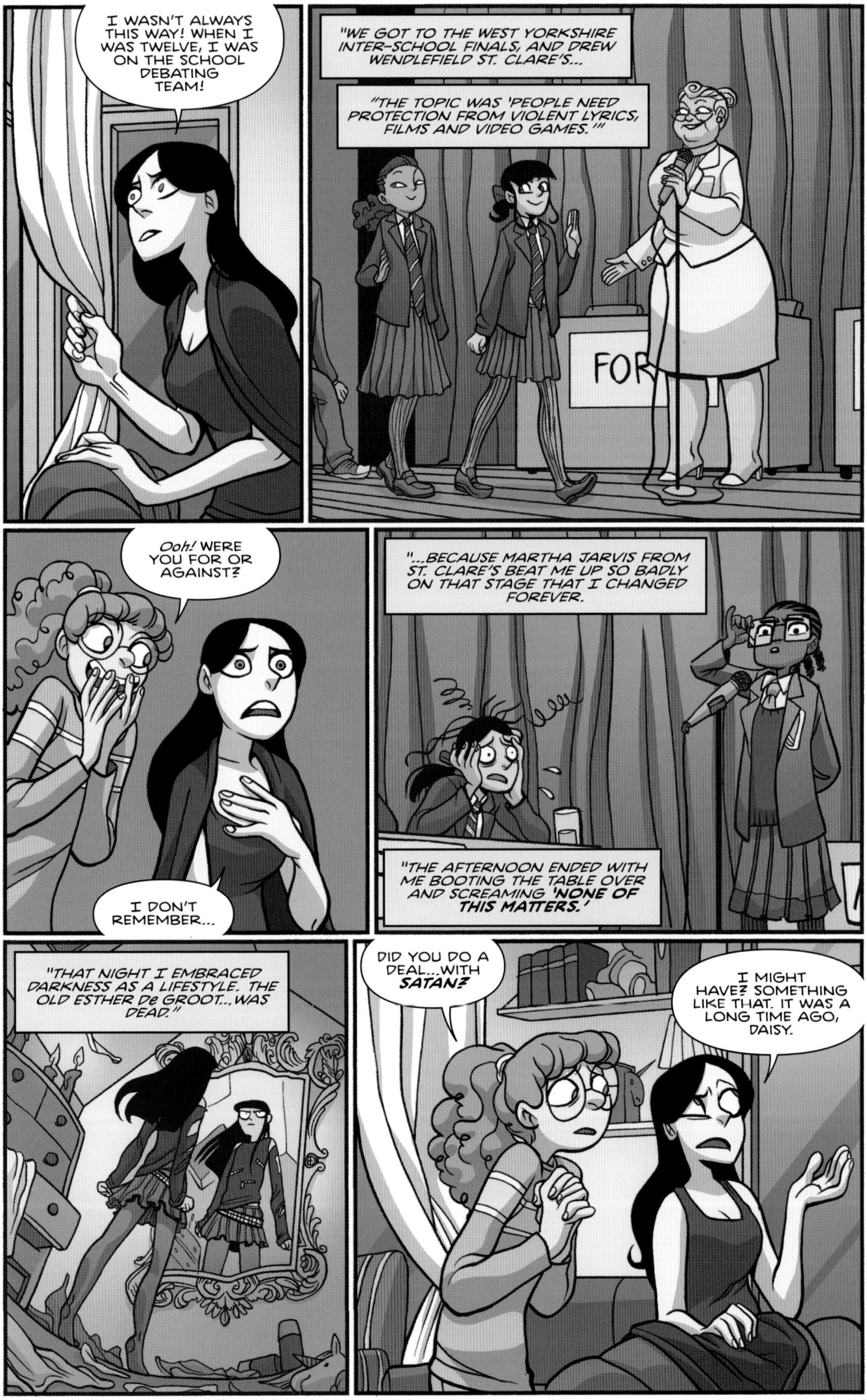

I WASN'T ALWAYS THIS WAY! WHEN I WAS TWELVE, I WAS ON THE SCHOOL DEBATING TEAM!
"WE GOT TO THE WEST YORKSHIRE INTER-SCHOOL FINALS, AND DREW WENDLEFIELD ST. CLARE'S...
"THE TOPIC WAS 'PEOPLE NEED PROTECTION FROM VIOLENT LYRICS, FILMS AND VIDEO GAMES.'"
FOR
Ooh! WERE YOU FOR OR AGAINST?
I DON'T REMEMBER...
"...BECAUSE MARTHA JARVIS FROM ST. CLARE'S BEAT ME UP SO BADLY ON THAT STAGE THAT I CHANGED FOREVER.
"THE AFTERNOON ENDED WITH ME BOOTING THE TABLE OVER AND SCREAMING 'NONE OF THIS MATTERS.'
"THAT NIGHT I EMBRACED DARKNESS AS A LIFESTYLE. THE OLD ESTHER De GROOT...WAS DEAD."
DID YOU DO A DEAL...WITH SATAN?
I MIGHT HAVE? SOMETHING LIKE THAT. IT WAS A LONG TIME AGO, DAISY.

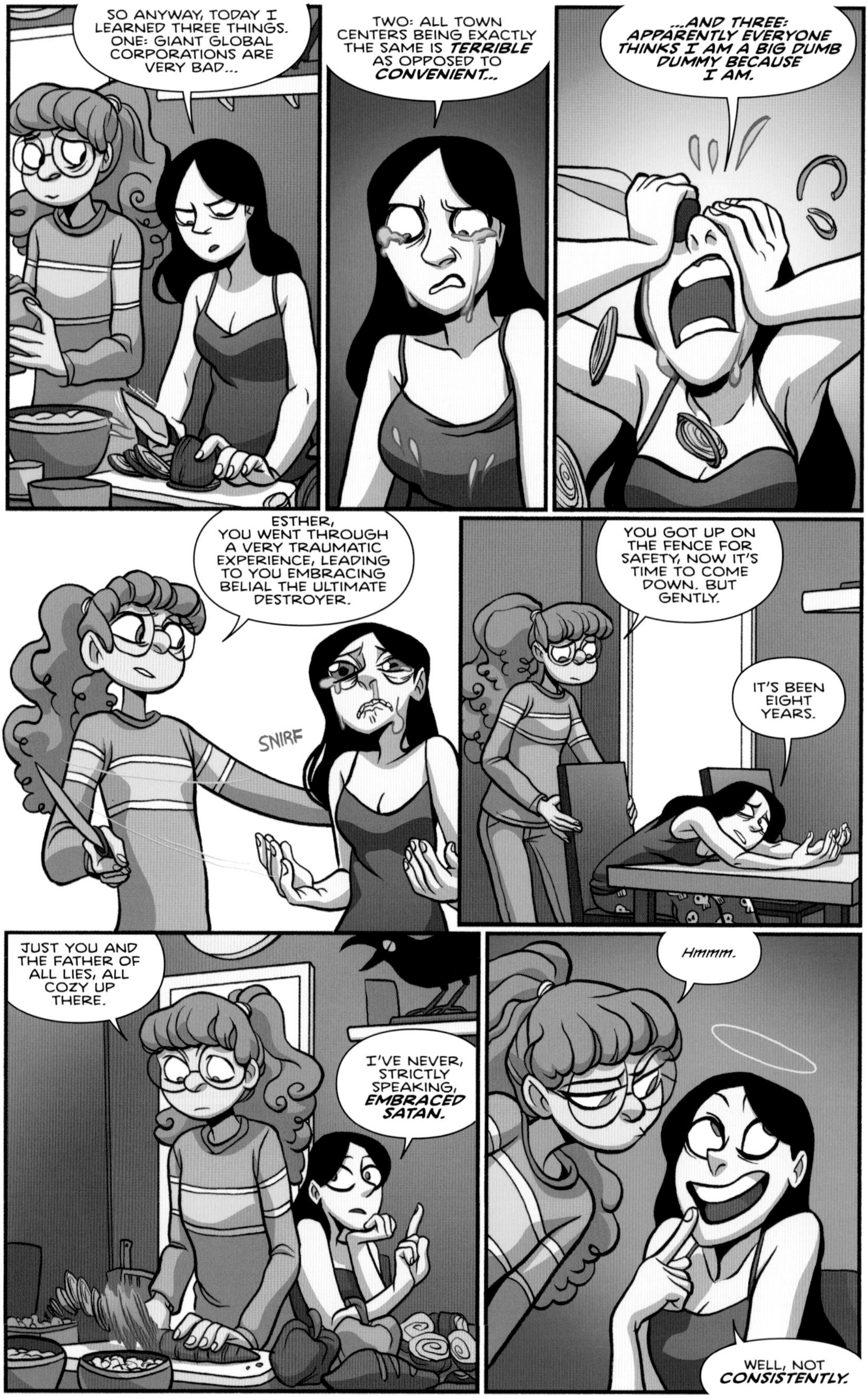

SO ANYWAY, TODAY I LEARNED THREE THINGS. ONE: GIANT GLOBAL CORPORATIONS ARE VERY BAD...
TWO: ALL TOWN CENTERS BEING EXACTLY THE SAME IS TERRIBLE AS OPPOSED TO CONVENIENT...
...AND THREE: APPARENTLY EVERYONE THINKS I AM A BIG DUMB DUMMY BECAUSE I AM.
ESTHER, YOU WENT THROUGH A VERY TRAUMATIC EXPERIENCE, LEADING TO YOU EMBRACING BELIAL THE ULTIMATE DESTROYER.
SNIRF
YOU GOT UP ON THE FENCE FOR SAFETY, NOW IT'S TIME TO COME DOWN. BUT GENTLY.
IT'S BEEN EIGHT YEARS.
JUST YOU AND THE FATHER OF ALL LIES, ALL COZY UP THERE.
I'VE NEVER, STRICTLY SPEAKING, EMBRACED SATAN.
Hmmm.
WELL, NOT CONSISTENTLY.

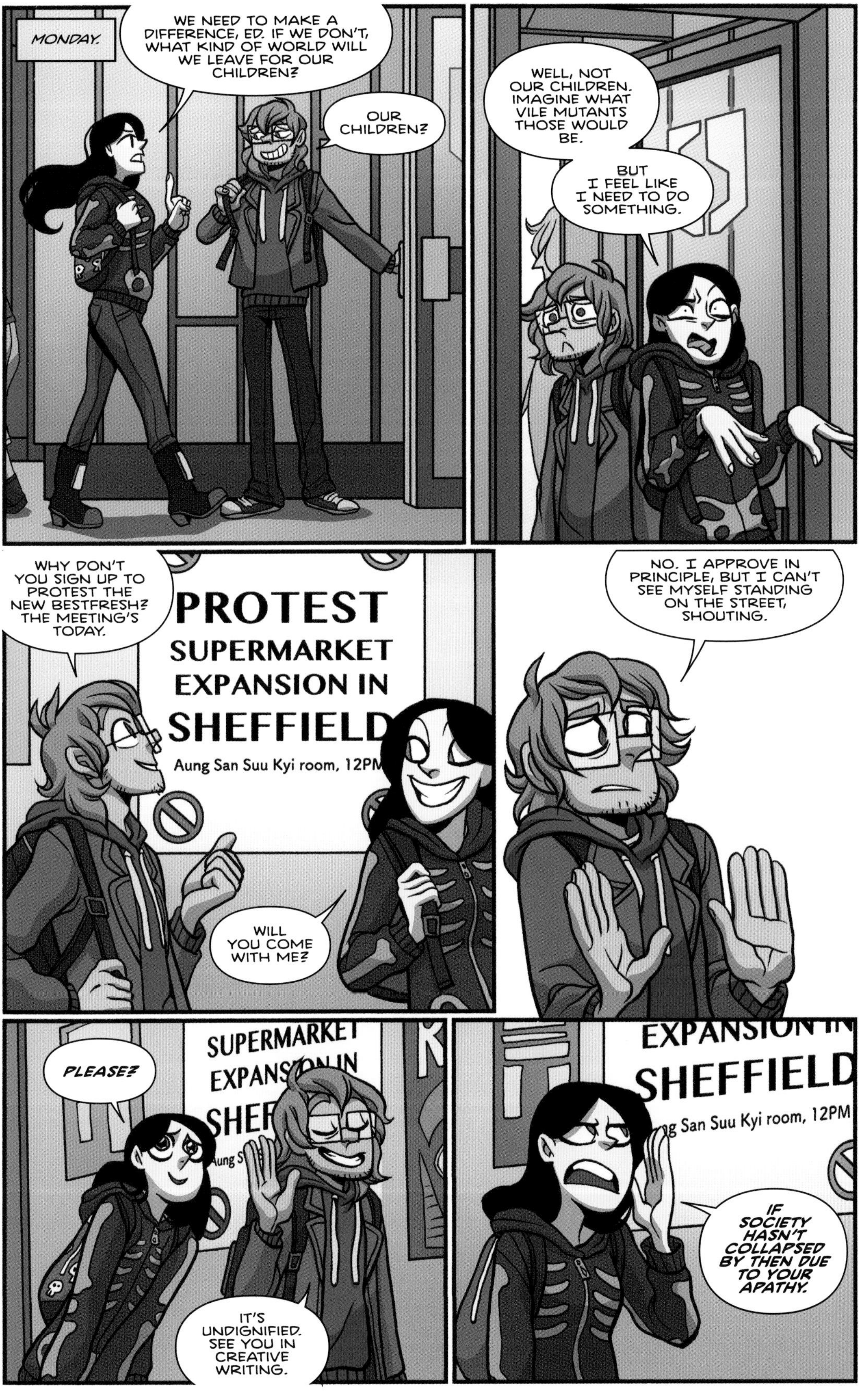
MONDAY.
WE NEED TO MAKE A DIFFERENCE, ED. IF WE DON'T, WHAT KIND OF WORLD WILL WE LEAVE FOR OUR CHILDREN?
OUR CHILDREN?
WELL, NOT OUR CHILDREN. IMAGINE WHAT VILE MUTANTS THOSE WOULD BE.
BUT I FEEL LIKE I NEED TO DO SOMETHING.
WHY DON'T YOU SIGN UP TO PROTEST THE NEW BESTFRESH? THE MEETING'S TODAY.
PROTEST
SUPERMARKET EXPANSION IN
SHEFFIELD
Aung San Suu Kyi room, 12PM
WILL YOU COME WITH ME?
NO. I APPROVE IN PRINCIPLE, BUT I CAN'T SEE MYSELF STANDING ON THE STREET, SHOUTING.
PLEASE?
IT'S UNDIGNIFIED. SEE YOU IN CREATIVE WRITING.
IF SOCIETY HASN'T COLLAPSED BY THEN DUE TO YOUR APATHY.

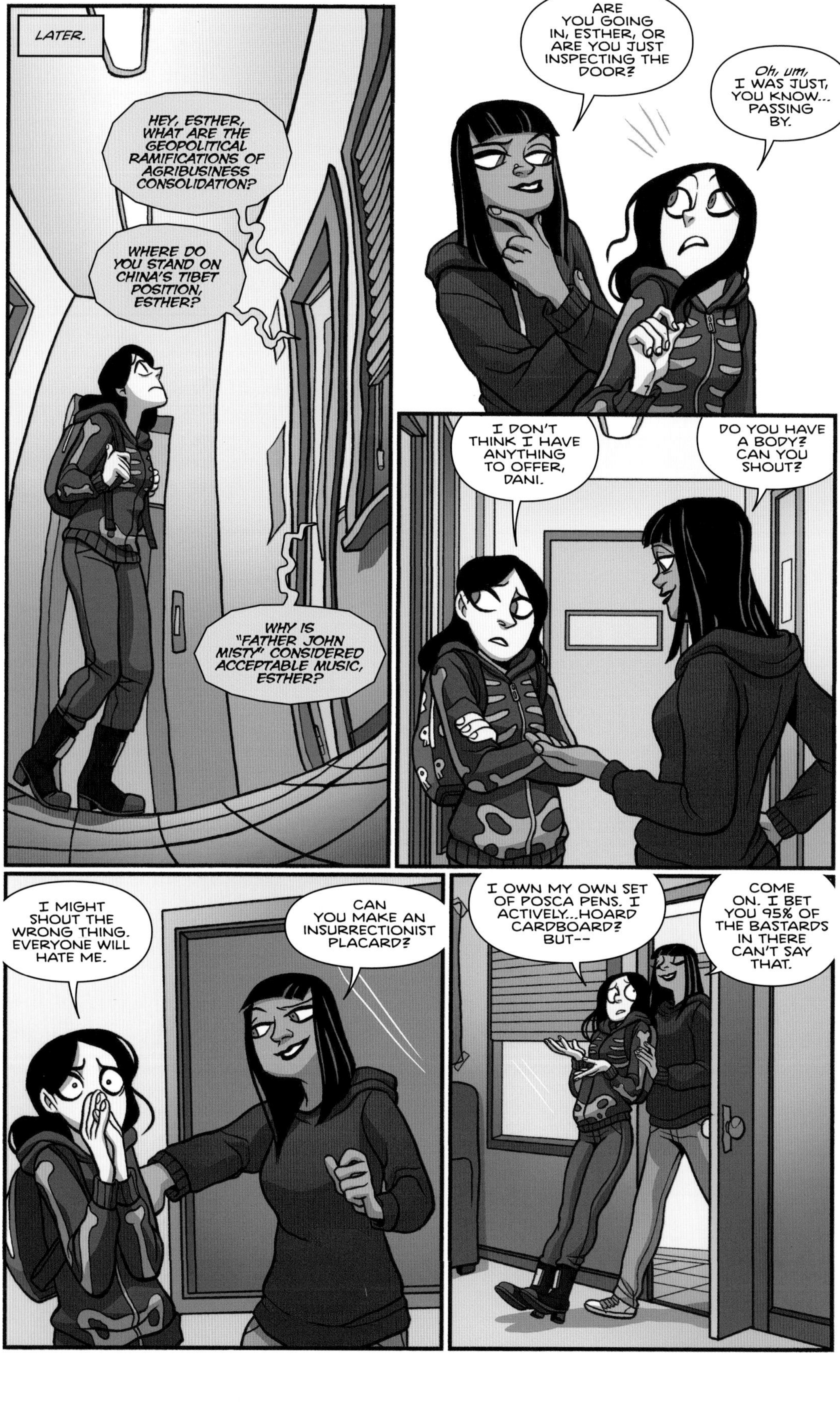
LATER.
HEY, ESTHER, WHAT ARE THE GEOPOLITICAL RAMIFICATIONS OF AGRIBUSINESS CONSOLIDATION?
WHERE DO YOU STAND ON CHINA'S TIBET POSITION, ESTHER?
WHY IS "FATHER JOHN MISTY" CONSIDERED ACCEPTABLE MUSIC, ESTHER?
ARE YOU GOING IN, ESTHER, OR ARE YOU JUST INSPECTING THE DOOR?
Oh, um, I WAS JUST, YOU KNOW... PASSING BY.
I DON'T THINK I HAVE ANYTHING TO OFFER, DANI.
DO YOU HAVE A BODY? CAN YOU SHOUT?
I MIGHT SHOUT THE WRONG THING. EVERYONE WILL HATE ME.
CAN YOU MAKE AN INSURRECTIONIST PLACARD?
I OWN MY OWN SET OF POSCA PENS. I ACTIVELY...HOARD CARDBOARD? BUT--
COME ON. I BET YOU 95% OF THE BASTARDS IN THERE CAN'T SAY THAT.

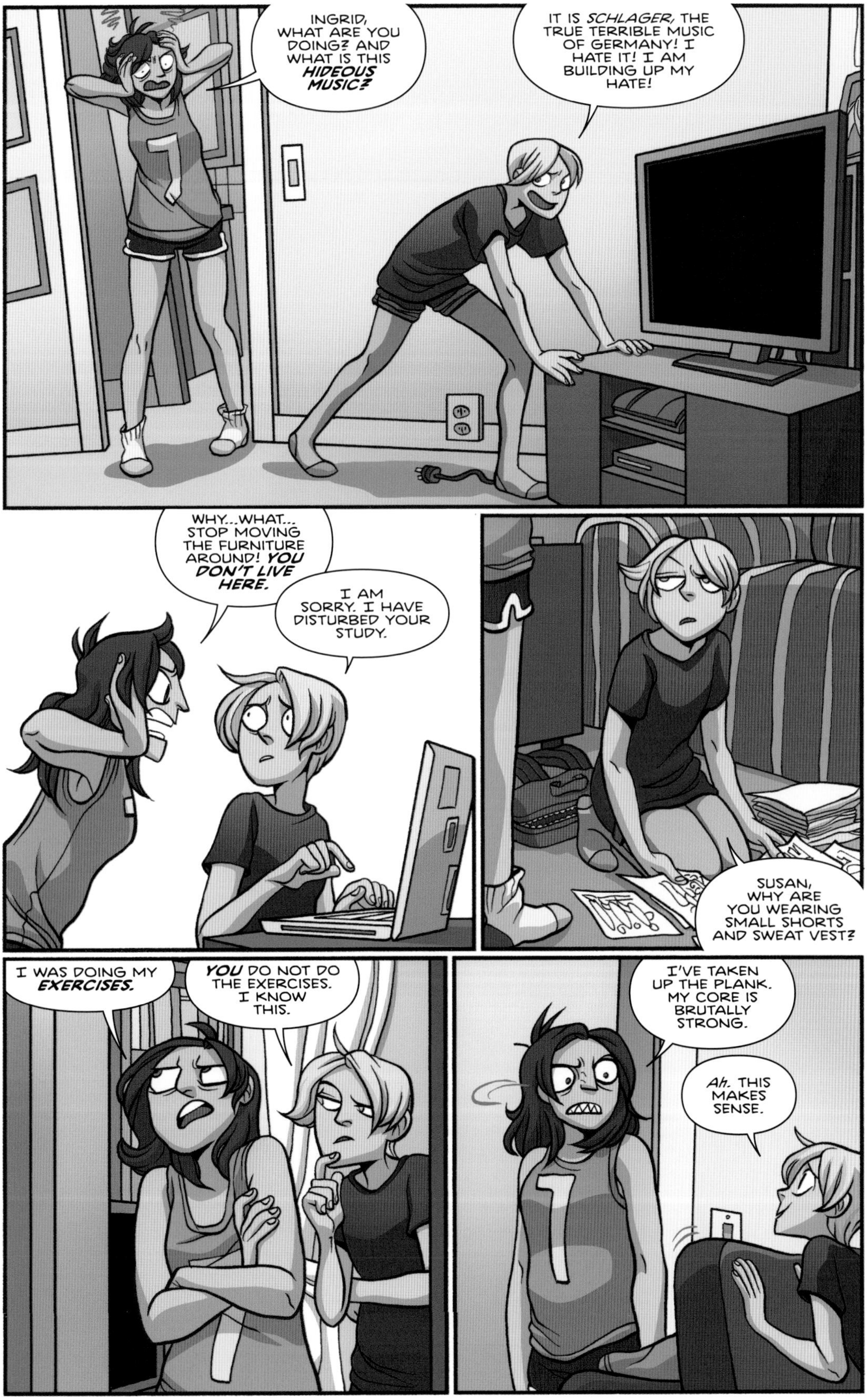
INGRID, WHAT ARE YOU DOING? AND WHAT IS THIS HIDEOUS MUSIC?
IT IS SCHLAGER, THE TRUE TERRIBLE MUSIC OF GERMANY! I HATE IT! I AM BUILDING UP MY HATE!
WHY...WHAT... STOP MOVING THE FURNITURE AROUND! YOU DON'T LIVE HERE.
I AM SORRY. I HAVE DISTURBED YOUR STUDY.
SUSAN, WHY ARE YOU WEARING SMALL SHORTS AND SWEAT VEST?
I WAS DOING MY EXERCISES.
YOU DO NOT DO THE EXERCISES. I KNOW THIS.
I'VE TAKEN UP THE PLANK. MY CORE IS BRUTALLY STRONG.
Ah. THIS MAKES SENSE.

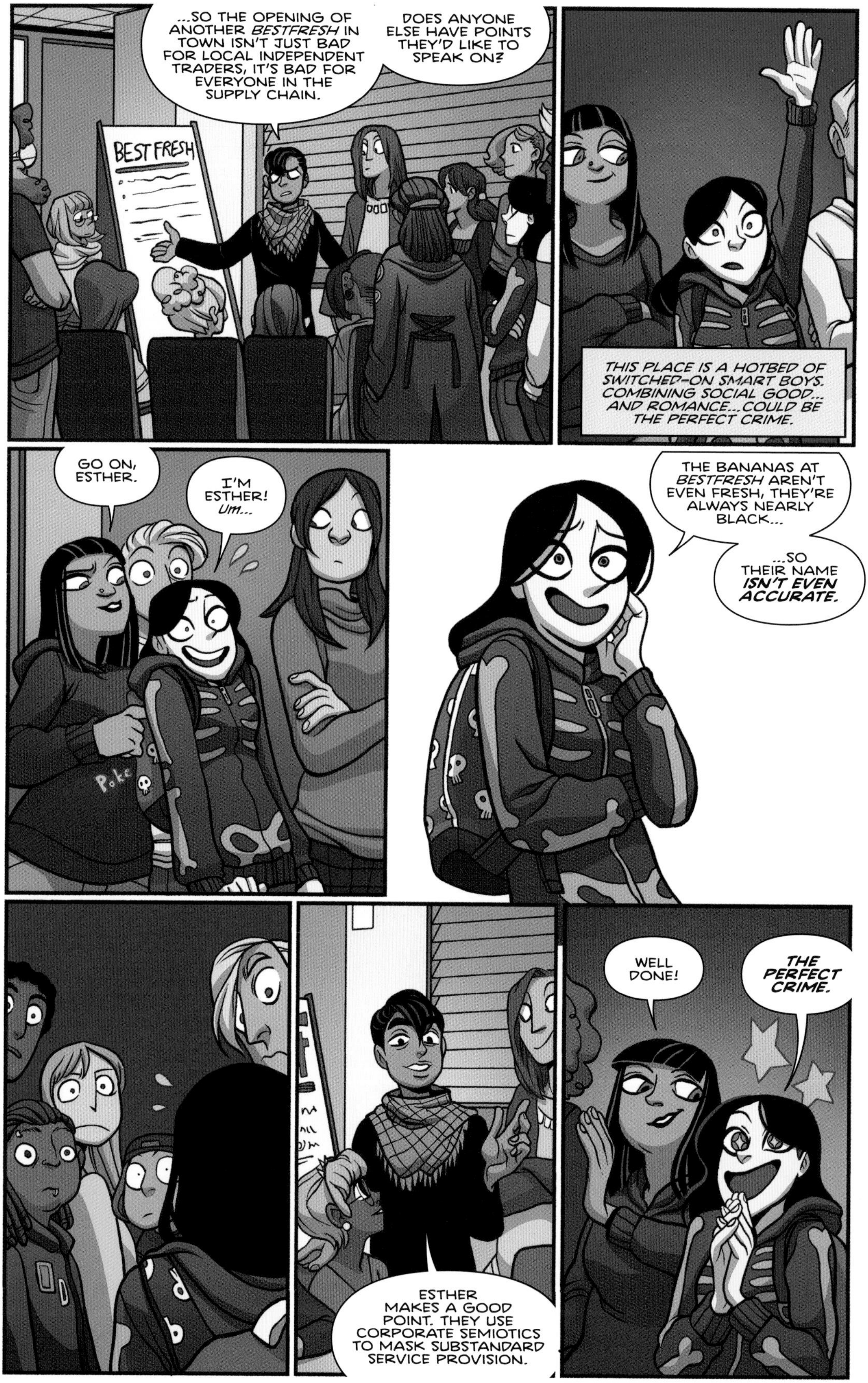
...SO THE OPENING OF ANOTHER *BESTFRESH* IN TOWN ISN'T JUST BAD FOR LOCAL INDEPENDENT TRADERS, IT'S BAD FOR EVERYONE IN THE SUPPLY CHAIN.
DOES ANYONE ELSE HAVE POINTS THEY'D LIKE TO SPEAK ON?
BEST FRESH
THIS PLACE IS A HOTBED OF SWITCHED-ON SMART BOYS. COMBINING SOCIAL GOOD... AND ROMANCE... COULD BE THE PERFECT CRIME.
GO ON, ESTHER.
I'M ESTHER! *Um...*
THE BANANAS AT *BESTFRESH* AREN'T EVEN FRESH, THEY'RE ALWAYS NEARLY BLACK...
...SO THEIR NAME ***ISN'T EVEN ACCURATE.***
ESTHER MAKES A GOOD POINT. THEY USE CORPORATE SEMIOTICS TO MASK SUBSTANDARD SERVICE PROVISION.
WELL DONE!
THE PERFECT CRIME.

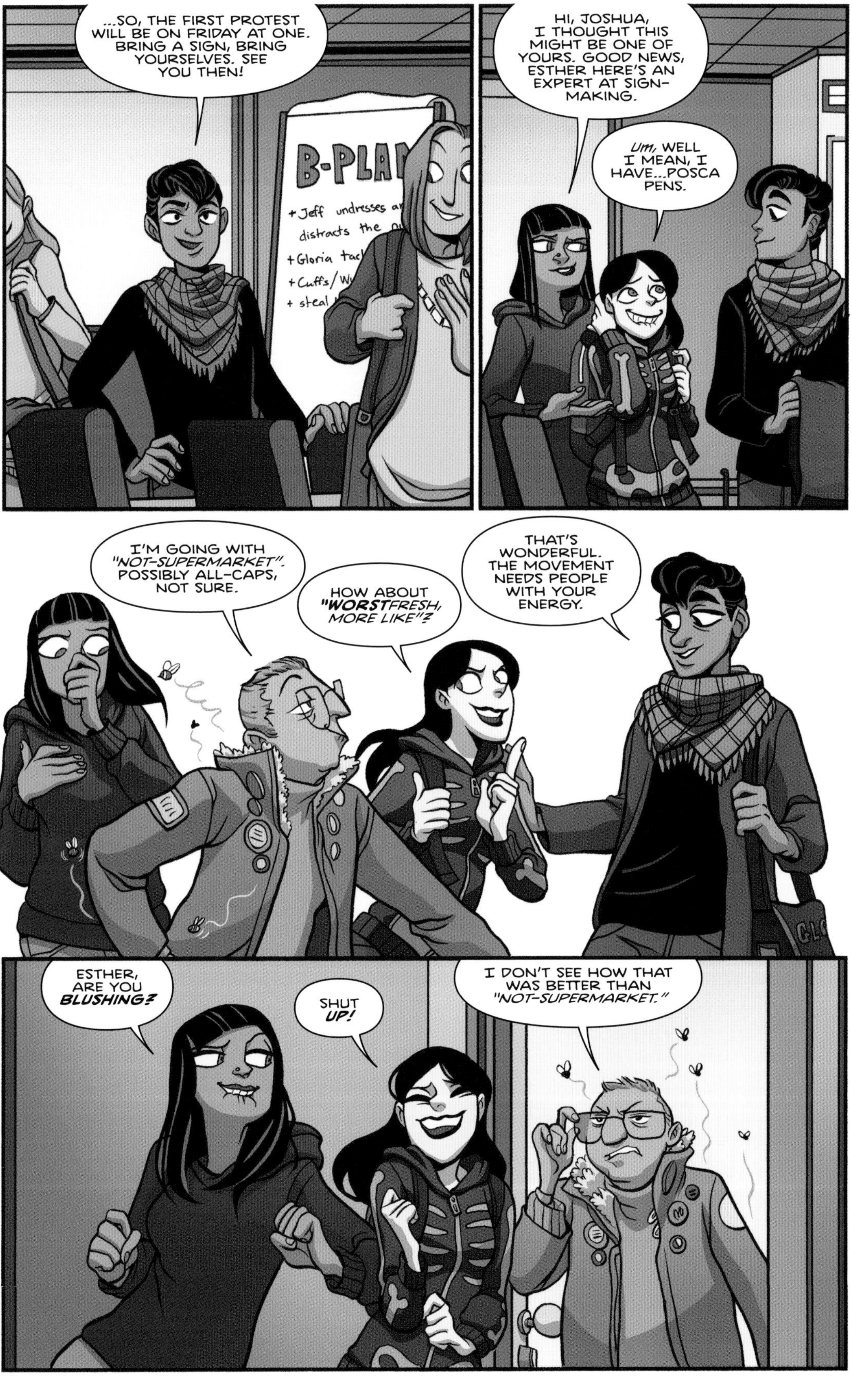
...SO, THE FIRST PROTEST WILL BE ON FRIDAY AT ONE. BRING A SIGN, BRING YOURSELVES. SEE YOU THEN!
HI, JOSHUA, I THOUGHT THIS MIGHT BE ONE OF YOURS. GOOD NEWS, ESTHER HERE'S AN EXPERT AT SIGN-MAKING.
UM, WELL I MEAN, I HAVE...POSCA PENS.
I'M GOING WITH *"NOT-SUPERMARKET"*. POSSIBLY ALL-CAPS, NOT SURE.
HOW ABOUT ***"WORST**FRESH, MORE LIKE"?*
THAT'S WONDERFUL. THE MOVEMENT NEEDS PEOPLE WITH YOUR ENERGY.
ESTHER, ARE YOU ***BLUSHING?***
SHUT ***UP!***
I DON'T SEE HOW THAT WAS BETTER THAN *"NOT-SUPERMARKET."*

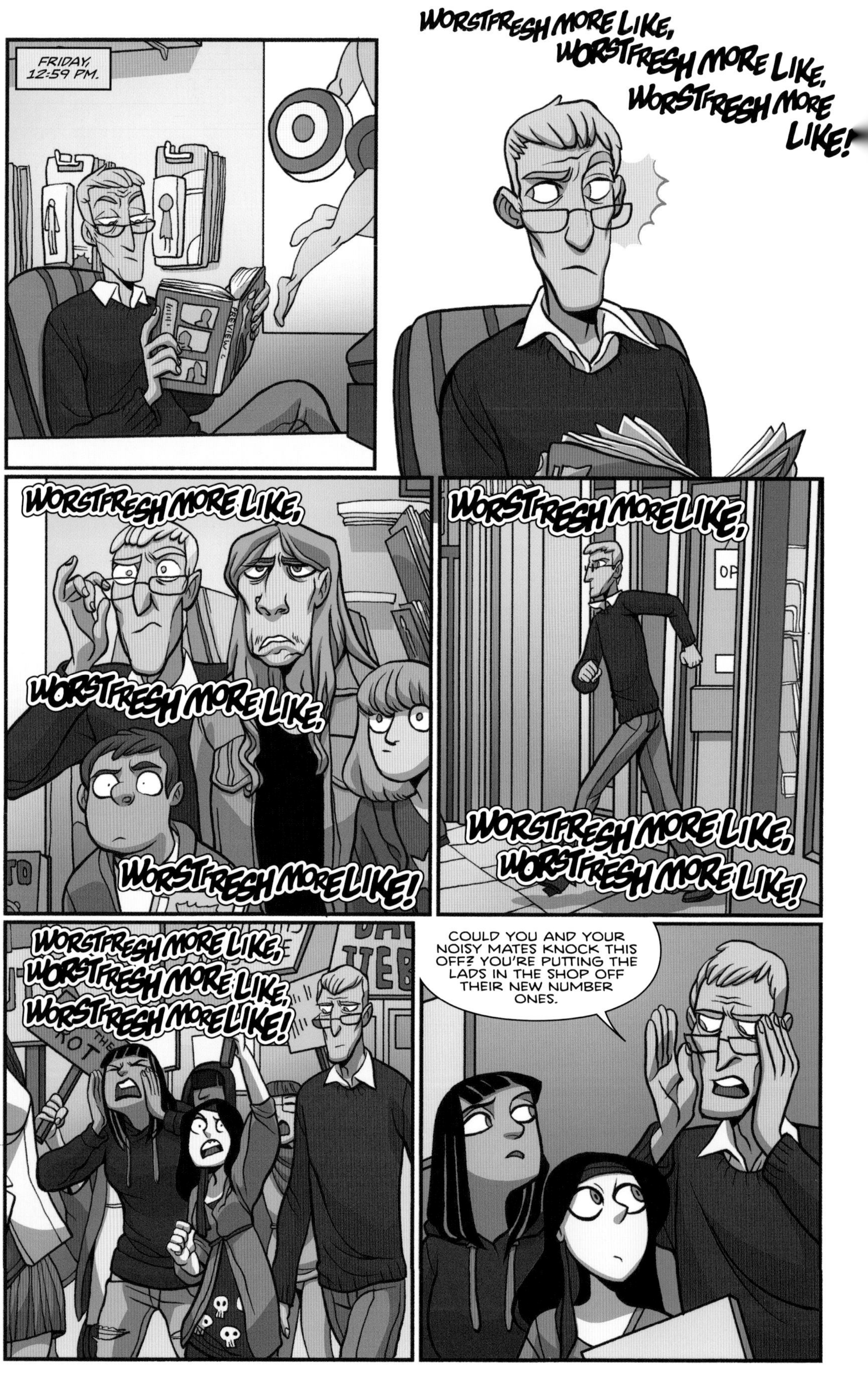
FRIDAY, 12:59 PM.
WORSTFRESH MORE LIKE,
WORSTFRESH MORE LIKE,
WORSTFRESH MORE LIKE!
WORSTFRESH MORE LIKE,
WORSTFRESH MORE LIKE,
WORSTFRESH MORE LIKE!
WORSTFRESH MORE LIKE,
WORSTFRESH MORE LIKE,
WORSTFRESH MORE LIKE!
WORSTFRESH MORE LIKE,
WORSTFRESH MORE LIKE,
WORSTFRESH MORE LIKE!
COULD YOU AND YOUR NOISY MATES KNOCK THIS OFF? YOU'RE PUTTING THE LADS IN THE SHOP OFF THEIR NEW NUMBER ONES.

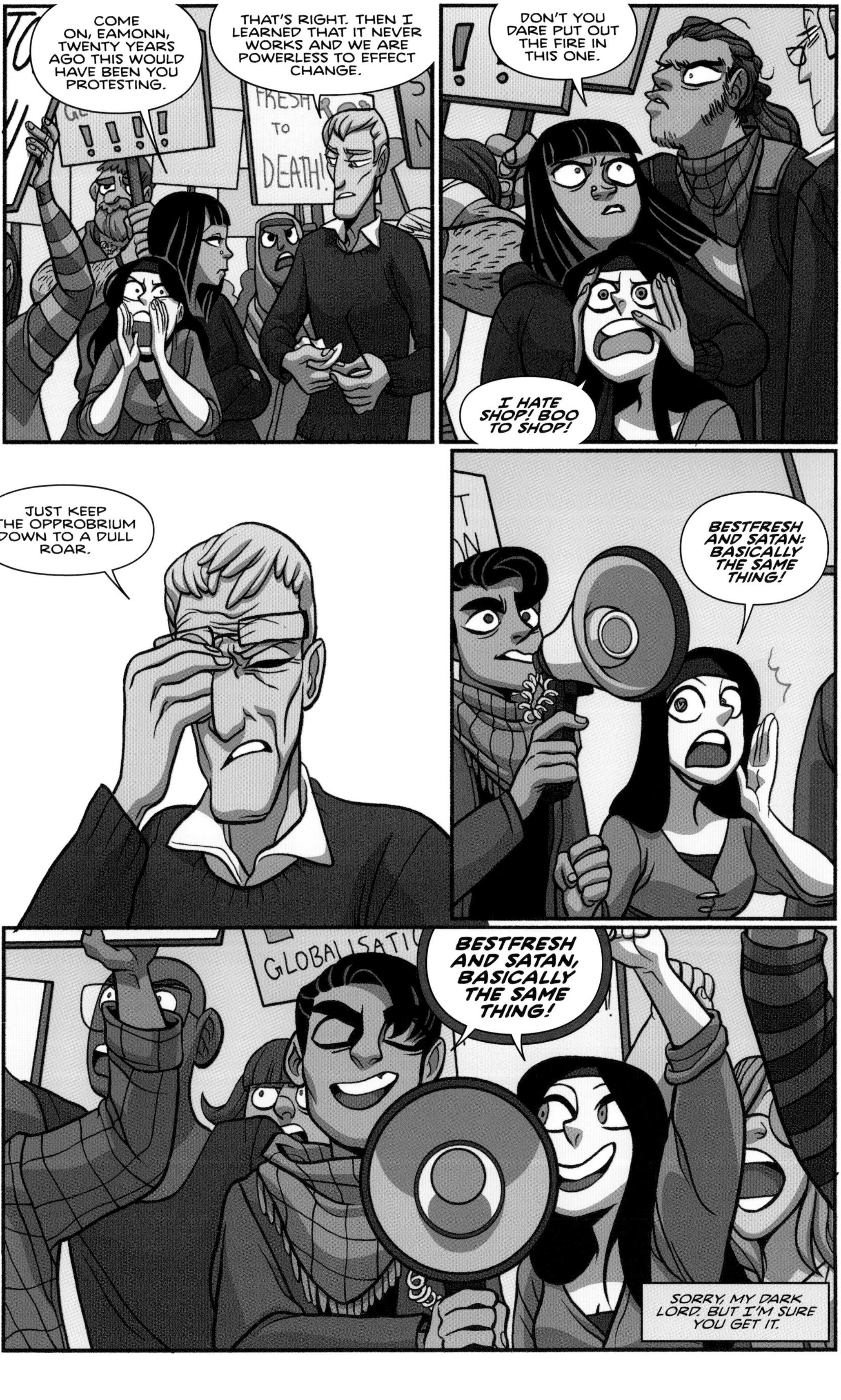
COME ON, EAMONN, TWENTY YEARS AGO THIS WOULD HAVE BEEN YOU PROTESTING.
THAT'S RIGHT. THEN I LEARNED THAT IT NEVER WORKS AND WE ARE POWERLESS TO EFFECT CHANGE.
FRESH TO DEATH!
DON'T YOU DARE PUT OUT THE FIRE IN THIS ONE.
I HATE SHOP! BOO TO SHOP!
JUST KEEP THE OPPROBRIUM DOWN TO A DULL ROAR.
BESTFRESH AND SATAN: BASICALLY THE SAME THING!
GLOBALISATI
BESTFRESH AND SATAN, BASICALLY THE SAME THING!
SORRY, MY DARK LORD, BUT I'M SURE YOU GET IT.

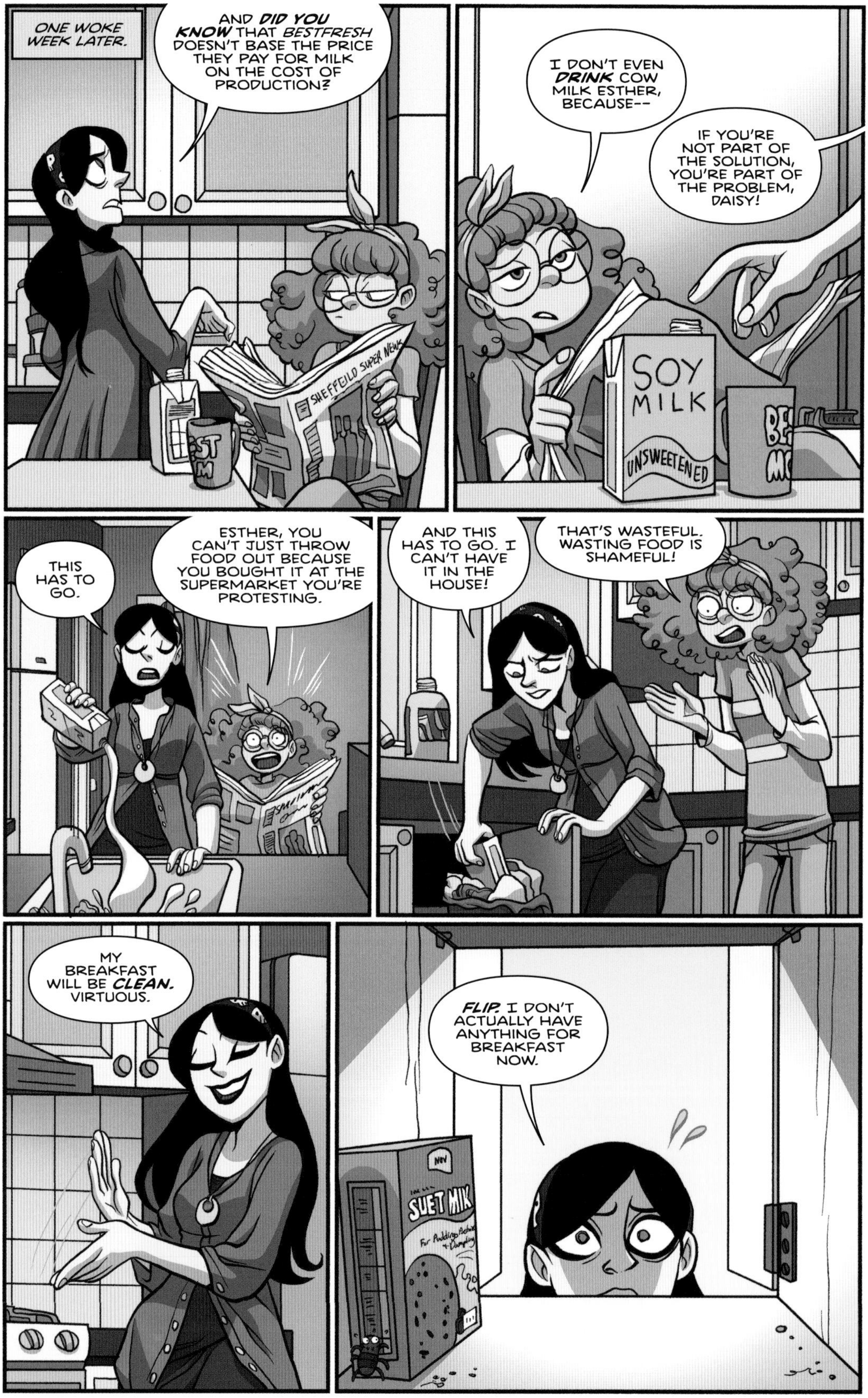
ONE WOKE WEEK LATER.
AND DID YOU KNOW THAT BESTFRESH DOESN'T BASE THE PRICE THEY PAY FOR MILK ON THE COST OF PRODUCTION?
SHEFFEILD SUPER NEWS
I DON'T EVEN DRINK COW MILK ESTHER, BECAUSE--
IF YOU'RE NOT PART OF THE SOLUTION, YOU'RE PART OF THE PROBLEM, DAISY!
SOY MILK
UNSWEETENED
THIS HAS TO GO.
ESTHER, YOU CAN'T JUST THROW FOOD OUT BECAUSE YOU BOUGHT IT AT THE SUPERMARKET YOU'RE PROTESTING.
AND THIS HAS TO GO. I CAN'T HAVE IT IN THE HOUSE!
THAT'S WASTEFUL. WASTING FOOD IS SHAMEFUL!
MY BREAKFAST WILL BE CLEAN. VIRTUOUS.
FLIP. I DON'T ACTUALLY HAVE ANYTHING FOR BREAKFAST NOW.
SUET MIX

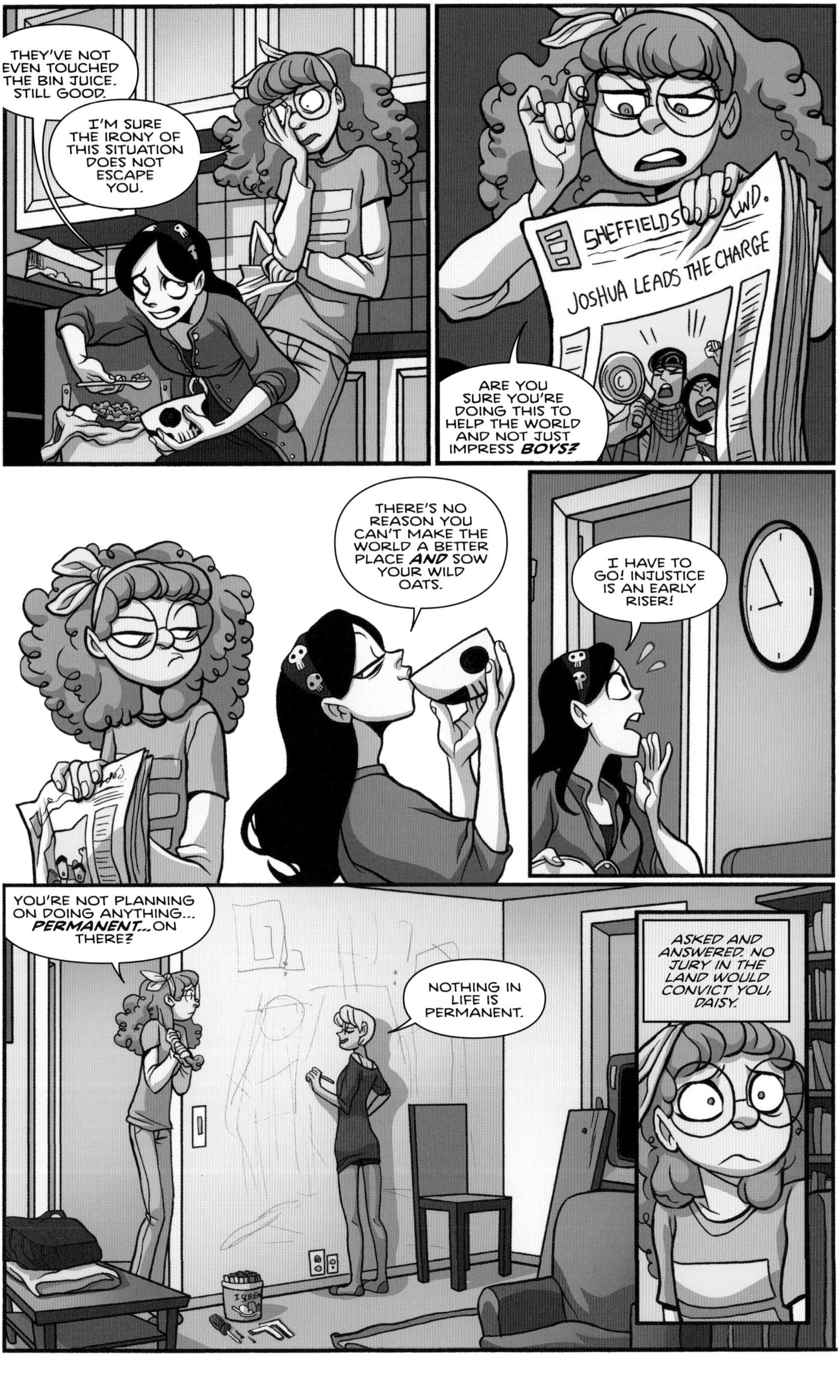

THEY'VE NOT EVEN TOUCHED THE BIN JUICE. STILL GOOD.
I'M SURE THE IRONY OF THIS SITUATION DOES NOT ESCAPE YOU.
SHEFFIELDS LWD.
JOSHUA LEADS THE CHARGE
ARE YOU SURE YOU'RE DOING THIS TO HELP THE WORLD AND NOT JUST IMPRESS *BOYS?*
THERE'S NO REASON YOU CAN'T MAKE THE WORLD A BETTER PLACE *AND* SOW YOUR WILD OATS.
I HAVE TO GO! INJUSTICE IS AN EARLY RISER!
YOU'RE NOT PLANNING ON DOING ANYTHING... *PERMANENT...* ON THERE?
NOTHING IN LIFE IS PERMANENT.
ASKED AND ANSWERED. NO JURY IN THE LAND WOULD CONVICT YOU, DAISY.

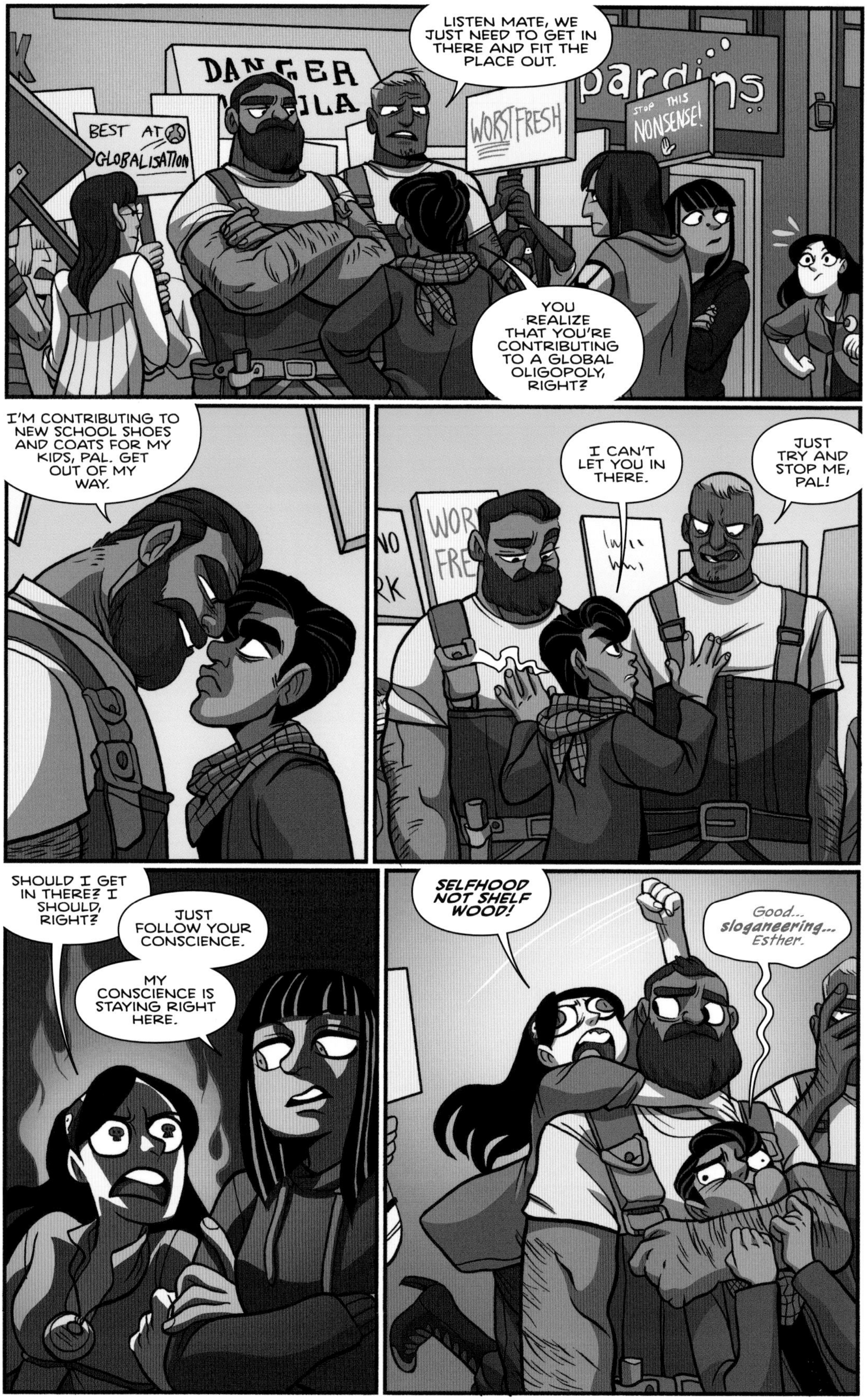
LISTEN MATE, WE JUST NEED TO GET IN THERE AND FIT THE PLACE OUT.
DANGER
BEST AT GLOBALISATION
WORSTFRESH
STOP THIS NONSENSE!
YOU REALIZE THAT YOU'RE CONTRIBUTING TO A GLOBAL OLIGOPOLY, RIGHT?
I'M CONTRIBUTING TO NEW SCHOOL SHOES AND COATS FOR MY KIDS, PAL. GET OUT OF MY WAY.
I CAN'T LET YOU IN THERE.
JUST TRY AND STOP ME, PAL!
SHOULD I GET IN THERE? I SHOULD, RIGHT?
JUST FOLLOW YOUR CONSCIENCE.
MY CONSCIENCE IS STAYING RIGHT HERE.
SELFHOOD NOT SHELF WOOD!
Good... sloganeering... Esther.

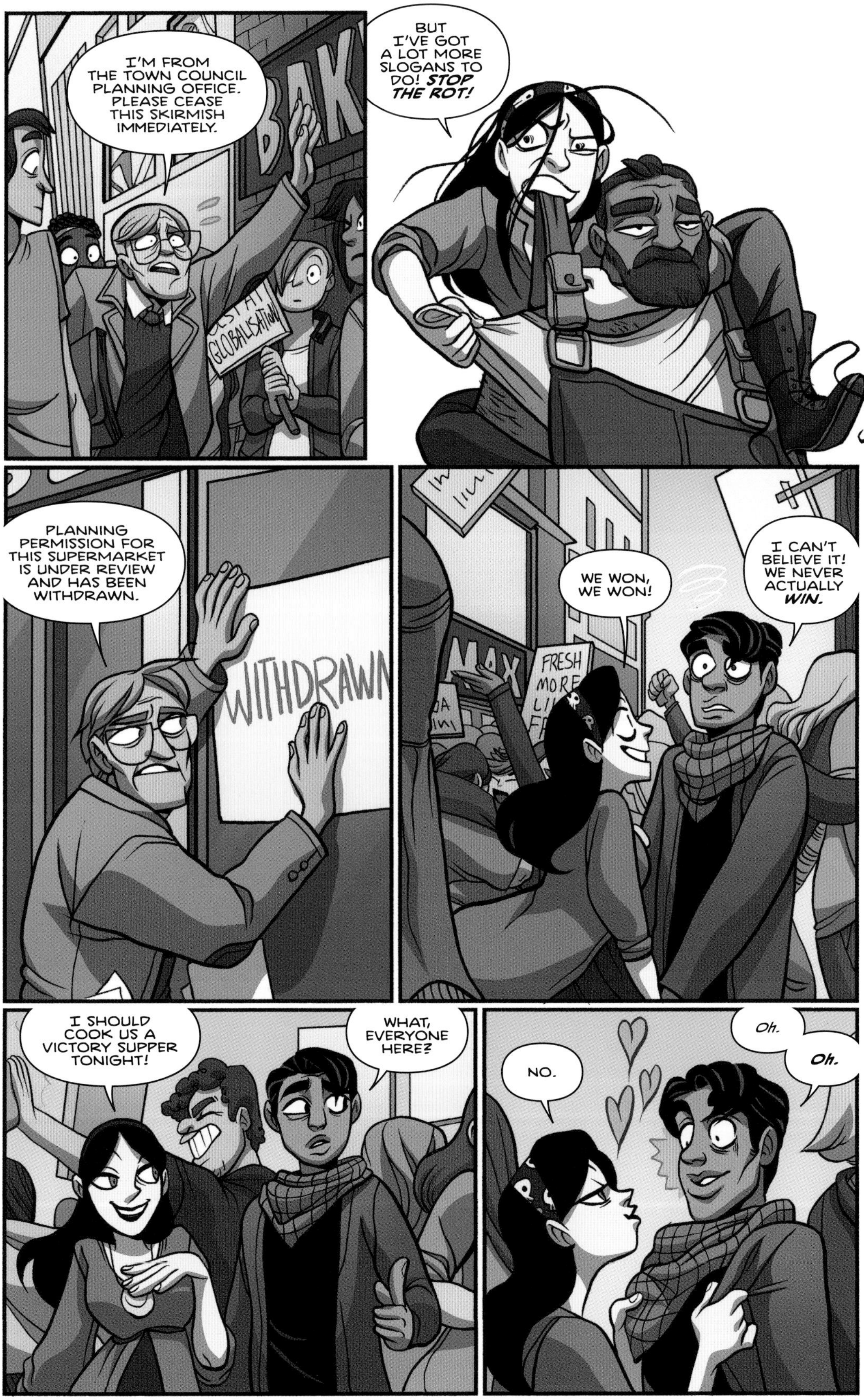
I'M FROM THE TOWN COUNCIL PLANNING OFFICE. PLEASE CEASE THIS SKIRMISH IMMEDIATELY.
GLOBALISATION
BUT I'VE GOT A LOT MORE SLOGANS TO DO! STOP THE ROT!
PLANNING PERMISSION FOR THIS SUPERMARKET IS UNDER REVIEW AND HAS BEEN WITHDRAWN.
WITHDRAWN
WE WON, WE WON!
I CAN'T BELIEVE IT! WE NEVER ACTUALLY WIN.
FRESH MORE
I SHOULD COOK US A VICTORY SUPPER TONIGHT!
WHAT, EVERYONE HERE?
NO.
Oh.
Oh.

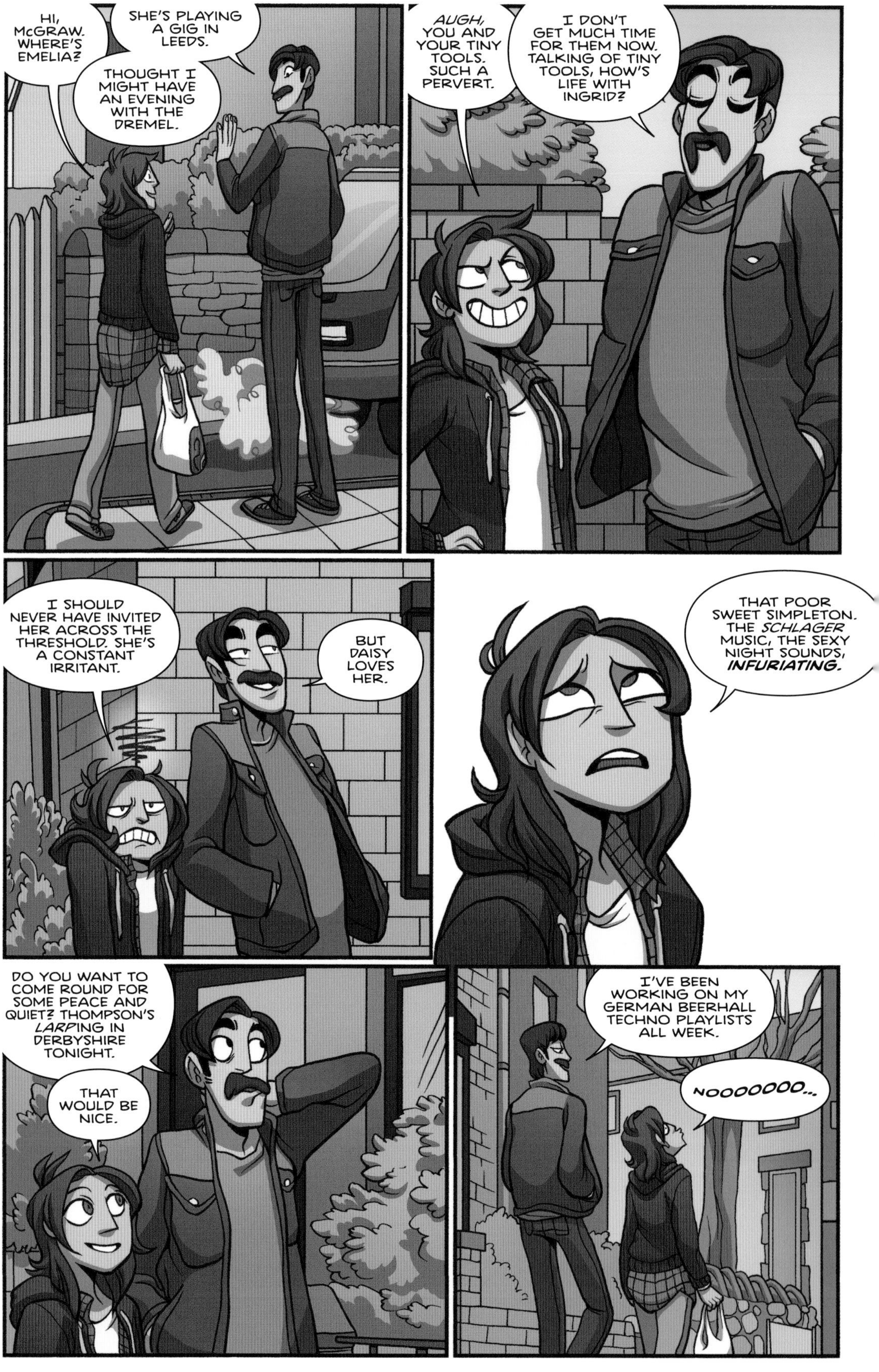
HI, McGRAW. WHERE'S EMELIA?
SHE'S PLAYING A GIG IN LEEDS.
THOUGHT I MIGHT HAVE AN EVENING WITH THE DREMEL.
AUGH, YOU AND YOUR TINY TOOLS. SUCH A PERVERT.
I DON'T GET MUCH TIME FOR THEM NOW. TALKING OF TINY TOOLS, HOW'S LIFE WITH INGRID?
I SHOULD NEVER HAVE INVITED HER ACROSS THE THRESHOLD. SHE'S A CONSTANT IRRITANT.
BUT DAISY LOVES HER.
THAT POOR SWEET SIMPLETON. THE *SCHLAGER* MUSIC, THE SEXY NIGHT SOUNDS, ***INFURIATING.***
DO YOU WANT TO COME ROUND FOR SOME PEACE AND QUIET? THOMPSON'S *LARP*ING IN DERBYSHIRE TONIGHT.
THAT WOULD BE NICE.
I'VE BEEN WORKING ON MY GERMAN BEERHALL TECHNO PLAYLISTS ALL WEEK.
NOOOOOOO...

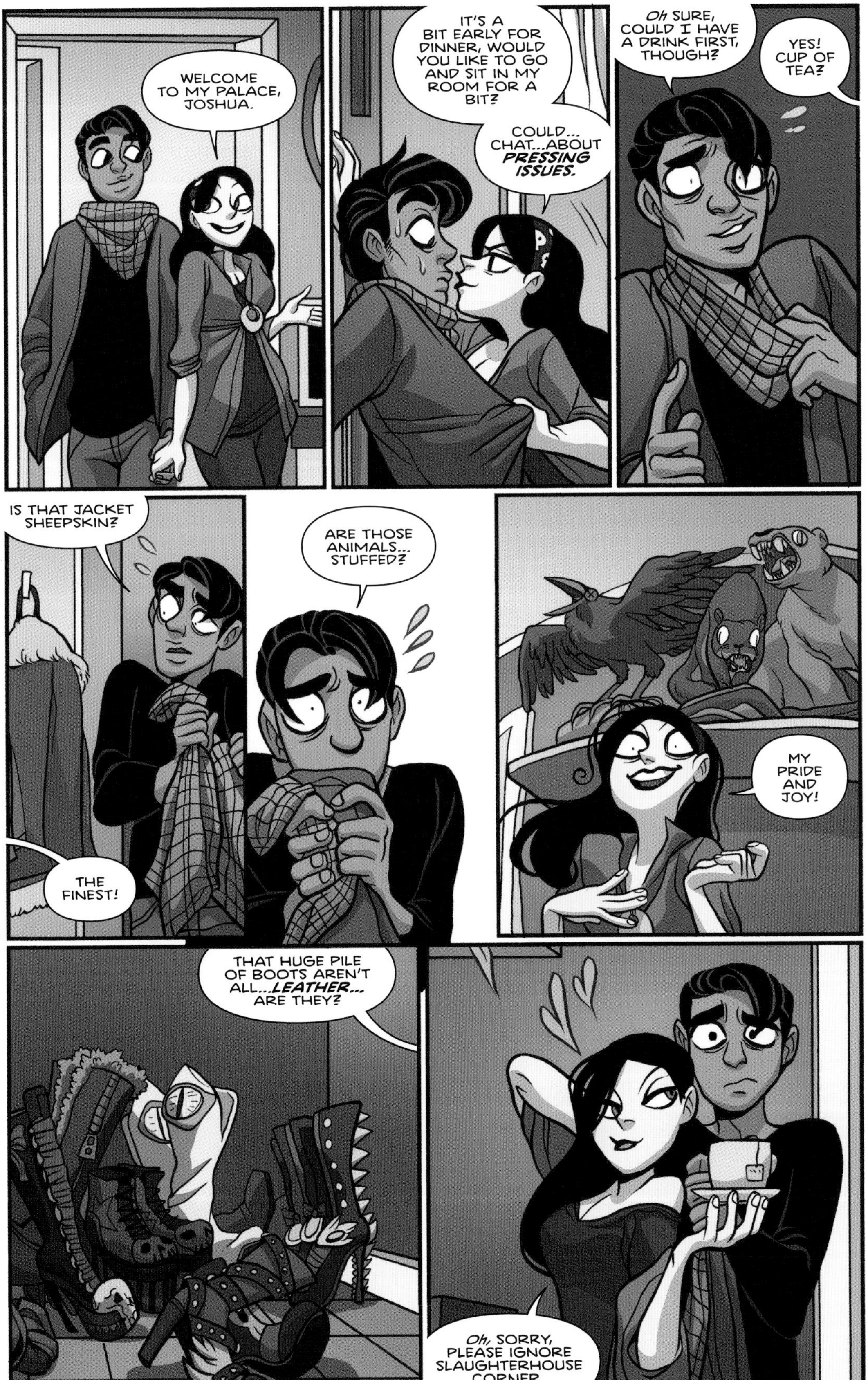
WELCOME TO MY PALACE, JOSHUA.
IT'S A BIT EARLY FOR DINNER, WOULD YOU LIKE TO GO AND SIT IN MY ROOM FOR A BIT?
COULD... CHAT... ABOUT *PRESSING ISSUES.*
Oh SURE, COULD I HAVE A DRINK FIRST, THOUGH?
YES! CUP OF TEA?
IS THAT JACKET SHEEPSKIN?
THE FINEST!
ARE THOSE ANIMALS... STUFFED?
MY PRIDE AND JOY!
THAT HUGE PILE OF BOOTS AREN'T ALL... *LEATHER...* ARE THEY?
Oh, SORRY, PLEASE IGNORE SLAUGHTERHOUSE CORNER.

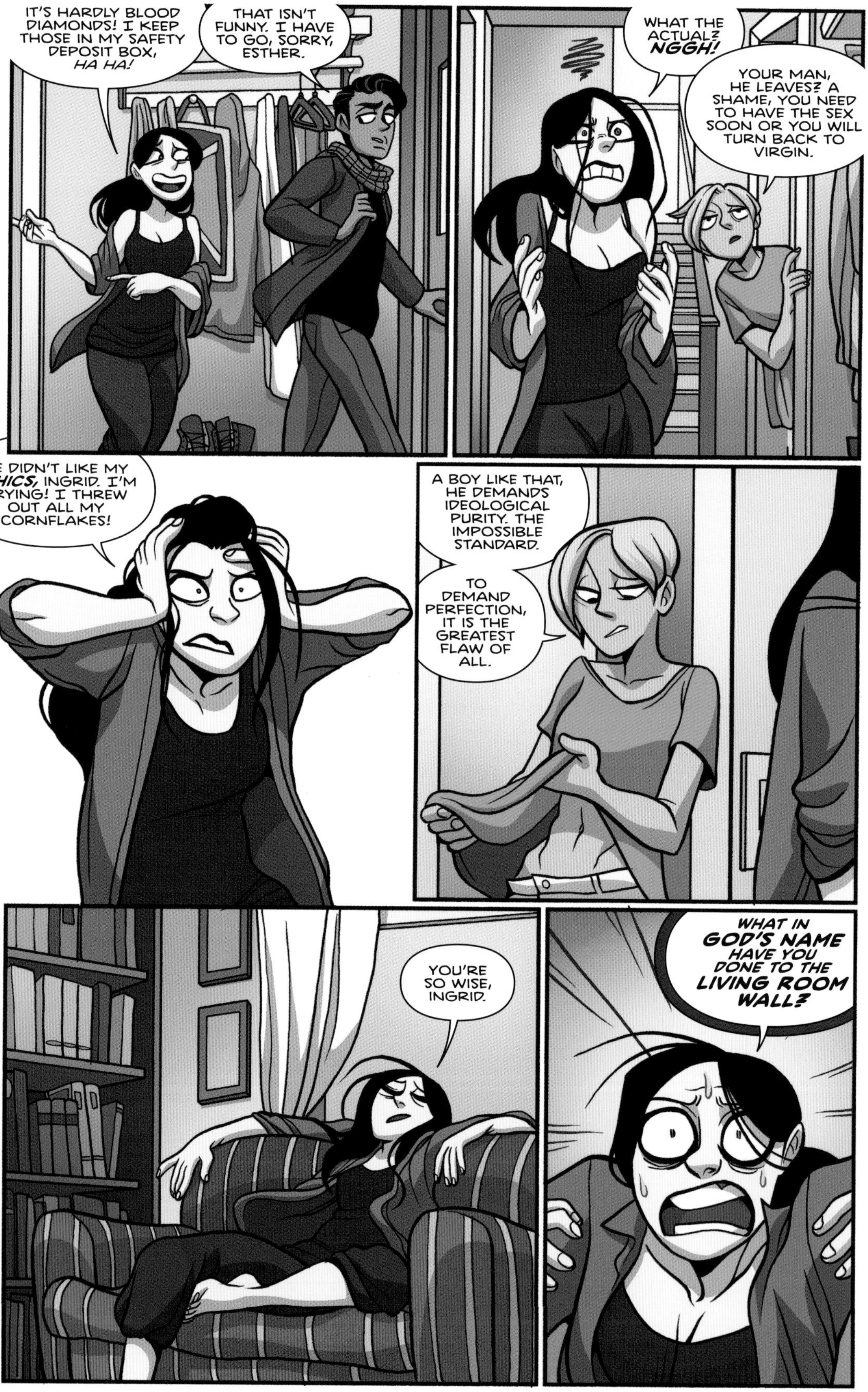
IT'S HARDLY BLOOD DIAMONDS! I KEEP THOSE IN MY SAFETY DEPOSIT BOX, HA HA!
THAT ISN'T FUNNY. I HAVE TO GO, SORRY, ESTHER.
WHAT THE ACTUAL? NGGH!
YOUR MAN, HE LEAVES? A SHAME, YOU NEED TO HAVE THE SEX SOON OR YOU WILL TURN BACK TO VIRGIN.
HE DIDN'T LIKE MY ETHICS, INGRID. I'M TRYING! I THREW OUT ALL MY CORNFLAKES!
A BOY LIKE THAT, HE DEMANDS IDEOLOGICAL PURITY. THE IMPOSSIBLE STANDARD.
TO DEMAND PERFECTION, IT IS THE GREATEST FLAW OF ALL.
YOU'RE SO WISE, INGRID.
WHAT IN GOD'S NAME HAVE YOU DONE TO THE LIVING ROOM WALL?

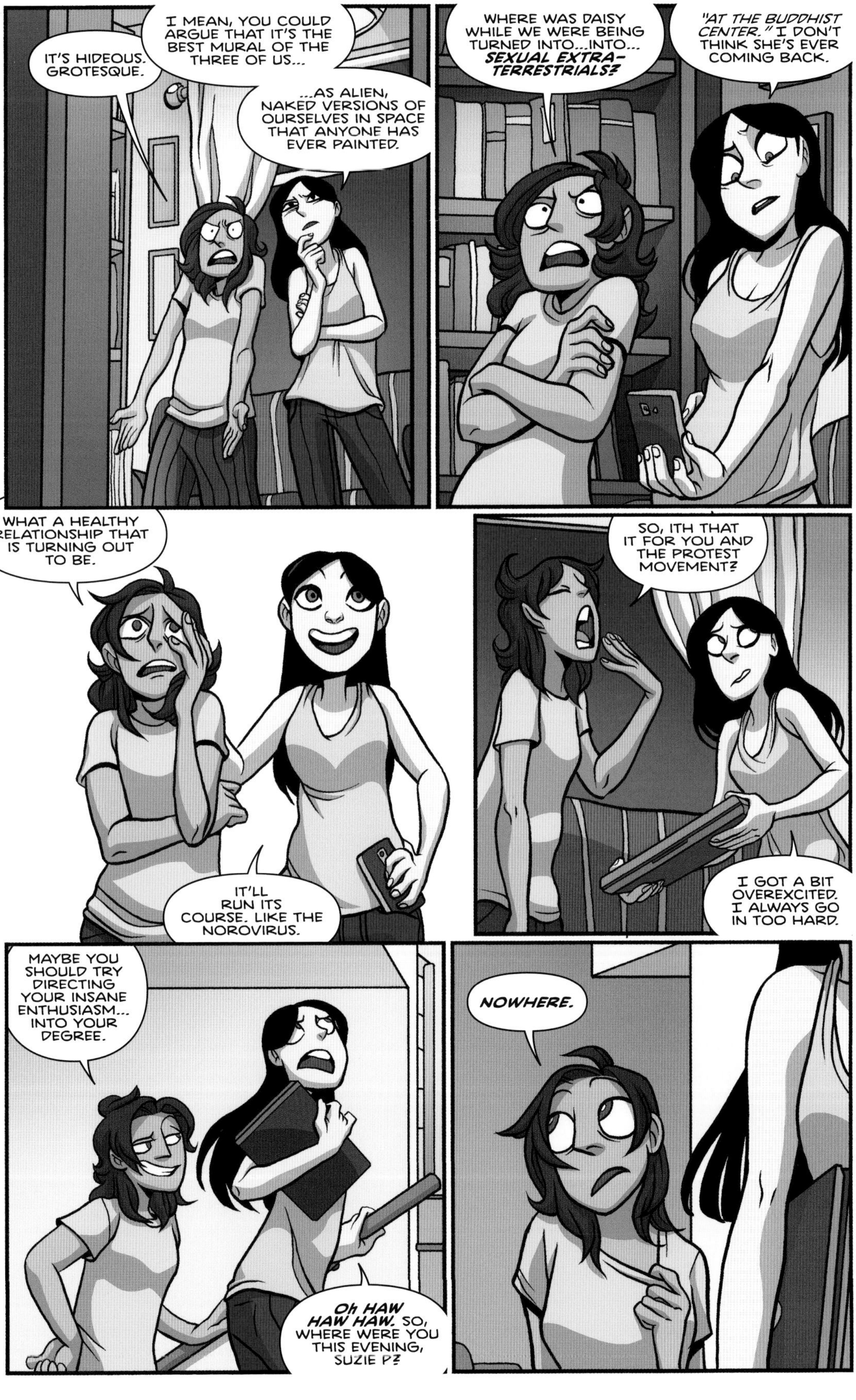
IT'S HIDEOUS. GROTESQUE.
I MEAN, YOU COULD ARGUE THAT IT'S THE BEST MURAL OF THE THREE OF US...
...AS ALIEN, NAKED VERSIONS OF OURSELVES IN SPACE THAT ANYONE HAS EVER PAINTED.
WHERE WAS DAISY WHILE WE WERE BEING TURNED INTO...INTO... SEXUAL EXTRA-TERRESTRIALS?
"AT THE BUDDHIST CENTER." I DON'T THINK SHE'S EVER COMING BACK.
WHAT A HEALTHY RELATIONSHIP THAT IS TURNING OUT TO BE.
IT'LL RUN ITS COURSE. LIKE THE NOROVIRUS.
SO, ITH THAT IT FOR YOU AND THE PROTEST MOVEMENT?
I GOT A BIT OVEREXCITED. I ALWAYS GO IN TOO HARD.
MAYBE YOU SHOULD TRY DIRECTING YOUR INSANE ENTHUSIASM... INTO YOUR DEGREE.
Oh HAW HAW HAW. SO, WHERE WERE YOU THIS EVENING, SUZIE P?
NOWHERE.

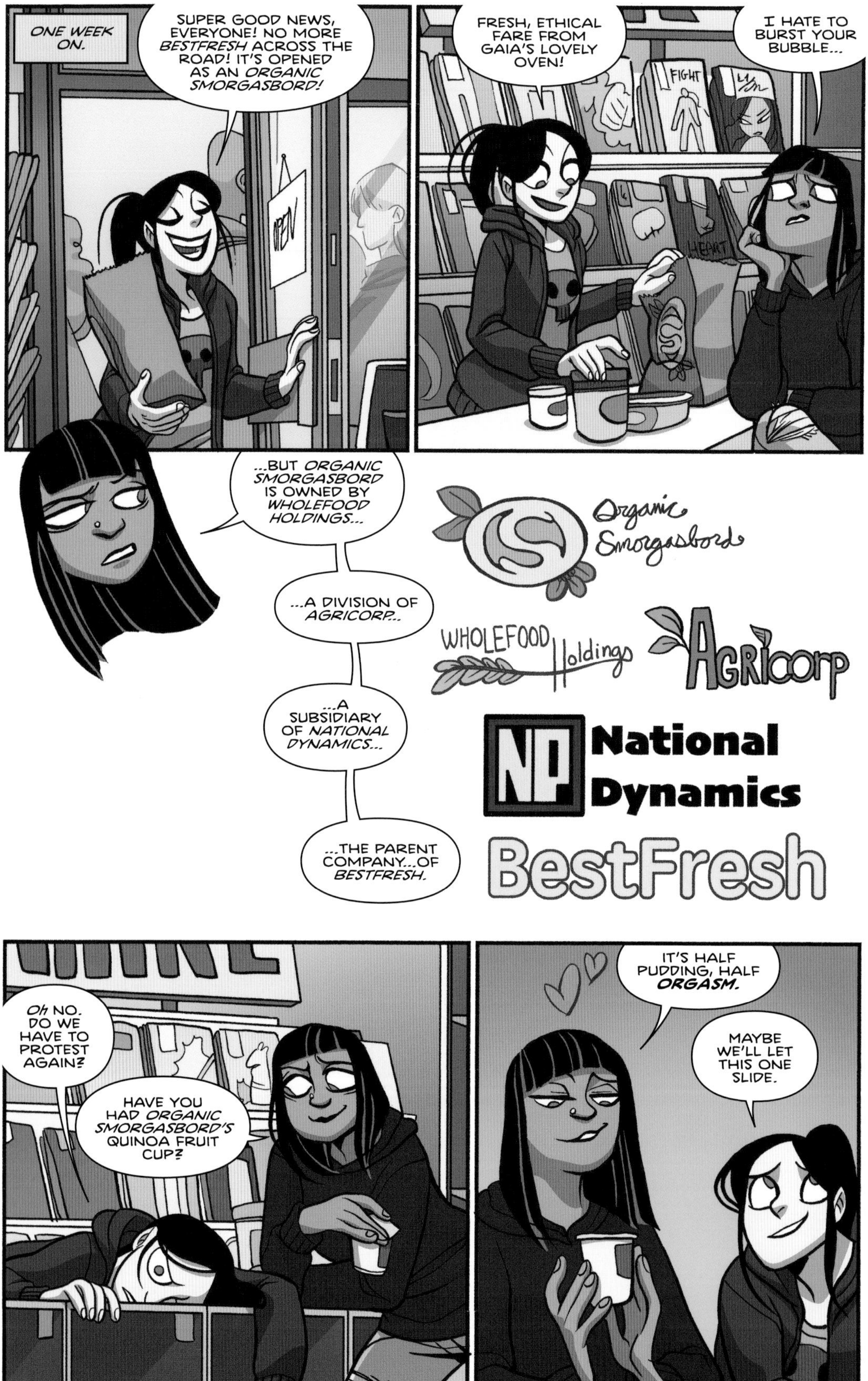
ONE WEEK ON.
SUPER GOOD NEWS, EVERYONE! NO MORE BESTFRESH ACROSS THE ROAD! IT'S OPENED AS AN ORGANIC SMORGASBORD!
OPEN
FRESH, ETHICAL FARE FROM GAIA'S LOVELY OVEN!
I HATE TO BURST YOUR BUBBLE...
FIGHT
HEART
...BUT ORGANIC SMORGASBORD IS OWNED BY WHOLEFOOD HOLDINGS...
Organic Smorgasbord
...A DIVISION OF AGRICORP...
WHOLEFOOD Holdings
Agricorp
...A SUBSIDIARY OF NATIONAL DYNAMICS...
ND National Dynamics
...THE PARENT COMPANY...OF BESTFRESH.
BestFresh
Oh NO. DO WE HAVE TO PROTEST AGAIN?
HAVE YOU HAD ORGANIC SMORGASBORD'S QUINOA FRUIT CUP?
IT'S HALF PUDDING, HALF ORGASM.
MAYBE WE'LL LET THIS ONE SLIDE.

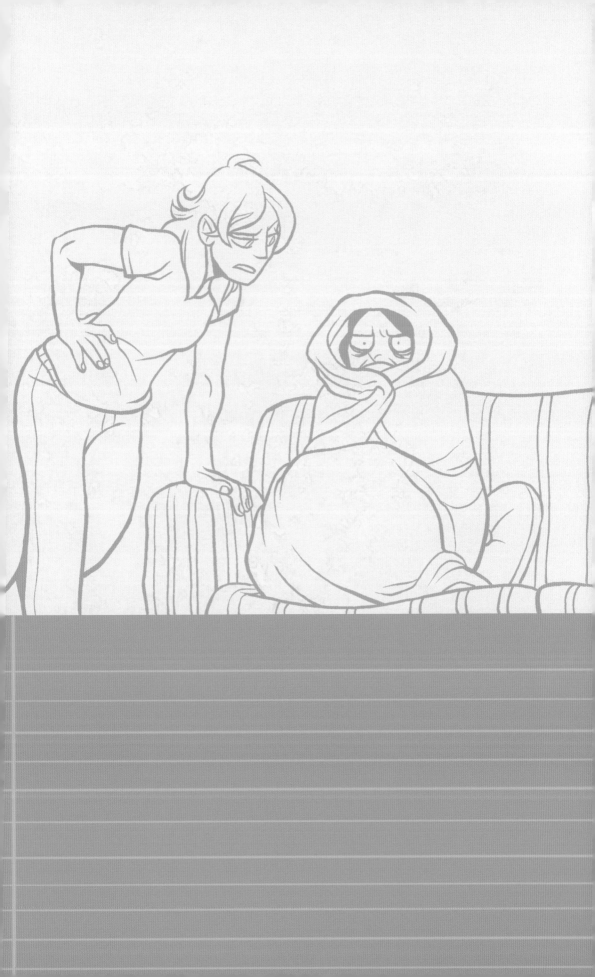

CHAPTER TWENTY-EIGHT

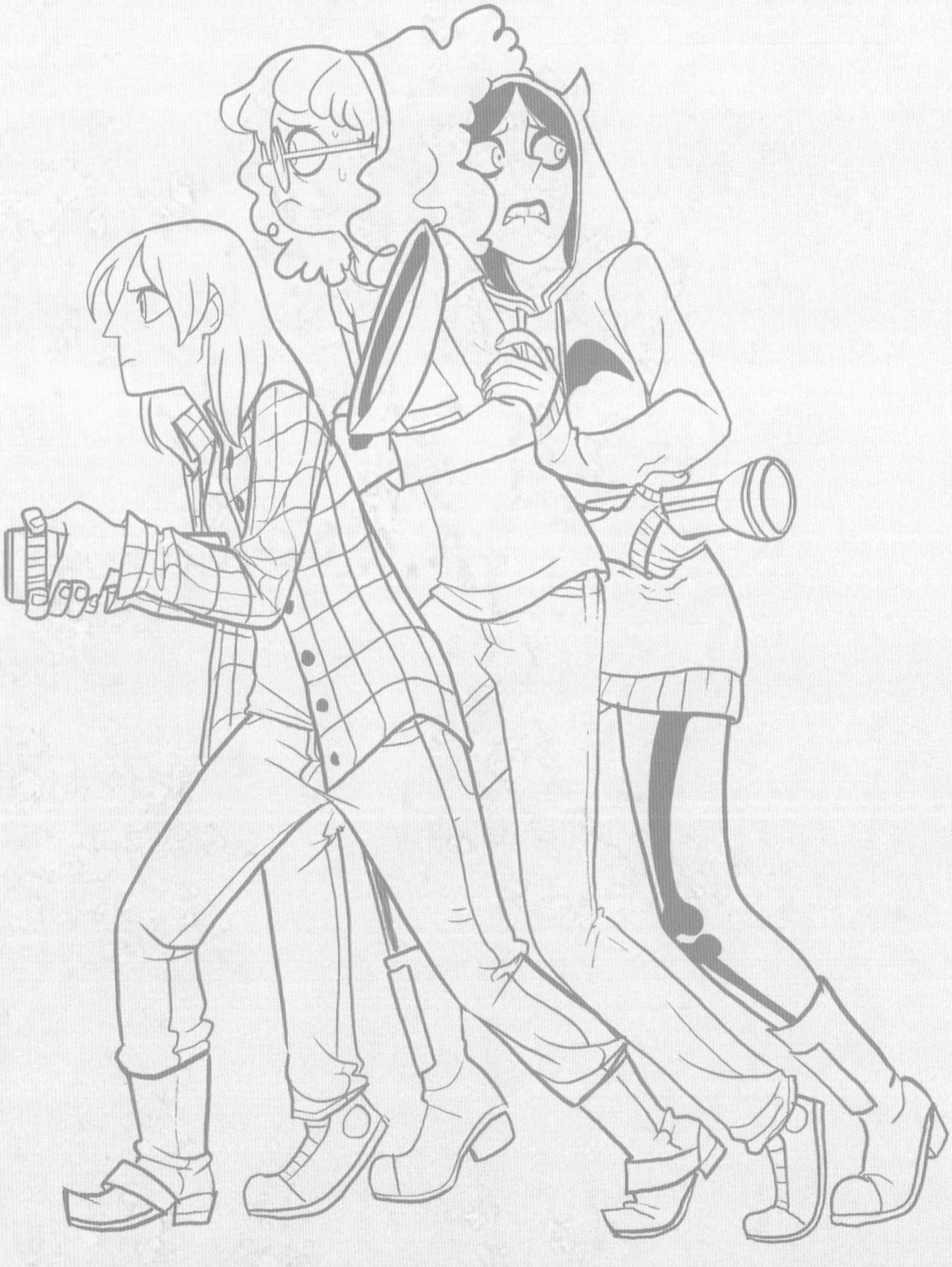

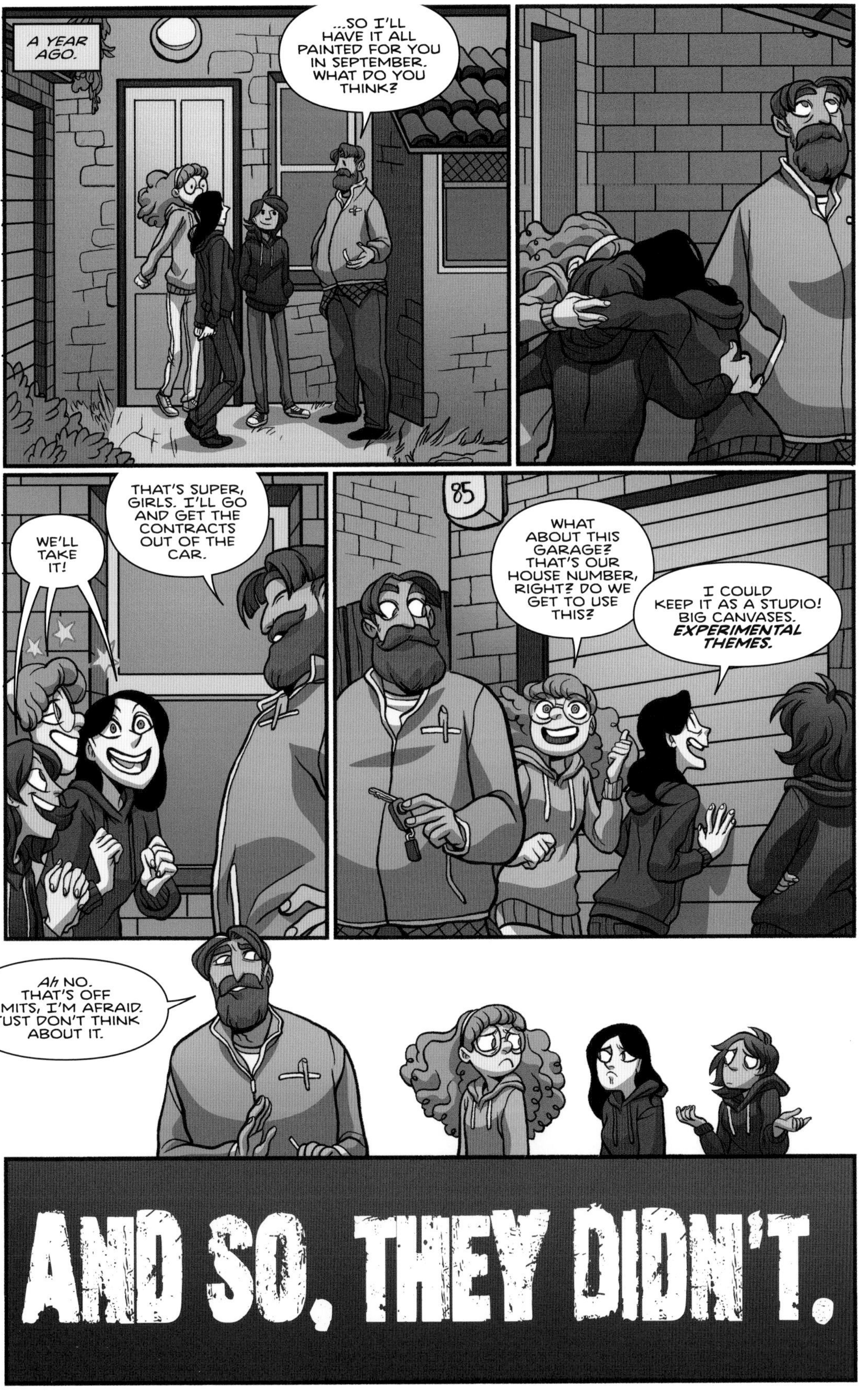
A YEAR AGO.
...SO I'LL HAVE IT ALL PAINTED FOR YOU IN SEPTEMBER. WHAT DO YOU THINK?
WE'LL TAKE IT!
THAT'S SUPER, GIRLS. I'LL GO AND GET THE CONTRACTS OUT OF THE CAR.
85
WHAT ABOUT THIS GARAGE? THAT'S OUR HOUSE NUMBER, RIGHT? DO WE GET TO USE THIS?
I COULD KEEP IT AS A STUDIO! BIG CANVASES. EXPERIMENTAL THEMES.
Ah NO. THAT'S OFF LIMITS, I'M AFRAID. JUST DON'T THINK ABOUT IT.
AND SO, THEY DIDN'T.

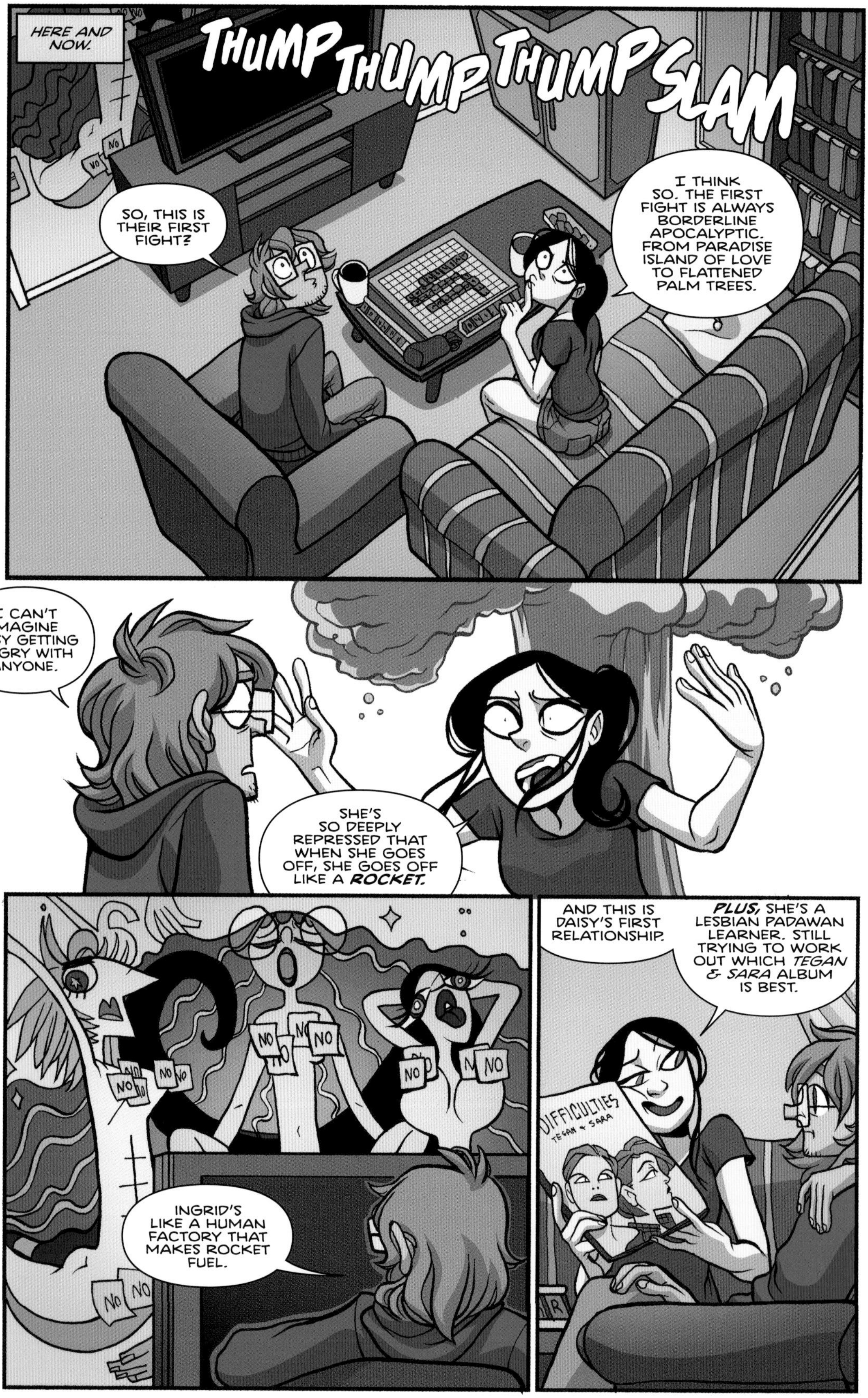
HERE AND NOW.
THUMP THUMP THUMP SLAM
SO, THIS IS THEIR FIRST FIGHT?
I THINK SO. THE FIRST FIGHT IS ALWAYS BORDERLINE APOCALYPTIC. FROM PARADISE ISLAND OF LOVE TO FLATTENED PALM TREES.
I CAN'T IMAGINE DAISY GETTING ANGRY WITH ANYONE.
SHE'S SO DEEPLY REPRESSED THAT WHEN SHE GOES OFF, SHE GOES OFF LIKE A ROCKET.
NO
NO
NO
INGRID'S LIKE A HUMAN FACTORY THAT MAKES ROCKET FUEL.
AND THIS IS DAISY'S FIRST RELATIONSHIP.
PLUS, SHE'S A LESBIAN PADAWAN LEARNER. STILL TRYING TO WORK OUT WHICH TEGAN & SARA ALBUM IS BEST.
DIFFICULTIES
TEGAN & SARA

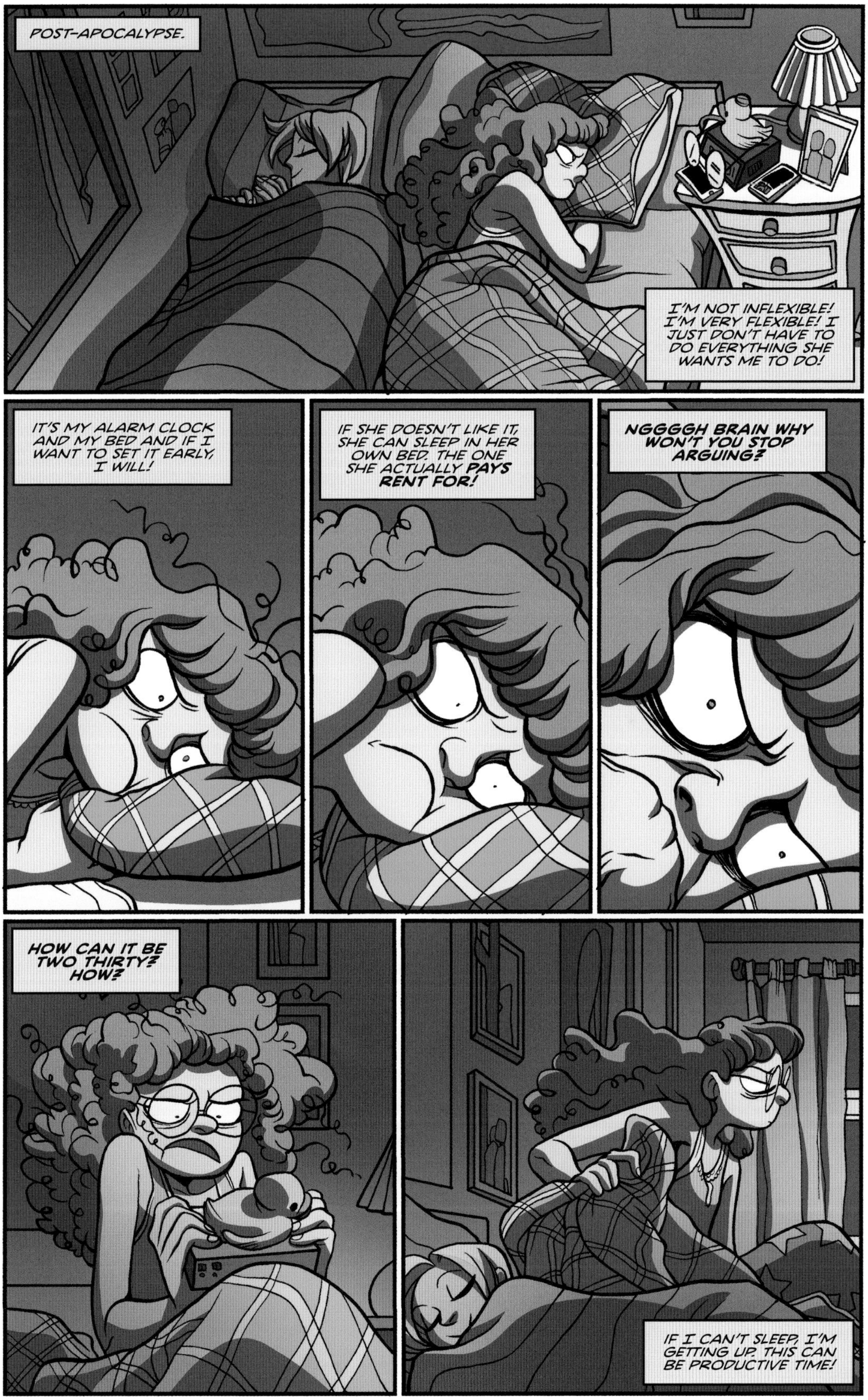
POST-APOCALYPSE.
I'M NOT INFLEXIBLE! I'M VERY FLEXIBLE! I JUST DON'T HAVE TO DO EVERYTHING SHE WANTS ME TO DO!
IT'S MY ALARM CLOCK AND MY BED AND IF I WANT TO SET IT EARLY, I WILL!
IF SHE DOESN'T LIKE IT, SHE CAN SLEEP IN HER OWN BED. THE ONE SHE ACTUALLY **PAYS RENT FOR!**
NGGGGH BRAIN WHY WON'T YOU STOP ARGUING?
HOW CAN IT BE TWO THIRTY? HOW?
IF I CAN'T SLEEP, I'M GETTING UP. THIS CAN BE PRODUCTIVE TIME!

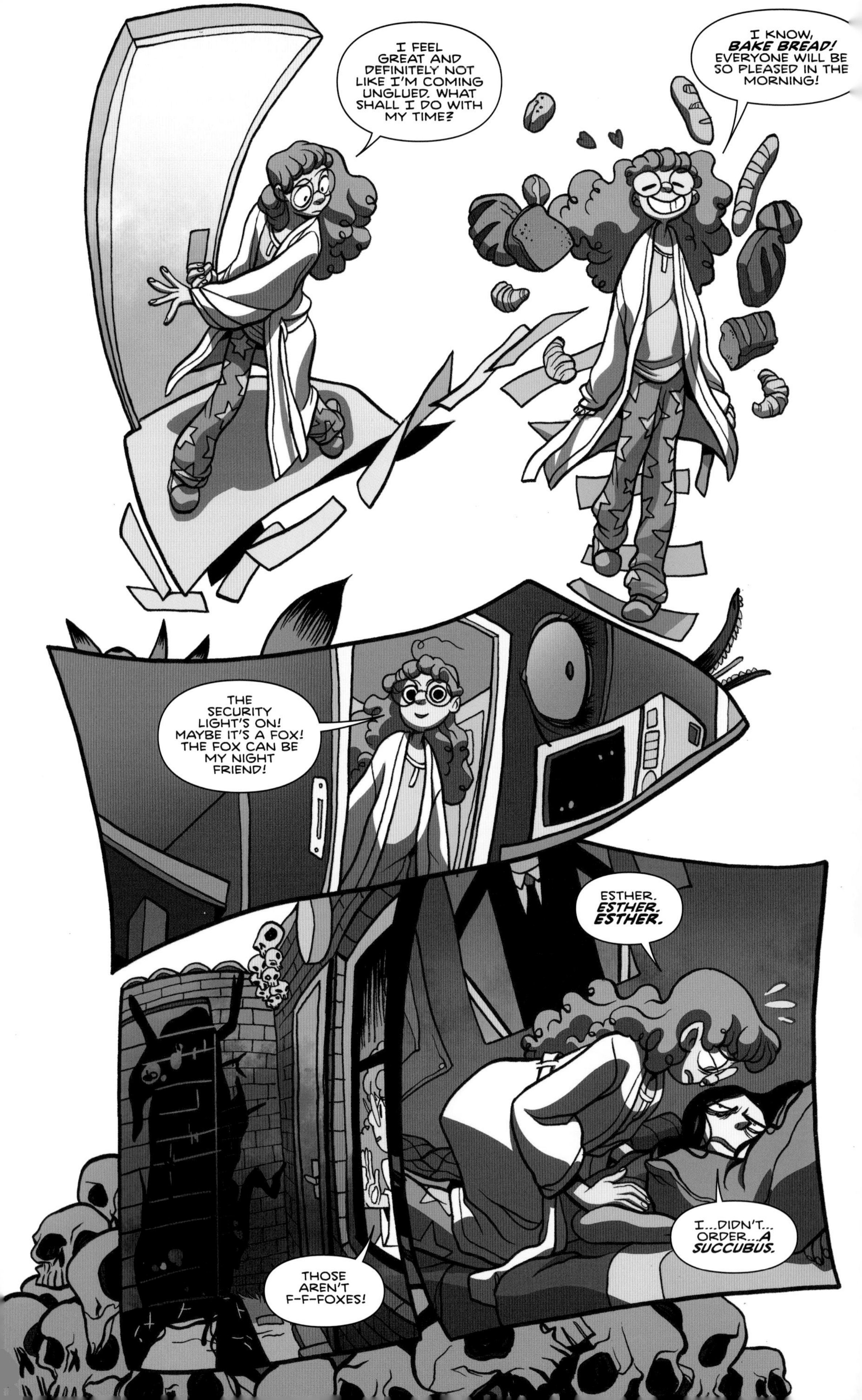
I FEEL GREAT AND DEFINITELY NOT LIKE I'M COMING UNGLUED. WHAT SHALL I DO WITH MY TIME?
I KNOW, BAKE BREAD! EVERYONE WILL BE SO PLEASED IN THE MORNING!
THE SECURITY LIGHT'S ON! MAYBE IT'S A FOX! THE FOX CAN BE MY NIGHT FRIEND!
ESTHER. ESTHER. ESTHER.
I...DIDN'T... ORDER...A SUCCUBUS.
THOSE AREN'T F-F-FOXES!

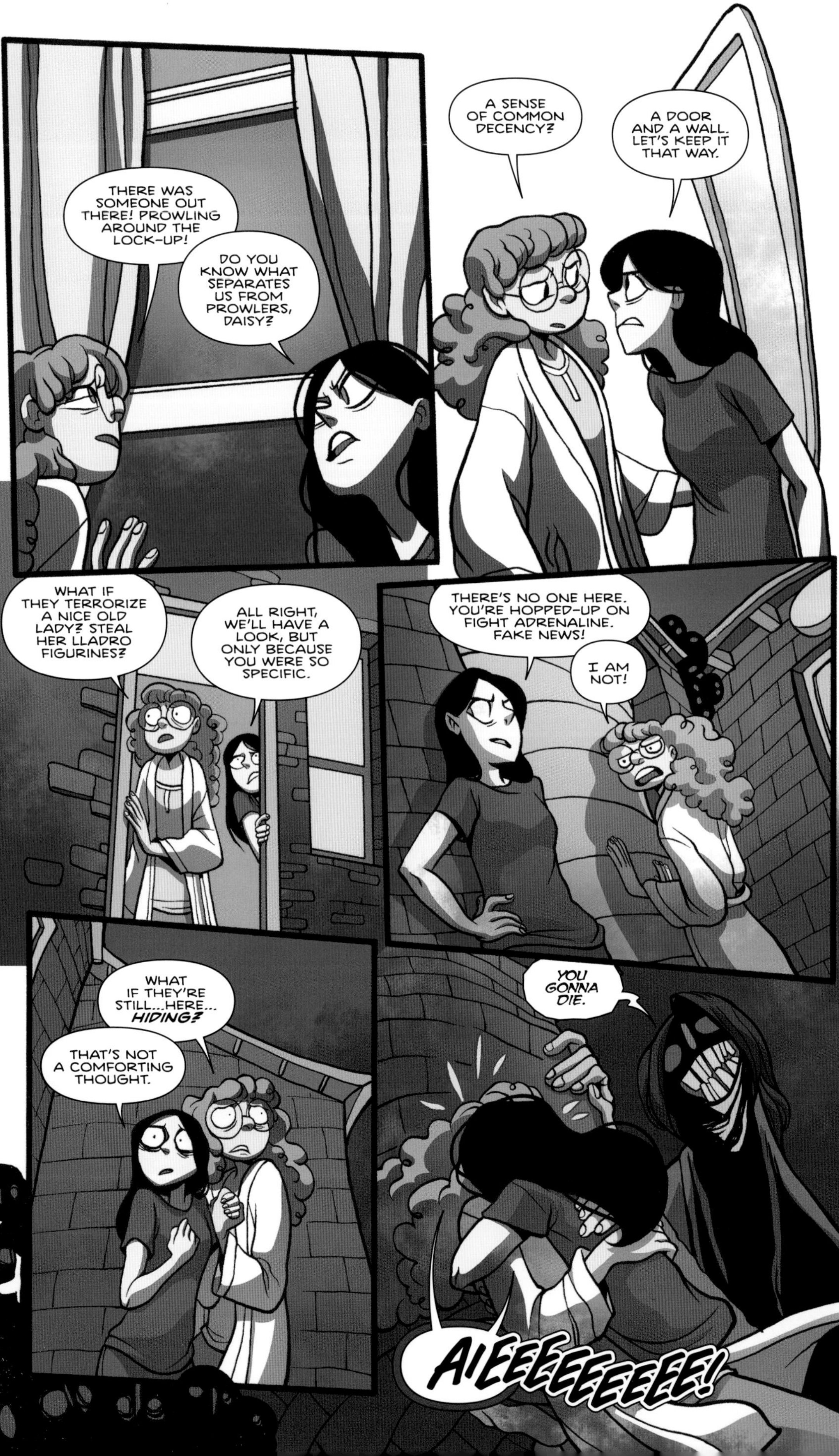
THERE WAS SOMEONE OUT THERE! PROWLING AROUND THE LOCK-UP!
DO YOU KNOW WHAT SEPARATES US FROM PROWLERS, DAISY?
A SENSE OF COMMON DECENCY?
A DOOR AND A WALL. LET'S KEEP IT THAT WAY.
WHAT IF THEY TERRORIZE A NICE OLD LADY? STEAL HER LLADRO FIGURINES?
ALL RIGHT, WE'LL HAVE A LOOK, BUT ONLY BECAUSE YOU WERE SO SPECIFIC.
THERE'S NO ONE HERE. YOU'RE HOPPED-UP ON FIGHT ADRENALINE. FAKE NEWS!
I AM NOT!
WHAT IF THEY'RE STILL...HERE... HIDING?
THAT'S NOT A COMFORTING THOUGHT.
YOU GONNA DIE.
AIEEEEEEEEEEE!

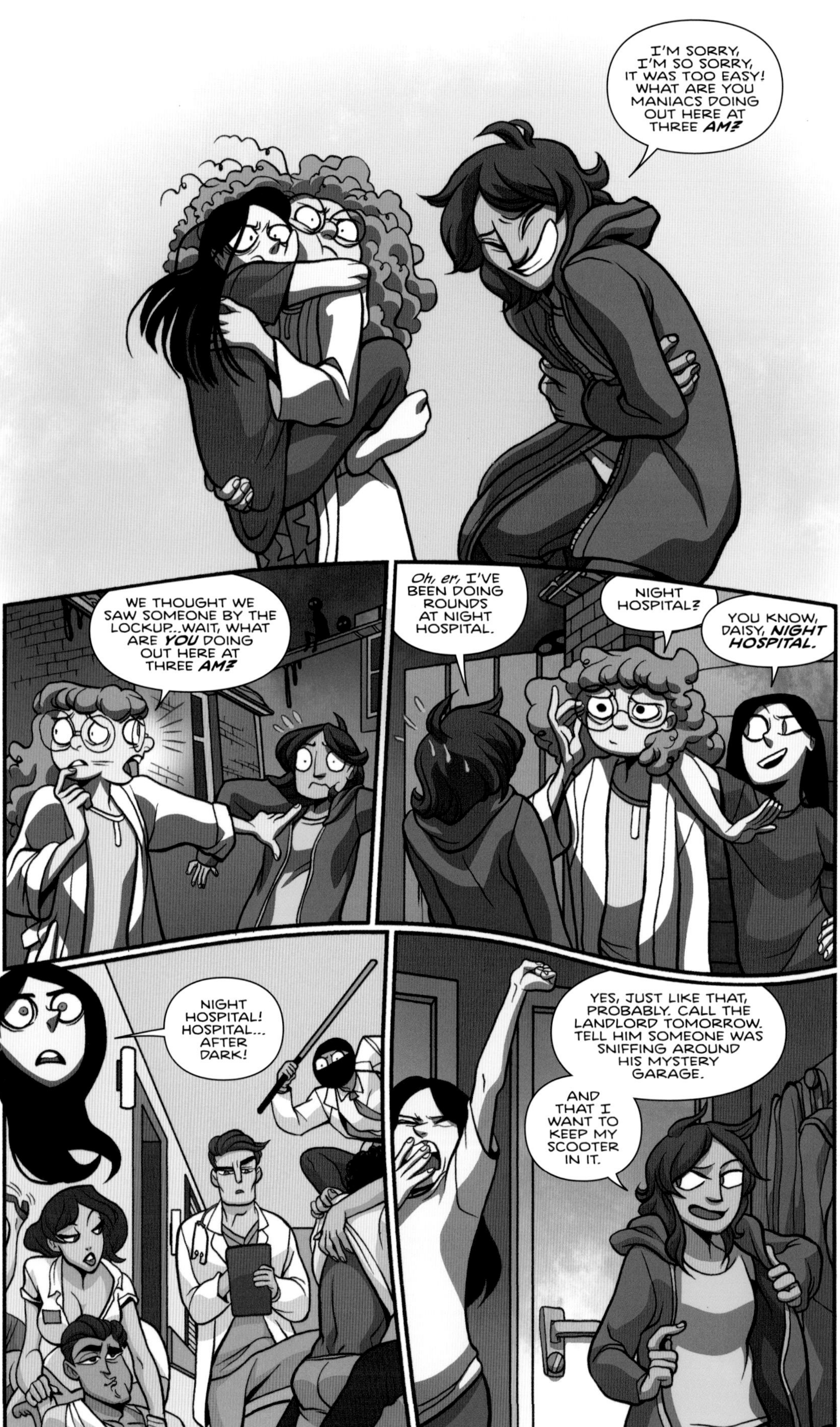

I'M SORRY, I'M SO SORRY, IT WAS TOO EASY! WHAT ARE YOU MANIACS DOING OUT HERE AT THREE AM?
WE THOUGHT WE SAW SOMEONE BY THE LOCKUP...WAIT, WHAT ARE YOU DOING OUT HERE AT THREE AM?
Oh, er, I'VE BEEN DOING ROUNDS AT NIGHT HOSPITAL.
NIGHT HOSPITAL?
YOU KNOW, DAISY, NIGHT HOSPITAL.
NIGHT HOSPITAL! HOSPITAL... AFTER DARK!
YES, JUST LIKE THAT, PROBABLY. CALL THE LANDLORD TOMORROW. TELL HIM SOMEONE WAS SNIFFING AROUND HIS MYSTERY GARAGE.
AND THAT I WANT TO KEEP MY SCOOTER IN IT.

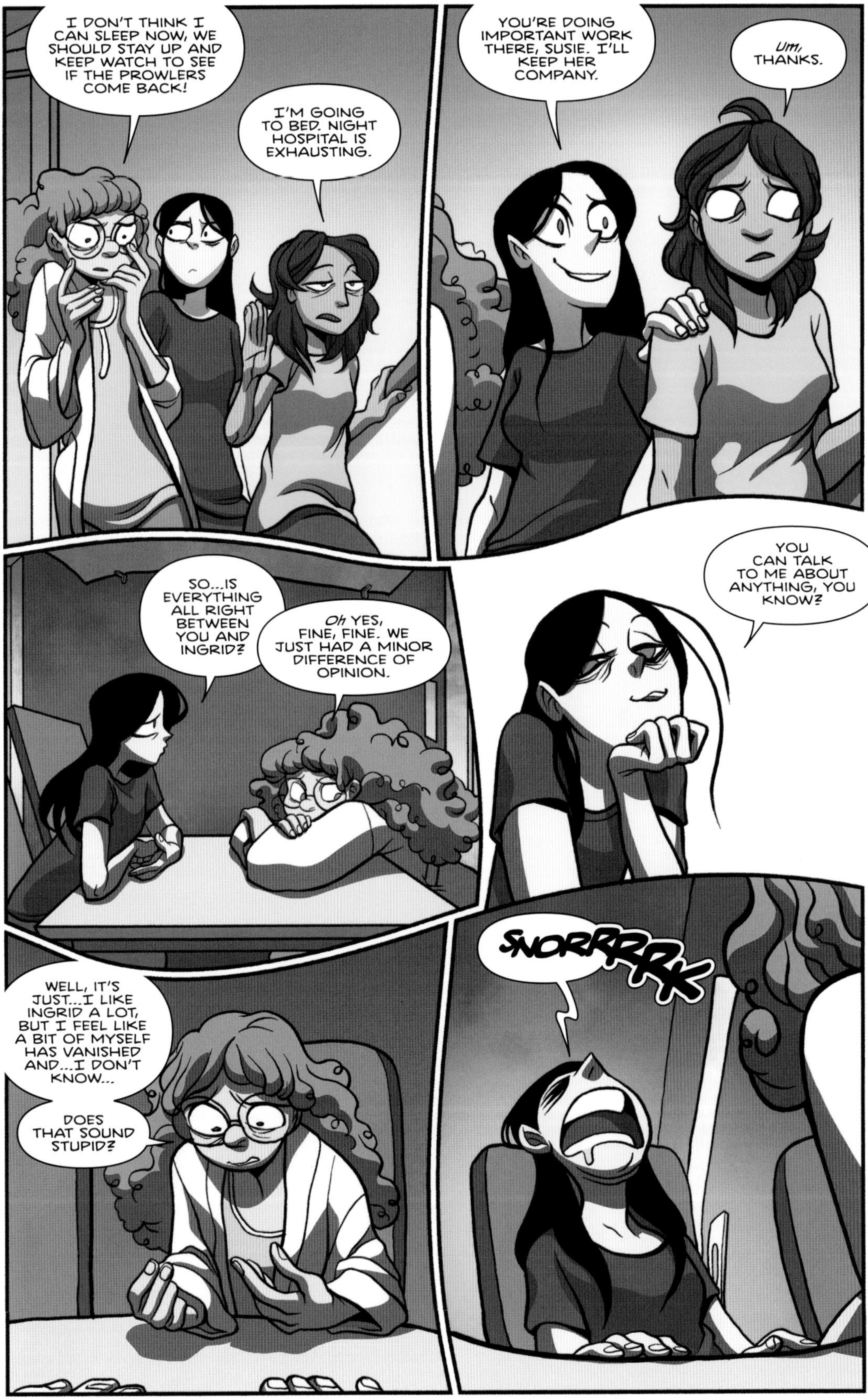
I DON'T THINK I CAN SLEEP NOW, WE SHOULD STAY UP AND KEEP WATCH TO SEE IF THE PROWLERS COME BACK!
I'M GOING TO BED. NIGHT HOSPITAL IS EXHAUSTING.
YOU'RE DOING IMPORTANT WORK THERE, SUSIE. I'LL KEEP HER COMPANY.
Um, THANKS.
SO...IS EVERYTHING ALL RIGHT BETWEEN YOU AND INGRID?
Oh YES, FINE, FINE. WE JUST HAD A MINOR DIFFERENCE OF OPINION.
YOU CAN TALK TO ME ABOUT ANYTHING, YOU KNOW?
WELL, IT'S JUST...I LIKE INGRID A LOT, BUT I FEEL LIKE A BIT OF MYSELF HAS VANISHED AND...I DON'T KNOW...
DOES THAT SOUND STUPID?
SNORRRRK

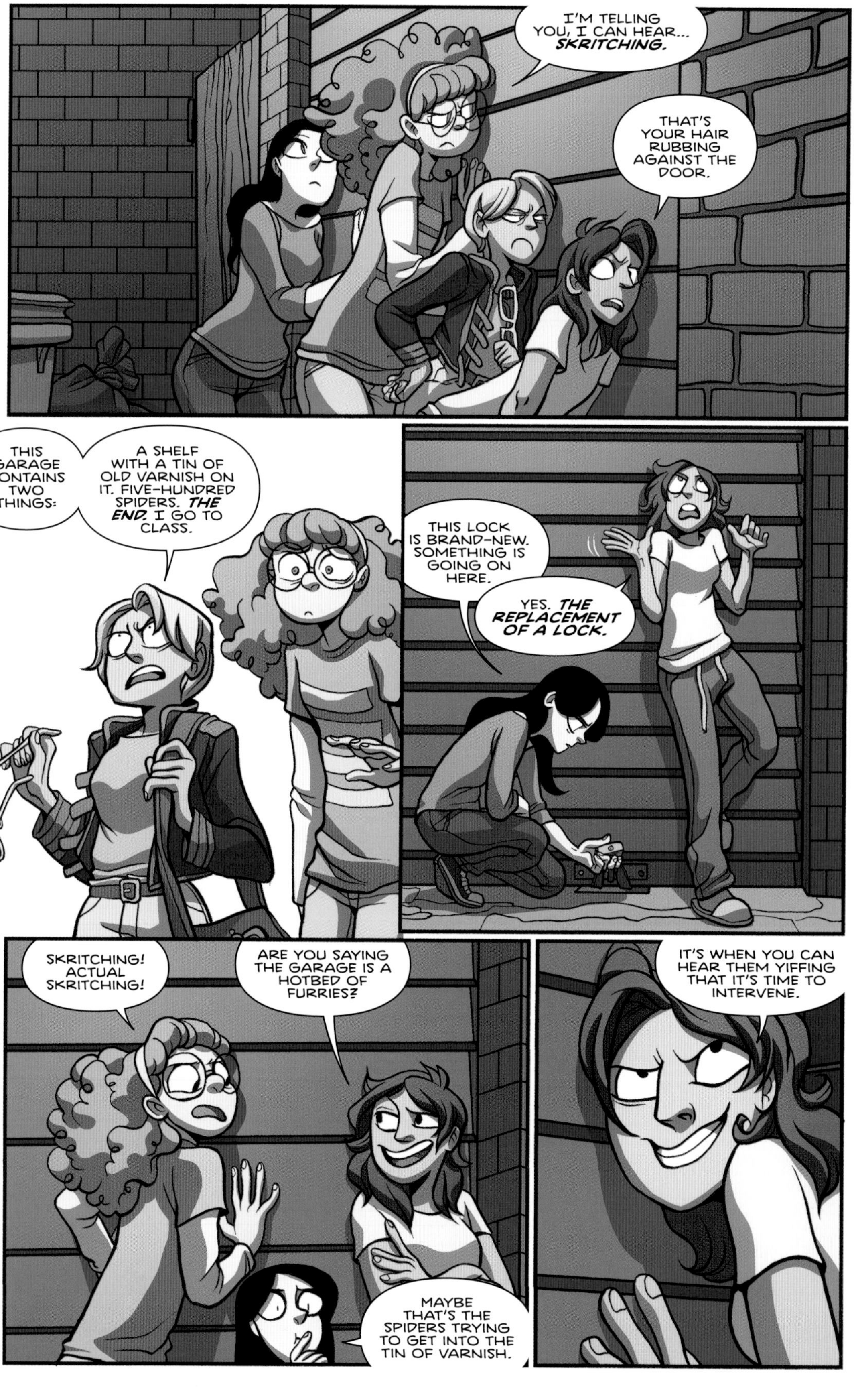
I'M TELLING YOU, I CAN HEAR... *SKRITCHING.*
THAT'S YOUR HAIR RUBBING AGAINST THE DOOR.
THIS GARAGE CONTAINS TWO THINGS:
A SHELF WITH A TIN OF OLD VARNISH ON IT. FIVE-HUNDRED SPIDERS. *THE END.* I GO TO CLASS.
THIS LOCK IS BRAND-NEW. SOMETHING IS GOING ON HERE.
YES. *THE REPLACEMENT OF A LOCK.*
SKRITCHING! ACTUAL SKRITCHING!
ARE YOU SAYING THE GARAGE IS A HOTBED OF FURRIES?
MAYBE THAT'S THE SPIDERS TRYING TO GET INTO THE TIN OF VARNISH.
IT'S WHEN YOU CAN HEAR THEM YIFFING THAT IT'S TIME TO INTERVENE.

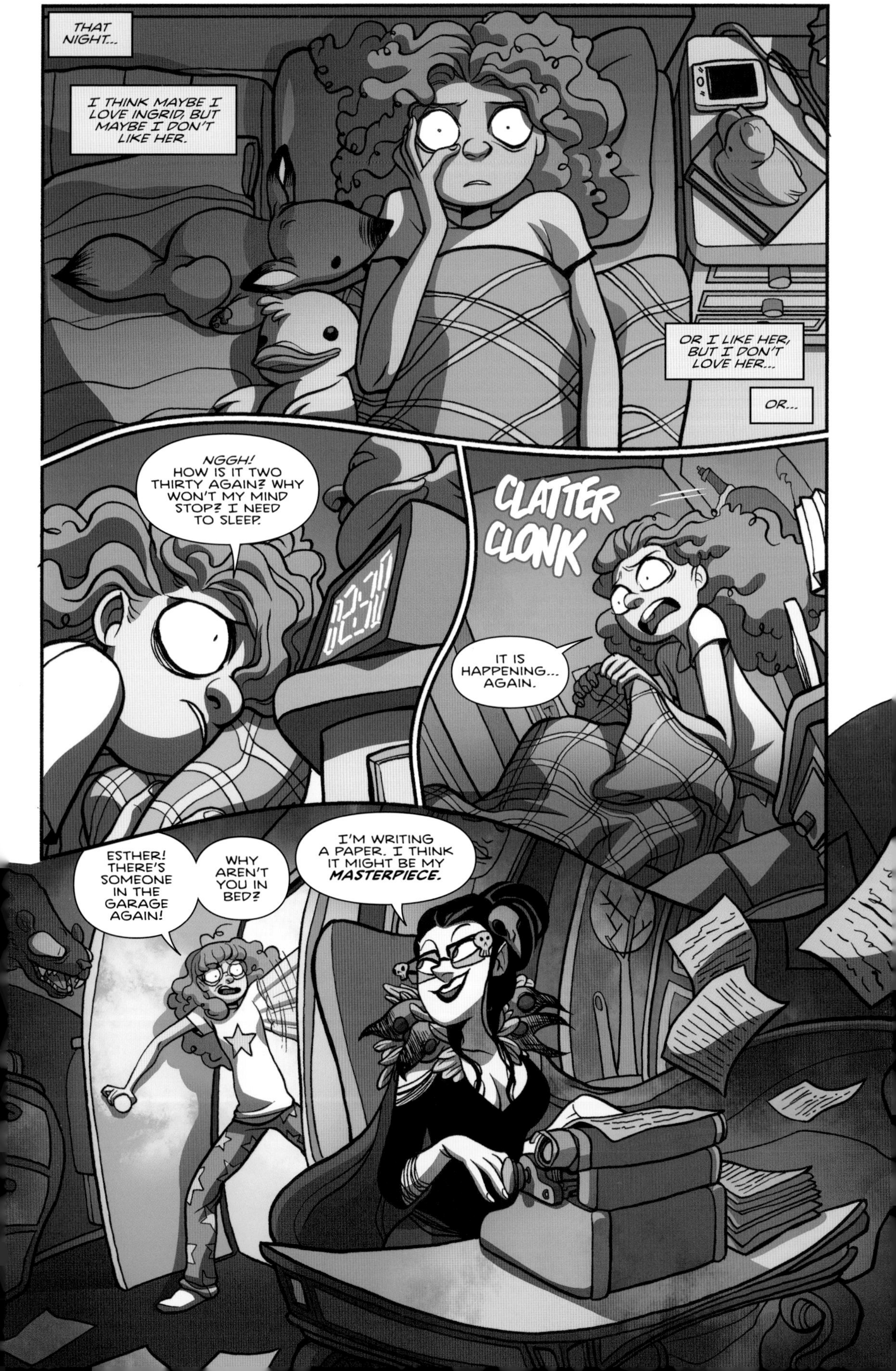
THAT NIGHT...
I THINK MAYBE I LOVE INGRID, BUT MAYBE I DON'T LIKE HER.
OR I LIKE HER, BUT I DON'T LOVE HER...
OR...
NGGH! HOW IS IT TWO THIRTY AGAIN? WHY WON'T MY MIND STOP? I NEED TO SLEEP.
CLATTER CLONK
IT IS HAPPENING... AGAIN.
ESTHER! THERE'S SOMEONE IN THE GARAGE AGAIN!
WHY AREN'T YOU IN BED?
I'M WRITING A PAPER. I THINK IT MIGHT BE MY MASTERPIECE.

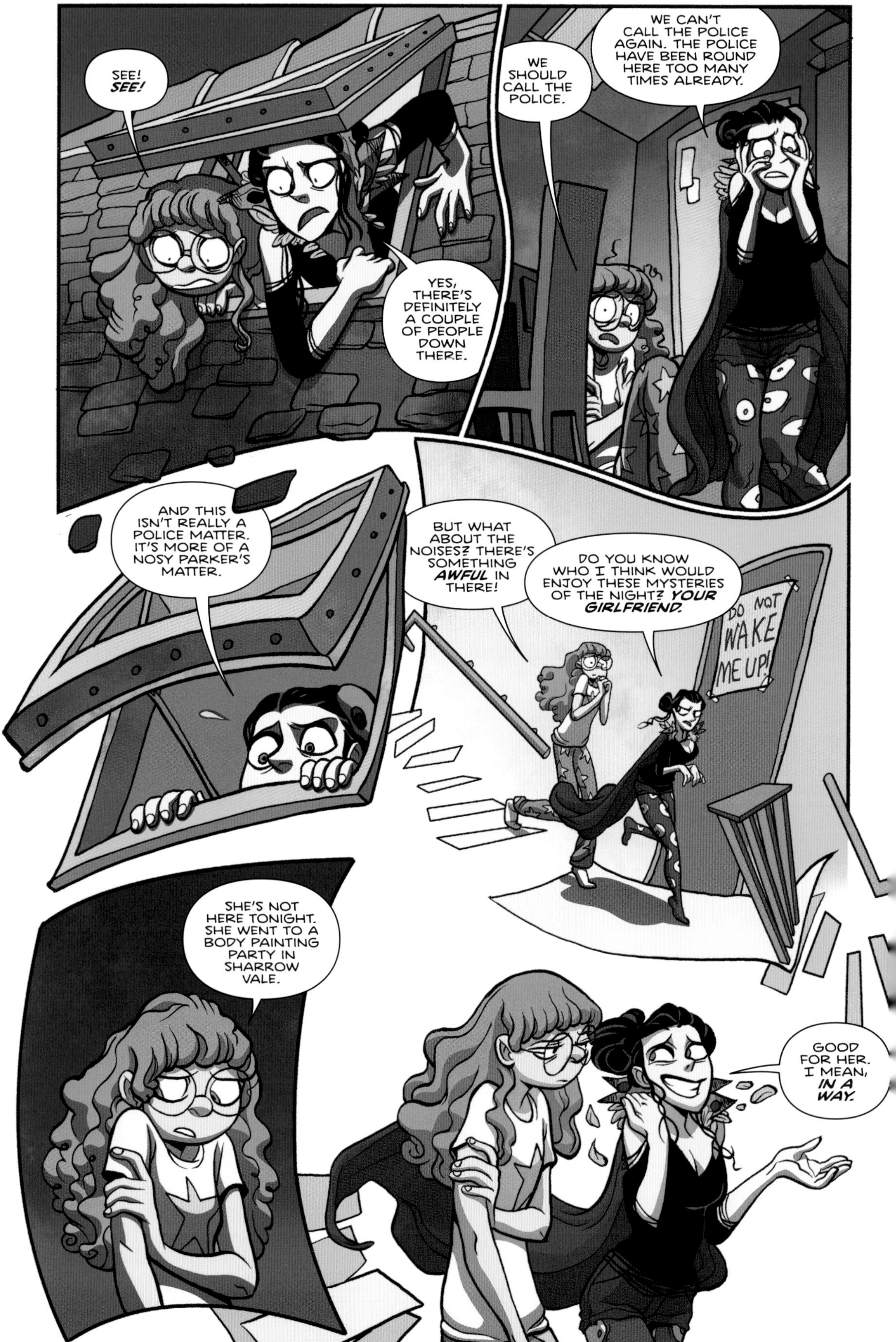
SEE! *SEE!*
YES, THERE'S DEFINITELY A COUPLE OF PEOPLE DOWN THERE.
WE SHOULD CALL THE POLICE.
WE CAN'T CALL THE POLICE AGAIN. THE POLICE HAVE BEEN ROUND HERE TOO MANY TIMES ALREADY.
AND THIS ISN'T REALLY A POLICE MATTER. IT'S MORE OF A NOSY PARKER'S MATTER.
BUT WHAT ABOUT THE NOISES? THERE'S SOMETHING *AWFUL* IN THERE!
DO YOU KNOW WHO I THINK WOULD ENJOY THESE MYSTERIES OF THE NIGHT? *YOUR GIRLFRIEND.*
DO NOT WAKE ME UP!
SHE'S NOT HERE TONIGHT. SHE WENT TO A BODY PAINTING PARTY IN SHARROW VALE.
GOOD FOR HER. I MEAN, *IN A WAY.*

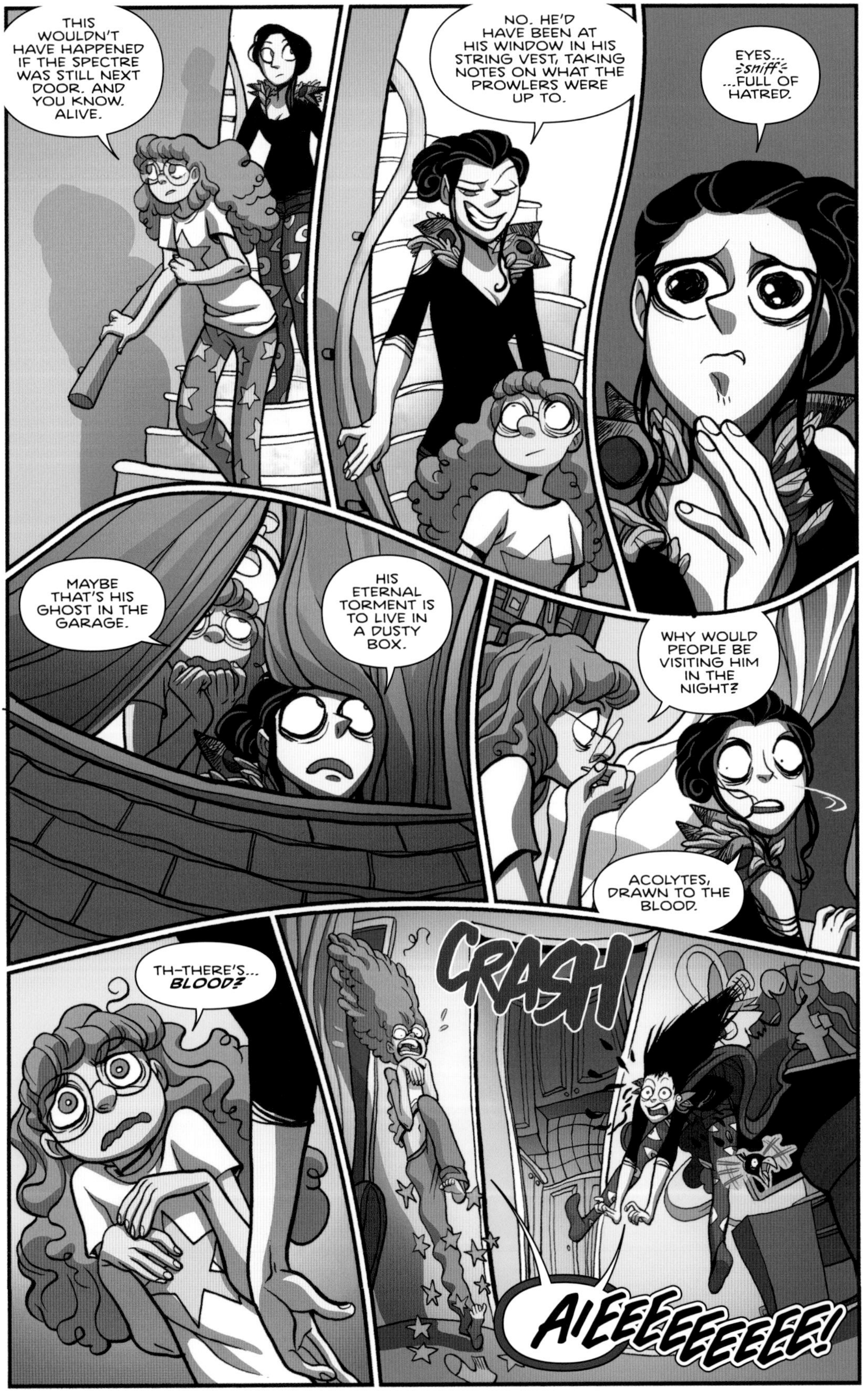
THIS WOULDN'T HAVE HAPPENED IF THE SPECTRE WAS STILL NEXT DOOR. AND YOU KNOW. ALIVE.
NO. HE'D HAVE BEEN AT HIS WINDOW IN HIS STRING VEST, TAKING NOTES ON WHAT THE PROWLERS WERE UP TO.
EYES... *sniff* ...FULL OF HATRED.
MAYBE THAT'S HIS GHOST IN THE GARAGE.
HIS ETERNAL TORMENT IS TO LIVE IN A DUSTY BOX.
WHY WOULD PEOPLE BE VISITING HIM IN THE NIGHT?
ACOLYTES, DRAWN TO THE BLOOD.
TH-THERE'S... BLOOD?
CRASH
AIEEEEEEEEEEE!

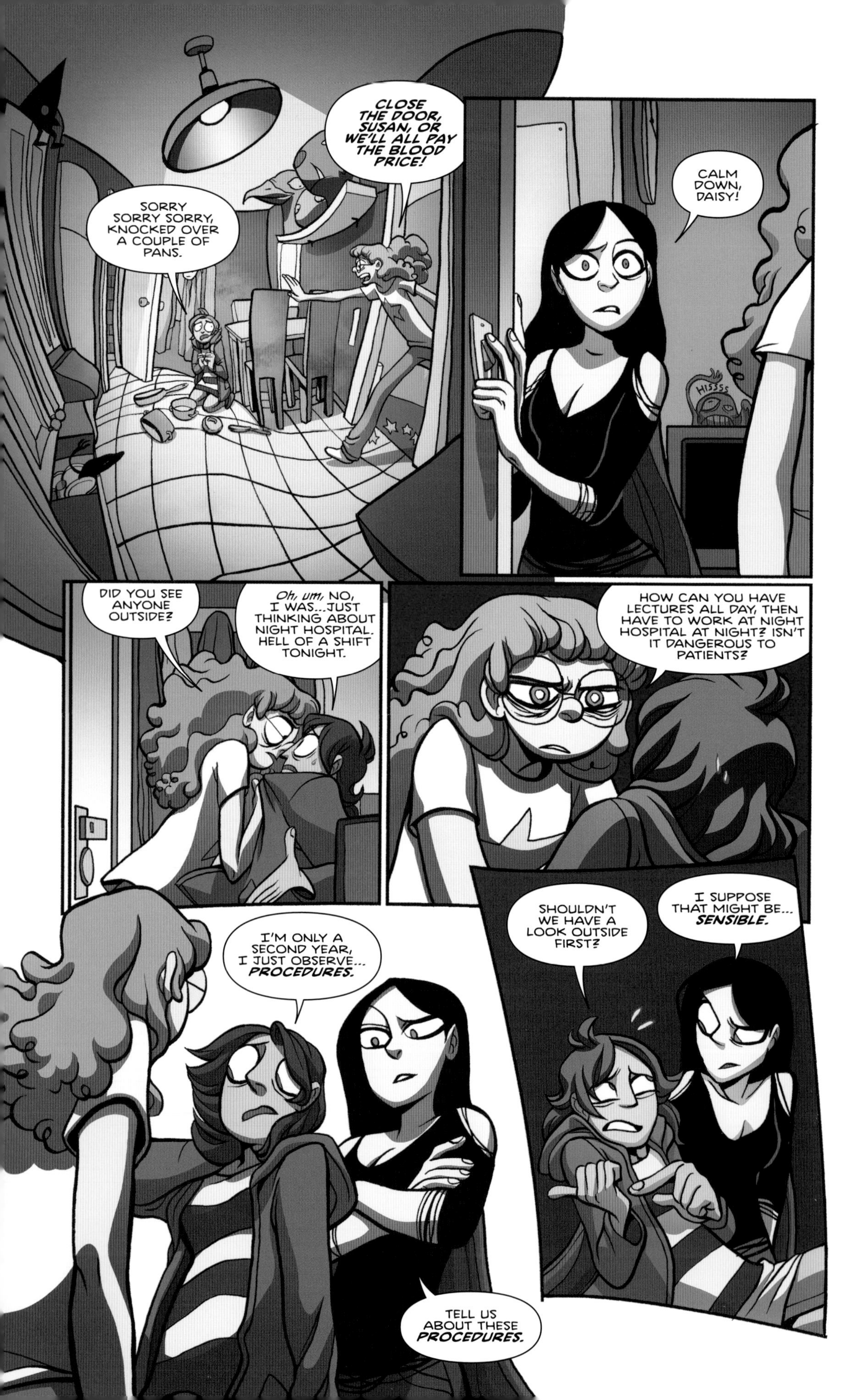
SORRY SORRY SORRY, KNOCKED OVER A COUPLE OF PANS.
CLOSE THE DOOR, SUSAN, OR WE'LL ALL PAY THE BLOOD PRICE!
CALM DOWN, DAISY!
HISSSS
DID YOU SEE ANYONE OUTSIDE?
Oh, um, NO, I WAS... JUST THINKING ABOUT NIGHT HOSPITAL. HELL OF A SHIFT TONIGHT.
HOW CAN YOU HAVE LECTURES ALL DAY, THEN HAVE TO WORK AT NIGHT HOSPITAL AT NIGHT? ISN'T IT DANGEROUS TO PATIENTS?
I'M ONLY A SECOND YEAR, I JUST OBSERVE... PROCEDURES.
TELL US ABOUT THESE PROCEDURES.
SHOULDN'T WE HAVE A LOOK OUTSIDE FIRST?
I SUPPOSE THAT MIGHT BE... SENSIBLE.

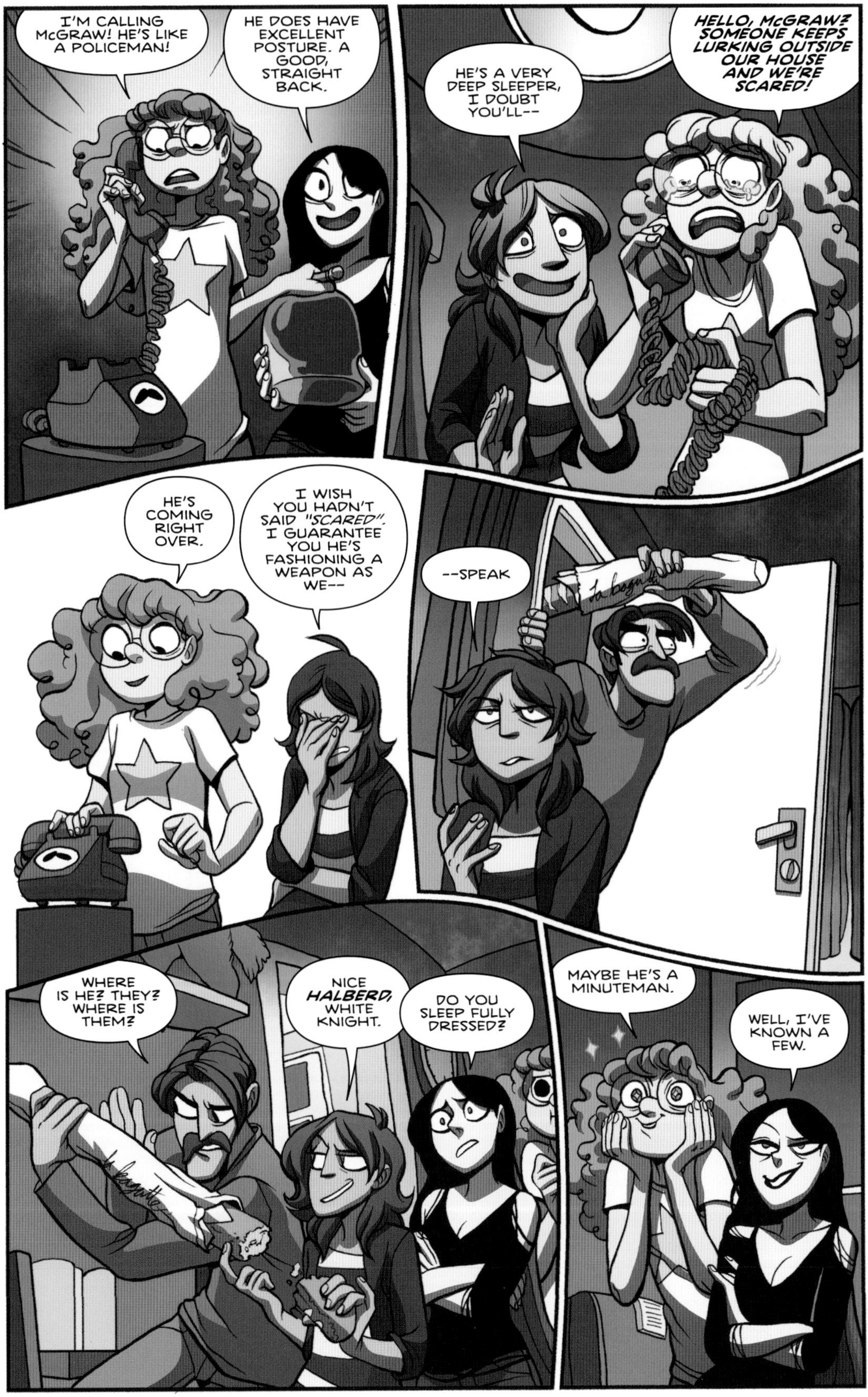
I'M CALLING McGRAW! HE'S LIKE A POLICEMAN!
HE DOES HAVE EXCELLENT POSTURE. A GOOD, STRAIGHT BACK.
HE'S A VERY DEEP SLEEPER, I DOUBT YOU'LL--
HELLO, McGRAW? SOMEONE KEEPS LURKING OUTSIDE OUR HOUSE AND WE'RE SCARED!
HE'S COMING RIGHT OVER.
I WISH YOU HADN'T SAID "SCARED". I GUARANTEE YOU HE'S FASHIONING A WEAPON AS WE--
--SPEAK
WHERE IS HE? THEY? WHERE IS THEM?
NICE HALBERD, WHITE KNIGHT.
DO YOU SLEEP FULLY DRESSED?
MAYBE HE'S A MINUTEMAN.
WELL, I'VE KNOWN A FEW.

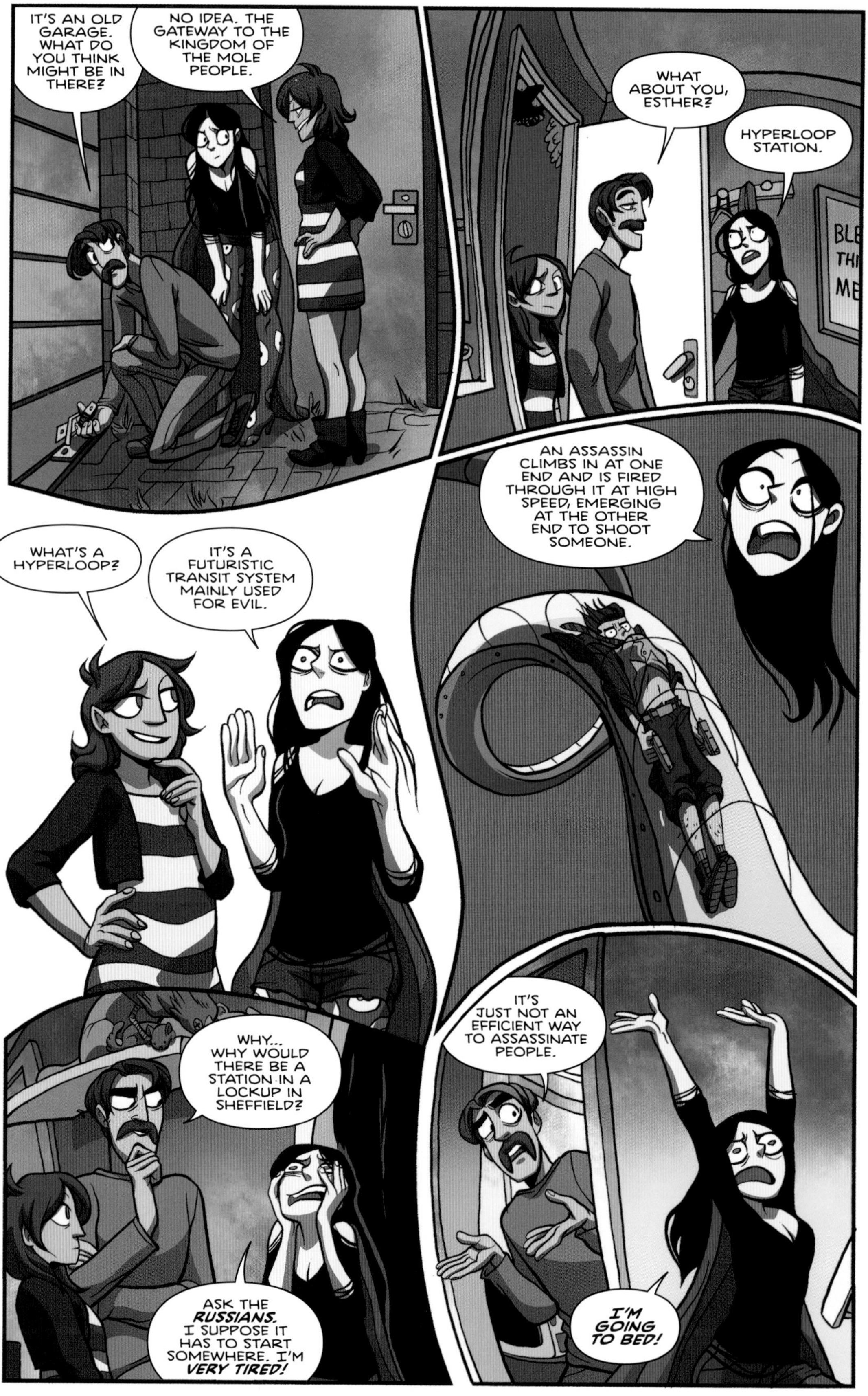
IT'S AN OLD GARAGE. WHAT DO YOU THINK MIGHT BE IN THERE?
NO IDEA. THE GATEWAY TO THE KINGDOM OF THE MOLE PEOPLE.
WHAT ABOUT YOU, ESTHER?
HYPERLOOP STATION.
BLE
THI
ME
WHAT'S A HYPERLOOP?
IT'S A FUTURISTIC TRANSIT SYSTEM MAINLY USED FOR EVIL.
AN ASSASSIN CLIMBS IN AT ONE END AND IS FIRED THROUGH IT AT HIGH SPEED, EMERGING AT THE OTHER END TO SHOOT SOMEONE.
WHY... WHY WOULD THERE BE A STATION IN A LOCKUP IN SHEFFIELD?
ASK THE ***RUSSIANS.*** I SUPPOSE IT HAS TO START SOMEWHERE. I'M ***VERY TIRED!***
IT'S JUST NOT AN EFFICIENT WAY TO ASSASSINATE PEOPLE.
I'M GOING TO BED!

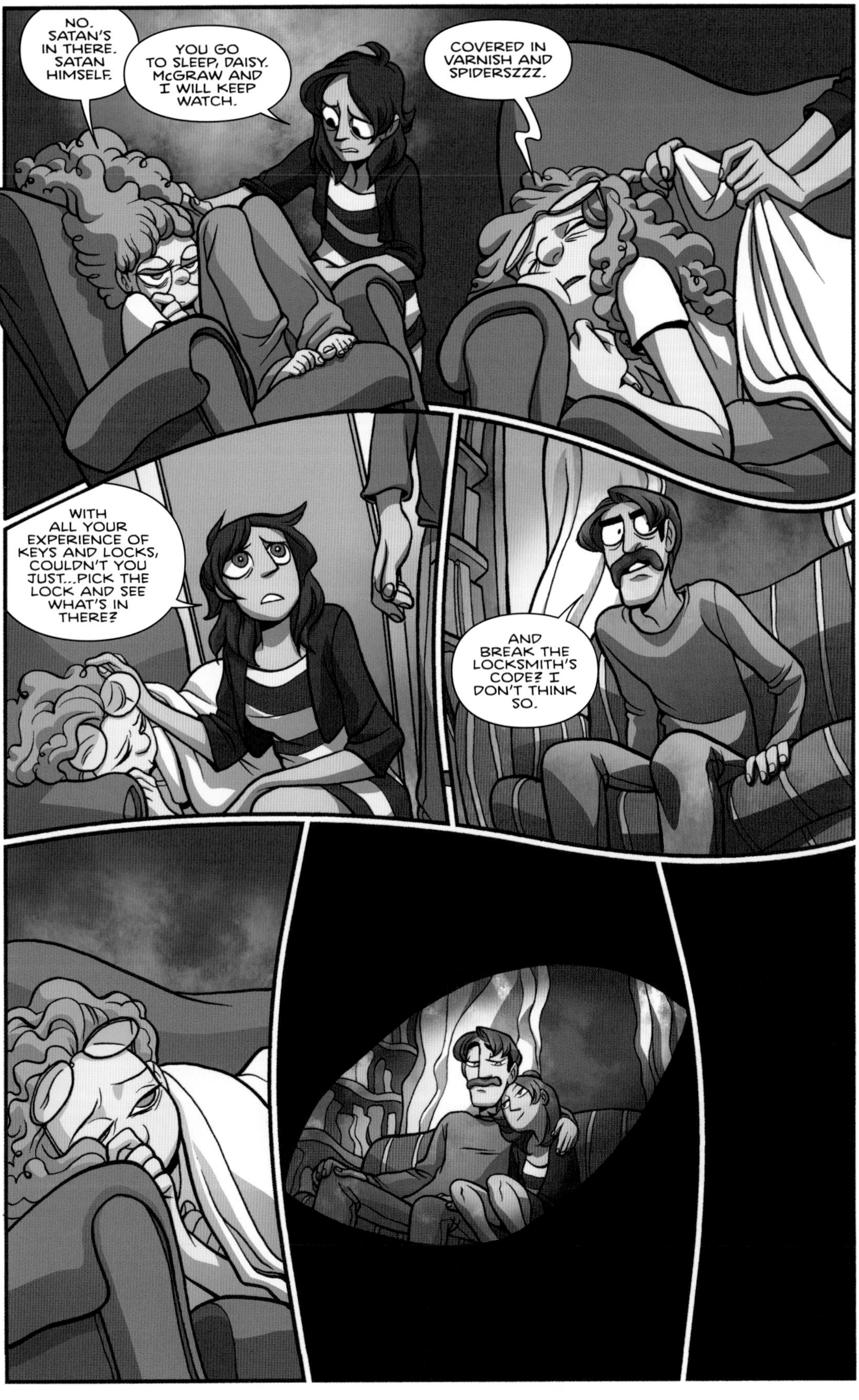
NO. SATAN'S IN THERE. SATAN HIMSELF.
YOU GO TO SLEEP, DAISY. McGRAW AND I WILL KEEP WATCH.
COVERED IN VARNISH AND SPIDERSZZZ.
WITH ALL YOUR EXPERIENCE OF KEYS AND LOCKS, COULDN'T YOU JUST...PICK THE LOCK AND SEE WHAT'S IN THERE?
AND BREAK THE LOCKSMITH'S CODE? I DON'T THINK SO.

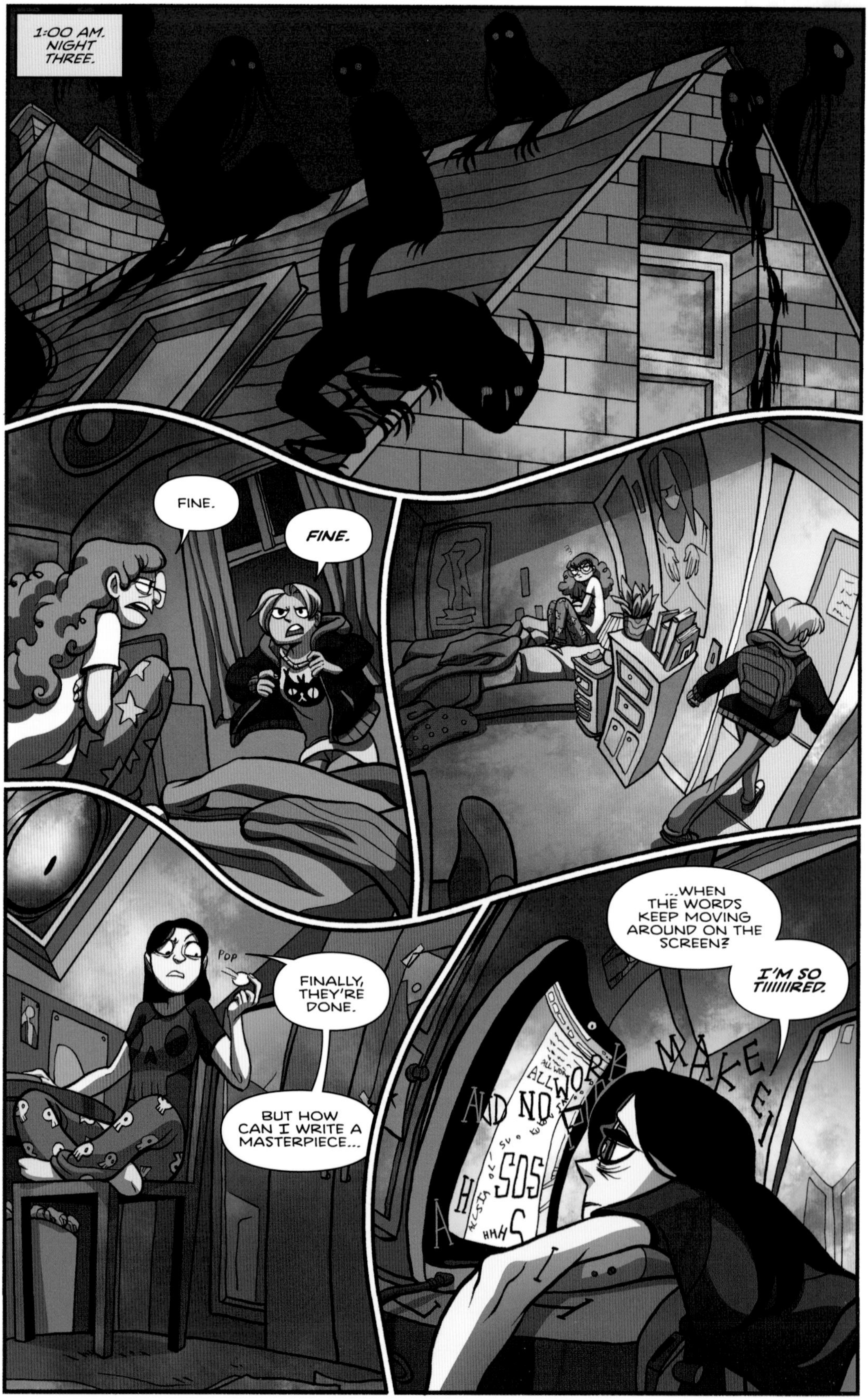
1:00 AM.
NIGHT
THREE.
FINE.
FINE.
POP
FINALLY, THEY'RE DONE.
BUT HOW CAN I WRITE A MASTERPIECE...
...WHEN THE WORDS KEEP MOVING AROUND ON THE SCREEN?
I'M SO TIIIIIRED.
AND NO
SOS

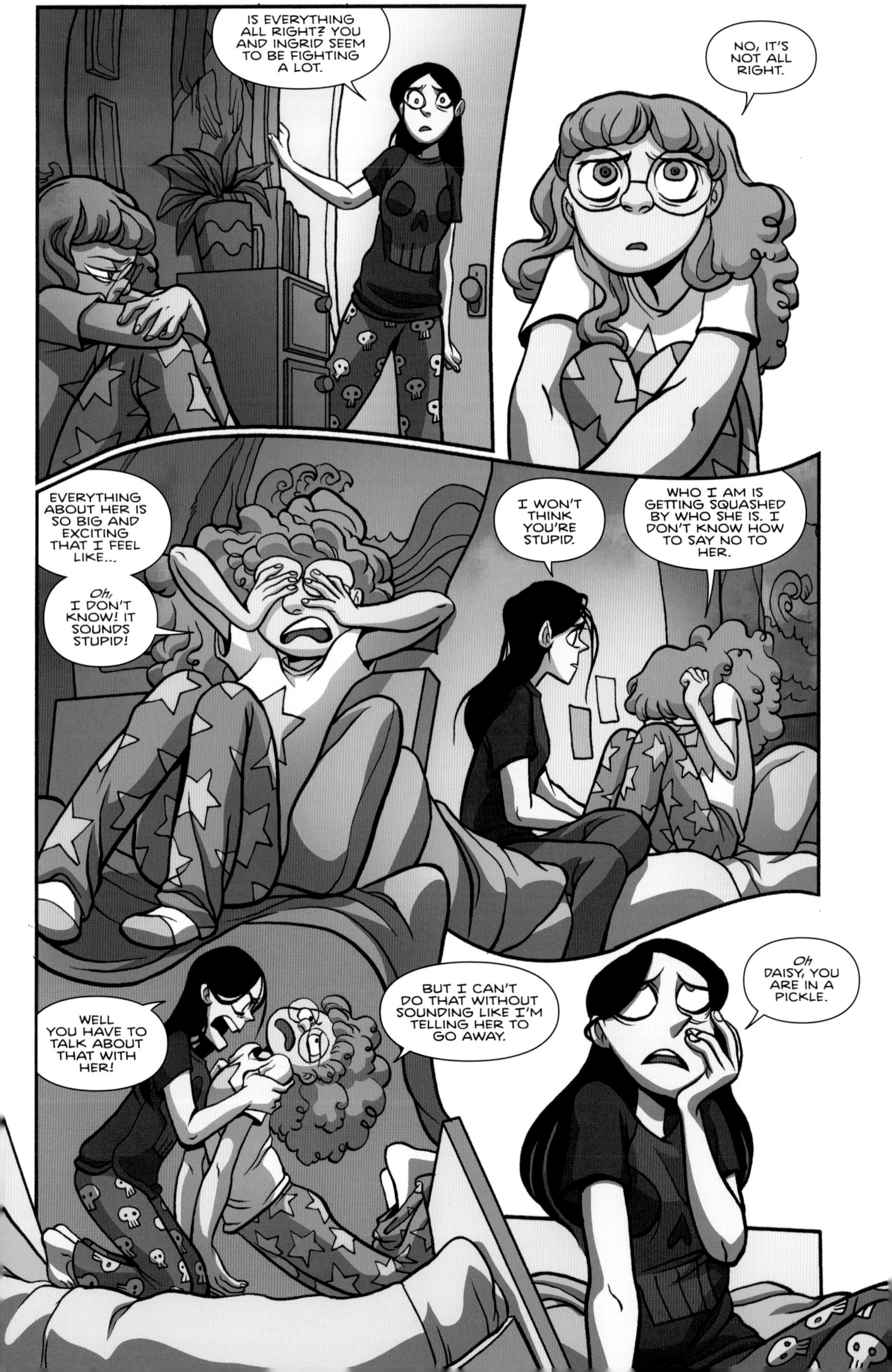
IS EVERYTHING ALL RIGHT? YOU AND INGRID SEEM TO BE FIGHTING A LOT.
NO, IT'S NOT ALL RIGHT.
EVERYTHING ABOUT HER IS SO BIG AND EXCITING THAT I FEEL LIKE...
Oh, I DON'T KNOW! IT SOUNDS STUPID!
I WON'T THINK YOU'RE STUPID.
WHO I AM IS GETTING SQUASHED BY WHO SHE IS. I DON'T KNOW HOW TO SAY NO TO HER.
WELL YOU HAVE TO TALK ABOUT THAT WITH HER!
BUT I CAN'T DO THAT WITHOUT SOUNDING LIKE I'M TELLING HER TO GO AWAY.
Oh DAISY, YOU ARE IN A PICKLE.

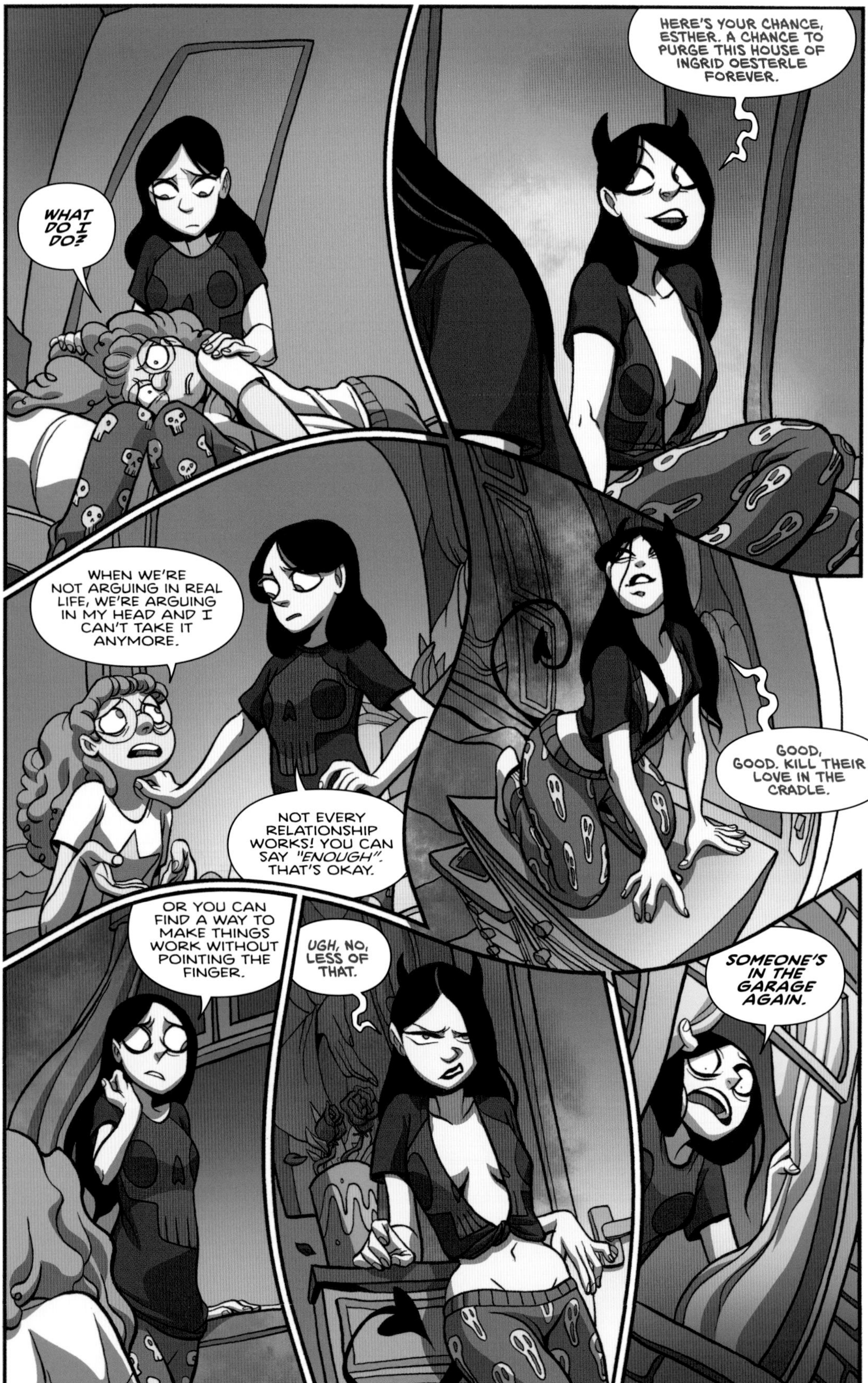
WHAT DO I DO?
HERE'S YOUR CHANCE, ESTHER. A CHANCE TO PURGE THIS HOUSE OF INGRID OESTERLE FOREVER.
WHEN WE'RE NOT ARGUING IN REAL LIFE, WE'RE ARGUING IN MY HEAD AND I CAN'T TAKE IT ANYMORE.
NOT EVERY RELATIONSHIP WORKS! YOU CAN SAY "ENOUGH". THAT'S OKAY.
GOOD, GOOD. KILL THEIR LOVE IN THE CRADLE.
OR YOU CAN FIND A WAY TO MAKE THINGS WORK WITHOUT POINTING THE FINGER.
UGH, NO, LESS OF THAT.
SOMEONE'S IN THE GARAGE AGAIN.

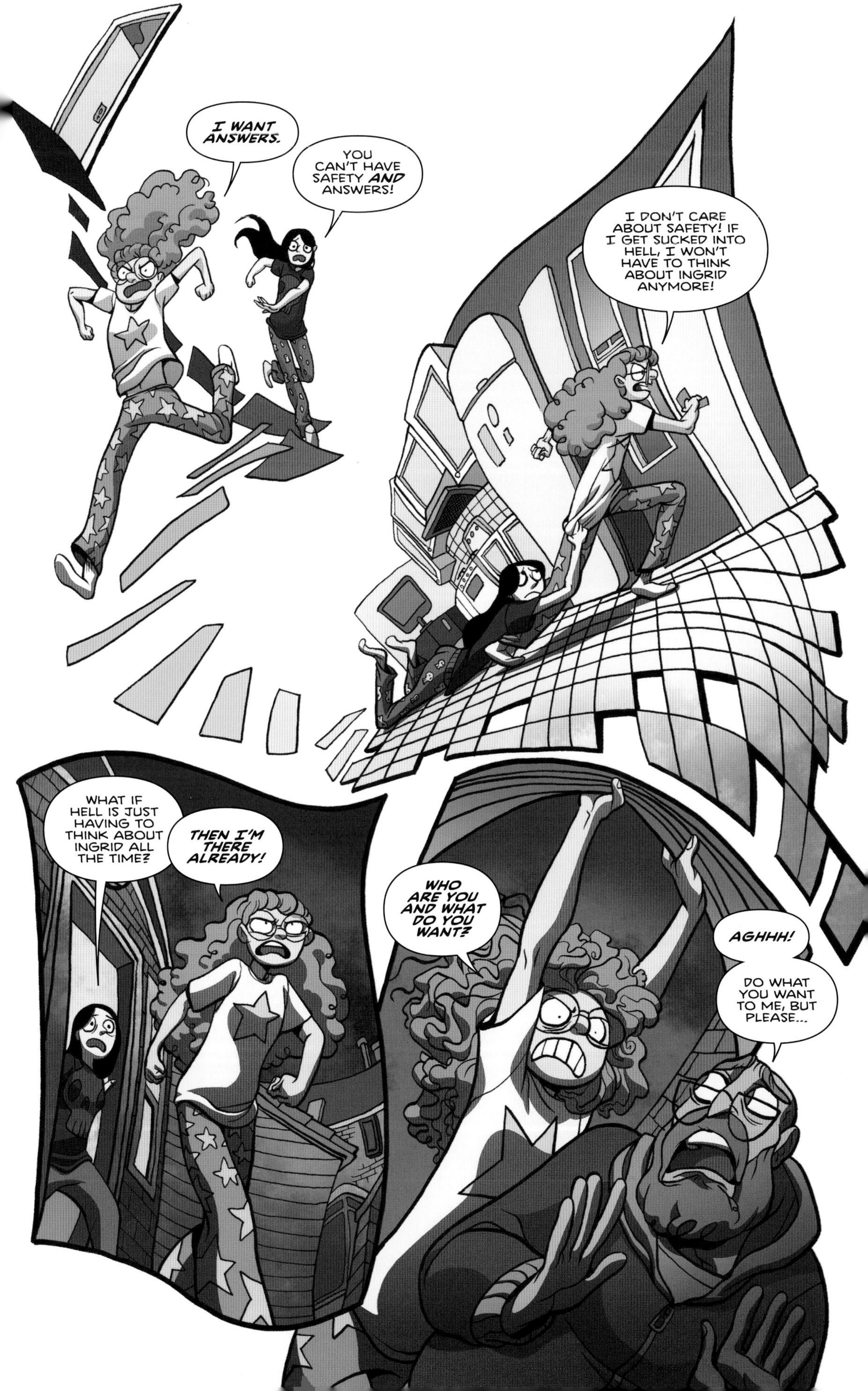
I WANT ANSWERS.
YOU CAN'T HAVE SAFETY AND ANSWERS!
I DON'T CARE ABOUT SAFETY! IF I GET SUCKED INTO HELL, I WON'T HAVE TO THINK ABOUT INGRID ANYMORE!
WHAT IF HELL IS JUST HAVING TO THINK ABOUT INGRID ALL THE TIME?
THEN I'M THERE ALREADY!
WHO ARE YOU AND WHAT DO YOU WANT?
AGHHH!
DO WHAT YOU WANT TO ME, BUT PLEASE...

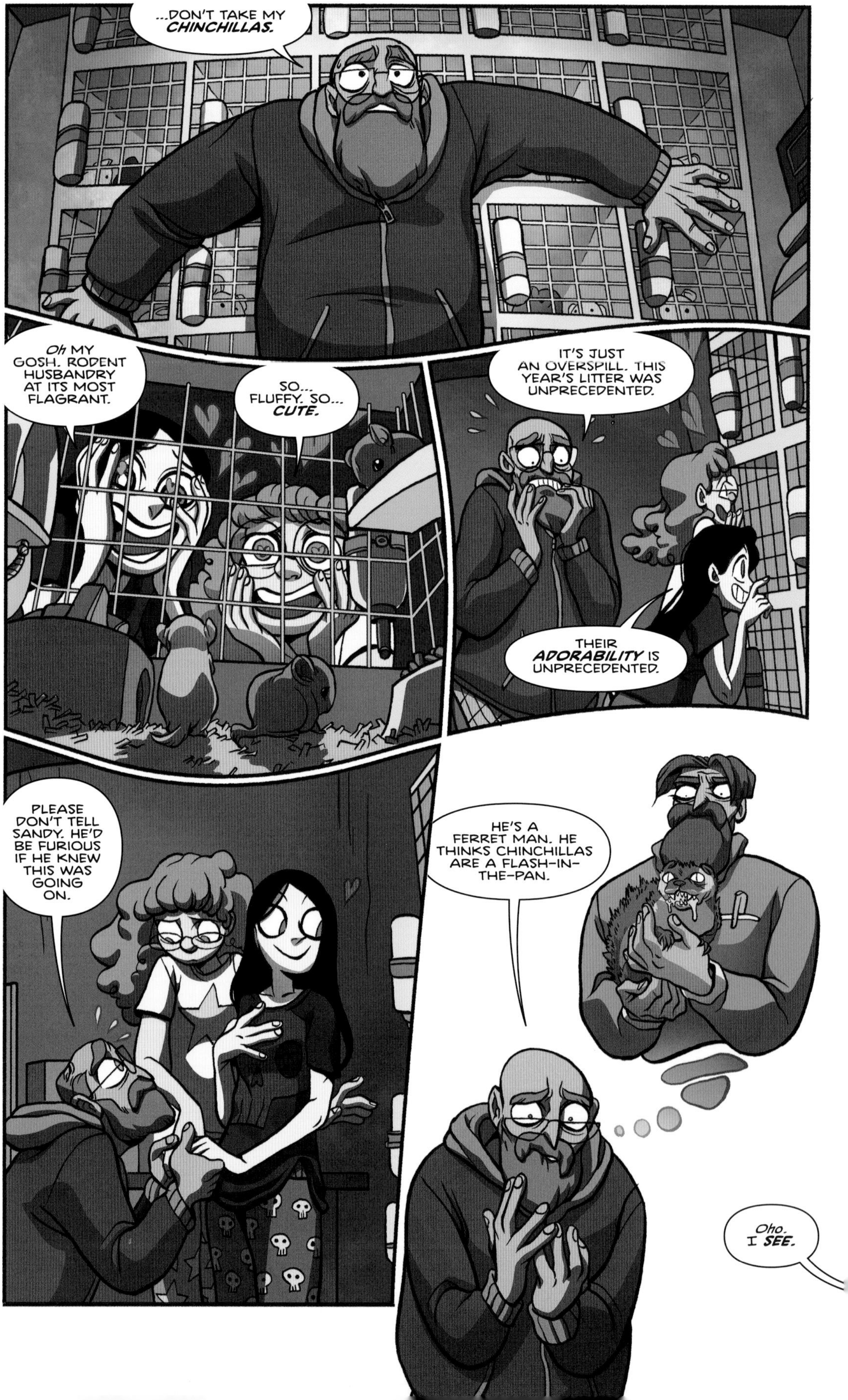
...DON'T TAKE MY *CHINCHILLAS.*
Oh MY GOSH. RODENT HUSBANDRY AT ITS MOST FLAGRANT.
SO... FLUFFY. SO... ***CUTE.***
IT'S JUST AN OVERSPILL. THIS YEAR'S LITTER WAS UNPRECEDENTED.
THEIR ***ADORABILITY*** IS UNPRECEDENTED.
PLEASE DON'T TELL SANDY. HE'D BE FURIOUS IF HE KNEW THIS WAS GOING ON.
HE'S A FERRET MAN. HE THINKS CHINCHILLAS ARE A FLASH-IN-THE-PAN.
Oho. I ***SEE.***

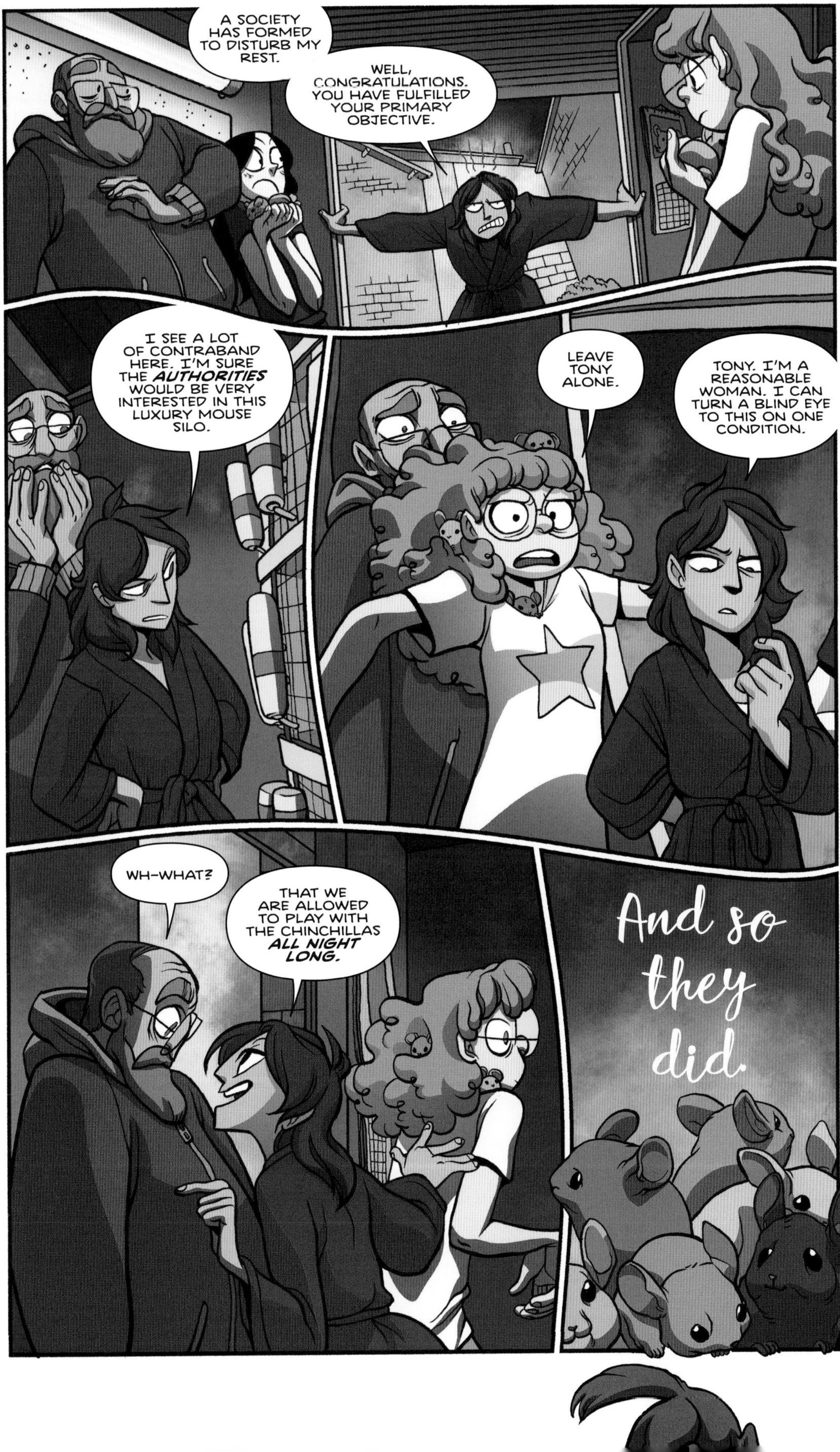
A SOCIETY HAS FORMED TO DISTURB MY REST.
WELL, CONGRATULATIONS. YOU HAVE FULFILLED YOUR PRIMARY OBJECTIVE.
I SEE A LOT OF CONTRABAND HERE. I'M SURE THE *AUTHORITIES* WOULD BE VERY INTERESTED IN THIS LUXURY MOUSE SILO.
LEAVE TONY ALONE.
TONY. I'M A REASONABLE WOMAN. I CAN TURN A BLIND EYE TO THIS ON ONE CONDITION.
WH-WHAT?
THAT WE ARE ALLOWED TO PLAY WITH THE CHINCHILLAS *ALL NIGHT LONG.*
And so they did.

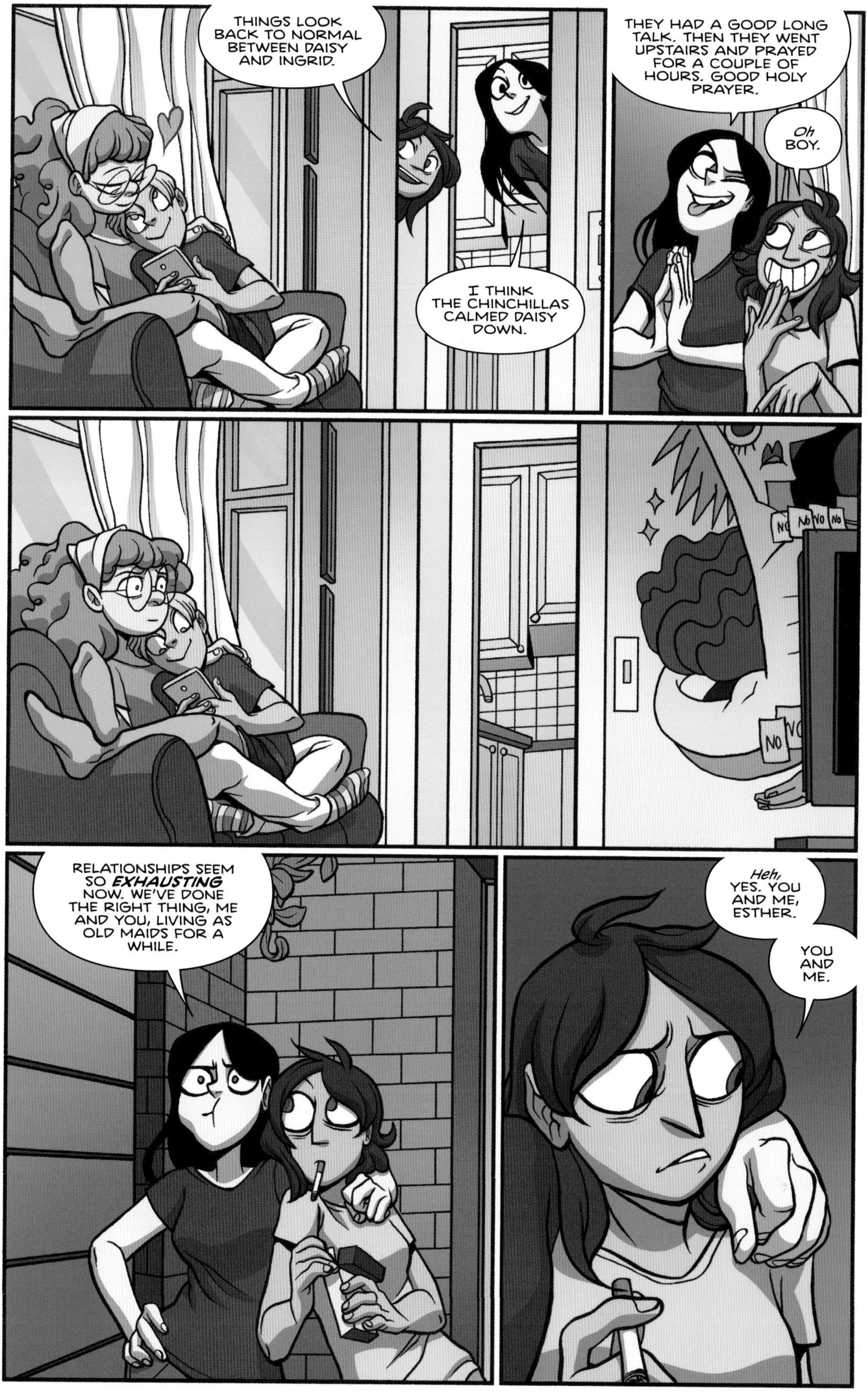
THINGS LOOK BACK TO NORMAL BETWEEN DAISY AND INGRID.
I THINK THE CHINCHILLAS CALMED DAISY DOWN.
THEY HAD A GOOD LONG TALK. THEN THEY WENT UPSTAIRS AND PRAYED FOR A COUPLE OF HOURS. GOOD HOLY PRAYER.
Oh BOY.
NO
NO
NO
NO
NO
NO
RELATIONSHIPS SEEM SO EXHAUSTING NOW. WE'VE DONE THE RIGHT THING, ME AND YOU, LIVING AS OLD MAIDS FOR A WHILE.
Heh, YES. YOU AND ME, ESTHER.
YOU AND ME.

CHAPTER
TWENTY-NINE

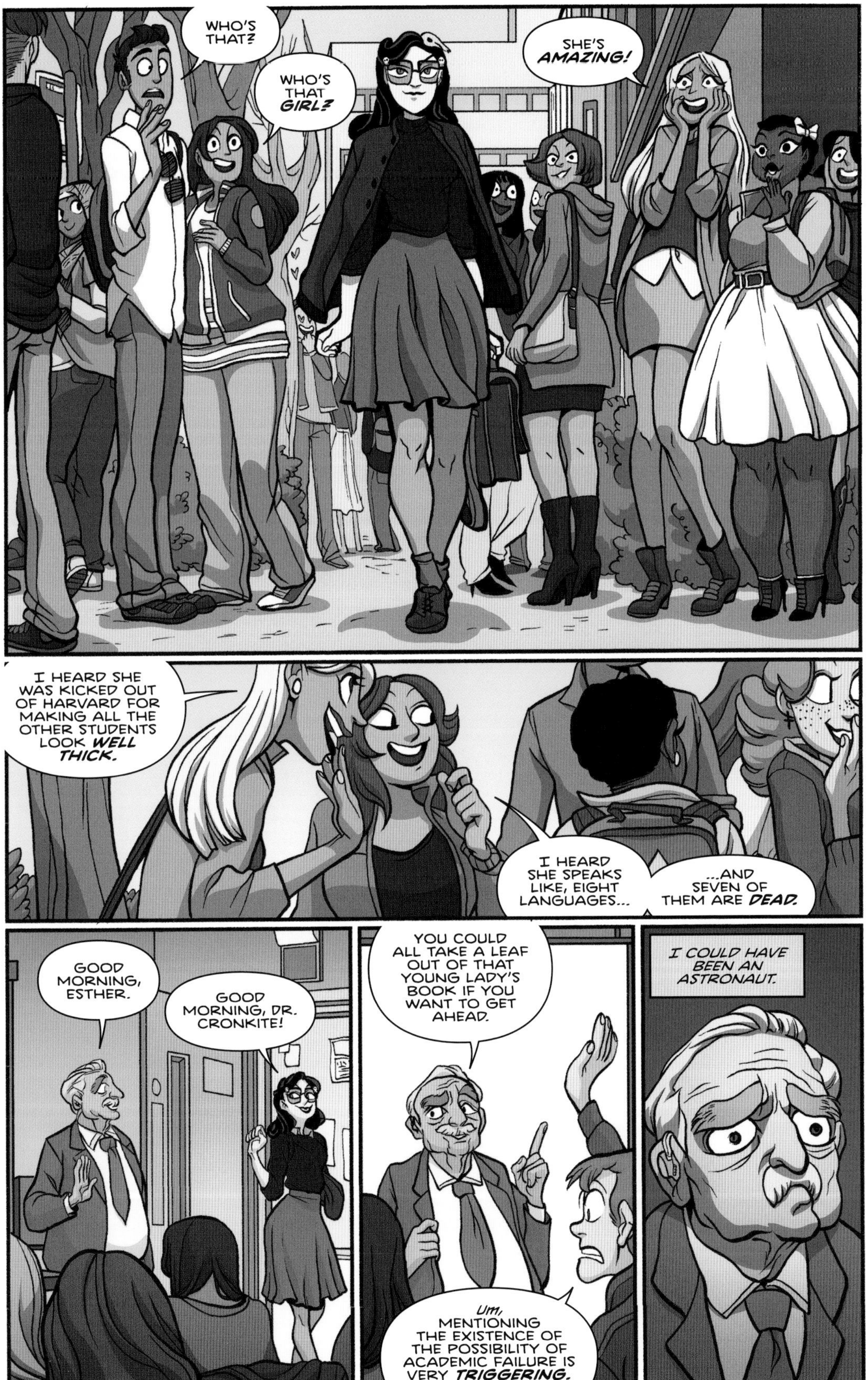
WHO'S THAT?
WHO'S THAT GIRL?
SHE'S AMAZING!
I HEARD SHE WAS KICKED OUT OF HARVARD FOR MAKING ALL THE OTHER STUDENTS LOOK WELL THICK.
I HEARD SHE SPEAKS LIKE, EIGHT LANGUAGES...
...AND SEVEN OF THEM ARE DEAD.
GOOD MORNING, ESTHER.
GOOD MORNING, DR. CRONKITE!
YOU COULD ALL TAKE A LEAF OUT OF THAT YOUNG LADY'S BOOK IF YOU WANT TO GET AHEAD.
Um, MENTIONING THE EXISTENCE OF THE POSSIBILITY OF ACADEMIC FAILURE IS VERY TRIGGERING.
I COULD HAVE BEEN AN ASTRONAUT.

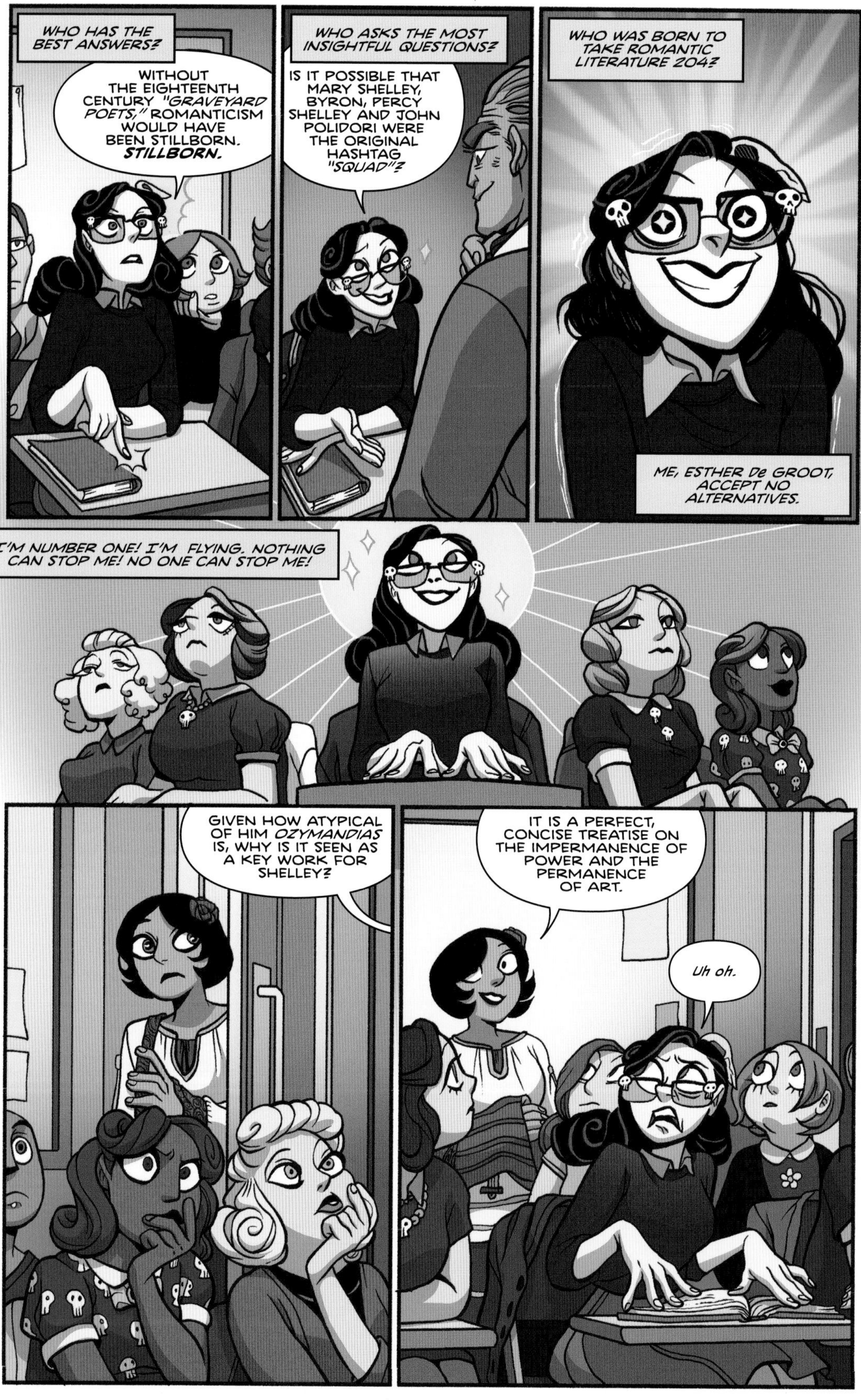

WHO HAS THE BEST ANSWERS?
WITHOUT THE EIGHTEENTH CENTURY "GRAVEYARD POETS," ROMANTICISM WOULD HAVE BEEN STILLBORN. STILLBORN.
WHO ASKS THE MOST INSIGHTFUL QUESTIONS?
IS IT POSSIBLE THAT MARY SHELLEY, BYRON, PERCY SHELLEY AND JOHN POLIDORI WERE THE ORIGINAL HASHTAG "SQUAD"?
WHO WAS BORN TO TAKE ROMANTIC LITERATURE 204?
ME, ESTHER De GROOT, ACCEPT NO ALTERNATIVES.
I'M NUMBER ONE! I'M FLYING. NOTHING CAN STOP ME! NO ONE CAN STOP ME!
GIVEN HOW ATYPICAL OF HIM OZYMANDIAS IS, WHY IS IT SEEN AS A KEY WORK FOR SHELLEY?
IT IS A PERFECT, CONCISE TREATISE ON THE IMPERMANENCE OF POWER AND THE PERMANENCE OF ART.
Uh oh.

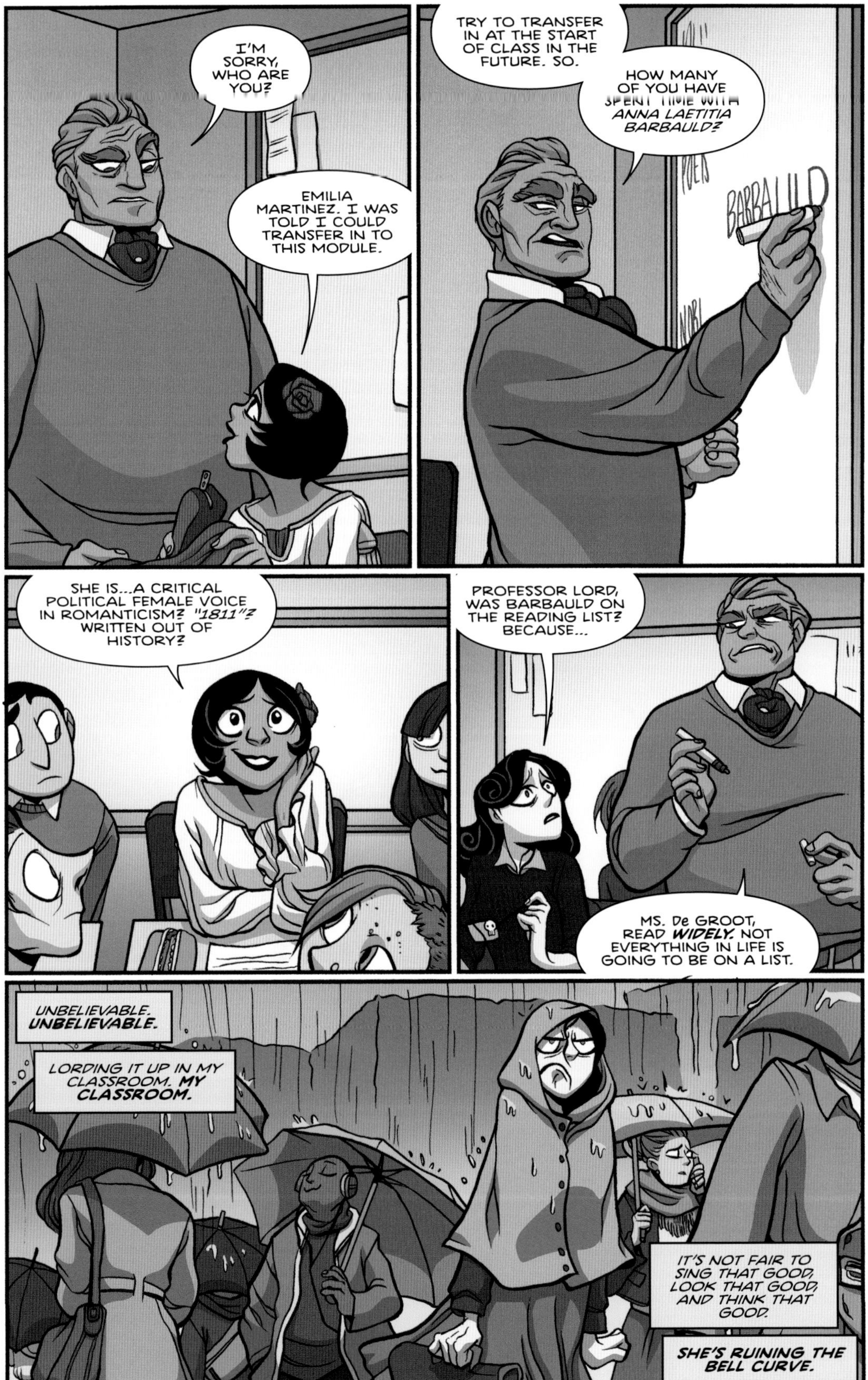
I'M SORRY, WHO ARE YOU?
EMILIA MARTINEZ. I WAS TOLD I COULD TRANSFER IN TO THIS MODULE.
TRY TO TRANSFER IN AT THE START OF CLASS IN THE FUTURE. SO.
HOW MANY OF YOU HAVE SPENT TIME WITH ANNA LAETITIA BARBAULD?
BARBAULD
SHE IS...A CRITICAL POLITICAL FEMALE VOICE IN ROMANTICISM? "1811"? WRITTEN OUT OF HISTORY?
PROFESSOR LORD, WAS BARBAULD ON THE READING LIST? BECAUSE...
MS. De GROOT, READ WIDELY. NOT EVERYTHING IN LIFE IS GOING TO BE ON A LIST.
UNBELIEVABLE. UNBELIEVABLE.
LORDING IT UP IN MY CLASSROOM. MY CLASSROOM.
IT'S NOT FAIR TO SING THAT GOOD, LOOK THAT GOOD, AND THINK THAT GOOD.
SHE'S RUINING THE BELL CURVE.

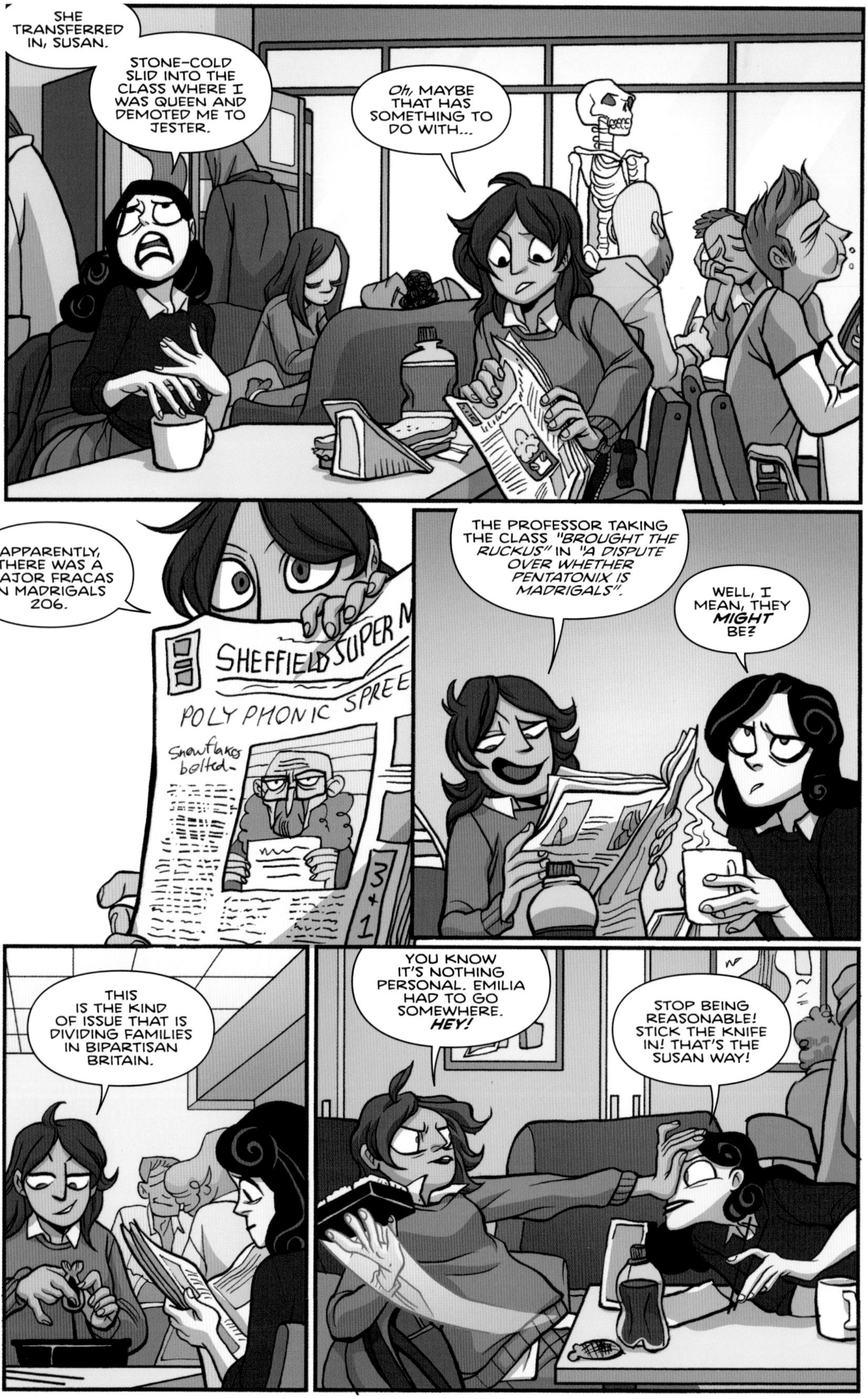

SHE TRANSFERRED IN, SUSAN.
STONE-COLD SLID INTO THE CLASS WHERE I WAS QUEEN AND DEMOTED ME TO JESTER.
Oh, MAYBE THAT HAS SOMETHING TO DO WITH...
APPARENTLY, THERE WAS A MAJOR FRACAS IN MADRIGALS 206.
SHEFFIELD SUPER M
POLYPHONIC SPREE
Snowflakes belted
THE PROFESSOR TAKING THE CLASS "BROUGHT THE RUCKUS" IN "A DISPUTE OVER WHETHER PENTATONIX IS MADRIGALS".
WELL, I MEAN, THEY MIGHT BE?
THIS IS THE KIND OF ISSUE THAT IS DIVIDING FAMILIES IN BIPARTISAN BRITAIN.
YOU KNOW IT'S NOTHING PERSONAL. EMILIA HAD TO GO SOMEWHERE. HEY!
STOP BEING REASONABLE! STICK THE KNIFE IN! THAT'S THE SUSAN WAY!

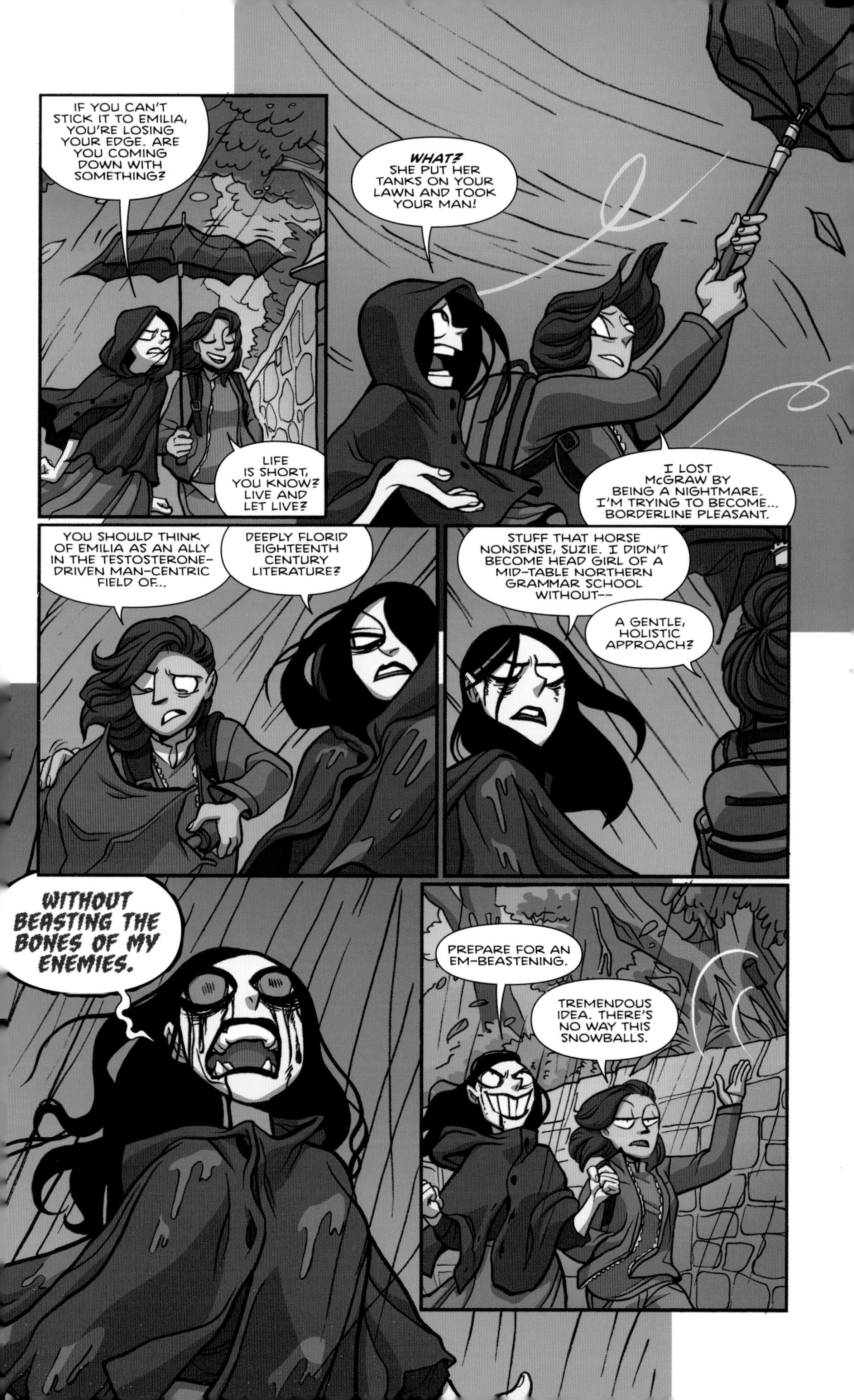
IF YOU CAN'T STICK IT TO EMILIA, YOU'RE LOSING YOUR EDGE. ARE YOU COMING DOWN WITH SOMETHING?
LIFE IS SHORT, YOU KNOW? LIVE AND LET LIVE?
WHAT? SHE PUT HER TANKS ON YOUR LAWN AND TOOK YOUR MAN!
I LOST McGRAW BY BEING A NIGHTMARE. I'M TRYING TO BECOME... BORDERLINE PLEASANT.
YOU SHOULD THINK OF EMILIA AS AN ALLY IN THE TESTOSTERONE-DRIVEN MAN-CENTRIC FIELD OF...
DEEPLY FLORID EIGHTEENTH CENTURY LITERATURE?
STUFF THAT HORSE NONSENSE, SUZIE. I DIDN'T BECOME HEAD GIRL OF A MID-TABLE NORTHERN GRAMMAR SCHOOL WITHOUT--
A GENTLE, HOLISTIC APPROACH?
WITHOUT BEASTING THE BONES OF MY ENEMIES.
PREPARE FOR AN EM-BEASTENING.
TREMENDOUS IDEA. THERE'S NO WAY THIS SNOWBALLS.

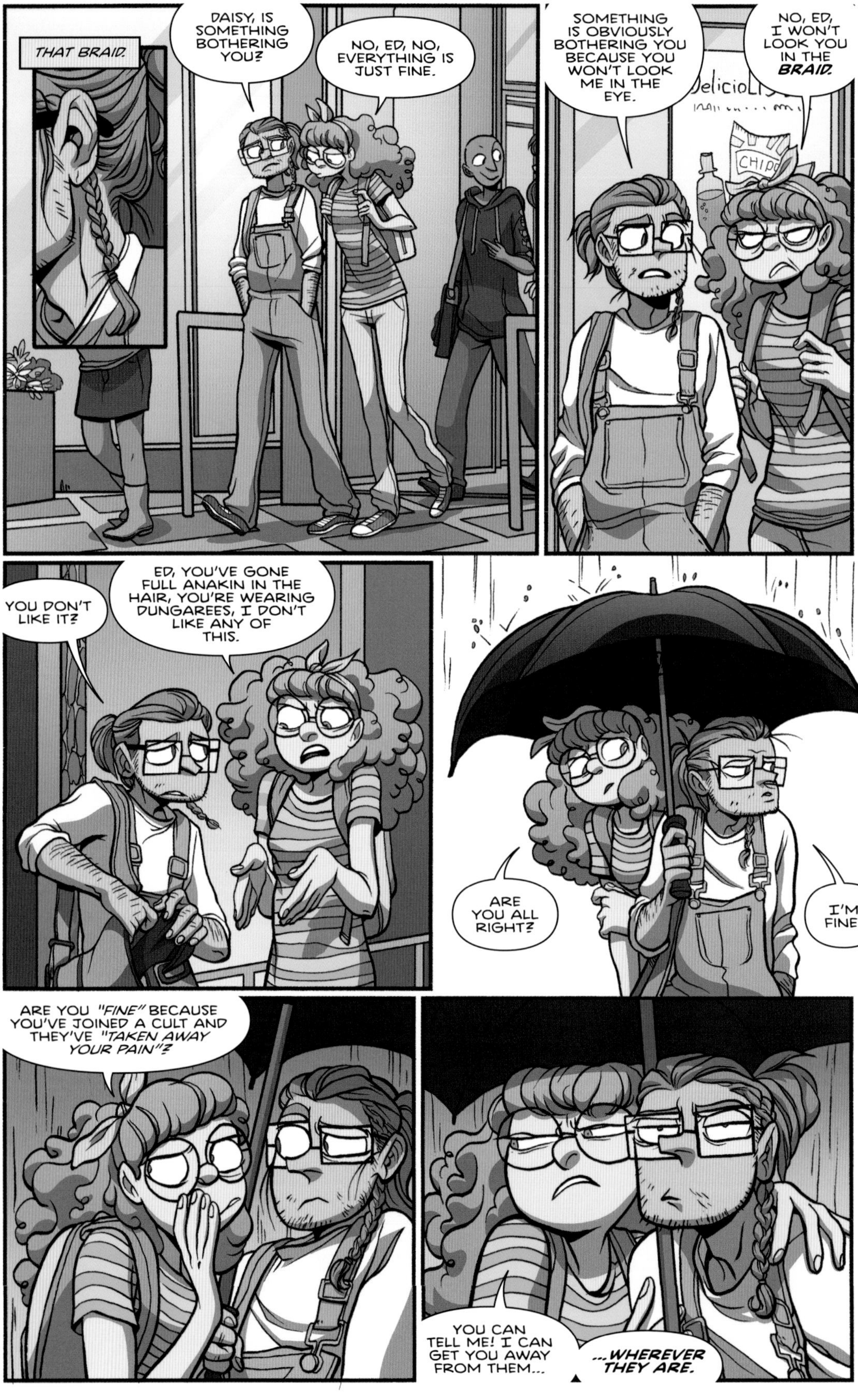
THAT BRAID.
DAISY, IS SOMETHING BOTHERING YOU?
NO, ED, NO, EVERYTHING IS JUST FINE.
SOMETHING IS OBVIOUSLY BOTHERING YOU BECAUSE YOU WON'T LOOK ME IN THE EYE.
NO, ED, I WON'T LOOK YOU IN THE BRAID.
CHIPS
YOU DON'T LIKE IT?
ED, YOU'VE GONE FULL ANAKIN IN THE HAIR, YOU'RE WEARING DUNGAREES, I DON'T LIKE ANY OF THIS.
ARE YOU ALL RIGHT?
I'M FINE.
ARE YOU "FINE" BECAUSE YOU'VE JOINED A CULT AND THEY'VE "TAKEN AWAY YOUR PAIN"?
YOU CAN TELL ME! I CAN GET YOU AWAY FROM THEM...
...WHEREVER THEY ARE.

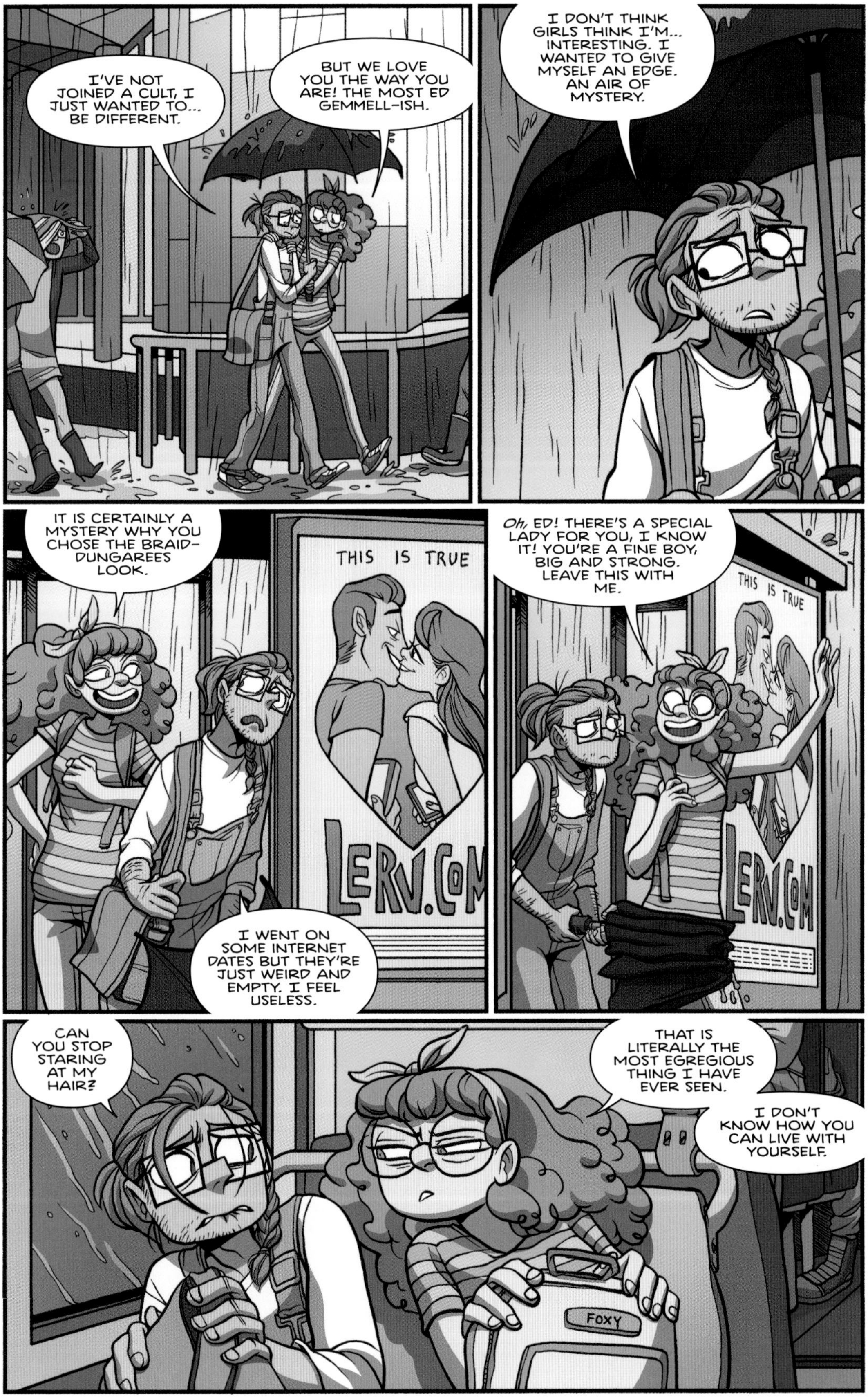
I'VE NOT JOINED A CULT, I JUST WANTED TO... BE DIFFERENT.
BUT WE LOVE YOU THE WAY YOU ARE! THE MOST ED GEMMELL-ISH.
I DON'T THINK GIRLS THINK I'M... INTERESTING. I WANTED TO GIVE MYSELF AN EDGE. AN AIR OF MYSTERY.
IT IS CERTAINLY A MYSTERY WHY YOU CHOSE THE BRAID-DUNGAREES LOOK.
THIS IS TRUE
LERV.COM
I WENT ON SOME INTERNET DATES BUT THEY'RE JUST WEIRD AND EMPTY. I FEEL USELESS.
Oh, ED! THERE'S A SPECIAL LADY FOR YOU, I KNOW IT! YOU'RE A FINE BOY, BIG AND STRONG. LEAVE THIS WITH ME.
THIS IS TRUE
LERV.COM
CAN YOU STOP STARING AT MY HAIR?
THAT IS LITERALLY THE MOST EGREGIOUS THING I HAVE EVER SEEN.
I DON'T KNOW HOW YOU CAN LIVE WITH YOURSELF.
FOXY

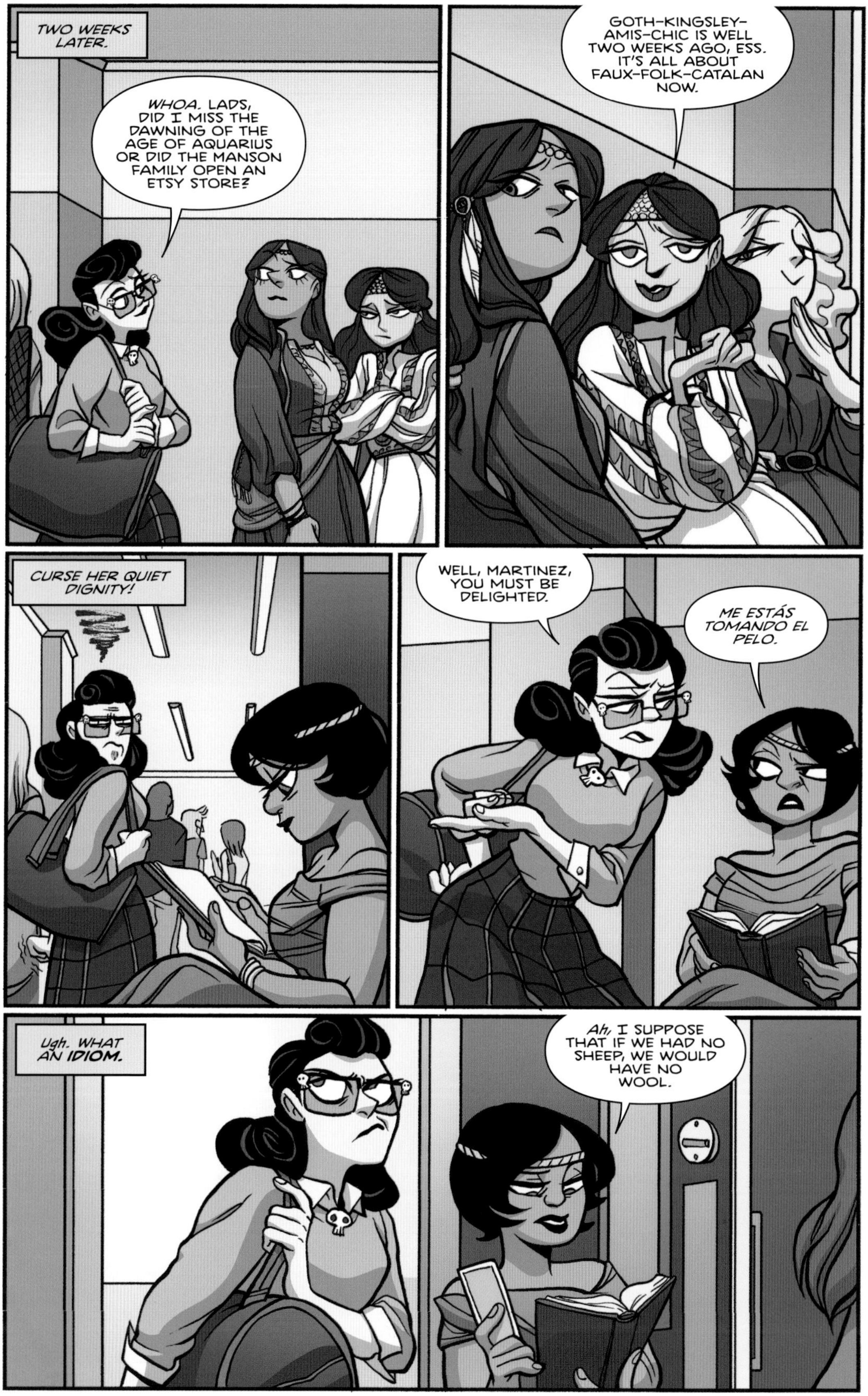

TWO WEEKS LATER.
WHOA. LADS, DID I MISS THE DAWNING OF THE AGE OF AQUARIUS OR DID THE MANSON FAMILY OPEN AN ETSY STORE?
GOTH-KINGSLEY-AMIS-CHIC IS WELL TWO WEEKS AGO, ESS. IT'S ALL ABOUT FAUX-FOLK-CATALAN NOW.
CURSE HER QUIET DIGNITY!
WELL, MARTINEZ, YOU MUST BE DELIGHTED.
ME ESTÁS TOMANDO EL PELO.
Ugh. WHAT AN IDIOM.
Ah, I SUPPOSE THAT IF WE HAD NO SHEEP, WE WOULD HAVE NO WOOL.

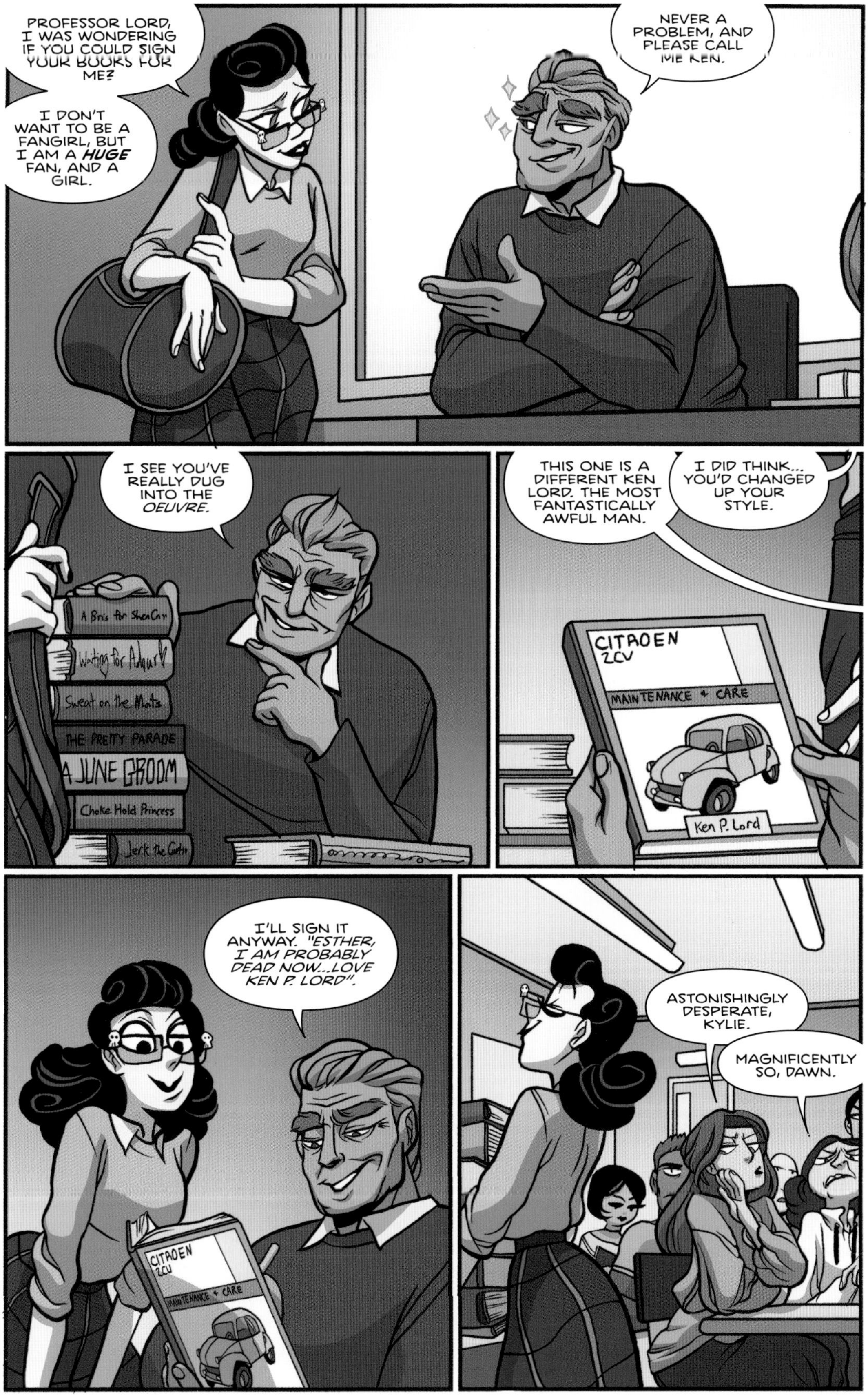
PROFESSOR LORD, I WAS WONDERING IF YOU COULD SIGN YOUR BOOKS FOR ME?
I DON'T WANT TO BE A FANGIRL, BUT I AM A *HUGE* FAN, AND A GIRL.
NEVER A PROBLEM, AND PLEASE CALL ME KEN.
I SEE YOU'VE REALLY DUG INTO THE *OEUVRE.*
A Bris for Shea Cir
Waiting for Adaur
Sweat on the Mats
THE PRETTY PARADE
A JUNE GROOM
Choke Hold Princess
Jerk the Gutts
THIS ONE IS A DIFFERENT KEN LORD. THE MOST FANTASTICALLY AWFUL MAN.
I DID THINK... YOU'D CHANGED UP YOUR STYLE.
CITROEN 2CV
MAINTENANCE & CARE
Ken P. Lord
I'LL SIGN IT ANYWAY. *"ESTHER, I AM PROBABLY DEAD NOW...LOVE KEN P. LORD".*
CITROEN 2CV
MAINTENANCE & CARE
ASTONISHINGLY DESPERATE, KYLIE.
MAGNIFICENTLY SO, DAWN.

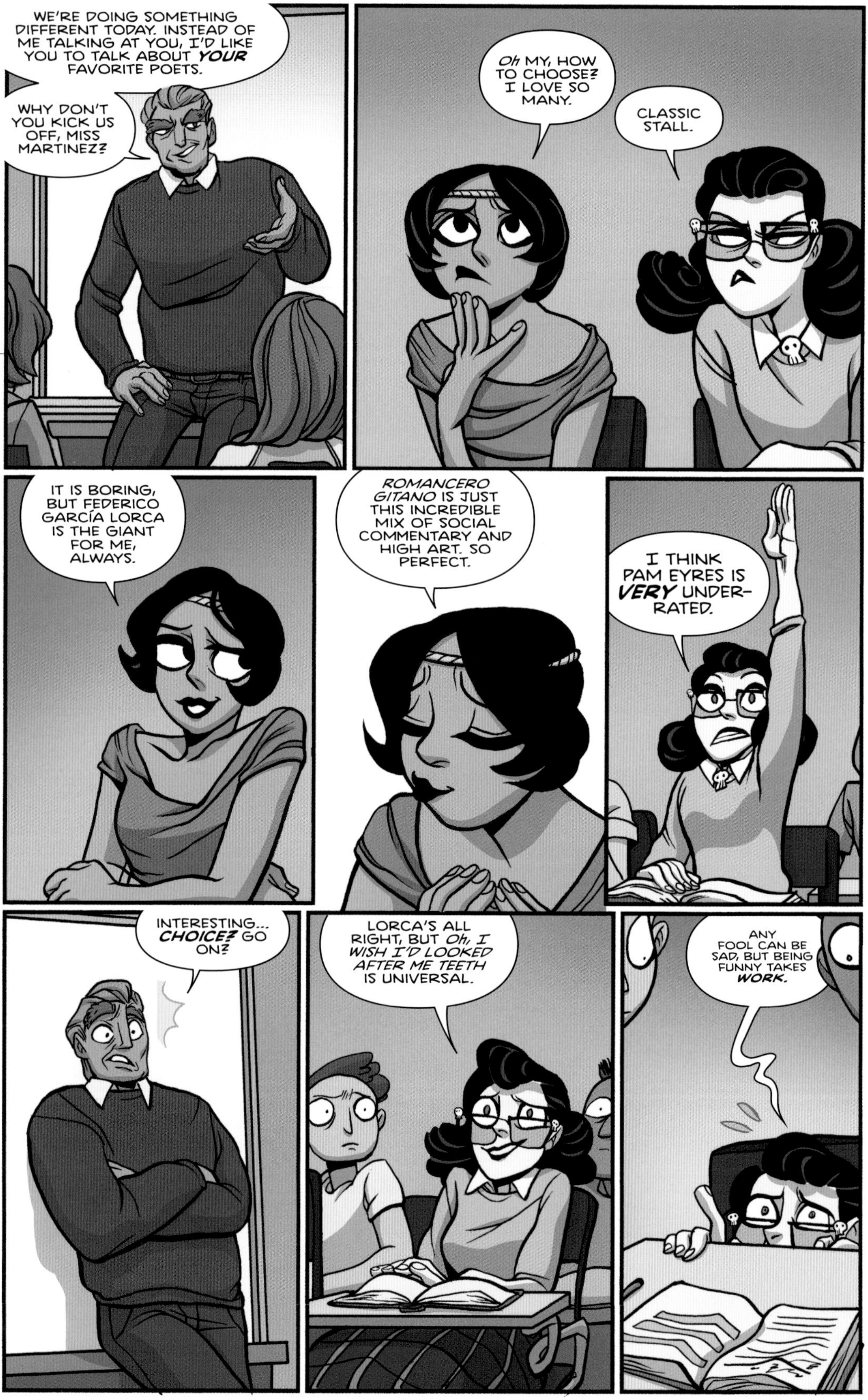

WE'RE DOING SOMETHING DIFFERENT TODAY. INSTEAD OF ME TALKING AT YOU, I'D LIKE YOU TO TALK ABOUT *YOUR* FAVORITE POETS.
WHY DON'T YOU KICK US OFF, MISS MARTINEZ?
Oh MY, HOW TO CHOOSE? I LOVE SO MANY.
CLASSIC STALL.
IT IS BORING, BUT FEDERICO GARCÍA LORCA IS THE GIANT FOR ME, ALWAYS.
ROMANCERO GITANO IS JUST THIS INCREDIBLE MIX OF SOCIAL COMMENTARY AND HIGH ART. SO PERFECT.
I THINK PAM EYRES IS ***VERY*** UNDER-RATED.
INTERESTING... ***CHOICE?*** GO ON?
LORCA'S ALL RIGHT, BUT *Oh, I WISH I'D LOOKED AFTER ME TEETH* IS UNIVERSAL.
ANY FOOL CAN BE SAD, BUT BEING FUNNY TAKES ***WORK.***

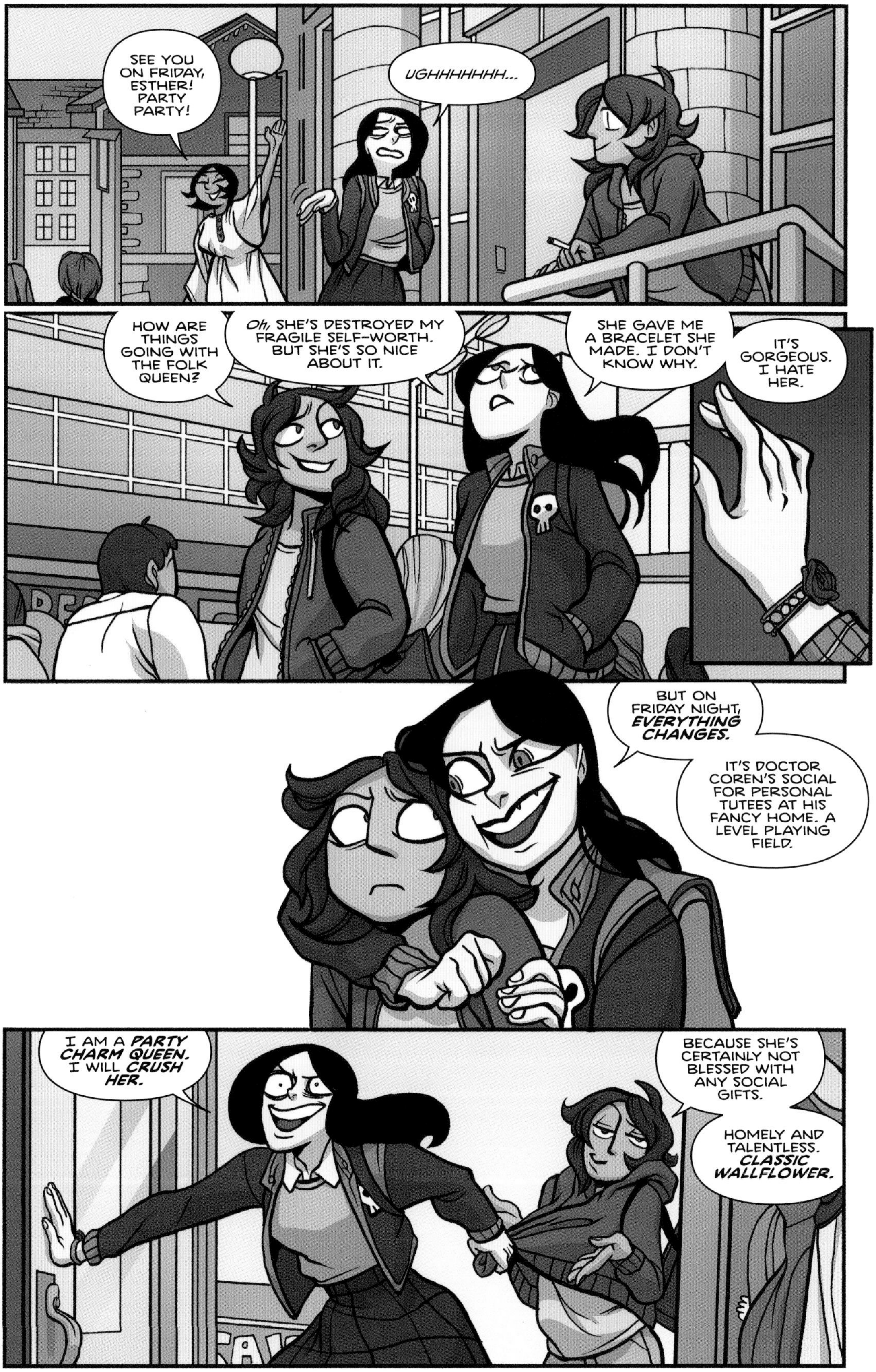
SEE YOU ON FRIDAY, ESTHER! PARTY PARTY!
UGHHHHHHH...
HOW ARE THINGS GOING WITH THE FOLK QUEEN?
Oh, SHE'S DESTROYED MY FRAGILE SELF-WORTH. BUT SHE'S SO NICE ABOUT IT.
SHE GAVE ME A BRACELET SHE MADE. I DON'T KNOW WHY.
IT'S GORGEOUS. I HATE HER.
BUT ON FRIDAY NIGHT, ***EVERYTHING CHANGES.***
IT'S DOCTOR COREN'S SOCIAL FOR PERSONAL TUTEES AT HIS FANCY HOME. A LEVEL PLAYING FIELD.
I AM A ***PARTY CHARM QUEEN.*** I WILL ***CRUSH HER.***
BECAUSE SHE'S CERTAINLY NOT BLESSED WITH ANY SOCIAL GIFTS.
HOMELY AND TALENTLESS. ***CLASSIC WALLFLOWER.***

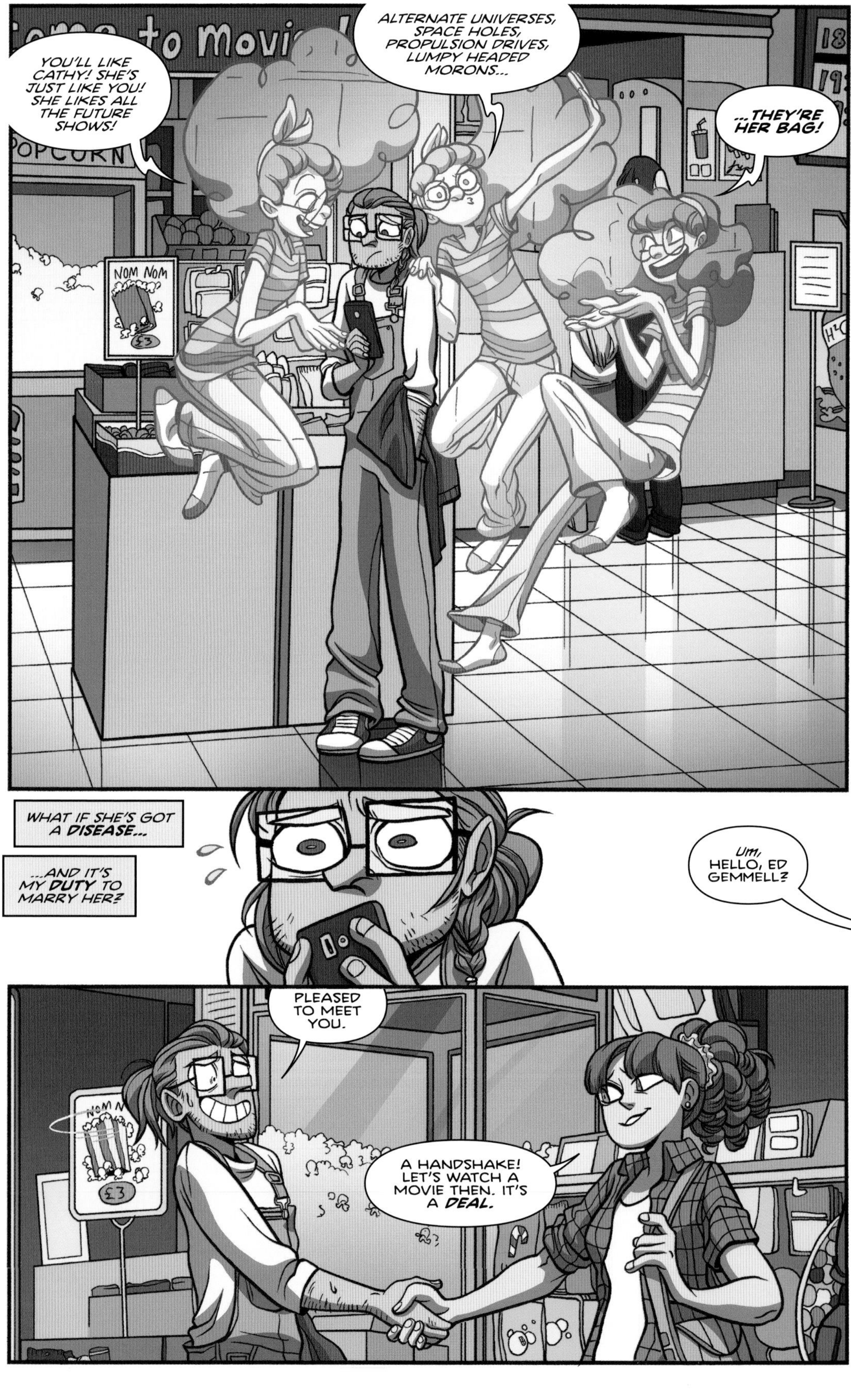
Come to Movi
POPCORN
YOU'LL LIKE CATHY! SHE'S JUST LIKE YOU! SHE LIKES ALL THE FUTURE SHOWS!
ALTERNATE UNIVERSES, SPACE HOLES, PROPULSION DRIVES, LUMPY HEADED MORONS...
...THEY'RE HER BAG!
NOM NOM
£3
WHAT IF SHE'S GOT A DISEASE...
...AND IT'S MY DUTY TO MARRY HER?
UM, HELLO, ED GEMMELL?
PLEASED TO MEET YOU.
A HANDSHAKE! LET'S WATCH A MOVIE THEN. IT'S A DEAL.
NOM N
£3

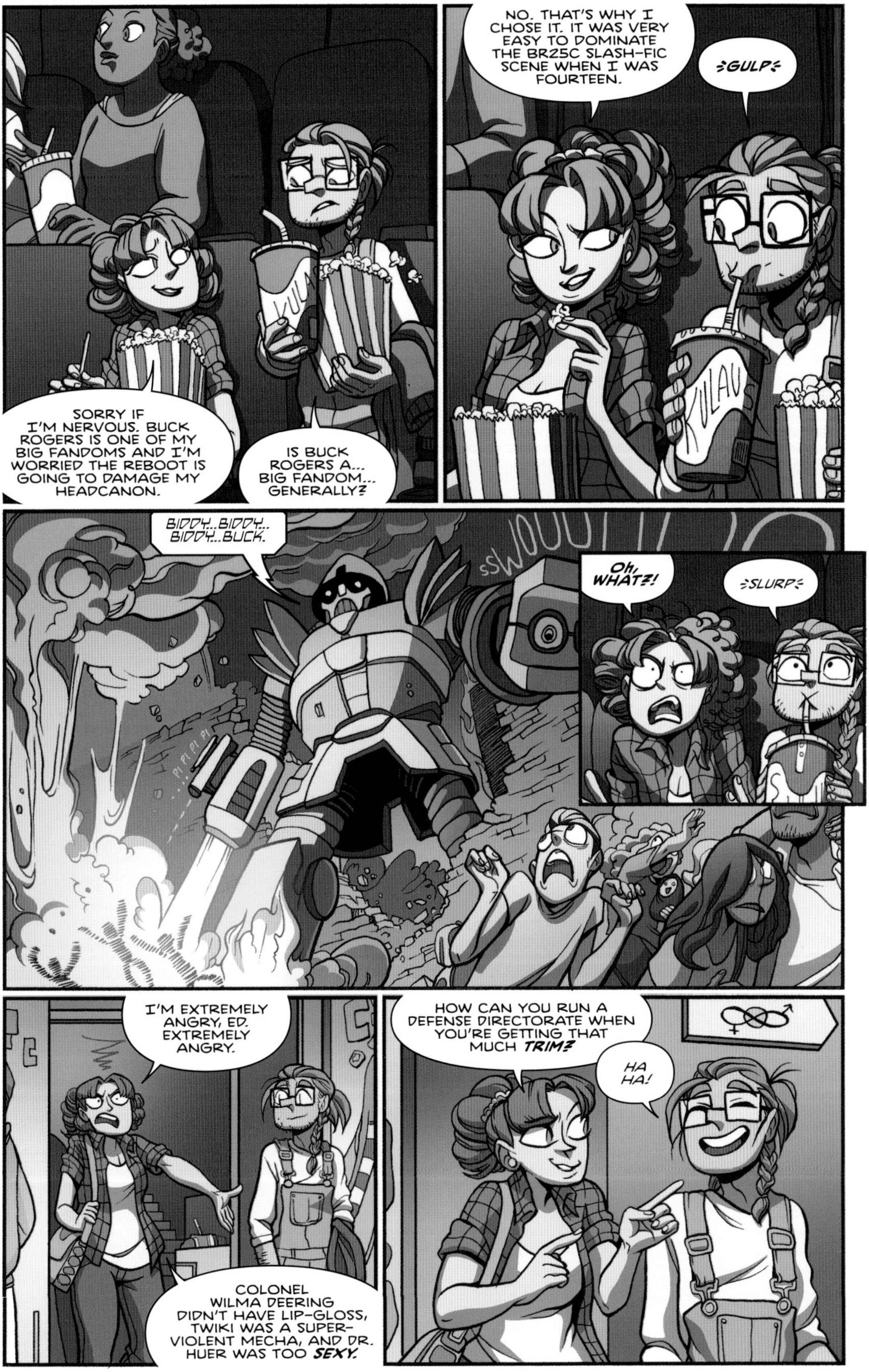
SORRY IF I'M NERVOUS. BUCK ROGERS IS ONE OF MY BIG FANDOMS AND I'M WORRIED THE REBOOT IS GOING TO DAMAGE MY HEADCANON.
IS BUCK ROGERS A... BIG FANDOM... GENERALLY?
NO. THAT'S WHY I CHOSE IT. IT WAS VERY EASY TO DOMINATE THE BR25C SLASH-FIC SCENE WHEN I WAS FOURTEEN.
GULP
BIDDY...BIDDY... BIDDY...BUCK.
SSWOOOO
PI PI PI PI
Oh, WHAT?!
SLURP
I'M EXTREMELY ANGRY, ED. EXTREMELY ANGRY.
COLONEL WILMA DEERING DIDN'T HAVE LIP-GLOSS, TWIKI WAS A SUPER-VIOLENT MECHA, AND DR. HUER WAS TOO SEXY.
HOW CAN YOU RUN A DEFENSE DIRECTORATE WHEN YOU'RE GETTING THAT MUCH TRIM?
HA HA!

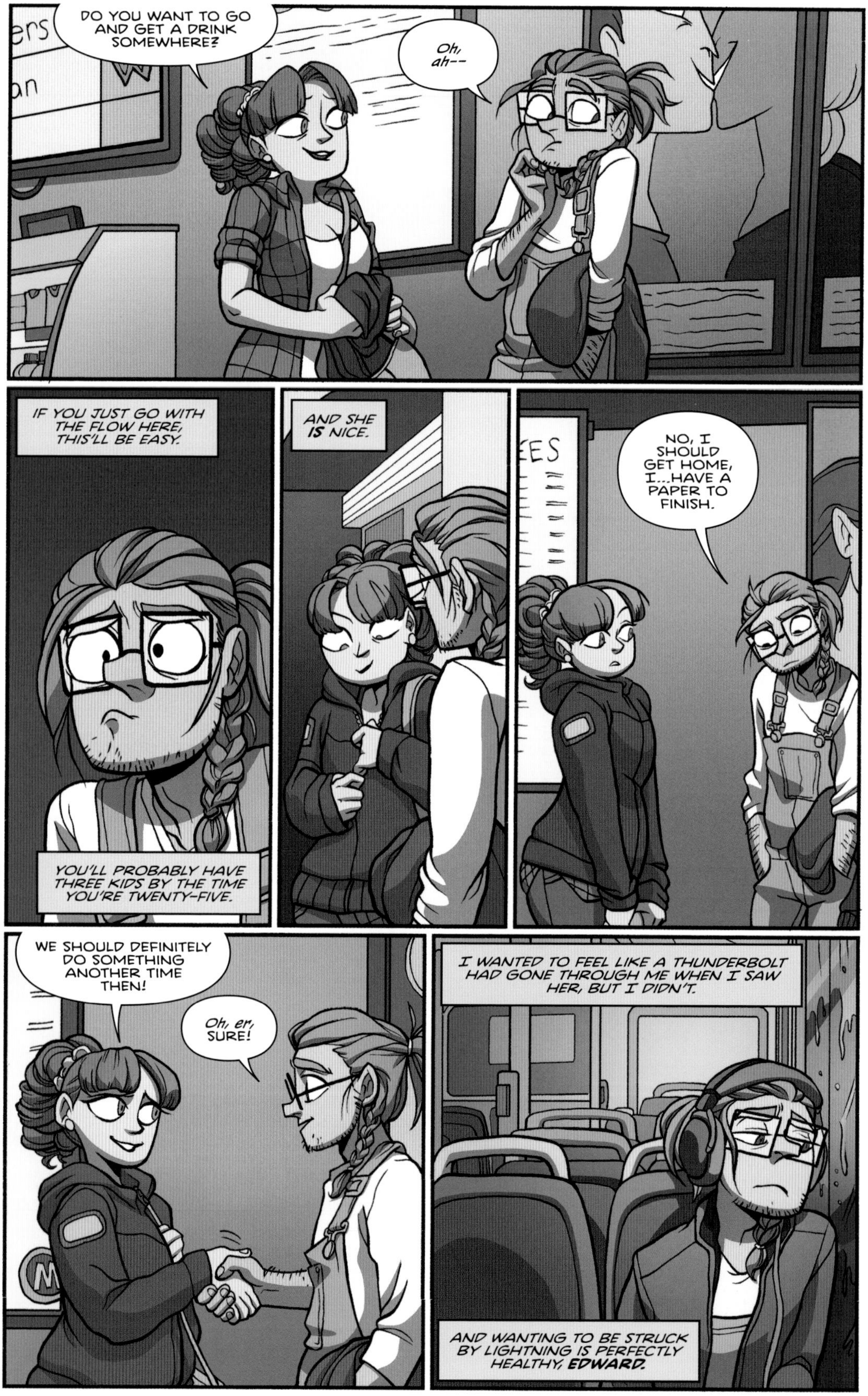

DO YOU WANT TO GO AND GET A DRINK SOMEWHERE?
Oh, ah--
IF YOU JUST GO WITH THE FLOW HERE, THIS'LL BE EASY.
YOU'LL PROBABLY HAVE THREE KIDS BY THE TIME YOU'RE TWENTY-FIVE.
AND SHE IS NICE.
NO, I SHOULD GET HOME, I...HAVE A PAPER TO FINISH.
WE SHOULD DEFINITELY DO SOMETHING ANOTHER TIME THEN!
Oh, er, SURE!
I WANTED TO FEEL LIKE A THUNDERBOLT HAD GONE THROUGH ME WHEN I SAW HER, BUT I DIDN'T.
AND WANTING TO BE STRUCK BY LIGHTNING IS PERFECTLY HEALTHY, EDWARD.

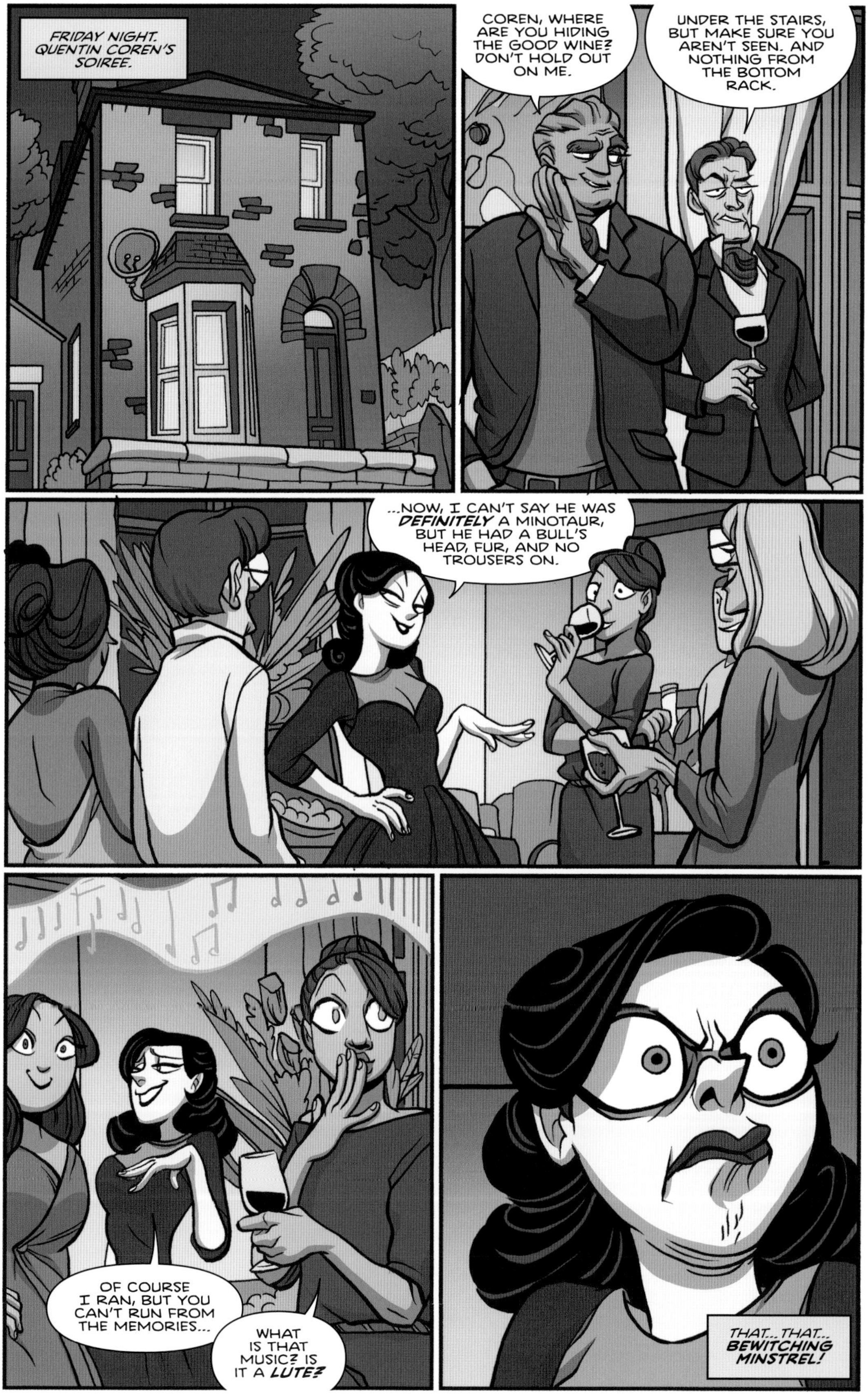
FRIDAY NIGHT. QUENTIN COREN'S SOIREE.
COREN, WHERE ARE YOU HIDING THE GOOD WINE? DON'T HOLD OUT ON ME.
UNDER THE STAIRS, BUT MAKE SURE YOU AREN'T SEEN. AND NOTHING FROM THE BOTTOM RACK.
...NOW, I CAN'T SAY HE WAS DEFINITELY A MINOTAUR, BUT HE HAD A BULL'S HEAD, FUR, AND NO TROUSERS ON.
OF COURSE I RAN, BUT YOU CAN'T RUN FROM THE MEMORIES...
WHAT IS THAT MUSIC? IS IT A LUTE?
THAT... THAT... BEWITCHING MINSTREL!

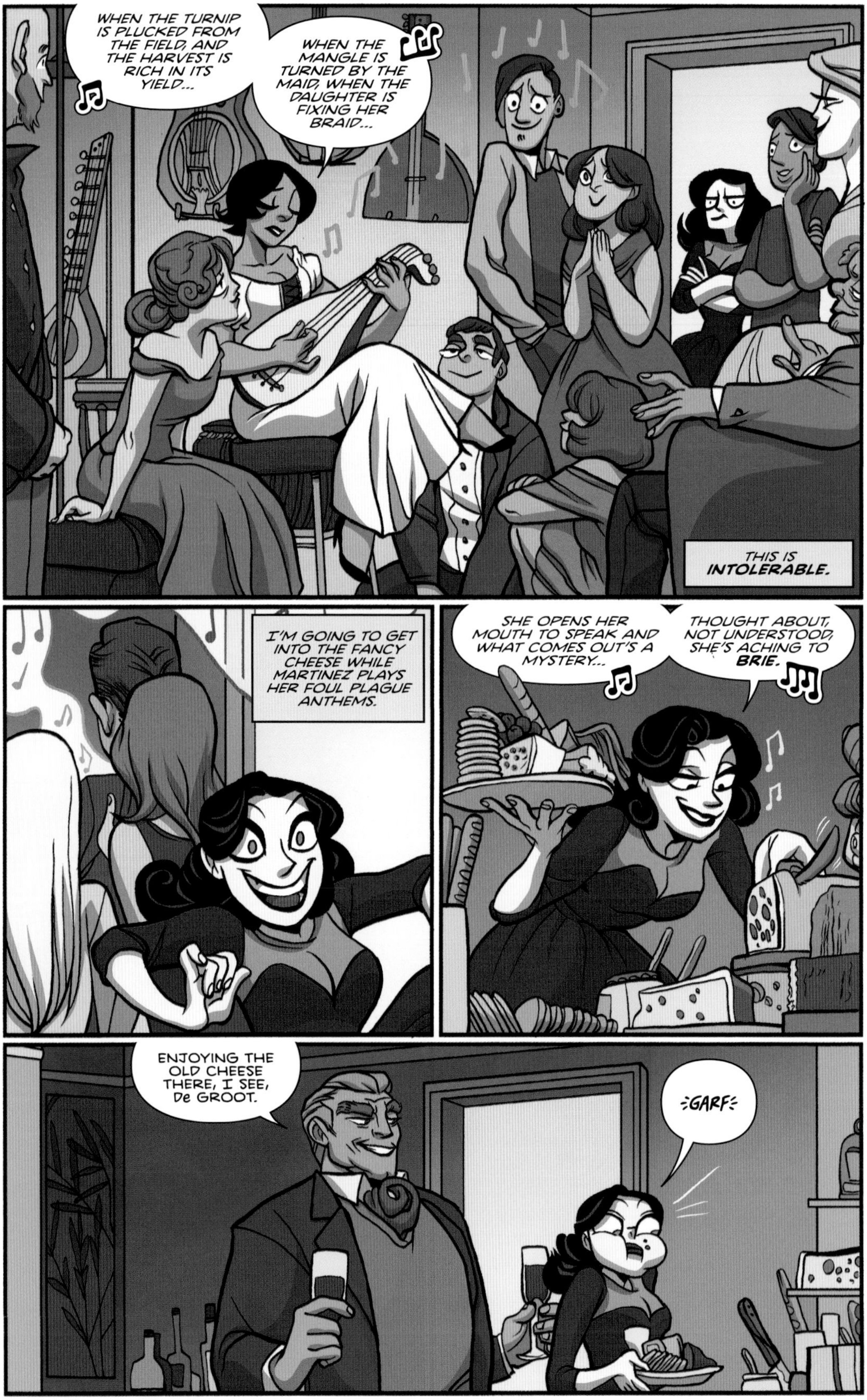
WHEN THE TURNIP IS PLUCKED FROM THE FIELD, AND THE HARVEST IS RICH IN ITS YIELD...
WHEN THE MANGLE IS TURNED BY THE MAID, WHEN THE DAUGHTER IS FIXING HER BRAID...
THIS IS INTOLERABLE.
I'M GOING TO GET INTO THE FANCY CHEESE WHILE MARTINEZ PLAYS HER FOUL PLAGUE ANTHEMS.
SHE OPENS HER MOUTH TO SPEAK AND WHAT COMES OUT'S A MYSTERY...
THOUGHT ABOUT, NOT UNDERSTOOD, SHE'S ACHING TO BRIE.
ENJOYING THE OLD CHEESE THERE, I SEE, De GROOT.
GARF

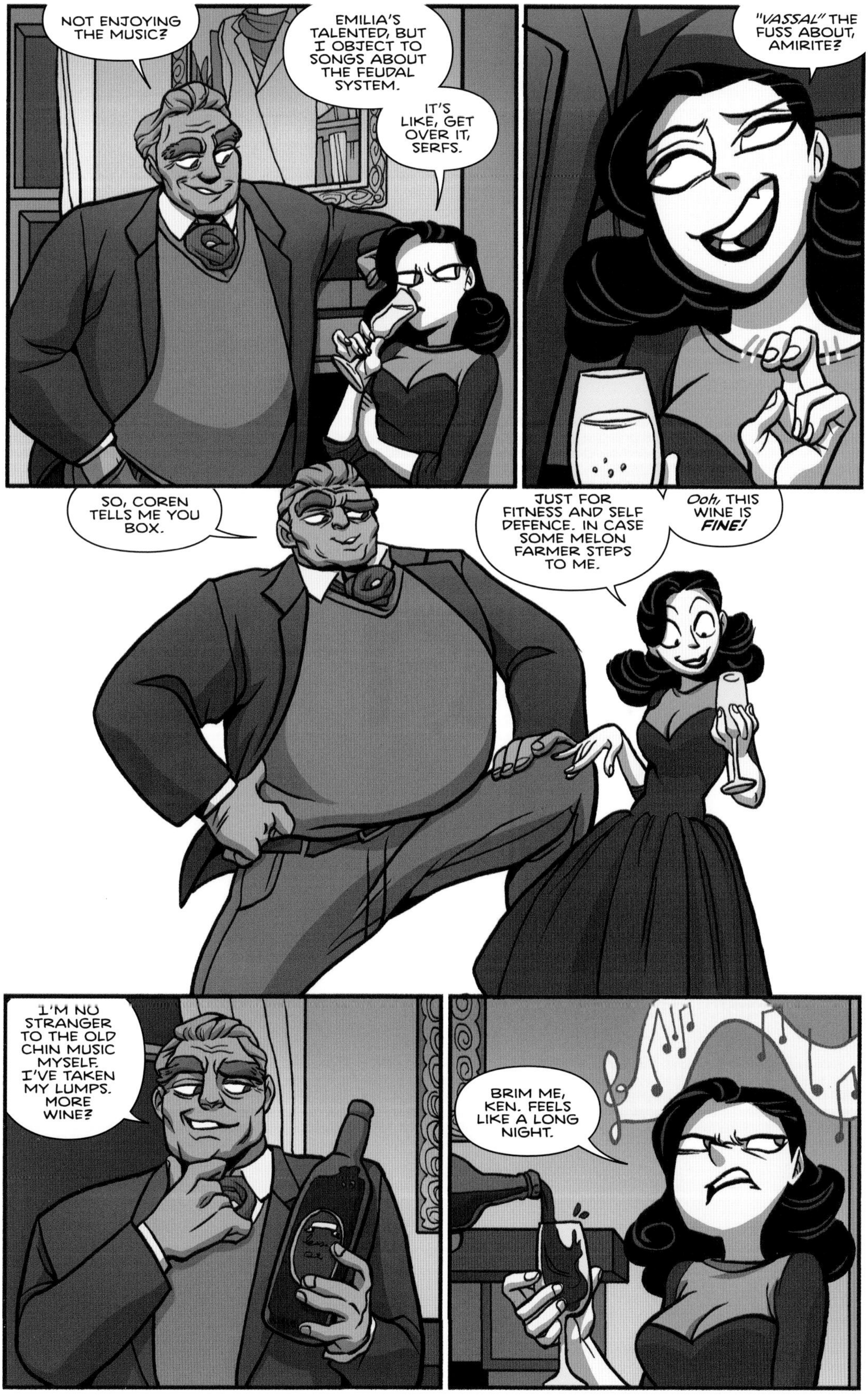
NOT ENJOYING THE MUSIC?
EMILIA'S TALENTED, BUT I OBJECT TO SONGS ABOUT THE FEUDAL SYSTEM.
IT'S LIKE, GET OVER IT, SERFS.
"VASSAL" THE FUSS ABOUT, AMIRITE?
SO, COREN TELLS ME YOU BOX.
JUST FOR FITNESS AND SELF DEFENCE. IN CASE SOME MELON FARMER STEPS TO ME.
Ooh, THIS WINE IS FINE!
I'M NO STRANGER TO THE OLD CHIN MUSIC MYSELF. I'VE TAKEN MY LUMPS. MORE WINE?
BRIM ME, KEN. FEELS LIKE A LONG NIGHT.

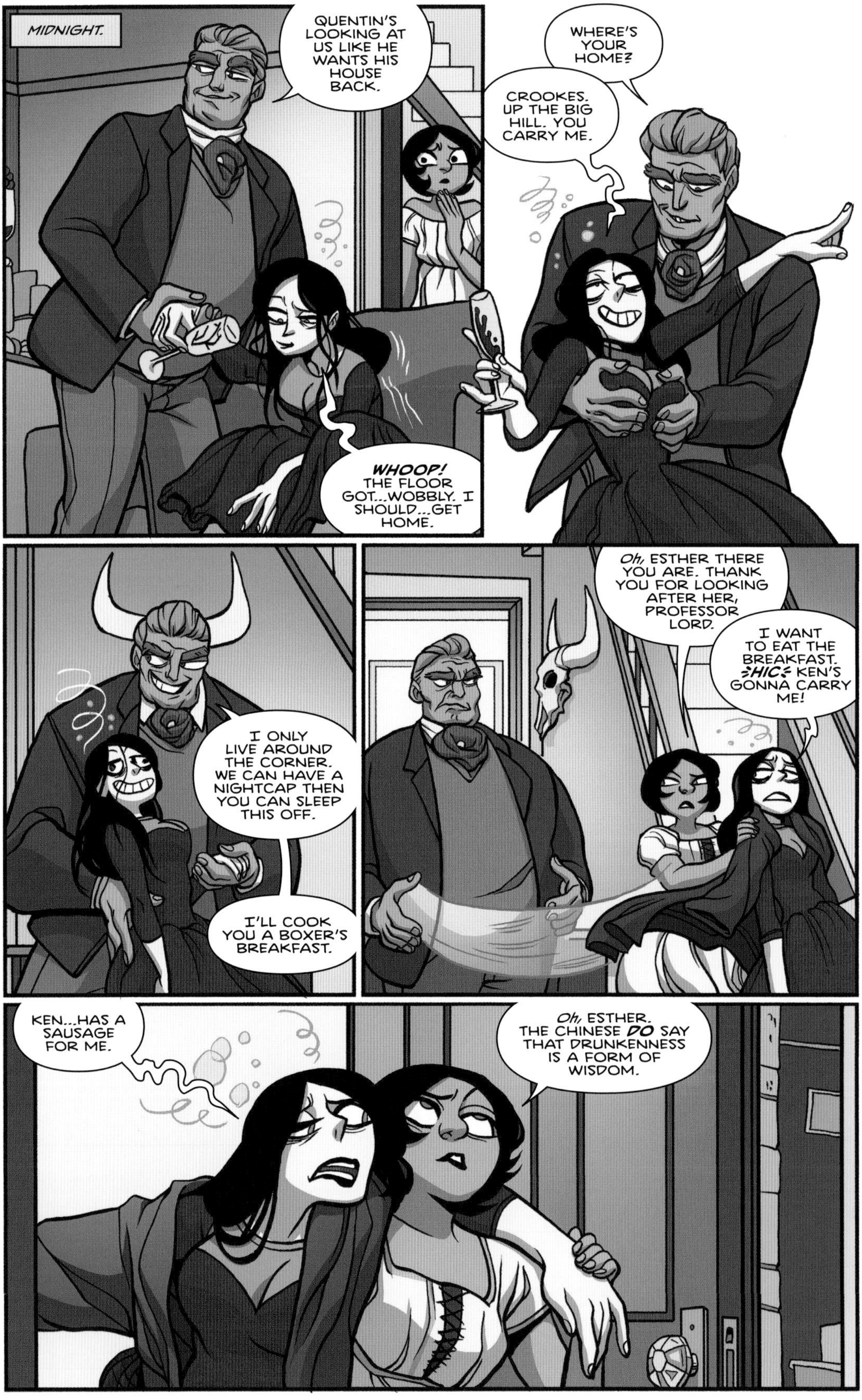
MIDNIGHT.
QUENTIN'S LOOKING AT US LIKE HE WANTS HIS HOUSE BACK.
WHOOP! THE FLOOR GOT...WOBBLY. I SHOULD...GET HOME.
WHERE'S YOUR HOME?
CROOKES. UP THE BIG HILL. YOU CARRY ME.
I ONLY LIVE AROUND THE CORNER. WE CAN HAVE A NIGHTCAP THEN YOU CAN SLEEP THIS OFF.
I'LL COOK YOU A BOXER'S BREAKFAST.
Oh, ESTHER THERE YOU ARE. THANK YOU FOR LOOKING AFTER HER, PROFESSOR LORD.
I WANT TO EAT THE BREAKFAST. HIC KEN'S GONNA CARRY ME!
KEN...HAS A SAUSAGE FOR ME.
Oh, ESTHER. THE CHINESE DO SAY THAT DRUNKENNESS IS A FORM OF WISDOM.

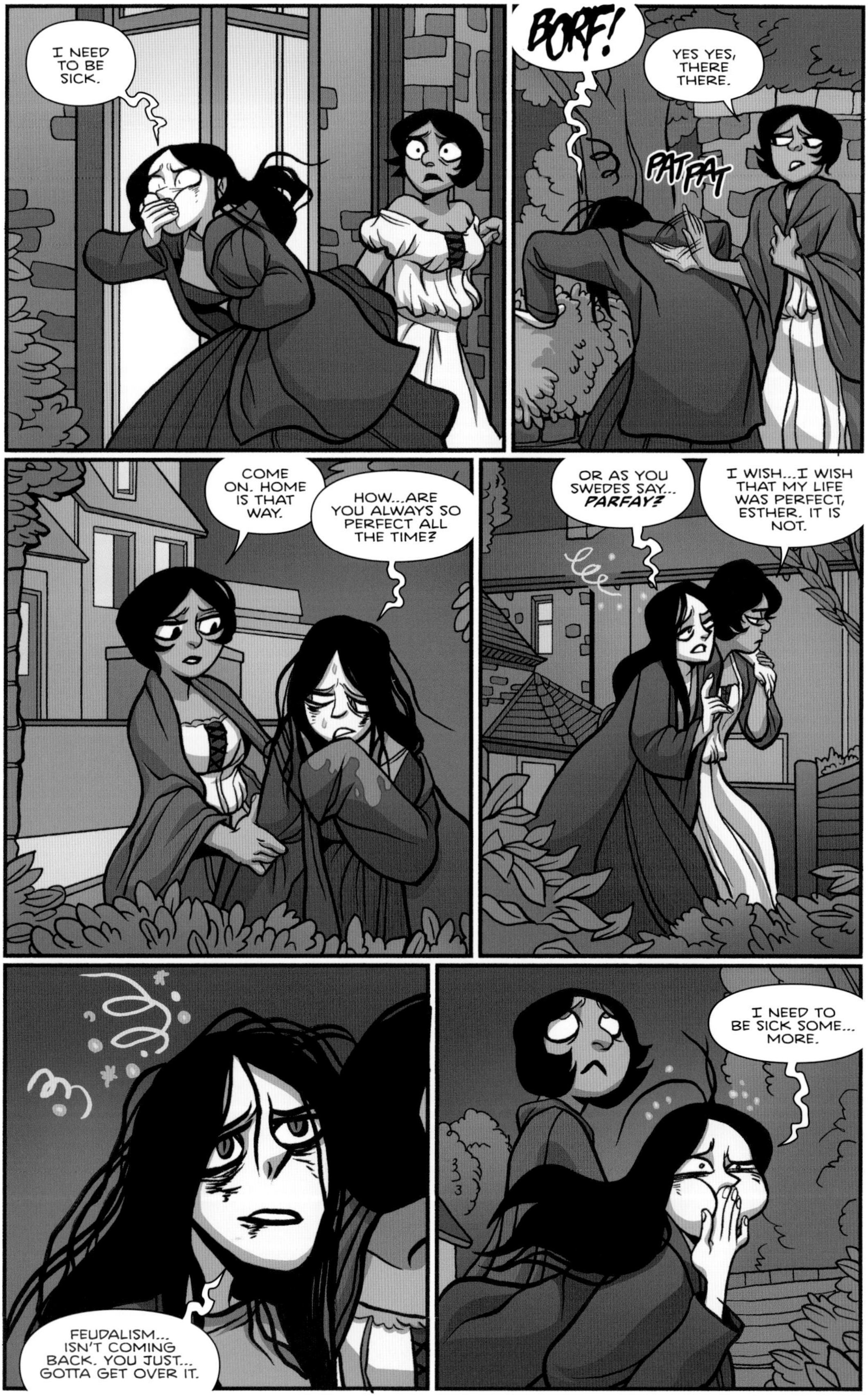
I NEED TO BE SICK.
BORF!
YES YES, THERE THERE.
PAT PAT
COME ON. HOME IS THAT WAY.
HOW...ARE YOU ALWAYS SO PERFECT ALL THE TIME?
OR AS YOU SWEDES SAY... *PARFAY?*
I WISH...I WISH THAT MY LIFE WAS PERFECT, ESTHER. IT IS NOT.
FEUDALISM... ISN'T COMING BACK. YOU JUST... GOTTA GET OVER IT.
I NEED TO BE SICK SOME... MORE.

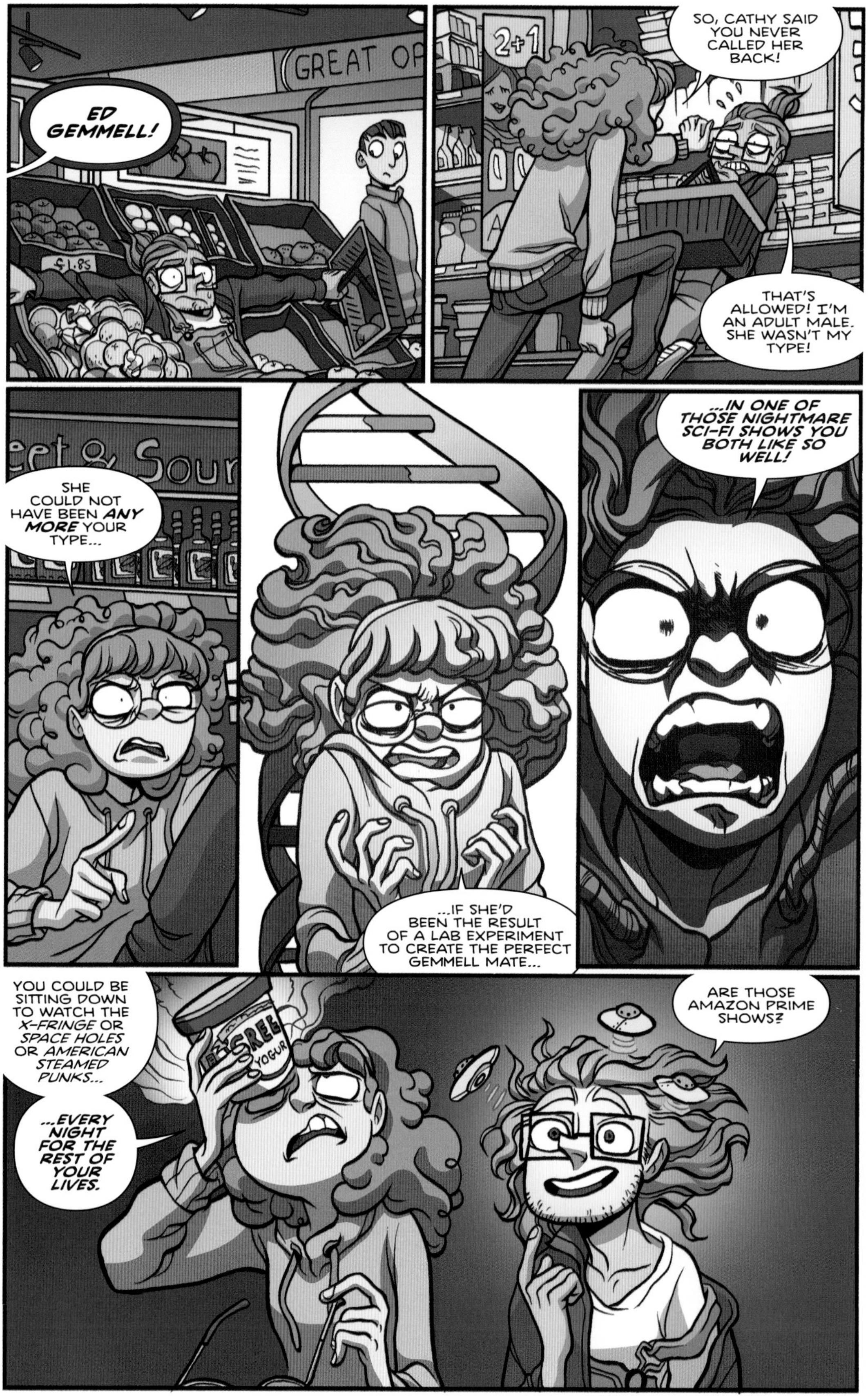
GREAT OP
£1.85
ED GEMMELL!
2+1
SO, CATHY SAID YOU NEVER CALLED HER BACK!
THAT'S ALLOWED! I'M AN ADULT MALE. SHE WASN'T MY TYPE!
eet & Sour
SHE COULD NOT HAVE BEEN ANY MORE YOUR TYPE...
...IF SHE'D BEEN THE RESULT OF A LAB EXPERIMENT TO CREATE THE PERFECT GEMMELL MATE...
...IN ONE OF THOSE NIGHTMARE SCI-FI SHOWS YOU BOTH LIKE SO WELL!
YOU COULD BE SITTING DOWN TO WATCH THE X-FRINGE OR SPACE HOLES OR AMERICAN STEAMED PUNKS...
...EVERY NIGHT FOR THE REST OF YOUR LIVES.
ARE THOSE AMAZON PRIME SHOWS?

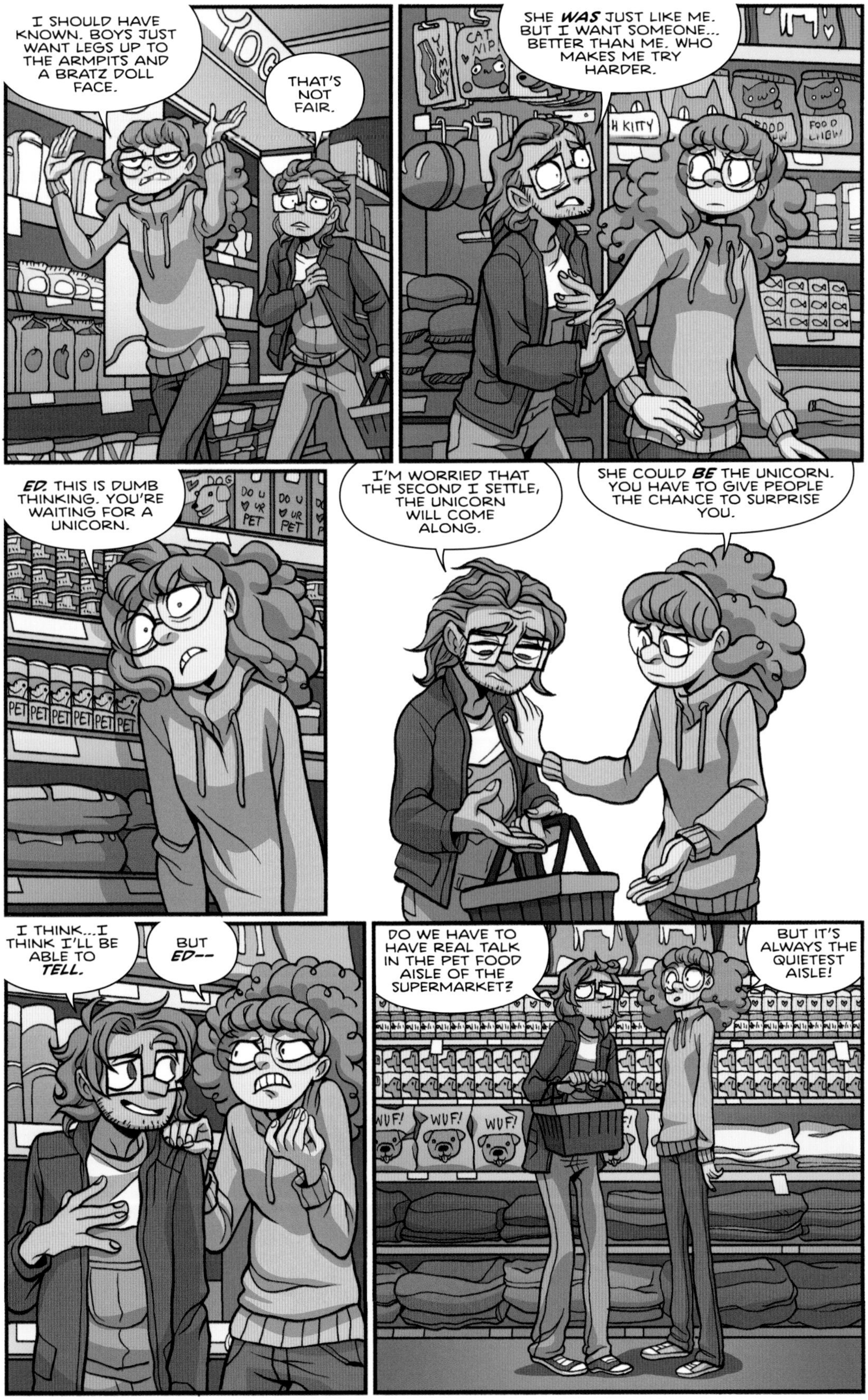
I SHOULD HAVE KNOWN. BOYS JUST WANT LEGS UP TO THE ARMPITS AND A BRATZ DOLL FACE.
THAT'S NOT FAIR.
SHE WAS JUST LIKE ME. BUT I WANT SOMEONE... BETTER THAN ME. WHO MAKES ME TRY HARDER.
ED. THIS IS DUMB THINKING. YOU'RE WAITING FOR A UNICORN.
I'M WORRIED THAT THE SECOND I SETTLE, THE UNICORN WILL COME ALONG.
SHE COULD BE THE UNICORN. YOU HAVE TO GIVE PEOPLE THE CHANCE TO SURPRISE YOU.
I THINK...I THINK I'LL BE ABLE TO TELL.
BUT ED--
DO WE HAVE TO HAVE REAL TALK IN THE PET FOOD AISLE OF THE SUPERMARKET?
BUT IT'S ALWAYS THE QUIETEST AISLE!
WUF!

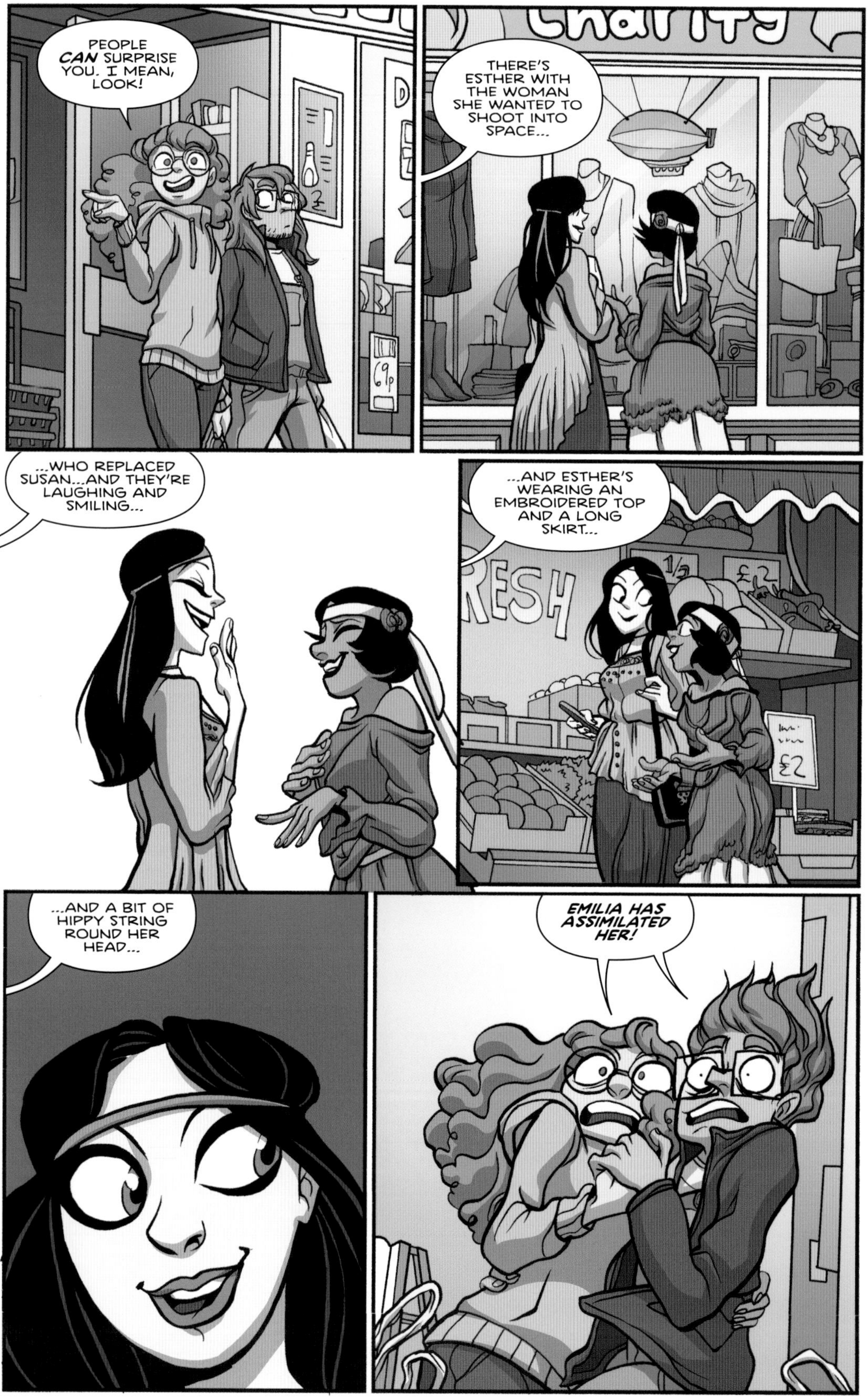

PEOPLE CAN SURPRISE YOU. I MEAN, LOOK!
Charity
THERE'S ESTHER WITH THE WOMAN SHE WANTED TO SHOOT INTO SPACE...
69p
...WHO REPLACED SUSAN...AND THEY'RE LAUGHING AND SMILING...
...AND ESTHER'S WEARING AN EMBROIDERED TOP AND A LONG SKIRT...
RESH
£2
£2
...AND A BIT OF HIPPY STRING ROUND HER HEAD...
EMILIA HAS ASSIMILATED HER!

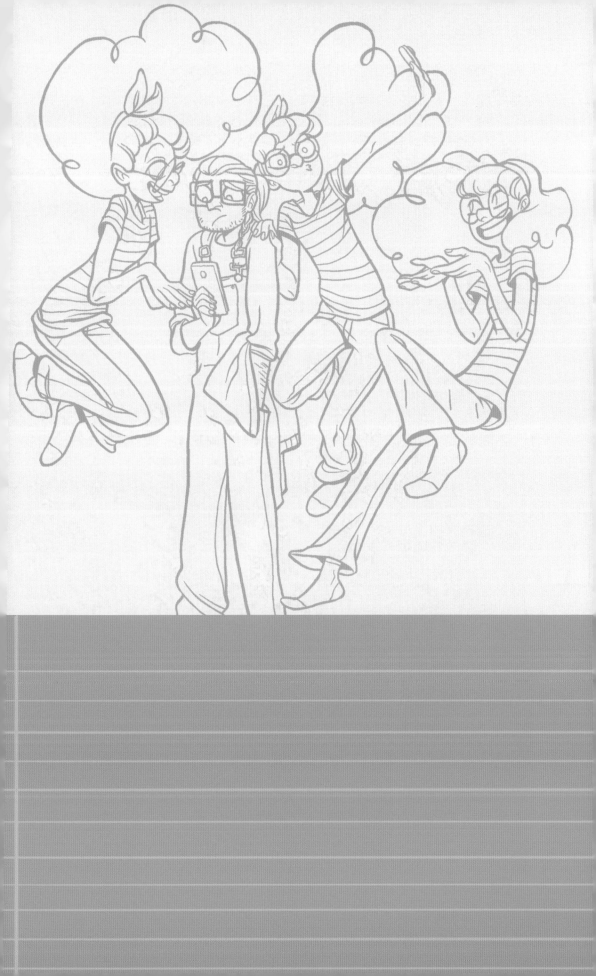

CHAPTER
THIRTY

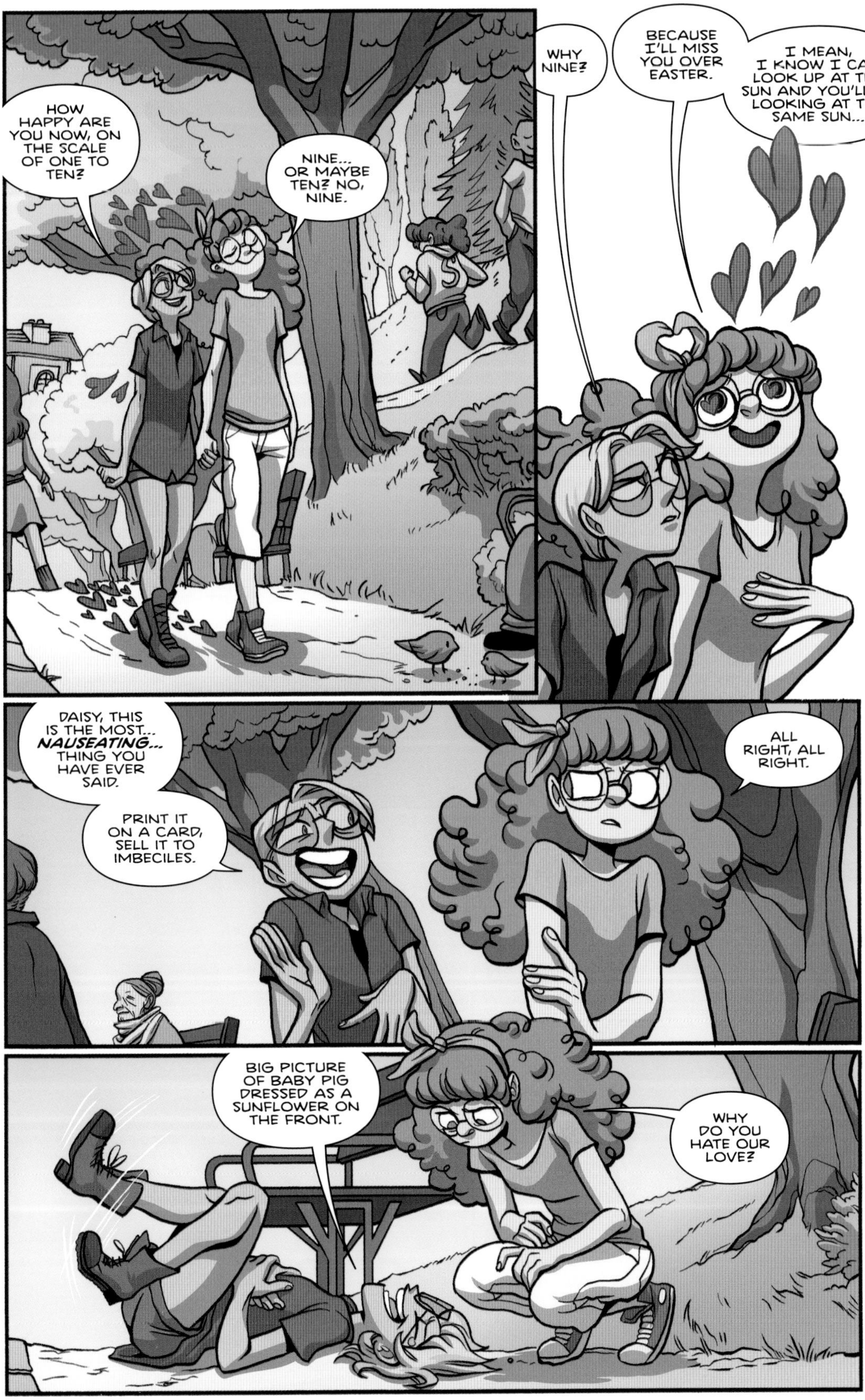
HOW HAPPY ARE YOU NOW, ON THE SCALE OF ONE TO TEN?
NINE... OR MAYBE TEN? NO, NINE.
WHY NINE?
BECAUSE I'LL MISS YOU OVER EASTER.
I MEAN, I KNOW I CAN LOOK UP AT THE SUN AND YOU'LL BE LOOKING AT THE SAME SUN...
DAISY, THIS IS THE MOST... NAUSEATING... THING YOU HAVE EVER SAID.
PRINT IT ON A CARD, SELL IT TO IMBECILES.
ALL RIGHT, ALL RIGHT.
BIG PICTURE OF BABY PIG DRESSED AS A SUNFLOWER ON THE FRONT.
WHY DO YOU HATE OUR LOVE?

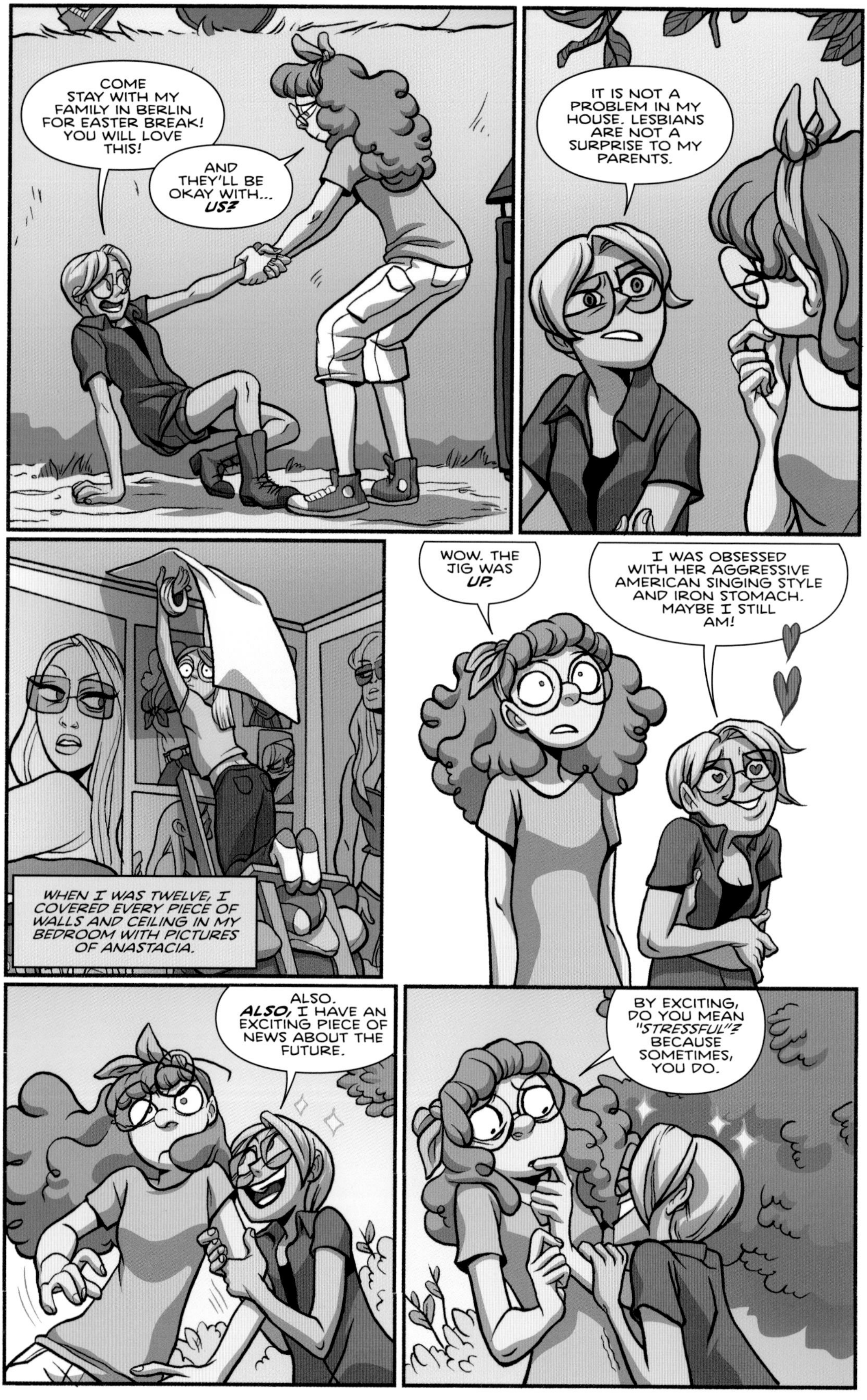
COME STAY WITH MY FAMILY IN BERLIN FOR EASTER BREAK! YOU WILL LOVE THIS!
AND THEY'LL BE OKAY WITH... US?
IT IS NOT A PROBLEM IN MY HOUSE. LESBIANS ARE NOT A SURPRISE TO MY PARENTS.
WHEN I WAS TWELVE, I COVERED EVERY PIECE OF WALLS AND CEILING IN MY BEDROOM WITH PICTURES OF ANASTACIA.
WOW. THE JIG WAS UP.
I WAS OBSESSED WITH HER AGGRESSIVE AMERICAN SINGING STYLE AND IRON STOMACH. MAYBE I STILL AM!
ALSO. ALSO, I HAVE AN EXCITING PIECE OF NEWS ABOUT THE FUTURE.
BY EXCITING, DO YOU MEAN "STRESSFUL"? BECAUSE SOMETIMES, YOU DO.

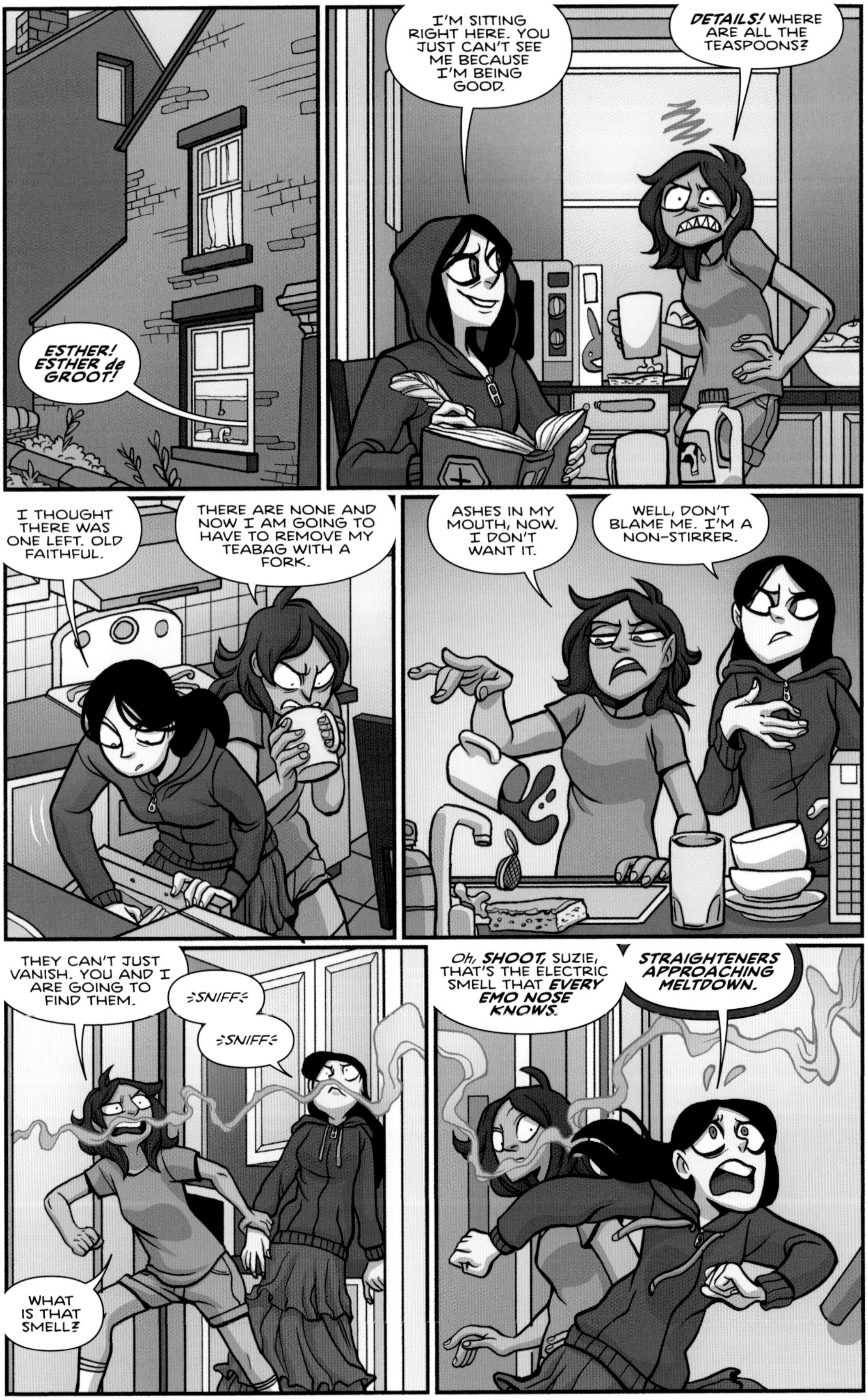
ESTHER! ESTHER de GROOT!
I'M SITTING RIGHT HERE. YOU JUST CAN'T SEE ME BECAUSE I'M BEING GOOD.
DETAILS! WHERE ARE ALL THE TEASPOONS?
I THOUGHT THERE WAS ONE LEFT. OLD FAITHFUL.
THERE ARE NONE AND NOW I AM GOING TO HAVE TO REMOVE MY TEABAG WITH A FORK.
ASHES IN MY MOUTH, NOW. I DON'T WANT IT.
WELL, DON'T BLAME ME. I'M A NON-STIRRER.
THEY CAN'T JUST VANISH. YOU AND I ARE GOING TO FIND THEM.
SNIFF
SNIFF
WHAT IS THAT SMELL?
Oh, SHOOT, SUZIE, THAT'S THE ELECTRIC SMELL THAT EVERY EMO NOSE KNOWS.
STRAIGHTENERS APPROACHING MELTDOWN.

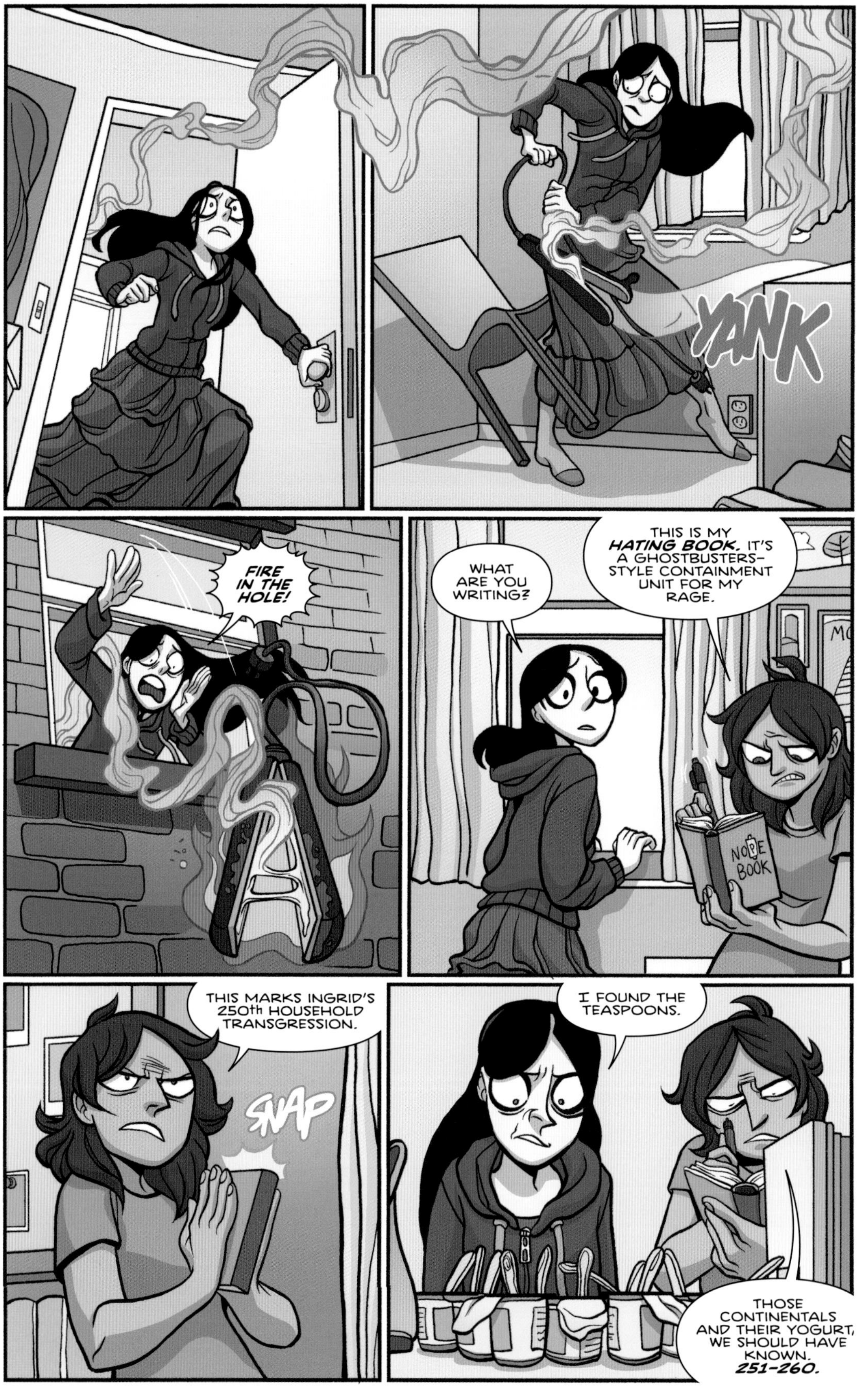
YANK
FIRE IN THE HOLE!
WHAT ARE YOU WRITING?
THIS IS MY *HATING BOOK.* IT'S A GHOSTBUSTERS-STYLE CONTAINMENT UNIT FOR MY RAGE.
NOPE BOOK
THIS MARKS INGRID'S 250th HOUSEHOLD TRANSGRESSION.
SNAP
I FOUND THE TEASPOONS.
THOSE CONTINENTALS AND THEIR YOGURT, WE SHOULD HAVE KNOWN. *251-260.*

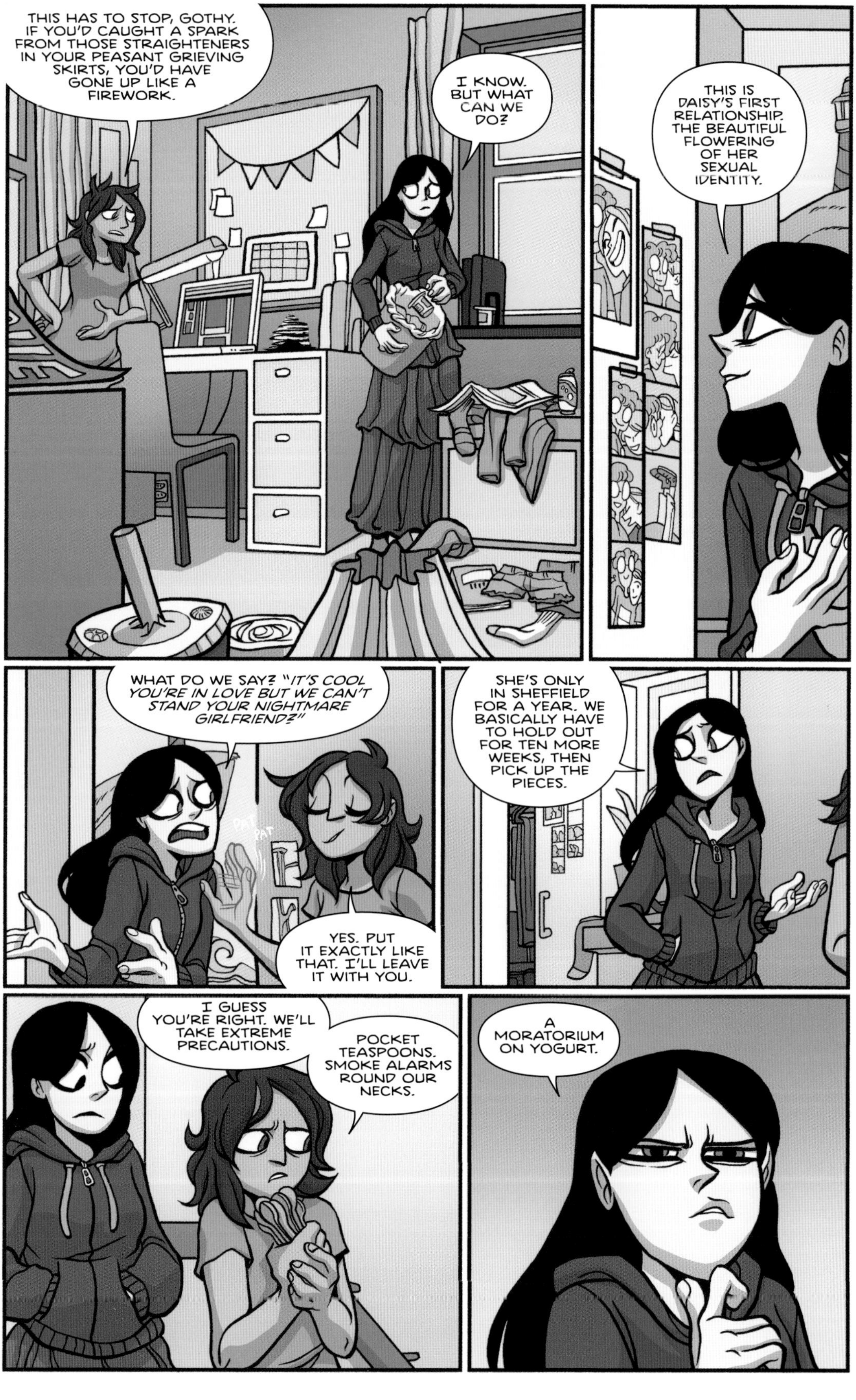

THIS HAS TO STOP, GOTHY. IF YOU'D CAUGHT A SPARK FROM THOSE STRAIGHTENERS IN YOUR PEASANT GRIEVING SKIRTS, YOU'D HAVE GONE UP LIKE A FIREWORK.
I KNOW. BUT WHAT CAN WE DO?
THIS IS DAISY'S FIRST RELATIONSHIP. THE BEAUTIFUL FLOWERING OF HER SEXUAL IDENTITY.
WHAT DO WE SAY? "IT'S COOL YOU'RE IN LOVE BUT WE CAN'T STAND YOUR NIGHTMARE GIRLFRIEND?"
PAT PAT
YES. PUT IT EXACTLY LIKE THAT. I'LL LEAVE IT WITH YOU.
SHE'S ONLY IN SHEFFIELD FOR A YEAR. WE BASICALLY HAVE TO HOLD OUT FOR TEN MORE WEEKS, THEN PICK UP THE PIECES.
I GUESS YOU'RE RIGHT. WE'LL TAKE EXTREME PRECAUTIONS.
POCKET TEASPOONS. SMOKE ALARMS ROUND OUR NECKS.
A MORATORIUM ON YOGURT.

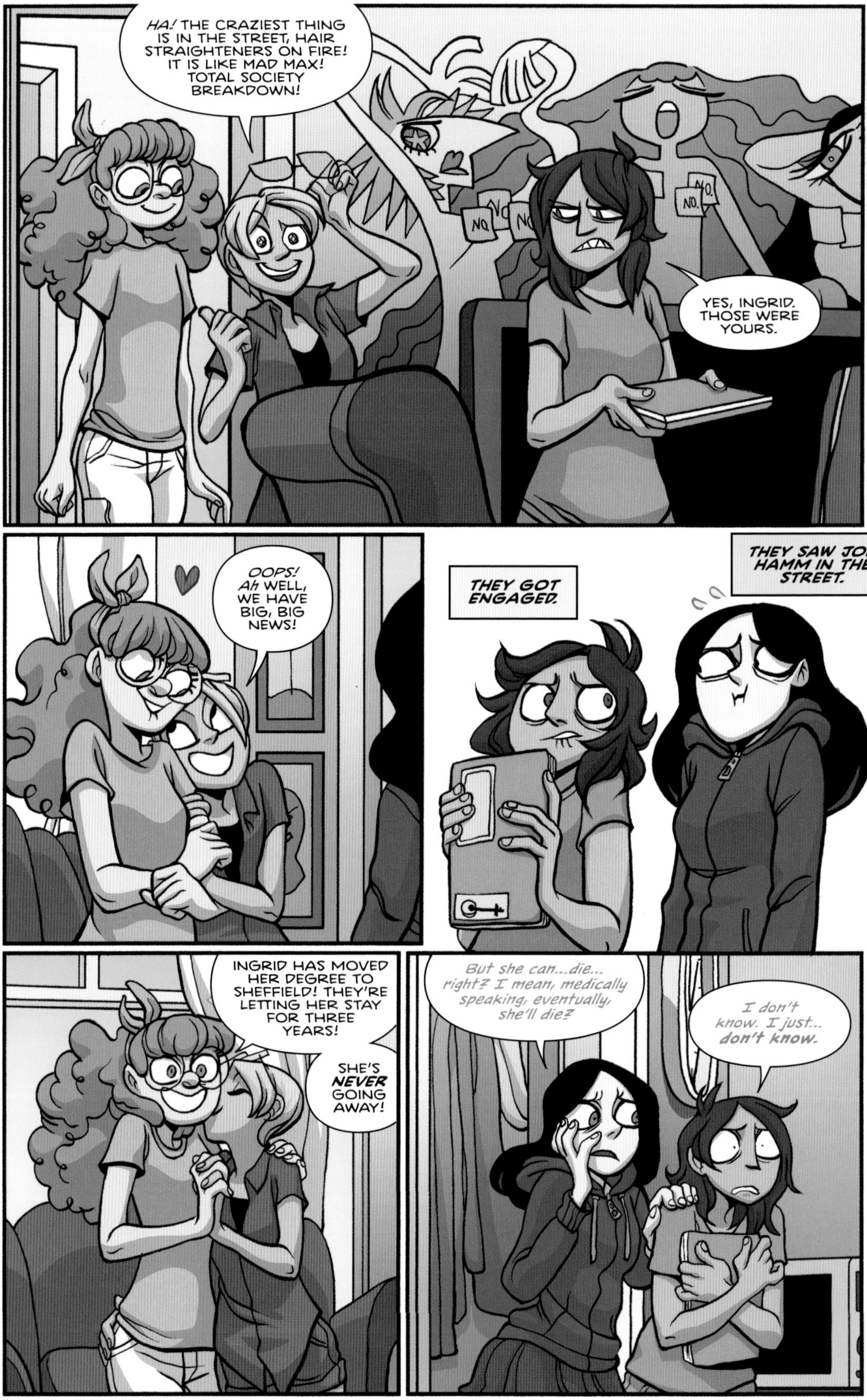
HA! THE CRAZIEST THING IS IN THE STREET, HAIR STRAIGHTENERS ON FIRE! IT IS LIKE MAD MAX! TOTAL SOCIETY BREAKDOWN!
NO.
NO.
NO.
NO.
NO.
YES, INGRID. THOSE WERE YOURS.
OOPS! Ah WELL, WE HAVE BIG, BIG NEWS!
THEY GOT ENGAGED.
THEY SAW JON HAMM IN THE STREET.
INGRID HAS MOVED HER DEGREE TO SHEFFIELD! THEY'RE LETTING HER STAY FOR THREE YEARS!
SHE'S NEVER GOING AWAY!
But she can...die... right? I mean, medically speaking, eventually, she'll die?
I don't know. I just... don't know.

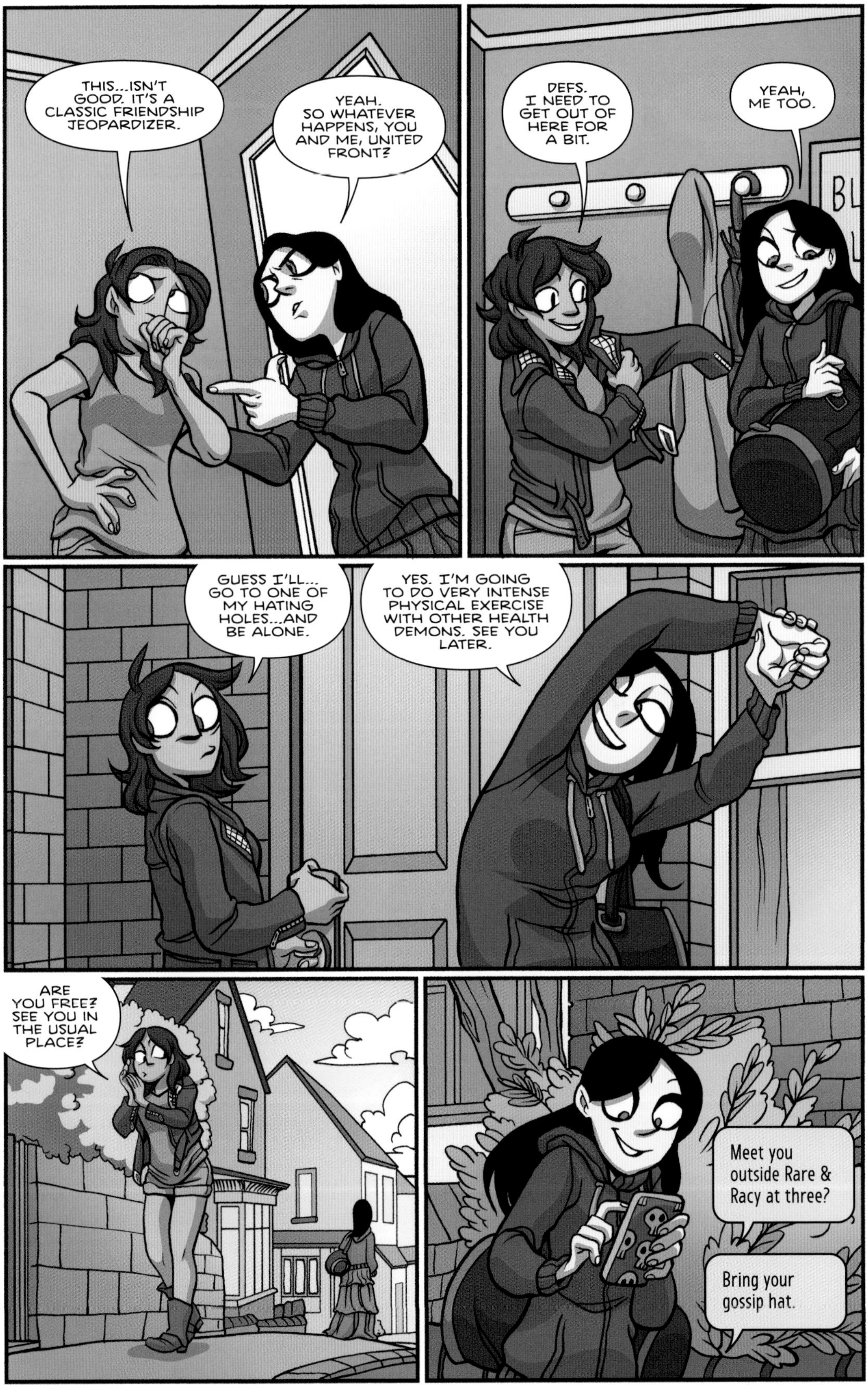
THIS...ISN'T GOOD. IT'S A CLASSIC FRIENDSHIP JEOPARDIZER.
YEAH. SO WHATEVER HAPPENS, YOU AND ME, UNITED FRONT?
DEFS. I NEED TO GET OUT OF HERE FOR A BIT.
YEAH, ME TOO.
GUESS I'LL... GO TO ONE OF MY HATING HOLES...AND BE ALONE.
YES. I'M GOING TO DO VERY INTENSE PHYSICAL EXERCISE WITH OTHER HEALTH DEMONS. SEE YOU LATER.
ARE YOU FREE? SEE YOU IN THE USUAL PLACE?
Meet you outside Rare & Racy at three?
Bring your gossip hat.

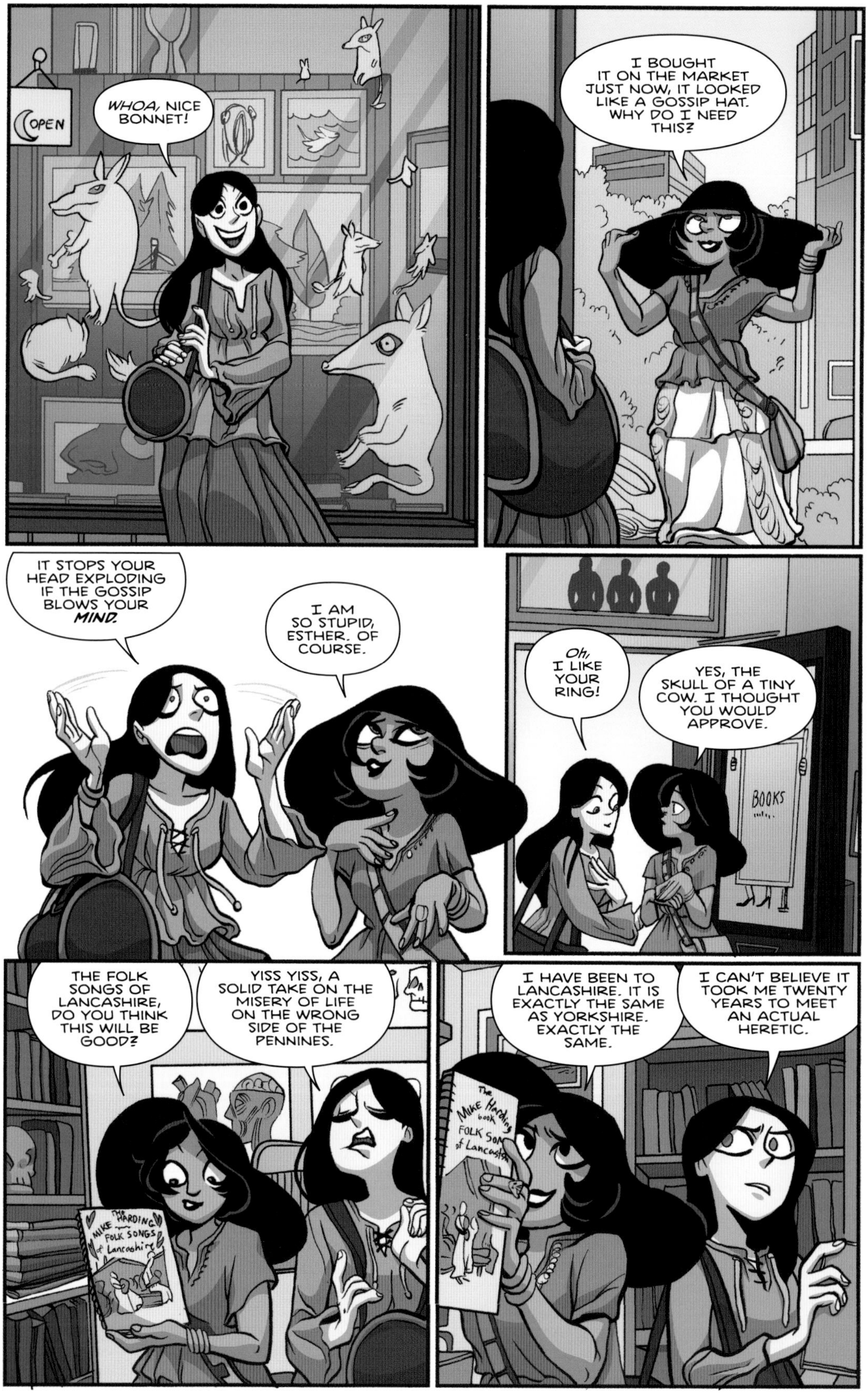
OPEN
WHOA, NICE BONNET!
I BOUGHT IT ON THE MARKET JUST NOW, IT LOOKED LIKE A GOSSIP HAT. WHY DO I NEED THIS?
IT STOPS YOUR HEAD EXPLODING IF THE GOSSIP BLOWS YOUR MIND.
I AM SO STUPID, ESTHER. OF COURSE.
Oh, I LIKE YOUR RING!
YES, THE SKULL OF A TINY COW. I THOUGHT YOU WOULD APPROVE.
BOOKS
THE FOLK SONGS OF LANCASHIRE, DO YOU THINK THIS WILL BE GOOD?
YISS YISS, A SOLID TAKE ON THE MISERY OF LIFE ON THE WRONG SIDE OF THE PENNINES.
The MIKE HARDING FOLK SONGS of Lancashire
I HAVE BEEN TO LANCASHIRE. IT IS EXACTLY THE SAME AS YORKSHIRE. EXACTLY THE SAME.
I CAN'T BELIEVE IT TOOK ME TWENTY YEARS TO MEET AN ACTUAL HERETIC.

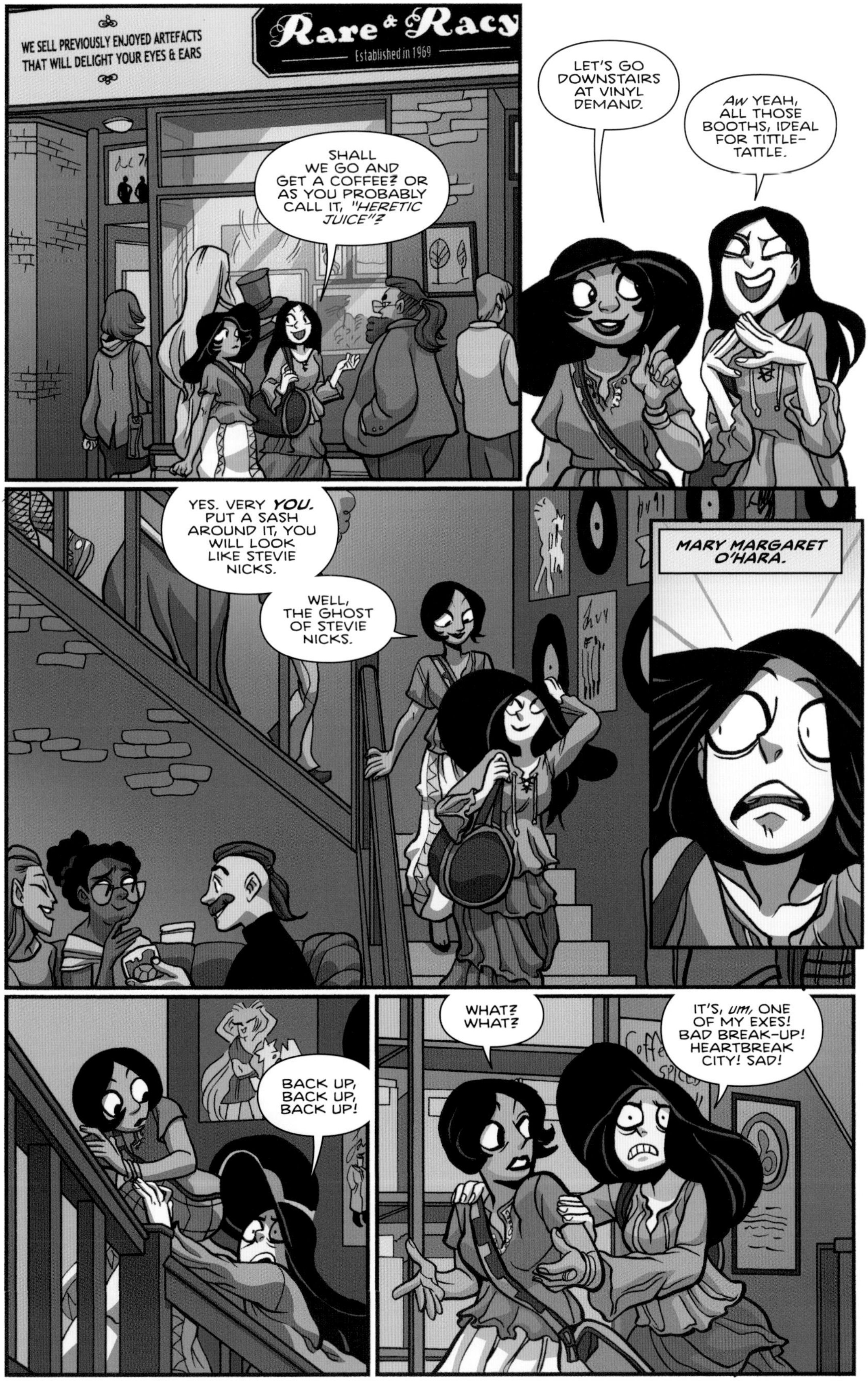
WE SELL PREVIOUSLY ENJOYED ARTEFACTS THAT WILL DELIGHT YOUR EYES & EARS
Rare & Racy
Established in 1969
SHALL WE GO AND GET A COFFEE? OR AS YOU PROBABLY CALL IT, "HERETIC JUICE"?
LET'S GO DOWNSTAIRS AT VINYL DEMAND.
AW YEAH, ALL THOSE BOOTHS, IDEAL FOR TITTLE-TATTLE.
YES. VERY YOU. PUT A SASH AROUND IT, YOU WILL LOOK LIKE STEVIE NICKS.
WELL, THE GHOST OF STEVIE NICKS.
MARY MARGARET O'HARA.
BACK UP, BACK UP, BACK UP!
WHAT? WHAT?
IT'S, UM, ONE OF MY EXES! BAD BREAK-UP! HEARTBREAK CITY! SAD!

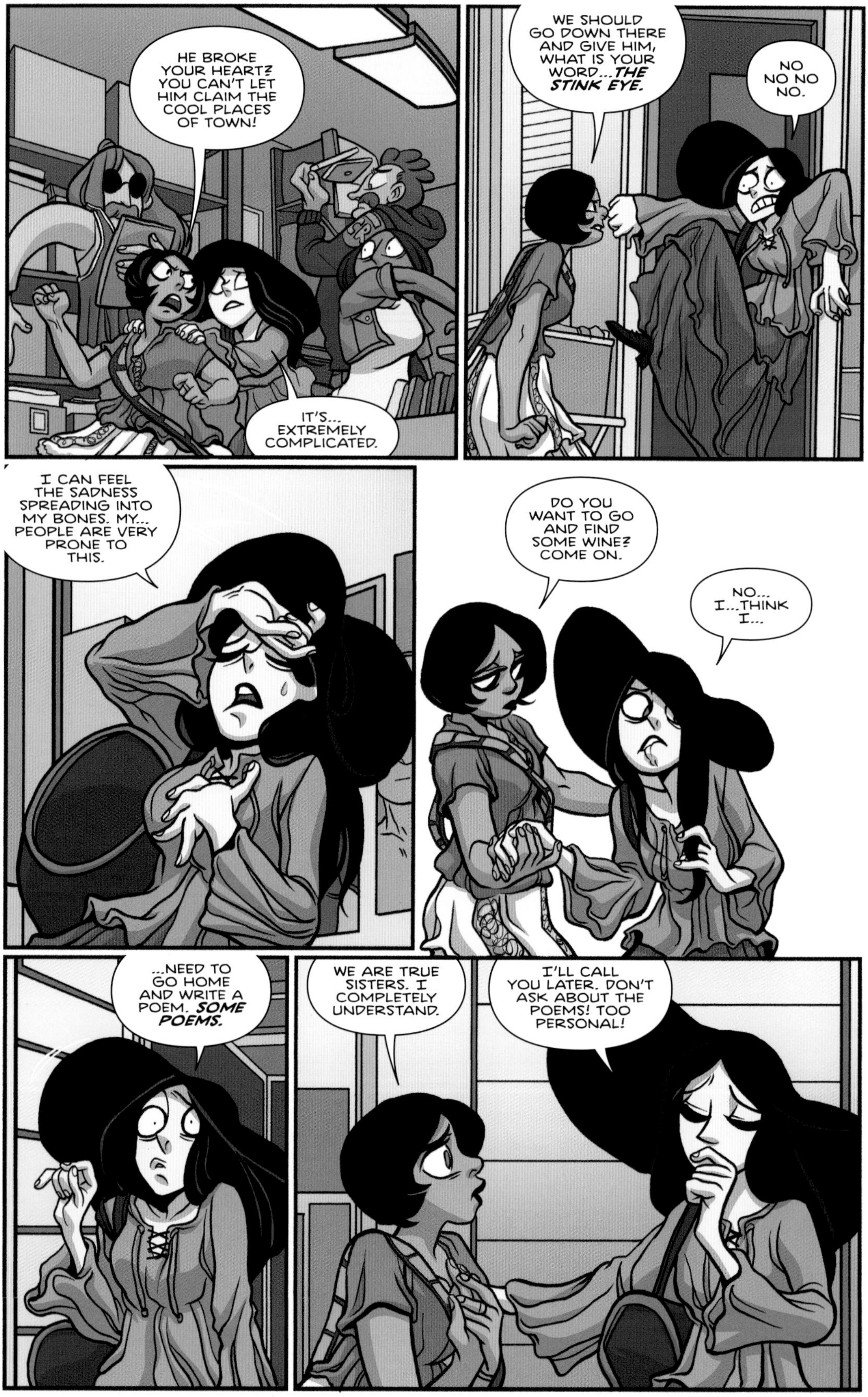
HE BROKE YOUR HEART? YOU CAN'T LET HIM CLAIM THE COOL PLACES OF TOWN!
IT'S... EXTREMELY COMPLICATED.
WE SHOULD GO DOWN THERE AND GIVE HIM, WHAT IS YOUR WORD... THE STINK EYE.
NO NO NO NO.
I CAN FEEL THE SADNESS SPREADING INTO MY BONES. MY... PEOPLE ARE VERY PRONE TO THIS.
DO YOU WANT TO GO AND FIND SOME WINE? COME ON.
NO... I...THINK I...
...NEED TO GO HOME AND WRITE A POEM. SOME POEMS.
WE ARE TRUE SISTERS. I COMPLETELY UNDERSTAND.
I'LL CALL YOU LATER. DON'T ASK ABOUT THE POEMS! TOO PERSONAL!

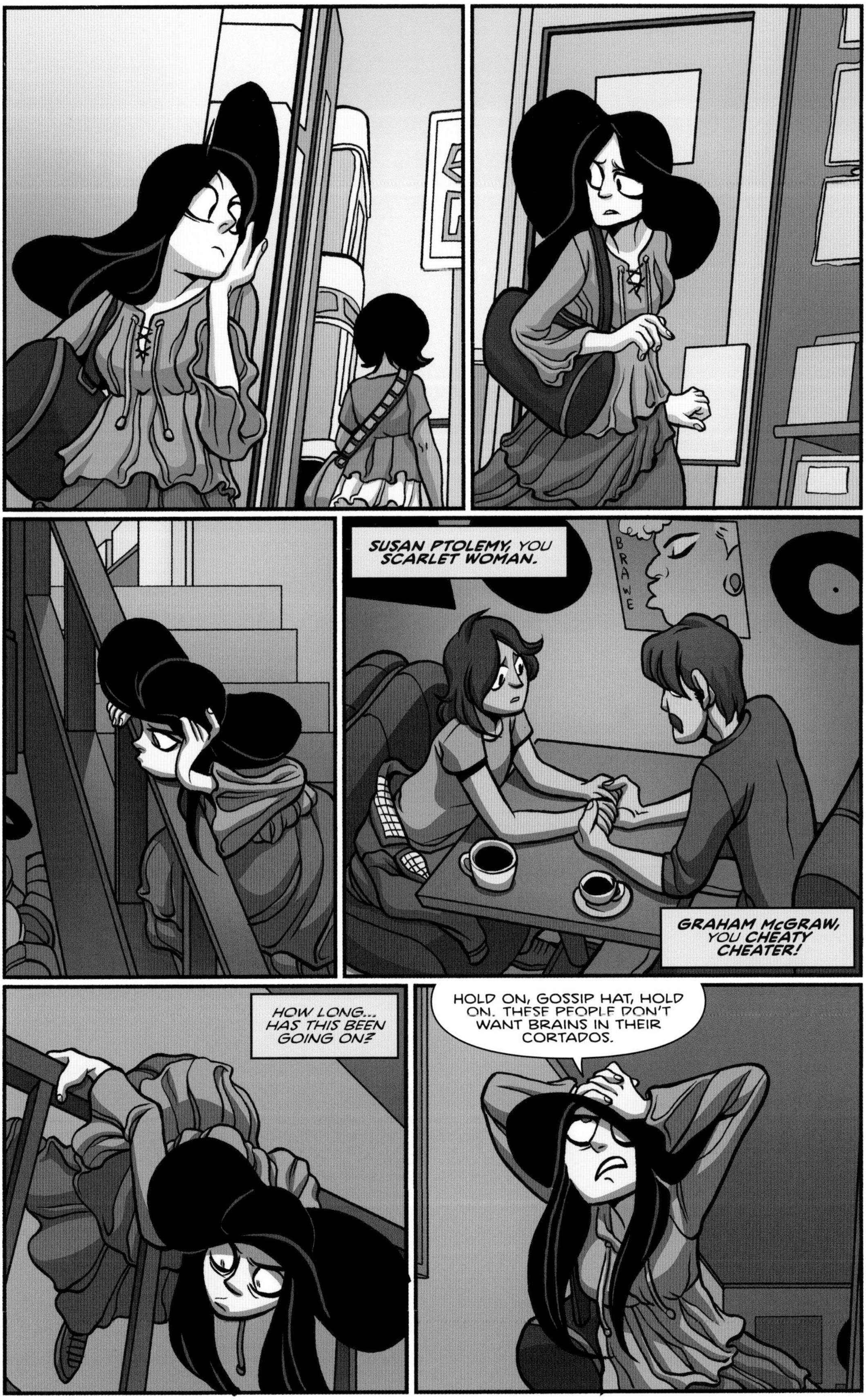
SUSAN PTOLEMY, YOU SCARLET WOMAN.
B R A W E
GRAHAM McGRAW, YOU CHEATY CHEATER!
HOW LONG... HAS THIS BEEN GOING ON?
HOLD ON, GOSSIP HAT, HOLD ON. THESE PEOPLE DON'T WANT BRAINS IN THEIR CORTADOS.

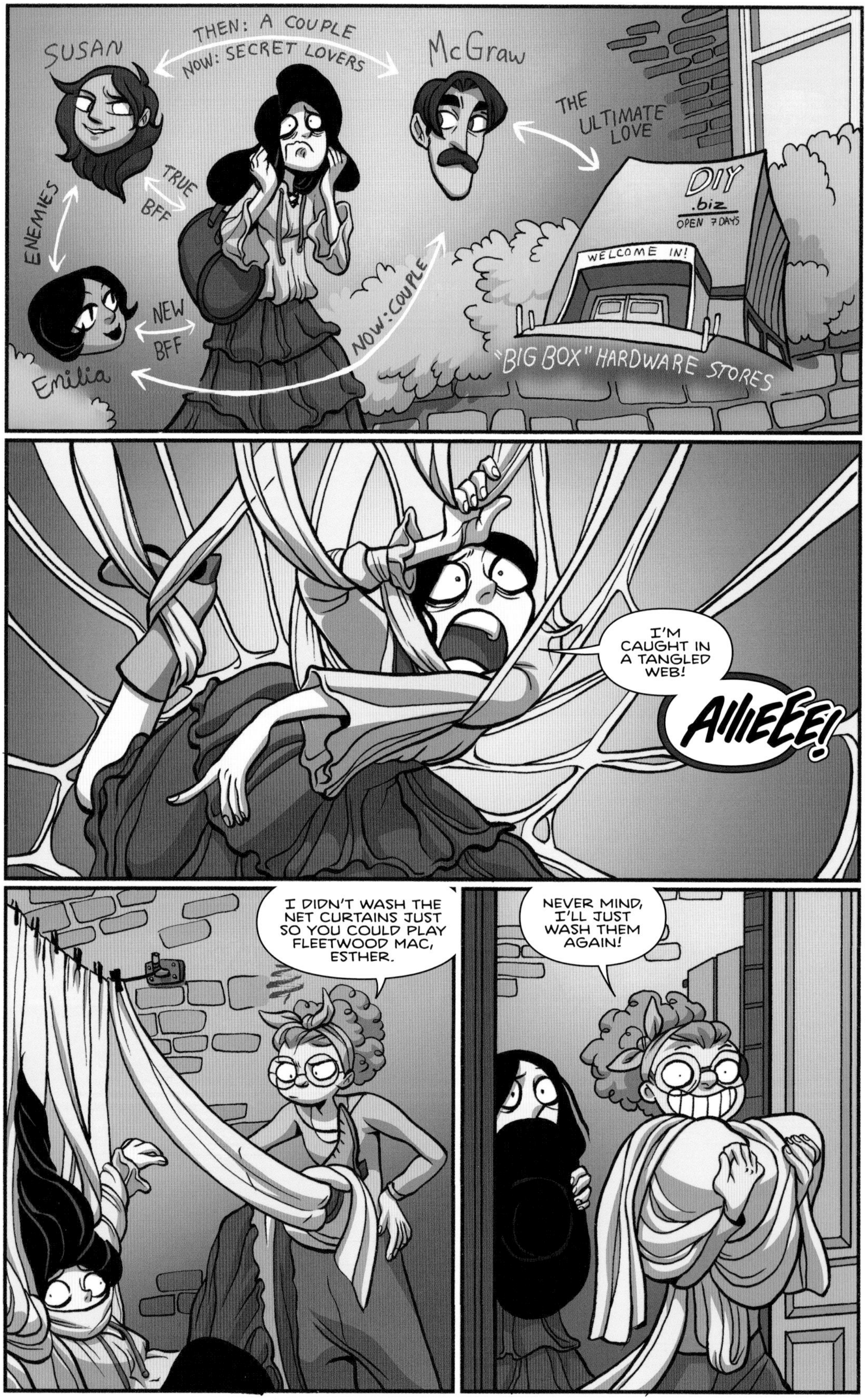
SUSAN
THEN: A COUPLE
NOW: SECRET LOVERS
McGraw
THE ULTIMATE LOVE
TRUE BFF
ENEMIES
DIY .biz
OPEN 7 DAYS
WELCOME IN!
NEW BFF
NOW: COUPLE
Emilia
"BIG BOX" HARDWARE STORES
I'M CAUGHT IN A TANGLED WEB!
AIIIEEE!
I DIDN'T WASH THE NET CURTAINS JUST SO YOU COULD PLAY FLEETWOOD MAC, ESTHER.
NEVER MIND, I'LL JUST WASH THEM AGAIN!

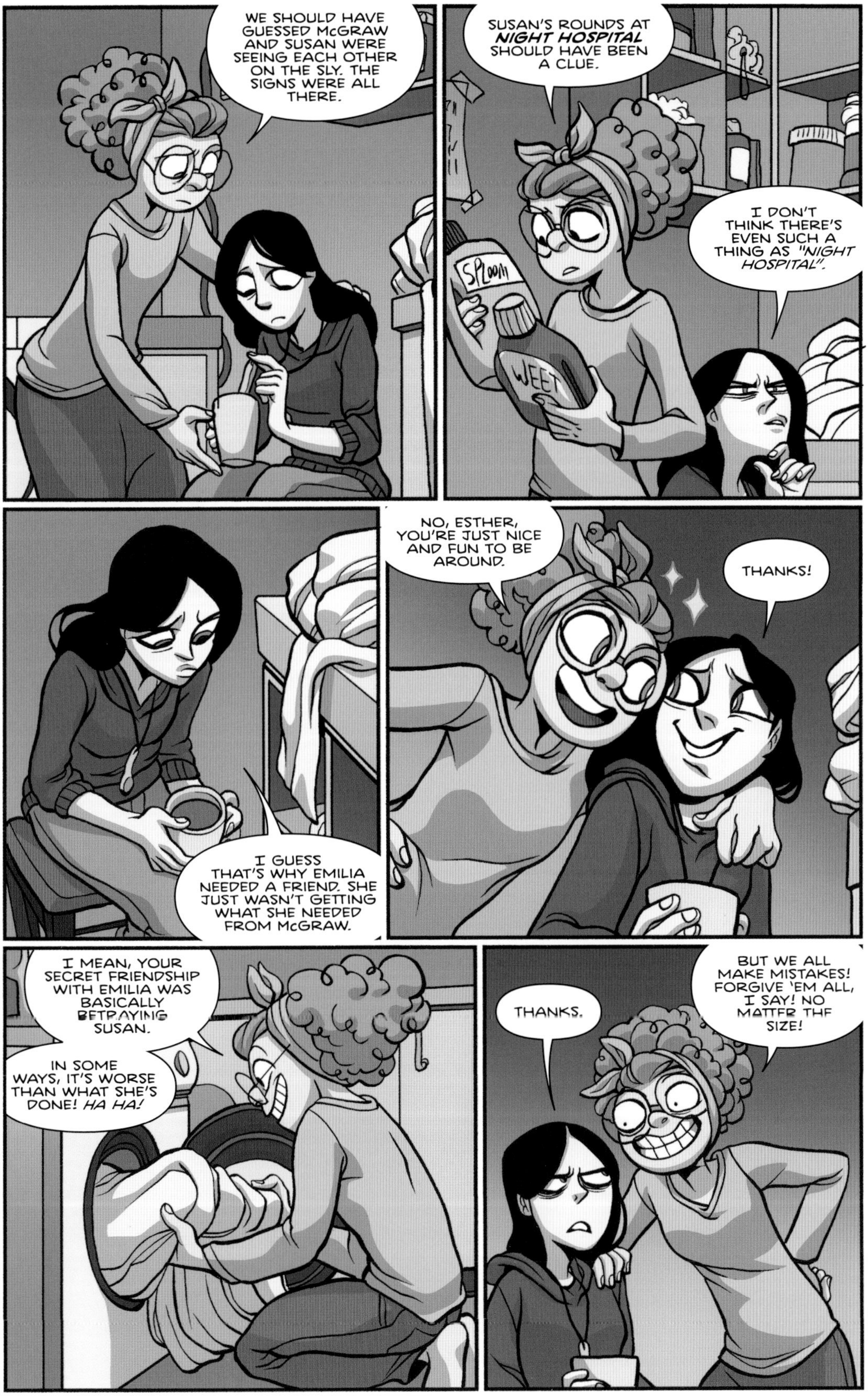
WE SHOULD HAVE GUESSED McGRAW AND SUSAN WERE SEEING EACH OTHER ON THE SLY. THE SIGNS WERE ALL THERE.
SUSAN'S ROUNDS AT *NIGHT HOSPITAL* SHOULD HAVE BEEN A CLUE.
SPLOOM
WEET
I DON'T THINK THERE'S EVEN SUCH A THING AS *"NIGHT HOSPITAL"*.
I GUESS THAT'S WHY EMILIA NEEDED A FRIEND. SHE JUST WASN'T GETTING WHAT SHE NEEDED FROM McGRAW.
NO, ESTHER, YOU'RE JUST NICE AND FUN TO BE AROUND.
THANKS!
I MEAN, YOUR SECRET FRIENDSHIP WITH EMILIA WAS BASICALLY BETRAYING SUSAN.
IN SOME WAYS, IT'S WORSE THAN WHAT SHE'S DONE! *HA HA!*
THANKS.
BUT WE ALL MAKE MISTAKES! FORGIVE 'EM ALL, I SAY! NO MATTER THE SIZE!

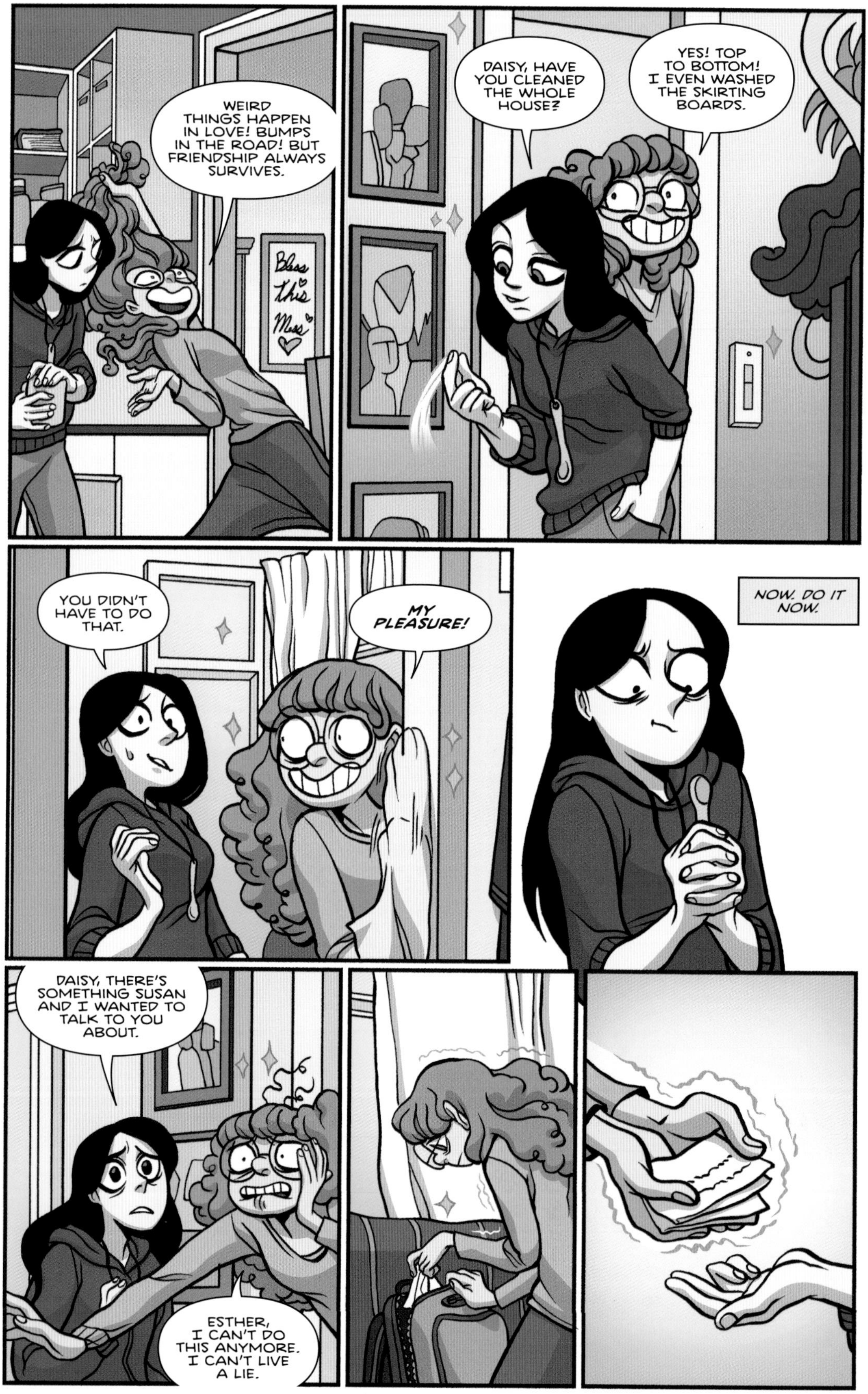

WEIRD THINGS HAPPEN IN LOVE! BUMPS IN THE ROAD! BUT FRIENDSHIP ALWAYS SURVIVES.
Bless This Mess
DAISY, HAVE YOU CLEANED THE WHOLE HOUSE?
YES! TOP TO BOTTOM! I EVEN WASHED THE SKIRTING BOARDS.
YOU DIDN'T HAVE TO DO THAT.
MY PLEASURE!
NOW. DO IT NOW.
DAISY, THERE'S SOMETHING SUSAN AND I WANTED TO TALK TO YOU ABOUT.
ESTHER, I CAN'T DO THIS ANYMORE. I CAN'T LIVE A LIE.

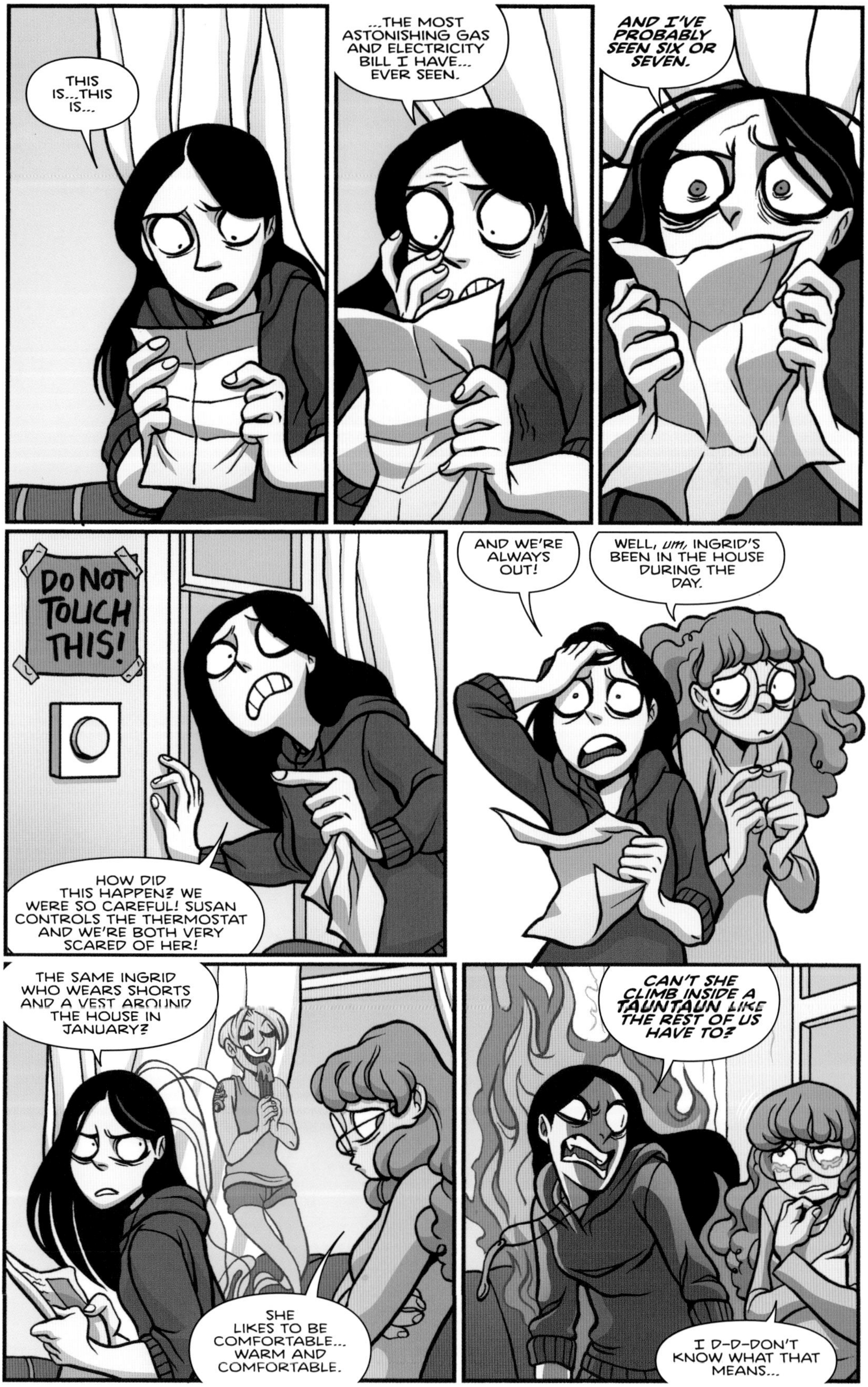
THIS IS...THIS IS...
...THE MOST ASTONISHING GAS AND ELECTRICITY BILL I HAVE... EVER SEEN.
AND I'VE PROBABLY SEEN SIX OR SEVEN.
DO NOT TOUCH THIS!
HOW DID THIS HAPPEN? WE WERE SO CAREFUL! SUSAN CONTROLS THE THERMOSTAT AND WE'RE BOTH VERY SCARED OF HER!
AND WE'RE ALWAYS OUT!
WELL, UM, INGRID'S BEEN IN THE HOUSE DURING THE DAY.
THE SAME INGRID WHO WEARS SHORTS AND A VEST AROUND THE HOUSE IN JANUARY?
SHE LIKES TO BE COMFORTABLE... WARM AND COMFORTABLE.
CAN'T SHE CLIMB INSIDE A TAUNTAUN LIKE THE REST OF US HAVE TO?
I D-D-DON'T KNOW WHAT THAT MEANS...

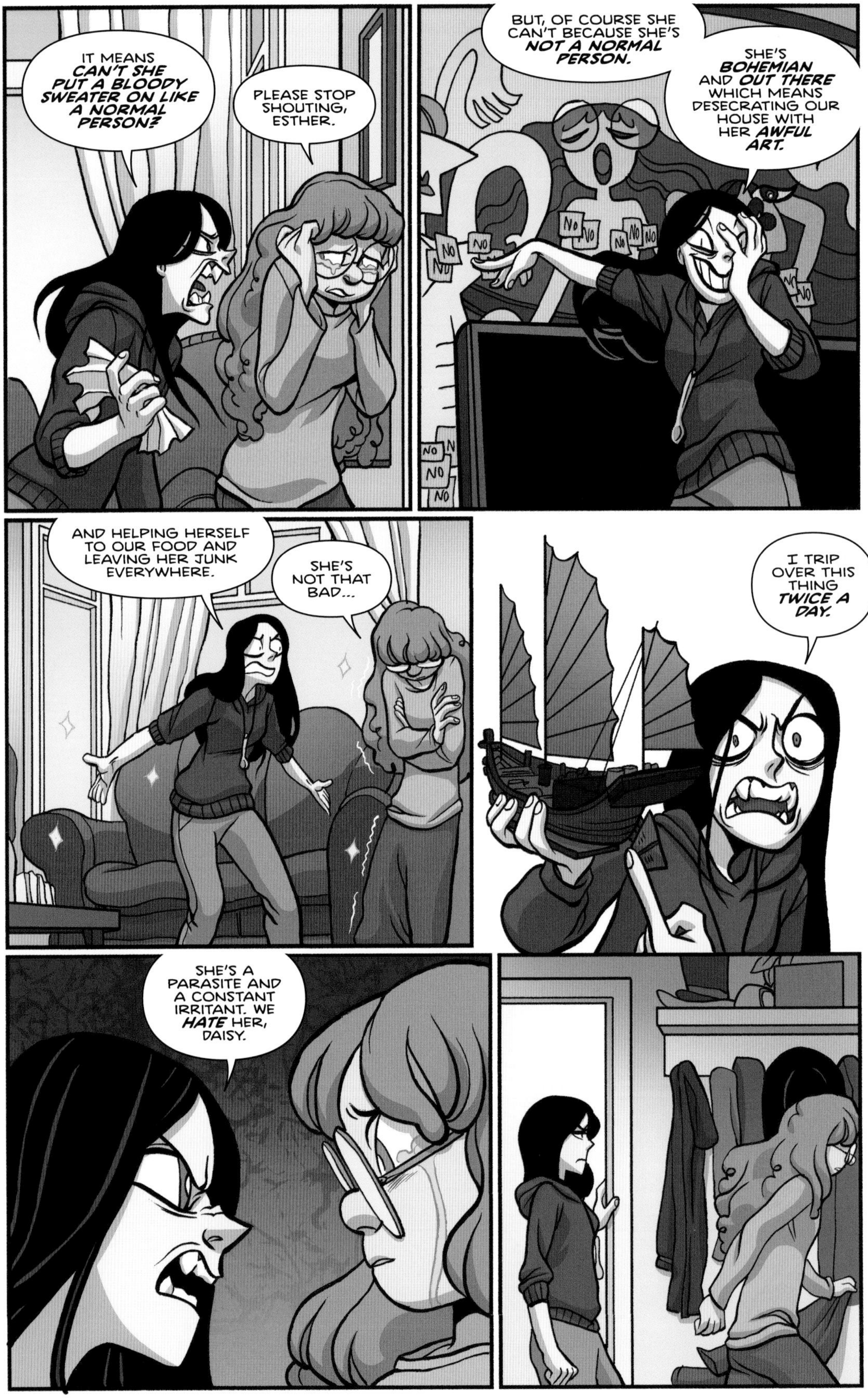
IT MEANS CAN'T SHE PUT A BLOODY SWEATER ON LIKE A NORMAL PERSON?
PLEASE STOP SHOUTING, ESTHER.
BUT, OF COURSE SHE CAN'T BECAUSE SHE'S NOT A NORMAL PERSON.
SHE'S BOHEMIAN AND OUT THERE WHICH MEANS DESECRATING OUR HOUSE WITH HER AWFUL ART.
NO
AND HELPING HERSELF TO OUR FOOD AND LEAVING HER JUNK EVERYWHERE.
SHE'S NOT THAT BAD...
I TRIP OVER THIS THING TWICE A DAY.
SHE'S A PARASITE AND A CONSTANT IRRITANT. WE HATE HER, DAISY.

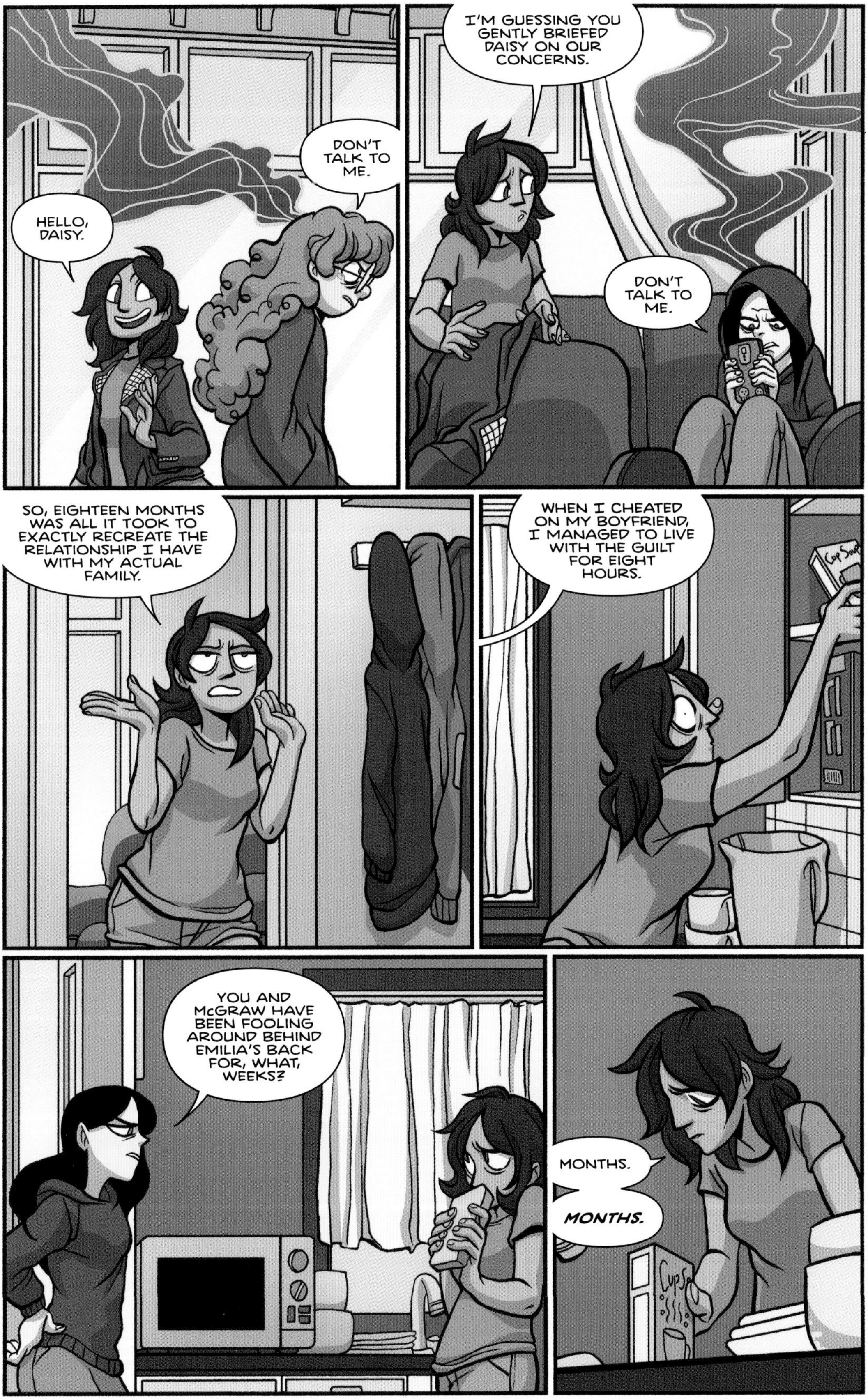
HELLO, DAISY.
DON'T TALK TO ME.
I'M GUESSING YOU GENTLY BRIEFED DAISY ON OUR CONCERNS.
DON'T TALK TO ME.
SO, EIGHTEEN MONTHS WAS ALL IT TOOK TO EXACTLY RECREATE THE RELATIONSHIP I HAVE WITH MY ACTUAL FAMILY.
WHEN I CHEATED ON MY BOYFRIEND, I MANAGED TO LIVE WITH THE GUILT FOR EIGHT HOURS.
YOU AND McGRAW HAVE BEEN FOOLING AROUND BEHIND EMILIA'S BACK FOR, WHAT, WEEKS?
MONTHS.
MONTHS.

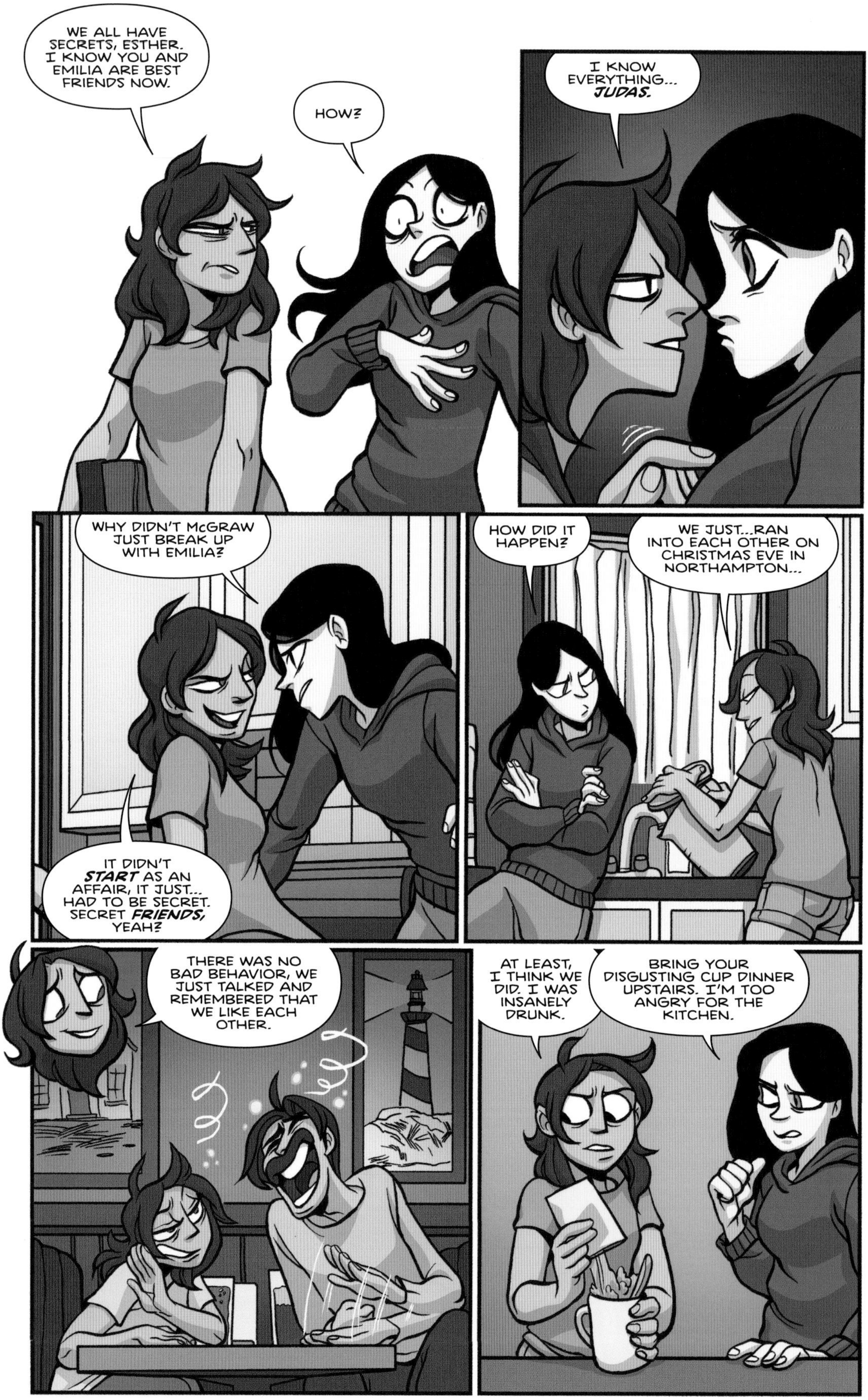

WE ALL HAVE SECRETS, ESTHER. I KNOW YOU AND EMILIA ARE BEST FRIENDS NOW.
HOW?
I KNOW EVERYTHING... *JUDAS.*
WHY DIDN'T McGRAW JUST BREAK UP WITH EMILIA?
IT DIDN'T **START** AS AN AFFAIR, IT JUST... HAD TO BE SECRET. SECRET **FRIENDS,** YEAH?
HOW DID IT HAPPEN?
WE JUST...RAN INTO EACH OTHER ON CHRISTMAS EVE IN NORTHAMPTON...
THERE WAS NO BAD BEHAVIOR, WE JUST TALKED AND REMEMBERED THAT WE LIKE EACH OTHER.
AT LEAST, I THINK WE DID. I WAS INSANELY DRUNK.
BRING YOUR DISGUSTING CUP DINNER UPSTAIRS. I'M TOO ANGRY FOR THE KITCHEN.

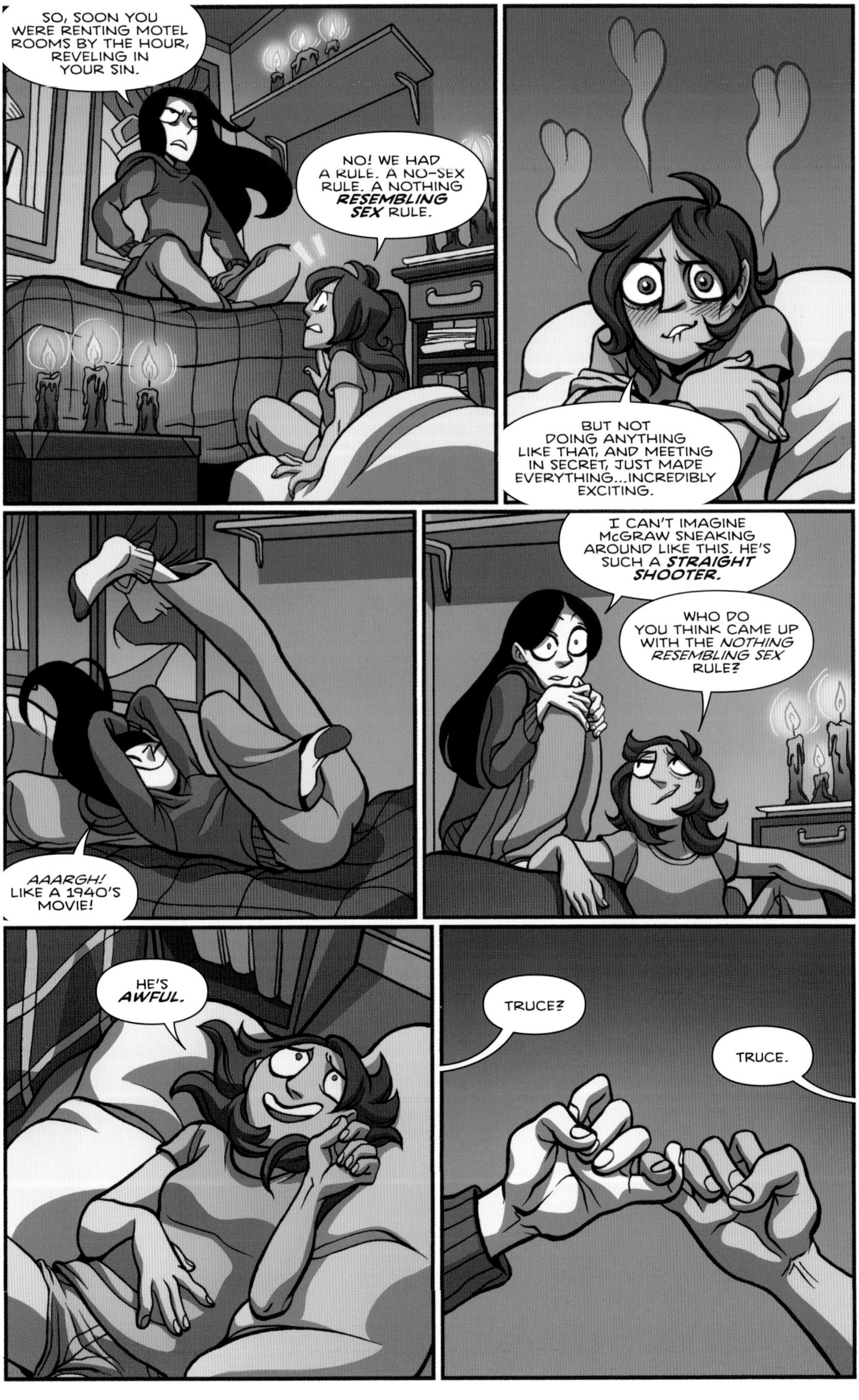
SO, SOON YOU WERE RENTING MOTEL ROOMS BY THE HOUR, REVELING IN YOUR SIN.
NO! WE HAD A RULE. A NO-SEX RULE. A NOTHING RESEMBLING SEX RULE.
BUT NOT DOING ANYTHING LIKE THAT, AND MEETING IN SECRET, JUST MADE EVERYTHING...INCREDIBLY EXCITING.
AAARGH! LIKE A 1940'S MOVIE!
I CAN'T IMAGINE McGRAW SNEAKING AROUND LIKE THIS. HE'S SUCH A STRAIGHT SHOOTER.
WHO DO YOU THINK CAME UP WITH THE NOTHING RESEMBLING SEX RULE?
HE'S AWFUL.
TRUCE?
TRUCE.

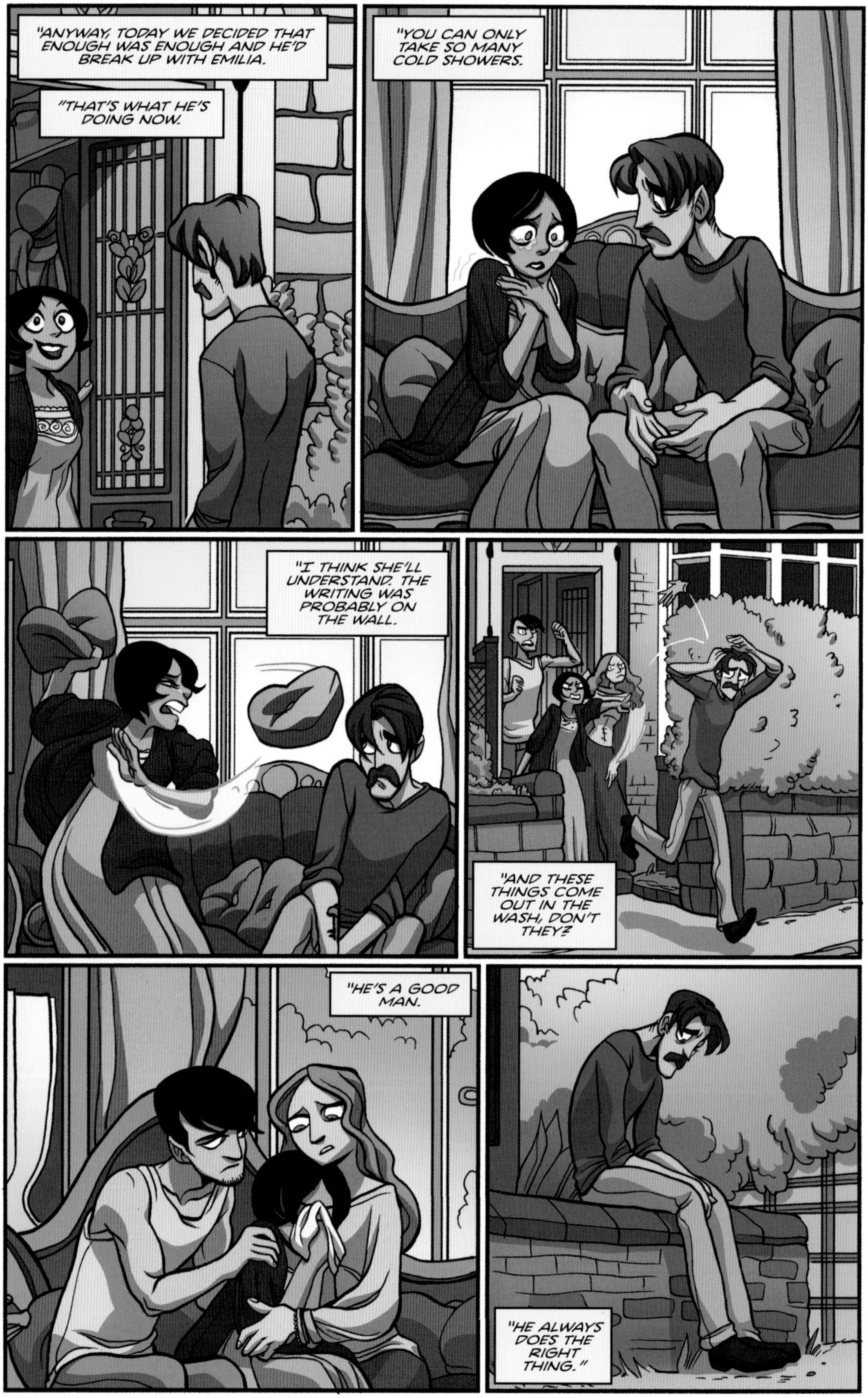
"ANYWAY, TODAY WE DECIDED THAT ENOUGH WAS ENOUGH AND HE'D BREAK UP WITH EMILIA.
"THAT'S WHAT HE'S DOING NOW.
"YOU CAN ONLY TAKE SO MANY COLD SHOWERS.
"I THINK SHE'LL UNDERSTAND. THE WRITING WAS PROBABLY ON THE WALL.
"AND THESE THINGS COME OUT IN THE WASH, DON'T THEY?
"HE'S A GOOD MAN.
"HE ALWAYS DOES THE RIGHT THING."

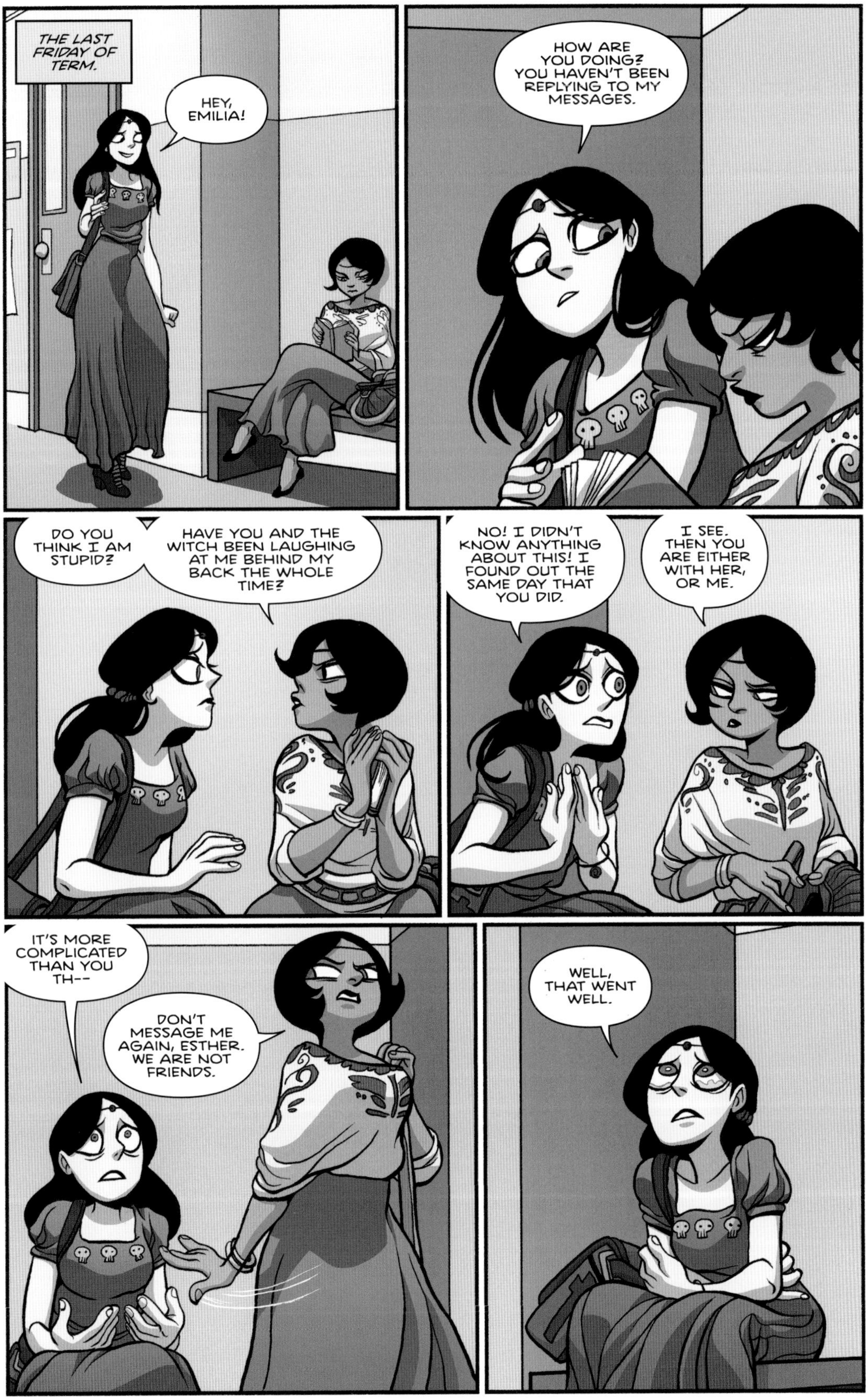
THE LAST FRIDAY OF TERM.
HEY, EMILIA!
HOW ARE YOU DOING? YOU HAVEN'T BEEN REPLYING TO MY MESSAGES.
DO YOU THINK I AM STUPID?
HAVE YOU AND THE WITCH BEEN LAUGHING AT ME BEHIND MY BACK THE WHOLE TIME?
NO! I DIDN'T KNOW ANYTHING ABOUT THIS! I FOUND OUT THE SAME DAY THAT YOU DID.
I SEE. THEN YOU ARE EITHER WITH HER, OR ME.
IT'S MORE COMPLICATED THAN YOU TH--
DON'T MESSAGE ME AGAIN, ESTHER. WE ARE NOT FRIENDS.
WELL, THAT WENT WELL.

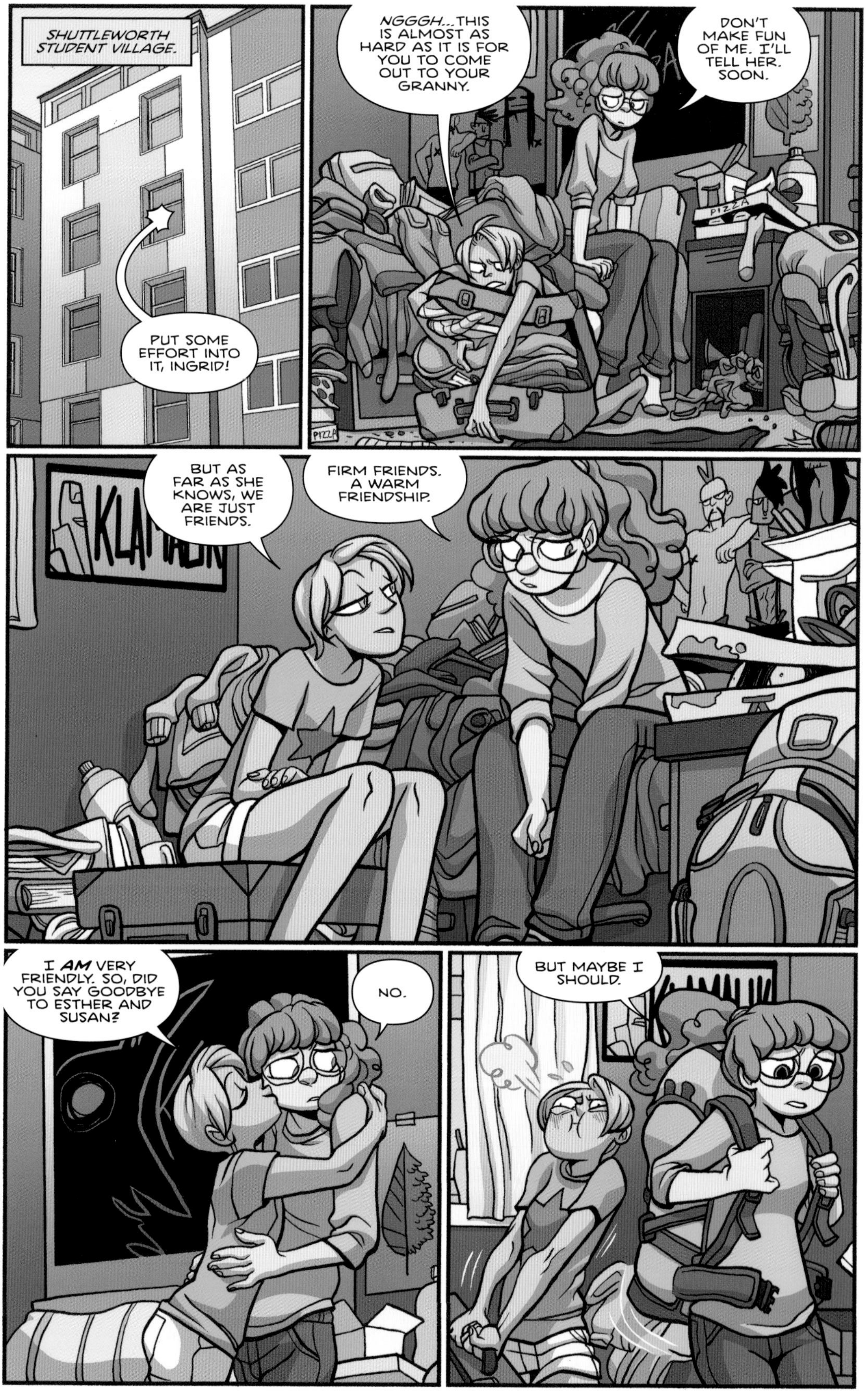
SHUTTLEWORTH STUDENT VILLAGE.
PUT SOME EFFORT INTO IT, INGRID!
NGGGH... THIS IS ALMOST AS HARD AS IT IS FOR YOU TO COME OUT TO YOUR GRANNY.
DON'T MAKE FUN OF ME. I'LL TELL HER. SOON.
PIZZA
PIZZA
BUT AS FAR AS SHE KNOWS, WE ARE JUST FRIENDS.
FIRM FRIENDS. A WARM FRIENDSHIP.
I AM VERY FRIENDLY. SO, DID YOU SAY GOODBYE TO ESTHER AND SUSAN?
NO.
BUT MAYBE I SHOULD.

CHAPTER
THIRTY-ONE

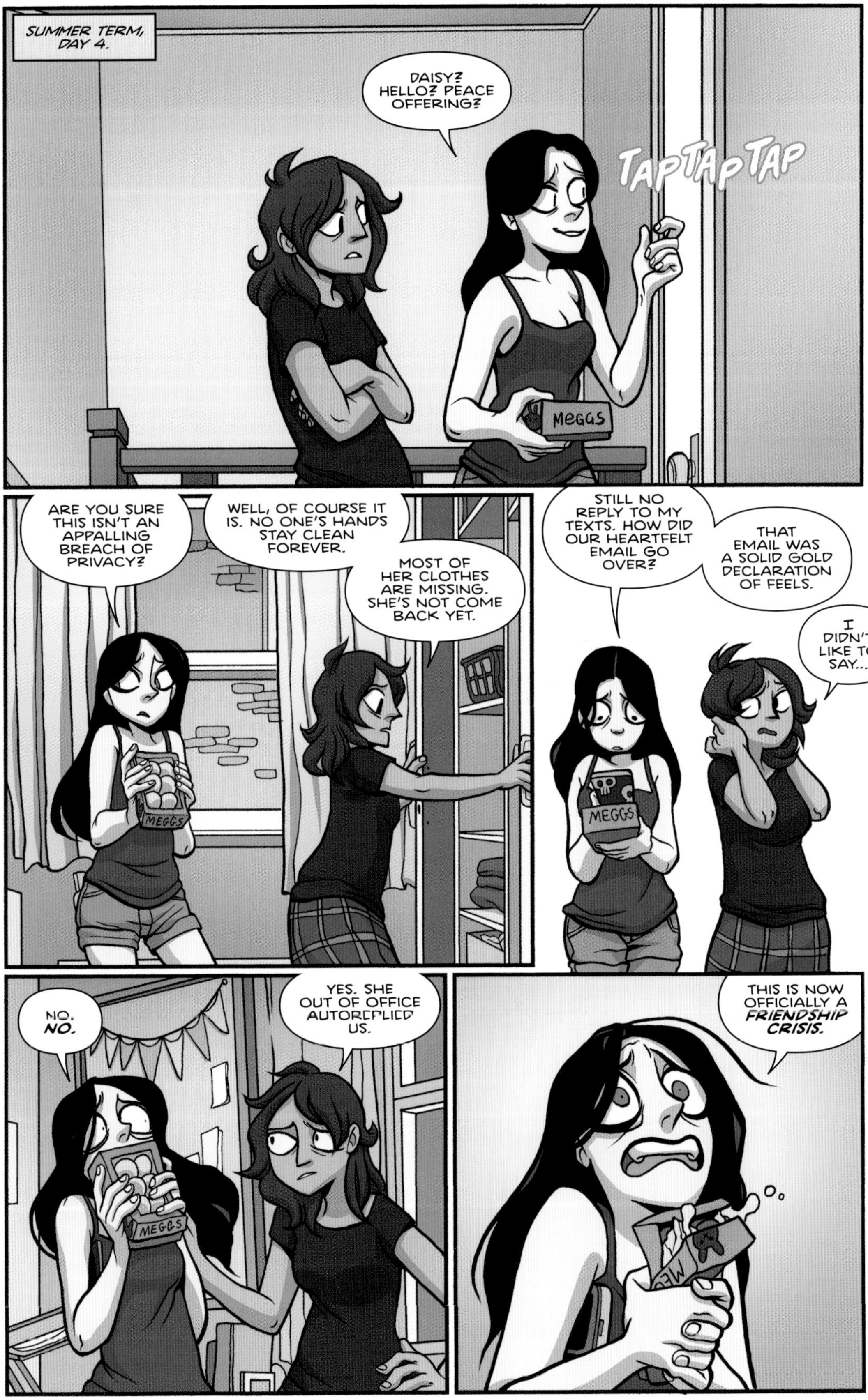

SUMMER TERM, DAY 4.
DAISY? HELLO? PEACE OFFERING?
TAPTAPTAP
MEGGS
ARE YOU SURE THIS ISN'T AN APPALLING BREACH OF PRIVACY?
WELL, OF COURSE IT IS. NO ONE'S HANDS STAY CLEAN FOREVER.
MOST OF HER CLOTHES ARE MISSING. SHE'S NOT COME BACK YET.
MEGGS
STILL NO REPLY TO MY TEXTS. HOW DID OUR HEARTFELT EMAIL GO OVER?
THAT EMAIL WAS A SOLID GOLD DECLARATION OF FEELS.
I DIDN'T LIKE TO SAY...
MEGGS
NO. NO.
YES. SHE OUT OF OFFICE AUTOREPLIED US.
MEGGS
THIS IS NOW OFFICIALLY A FRIENDSHIP CRISIS.

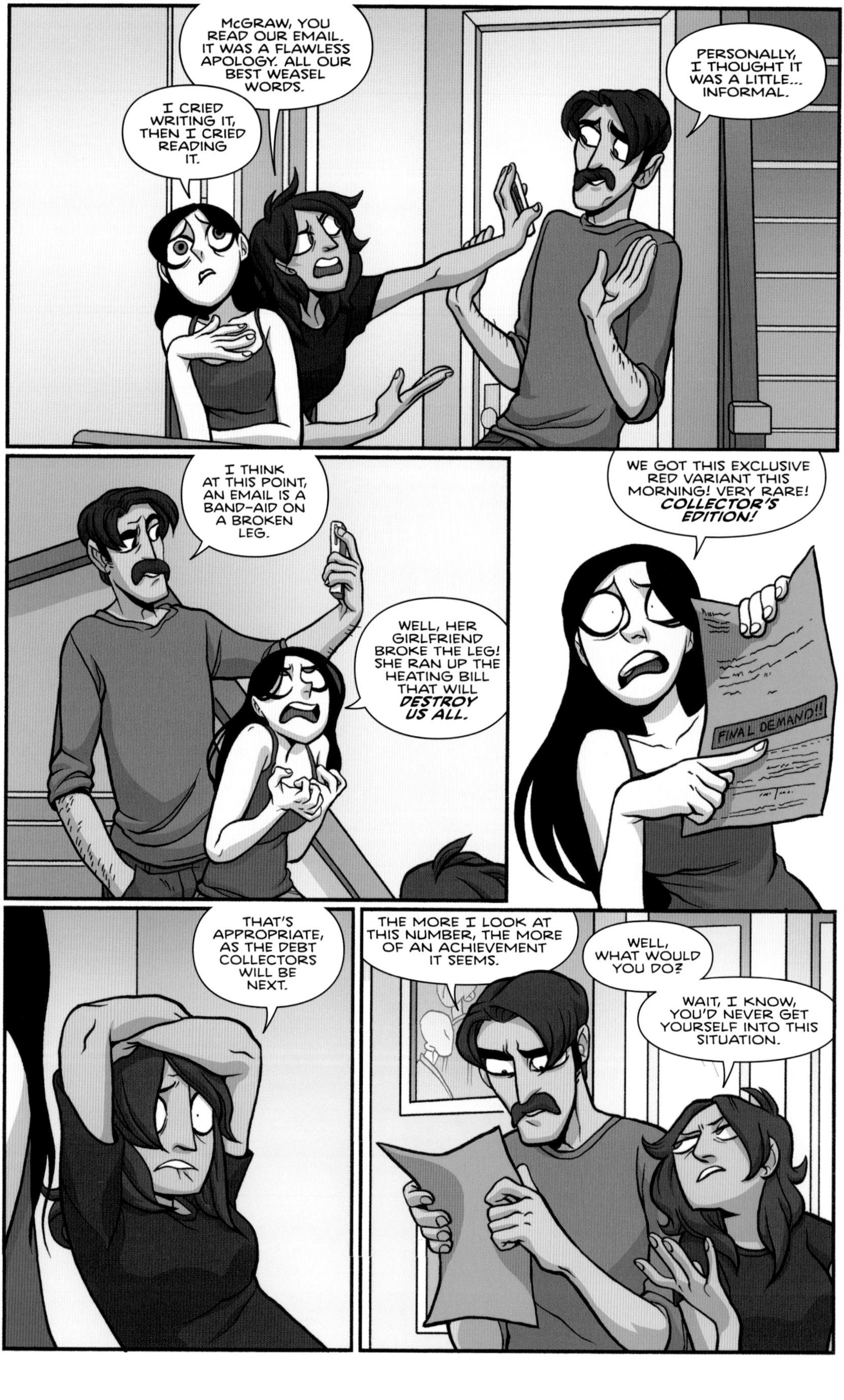
McGRAW, YOU READ OUR EMAIL. IT WAS A FLAWLESS APOLOGY. ALL OUR BEST WEASEL WORDS.
I CRIED WRITING IT, THEN I CRIED READING IT.
PERSONALLY, I THOUGHT IT WAS A LITTLE... INFORMAL.
I THINK AT THIS POINT, AN EMAIL IS A BAND-AID ON A BROKEN LEG.
WELL, HER GIRLFRIEND BROKE THE LEG! SHE RAN UP THE HEATING BILL THAT WILL ***DESTROY US ALL.***
WE GOT THIS EXCLUSIVE RED VARIANT THIS MORNING! VERY RARE! ***COLLECTOR'S EDITION!***
FINAL DEMAND!!
THAT'S APPROPRIATE, AS THE DEBT COLLECTORS WILL BE NEXT.
THE MORE I LOOK AT THIS NUMBER, THE MORE OF AN ACHIEVEMENT IT SEEMS.
WELL, WHAT WOULD YOU DO?
WAIT, I KNOW, YOU'D NEVER GET YOURSELF INTO THIS SITUATION.

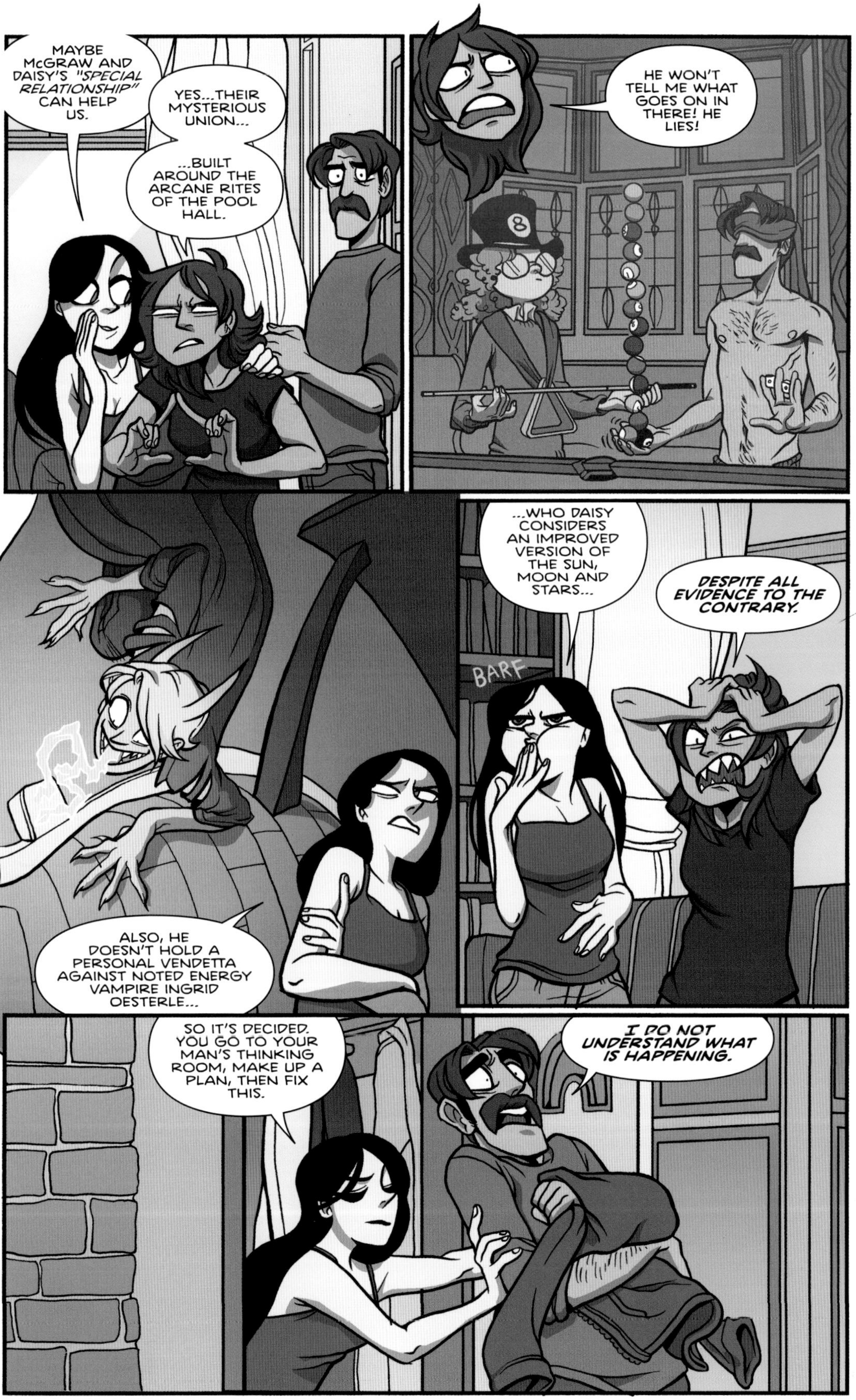
MAYBE McGRAW AND DAISY'S *"SPECIAL RELATIONSHIP"* CAN HELP US.
YES... THEIR MYSTERIOUS UNION...
...BUILT AROUND THE ARCANE RITES OF THE POOL HALL.
HE WON'T TELL ME WHAT GOES ON IN THERE! HE LIES!
ALSO, HE DOESN'T HOLD A PERSONAL VENDETTA AGAINST NOTED ENERGY VAMPIRE INGRID OESTERLE...
...WHO DAISY CONSIDERS AN IMPROVED VERSION OF THE SUN, MOON AND STARS...
DESPITE ALL EVIDENCE TO THE CONTRARY.
BARF
SO IT'S DECIDED. YOU GO TO YOUR MAN'S THINKING ROOM, MAKE UP A PLAN, THEN FIX THIS.
I DO NOT UNDERSTAND WHAT IS HAPPENING.

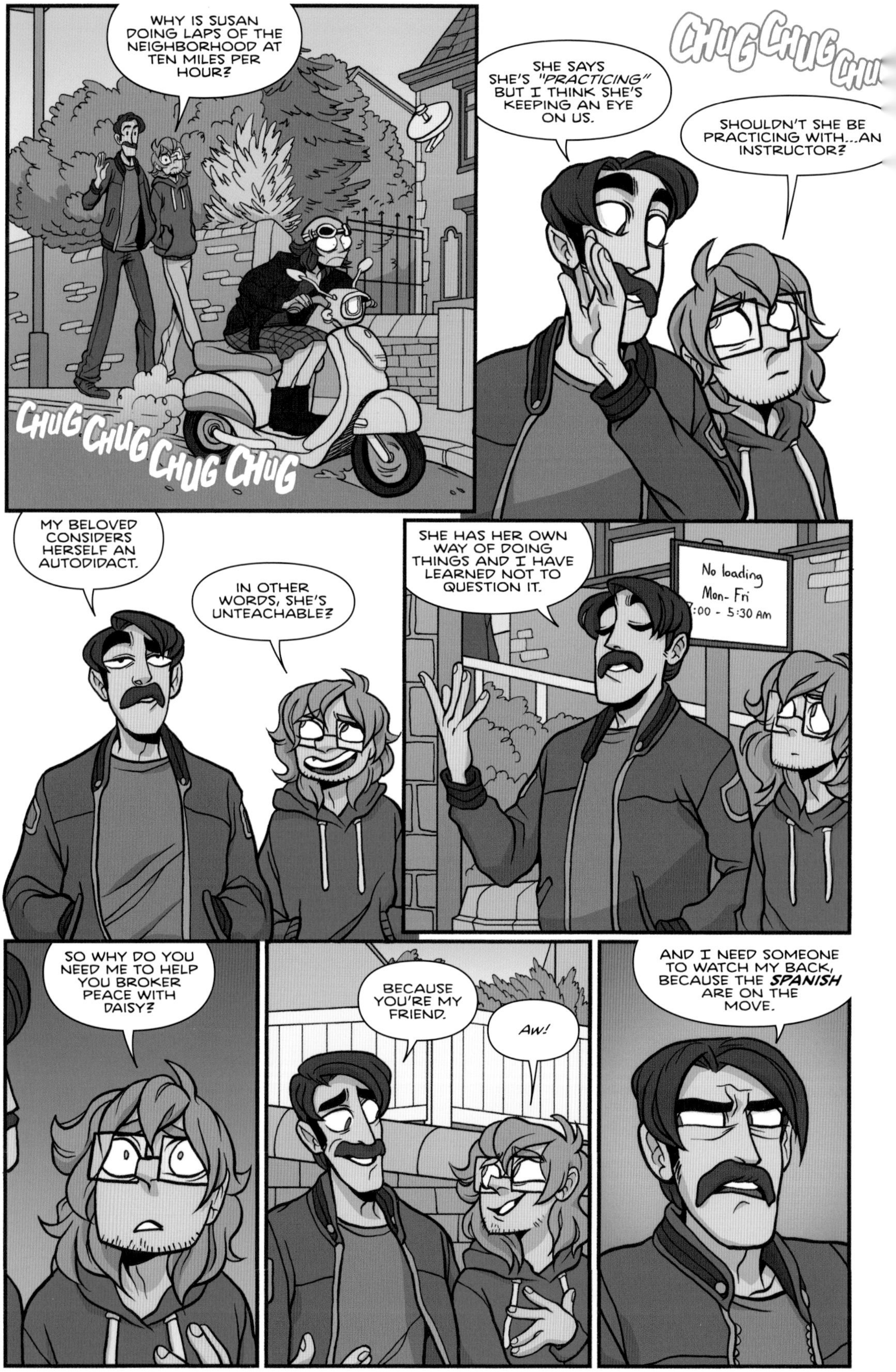

WHY IS SUSAN DOING LAPS OF THE NEIGHBORHOOD AT TEN MILES PER HOUR?
CHUG CHUG CHUG CHUG
SHE SAYS SHE'S "PRACTICING" BUT I THINK SHE'S KEEPING AN EYE ON US.
CHUG CHUG CHU
SHOULDN'T SHE BE PRACTICING WITH...AN INSTRUCTOR?
MY BELOVED CONSIDERS HERSELF AN AUTODIDACT.
IN OTHER WORDS, SHE'S UNTEACHABLE?
SHE HAS HER OWN WAY OF DOING THINGS AND I HAVE LEARNED NOT TO QUESTION IT.
No loading
Mon- Fri
:00 - 5:30 AM
SO WHY DO YOU NEED ME TO HELP YOU BROKER PEACE WITH DAISY?
BECAUSE YOU'RE MY FRIEND.
AW!
AND I NEED SOMEONE TO WATCH MY BACK, BECAUSE THE SPANISH ARE ON THE MOVE.

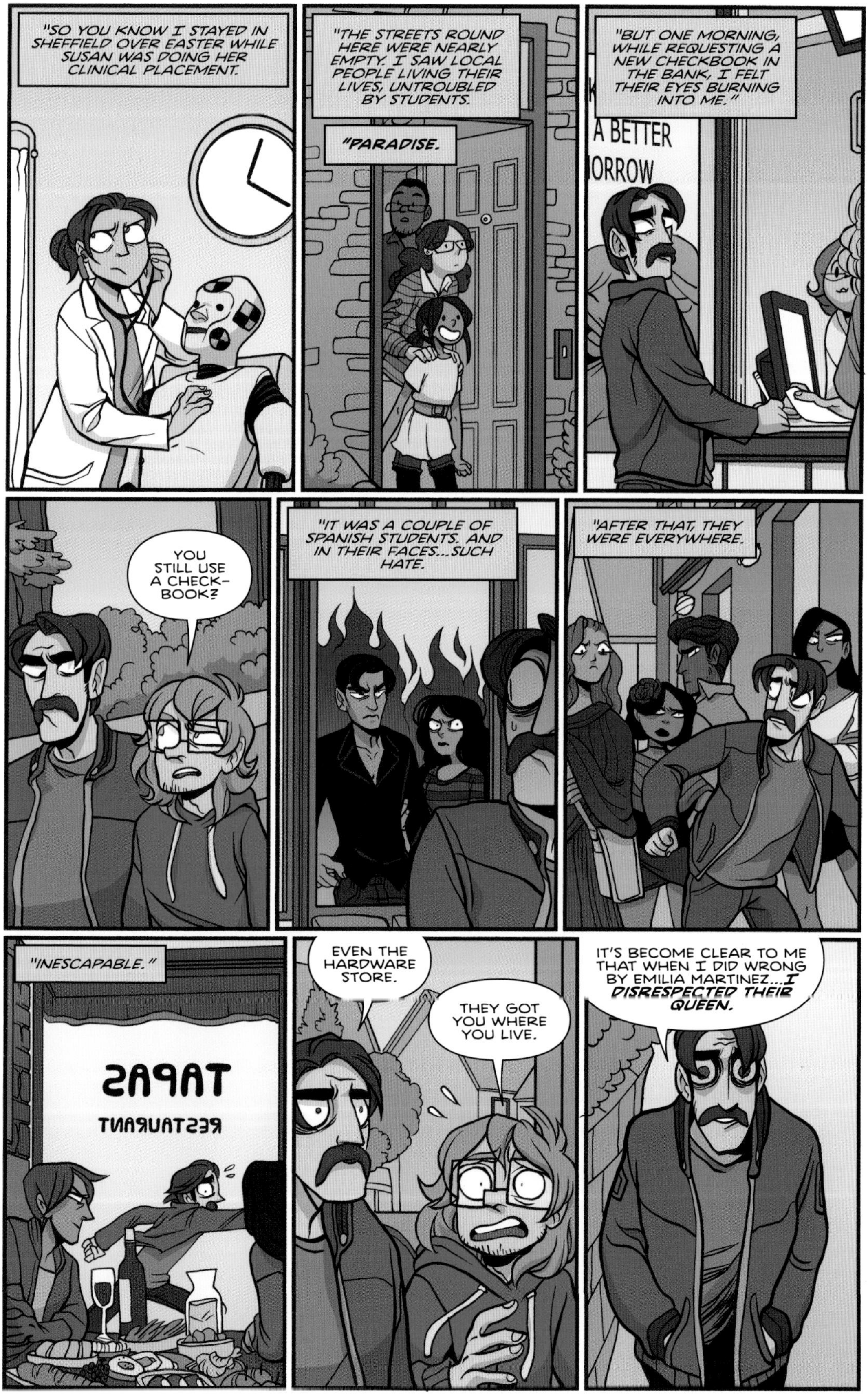
"SO YOU KNOW I STAYED IN SHEFFIELD OVER EASTER WHILE SUSAN WAS DOING HER CLINICAL PLACEMENT.
"THE STREETS ROUND HERE WERE NEARLY EMPTY. I SAW LOCAL PEOPLE LIVING THEIR LIVES, UNTROUBLED BY STUDENTS.
"PARADISE.
"BUT ONE MORNING, WHILE REQUESTING A NEW CHECKBOOK IN THE BANK, I FELT THEIR EYES BURNING INTO ME."
A BETTER
ORROW
YOU STILL USE A CHECK-BOOK?
"IT WAS A COUPLE OF SPANISH STUDENTS. AND IN THEIR FACES...SUCH HATE.
"AFTER THAT, THEY WERE EVERYWHERE.
"INESCAPABLE."
TAPAS
RESTAURANT
EVEN THE HARDWARE STORE.
THEY GOT YOU WHERE YOU LIVE.
IT'S BECOME CLEAR TO ME THAT WHEN I DID WRONG BY EMILIA MARTINEZ... I DISRESPECTED THEIR QUEEN.

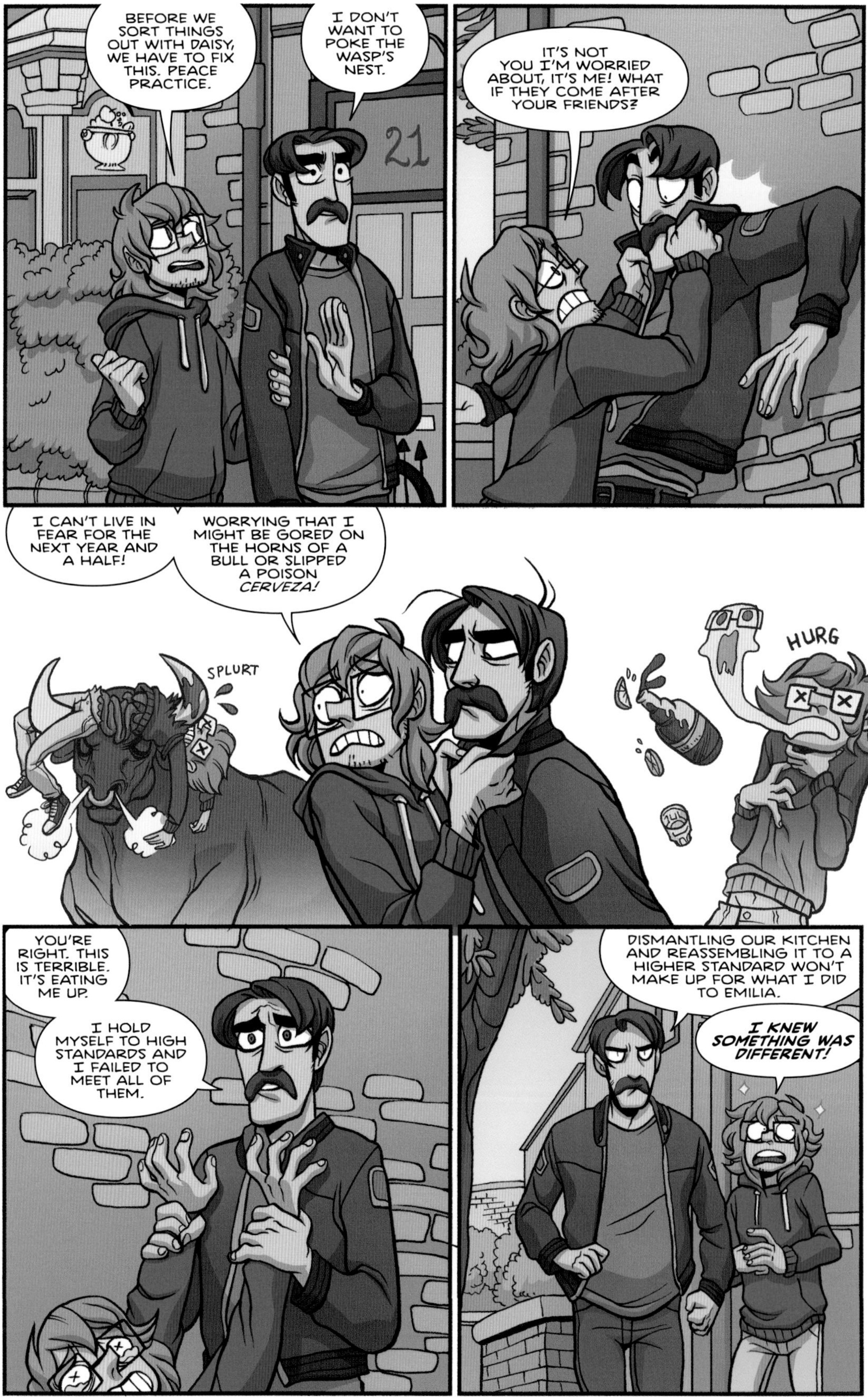
BEFORE WE SORT THINGS OUT WITH DAISY, WE HAVE TO FIX THIS. PEACE PRACTICE.
I DON'T WANT TO POKE THE WASP'S NEST.
21
IT'S NOT YOU I'M WORRIED ABOUT, IT'S ME! WHAT IF THEY COME AFTER YOUR FRIENDS?
I CAN'T LIVE IN FEAR FOR THE NEXT YEAR AND A HALF!
WORRYING THAT I MIGHT BE GORED ON THE HORNS OF A BULL OR SLIPPED A POISON *CERVEZA!*
SPLURT
HURG
YOU'RE RIGHT. THIS IS TERRIBLE. IT'S EATING ME UP.
I HOLD MYSELF TO HIGH STANDARDS AND I FAILED TO MEET ALL OF THEM.
DISMANTLING OUR KITCHEN AND REASSEMBLING IT TO A HIGHER STANDARD WON'T MAKE UP FOR WHAT I DID TO EMILIA.
I KNEW SOMETHING WAS DIFFERENT!

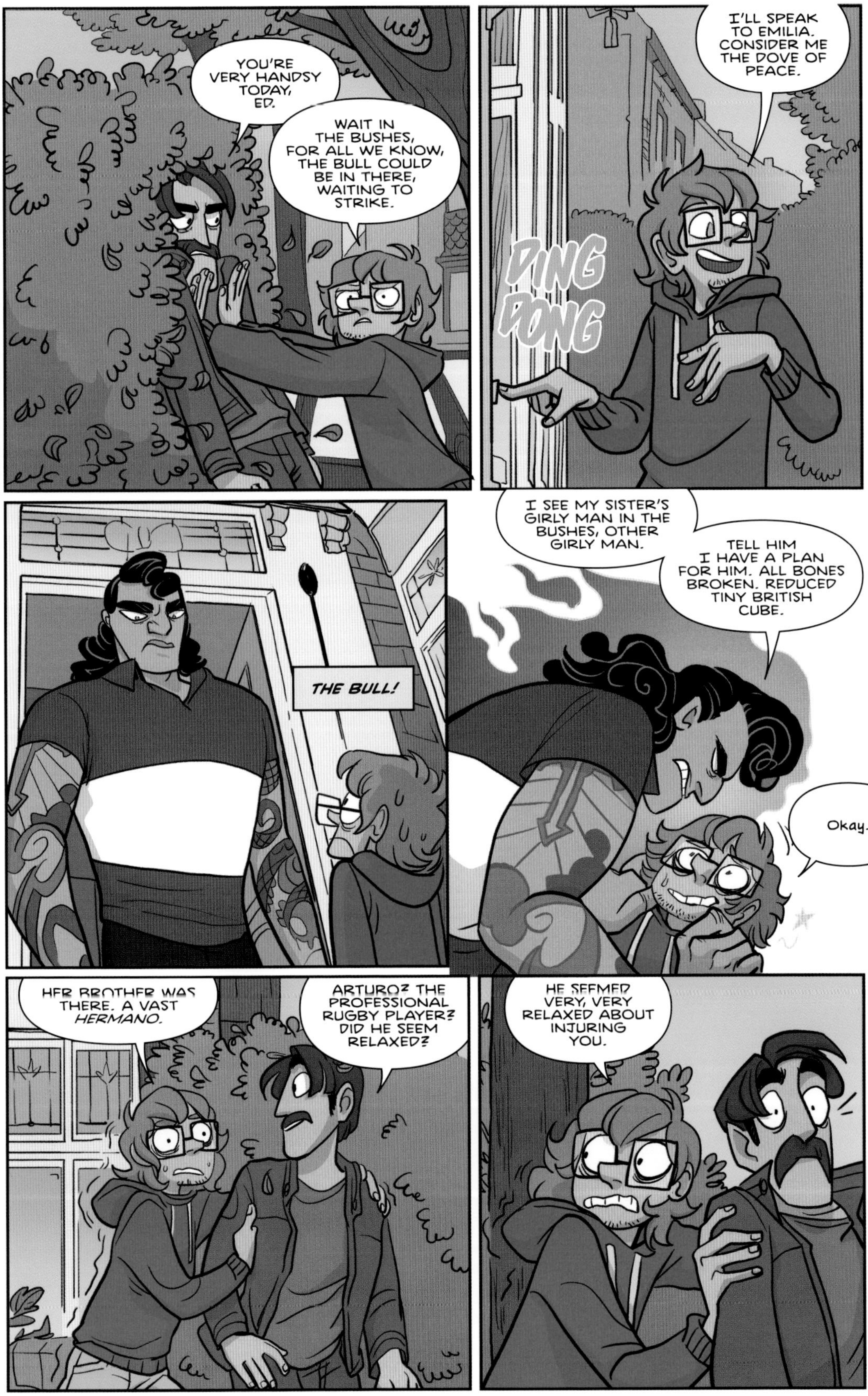
YOU'RE VERY HANDSY TODAY, ED.
WAIT IN THE BUSHES, FOR ALL WE KNOW, THE BULL COULD BE IN THERE, WAITING TO STRIKE.
I'LL SPEAK TO EMILIA. CONSIDER ME THE DOVE OF PEACE.
DING DONG
THE BULL!
I SEE MY SISTER'S GIRLY MAN IN THE BUSHES, OTHER GIRLY MAN.
TELL HIM I HAVE A PLAN FOR HIM. ALL BONES BROKEN. REDUCED TINY BRITISH CUBE.
Okay.
HER BROTHER WAS THERE. A VAST *HERMANO.*
ARTURO? THE PROFESSIONAL RUGBY PLAYER? DID HE SEEM RELAXED?
HE SEEMED VERY, VERY RELAXED ABOUT INJURING YOU.

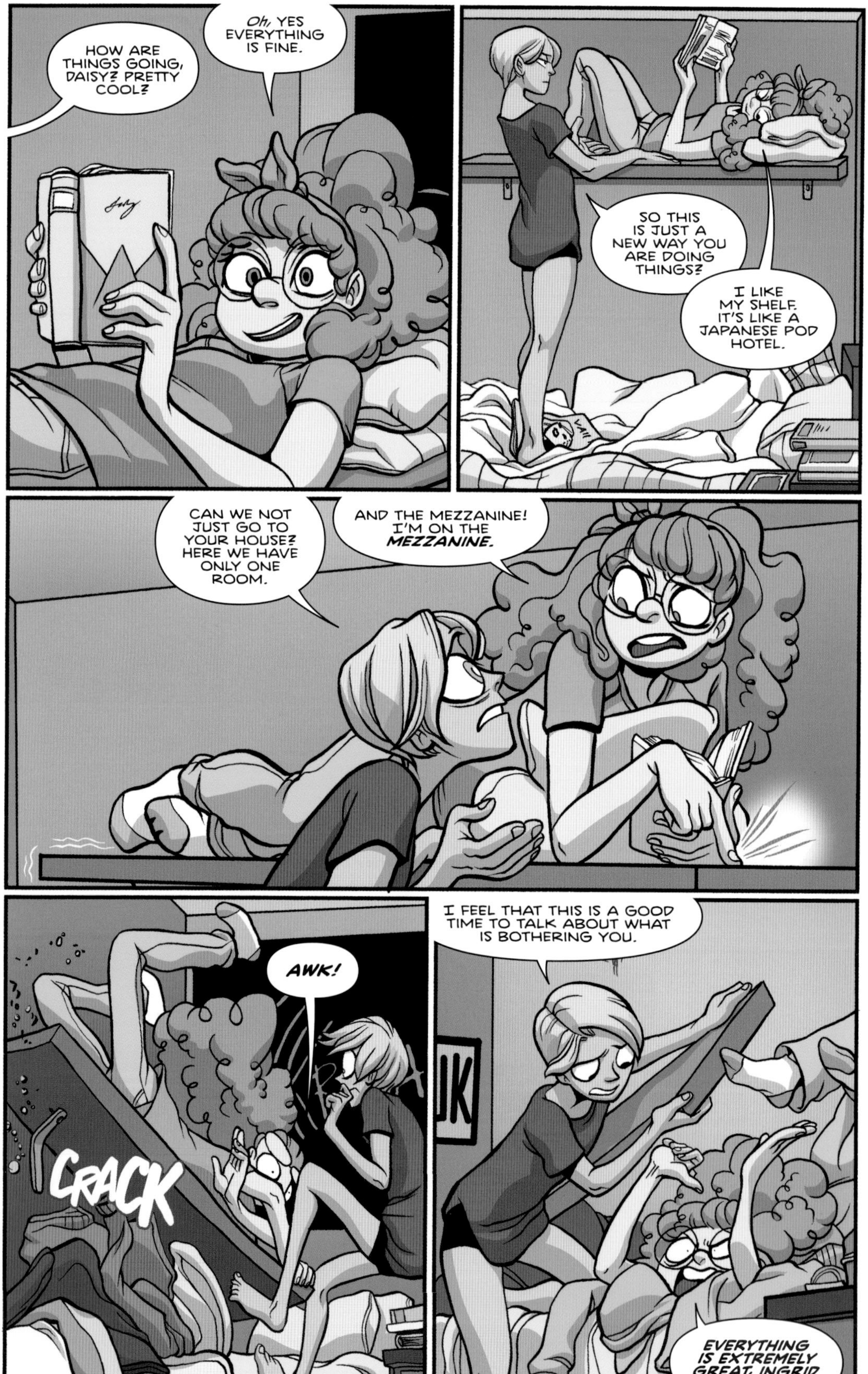

HOW ARE THINGS GOING, DAISY? PRETTY COOL?
Oh, YES EVERYTHING IS FINE.
SO THIS IS JUST A NEW WAY YOU ARE DOING THINGS?
I LIKE MY SHELF. IT'S LIKE A JAPANESE POD HOTEL.
CAN WE NOT JUST GO TO YOUR HOUSE? HERE WE HAVE ONLY ONE ROOM.
AND THE MEZZANINE! I'M ON THE MEZZANINE.
AWK!
CRACK
I FEEL THAT THIS IS A GOOD TIME TO TALK ABOUT WHAT IS BOTHERING YOU.
EVERYTHING IS EXTREMELY GREAT, INGRID.

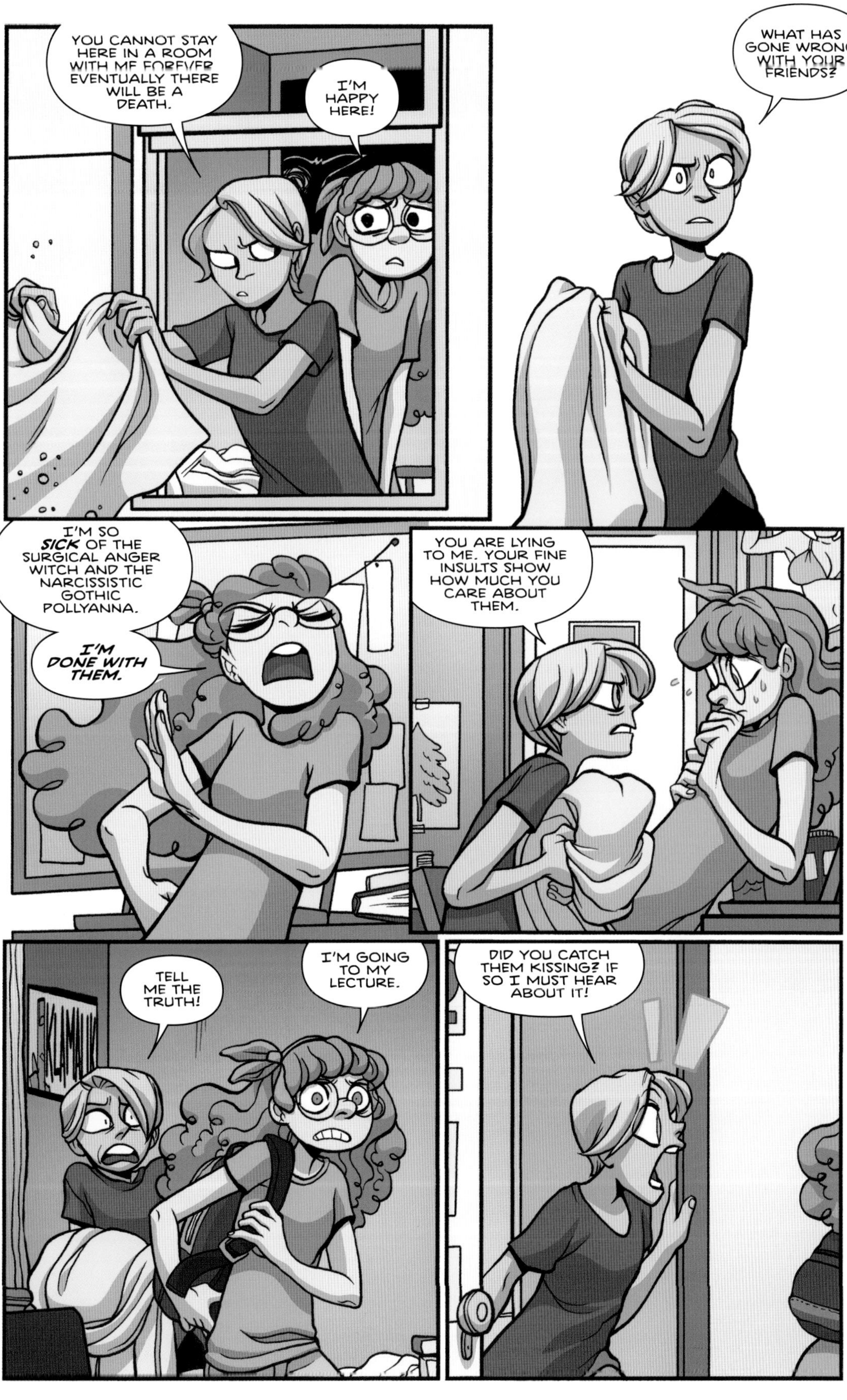
YOU CANNOT STAY HERE IN A ROOM WITH ME FOREVER EVENTUALLY THERE WILL BE A DEATH.
I'M HAPPY HERE!
WHAT HAS GONE WRONG WITH YOUR FRIENDS?
I'M SO SICK OF THE SURGICAL ANGER WITCH AND THE NARCISSISTIC GOTHIC POLLYANNA.
I'M DONE WITH THEM.
YOU ARE LYING TO ME. YOUR FINE INSULTS SHOW HOW MUCH YOU CARE ABOUT THEM.
TELL ME THE TRUTH!
I'M GOING TO MY LECTURE.
DID YOU CATCH THEM KISSING? IF SO I MUST HEAR ABOUT IT!
!!

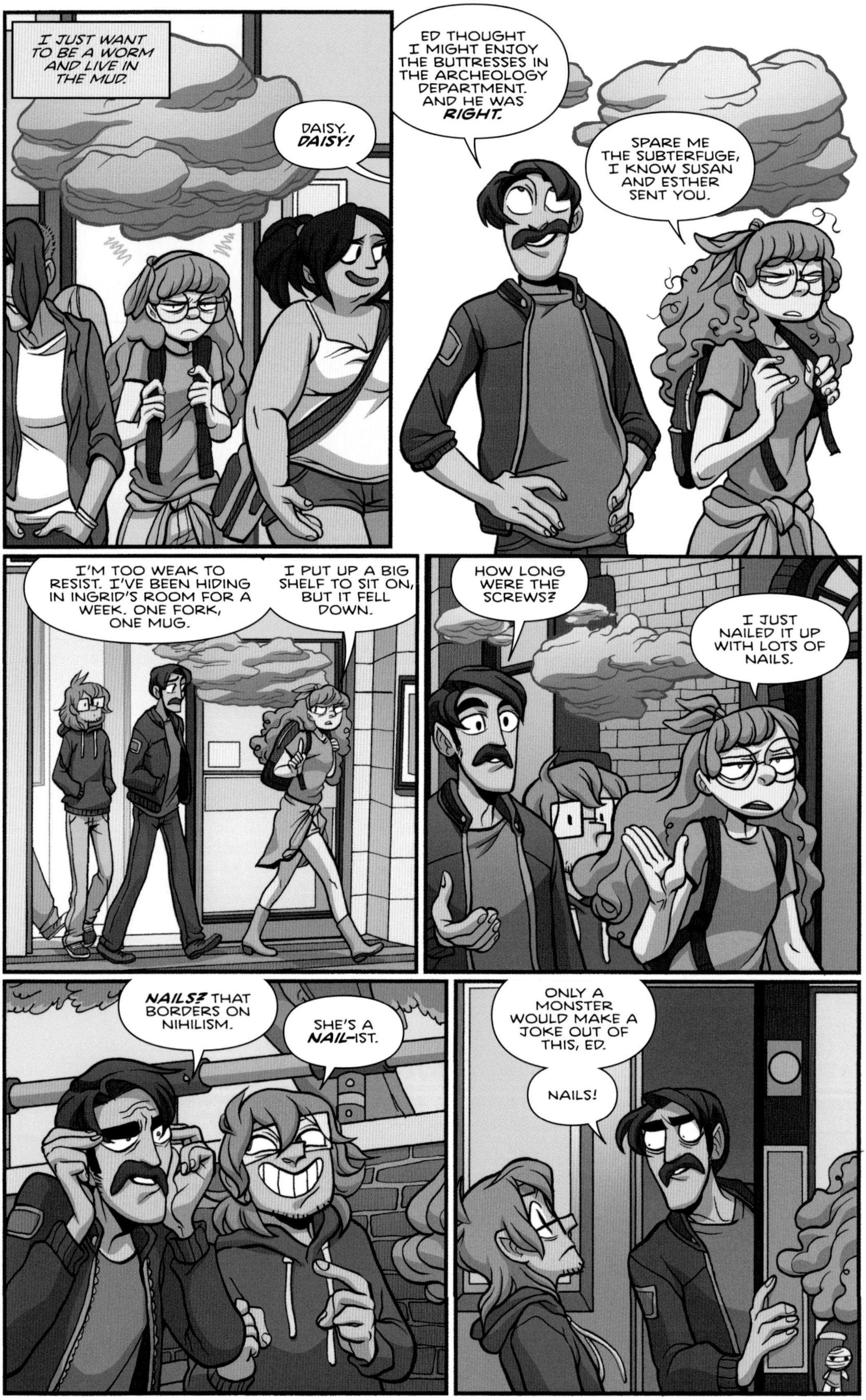
I JUST WANT TO BE A WORM AND LIVE IN THE MUD.
DAISY. DAISY!
ED THOUGHT I MIGHT ENJOY THE BUTTRESSES IN THE ARCHEOLOGY DEPARTMENT. AND HE WAS RIGHT.
SPARE ME THE SUBTERFUGE, I KNOW SUSAN AND ESTHER SENT YOU.
I'M TOO WEAK TO RESIST. I'VE BEEN HIDING IN INGRID'S ROOM FOR A WEEK. ONE FORK, ONE MUG.
I PUT UP A BIG SHELF TO SIT ON, BUT IT FELL DOWN.
HOW LONG WERE THE SCREWS?
I JUST NAILED IT UP WITH LOTS OF NAILS.
NAILS? THAT BORDERS ON NIHILISM.
SHE'S A NAIL-IST.
ONLY A MONSTER WOULD MAKE A JOKE OUT OF THIS, ED.
NAILS!

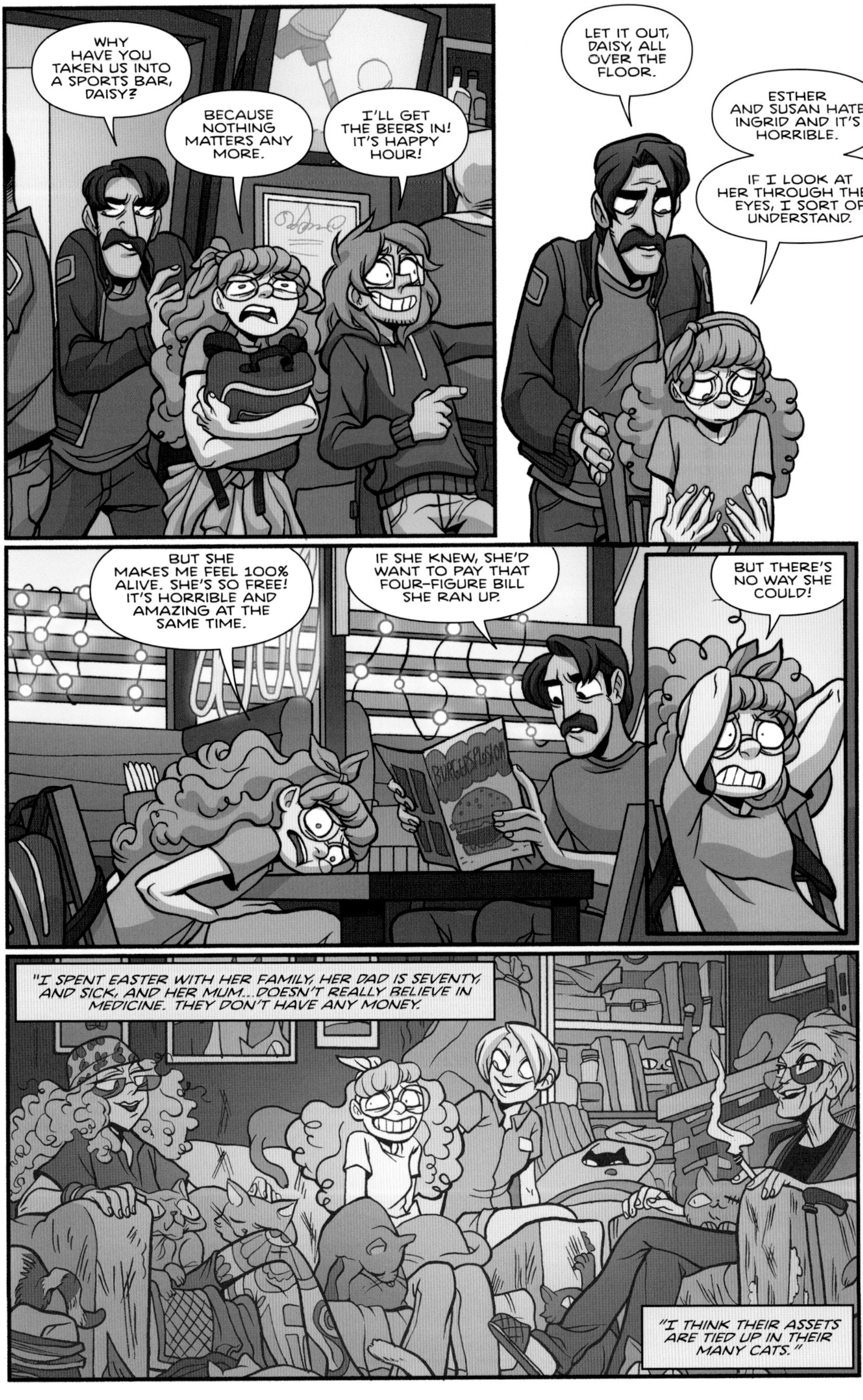
WHY HAVE YOU TAKEN US INTO A SPORTS BAR, DAISY?
BECAUSE NOTHING MATTERS ANY MORE.
I'LL GET THE BEERS IN! IT'S HAPPY HOUR!
LET IT OUT, DAISY, ALL OVER THE FLOOR.
ESTHER AND SUSAN HATE INGRID AND IT'S HORRIBLE.
IF I LOOK AT HER THROUGH THEIR EYES, I SORT OF UNDERSTAND.
BUT SHE MAKES ME FEEL 100% ALIVE. SHE'S SO FREE! IT'S HORRIBLE AND AMAZING AT THE SAME TIME.
IF SHE KNEW, SHE'D WANT TO PAY THAT FOUR-FIGURE BILL SHE RAN UP.
BURGERSPLOSION
BUT THERE'S NO WAY SHE COULD!
"I SPENT EASTER WITH HER FAMILY, HER DAD IS SEVENTY, AND SICK, AND HER MUM...DOESN'T REALLY BELIEVE IN MEDICINE. THEY DON'T HAVE ANY MONEY.
"I THINK THEIR ASSETS ARE TIED UP IN THEIR MANY CATS."

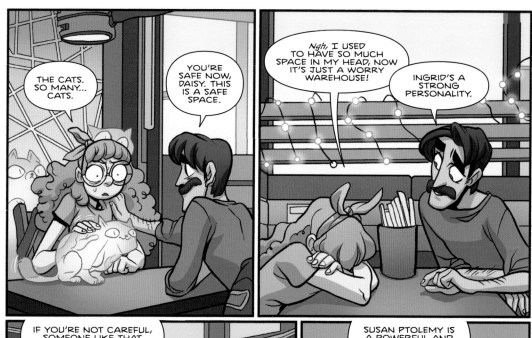

THE CATS. SO MANY... CATS.

YOU'RE SAFE NOW, DAISY. THIS IS A SAFE SPACE.

Ngh, I USED TO HAVE SO MUCH SPACE IN MY HEAD, NOW IT'S JUST A WORRY WAREHOUSE!

INGRID'S A STRONG PERSONALITY.

IF YOU'RE NOT CAREFUL, SOMEONE LIKE THAT CAN COMPLETELY OVERWHELM YOUR EXISTENCE.

Oh, LIKE SUSAN HAS DESTROYED YOURS?

SUSAN PTOLEMY IS A POWERFUL AND COMPLICATED WOMAN, BUT WE EXIST IN HARMONY.

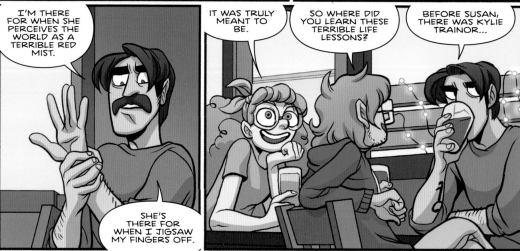

I'M THERE FOR WHEN SHE PERCEIVES THE WORLD AS A TERRIBLE RED MIST.

SHE'S THERE FOR WHEN I JIGSAW MY FINGERS OFF.

IT WAS TRULY MEANT TO BE.

SO WHERE DID YOU LEARN THESE TERRIBLE LIFE LESSONS?

BEFORE SUSAN, THERE WAS KYLIE TRAINOR...

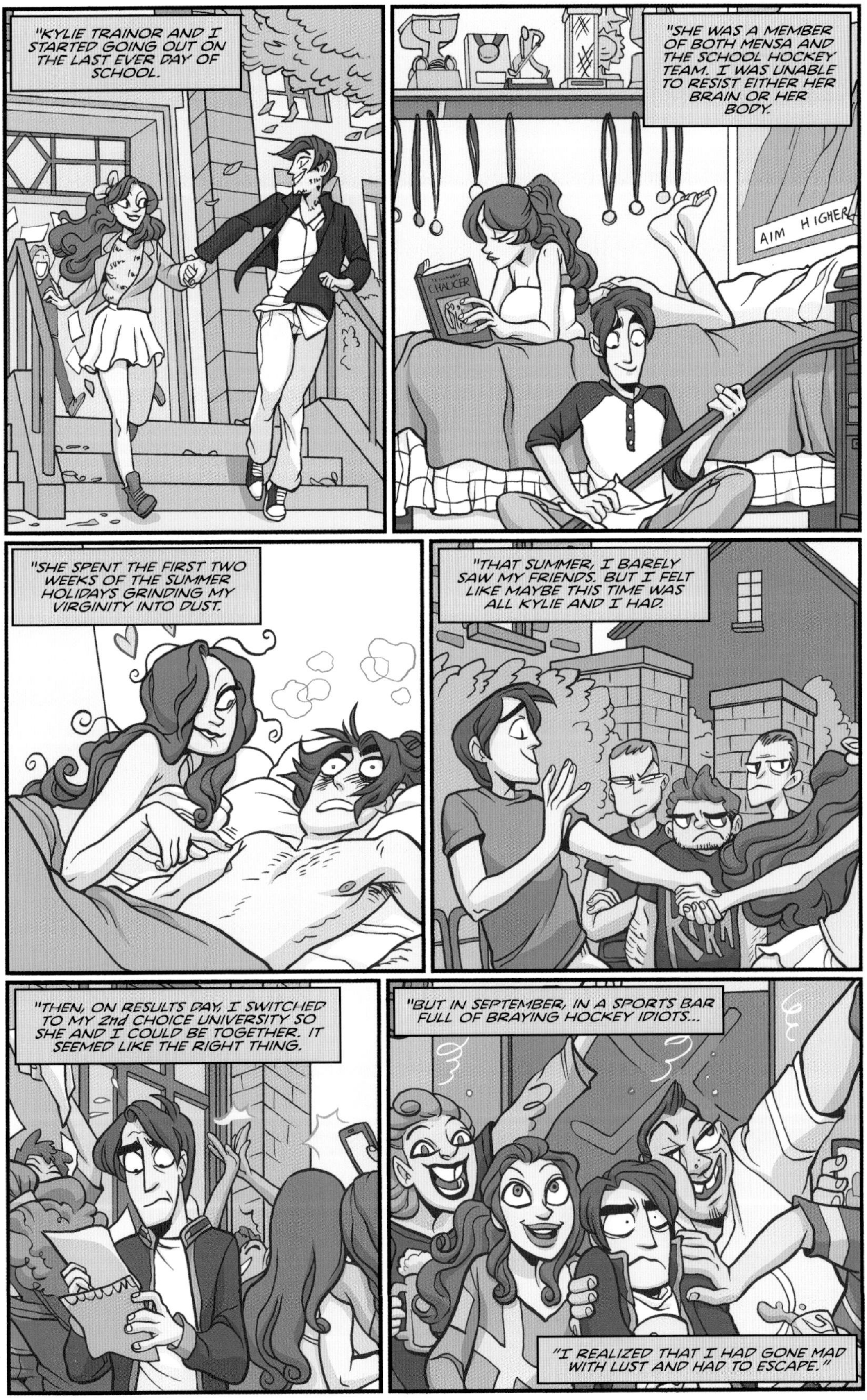
"KYLIE TRAINOR AND I STARTED GOING OUT ON THE LAST EVER DAY OF SCHOOL.
"SHE WAS A MEMBER OF BOTH MENSA AND THE SCHOOL HOCKEY TEAM. I WAS UNABLE TO RESIST EITHER HER BRAIN OR HER BODY.
CHAUCER
AIM HIGHER
"SHE SPENT THE FIRST TWO WEEKS OF THE SUMMER HOLIDAYS GRINDING MY VIRGINITY INTO DUST.
"THAT SUMMER, I BARELY SAW MY FRIENDS. BUT I FELT LIKE MAYBE THIS TIME WAS ALL KYLIE AND I HAD.
"THEN, ON RESULTS DAY, I SWITCHED TO MY 2nd CHOICE UNIVERSITY SO SHE AND I COULD BE TOGETHER. IT SEEMED LIKE THE RIGHT THING.
"BUT IN SEPTEMBER, IN A SPORTS BAR FULL OF BRAYING HOCKEY IDIOTS...
"I REALIZED THAT I HAD GONE MAD WITH LUST AND HAD TO ESCAPE."

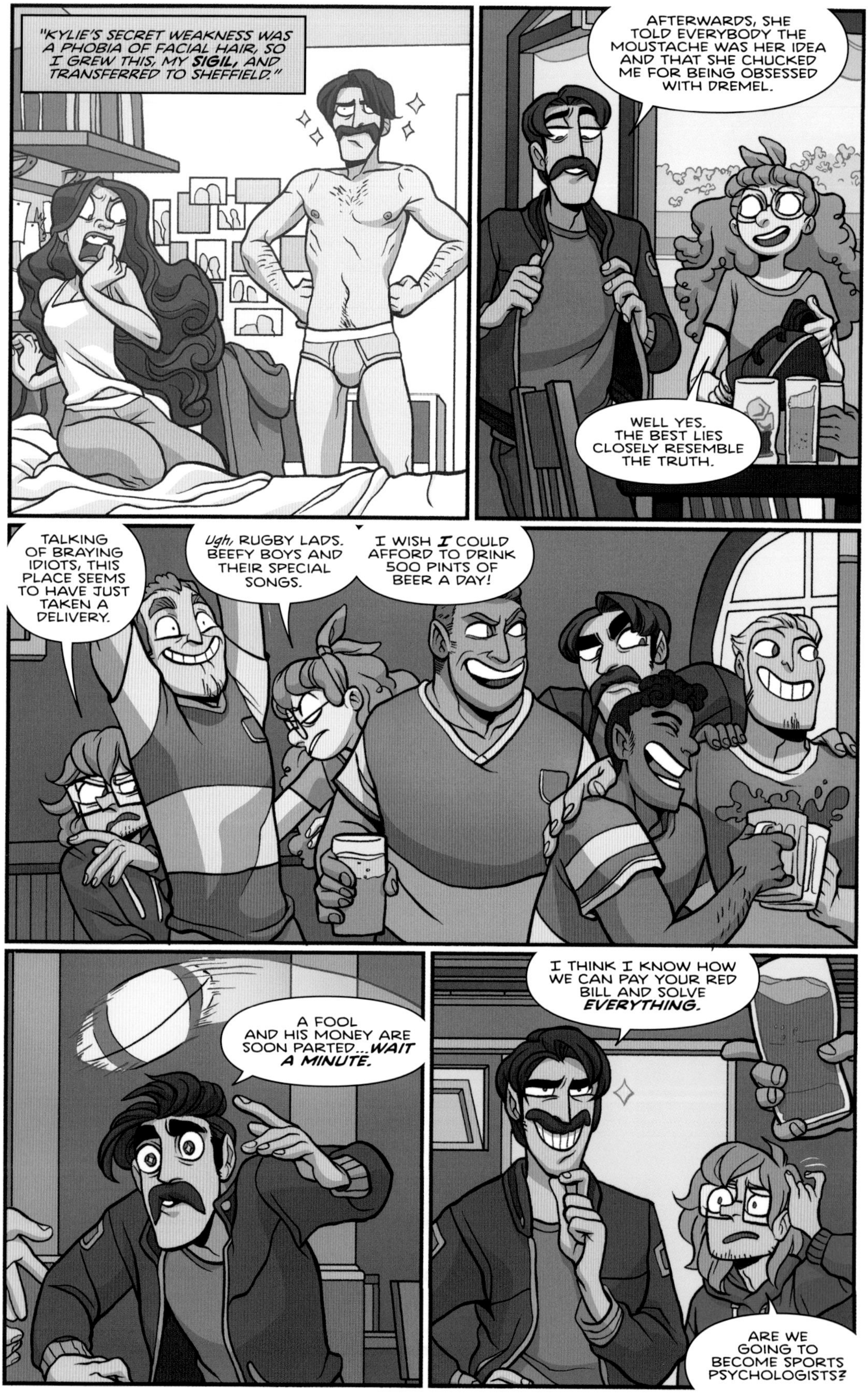
"KYLIE'S SECRET WEAKNESS WAS A PHOBIA OF FACIAL HAIR, SO I GREW THIS, MY SIGIL, AND TRANSFERRED TO SHEFFIELD."
AFTERWARDS, SHE TOLD EVERYBODY THE MOUSTACHE WAS HER IDEA AND THAT SHE CHUCKED ME FOR BEING OBSESSED WITH DREMEL.
WELL YES. THE BEST LIES CLOSELY RESEMBLE THE TRUTH.
TALKING OF BRAYING IDIOTS, THIS PLACE SEEMS TO HAVE JUST TAKEN A DELIVERY.
Ugh, RUGBY LADS. BEEFY BOYS AND THEIR SPECIAL SONGS.
I WISH I COULD AFFORD TO DRINK 500 PINTS OF BEER A DAY!
A FOOL AND HIS MONEY ARE SOON PARTED... WAIT A MINUTE.
I THINK I KNOW HOW WE CAN PAY YOUR RED BILL AND SOLVE EVERYTHING.
ARE WE GOING TO BECOME SPORTS PSYCHOLOGISTS?

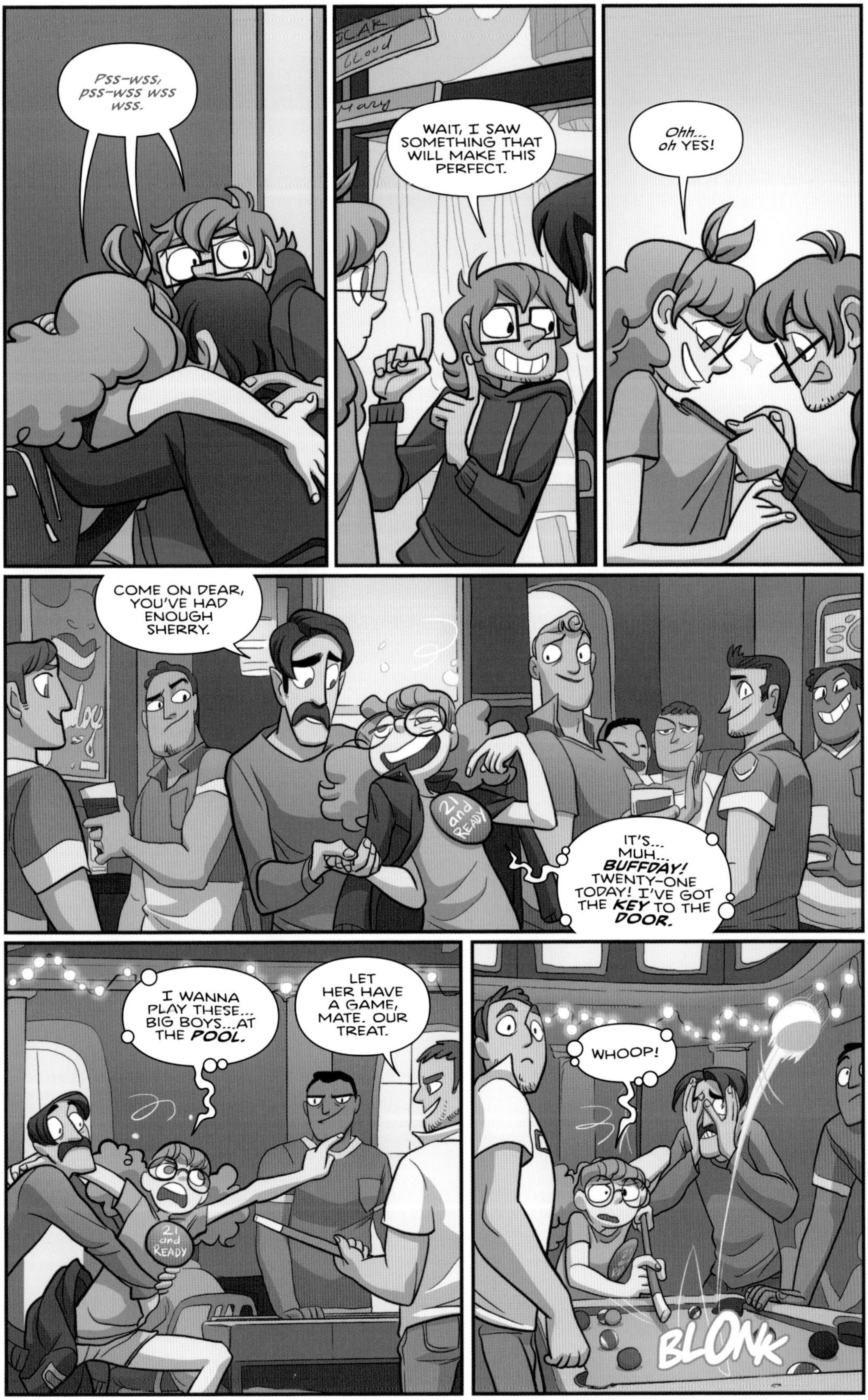
Pss–wss, pss–wss wss wss.
WAIT, I SAW SOMETHING THAT WILL MAKE THIS PERFECT.
Ohh... oh YES!
COME ON DEAR, YOU'VE HAD ENOUGH SHERRY.
21 and READY
IT'S... MUH... BUFFDAY! TWENTY-ONE TODAY! I'VE GOT THE KEY TO THE DOOR.
I WANNA PLAY THESE... BIG BOYS... AT THE POOL.
LET HER HAVE A GAME, MATE. OUR TREAT.
21 and READY
WHOOP!
BLONK

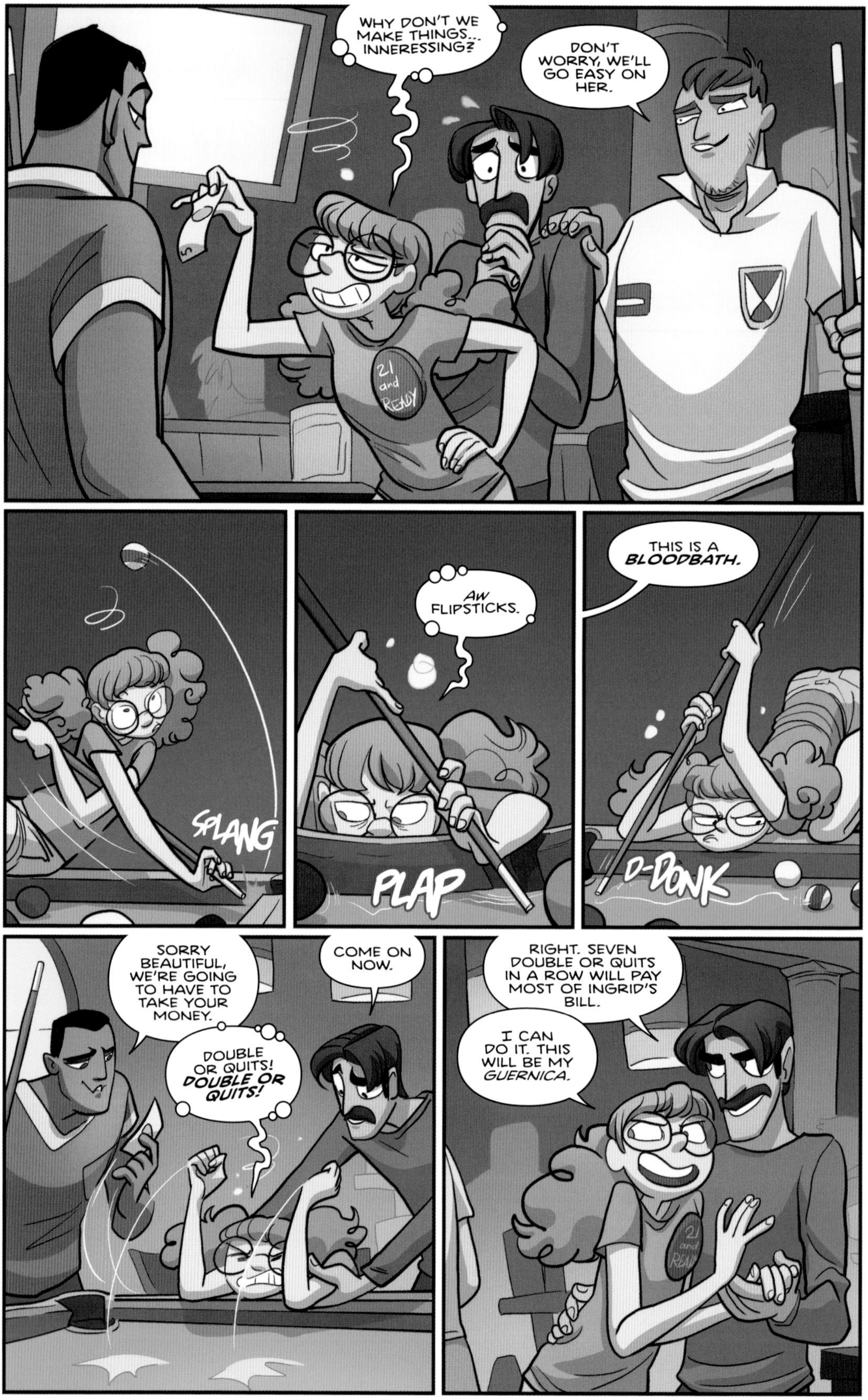
WHY DON'T WE MAKE THINGS... INNERESSING?
DON'T WORRY, WE'LL GO EASY ON HER.
21 and READY
SPLANG
AW FLIPSTICKS.
PLAP
THIS IS A BLOODBATH.
D-DONK
SORRY BEAUTIFUL, WE'RE GOING TO HAVE TO TAKE YOUR MONEY.
COME ON NOW.
DOUBLE OR QUITS! DOUBLE OR QUITS!
RIGHT. SEVEN DOUBLE OR QUITS IN A ROW WILL PAY MOST OF INGRID'S BILL.
I CAN DO IT. THIS WILL BE MY GUERNICA.

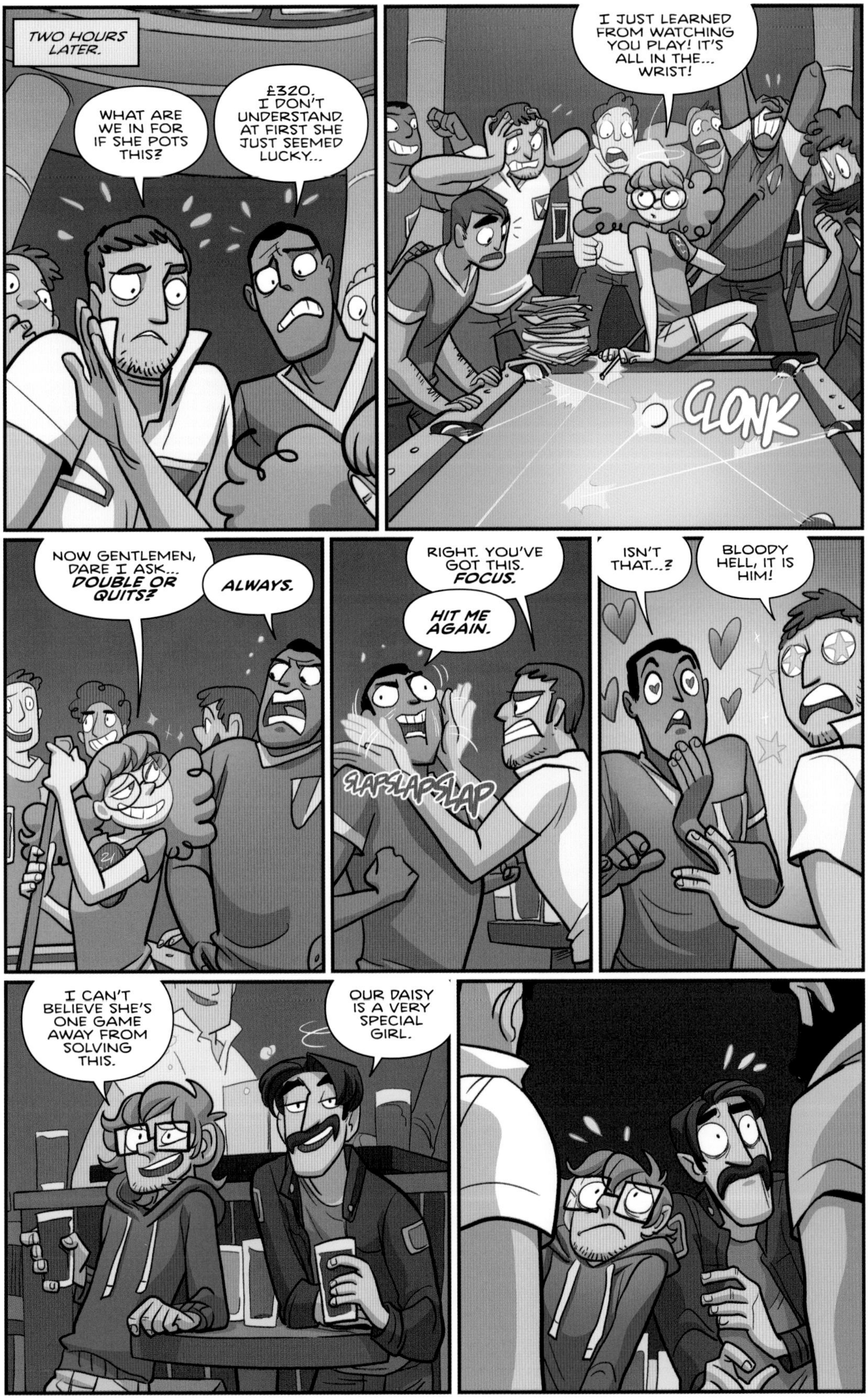
TWO HOURS LATER.
WHAT ARE WE IN FOR IF SHE POTS THIS?
£320. I DON'T UNDERSTAND. AT FIRST SHE JUST SEEMED LUCKY...
I JUST LEARNED FROM WATCHING YOU PLAY! IT'S ALL IN THE... WRIST!
CLONK
NOW GENTLEMEN, DARE I ASK... DOUBLE OR QUITS?
ALWAYS.
RIGHT. YOU'VE GOT THIS. FOCUS.
HIT ME AGAIN.
SLAPSLAPSLAP
ISN'T THAT...?
BLOODY HELL, IT IS HIM!
I CAN'T BELIEVE SHE'S ONE GAME AWAY FROM SOLVING THIS.
OUR DAISY IS A VERY SPECIAL GIRL.

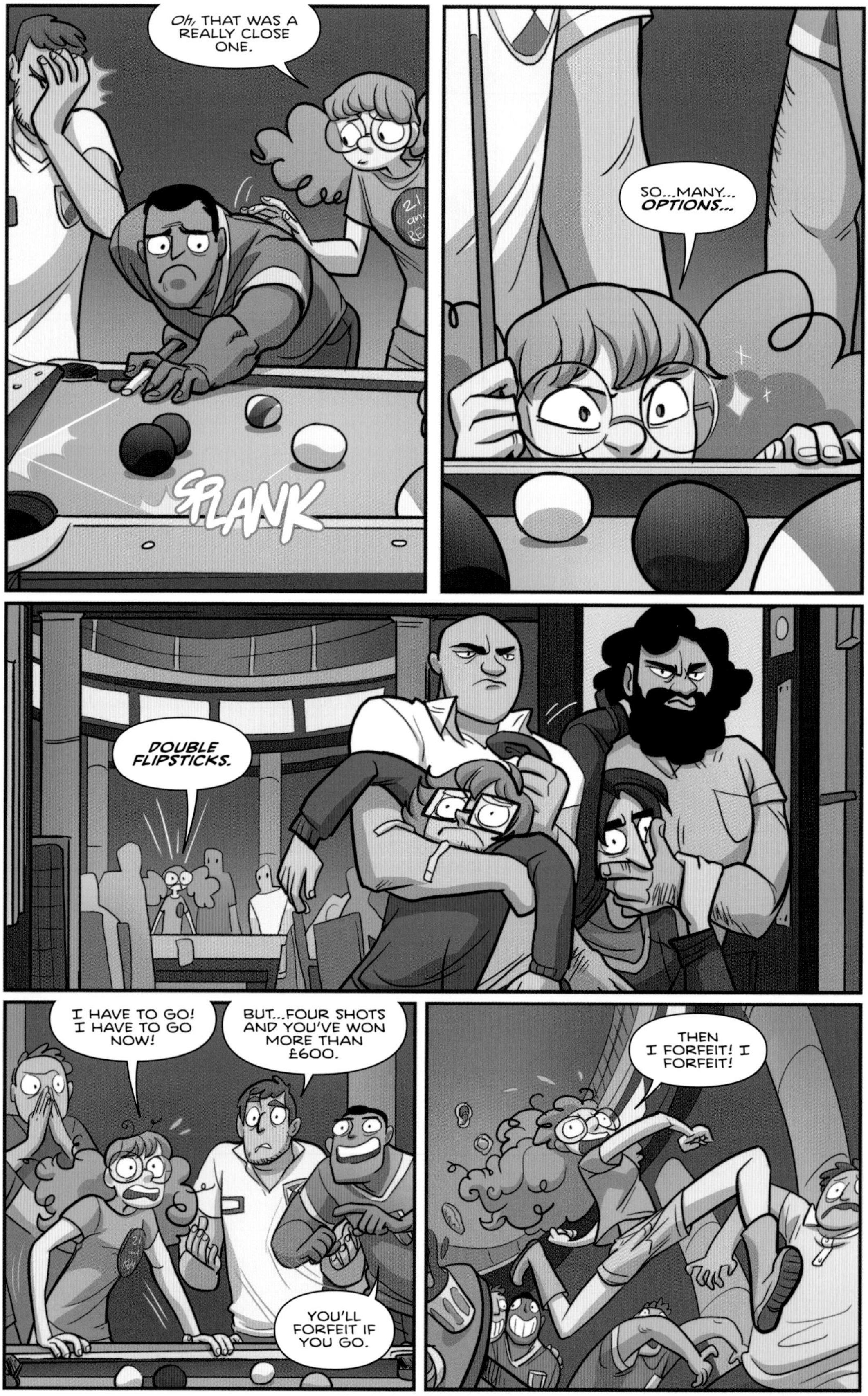

Oh, THAT WAS A REALLY CLOSE ONE.
SPLANK
SO...MANY... OPTIONS...
DOUBLE FLIPSTICKS.
I HAVE TO GO! I HAVE TO GO NOW!
BUT...FOUR SHOTS AND YOU'VE WON MORE THAN £600.
YOU'LL FORFEIT IF YOU GO.
THEN I FORFEIT! I FORFEIT!

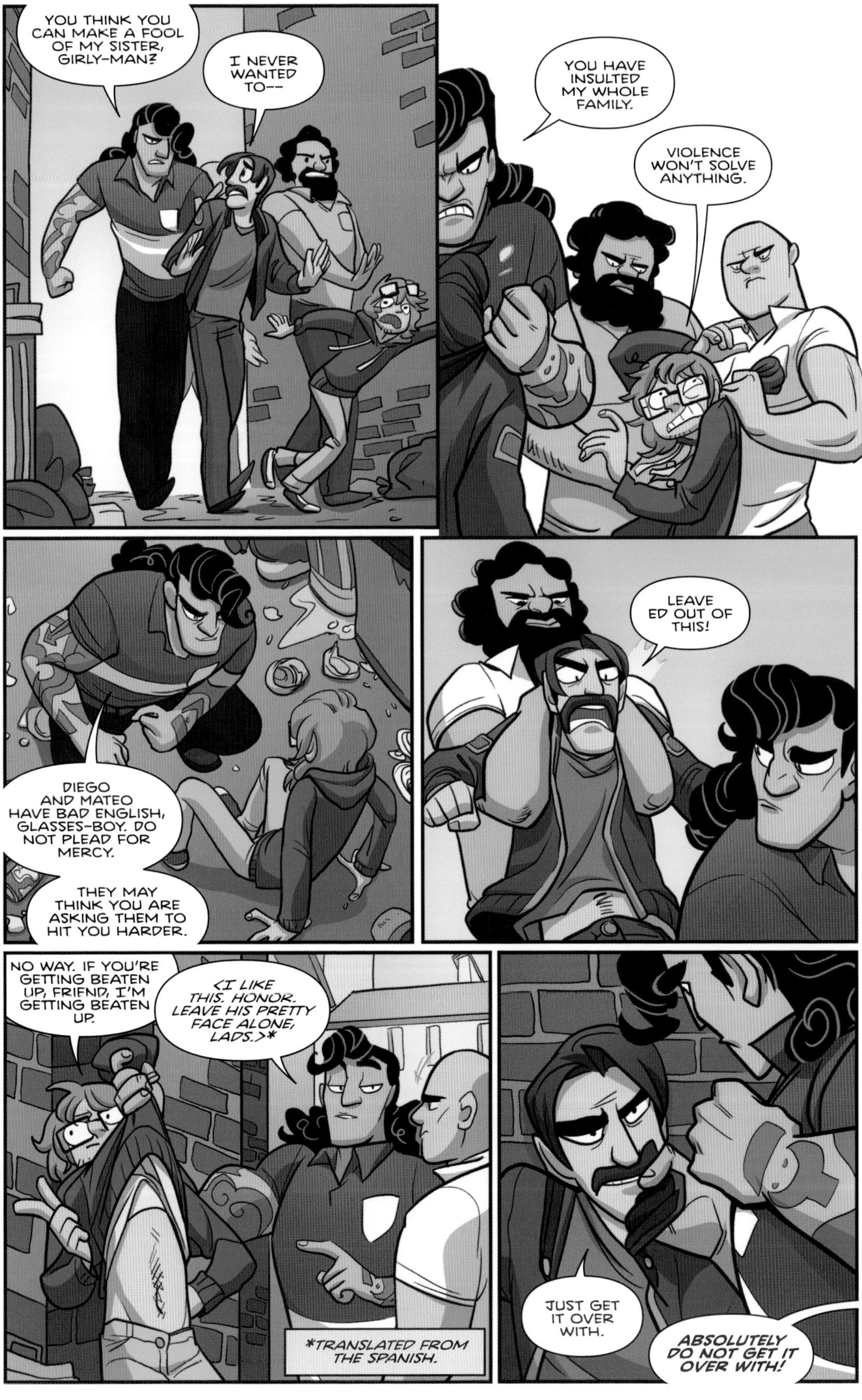
YOU THINK YOU CAN MAKE A FOOL OF MY SISTER, GIRLY-MAN?
I NEVER WANTED TO--
YOU HAVE INSULTED MY WHOLE FAMILY.
VIOLENCE WON'T SOLVE ANYTHING.
DIEGO AND MATEO HAVE BAD ENGLISH, GLASSES-BOY. DO NOT PLEAD FOR MERCY.
THEY MAY THINK YOU ARE ASKING THEM TO HIT YOU HARDER.
LEAVE ED OUT OF THIS!
NO WAY. IF YOU'RE GETTING BEATEN UP, FRIEND, I'M GETTING BEATEN UP.
<I LIKE THIS. HONOR. LEAVE HIS PRETTY FACE ALONE, LADS.>*
*TRANSLATED FROM THE SPANISH.
JUST GET IT OVER WITH.
ABSOLUTELY DO NOT GET IT OVER WITH!

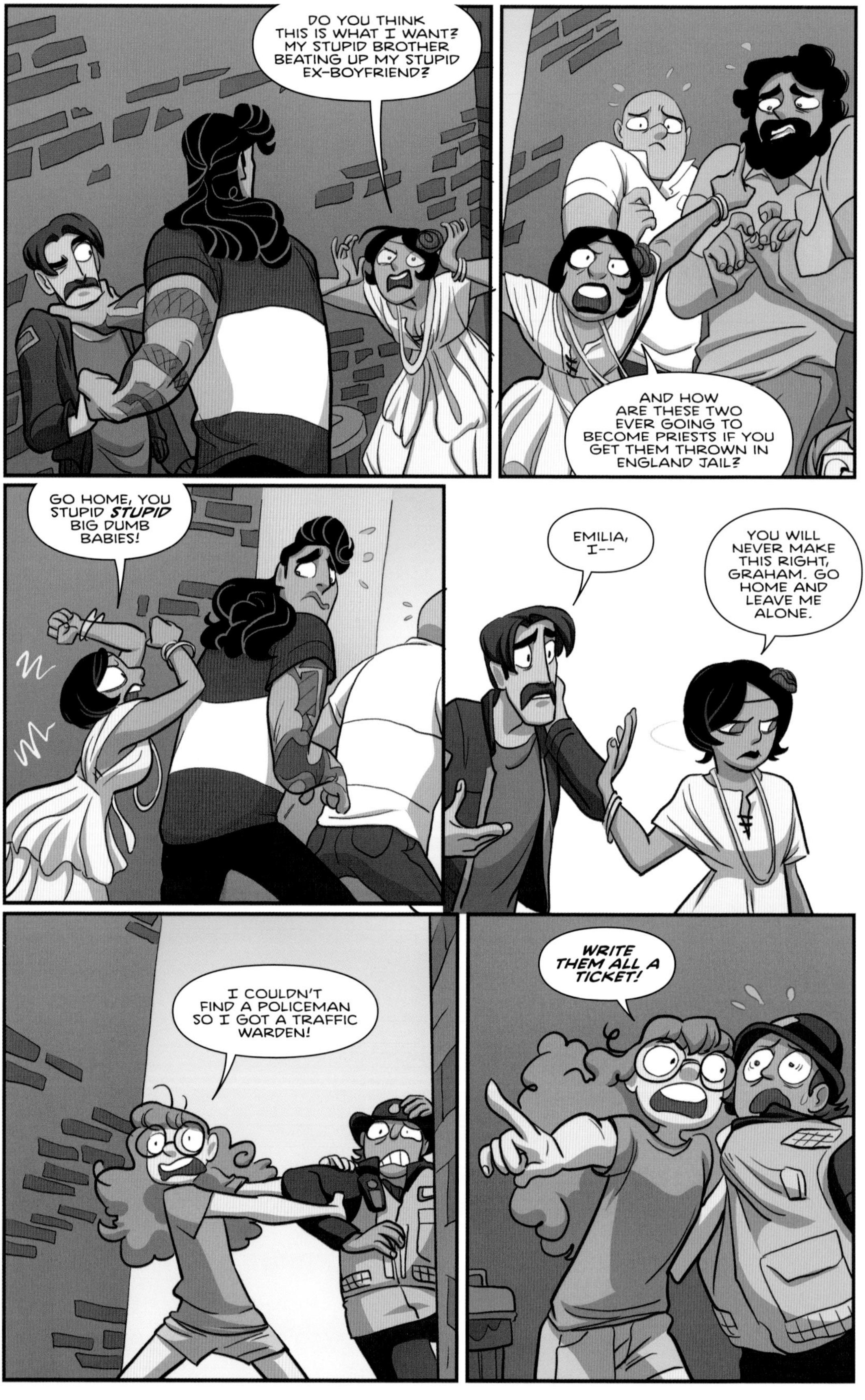
DO YOU THINK THIS IS WHAT I WANT? MY STUPID BROTHER BEATING UP MY STUPID EX-BOYFRIEND?
AND HOW ARE THESE TWO EVER GOING TO BECOME PRIESTS IF YOU GET THEM THROWN IN ENGLAND JAIL?
GO HOME, YOU STUPID ***STUPID*** BIG DUMB BABIES!
EMILIA, I--
YOU WILL NEVER MAKE THIS RIGHT, GRAHAM. GO HOME AND LEAVE ME ALONE.
I COULDN'T FIND A POLICEMAN SO I GOT A TRAFFIC WARDEN!
WRITE THEM ALL A TICKET!

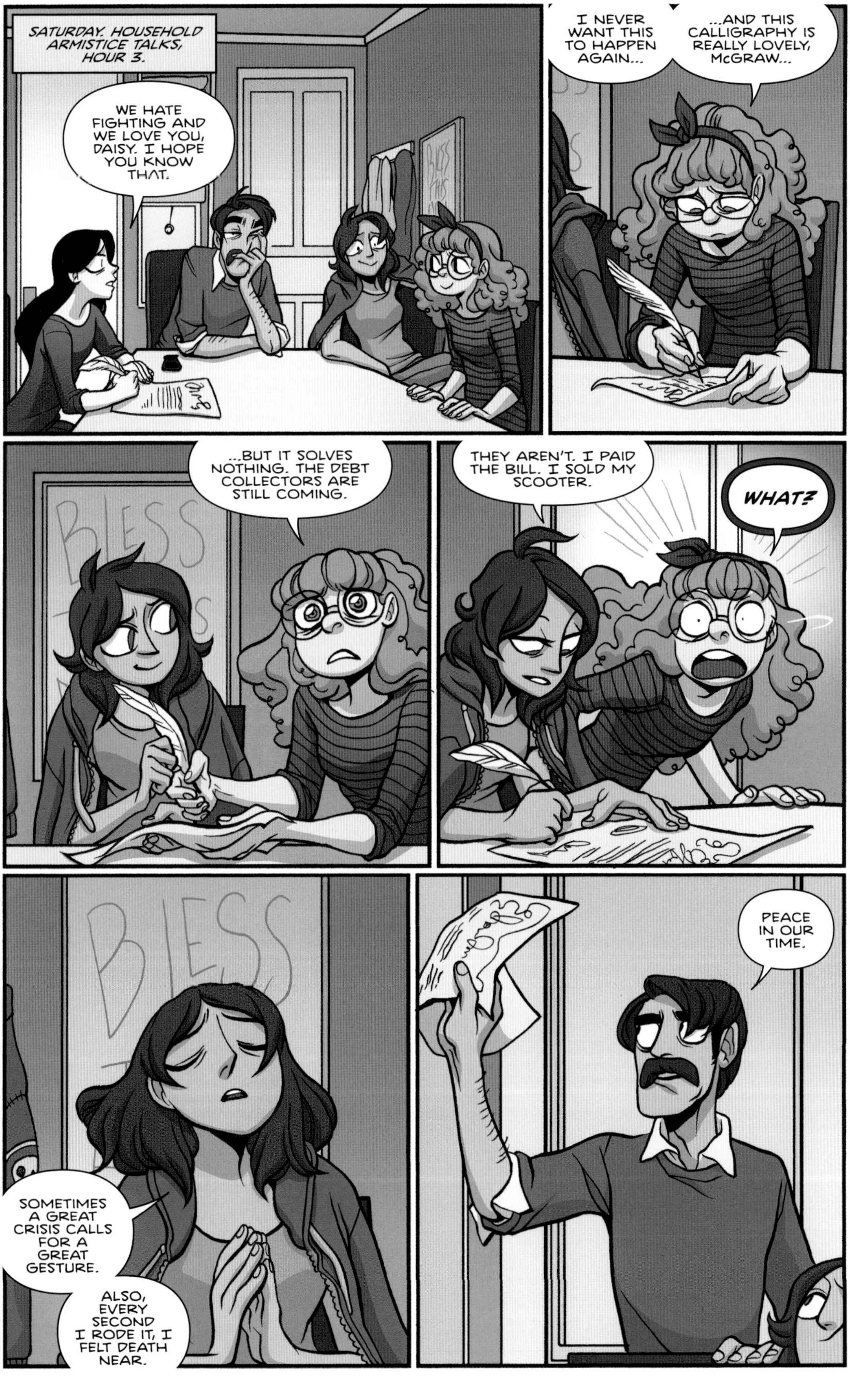
SATURDAY. HOUSEHOLD ARMISTICE TALKS, HOUR 3.
WE HATE FIGHTING AND WE LOVE YOU, DAISY. I HOPE YOU KNOW THAT.
I NEVER WANT THIS TO HAPPEN AGAIN...
...AND THIS CALLIGRAPHY IS REALLY LOVELY, McGRAW...
BLESS
...BUT IT SOLVES NOTHING. THE DEBT COLLECTORS ARE STILL COMING.
THEY AREN'T. I PAID THE BILL. I SOLD MY SCOOTER.
WHAT?
BLESS
SOMETIMES A GREAT CRISIS CALLS FOR A GREAT GESTURE.
ALSO, EVERY SECOND I RODE IT, I FELT DEATH NEAR.
PEACE IN OUR TIME.

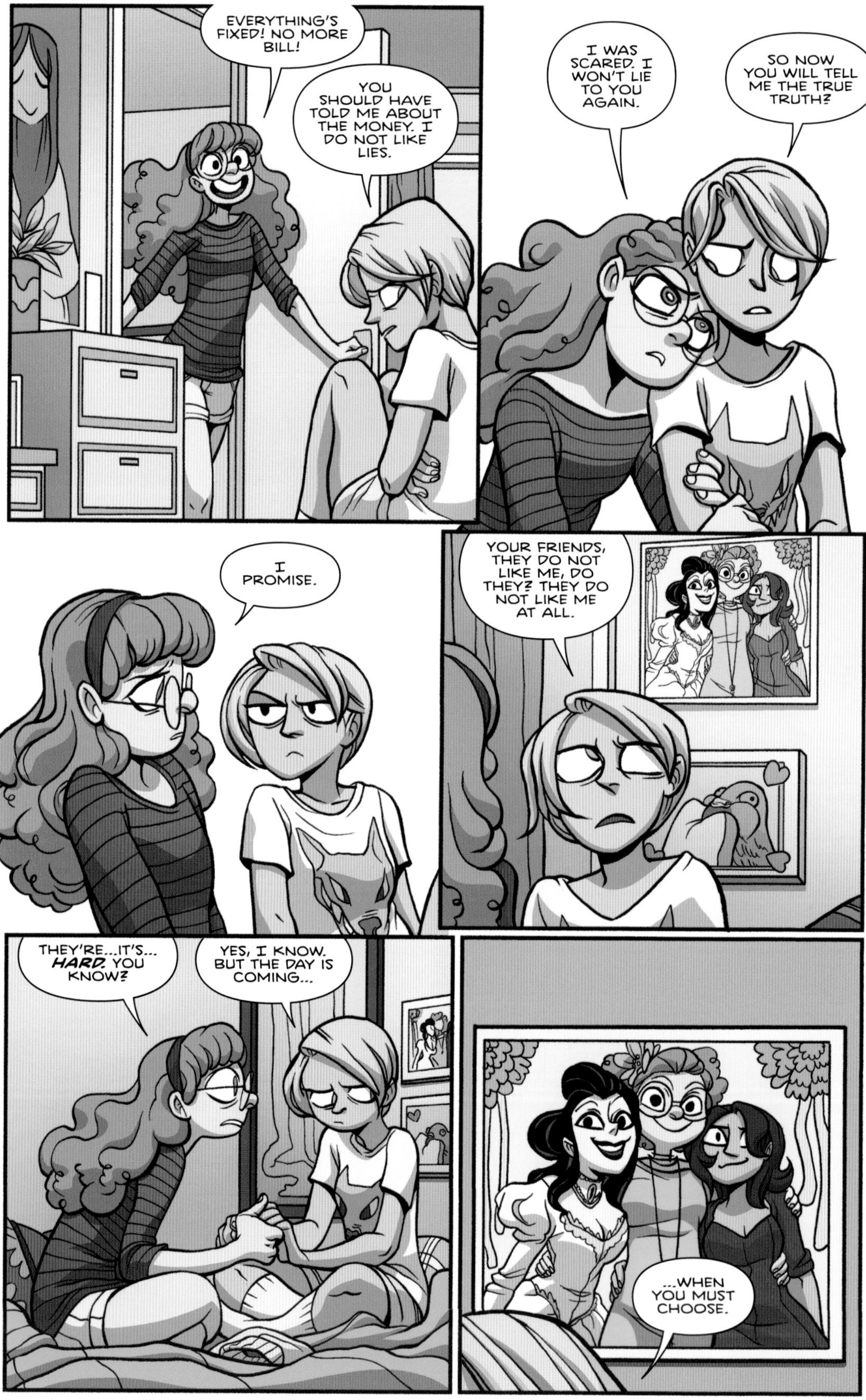
EVERYTHING'S FIXED! NO MORE BILL!
YOU SHOULD HAVE TOLD ME ABOUT THE MONEY. I DO NOT LIKE LIES.
I WAS SCARED. I WON'T LIE TO YOU AGAIN.
SO NOW YOU WILL TELL ME THE TRUE TRUTH?
I PROMISE.
YOUR FRIENDS, THEY DO NOT LIKE ME, DO THEY? THEY DO NOT LIKE ME AT ALL.
THEY'RE...IT'S... **HARD.** YOU KNOW?
YES, I KNOW. BUT THE DAY IS COMING...
...WHEN YOU MUST CHOOSE.

CHAPTER THIRTY-TWO

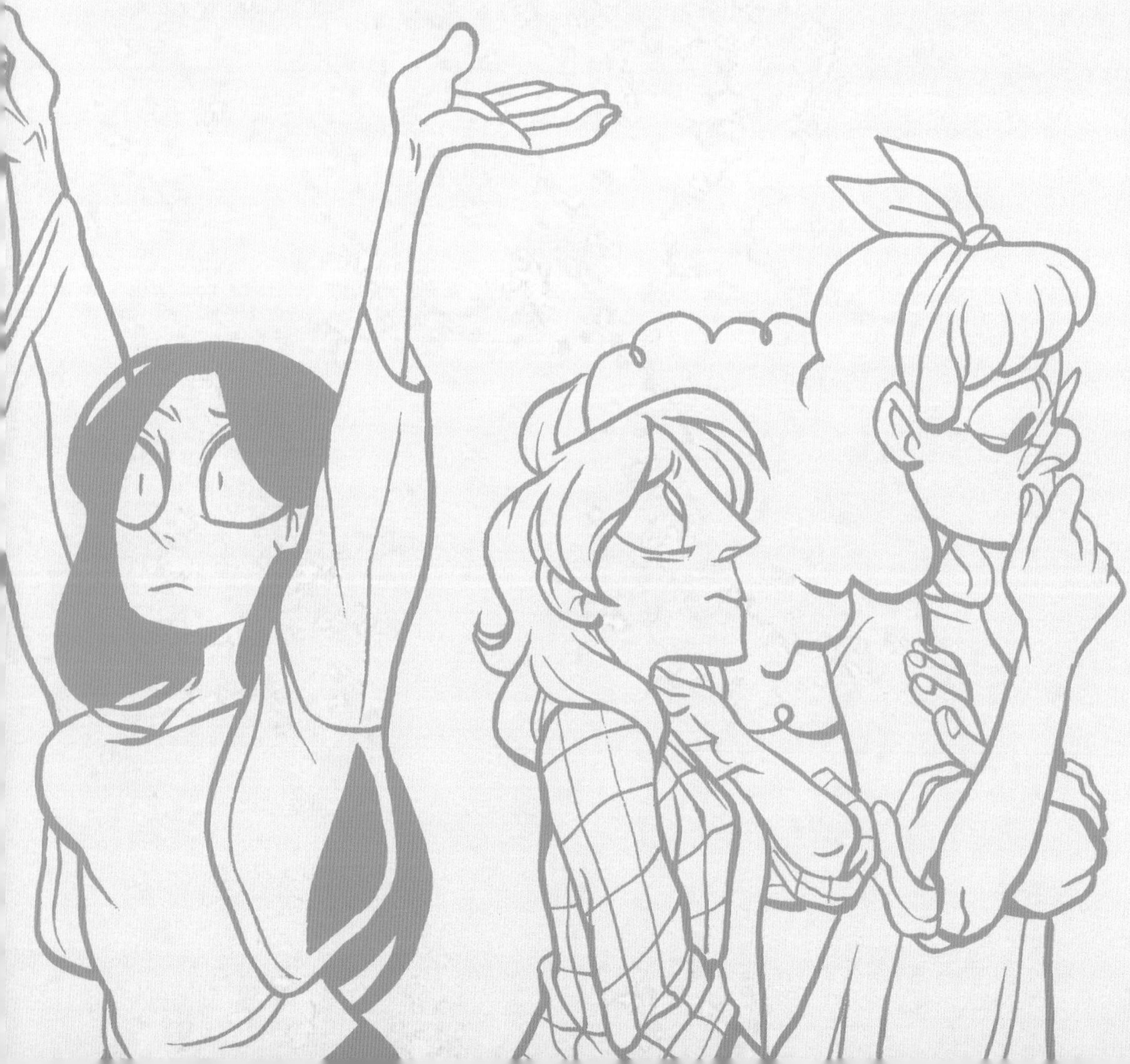

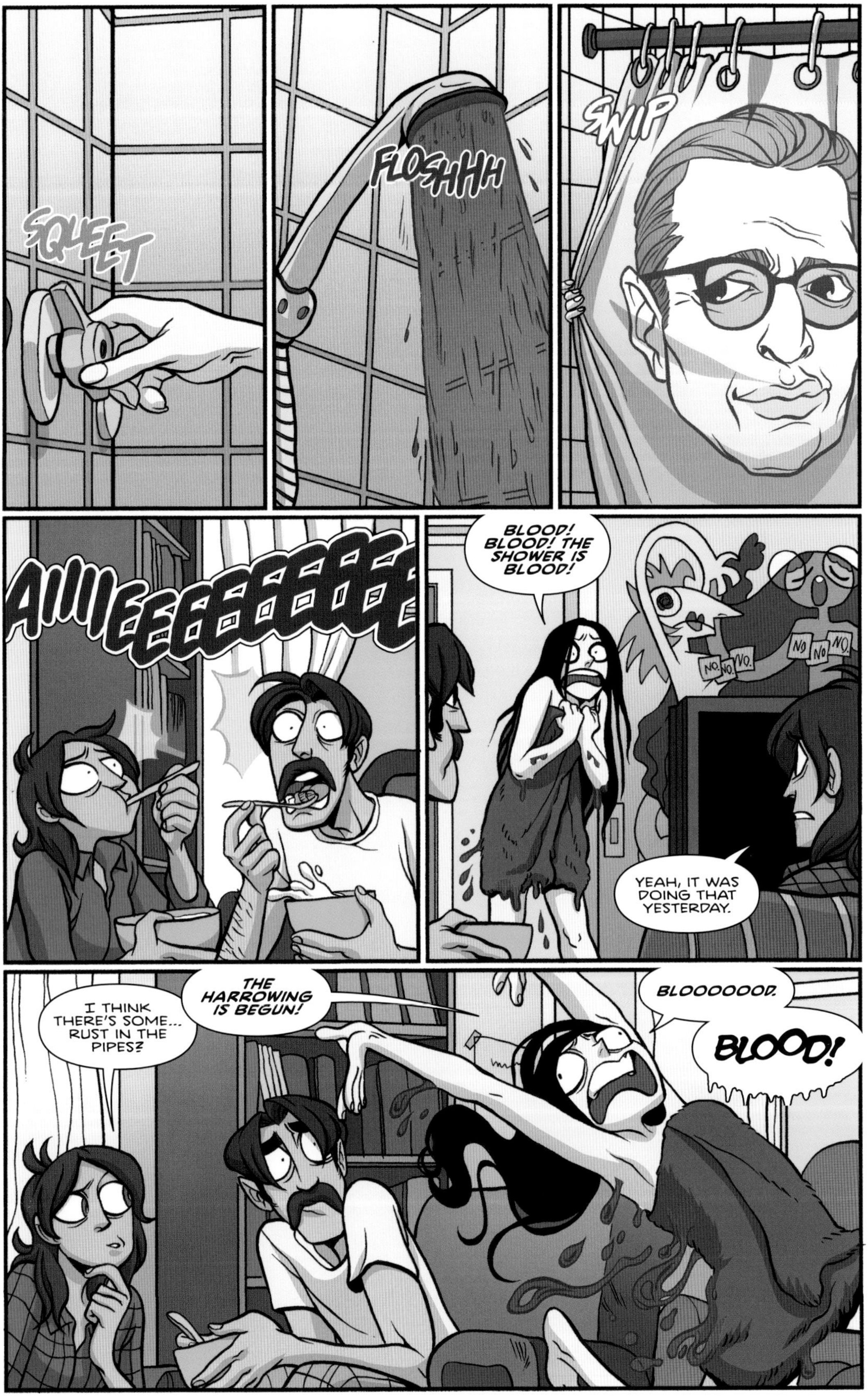
SQUEET
FLOSHHH
SWIP
AIIIIEEEEEEEEEEEE
BLOOD! BLOOD! THE SHOWER IS BLOOD!
NO.
NO.
NO.
NO.
NO
NO.
YEAH, IT WAS DOING THAT YESTERDAY.
I THINK THERE'S SOME... RUST IN THE PIPES?
THE HARROWING IS BEGUN!
BLOOOOOOD.
BLOOD!

I HAVE TO GO TO WORK AND I LOOK LIKE *CARRIE.*
IT DRIES TO A PLEASING OXIDE CRUST THAT YOU CAN PICK OFF. VERY SATISFYING.
I'M GOING TO WASH MYSELF THE WAY WE DID BETWEEN THE WARS.
FROM A JUG.
WILL YOU STOP INSPECTING THINGS? YOU'RE MAKING ME NERVOUS.
YOU SHOULD BE NERVOUS. THIS TIMBER IS RIDDLED WITH WOODWORM.
ELLO
HI
IT ME
CAN'T YOU WAVE YOUR MAGIC FIXING STICK AT IT?
NO. THESE ARE LANDLORD ISSUES.
THE MAIN ISSUE BEING THAT THIS IS THE HOUSE EQUIVALENT OF A RESCUE DOG IN ITS *"BEFORE"* PHOTO.
Shhh shh, DON'T LISTEN TO THE NASTY OLD MAN.

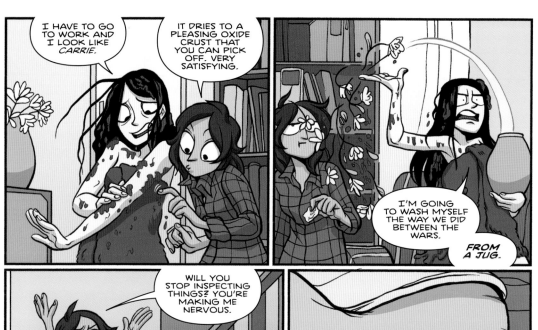

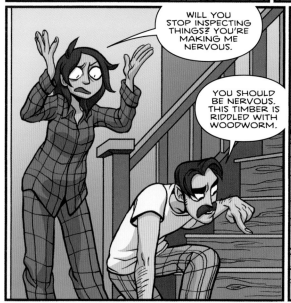

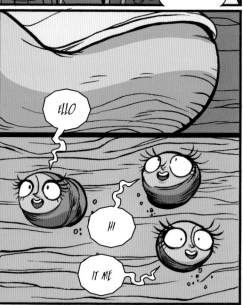

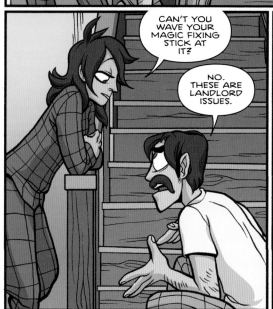

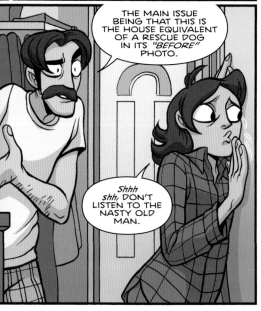

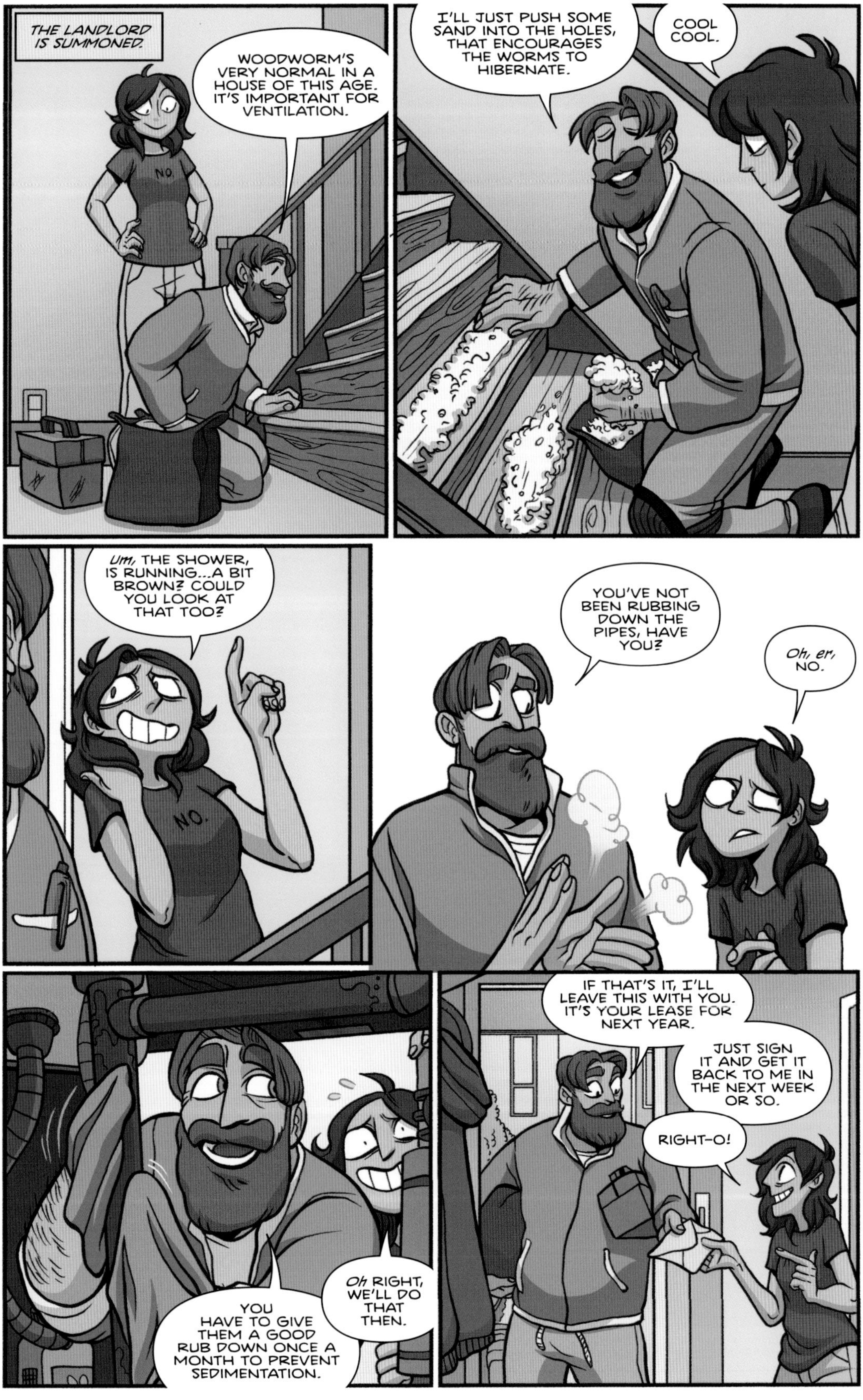
THE LANDLORD IS SUMMONED.
WOODWORM'S VERY NORMAL IN A HOUSE OF THIS AGE. IT'S IMPORTANT FOR VENTILATION.
NO.
I'LL JUST PUSH SOME SAND INTO THE HOLES, THAT ENCOURAGES THE WORMS TO HIBERNATE.
COOL COOL.
Um, THE SHOWER, IS RUNNING...A BIT BROWN? COULD YOU LOOK AT THAT TOO?
NO.
YOU'VE NOT BEEN RUBBING DOWN THE PIPES, HAVE YOU?
Oh, er, NO.
YOU HAVE TO GIVE THEM A GOOD RUB DOWN ONCE A MONTH TO PREVENT SEDIMENTATION.
Oh RIGHT, WE'LL DO THAT THEN.
IF THAT'S IT, I'LL LEAVE THIS WITH YOU. IT'S YOUR LEASE FOR NEXT YEAR.
JUST SIGN IT AND GET IT BACK TO ME IN THE NEXT WEEK OR SO.
RIGHT-O!

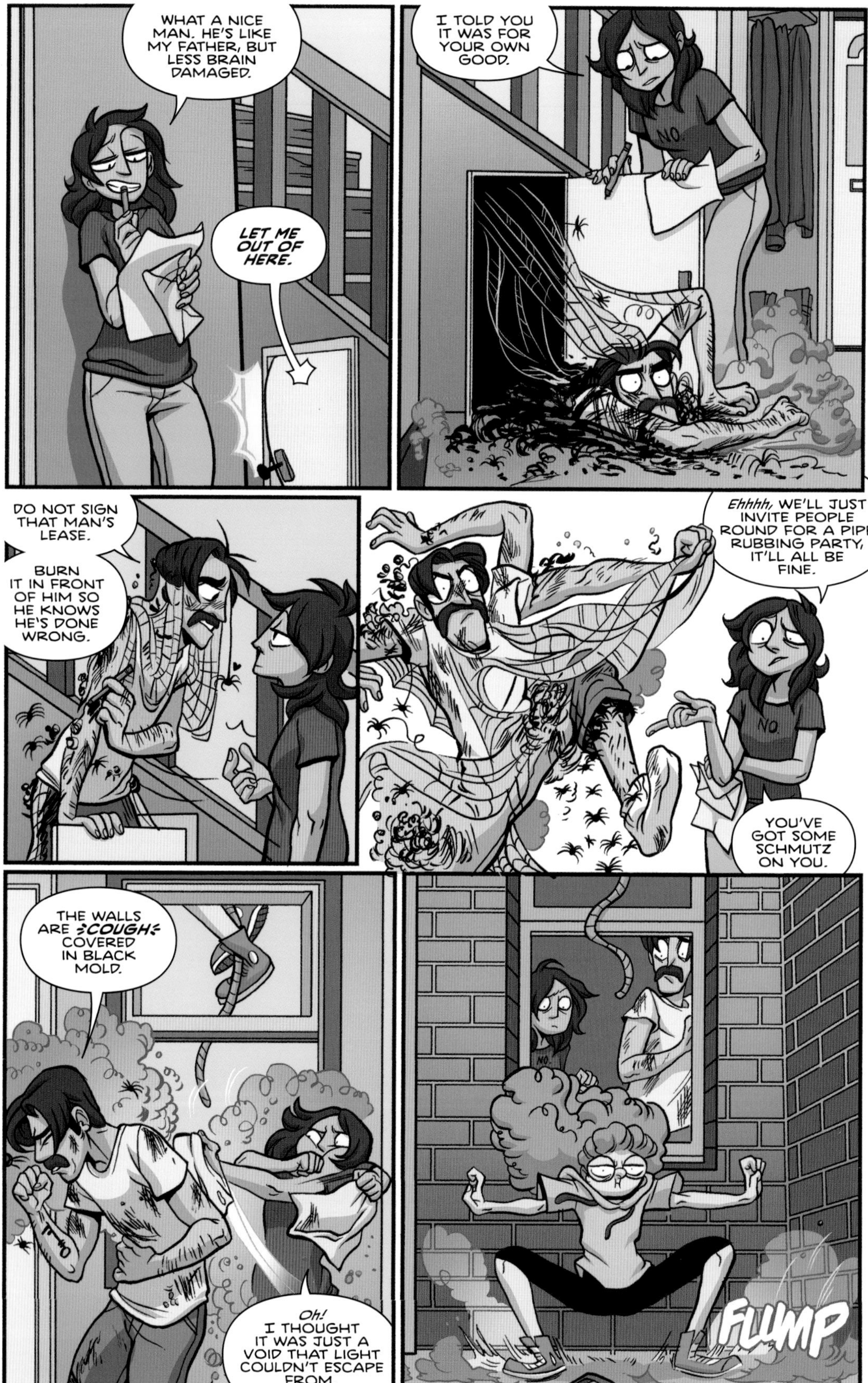

WHAT A NICE MAN. HE'S LIKE MY FATHER, BUT LESS BRAIN DAMAGED.
LET ME OUT OF HERE.
I TOLD YOU IT WAS FOR YOUR OWN GOOD.
NO.
DO NOT SIGN THAT MAN'S LEASE.
BURN IT IN FRONT OF HIM SO HE KNOWS HE'S DONE WRONG.
Ehhhh, WE'LL JUST INVITE PEOPLE ROUND FOR A PIPE RUBBING PARTY, IT'LL ALL BE FINE.
NO.
YOU'VE GOT SOME SCHMUTZ ON YOU.
THE WALLS ARE *COUGH* COVERED IN BLACK MOLD.
Oh! I THOUGHT IT WAS JUST A VOID THAT LIGHT COULDN'T ESCAPE FROM.
NO.
FLUMP

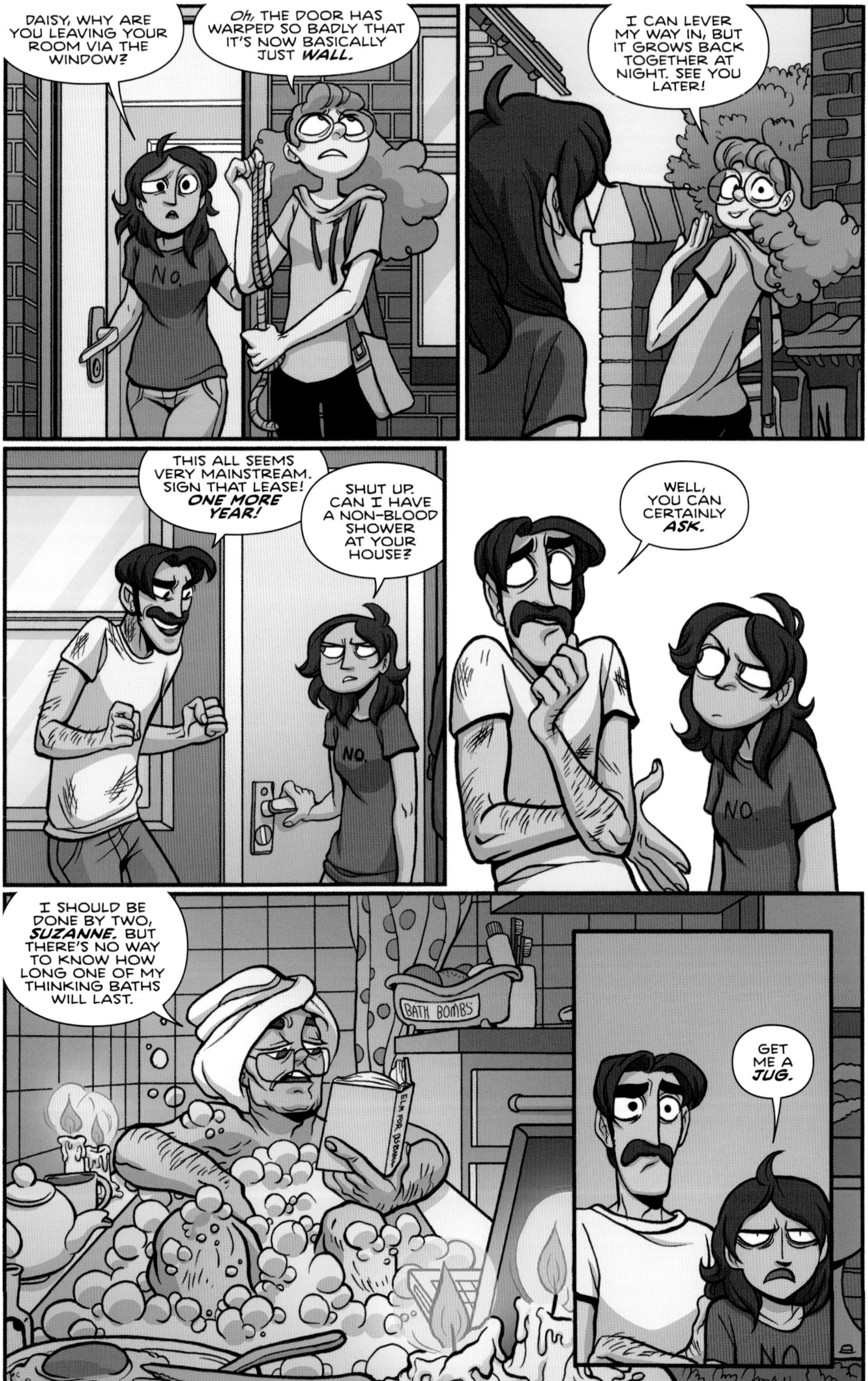
DAISY, WHY ARE YOU LEAVING YOUR ROOM VIA THE WINDOW?
Oh, THE DOOR HAS WARPED SO BADLY THAT IT'S NOW BASICALLY JUST ***WALL.***
NO.
I CAN LEVER MY WAY IN, BUT IT GROWS BACK TOGETHER AT NIGHT. SEE YOU LATER!
THIS ALL SEEMS VERY MAINSTREAM. SIGN THAT LEASE! ***ONE MORE YEAR!***
SHUT UP. CAN I HAVE A NON-BLOOD SHOWER AT YOUR HOUSE?
NO.
WELL, YOU CAN CERTAINLY ***ASK.***
NO.
I SHOULD BE DONE BY TWO, ***SUZANNE.*** BUT THERE'S NO WAY TO KNOW HOW LONG ONE OF MY THINKING BATHS WILL LAST.
BATH BOMBS
GET ME A ***JUG.***
NO

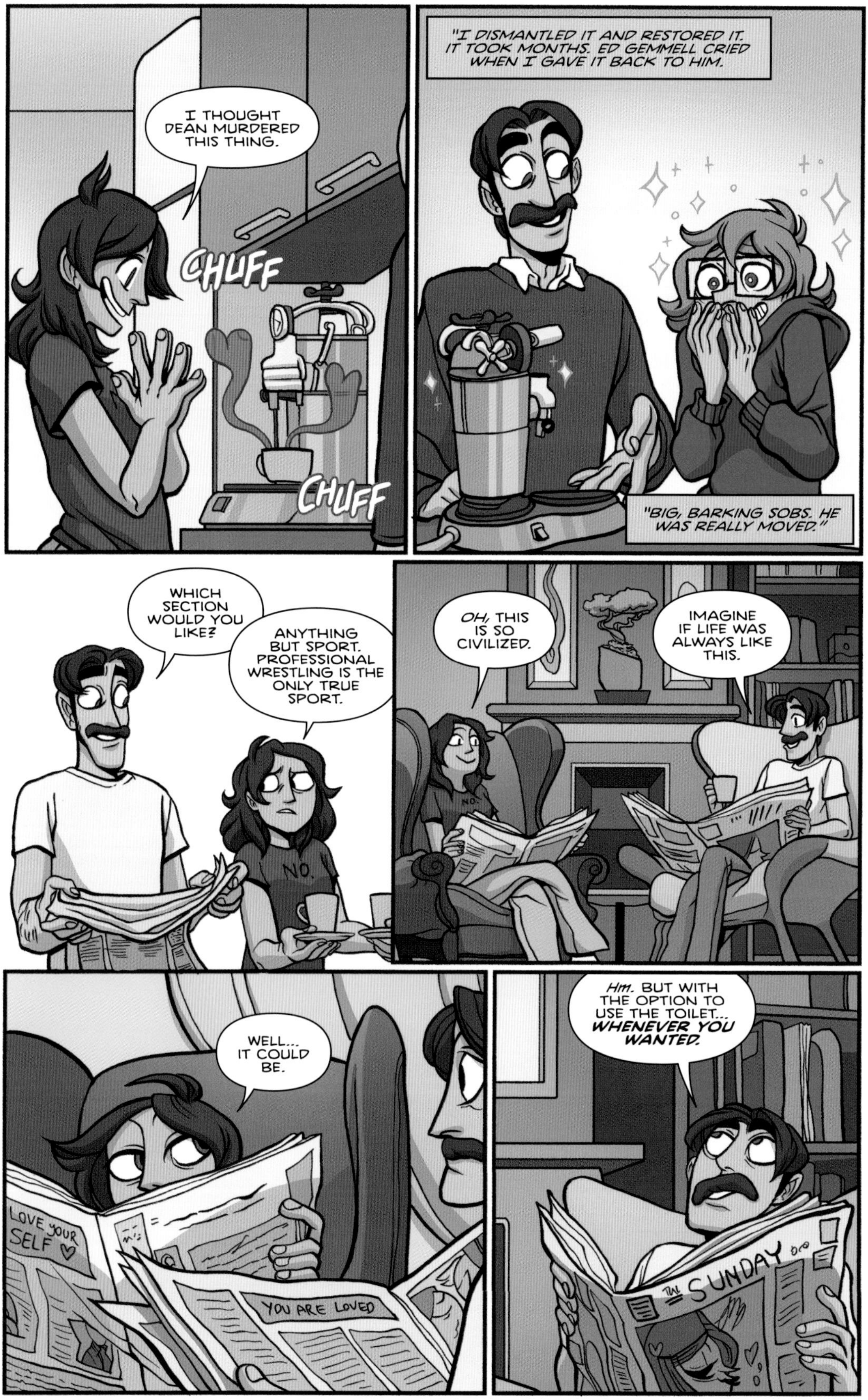
I THOUGHT DEAN MURDERED THIS THING.
CHUFF
CHUFF
"I DISMANTLED IT AND RESTORED IT. IT TOOK MONTHS. ED GEMMELL CRIED WHEN I GAVE IT BACK TO HIM.
"BIG, BARKING SOBS. HE WAS REALLY MOVED."
WHICH SECTION WOULD YOU LIKE?
ANYTHING BUT SPORT. PROFESSIONAL WRESTLING IS THE ONLY TRUE SPORT.
NO.
OH, THIS IS SO CIVILIZED.
IMAGINE IF LIFE WAS ALWAYS LIKE THIS.
WELL... IT COULD BE.
LOVE YOUR SELF ♡
YOU ARE LOVED
Hm. BUT WITH THE OPTION TO USE THE TOILET... WHENEVER YOU WANTED.
THE SUNDAY

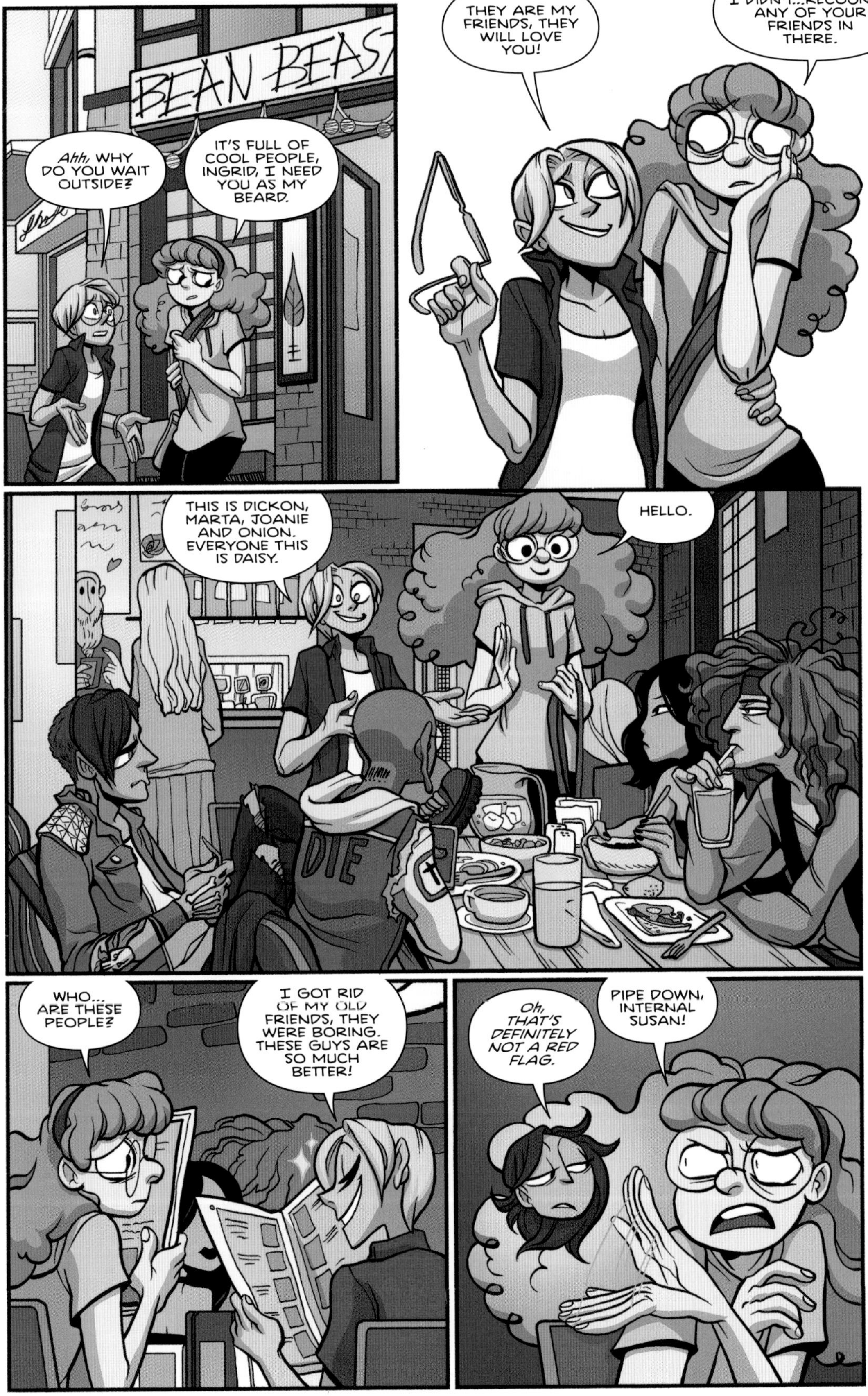
BEAN BEAST
Ahh, WHY DO YOU WAIT OUTSIDE?
IT'S FULL OF COOL PEOPLE, INGRID, I NEED YOU AS MY BEARD.
THEY ARE MY FRIENDS, THEY WILL LOVE YOU!
I LOOKED, I DIDN'T...RECOGNIZE ANY OF YOUR FRIENDS IN THERE.
THIS IS DICKON, MARTA, JOANIE AND ONION. EVERYONE THIS IS DAISY.
HELLO.
DIE
WHO... ARE THESE PEOPLE?
I GOT RID OF MY OLD FRIENDS, THEY WERE BORING. THESE GUYS ARE SO MUCH BETTER!
Oh, THAT'S DEFINITELY NOT A RED FLAG.
PIPE DOWN, INTERNAL SUSAN!

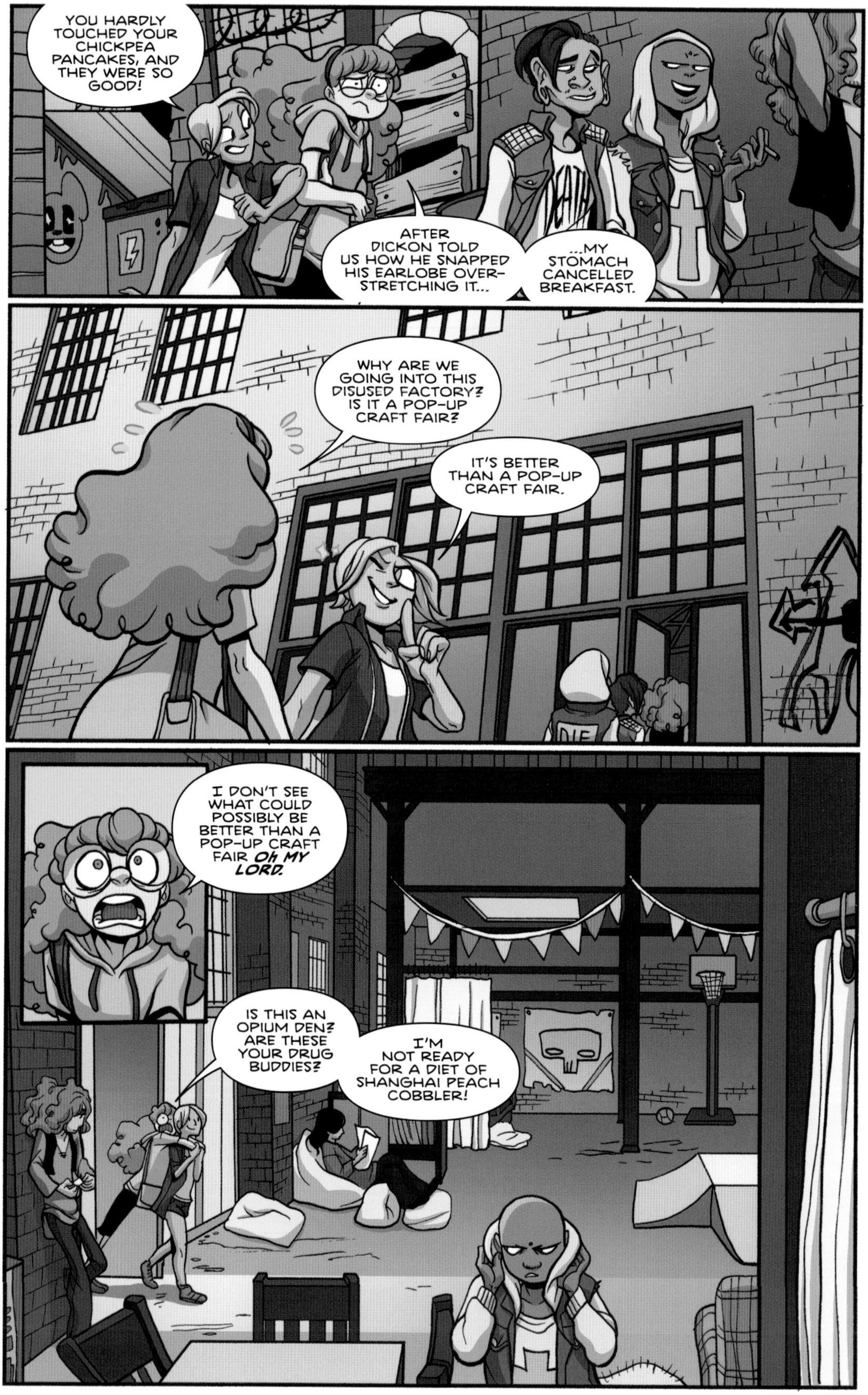
YOU HARDLY TOUCHED YOUR CHICKPEA PANCAKES, AND THEY WERE SO GOOD!
AFTER DICKON TOLD US HOW HE SNAPPED HIS EARLOBE OVER-STRETCHING IT...
...MY STOMACH CANCELLED BREAKFAST.
WHY ARE WE GOING INTO THIS DISUSED FACTORY? IS IT A POP-UP CRAFT FAIR?
IT'S BETTER THAN A POP-UP CRAFT FAIR.
DIE
I DON'T SEE WHAT COULD POSSIBLY BE BETTER THAN A POP-UP CRAFT FAIR *Oh MY LORD.*
IS THIS AN OPIUM DEN? ARE THESE YOUR DRUG BUDDIES?
I'M NOT READY FOR A DIET OF SHANGHAI PEACH COBBLER!

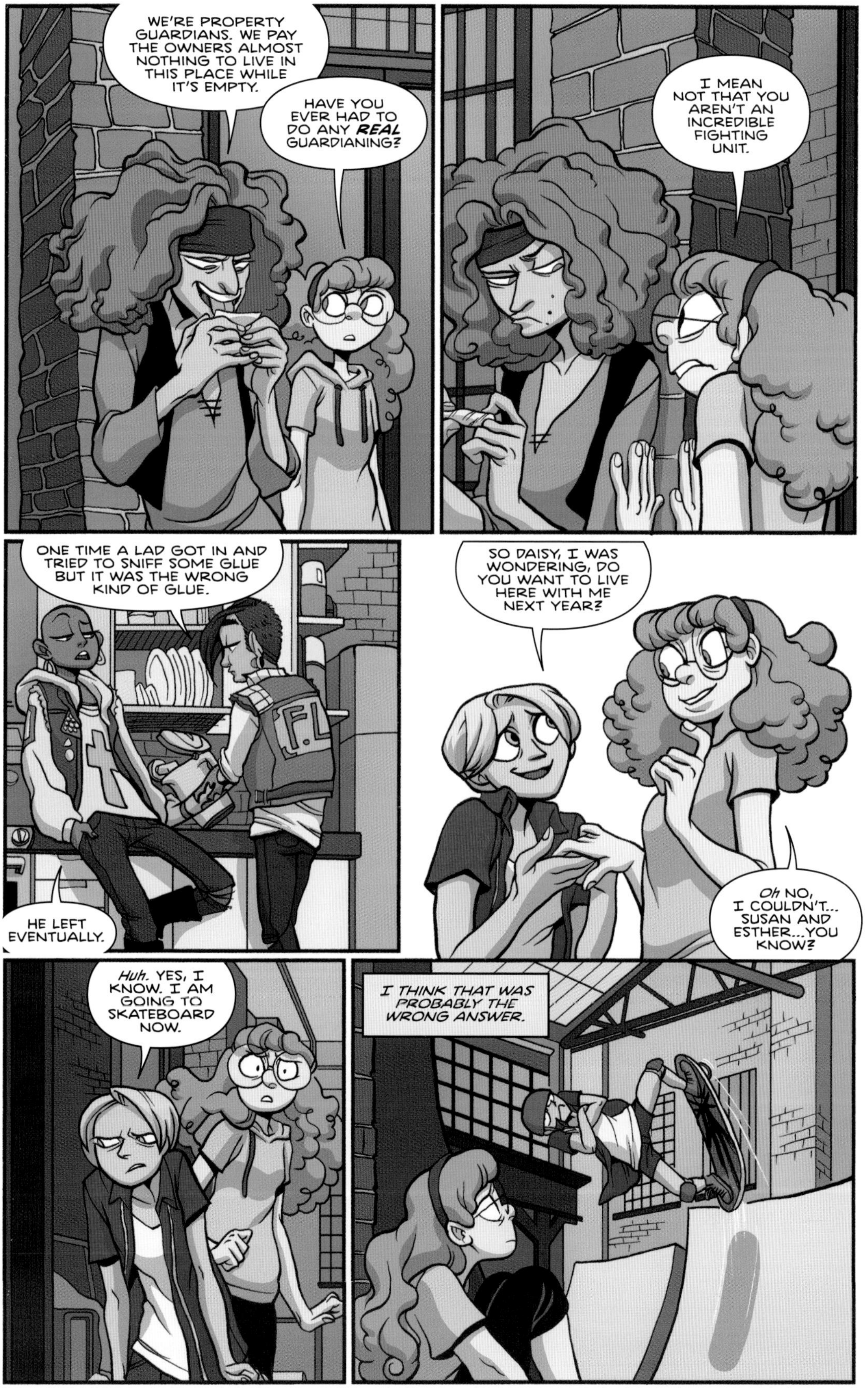
WE'RE PROPERTY GUARDIANS. WE PAY THE OWNERS ALMOST NOTHING TO LIVE IN THIS PLACE WHILE IT'S EMPTY.
HAVE YOU EVER HAD TO DO ANY *REAL* GUARDIANING?
I MEAN NOT THAT YOU AREN'T AN INCREDIBLE FIGHTING UNIT.
ONE TIME A LAD GOT IN AND TRIED TO SNIFF SOME GLUE BUT IT WAS THE WRONG KIND OF GLUE.
HE LEFT EVENTUALLY.
SO DAISY, I WAS WONDERING, DO YOU WANT TO LIVE HERE WITH ME NEXT YEAR?
Oh NO, I COULDN'T... SUSAN AND ESTHER...YOU KNOW?
Huh. YES, I KNOW. I AM GOING TO SKATEBOARD NOW.
I THINK THAT WAS PROBABLY THE WRONG ANSWER.

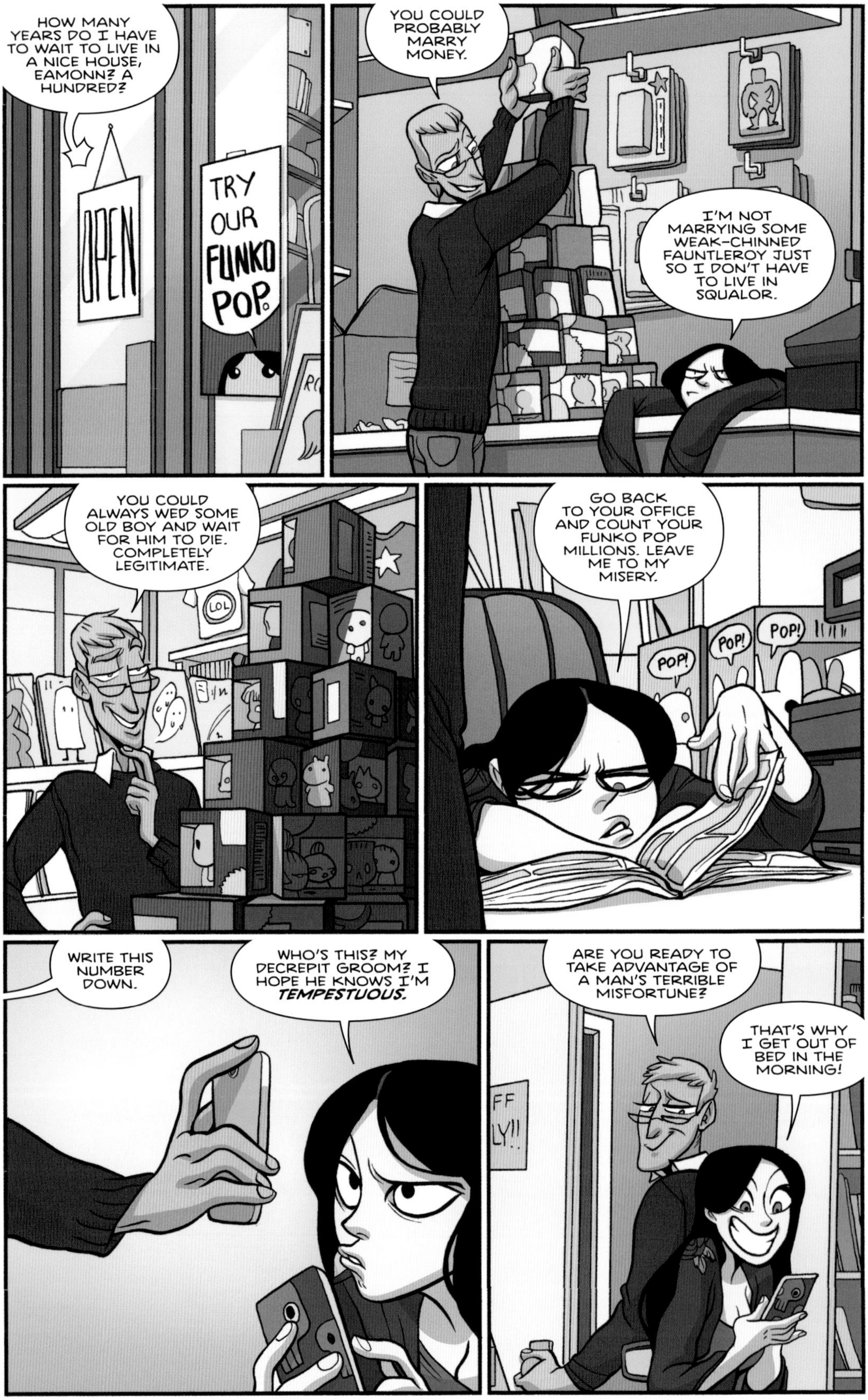
HOW MANY YEARS DO I HAVE TO WAIT TO LIVE IN A NICE HOUSE, EAMONN? A HUNDRED?
OPEN
TRY OUR FUNKO POP.
YOU COULD PROBABLY MARRY MONEY.
I'M NOT MARRYING SOME WEAK-CHINNED FAUNTLEROY JUST SO I DON'T HAVE TO LIVE IN SQUALOR.
YOU COULD ALWAYS WED SOME OLD BOY AND WAIT FOR HIM TO DIE. COMPLETELY LEGITIMATE.
LOL
GO BACK TO YOUR OFFICE AND COUNT YOUR FUNKO POP MILLIONS. LEAVE ME TO MY MISERY.
POP!
POP!
POP!
WRITE THIS NUMBER DOWN.
WHO'S THIS? MY DECREPIT GROOM? I HOPE HE KNOWS I'M *TEMPESTUOUS.*
ARE YOU READY TO TAKE ADVANTAGE OF A MAN'S TERRIBLE MISFORTUNE?
THAT'S WHY I GET OUT OF BED IN THE MORNING!

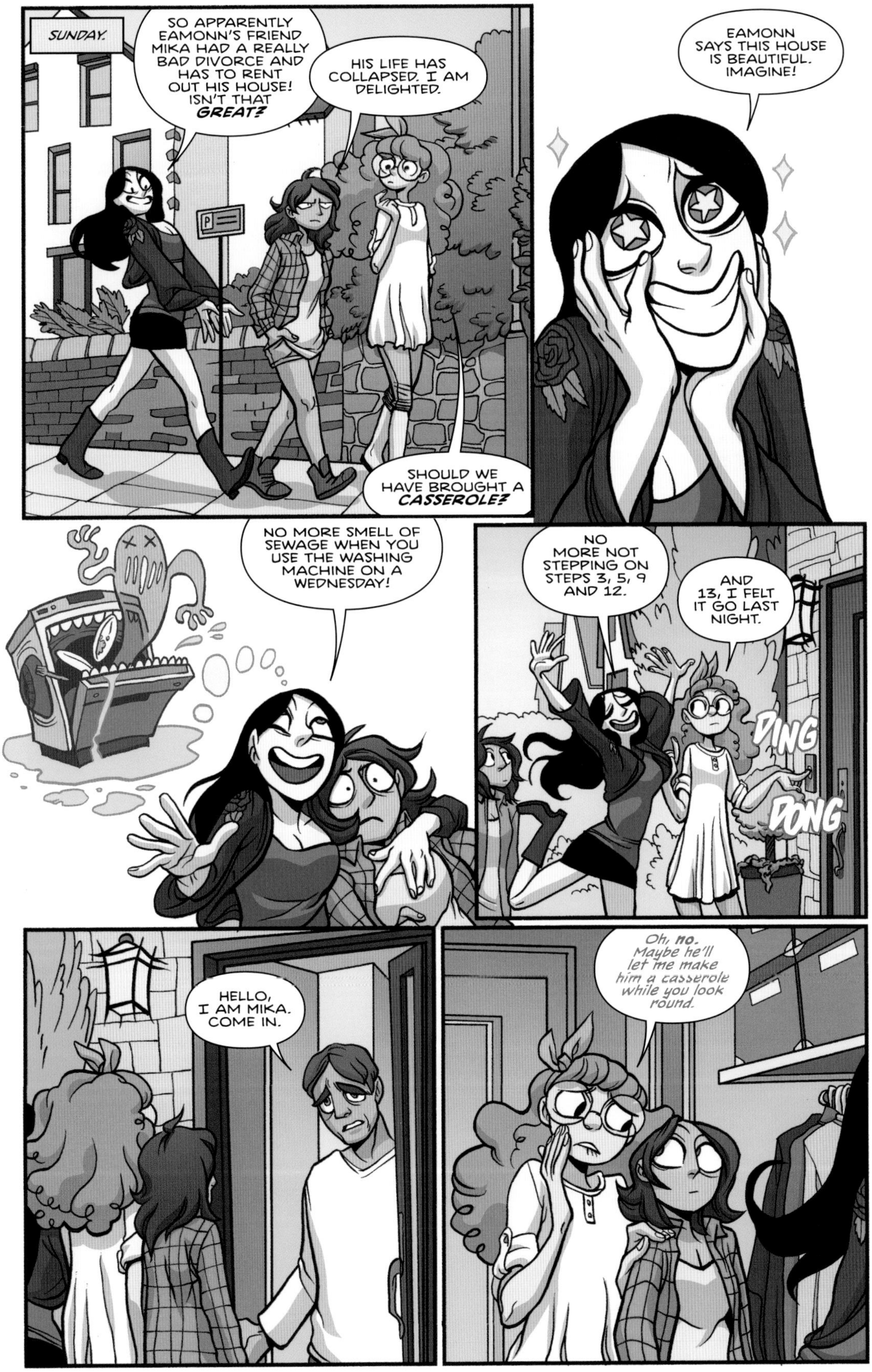

SUNDAY.
SO APPARENTLY EAMONN'S FRIEND MIKA HAD A REALLY BAD DIVORCE AND HAS TO RENT OUT HIS HOUSE! ISN'T THAT GREAT?
HIS LIFE HAS COLLAPSED. I AM DELIGHTED.
SHOULD WE HAVE BROUGHT A CASSEROLE?
EAMONN SAYS THIS HOUSE IS BEAUTIFUL. IMAGINE!
NO MORE SMELL OF SEWAGE WHEN YOU USE THE WASHING MACHINE ON A WEDNESDAY!
NO MORE NOT STEPPING ON STEPS 3, 5, 9 AND 12.
AND 13, I FELT IT GO LAST NIGHT.
DING
DONG
HELLO, I AM MIKA. COME IN.
Oh, no. Maybe he'll let me make him a casserole while you look round.

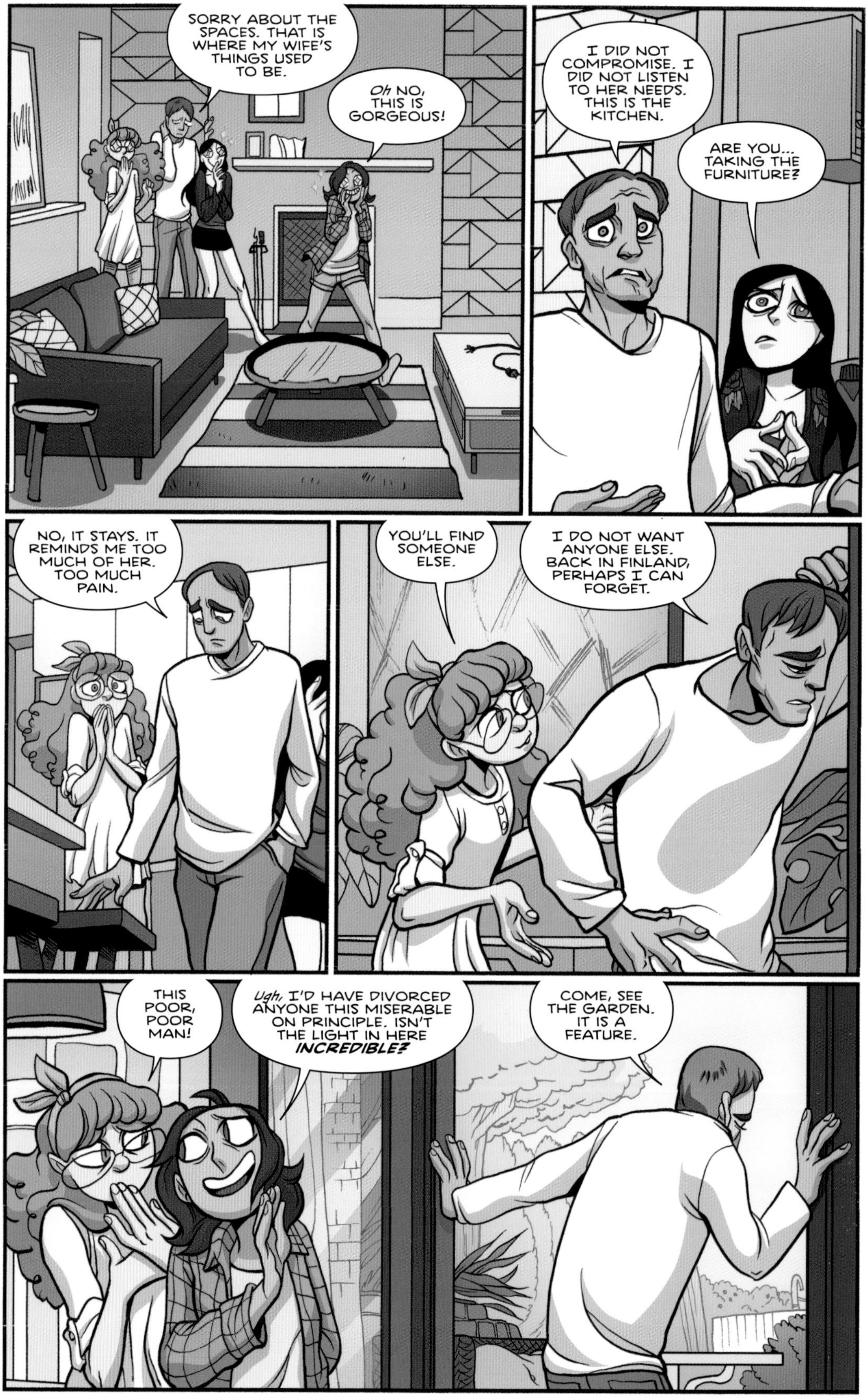

SORRY ABOUT THE SPACES. THAT IS WHERE MY WIFE'S THINGS USED TO BE.
Oh NO, THIS IS GORGEOUS!
I DID NOT COMPROMISE. I DID NOT LISTEN TO HER NEEDS. THIS IS THE KITCHEN.
ARE YOU... TAKING THE FURNITURE?
NO, IT STAYS. IT REMINDS ME TOO MUCH OF HER. TOO MUCH PAIN.
YOU'LL FIND SOMEONE ELSE.
I DO NOT WANT ANYONE ELSE. BACK IN FINLAND, PERHAPS I CAN FORGET.
THIS POOR, POOR MAN!
Ugh, I'D HAVE DIVORCED ANYONE THIS MISERABLE ON PRINCIPLE. ISN'T THE LIGHT IN HERE ***INCREDIBLE?***
COME, SEE THE GARDEN. IT IS A FEATURE.

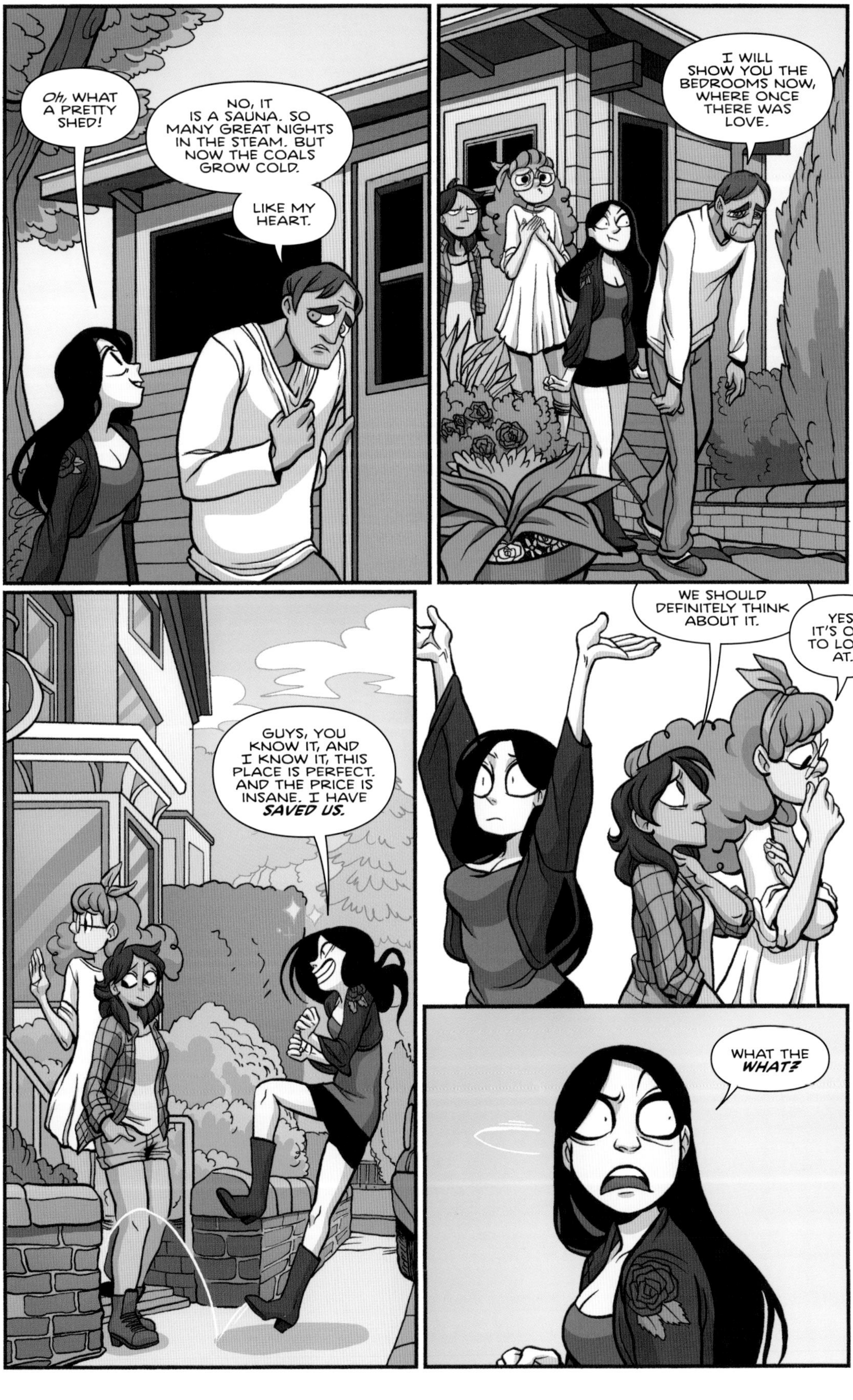
Oh, WHAT A PRETTY SHED!
NO, IT IS A SAUNA. SO MANY GREAT NIGHTS IN THE STEAM. BUT NOW THE COALS GROW COLD.
LIKE MY HEART.
I WILL SHOW YOU THE BEDROOMS NOW, WHERE ONCE THERE WAS LOVE.
GUYS, YOU KNOW IT, AND I KNOW IT, THIS PLACE IS PERFECT. AND THE PRICE IS INSANE. I HAVE ***SAVED US.***
WE SHOULD DEFINITELY THINK ABOUT IT.
YES. IT'S ONE TO LOOK AT.
WHAT THE ***WHAT?***

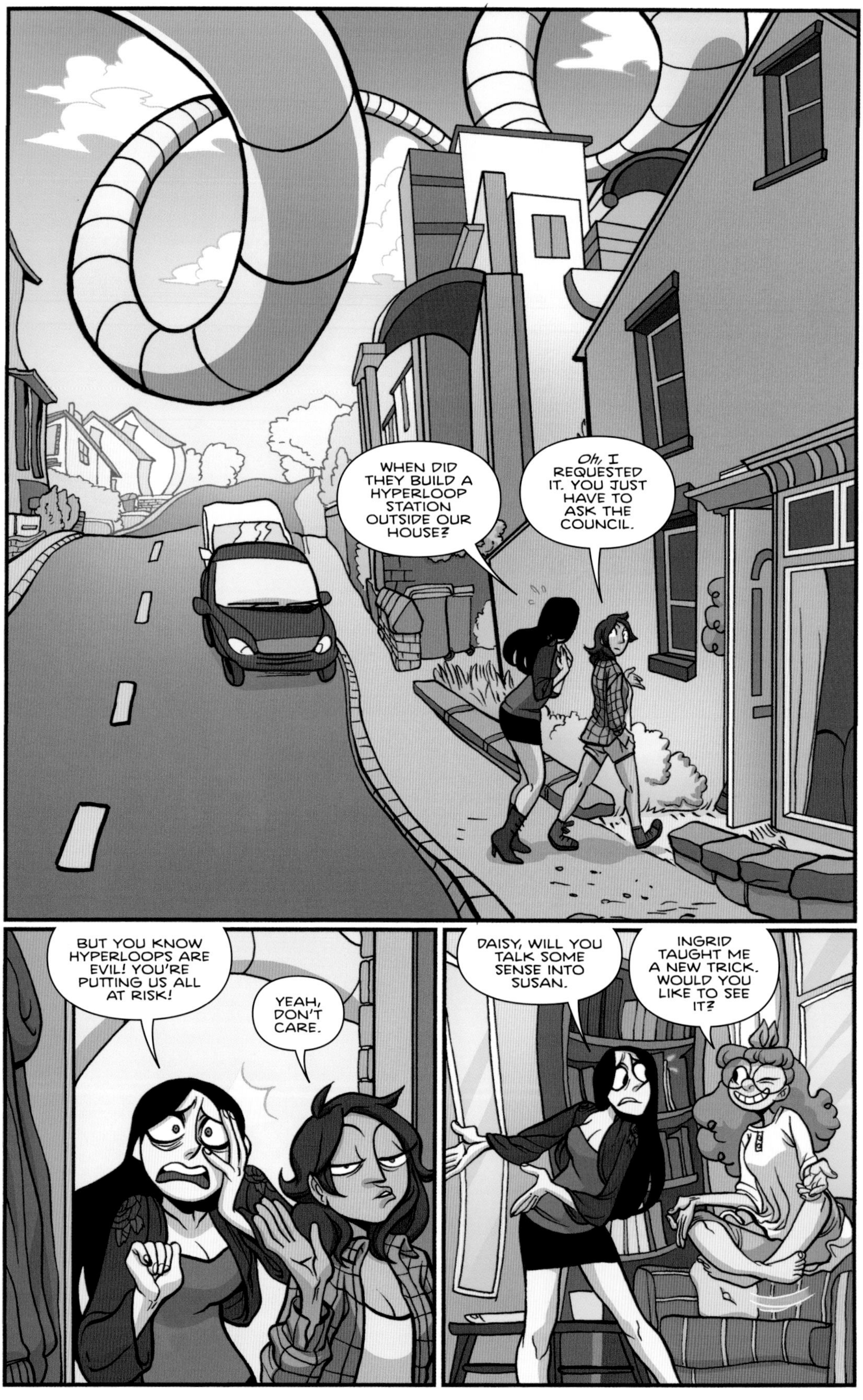
WHEN DID THEY BUILD A HYPERLOOP STATION OUTSIDE OUR HOUSE?
Oh, I REQUESTED IT. YOU JUST HAVE TO ASK THE COUNCIL.
BUT YOU KNOW HYPERLOOPS ARE EVIL! YOU'RE PUTTING US ALL AT RISK!
YEAH, DON'T CARE.
DAISY, WILL YOU TALK SOME SENSE INTO SUSAN.
INGRID TAUGHT ME A NEW TRICK. WOULD YOU LIKE TO SEE IT?

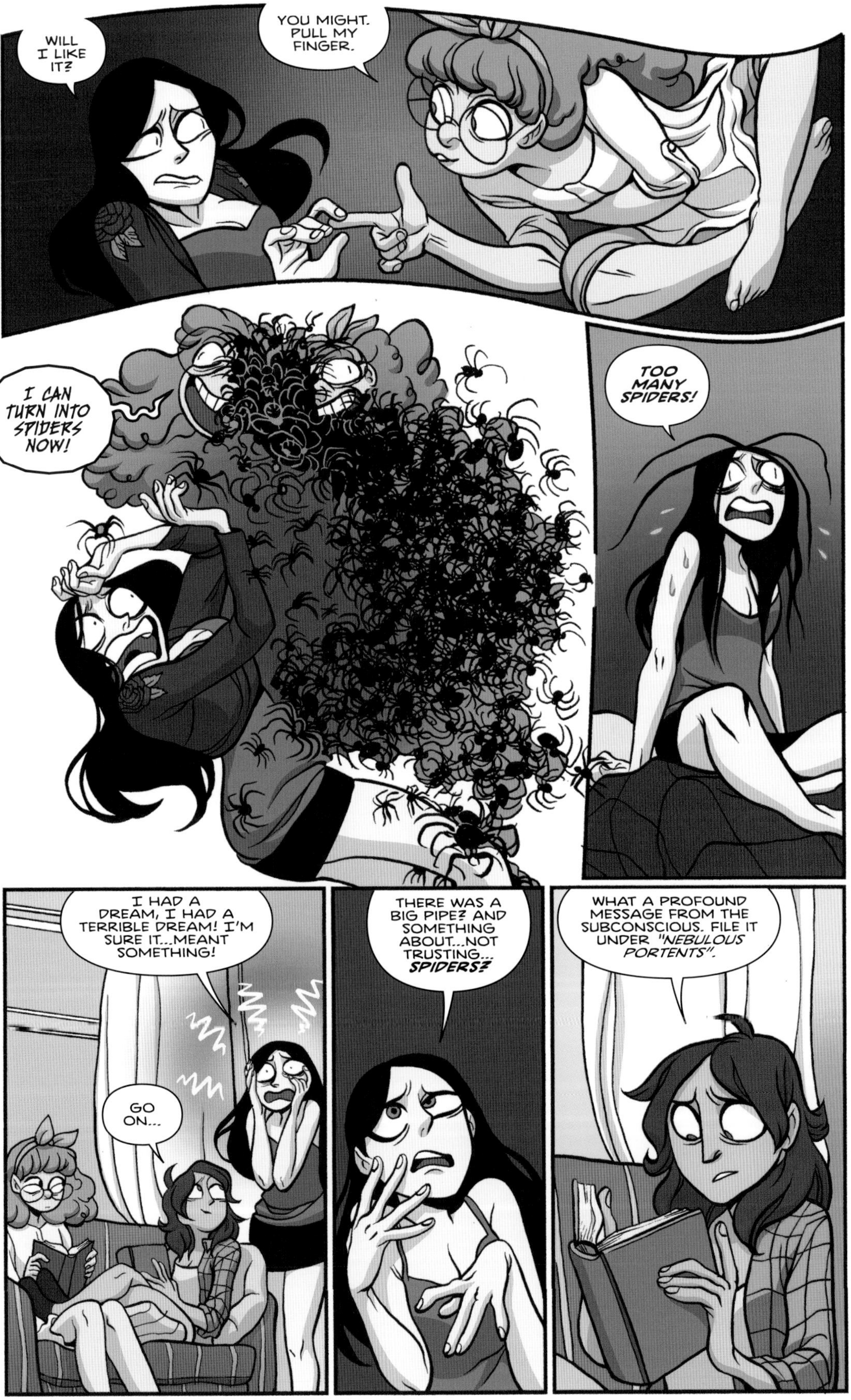
WILL I LIKE IT?
YOU MIGHT. PULL MY FINGER.
I CAN TURN INTO SPIDERS NOW!
TOO MANY SPIDERS!
I HAD A DREAM, I HAD A TERRIBLE DREAM! I'M SURE IT...MEANT SOMETHING!
GO ON...
THERE WAS A BIG PIPE? AND SOMETHING ABOUT...NOT TRUSTING... SPIDERS?
WHAT A PROFOUND MESSAGE FROM THE SUBCONSCIOUS. FILE IT UNDER "NEBULOUS PORTENTS".

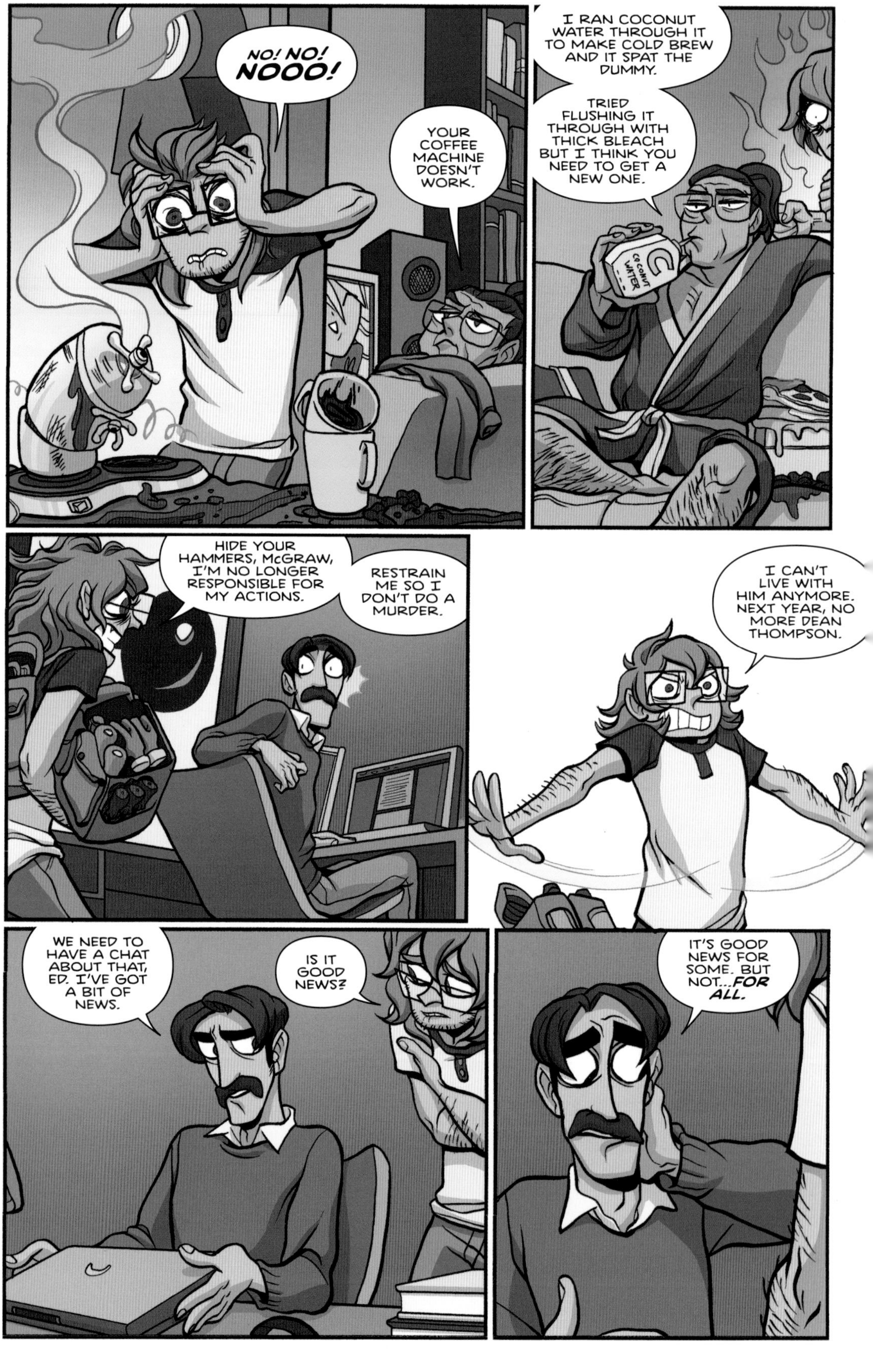
NO! NO! NOOO!
YOUR COFFEE MACHINE DOESN'T WORK.
I RAN COCONUT WATER THROUGH IT TO MAKE COLD BREW AND IT SPAT THE DUMMY.
TRIED FLUSHING IT THROUGH WITH THICK BLEACH BUT I THINK YOU NEED TO GET A NEW ONE.
COCONUT WATER
HIDE YOUR HAMMERS, McGRAW, I'M NO LONGER RESPONSIBLE FOR MY ACTIONS.
RESTRAIN ME SO I DON'T DO A MURDER.
I CAN'T LIVE WITH HIM ANYMORE. NEXT YEAR, NO MORE DEAN THOMPSON.
WE NEED TO HAVE A CHAT ABOUT THAT, ED. I'VE GOT A BIT OF NEWS.
IS IT GOOD NEWS?
IT'S GOOD NEWS FOR SOME. BUT NOT...FOR ALL.

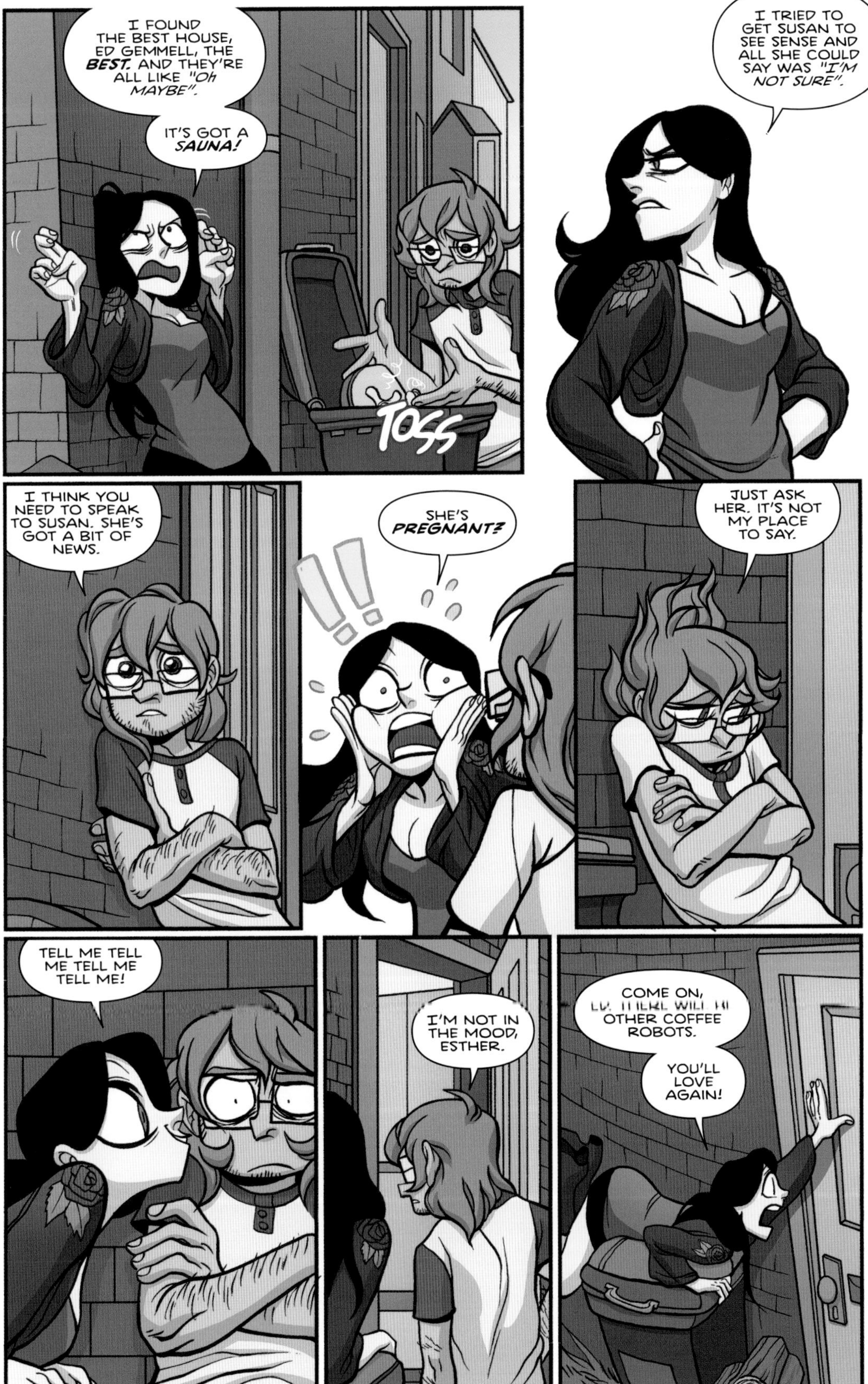
I FOUND THE BEST HOUSE, ED GEMMELL, THE **BEST.** AND THEY'RE ALL LIKE *"Oh MAYBE"*.
IT'S GOT A ***SAUNA!***
TOSS
I TRIED TO GET SUSAN TO SEE SENSE AND ALL SHE COULD SAY WAS *"I'M NOT SURE"*.
I THINK YOU NEED TO SPEAK TO SUSAN. SHE'S GOT A BIT OF NEWS.
SHE'S ***PREGNANT?***
JUST ASK HER. IT'S NOT MY PLACE TO SAY.
TELL ME TELL ME TELL ME TELL ME!
I'M NOT IN THE MOOD, ESTHER.
COME ON,
OTHER COFFEE ROBOTS.
YOU'LL LOVE AGAIN!

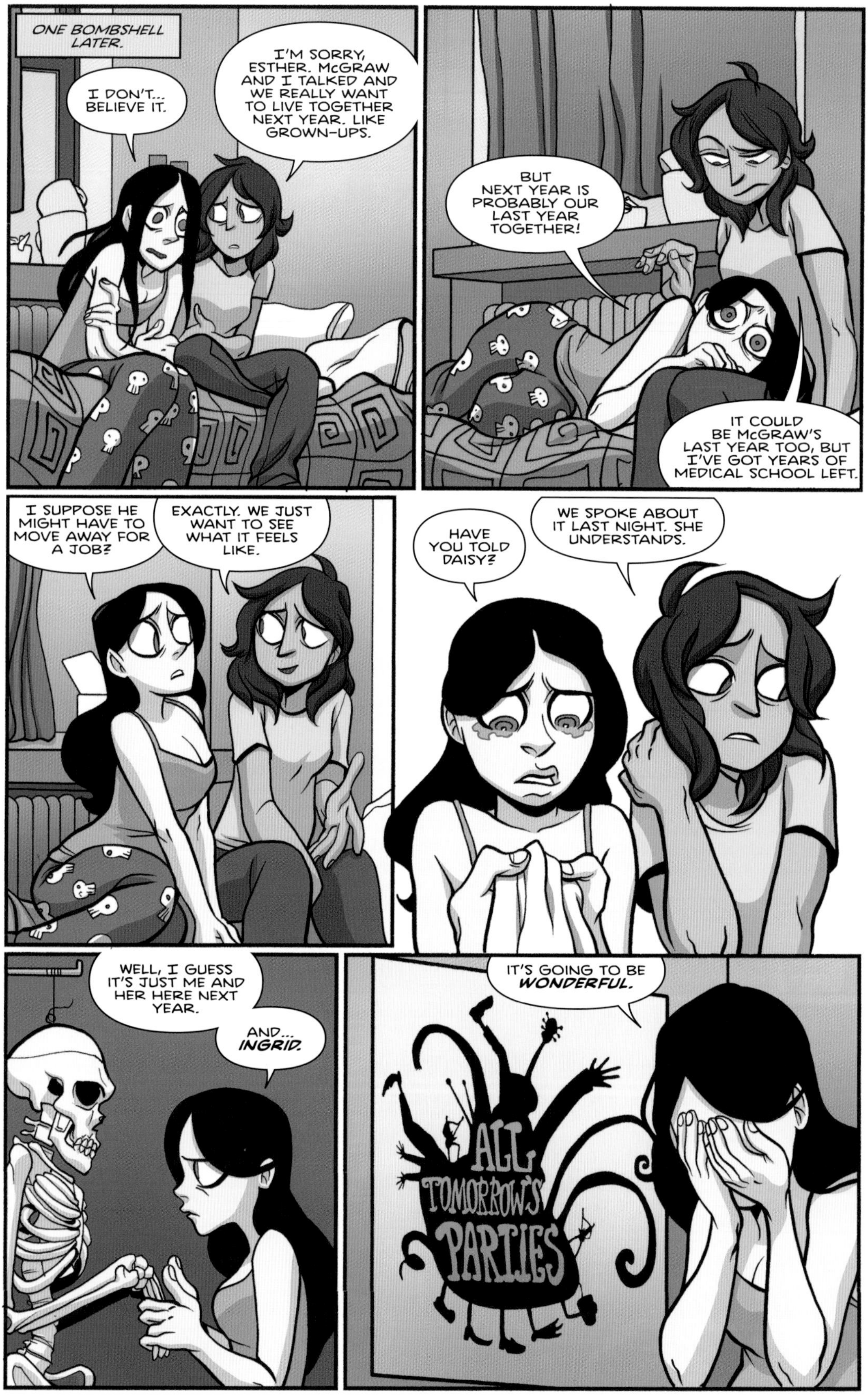
ONE BOMBSHELL LATER.
I DON'T... BELIEVE IT.
I'M SORRY, ESTHER. McGRAW AND I TALKED AND WE REALLY WANT TO LIVE TOGETHER NEXT YEAR. LIKE GROWN-UPS.
BUT NEXT YEAR IS PROBABLY OUR LAST YEAR TOGETHER!
IT COULD BE McGRAW'S LAST YEAR TOO, BUT I'VE GOT YEARS OF MEDICAL SCHOOL LEFT.
I SUPPOSE HE MIGHT HAVE TO MOVE AWAY FOR A JOB?
EXACTLY. WE JUST WANT TO SEE WHAT IT FEELS LIKE.
HAVE YOU TOLD DAISY?
WE SPOKE ABOUT IT LAST NIGHT. SHE UNDERSTANDS.
WELL, I GUESS IT'S JUST ME AND HER HERE NEXT YEAR.
AND... *INGRID.*
IT'S GOING TO BE ***WONDERFUL.***
ALL TOMORROW'S PARTIES

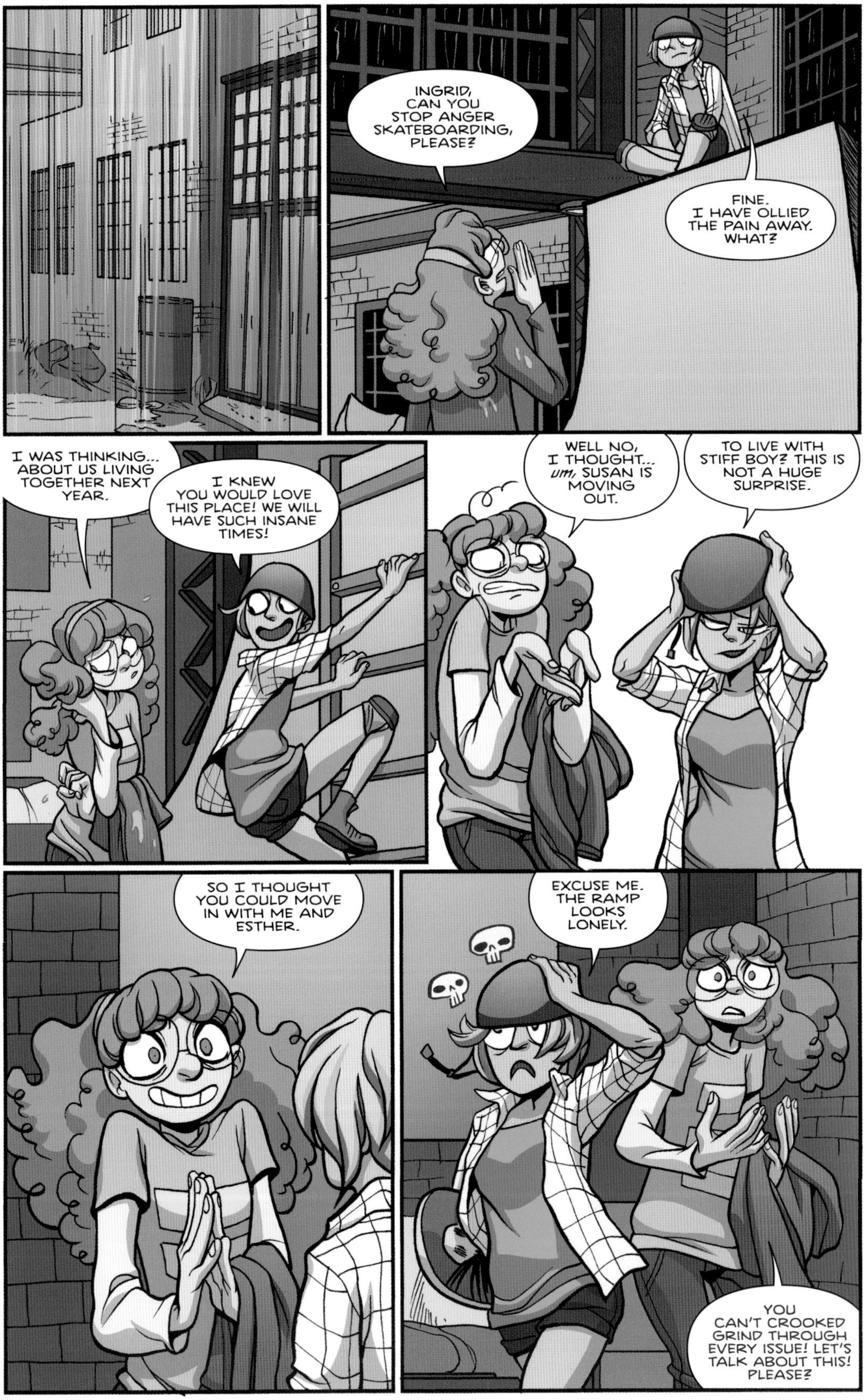
INGRID, CAN YOU STOP ANGER SKATEBOARDING, PLEASE?
FINE. I HAVE OLLIED THE PAIN AWAY. WHAT?
I WAS THINKING... ABOUT US LIVING TOGETHER NEXT YEAR.
I KNEW YOU WOULD LOVE THIS PLACE! WE WILL HAVE SUCH INSANE TIMES!
WELL NO, I THOUGHT... UM, SUSAN IS MOVING OUT.
TO LIVE WITH STIFF BOY? THIS IS NOT A HUGE SURPRISE.
SO I THOUGHT YOU COULD MOVE IN WITH ME AND ESTHER.
EXCUSE ME. THE RAMP LOOKS LONELY.
YOU CAN'T CROOKED GRIND THROUGH EVERY ISSUE! LET'S TALK ABOUT THIS! PLEASE?

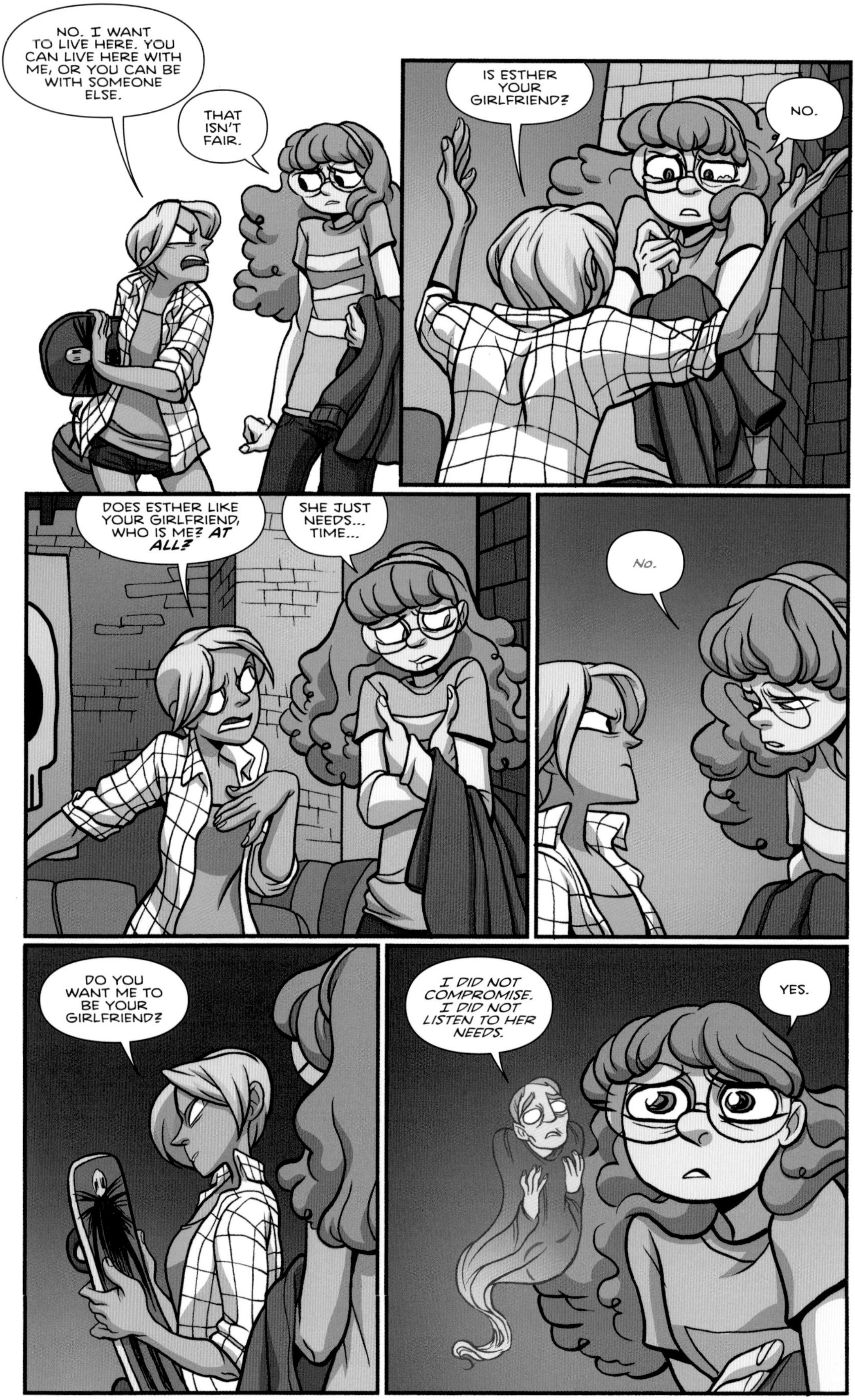
NO. I WANT TO LIVE HERE. YOU CAN LIVE HERE WITH ME, OR YOU CAN BE WITH SOMEONE ELSE.
THAT ISN'T FAIR.
IS ESTHER YOUR GIRLFRIEND?
NO.
DOES ESTHER LIKE YOUR GIRLFRIEND, WHO IS ME? AT ALL?
SHE JUST NEEDS... TIME...
No.
DO YOU WANT ME TO BE YOUR GIRLFRIEND?
I DID NOT COMPROMISE. I DID NOT LISTEN TO HER NEEDS.
YES.

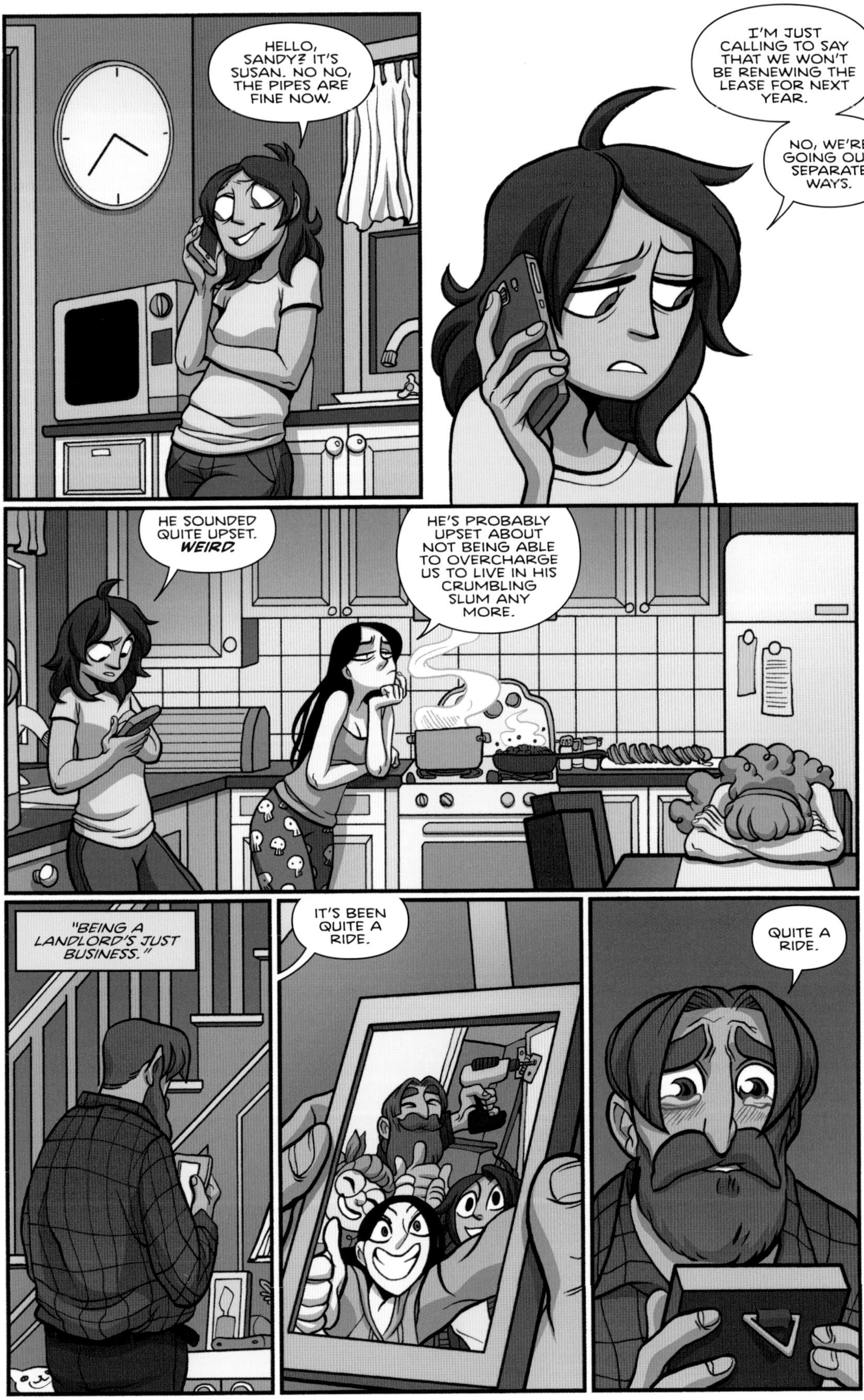
HELLO, SANDY? IT'S SUSAN. NO NO, THE PIPES ARE FINE NOW.
I'M JUST CALLING TO SAY THAT WE WON'T BE RENEWING THE LEASE FOR NEXT YEAR.
NO, WE'RE GOING OUR SEPARATE WAYS.
HE SOUNDED QUITE UPSET. *WEIRD.*
HE'S PROBABLY UPSET ABOUT NOT BEING ABLE TO OVERCHARGE US TO LIVE IN HIS CRUMBLING SLUM ANY MORE.
"BEING A LANDLORD'S JUST BUSINESS."
IT'S BEEN QUITE A RIDE.
QUITE A RIDE.

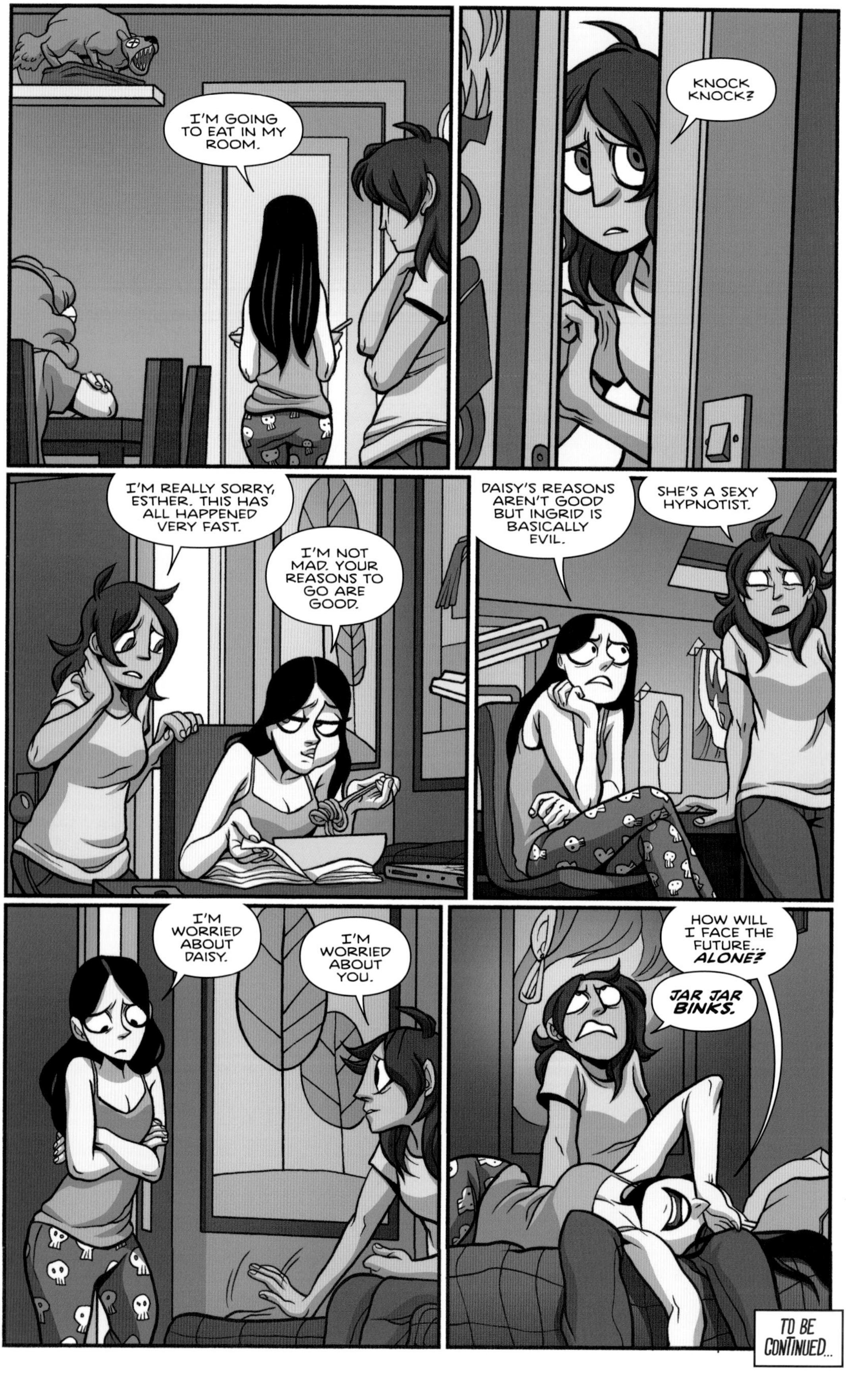
I'M GOING TO EAT IN MY ROOM.
KNOCK KNOCK?
I'M REALLY SORRY, ESTHER. THIS HAS ALL HAPPENED VERY FAST.
I'M NOT MAD. YOUR REASONS TO GO ARE GOOD.
DAISY'S REASONS AREN'T GOOD BUT INGRID IS BASICALLY EVIL.
SHE'S A SEXY HYPNOTIST.
I'M WORRIED ABOUT DAISY.
I'M WORRIED ABOUT YOU.
HOW WILL I FACE THE FUTURE... *ALONE?*
JAR JAR BINKS.
TO BE CONTINUED...

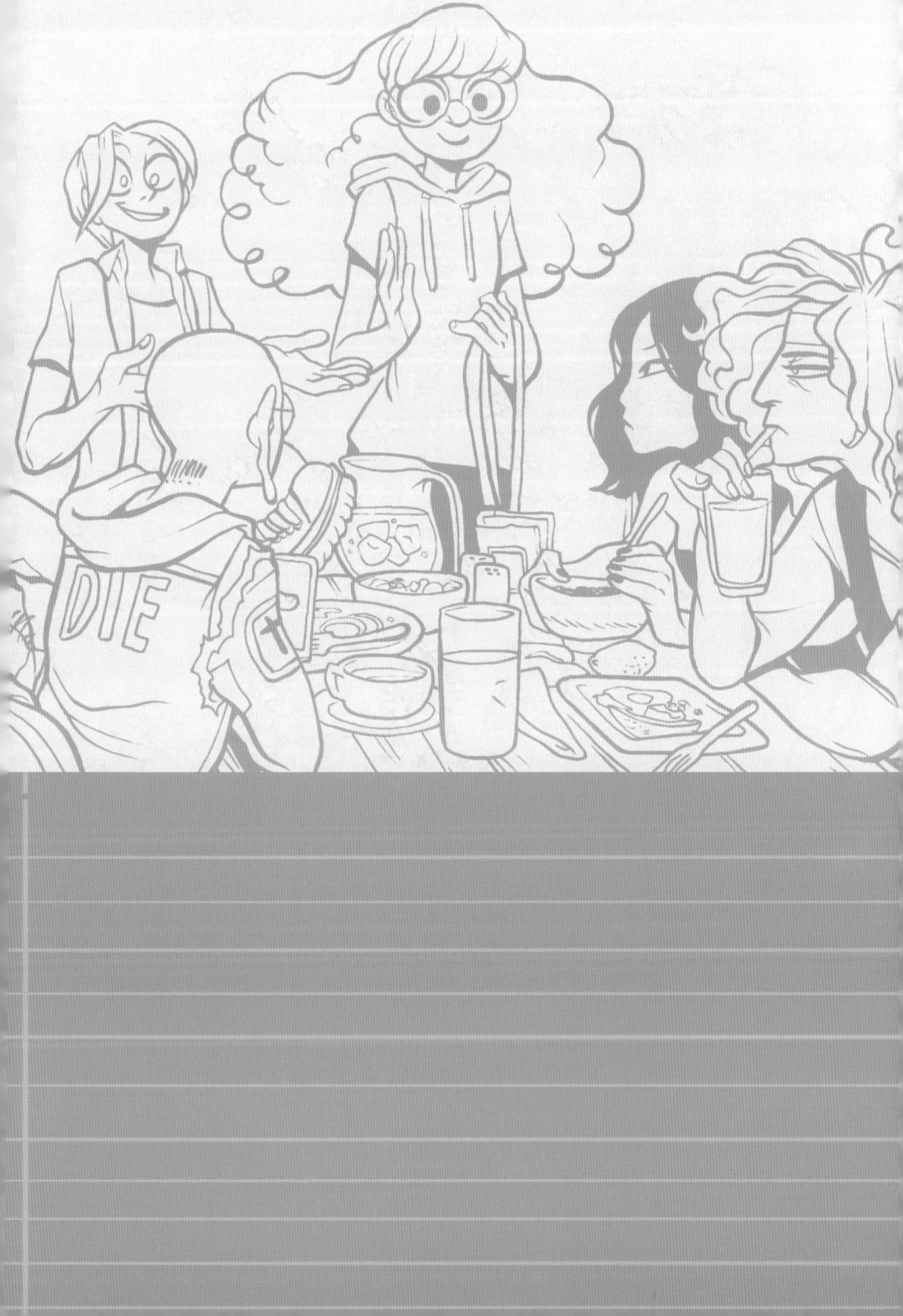
DIE

WHAT WOULD HAVE HAPPENED IF ESTHER, DAISY, AND SUSAN HADN'T BECOME FRIENDS (AND IT WAS CHRISTMAS)?

CREATED & WRITTEN BY
JOHN ALLISON

ILLUSTRATED BY
LISSA TREIMAN

COLORS BY
SARAH STERN

LETTERS BY
JIM CAMPBELL

HOW THE FISHMAN DESPOILED CHRISTMAS

CREATED & WRITTEN BY
JOHN ALLISON

ILLUSTRATED BY
CANAAN GRALL

COLORS BY
JEREMY LAWSON

LETTERS BY
JIM CAMPBELL

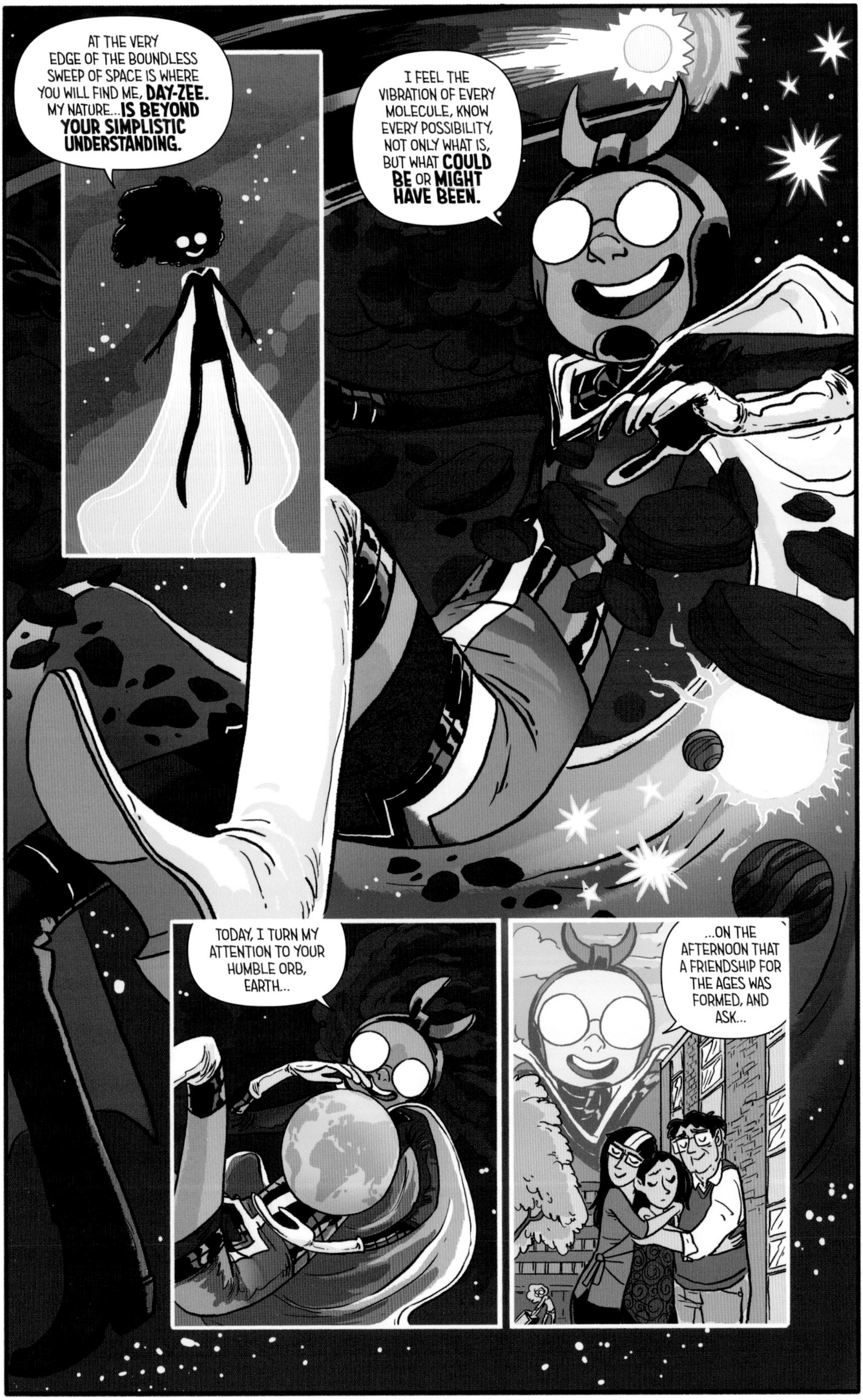
AT THE VERY EDGE OF THE BOUNDLESS SWEEP OF SPACE IS WHERE YOU WILL FIND ME, DAY-ZEE. MY NATURE... IS BEYOND YOUR SIMPLISTIC UNDERSTANDING.
I FEEL THE VIBRATION OF EVERY MOLECULE, KNOW EVERY POSSIBILITY, NOT ONLY WHAT IS, BUT WHAT COULD BE OR MIGHT HAVE BEEN.
TODAY, I TURN MY ATTENTION TO YOUR HUMBLE ORB, EARTH...
...ON THE AFTERNOON THAT A FRIENDSHIP FOR THE AGES WAS FORMED, AND ASK...

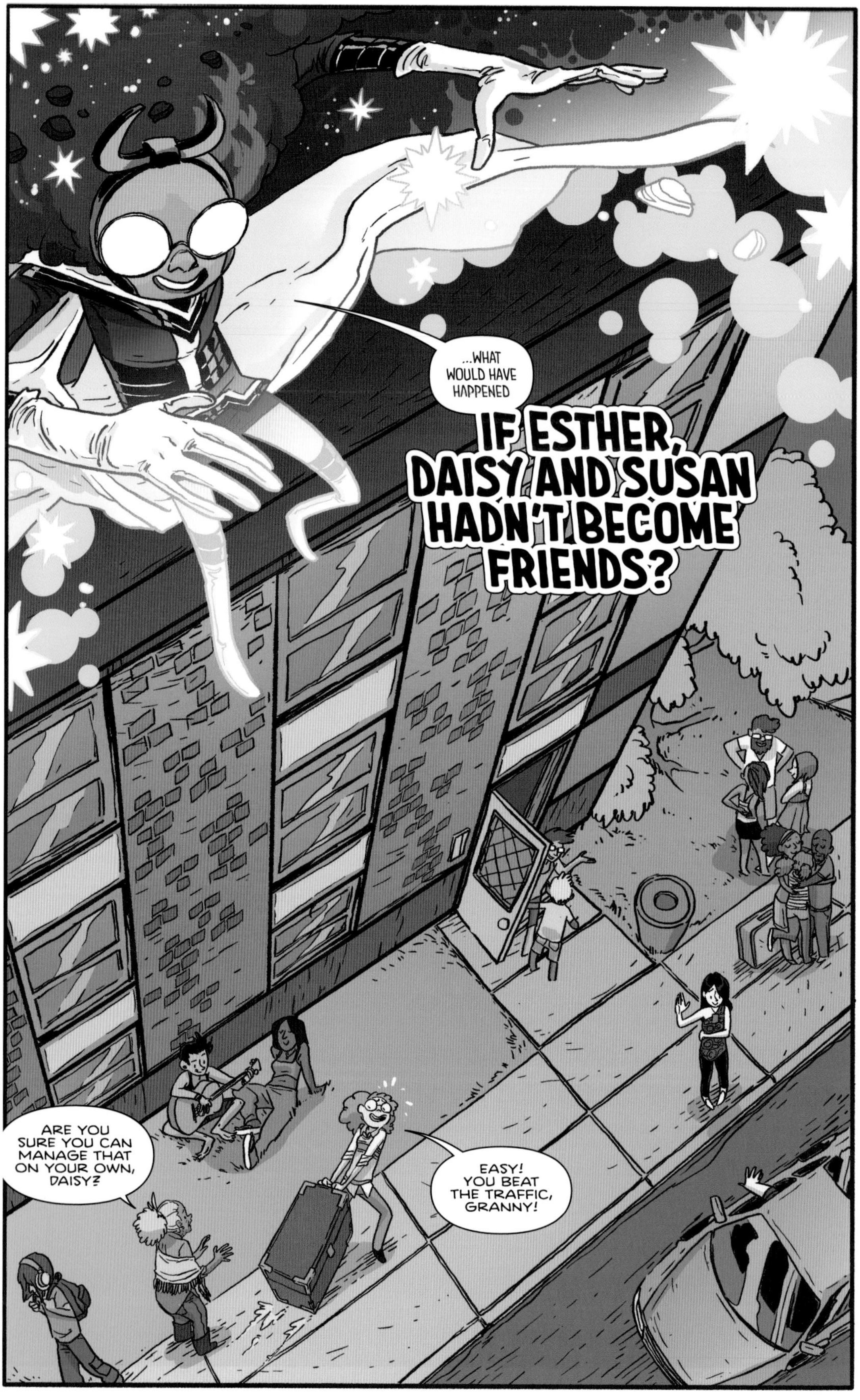
...WHAT WOULD HAVE HAPPENED
IF ESTHER, DAISY AND SUSAN HADN'T BECOME FRIENDS?
ARE YOU SURE YOU CAN MANAGE THAT ON YOUR OWN, DAISY?
EASY! YOU BEAT THE TRAFFIC, GRANNY!

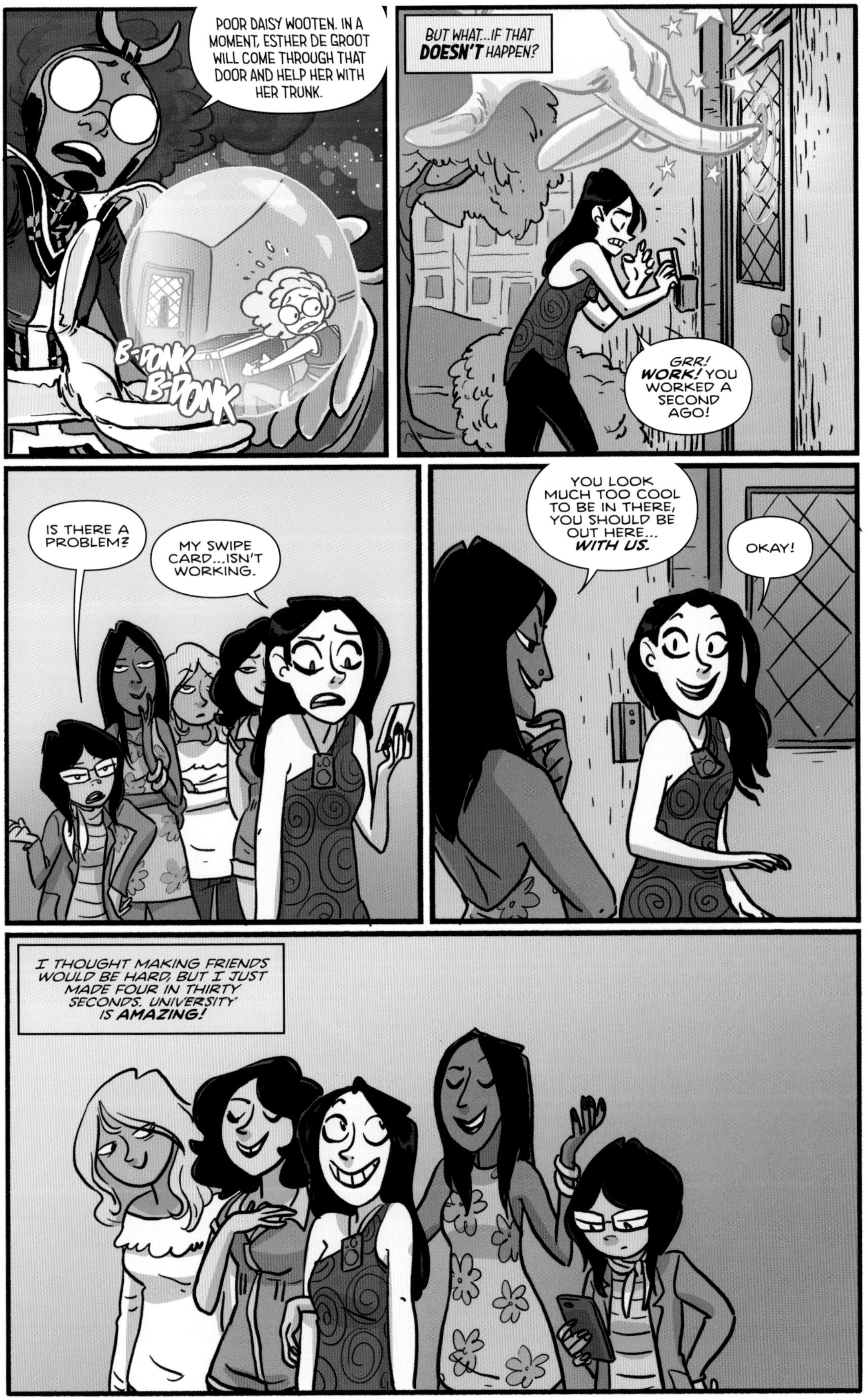
POOR DAISY WOOTEN. IN A MOMENT, ESTHER DE GROOT WILL COME THROUGH THAT DOOR AND HELP HER WITH HER TRUNK.
B-DONK B-DONK
BUT WHAT...IF THAT DOESN'T HAPPEN?
GRR! WORK! YOU WORKED A SECOND AGO!
IS THERE A PROBLEM?
MY SWIPE CARD...ISN'T WORKING.
YOU LOOK MUCH TOO COOL TO BE IN THERE, YOU SHOULD BE OUT HERE... WITH US.
OKAY!
I THOUGHT MAKING FRIENDS WOULD BE HARD, BUT I JUST MADE FOUR IN THIRTY SECONDS. UNIVERSITY IS AMAZING!

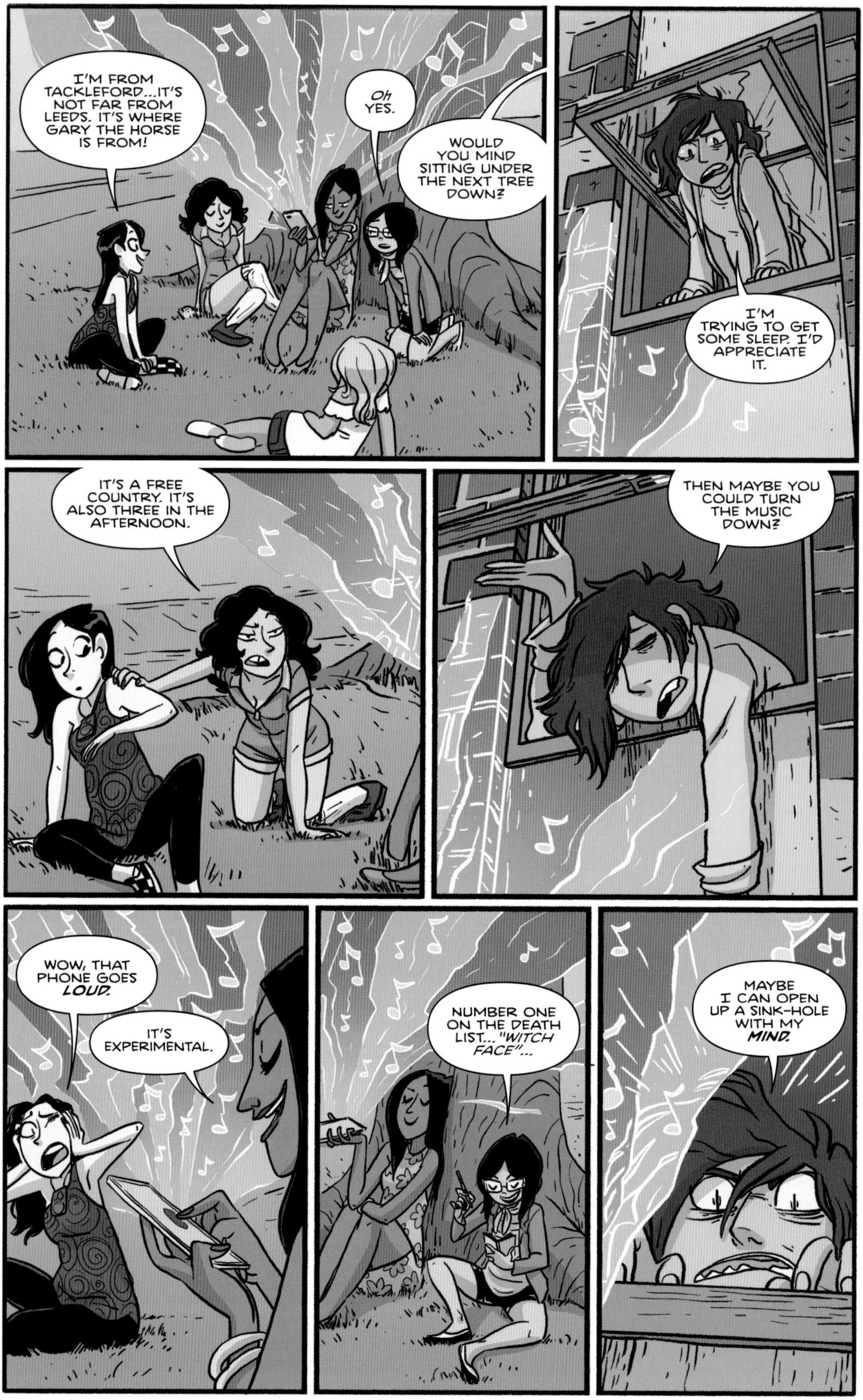
I'M FROM TACKLEFORD...IT'S NOT FAR FROM LEEDS. IT'S WHERE GARY THE HORSE IS FROM!
Oh YES.
WOULD YOU MIND SITTING UNDER THE NEXT TREE DOWN?
I'M TRYING TO GET SOME SLEEP. I'D APPRECIATE IT.
IT'S A FREE COUNTRY. IT'S ALSO THREE IN THE AFTERNOON.
THEN MAYBE YOU COULD TURN THE MUSIC DOWN?
WOW, THAT PHONE GOES ***LOUD.***
IT'S EXPERIMENTAL.
NUMBER ONE ON THE DEATH LIST... *"WITCH FACE"*...
MAYBE I CAN OPEN UP A SINK-HOLE WITH MY ***MIND.***

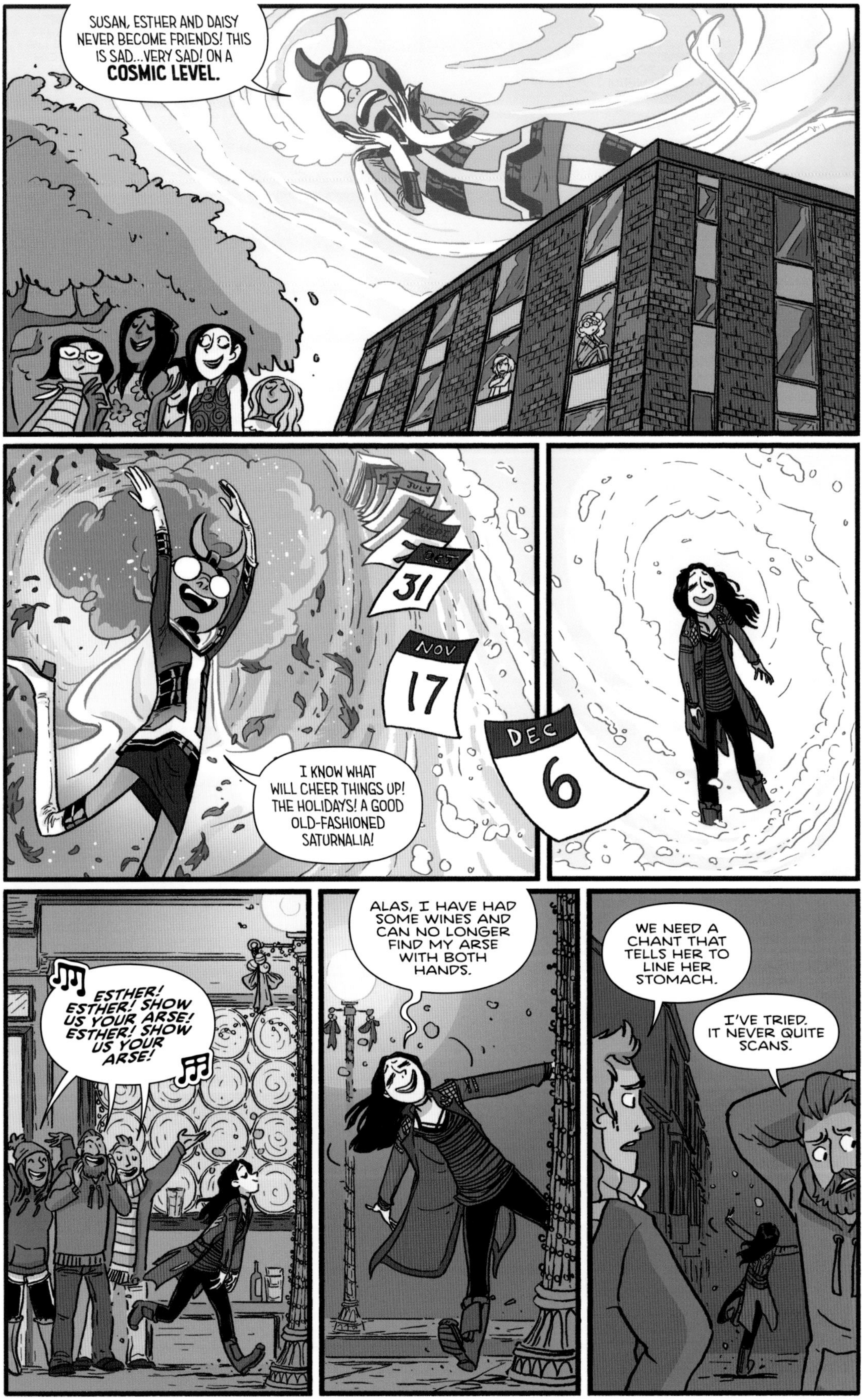
SUSAN, ESTHER AND DAISY NEVER BECOME FRIENDS! THIS IS SAD...VERY SAD! ON A **COSMIC LEVEL.**
JULY
OCT
31
NOV
17
DEC
6
I KNOW WHAT WILL CHEER THINGS UP! THE HOLIDAYS! A GOOD OLD-FASHIONED SATURNALIA!
ESTHER! ESTHER! SHOW US YOUR ARSE! ESTHER! SHOW US YOUR ARSE!
ALAS, I HAVE HAD SOME WINES AND CAN NO LONGER FIND MY ARSE WITH BOTH HANDS.
WE NEED A CHANT THAT TELLS HER TO LINE HER STOMACH.
I'VE TRIED. IT NEVER QUITE SCANS.

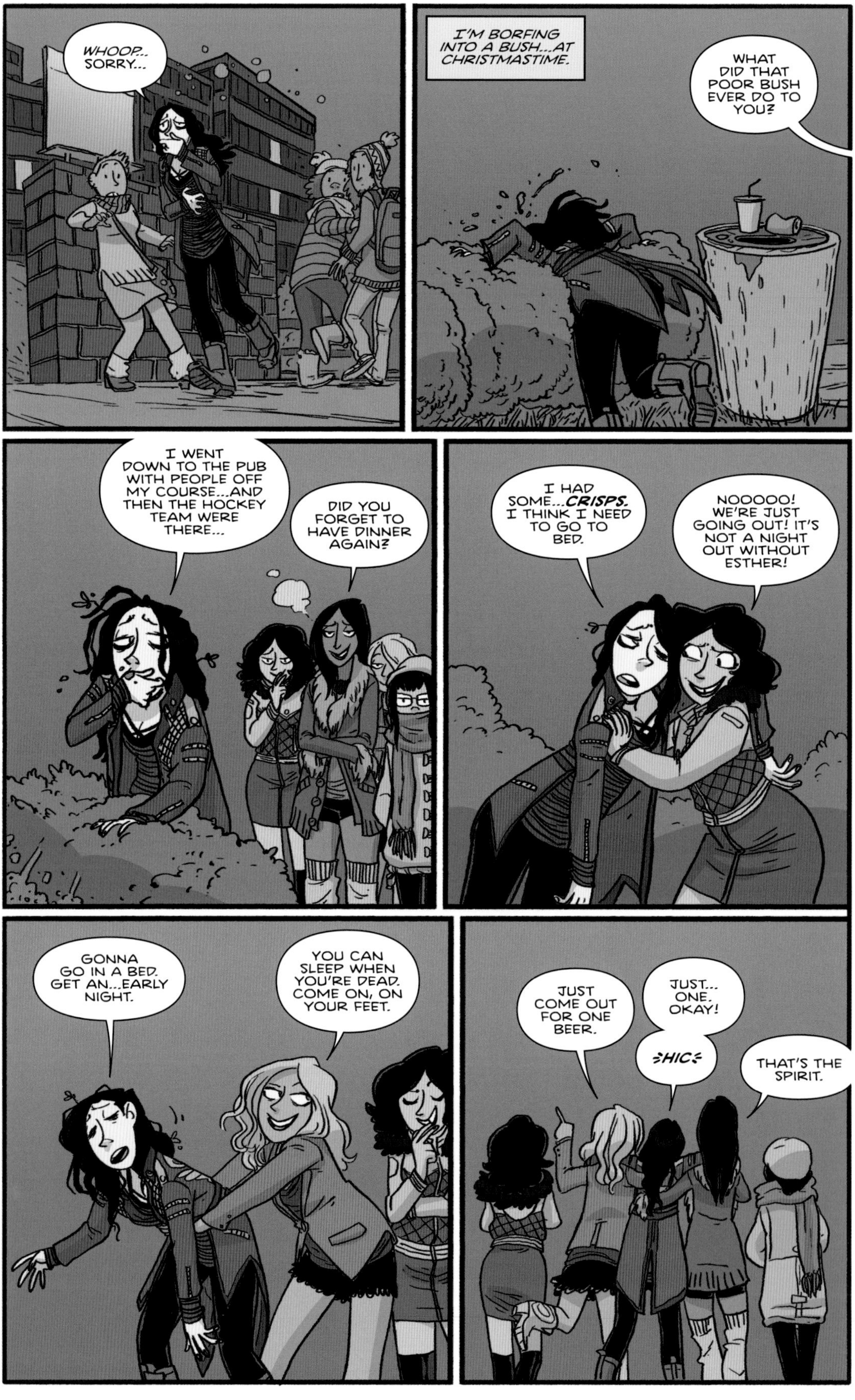
WHOOP.. SORRY...
I'M BORFING INTO A BUSH...AT CHRISTMASTIME.
WHAT DID THAT POOR BUSH EVER DO TO YOU?
I WENT DOWN TO THE PUB WITH PEOPLE OFF MY COURSE...AND THEN THE HOCKEY TEAM WERE THERE...
DID YOU FORGET TO HAVE DINNER AGAIN?
I HAD SOME...CRISPS. I THINK I NEED TO GO TO BED.
NOOOOO! WE'RE JUST GOING OUT! IT'S NOT A NIGHT OUT WITHOUT ESTHER!
GONNA GO IN A BED. GET AN...EARLY NIGHT.
YOU CAN SLEEP WHEN YOU'RE DEAD. COME ON, ON YOUR FEET.
JUST COME OUT FOR ONE BEER.
JUST... ONE. OKAY!
HIC
THAT'S THE SPIRIT.

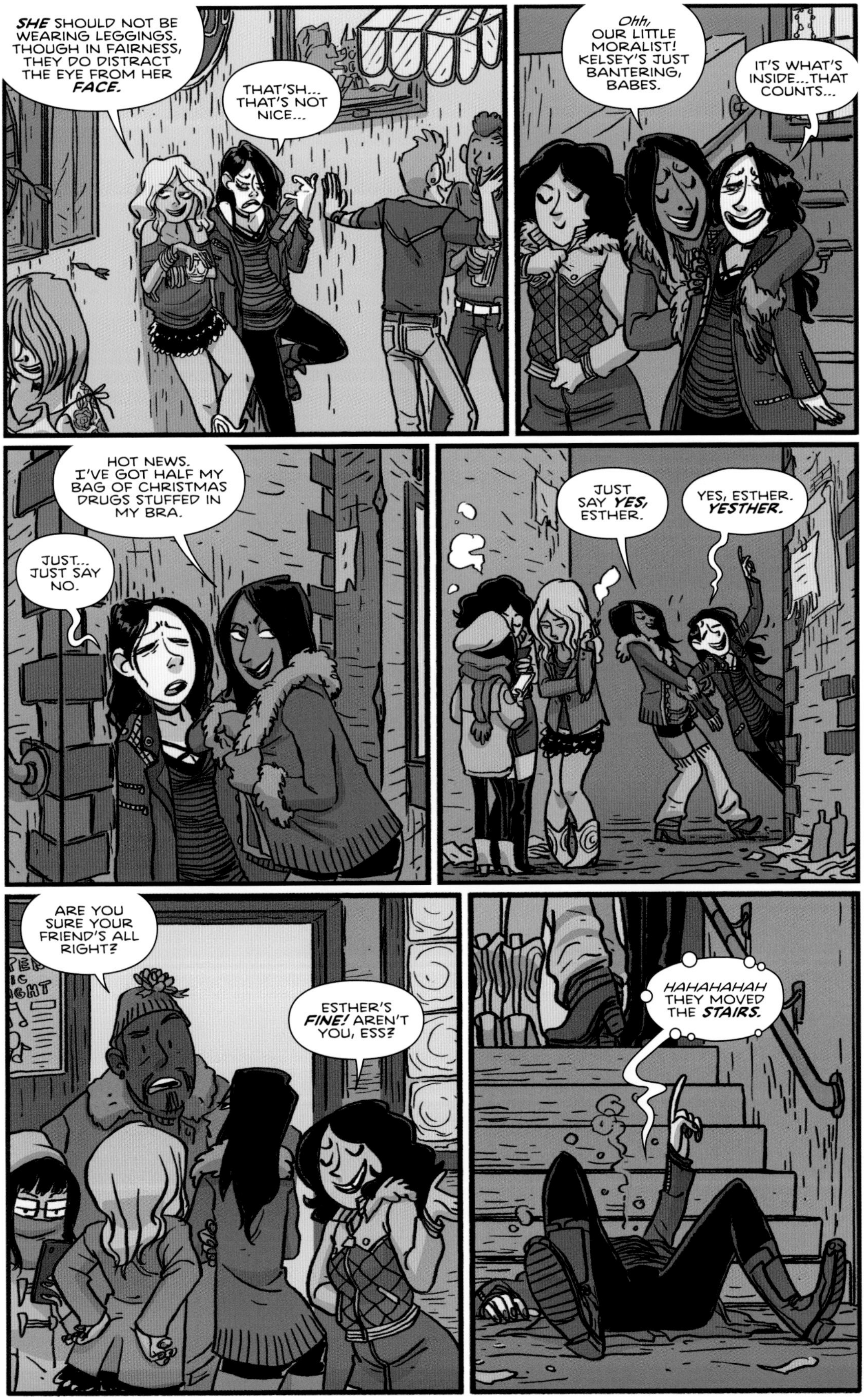
SHE SHOULD NOT BE WEARING LEGGINGS. THOUGH IN FAIRNESS, THEY DO DISTRACT THE EYE FROM HER FACE.
THAT'SH... THAT'S NOT NICE...
Ohh, OUR LITTLE MORALIST! KELSEY'S JUST BANTERING, BABES.
IT'S WHAT'S INSIDE...THAT COUNTS...
HOT NEWS. I'VE GOT HALF MY BAG OF CHRISTMAS DRUGS STUFFED IN MY BRA.
JUST... JUST SAY NO.
JUST SAY YES, ESTHER.
YES, ESTHER. YESTHER.
ARE YOU SURE YOUR FRIEND'S ALL RIGHT?
ESTHER'S FINE! AREN'T YOU, ESS?
HAHAHAHAH THEY MOVED THE STAIRS.

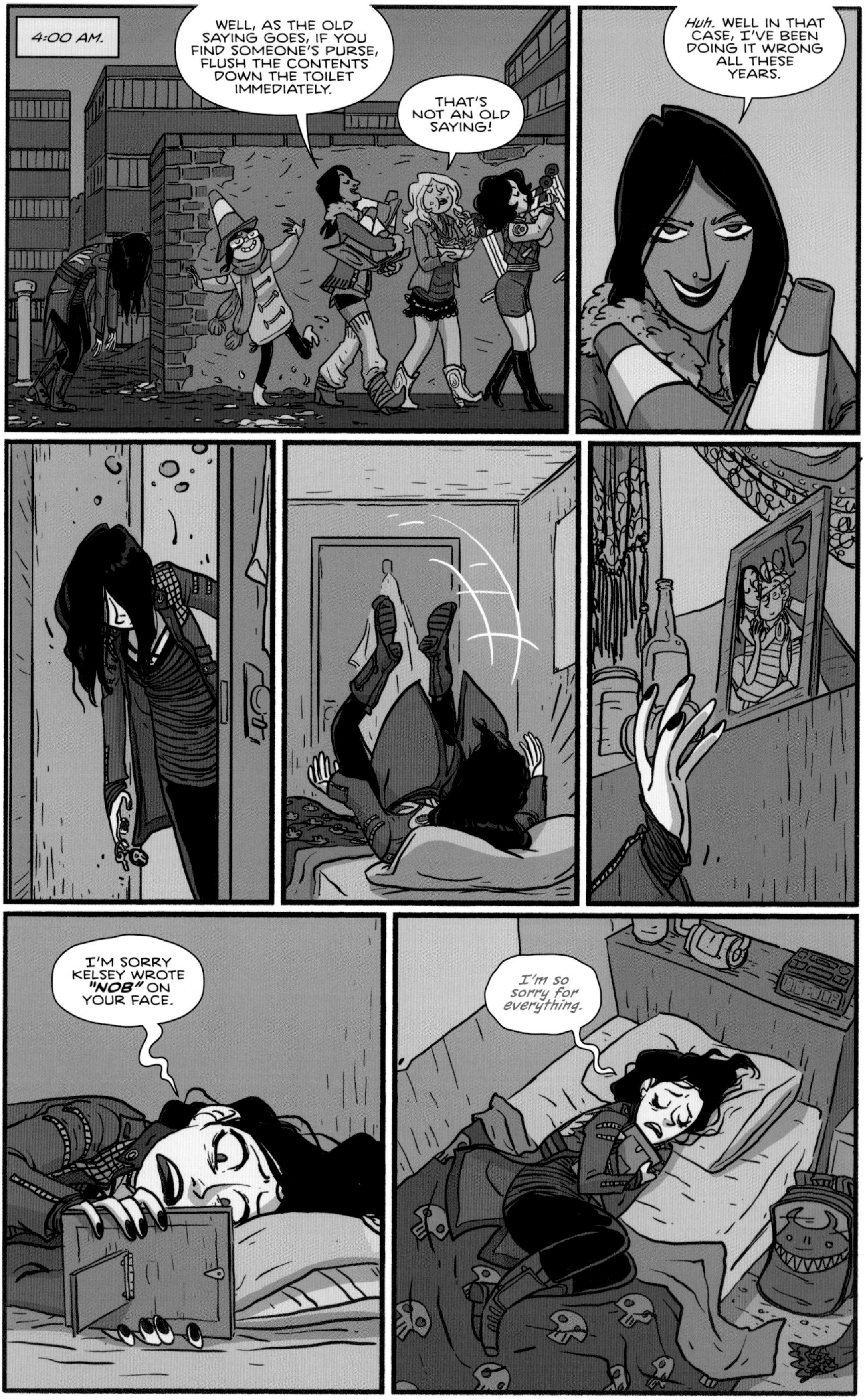
4:00 AM.
WELL, AS THE OLD SAYING GOES, IF YOU FIND SOMEONE'S PURSE, FLUSH THE CONTENTS DOWN THE TOILET IMMEDIATELY.
THAT'S NOT AN OLD SAYING!
Huh. WELL IN THAT CASE, I'VE BEEN DOING IT WRONG ALL THESE YEARS.
I'M SORRY KELSEY WROTE "NOB" ON YOUR FACE.
I'm so sorry for everything.

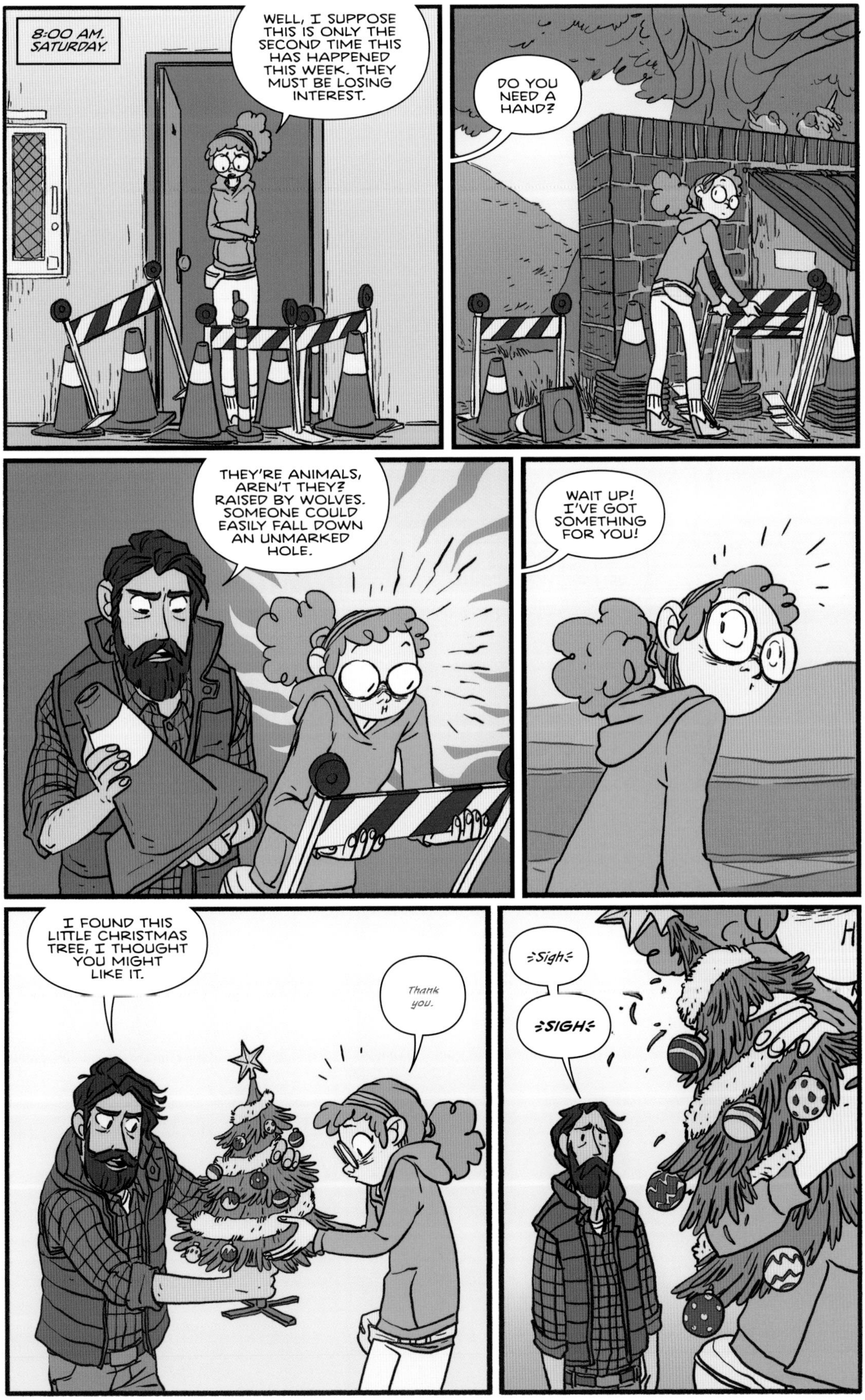
8:00 AM. SATURDAY.
WELL, I SUPPOSE THIS IS ONLY THE SECOND TIME THIS HAS HAPPENED THIS WEEK. THEY MUST BE LOSING INTEREST.
DO YOU NEED A HAND?
THEY'RE ANIMALS, AREN'T THEY? RAISED BY WOLVES. SOMEONE COULD EASILY FALL DOWN AN UNMARKED HOLE.
WAIT UP! I'VE GOT SOMETHING FOR YOU!
I FOUND THIS LITTLE CHRISTMAS TREE, I THOUGHT YOU MIGHT LIKE IT.
Thank you.
Sigh
SIGH

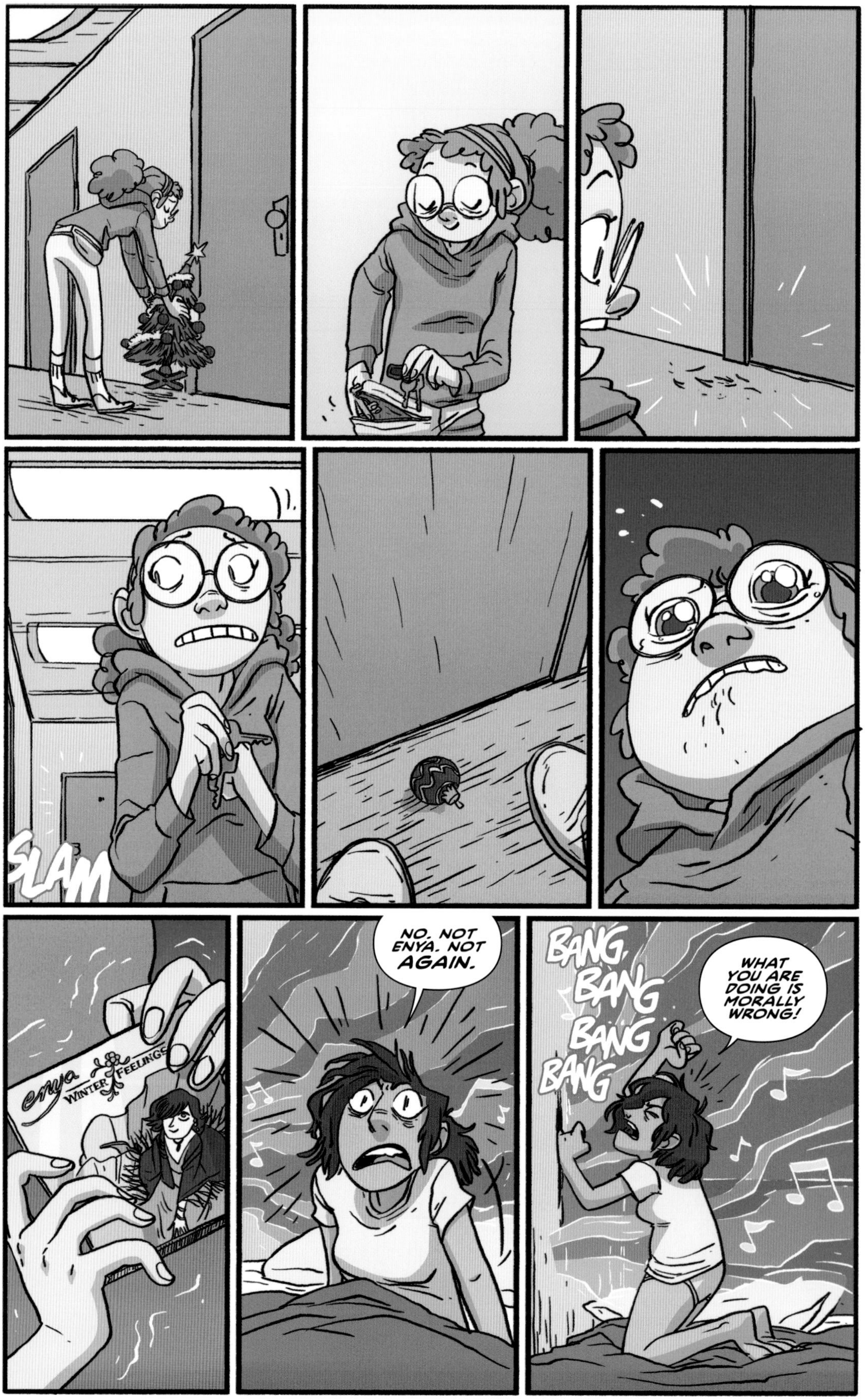
SLAM
enya
WINTER FEELINGS
NO. NOT ENYA. NOT AGAIN.
BANG BANG BANG BANG
WHAT YOU ARE DOING IS MORALLY WRONG!

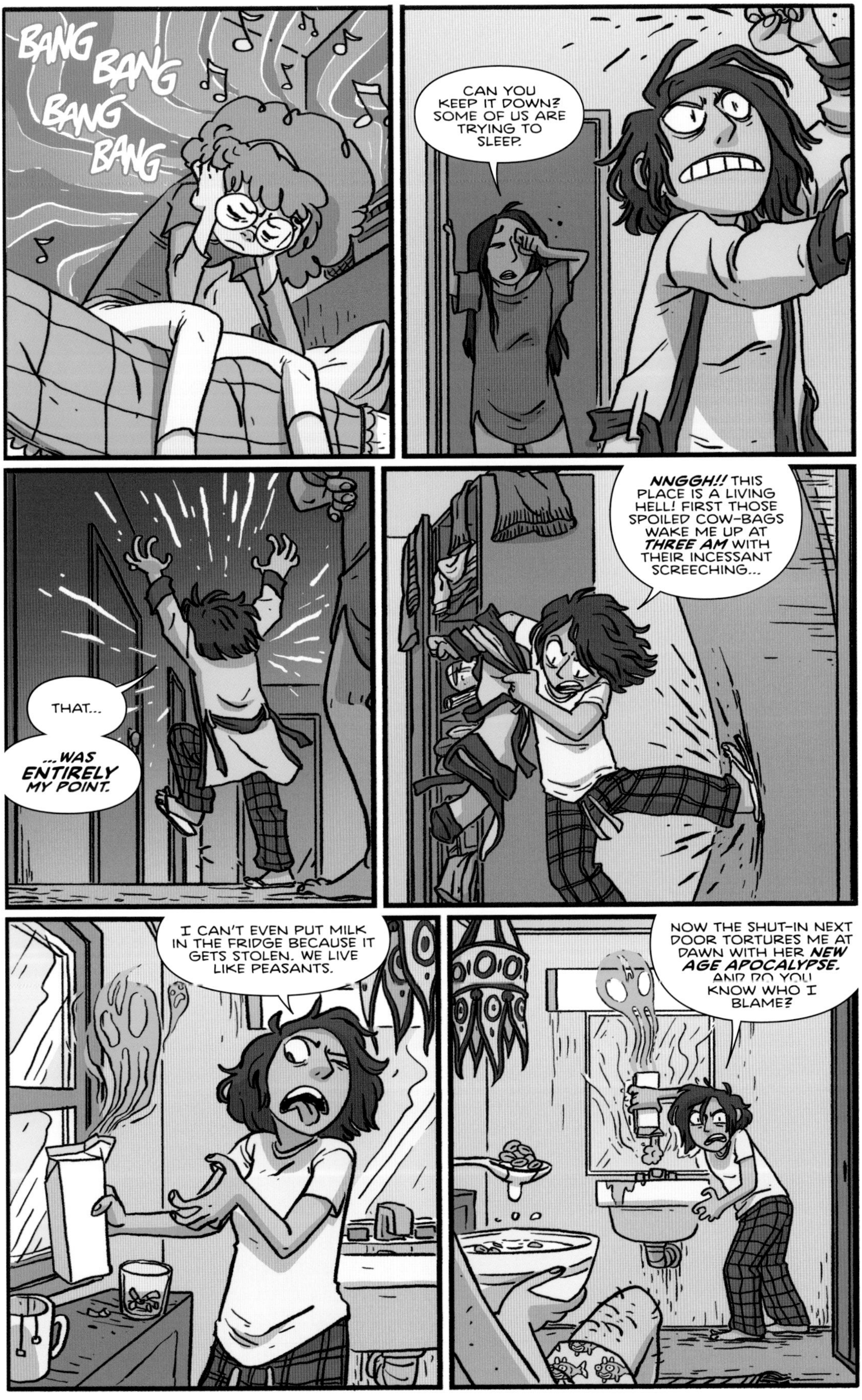
BANG BANG BANG BANG
CAN YOU KEEP IT DOWN? SOME OF US ARE TRYING TO SLEEP.
THAT...
...WAS ENTIRELY MY POINT.
NNGGH!! THIS PLACE IS A LIVING HELL! FIRST THOSE SPOILED COW-BAGS WAKE ME UP AT THREE AM WITH THEIR INCESSANT SCREECHING...
I CAN'T EVEN PUT MILK IN THE FRIDGE BECAUSE IT GETS STOLEN. WE LIVE LIKE PEASANTS.
NOW THE SHUT-IN NEXT DOOR TORTURES ME AT DAWN WITH HER NEW AGE APOCALYPSE. AND DO YOU KNOW WHO I BLAME?

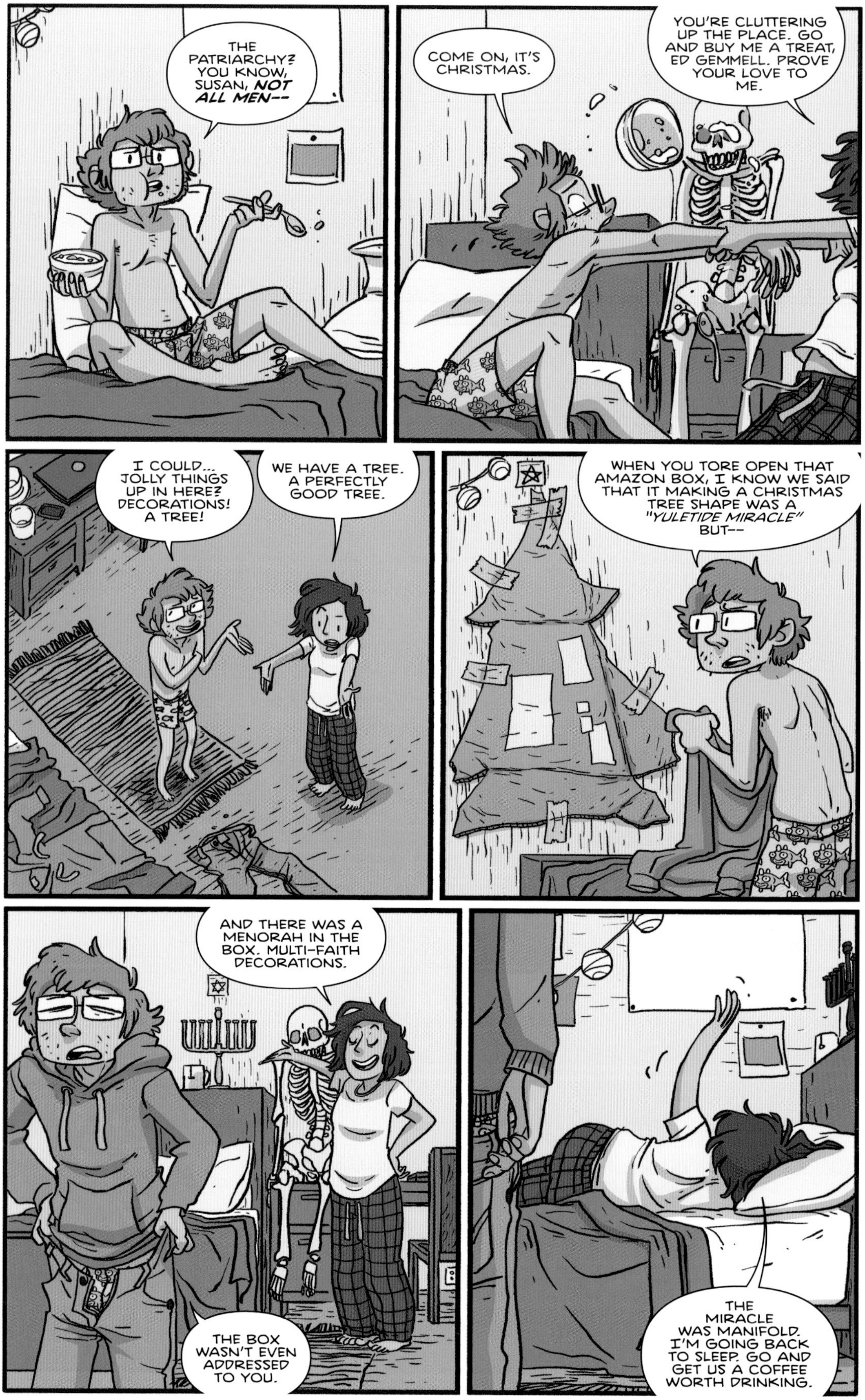
THE PATRIARCHY? YOU KNOW, SUSAN, **NOT ALL MEN--**
COME ON, IT'S CHRISTMAS.
YOU'RE CLUTTERING UP THE PLACE. GO AND BUY ME A TREAT, ED GEMMELL. PROVE YOUR LOVE TO ME.
I COULD... JOLLY THINGS UP IN HERE? DECORATIONS! A TREE!
WE HAVE A TREE. A PERFECTLY GOOD TREE.
WHEN YOU TORE OPEN THAT AMAZON BOX, I KNOW WE SAID THAT IT MAKING A CHRISTMAS TREE SHAPE WAS A *"YULETIDE MIRACLE"* BUT--
AND THERE WAS A MENORAH IN THE BOX. MULTI-FAITH DECORATIONS.
THE BOX WASN'T EVEN ADDRESSED TO YOU.
THE MIRACLE WAS MANIFOLD. I'M GOING BACK TO SLEEP. GO AND GET US A COFFEE WORTH DRINKING.

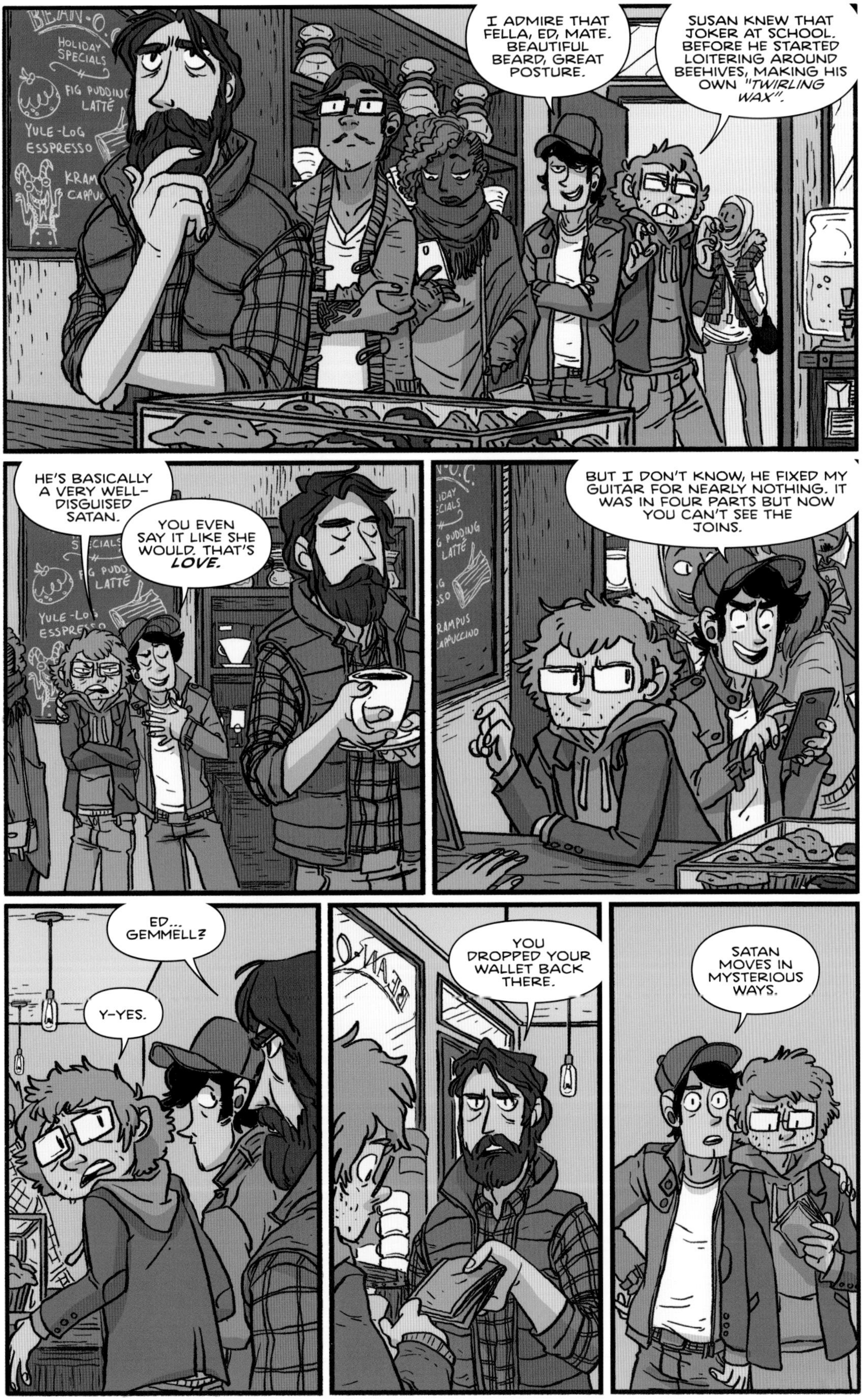
BEAN-O.C.
HOLIDAY SPECIALS
FIG PUDDING LATTÉ
YULE-LOG ESSPRESSO
I ADMIRE THAT FELLA, ED, MATE. BEAUTIFUL BEARD, GREAT POSTURE.
SUSAN KNEW THAT JOKER AT SCHOOL. BEFORE HE STARTED LOITERING AROUND BEEHIVES, MAKING HIS OWN *"TWIRLING WAX"*.
HE'S BASICALLY A VERY WELL-DISGUISED SATAN.
YOU EVEN SAY IT LIKE SHE WOULD. THAT'S ***LOVE.***
BUT I DON'T KNOW, HE FIXED MY GUITAR FOR NEARLY NOTHING. IT WAS IN FOUR PARTS BUT NOW YOU CAN'T SEE THE JOINS.
KRAMPUS CAPPUCCINO
ED... GEMMELL?
Y-YES.
YOU DROPPED YOUR WALLET BACK THERE.
SATAN MOVES IN MYSTERIOUS WAYS.

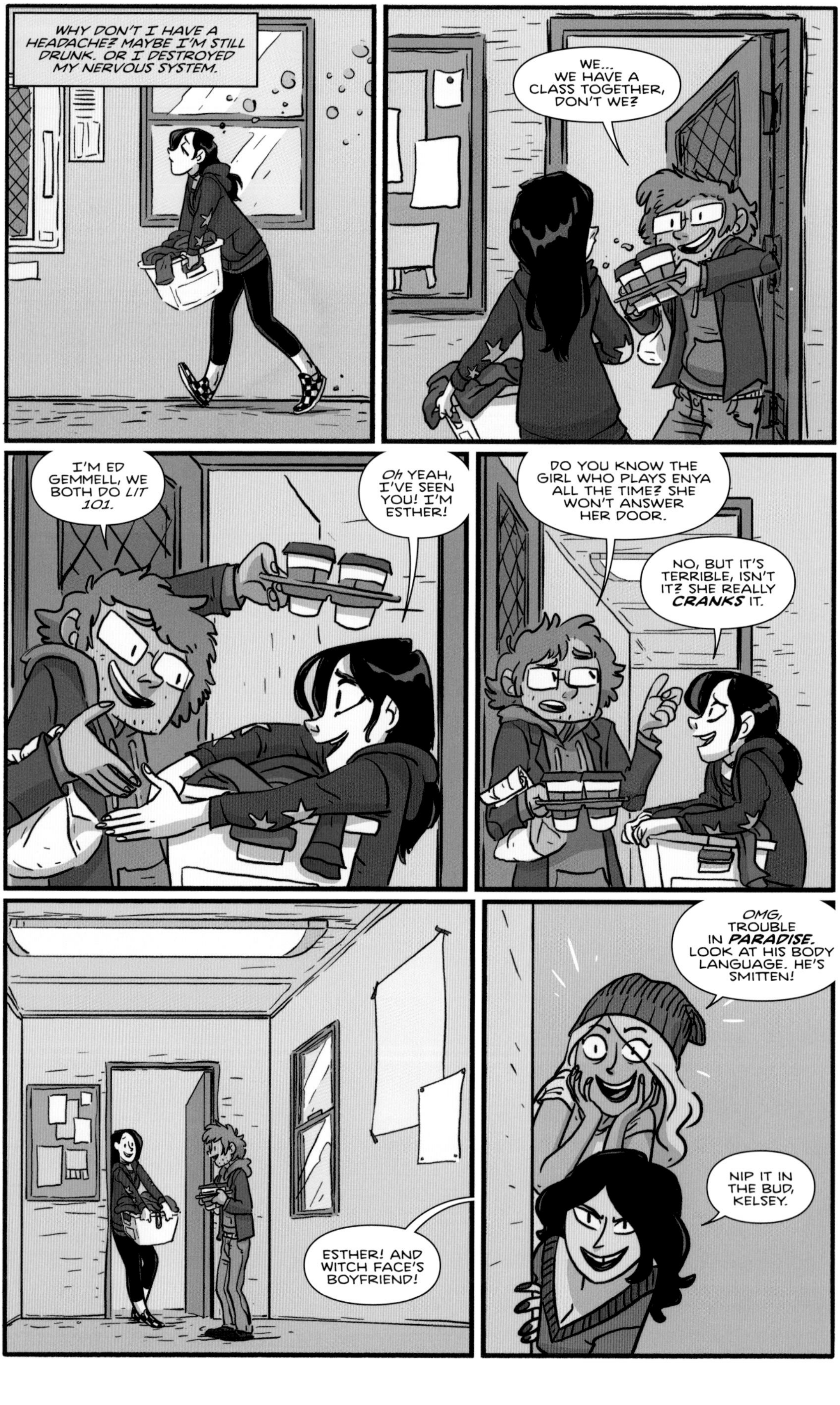
WHY DON'T I HAVE A HEADACHE? MAYBE I'M STILL DRUNK. OR I DESTROYED MY NERVOUS SYSTEM.
WE... WE HAVE A CLASS TOGETHER, DON'T WE?
I'M ED GEMMELL, WE BOTH DO LIT 101.
Oh YEAH, I'VE SEEN YOU! I'M ESTHER!
DO YOU KNOW THE GIRL WHO PLAYS ENYA ALL THE TIME? SHE WON'T ANSWER HER DOOR.
NO, BUT IT'S TERRIBLE, ISN'T IT? SHE REALLY CRANKS IT.
ESTHER! AND WITCH FACE'S BOYFRIEND!
OMG, TROUBLE IN PARADISE. LOOK AT HIS BODY LANGUAGE. HE'S SMITTEN!
NIP IT IN THE BUD, KELSEY.

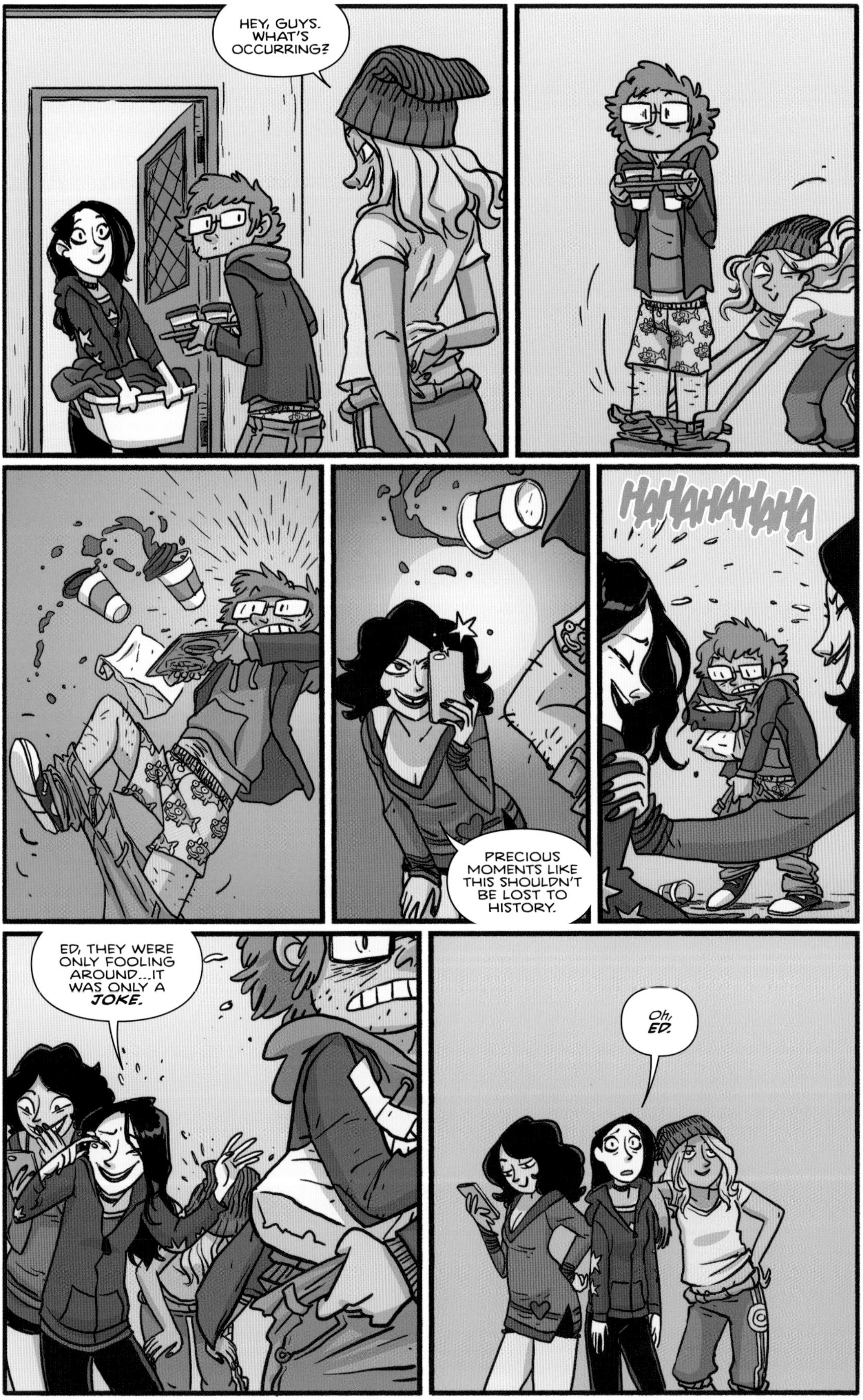
HEY, GUYS. WHAT'S OCCURRING?
HAHAHAHAHA
PRECIOUS MOMENTS LIKE THIS SHOULDN'T BE LOST TO HISTORY.
ED, THEY WERE ONLY FOOLING AROUND... IT WAS ONLY A JOKE.
Oh, ED.

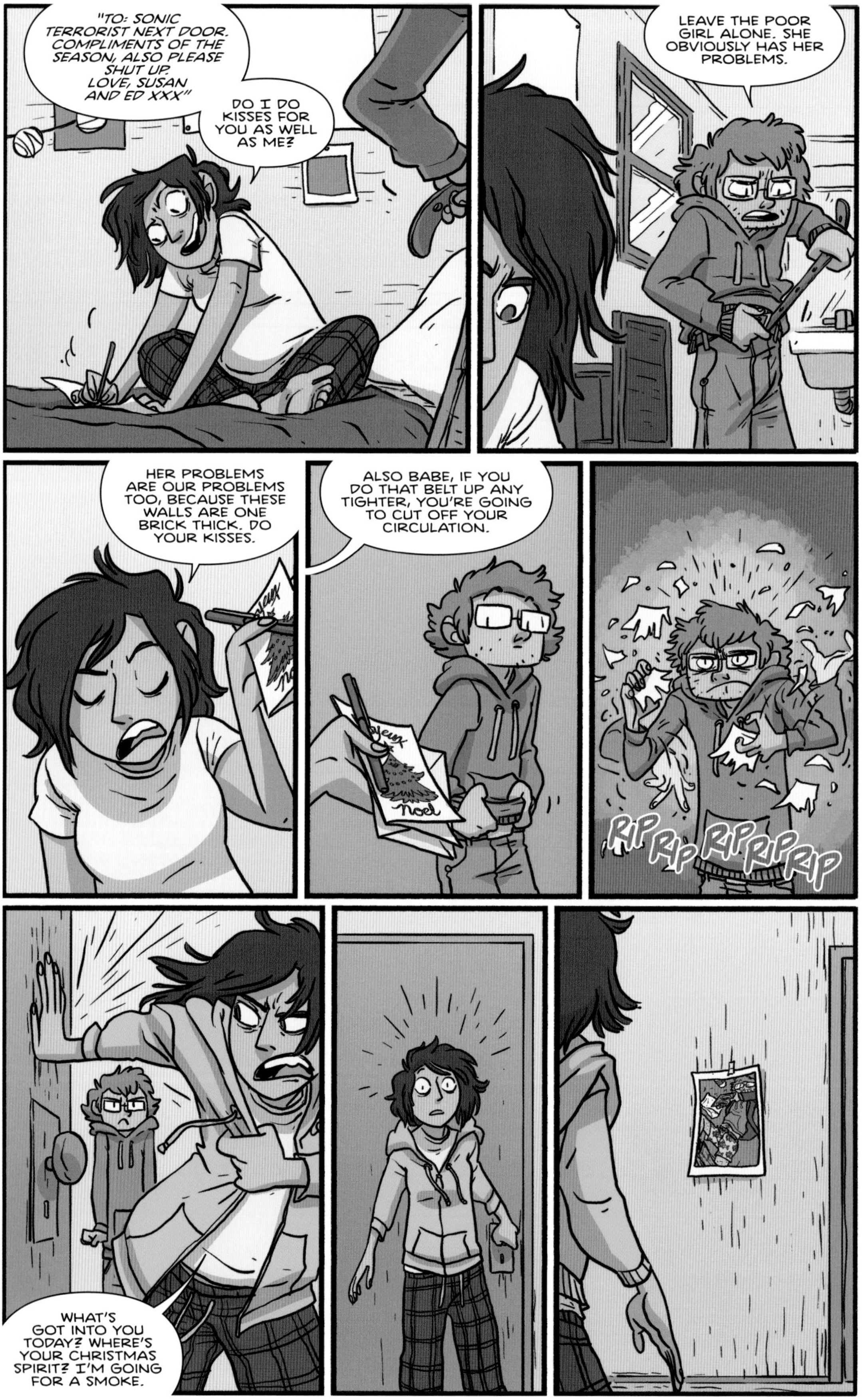
"TO: SONIC TERRORIST NEXT DOOR. COMPLIMENTS OF THE SEASON, ALSO PLEASE SHUT UP. LOVE, SUSAN AND ED XXX"
DO I DO KISSES FOR YOU AS WELL AS ME?
LEAVE THE POOR GIRL ALONE. SHE OBVIOUSLY HAS HER PROBLEMS.
HER PROBLEMS ARE OUR PROBLEMS TOO, BECAUSE THESE WALLS ARE ONE BRICK THICK. DO YOUR KISSES.
ALSO BABE, IF YOU DO THAT BELT UP ANY TIGHTER, YOU'RE GOING TO CUT OFF YOUR CIRCULATION.
RIP RIP RIP RIP RIP
WHAT'S GOT INTO YOU TODAY? WHERE'S YOUR CHRISTMAS SPIRIT? I'M GOING FOR A SMOKE.

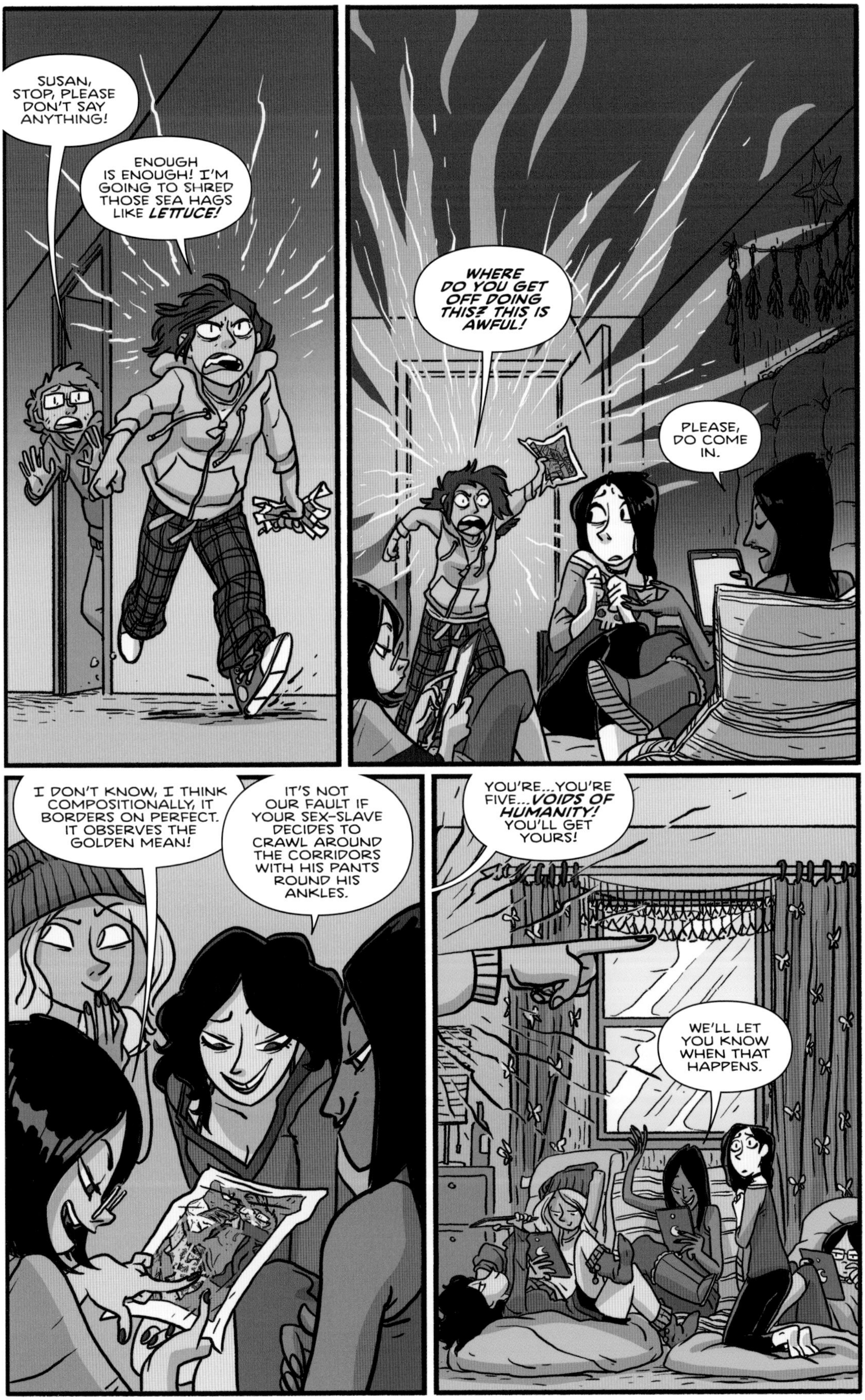
SUSAN, STOP, PLEASE DON'T SAY ANYTHING!
ENOUGH IS ENOUGH! I'M GOING TO SHRED THOSE SEA HAGS LIKE *LETTUCE!*
WHERE DO YOU GET OFF DOING THIS? THIS IS AWFUL!
PLEASE, DO COME IN.
I DON'T KNOW, I THINK COMPOSITIONALLY, IT BORDERS ON PERFECT. IT OBSERVES THE GOLDEN MEAN!
IT'S NOT OUR FAULT IF YOUR SEX-SLAVE DECIDES TO CRAWL AROUND THE CORRIDORS WITH HIS PANTS ROUND HIS ANKLES.
YOU'RE...YOU'RE FIVE...*VOIDS OF HUMANITY!* YOU'LL GET YOURS!
WE'LL LET YOU KNOW WHEN THAT HAPPENS.

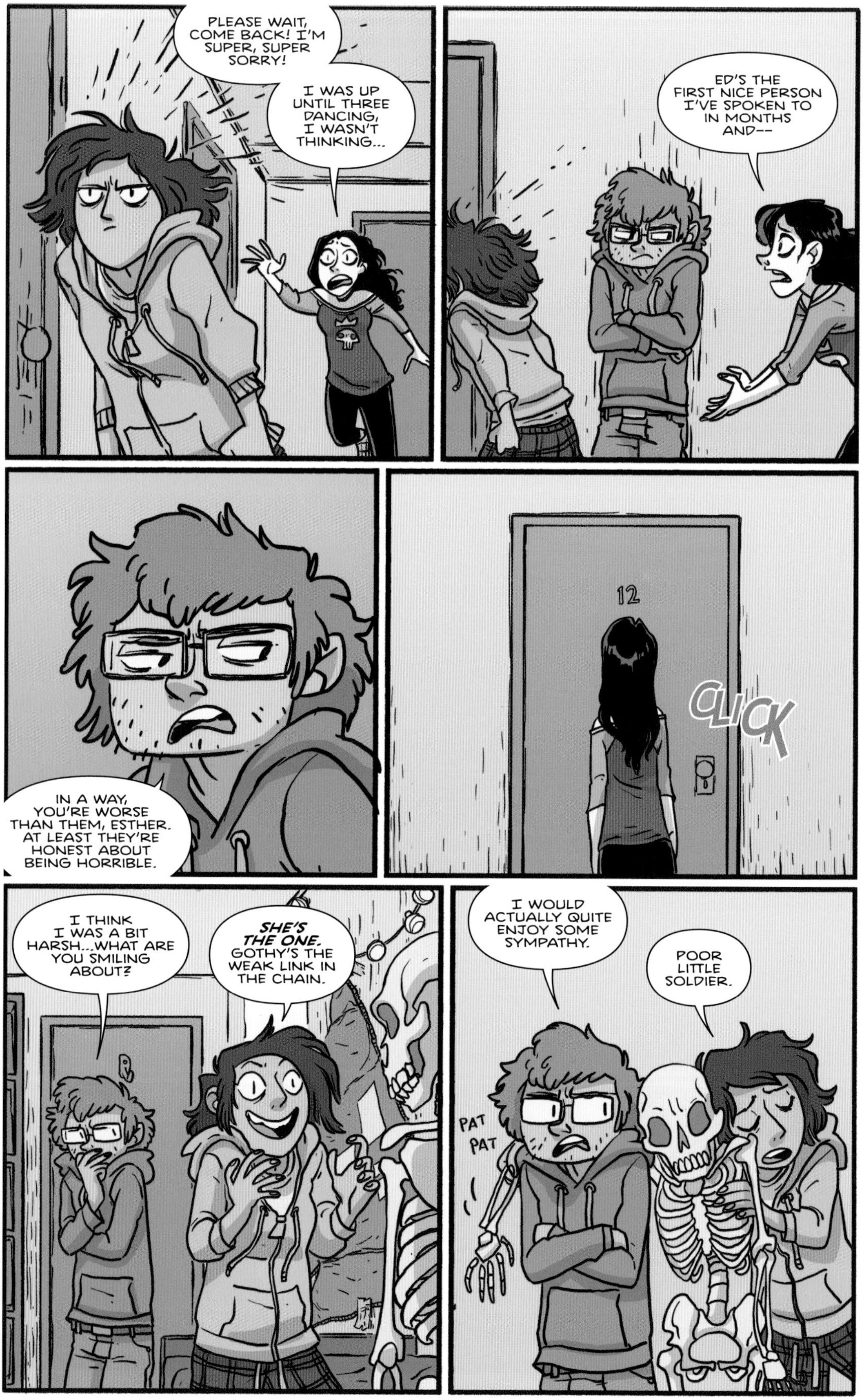
PLEASE WAIT, COME BACK! I'M SUPER, SUPER SORRY!
I WAS UP UNTIL THREE DANCING, I WASN'T THINKING...
ED'S THE FIRST NICE PERSON I'VE SPOKEN TO IN MONTHS AND--
IN A WAY, YOU'RE WORSE THAN THEM, ESTHER. AT LEAST THEY'RE HONEST ABOUT BEING HORRIBLE.
12
CLICK
I THINK I WAS A BIT HARSH...WHAT ARE YOU SMILING ABOUT?
SHE'S THE ONE. GOTHY'S THE WEAK LINK IN THE CHAIN.
I WOULD ACTUALLY QUITE ENJOY SOME SYMPATHY.
POOR LITTLE SOLDIER.
PAT PAT

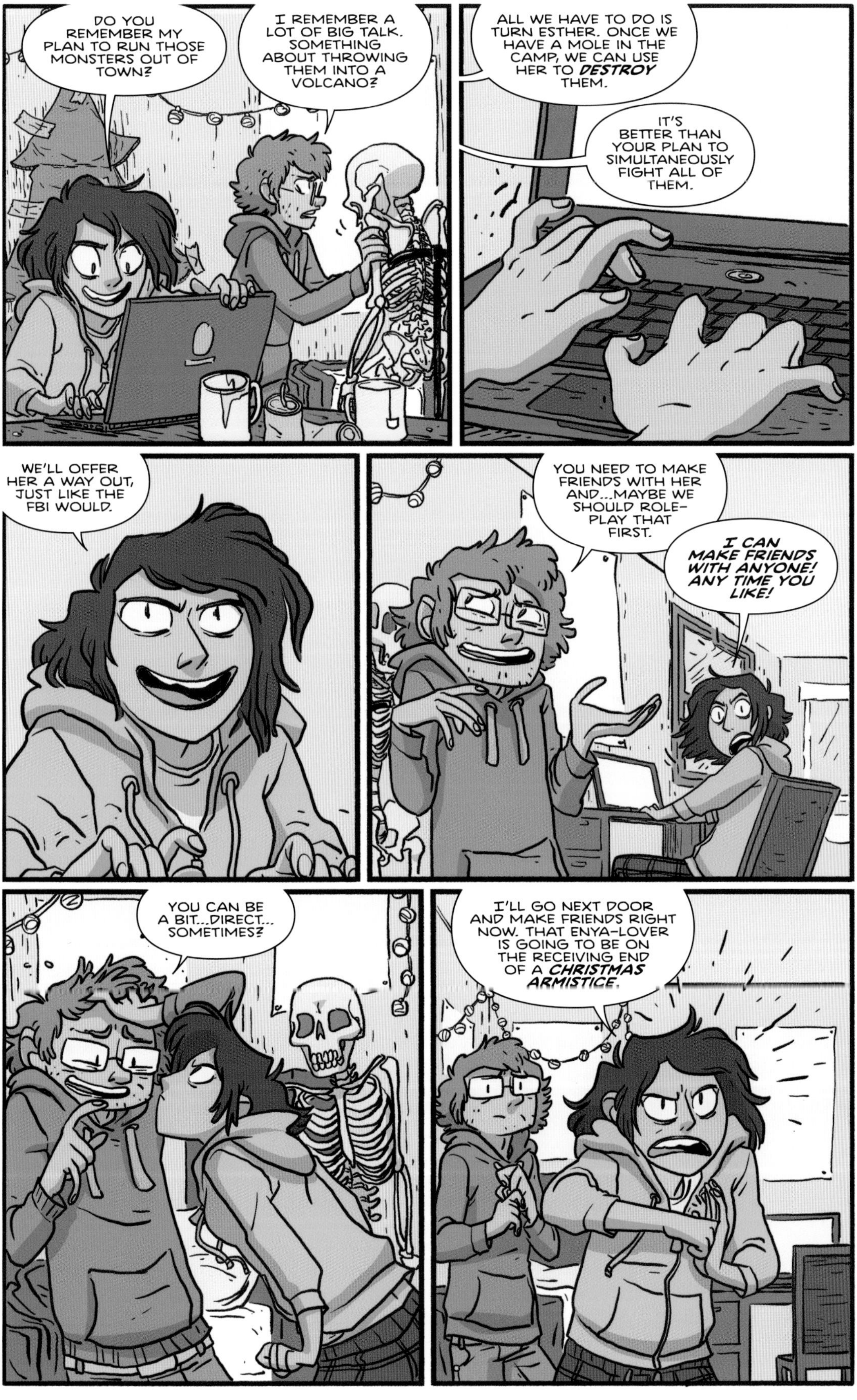
DO YOU REMEMBER MY PLAN TO RUN THOSE MONSTERS OUT OF TOWN?
I REMEMBER A LOT OF BIG TALK. SOMETHING ABOUT THROWING THEM INTO A VOLCANO?
ALL WE HAVE TO DO IS TURN ESTHER. ONCE WE HAVE A MOLE IN THE CAMP, WE CAN USE HER TO *DESTROY* THEM.
IT'S BETTER THAN YOUR PLAN TO SIMULTANEOUSLY FIGHT ALL OF THEM.
WE'LL OFFER HER A WAY OUT, JUST LIKE THE FBI WOULD.
YOU NEED TO MAKE FRIENDS WITH HER AND...MAYBE WE SHOULD ROLE-PLAY THAT FIRST.
I CAN MAKE FRIENDS WITH ANYONE! ANY TIME YOU LIKE!
YOU CAN BE A BIT...DIRECT... SOMETIMES?
I'LL GO NEXT DOOR AND MAKE FRIENDS RIGHT NOW. THAT ENYA-LOVER IS GOING TO BE ON THE RECEIVING END OF A *CHRISTMAS ARMISTICE*.

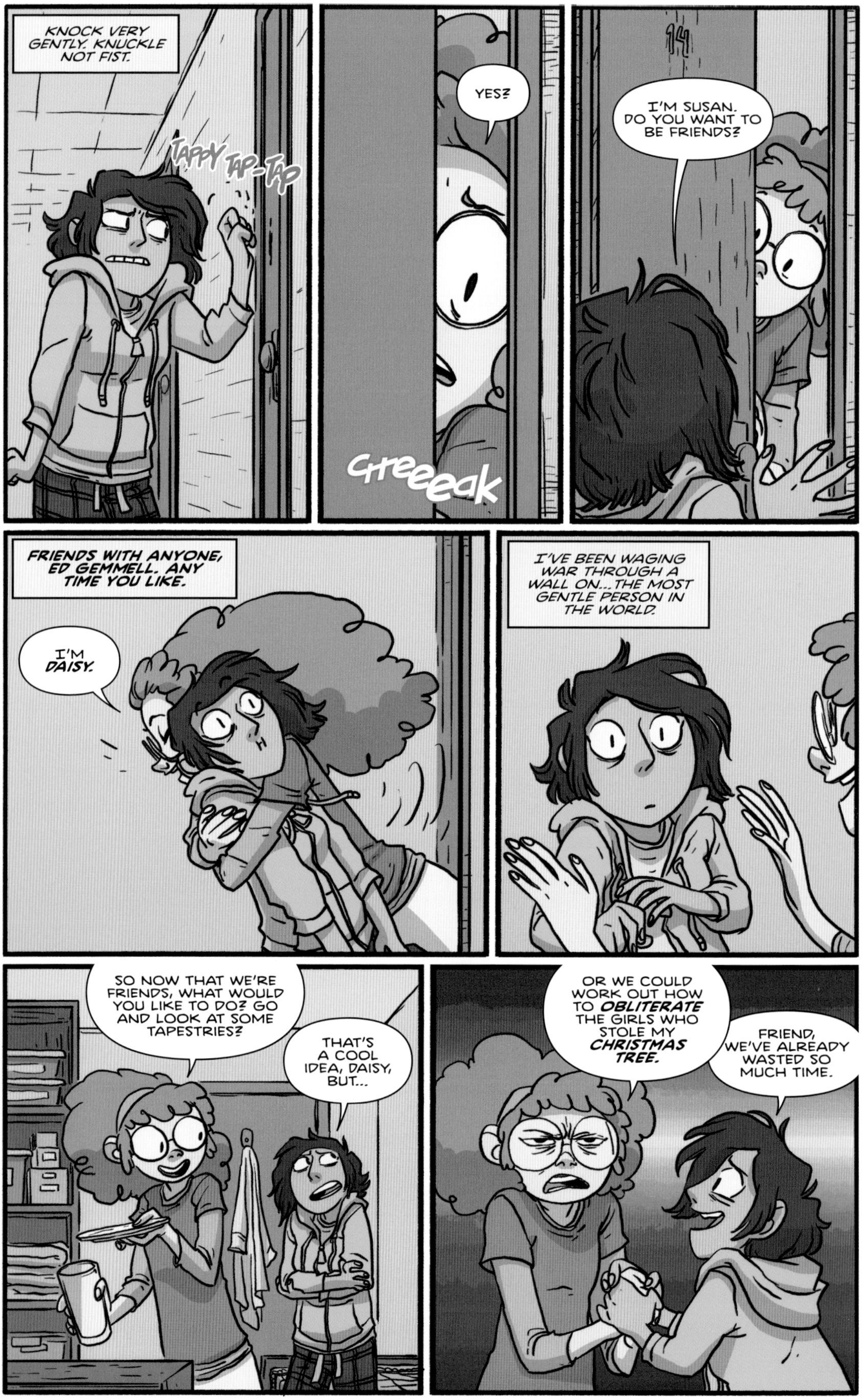

KNOCK VERY GENTLY. KNUCKLE NOT FIST.
TAPPY TAP-TAP
YES?
CREEEAK
I'M SUSAN. DO YOU WANT TO BE FRIENDS?
FRIENDS WITH ANYONE, ED GEMMELL. ANY TIME YOU LIKE.
I'M DAISY.
I'VE BEEN WAGING WAR THROUGH A WALL ON... THE MOST GENTLE PERSON IN THE WORLD.
SO NOW THAT WE'RE FRIENDS, WHAT WOULD YOU LIKE TO DO? GO AND LOOK AT SOME TAPESTRIES?
THAT'S A COOL IDEA, DAISY, BUT...
OR WE COULD WORK OUT HOW TO OBLITERATE THE GIRLS WHO STOLE MY CHRISTMAS TREE.
FRIEND, WE'VE ALREADY WASTED SO MUCH TIME.

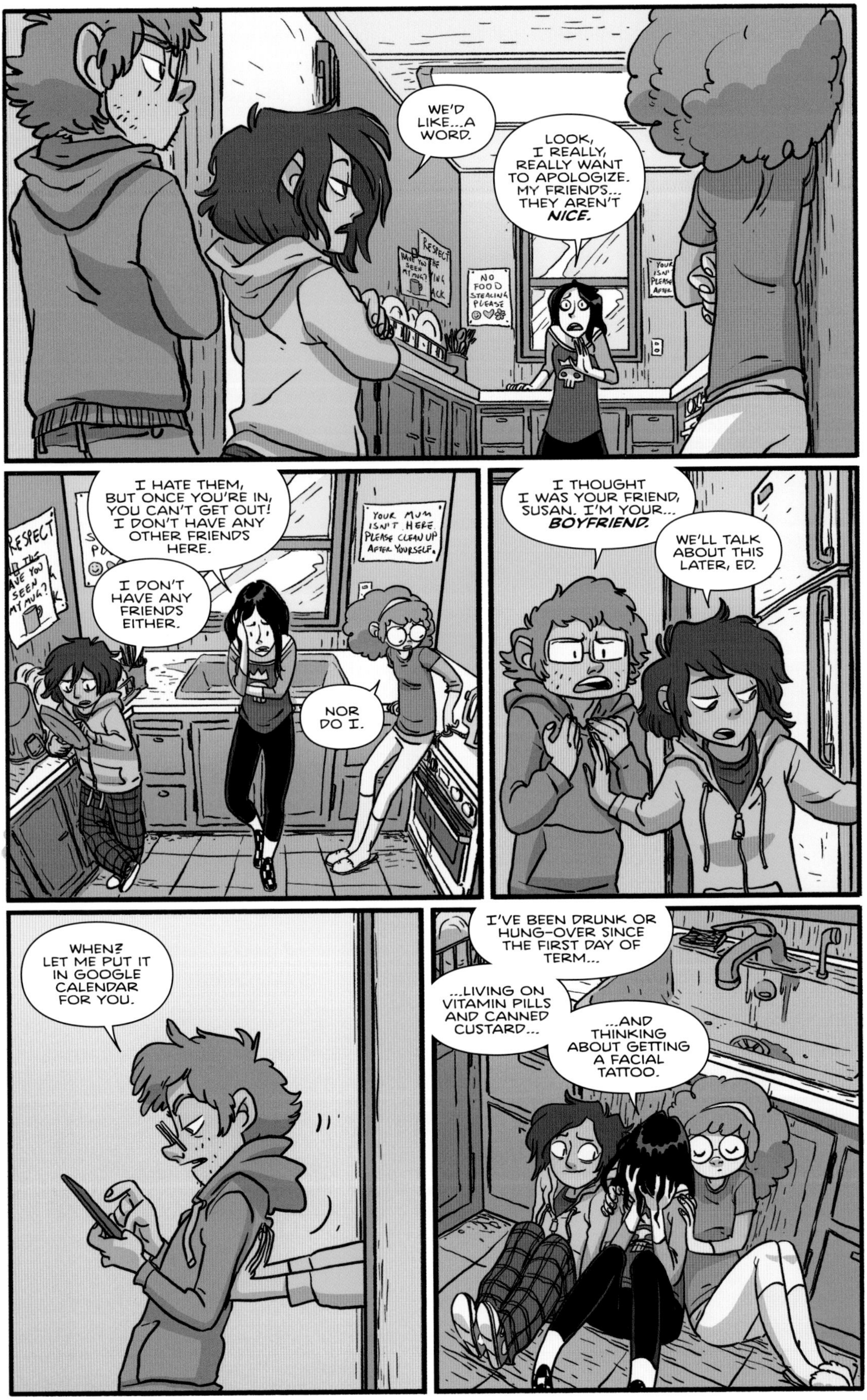
WE'D LIKE...A WORD.
LOOK, I REALLY, REALLY WANT TO APOLOGIZE. MY FRIENDS... THEY AREN'T NICE.
NO FOOD STEALING PLEASE
I HATE THEM, BUT ONCE YOU'RE IN, YOU CAN'T GET OUT! I DON'T HAVE ANY OTHER FRIENDS HERE.
YOUR MUM ISN'T HERE. PLEASE CLEAN UP AFTER YOURSELF.
I DON'T HAVE ANY FRIENDS EITHER.
NOR DO I.
I THOUGHT I WAS YOUR FRIEND, SUSAN. I'M YOUR... BOYFRIEND.
WE'LL TALK ABOUT THIS LATER, ED.
WHEN? LET ME PUT IT IN GOOGLE CALENDAR FOR YOU.
I'VE BEEN DRUNK OR HUNG-OVER SINCE THE FIRST DAY OF TERM...
...LIVING ON VITAMIN PILLS AND CANNED CUSTARD...
...AND THINKING ABOUT GETTING A FACIAL TATTOO.

THIS IS...A *TOXIC ENVIRONMENT*, ESTHER.

MOTHER MARY, WHAT A *CRYPT*.

WE'RE GOING TO THROW AWAY ALL THE EFFLUVIA OF YOUR EVIL LIFESTYLE.

THIS IS SO KIND. YOU'RE BEING SO KIND TO ME.

WHAT DID YOU USE THESE FOR? TO BEAT UP THE INNOCENT?

I USED... TO BOX.

THE LITTLE GOTH BOXES! HILARIOUS.

IT'S SO SAD BEING AWAY FROM HOME AT CHRISTMAS. WE'D BE PUTTING UP THE TREE TODAY...

HAVE A MENORAH! HAPPY HANNUKAH!

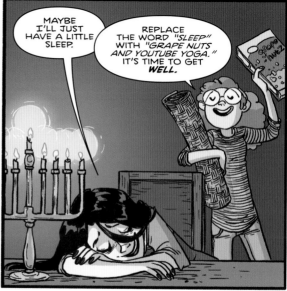

MAYBE I'LL JUST HAVE A LITTLE SLEEP.

REPLACE THE WORD *"SLEEP"* WITH *"GRAPE NUTS AND YOUTUBE YOGA."* IT'S TIME TO GET *WELL*.

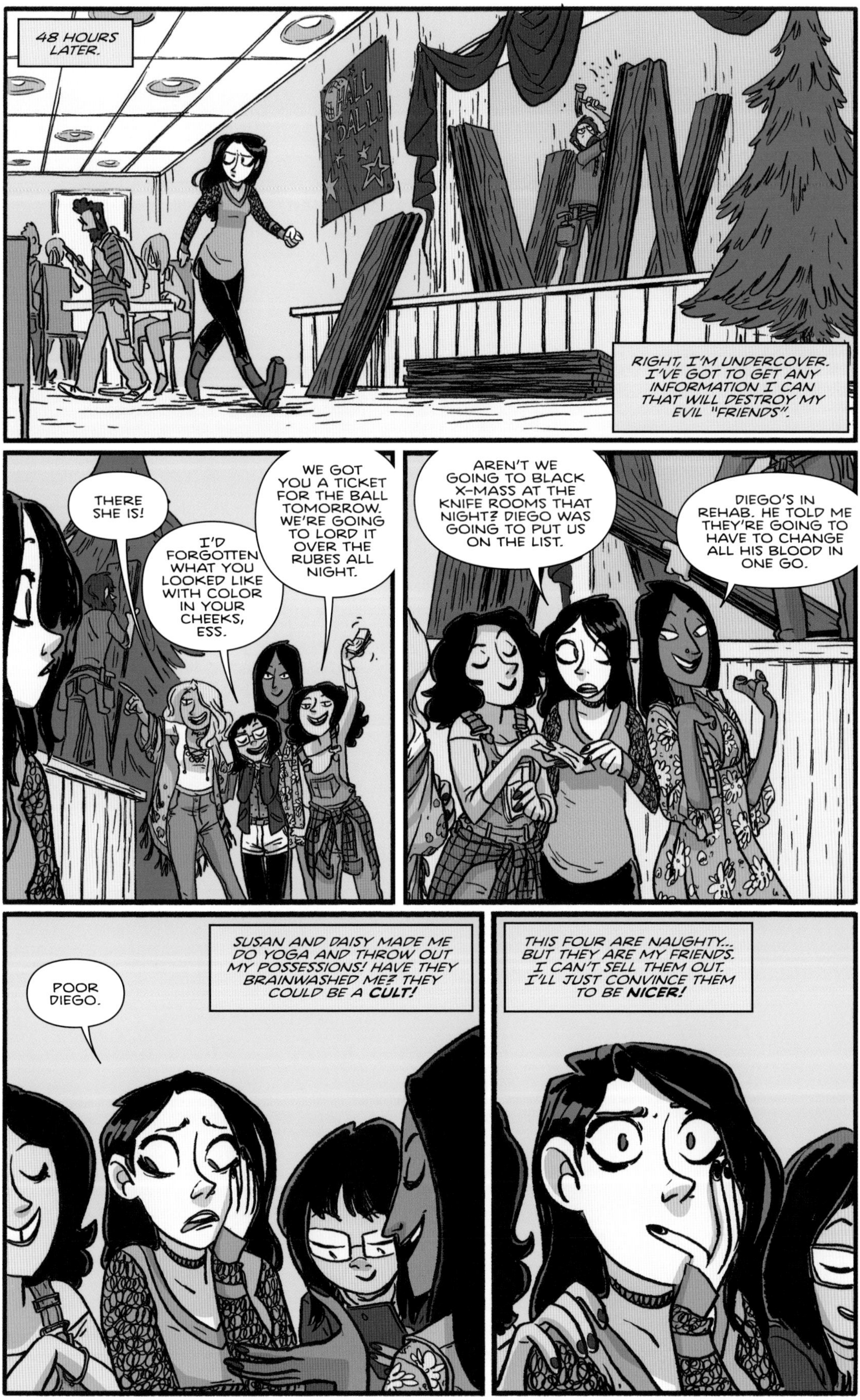
48 HOURS LATER.
HALL BALL!
RIGHT, I'M UNDERCOVER. I'VE GOT TO GET ANY INFORMATION I CAN THAT WILL DESTROY MY EVIL "FRIENDS".
THERE SHE IS!
I'D FORGOTTEN WHAT YOU LOOKED LIKE WITH COLOR IN YOUR CHEEKS, ESS.
WE GOT YOU A TICKET FOR THE BALL TOMORROW. WE'RE GOING TO LORD IT OVER THE RUBES ALL NIGHT.
AREN'T WE GOING TO BLACK X-MASS AT THE KNIFE ROOMS THAT NIGHT? DIEGO WAS GOING TO PUT US ON THE LIST.
DIEGO'S IN REHAB. HE TOLD ME THEY'RE GOING TO HAVE TO CHANGE ALL HIS BLOOD IN ONE GO.
POOR DIEGO.
SUSAN AND DAISY MADE ME DO YOGA AND THROW OUT MY POSSESSIONS! HAVE THEY BRAINWASHED ME? THEY COULD BE A CULT!
THIS FOUR ARE NAUGHTY... BUT THEY ARE MY FRIENDS. I CAN'T SELL THEM OUT. I'LL JUST CONVINCE THEM TO BE NICER!

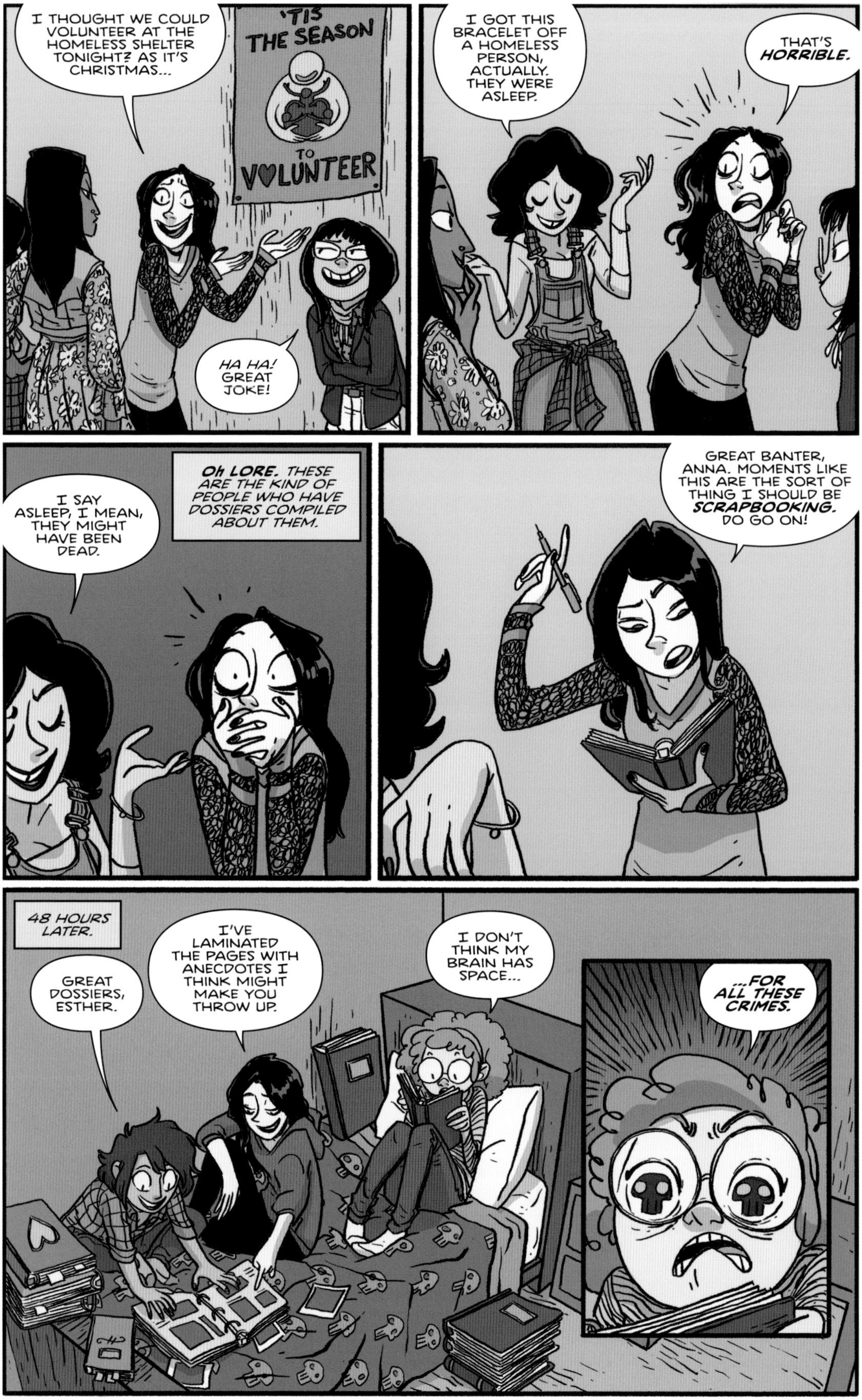

I THOUGHT WE COULD VOLUNTEER AT THE HOMELESS SHELTER TONIGHT? AS IT'S CHRISTMAS...
'TIS THE SEASON TO VOLUNTEER
HA HA! GREAT JOKE!
I GOT THIS BRACELET OFF A HOMELESS PERSON, ACTUALLY. THEY WERE ASLEEP.
THAT'S *HORRIBLE.*
I SAY ASLEEP, I MEAN, THEY MIGHT HAVE BEEN DEAD.
Oh LORE. THESE ARE THE KIND OF PEOPLE WHO HAVE DOSSIERS COMPILED ABOUT THEM.
GREAT BANTER, ANNA. MOMENTS LIKE THIS ARE THE SORT OF THING I SHOULD BE *SCRAPBOOKING.* DO GO ON!
48 HOURS LATER.
GREAT DOSSIERS, ESTHER.
I'VE LAMINATED THE PAGES WITH ANECDOTES I THINK MIGHT MAKE YOU THROW UP.
I DON'T THINK MY BRAIN HAS SPACE...
...FOR ALL THESE CRIMES.

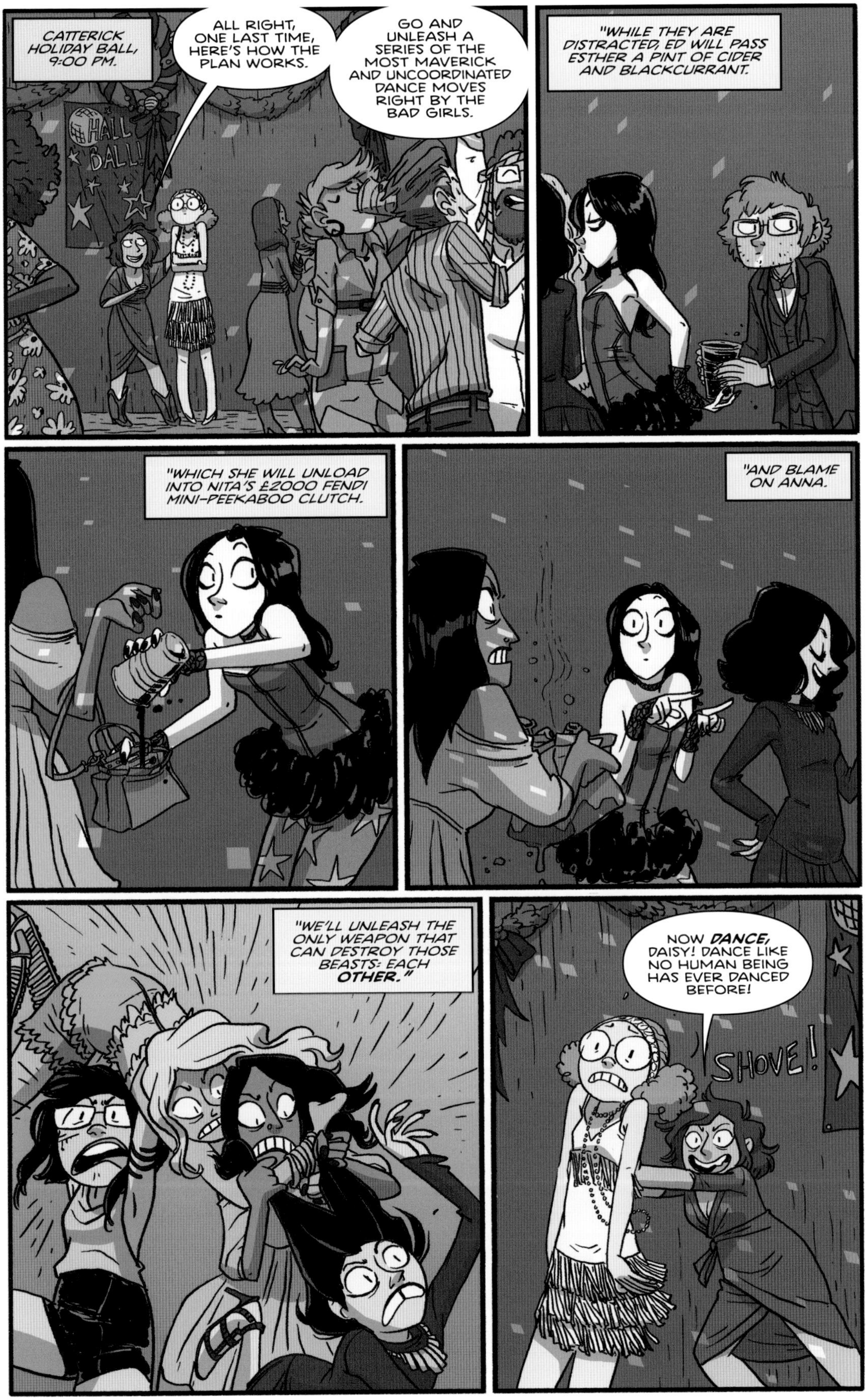
CATTERICK HOLIDAY BALL, 9:00 PM.
ALL RIGHT, ONE LAST TIME, HERE'S HOW THE PLAN WORKS.
GO AND UNLEASH A SERIES OF THE MOST MAVERICK AND UNCOORDINATED DANCE MOVES RIGHT BY THE BAD GIRLS.
HALL BALL!
"WHILE THEY ARE DISTRACTED, ED WILL PASS ESTHER A PINT OF CIDER AND BLACKCURRANT.
"WHICH SHE WILL UNLOAD INTO NITA'S £2000 FENDI MINI-PEEKABOO CLUTCH.
"AND BLAME ON ANNA.
"WE'LL UNLEASH THE ONLY WEAPON THAT CAN DESTROY THOSE BEASTS: EACH OTHER."
NOW DANCE, DAISY! DANCE LIKE NO HUMAN BEING HAS EVER DANCED BEFORE!
SHOVE!

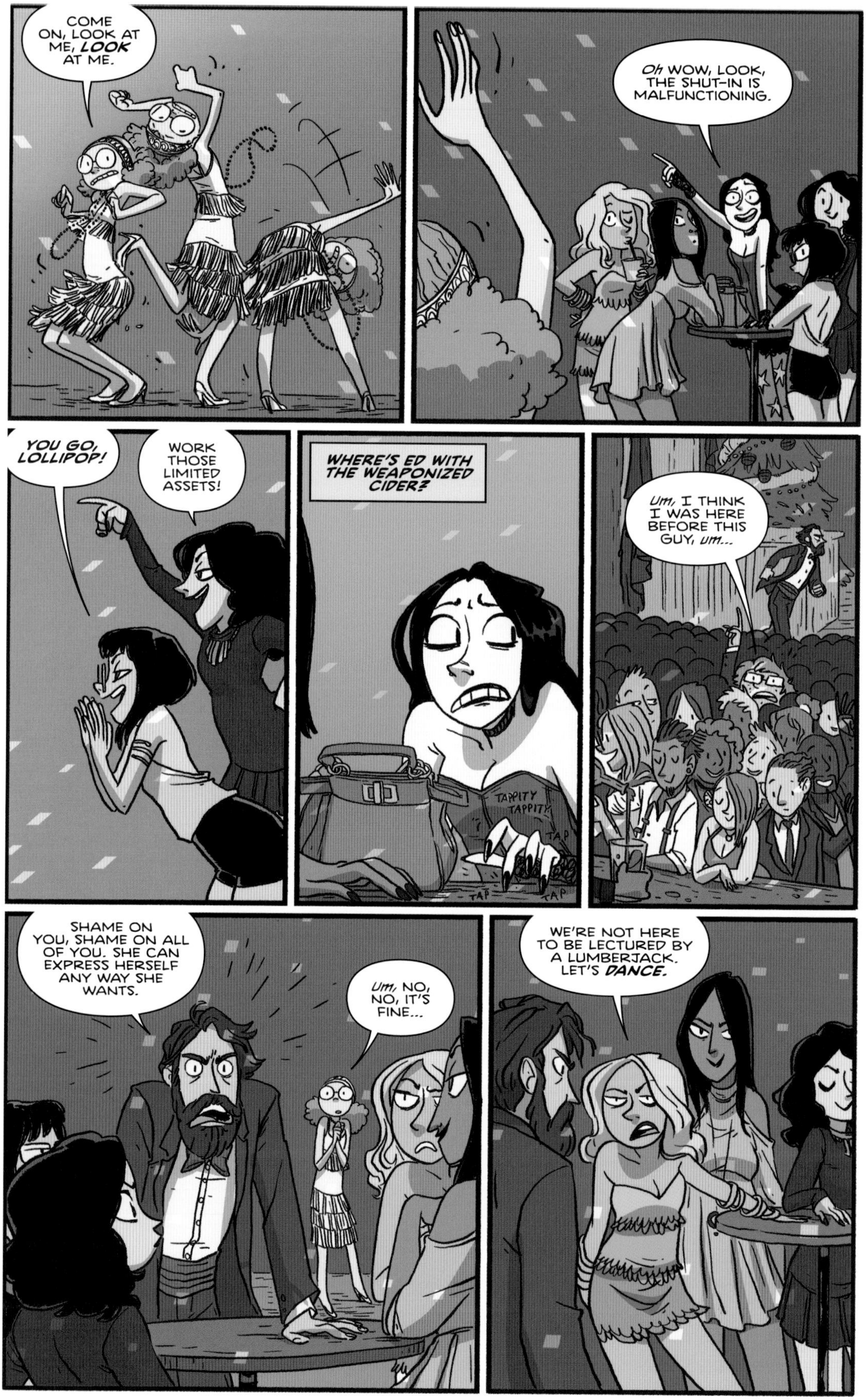
COME ON, LOOK AT ME, LOOK AT ME.
Oh WOW, LOOK, THE SHUT-IN IS MALFUNCTIONING.
YOU GO, LOLLIPOP!
WORK THOSE LIMITED ASSETS!
WHERE'S ED WITH THE WEAPONIZED CIDER?
TAPPITY TAPPITY TAP
TAP TAP
Um, I THINK I WAS HERE BEFORE THIS GUY, um...
SHAME ON YOU, SHAME ON ALL OF YOU. SHE CAN EXPRESS HERSELF ANY WAY SHE WANTS.
Um, NO, NO, IT'S FINE...
WE'RE NOT HERE TO BE LECTURED BY A LUMBERJACK. LET'S DANCE.

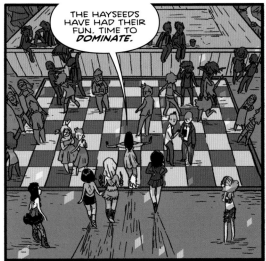

THE HAYSEEDS HAVE HAD THEIR FUN. TIME TO *DOMINATE.*

OUT OF OUR WAY, NORMS!

NO RANDOS ON STAGE WHILE WE *GO OFF.*

THOSE... *MOVES.*

WHERE WAS ED? WHO WAS THAT POLITE WEREWOLF BOY? WHAT DO WE DO NOW?

NEW PLAN.

LET'S GET DRUNK ENOUGH TO FIGHT THEM IN THE QUADRANGLE. IF YOU CAN'T *FEEL* THE BEATING, IT CAN'T *HURT* YOU.

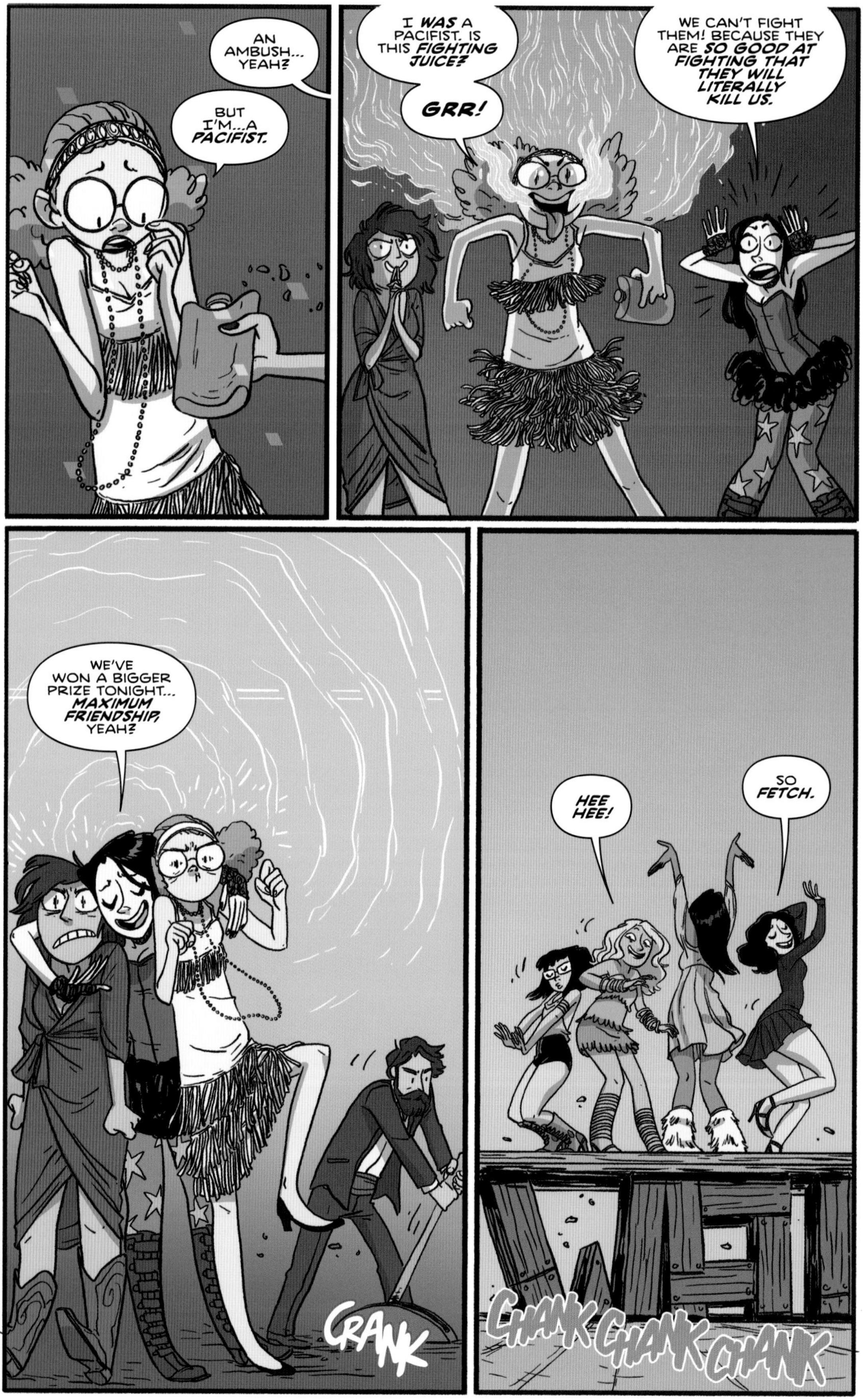
AN AMBUSH... YEAH?
BUT I'M...A PACIFIST.
I WAS A PACIFIST. IS THIS FIGHTING JUICE?
GRR!
WE CAN'T FIGHT THEM! BECAUSE THEY ARE SO GOOD AT FIGHTING THAT THEY WILL LITERALLY KILL US.
WE'VE WON A BIGGER PRIZE TONIGHT... MAXIMUM FRIENDSHIP, YEAH?
CRANK
HEE HEE!
SO FETCH.
CHANK CHANK CHANK

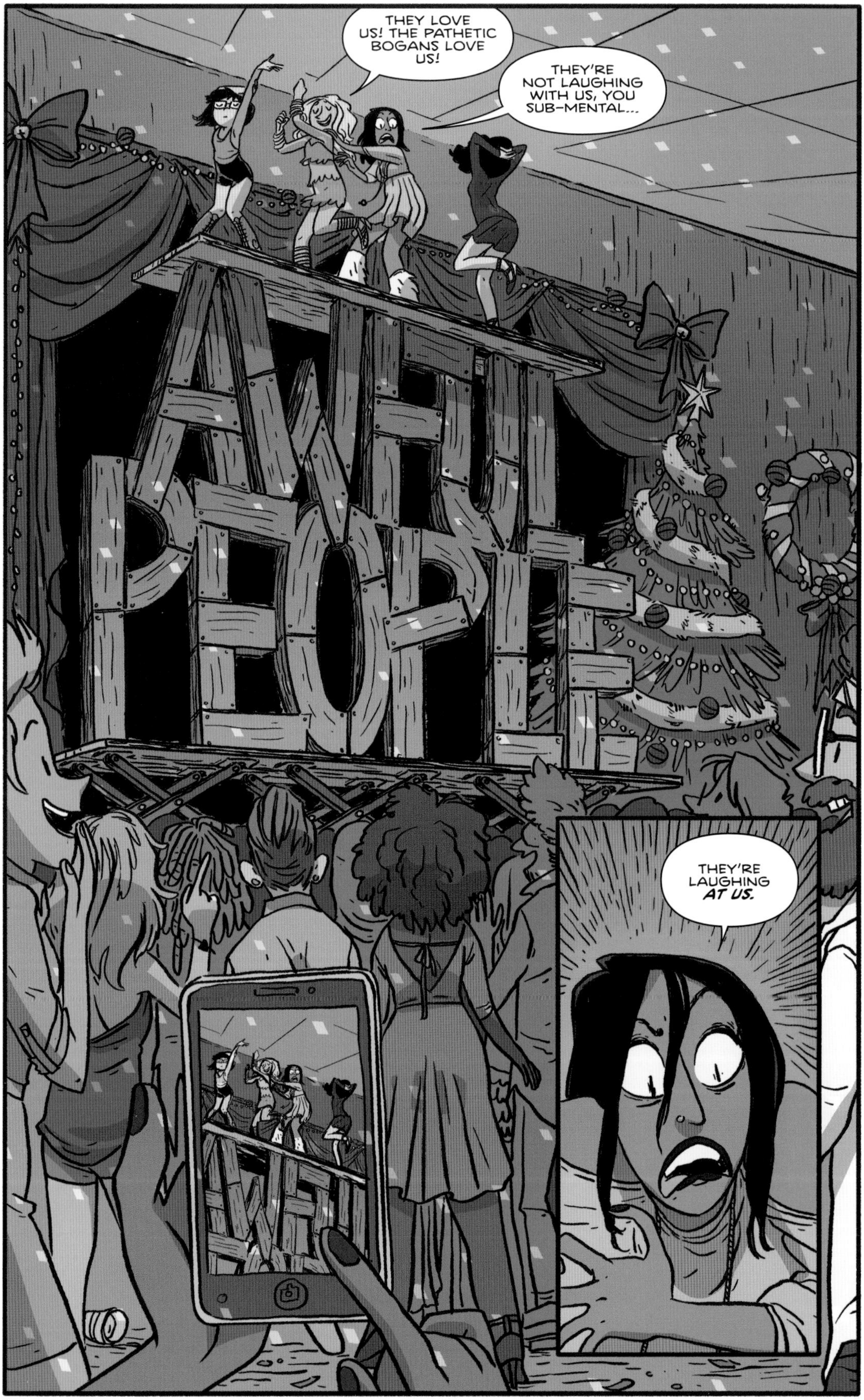
THEY LOVE US! THE PATHETIC BOGANS LOVE US!
THEY'RE NOT LAUGHING WITH US, YOU SUB-MENTAL...
THEY'RE LAUGHING *AT US.*

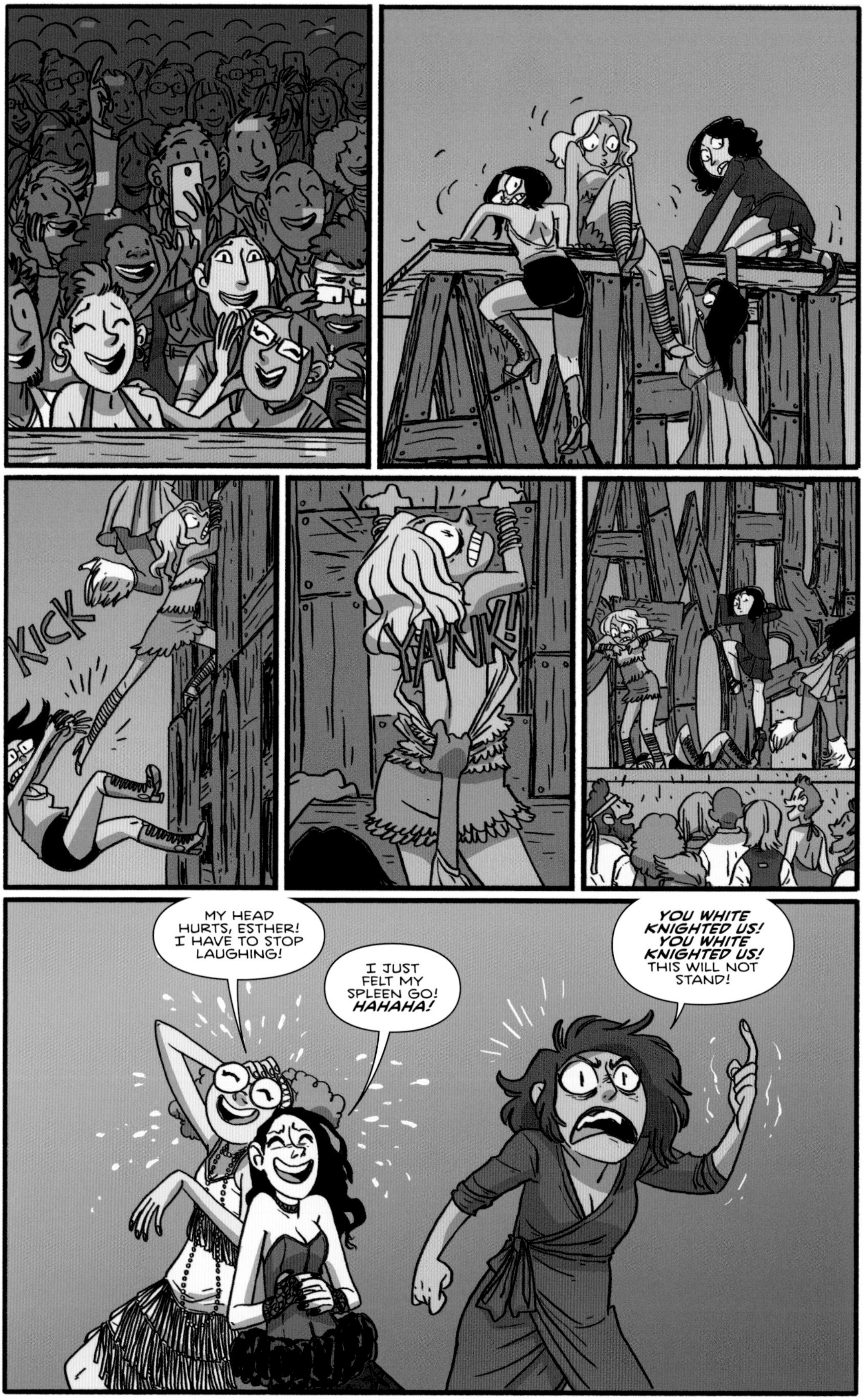
KICK
YANK!
MY HEAD HURTS, ESTHER! I HAVE TO STOP LAUGHING!
I JUST FELT MY SPLEEN GO! *HAHAHA!*
YOU WHITE KNIGHTED US! YOU WHITE KNIGHTED US! THIS WILL NOT STAND!

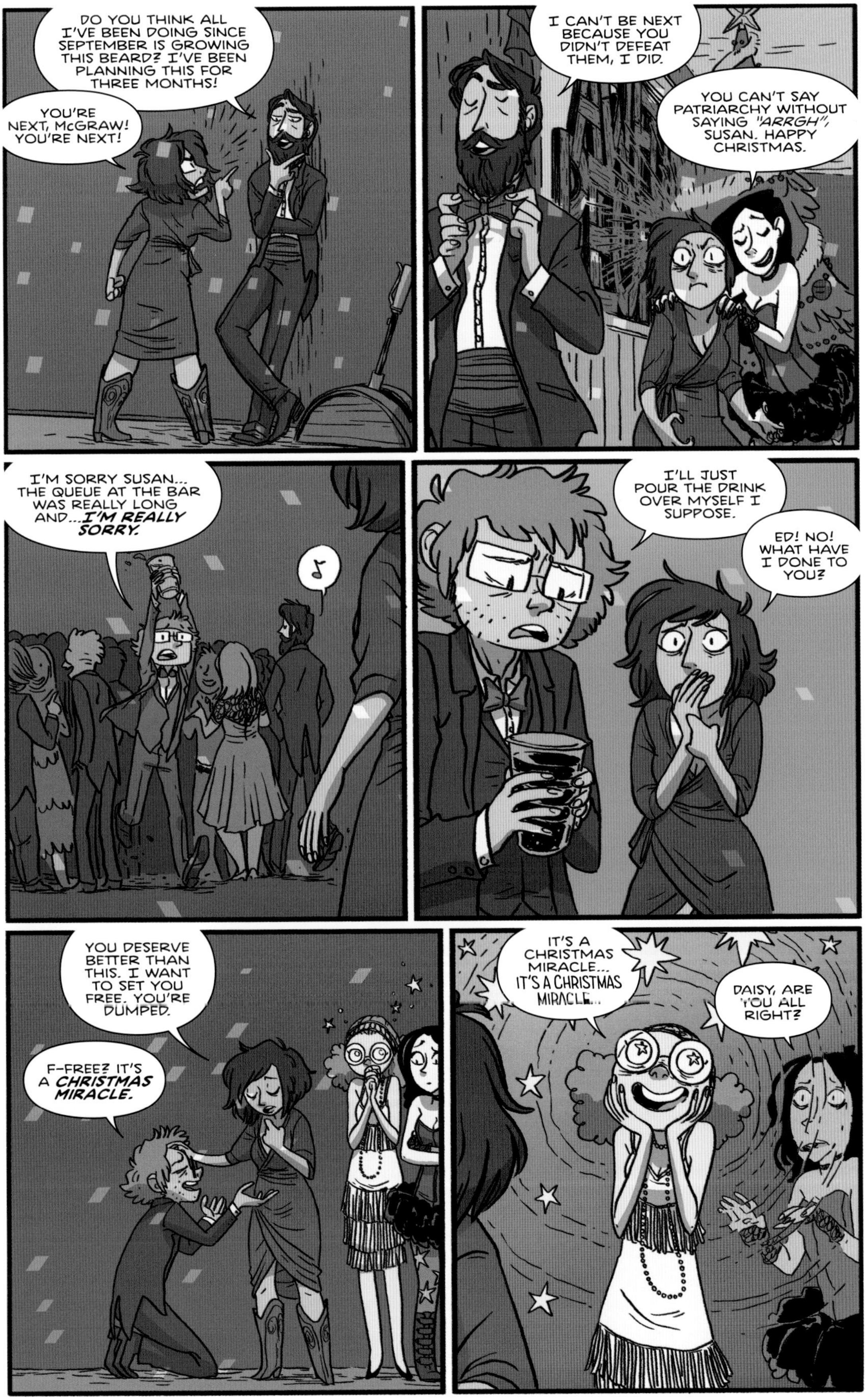

DO YOU THINK ALL I'VE BEEN DOING SINCE SEPTEMBER IS GROWING THIS BEARD? I'VE BEEN PLANNING THIS FOR THREE MONTHS!
YOU'RE NEXT, McGRAW! YOU'RE NEXT!
I CAN'T BE NEXT BECAUSE YOU DIDN'T DEFEAT THEM, I DID.
YOU CAN'T SAY PATRIARCHY WITHOUT SAYING "ARRGH", SUSAN. HAPPY CHRISTMAS.
I'M SORRY SUSAN... THE QUEUE AT THE BAR WAS REALLY LONG AND...I'M REALLY SORRY.
♪
I'LL JUST POUR THE DRINK OVER MYSELF I SUPPOSE.
ED! NO! WHAT HAVE I DONE TO YOU?
YOU DESERVE BETTER THAN THIS. I WANT TO SET YOU FREE. YOU'RE DUMPED.
F-FREE? IT'S A CHRISTMAS MIRACLE.
IT'S A CHRISTMAS MIRACLE... IT'S A CHRISTMAS MIRACLE...
DAISY, ARE YOU ALL RIGHT?

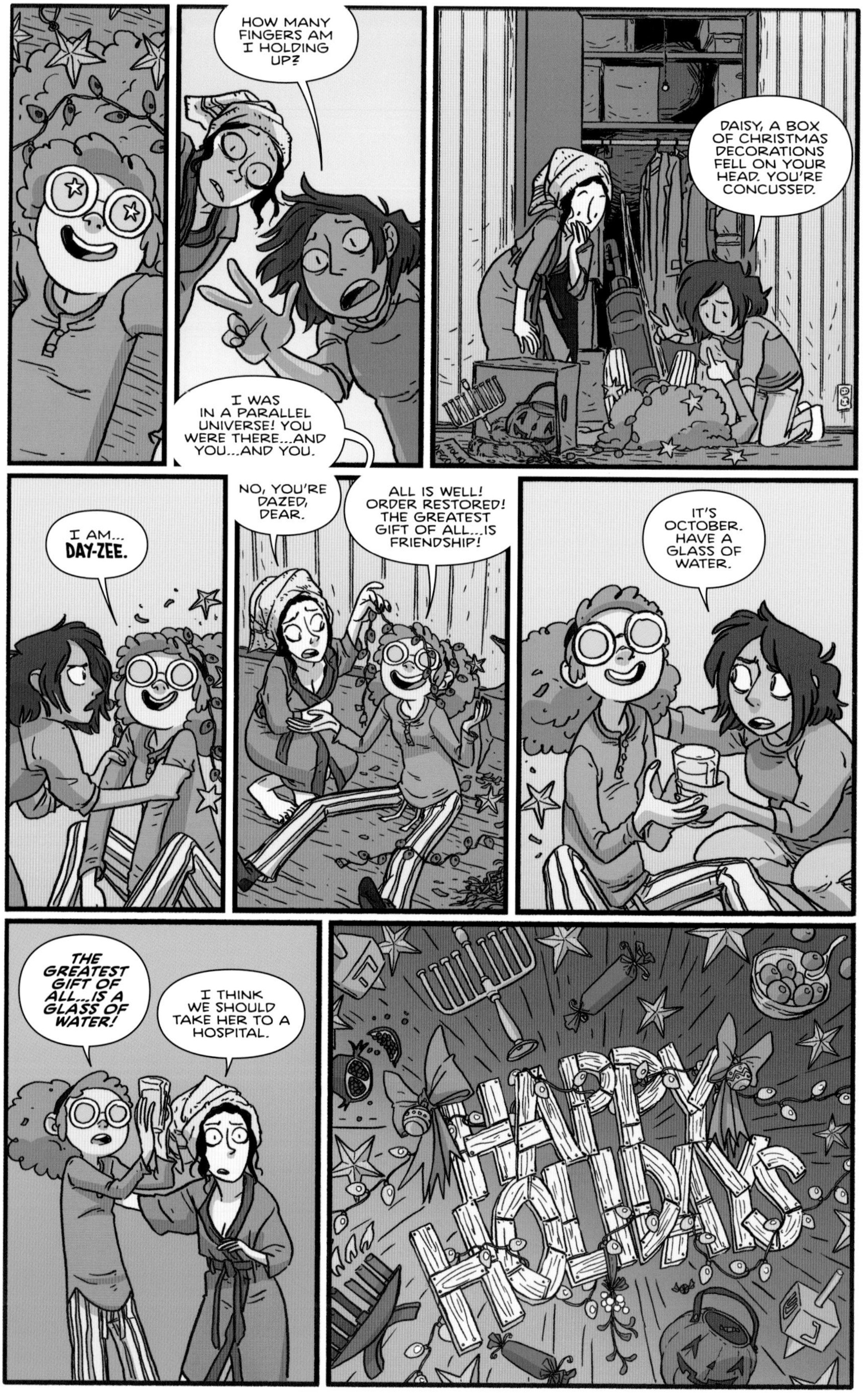
HOW MANY FINGERS AM I HOLDING UP?
DAISY, A BOX OF CHRISTMAS DECORATIONS FELL ON YOUR HEAD. YOU'RE CONCUSSED.
I WAS IN A PARALLEL UNIVERSE! YOU WERE THERE...AND YOU...AND YOU.
I AM... DAY-ZEE.
NO, YOU'RE DAZED, DEAR.
ALL IS WELL! ORDER RESTORED! THE GREATEST GIFT OF ALL...IS FRIENDSHIP!
IT'S OCTOBER. HAVE A GLASS OF WATER.
THE GREATEST GIFT OF ALL...IS A GLASS OF WATER!
I THINK WE SHOULD TAKE HER TO A HOSPITAL.
HAPPY HOLIDAYS

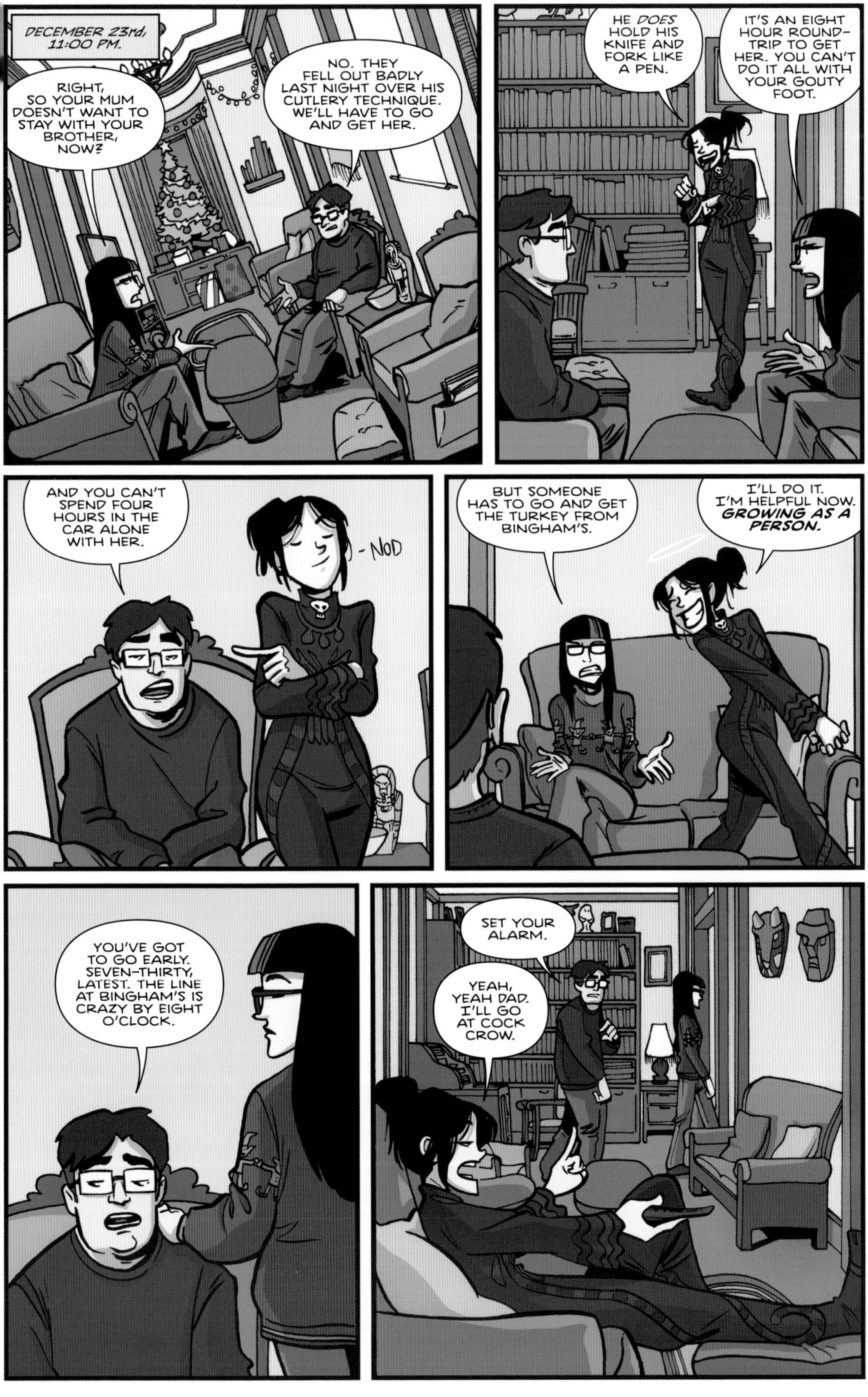
DECEMBER 23rd, 11:00 PM.
RIGHT, SO YOUR MUM DOESN'T WANT TO STAY WITH YOUR BROTHER, NOW?
NO. THEY FELL OUT BADLY LAST NIGHT OVER HIS CUTLERY TECHNIQUE. WE'LL HAVE TO GO AND GET HER.
HE DOES HOLD HIS KNIFE AND FORK LIKE A PEN.
IT'S AN EIGHT HOUR ROUND-TRIP TO GET HER. YOU CAN'T DO IT ALL WITH YOUR GOUTY FOOT.
AND YOU CAN'T SPEND FOUR HOURS IN THE CAR ALONE WITH HER.
- NOD
BUT SOMEONE HAS TO GO AND GET THE TURKEY FROM BINGHAM'S.
I'LL DO IT. I'M HELPFUL NOW. GROWING AS A PERSON.
YOU'VE GOT TO GO EARLY. SEVEN-THIRTY, LATEST. THE LINE AT BINGHAM'S IS CRAZY BY EIGHT O'CLOCK.
SET YOUR ALARM.
YEAH, YEAH DAD. I'LL GO AT COCK CROW.

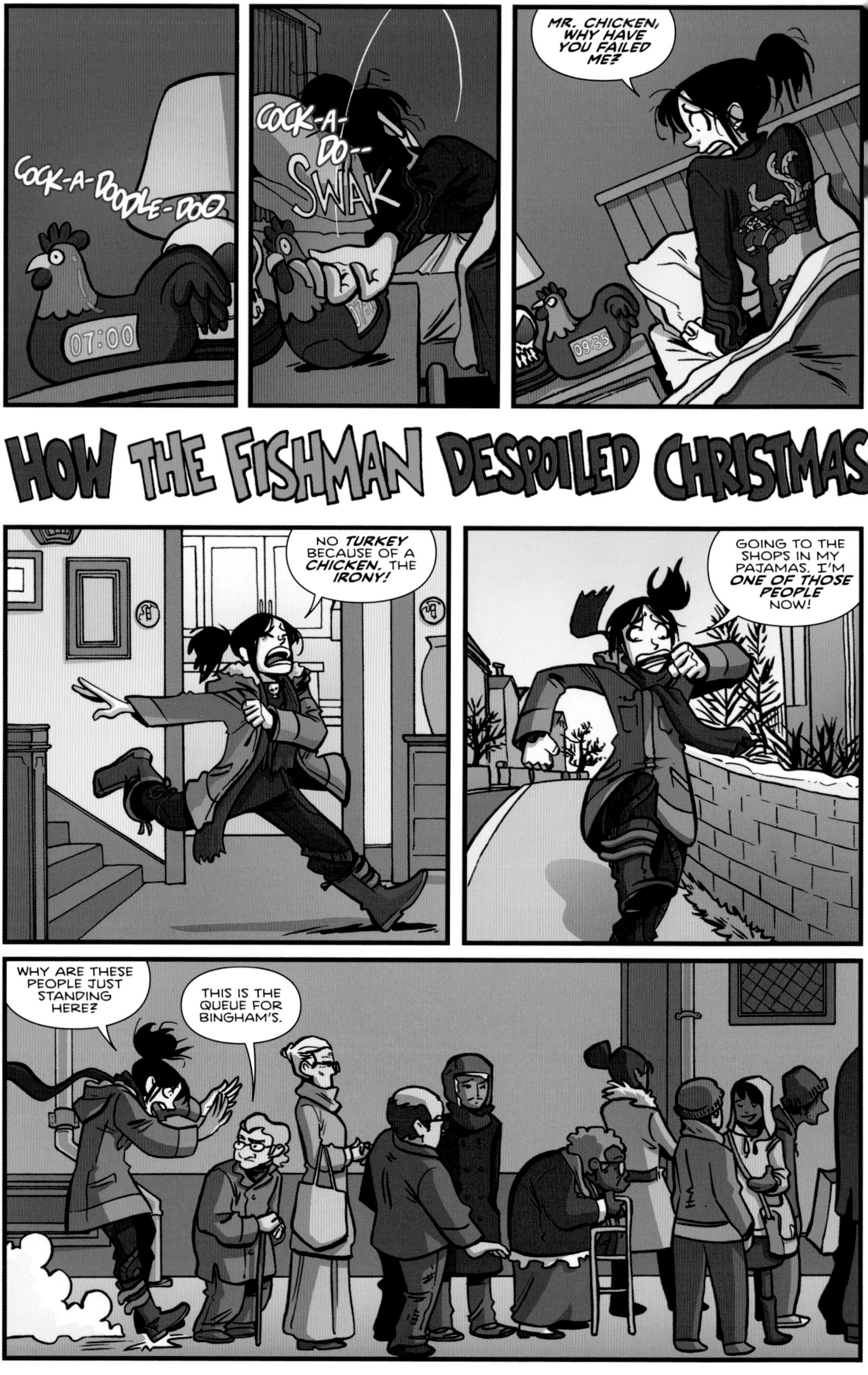
COCK-A-DOODLE-DOO
07:00
COCK-A-DO--
SWAK
MR. CHICKEN, WHY HAVE YOU FAILED ME?
09:35
HOW THE FISHMAN DESPOILED CHRISTMAS
NO TURKEY BECAUSE OF A CHICKEN. THE IRONY!
GOING TO THE SHOPS IN MY PAJAMAS. I'M ONE OF THOSE PEOPLE NOW!
WHY ARE THESE PEOPLE JUST STANDING HERE?
THIS IS THE QUEUE FOR BINGHAM'S.

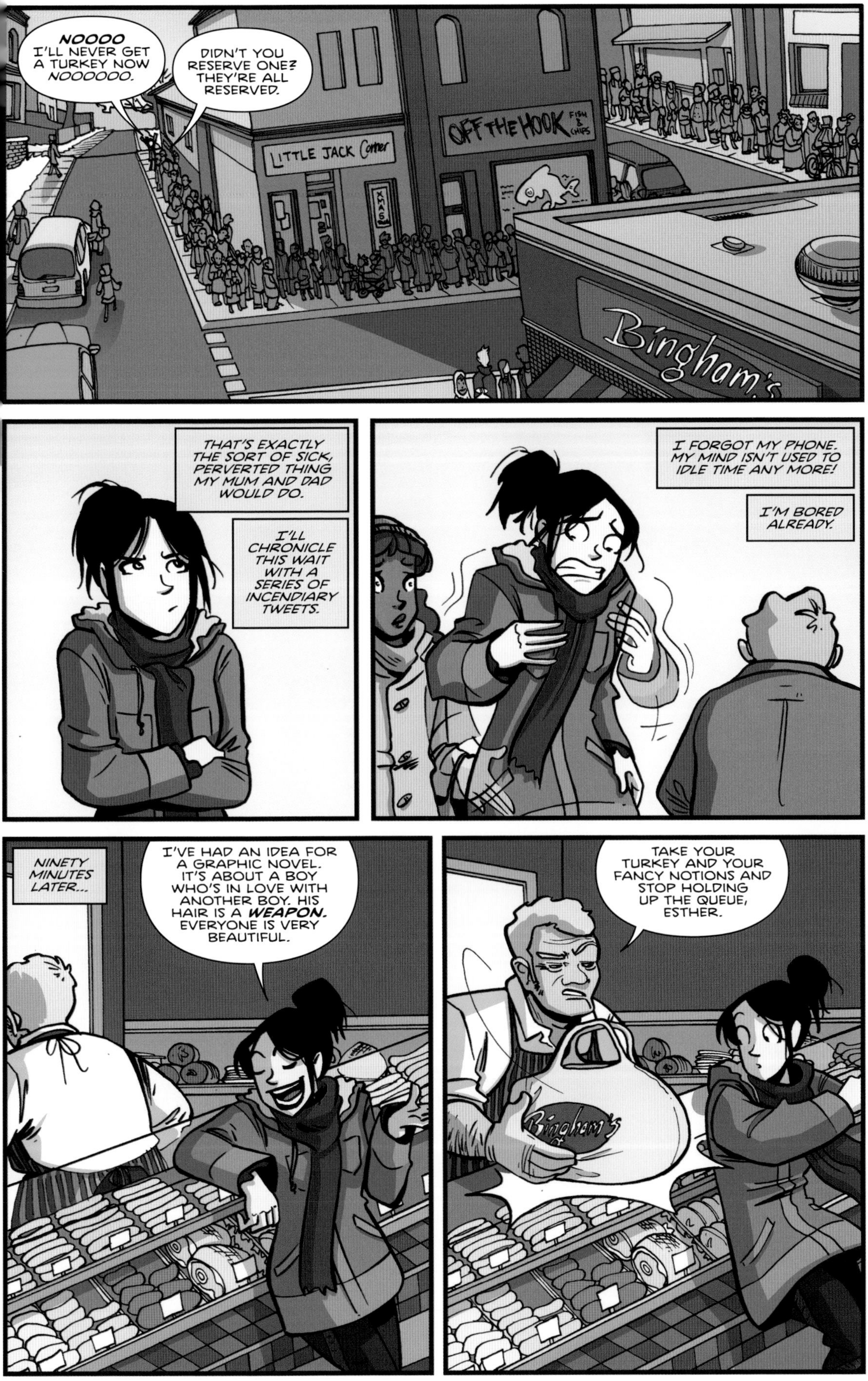
NOOOO I'LL NEVER GET A TURKEY NOW NOOOOOO.
DIDN'T YOU RESERVE ONE? THEY'RE ALL RESERVED.
LITTLE JACK Corner
OFF THE HOOK FISH & CHIPS
XMAS
Bingham's
THAT'S EXACTLY THE SORT OF SICK, PERVERTED THING MY MUM AND DAD WOULD DO.
I'LL CHRONICLE THIS WAIT WITH A SERIES OF INCENDIARY TWEETS.
I FORGOT MY PHONE. MY MIND ISN'T USED TO IDLE TIME ANY MORE!
I'M BORED ALREADY.
NINETY MINUTES LATER...
I'VE HAD AN IDEA FOR A GRAPHIC NOVEL. IT'S ABOUT A BOY WHO'S IN LOVE WITH ANOTHER BOY. HIS HAIR IS A WEAPON. EVERYONE IS VERY BEAUTIFUL.
TAKE YOUR TURKEY AND YOUR FANCY NOTIONS AND STOP HOLDING UP THE QUEUE, ESTHER.
Bingham's

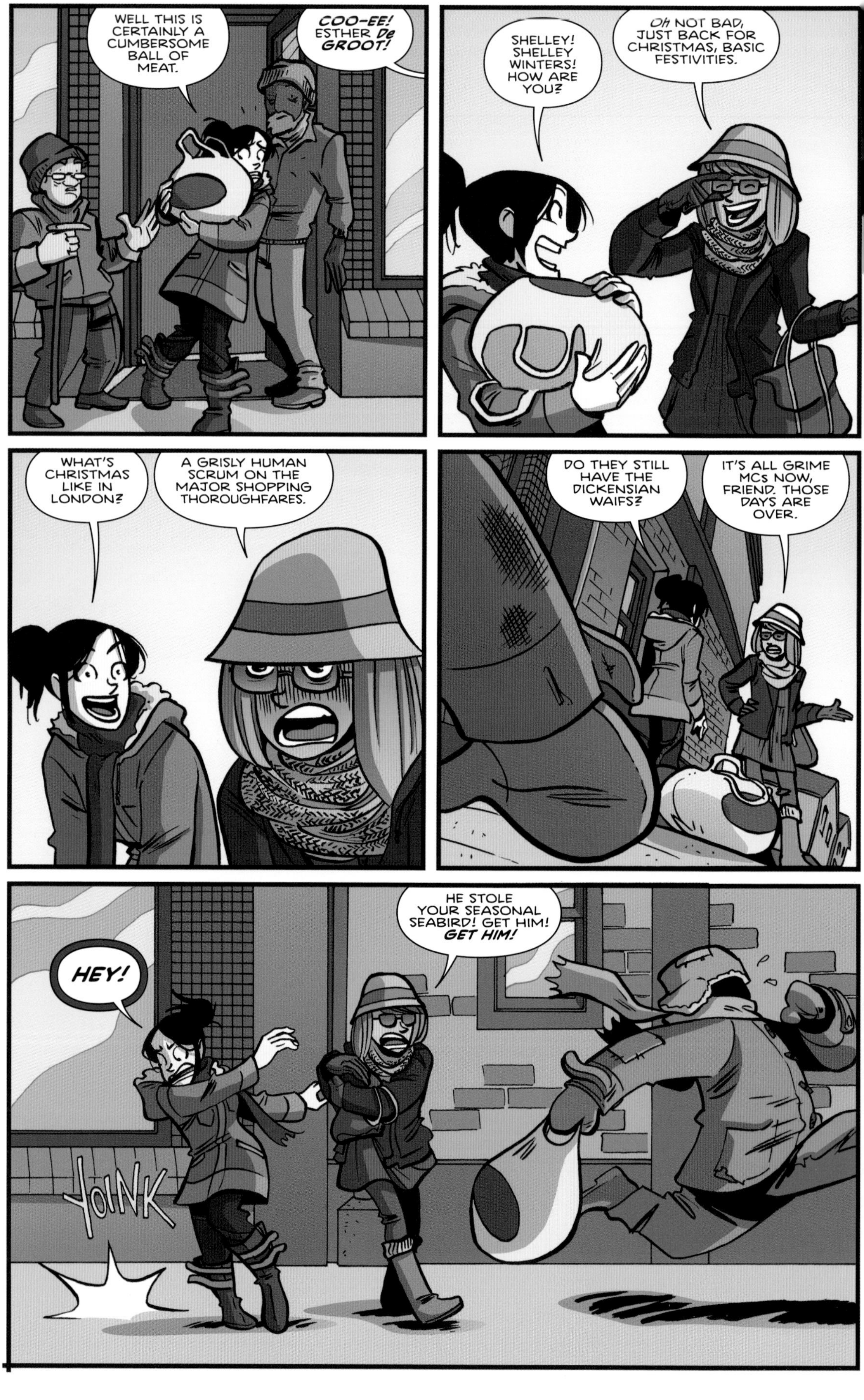
WELL THIS IS CERTAINLY A CUMBERSOME BALL OF MEAT.
COO-EE! ESTHER De GROOT!
SHELLEY! SHELLEY WINTERS! HOW ARE YOU?
Oh NOT BAD, JUST BACK FOR CHRISTMAS, BASIC FESTIVITIES.
WHAT'S CHRISTMAS LIKE IN LONDON?
A GRISLY HUMAN SCRUM ON THE MAJOR SHOPPING THOROUGHFARES.
DO THEY STILL HAVE THE DICKENSIAN WAIFS?
IT'S ALL GRIME MCs NOW, FRIEND. THOSE DAYS ARE OVER.
HEY!
HE STOLE YOUR SEASONAL SEABIRD! GET HIM! GET HIM!
YOINK

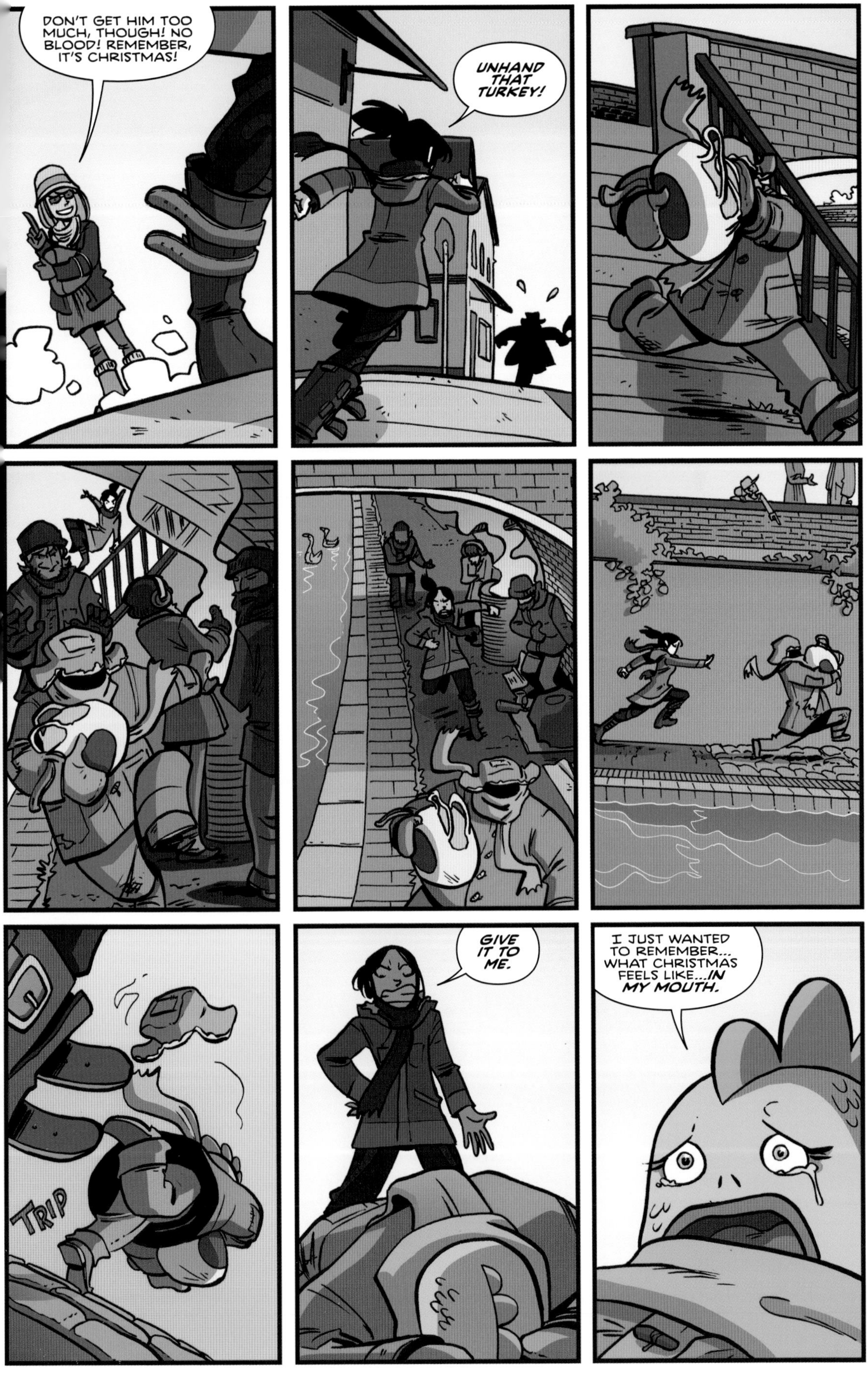
DON'T GET HIM TOO MUCH, THOUGH! NO BLOOD! REMEMBER, IT'S CHRISTMAS!
UNHAND THAT TURKEY!
TRIP
GIVE IT TO ME.
I JUST WANTED TO REMEMBER... WHAT CHRISTMAS FEELS LIKE... IN MY MOUTH.

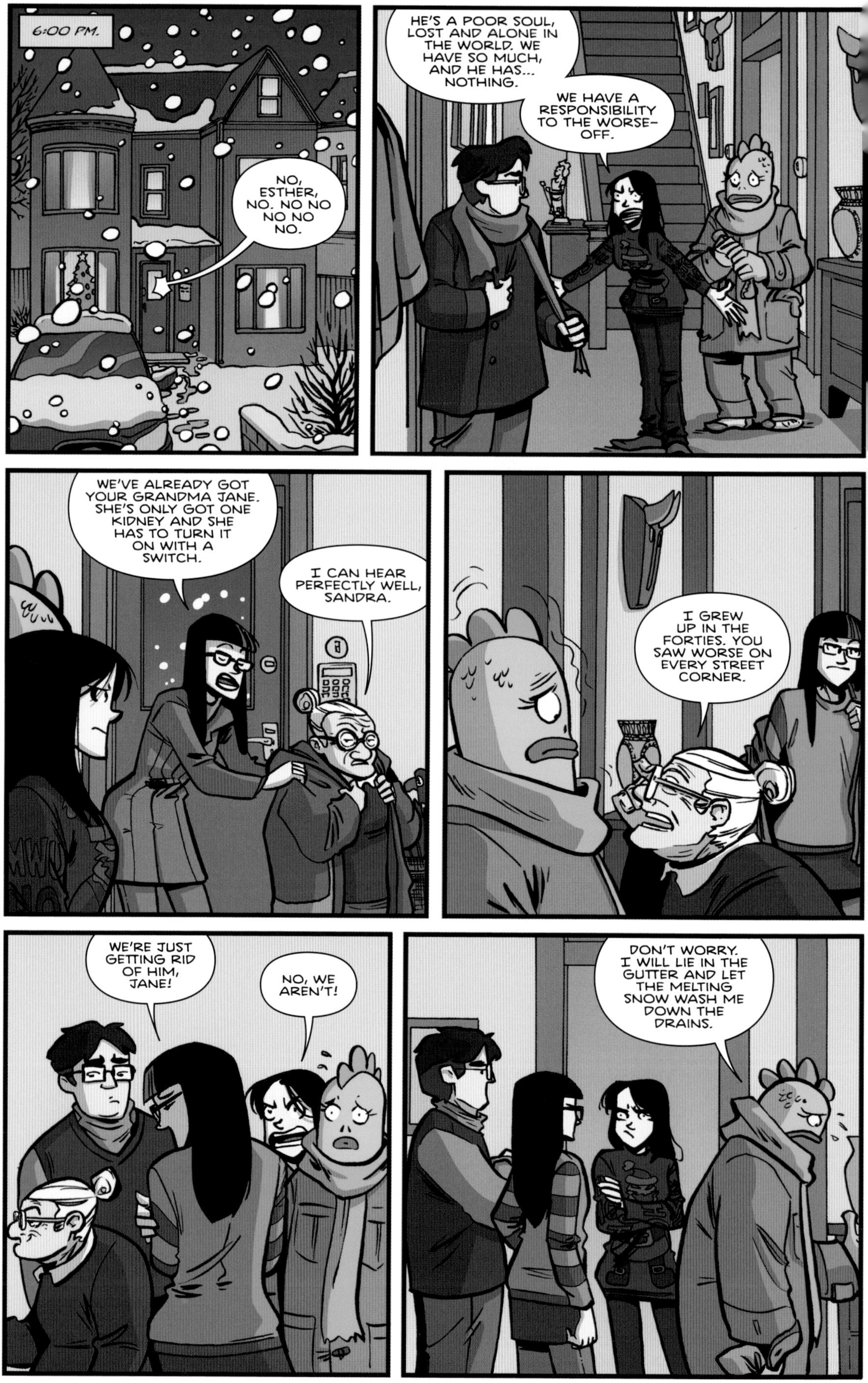
6:00 PM.
NO, ESTHER, NO. NO NO NO NO NO.
HE'S A POOR SOUL, LOST AND ALONE IN THE WORLD. WE HAVE SO MUCH, AND HE HAS... NOTHING.
WE HAVE A RESPONSIBILITY TO THE WORSE-OFF.
WE'VE ALREADY GOT YOUR GRANDMA JANE. SHE'S ONLY GOT ONE KIDNEY AND SHE HAS TO TURN IT ON WITH A SWITCH.
I CAN HEAR PERFECTLY WELL, SANDRA.
I GREW UP IN THE FORTIES. YOU SAW WORSE ON EVERY STREET CORNER.
WE'RE JUST GETTING RID OF HIM, JANE!
NO, WE AREN'T!
DON'T WORRY. I WILL LIE IN THE GUTTER AND LET THE MELTING SNOW WASH ME DOWN THE DRAINS.

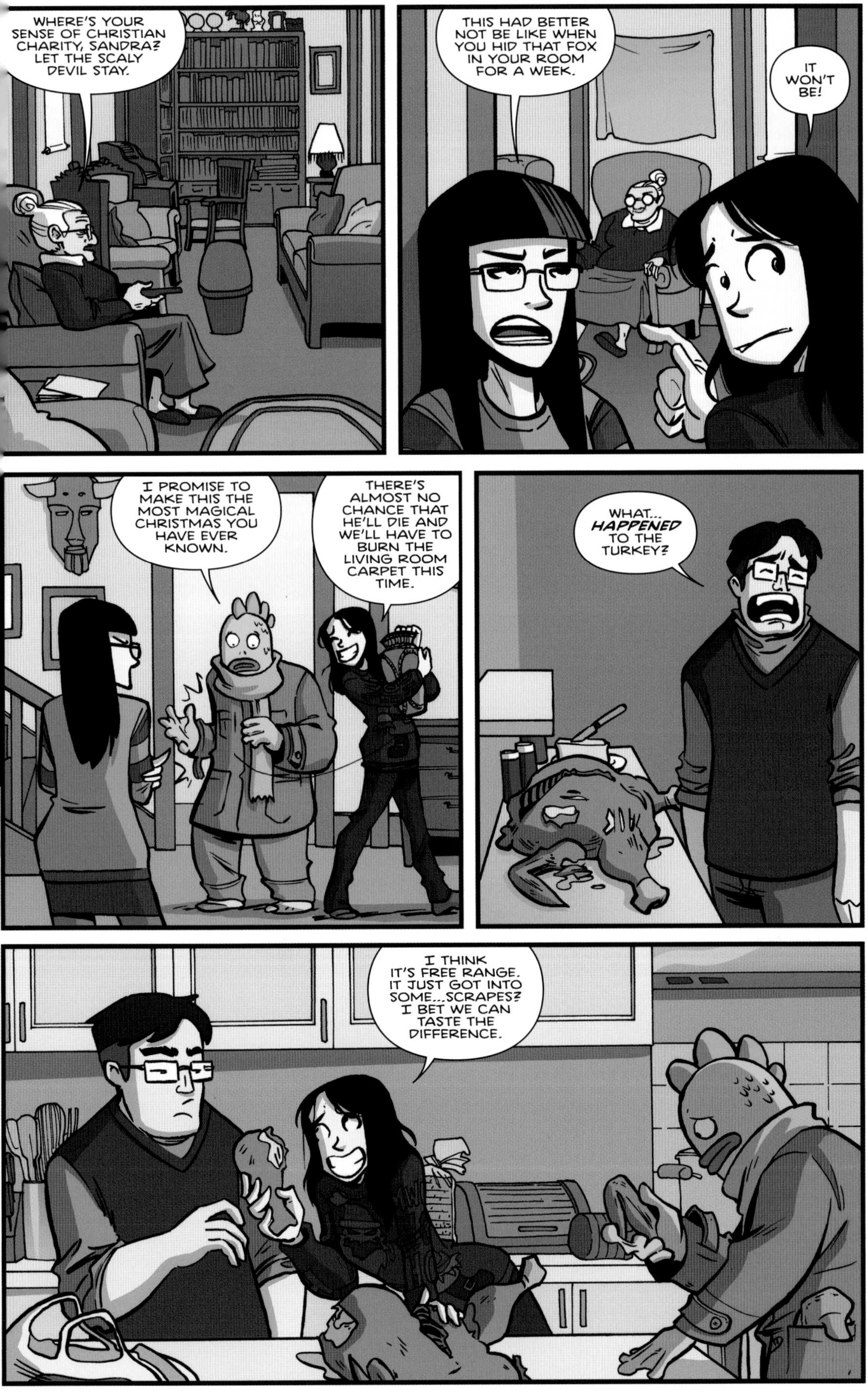

WHERE'S YOUR SENSE OF CHRISTIAN CHARITY, SANDRA? LET THE SCALY DEVIL STAY.
THIS HAD BETTER NOT BE LIKE WHEN YOU HID THAT FOX IN YOUR ROOM FOR A WEEK.
IT WON'T BE!
I PROMISE TO MAKE THIS THE MOST MAGICAL CHRISTMAS YOU HAVE EVER KNOWN.
THERE'S ALMOST NO CHANCE THAT HE'LL DIE AND WE'LL HAVE TO BURN THE LIVING ROOM CARPET THIS TIME.
WHAT... HAPPENED TO THE TURKEY?
I THINK IT'S FREE RANGE. IT JUST GOT INTO SOME... SCRAPES? I BET WE CAN TASTE THE DIFFERENCE.

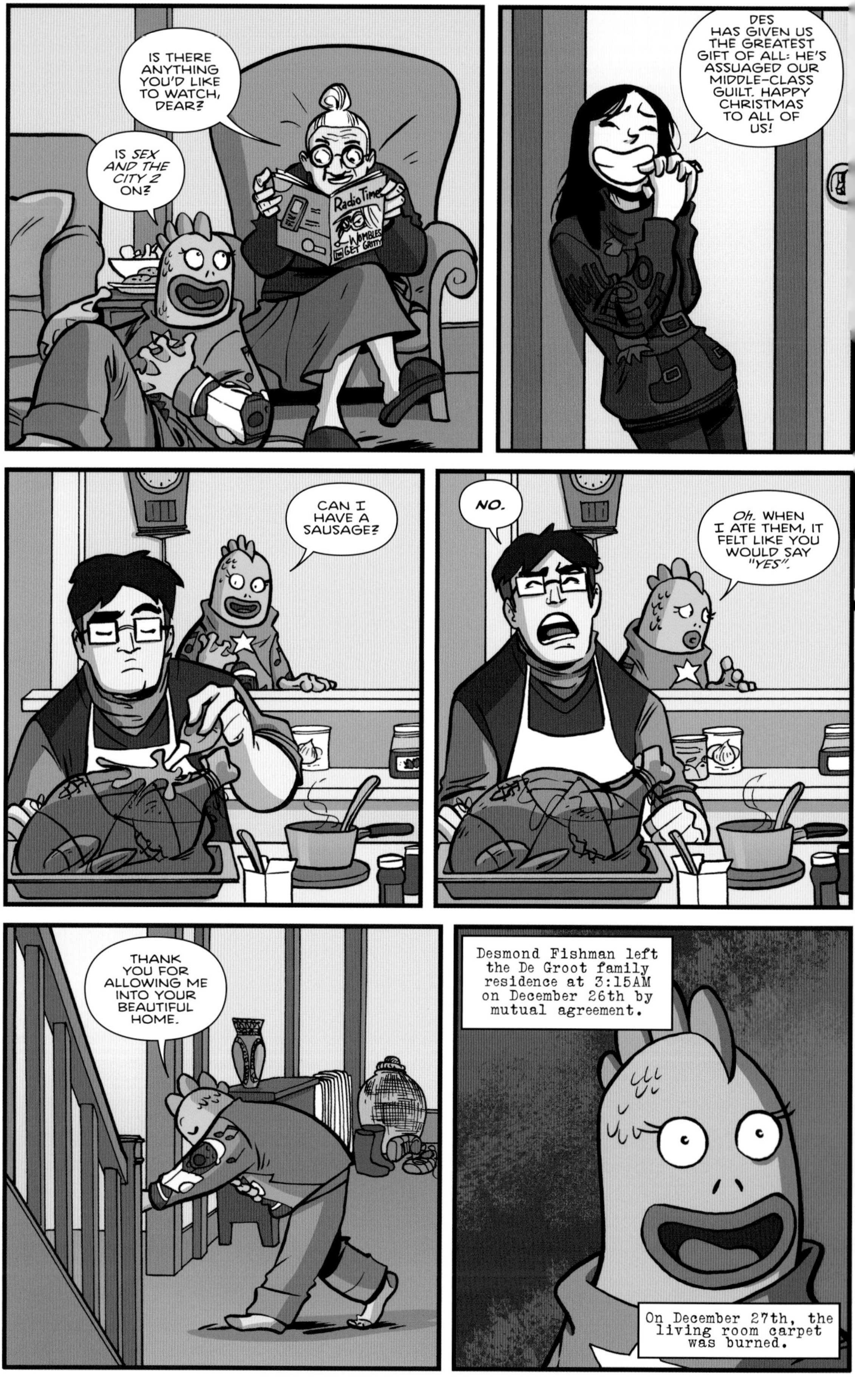
IS THERE ANYTHING YOU'D LIKE TO WATCH, DEAR?
IS *SEX AND THE CITY 2* ON?
Radio Times
WOMBLES GET GRITTY
DES HAS GIVEN US THE GREATEST GIFT OF ALL: HE'S ASSUAGED OUR MIDDLE-CLASS GUILT. HAPPY CHRISTMAS TO ALL OF US!
CAN I HAVE A SAUSAGE?
NO.
Oh. WHEN I ATE THEM, IT FELT LIKE YOU WOULD SAY *"YES"*.
THANK YOU FOR ALLOWING ME INTO YOUR BEAUTIFUL HOME.
Desmond Fishman left the De Groot family residence at 3:15AM on December 26th by mutual agreement.
On December 27th, the living room carpet was burned.

GIANT DAYS:
COVER GALLERY

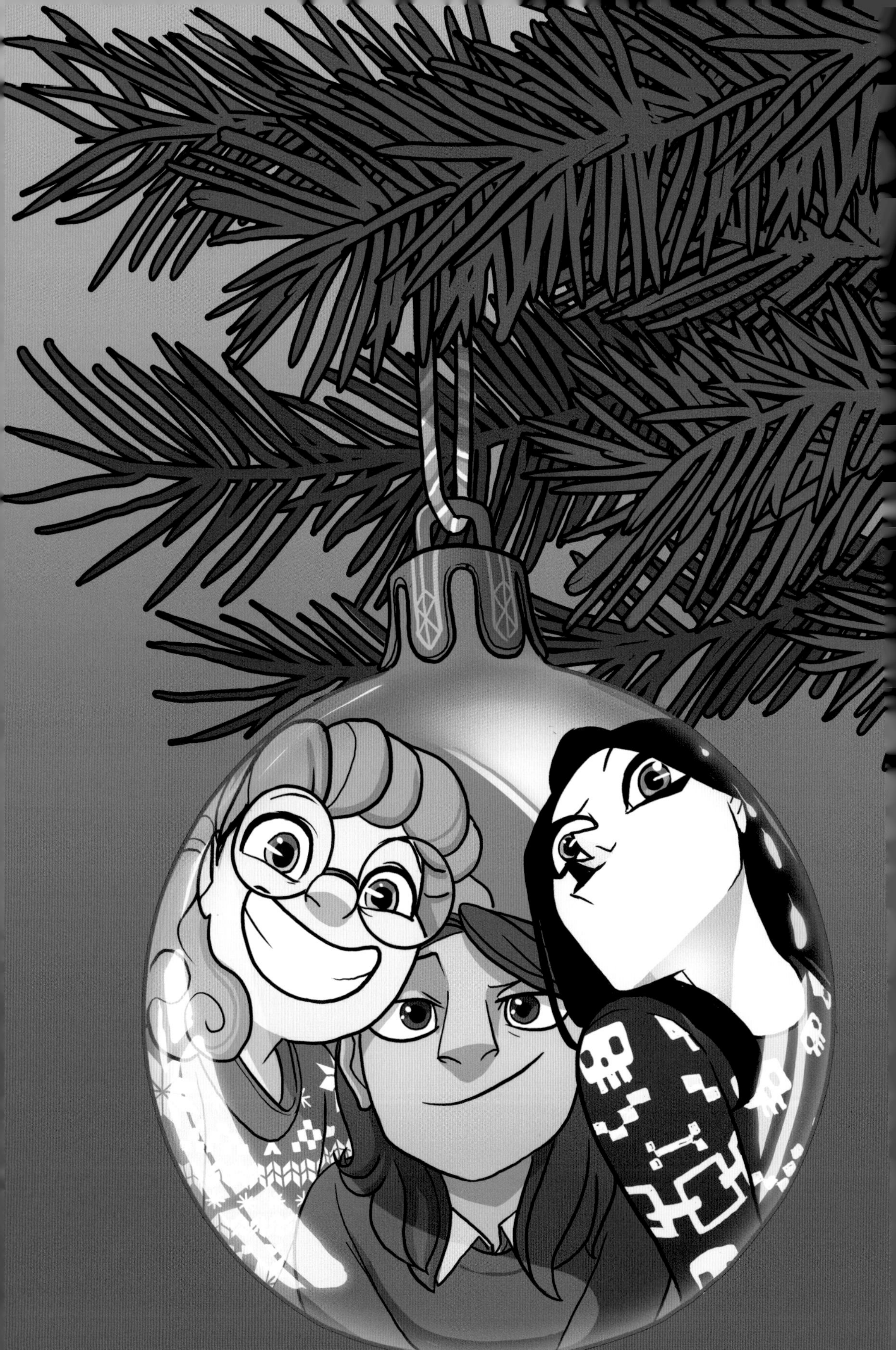

ISSUE #25 COVER
MAX SARIN

ISSUE #26 COVER
MAX SARIN

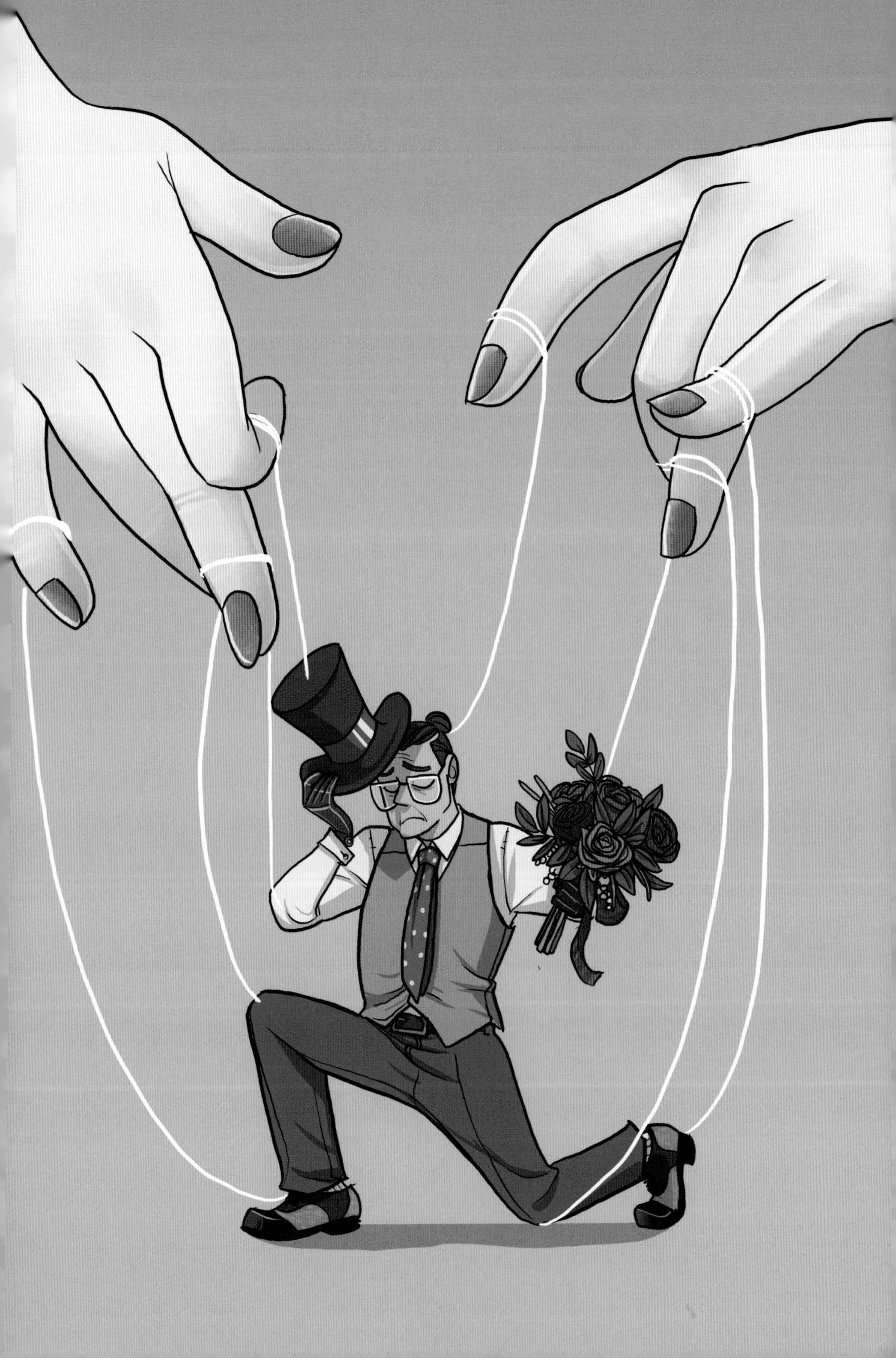

ISSUE #27 COVER
MAX SARIN

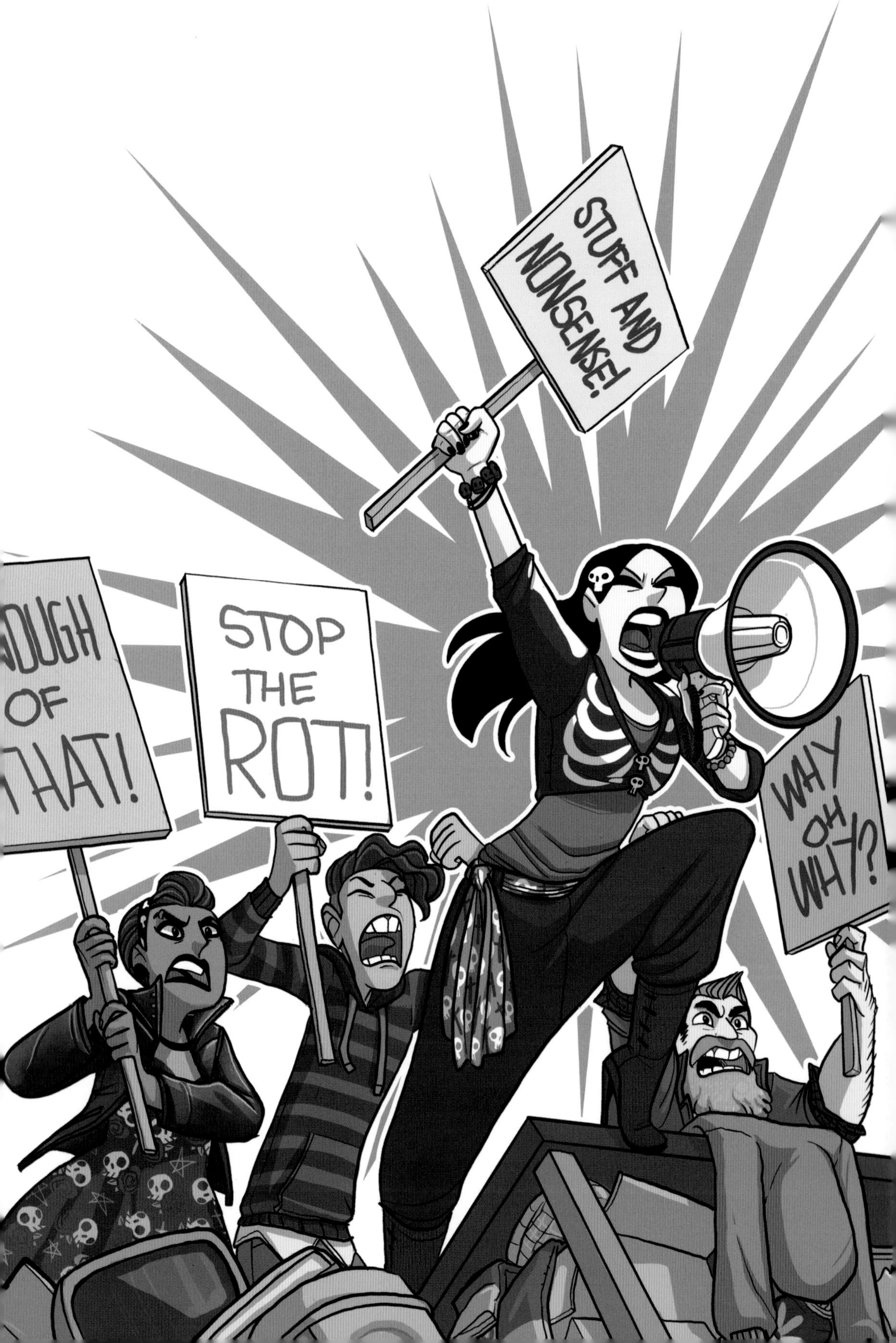
STUFF AND NONSENSE!
OUGH OF HAT!
STOP THE ROT!
WHY OH WHY?

ISSUE #28 COVER
MAX SARIN

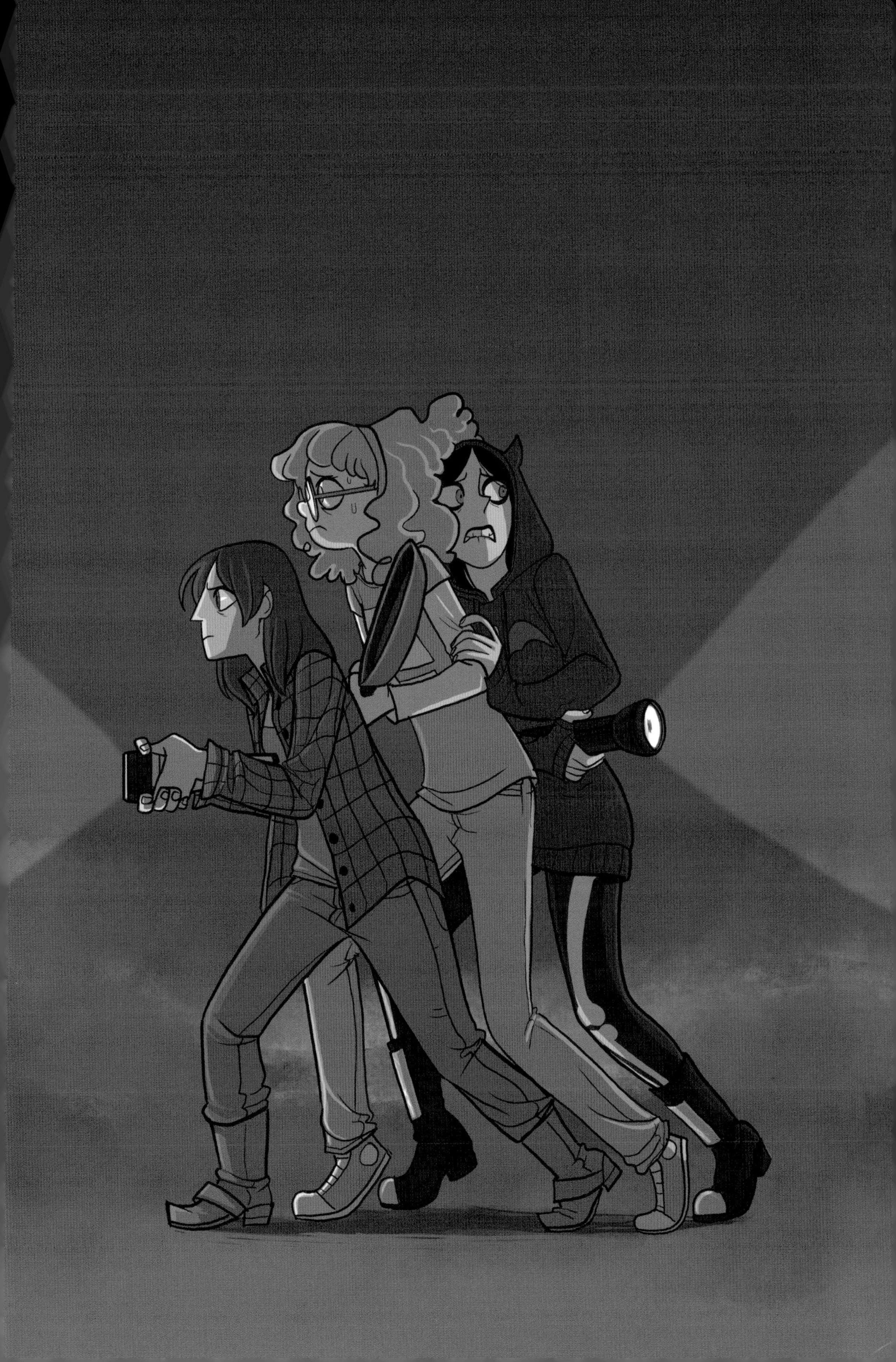

ISSUE #29 COVER
MAX SARIN

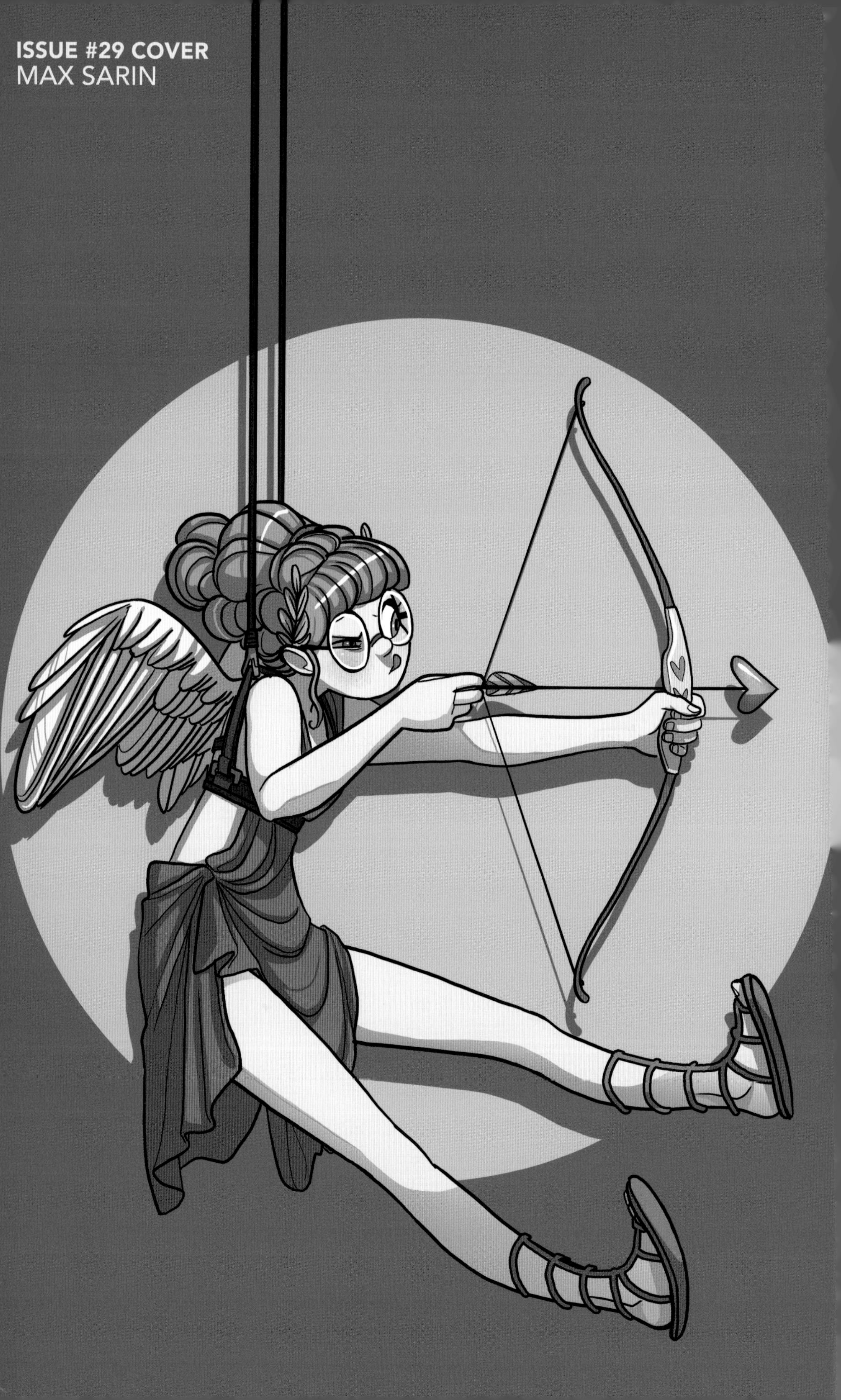

ISSUE #30 COVER
MAX SARIN

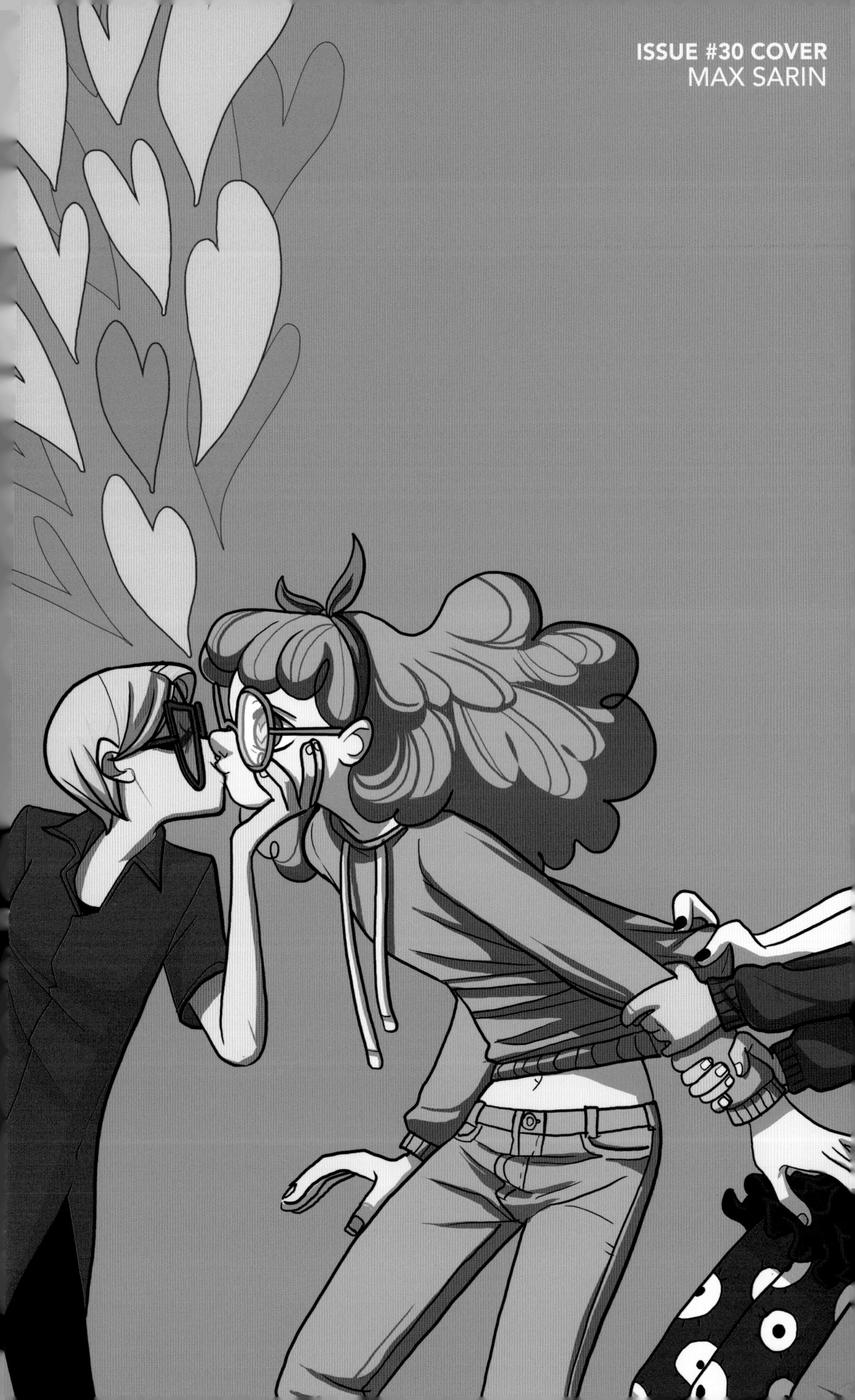

ISSUE #31 COVER
MAX SARIN

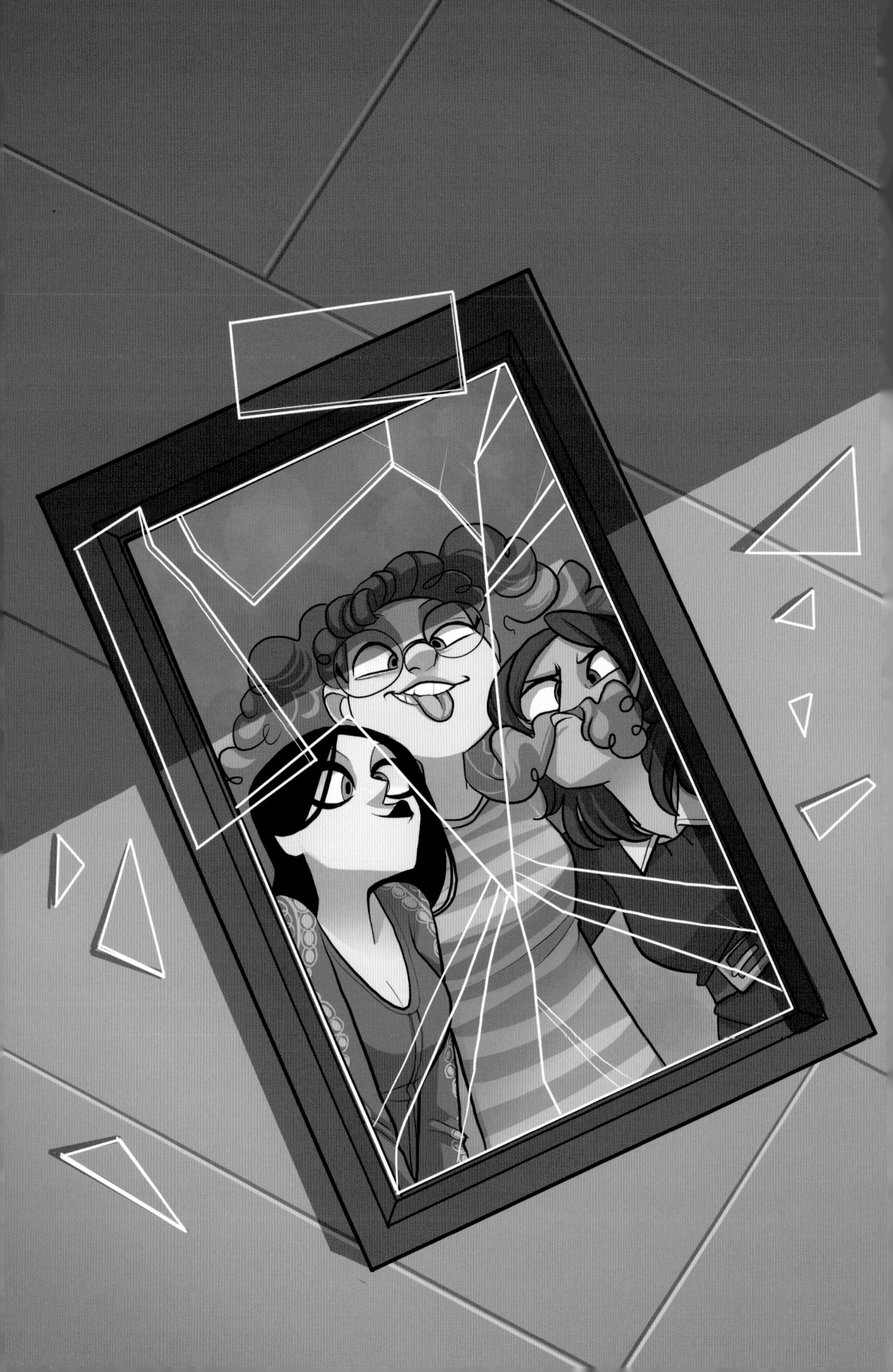

ISSUE #32 COVER
MAX SARIN

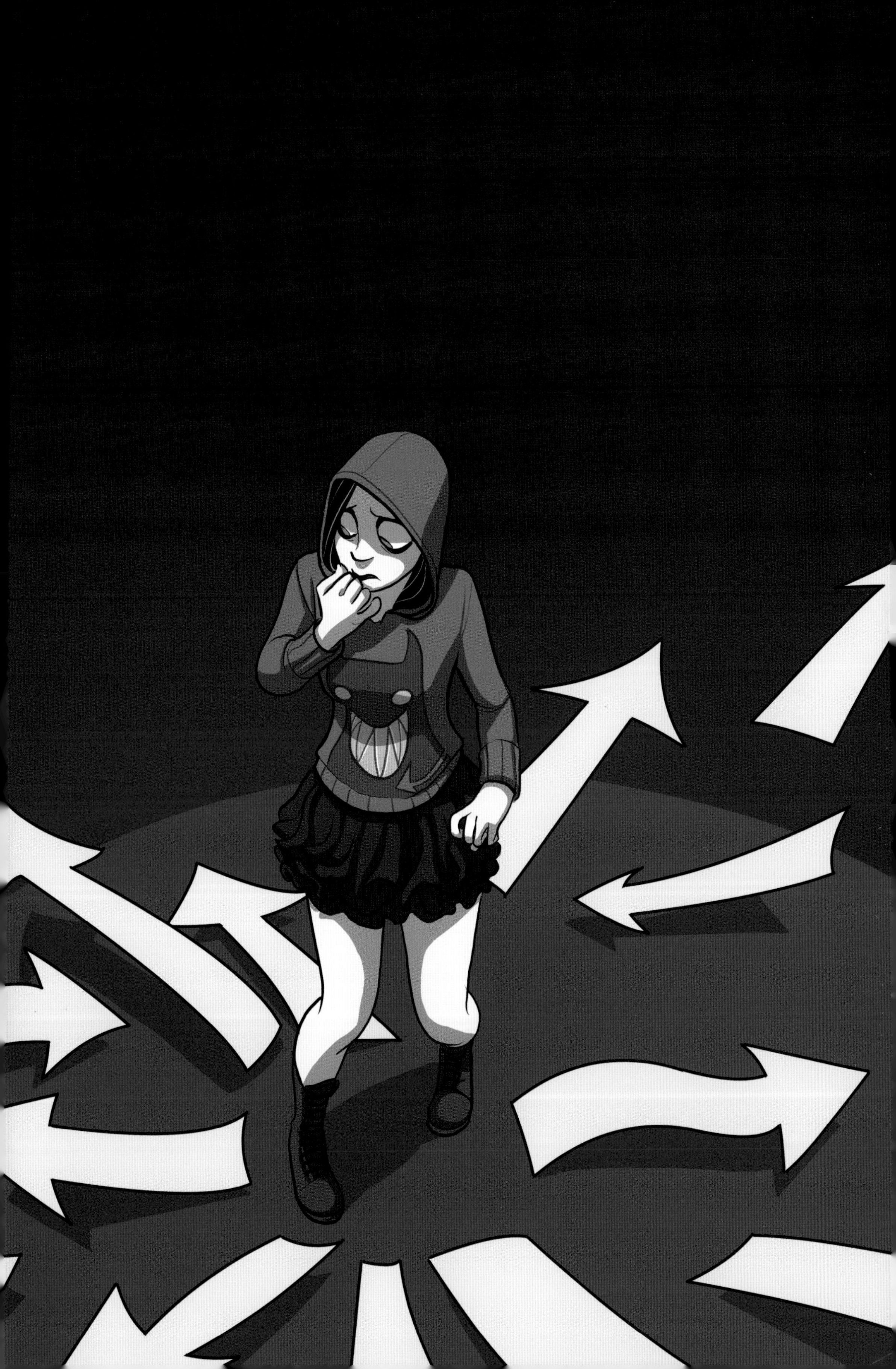

2016 HOLIDAY SPECIAL COVER BY
LISSA TREIMAN

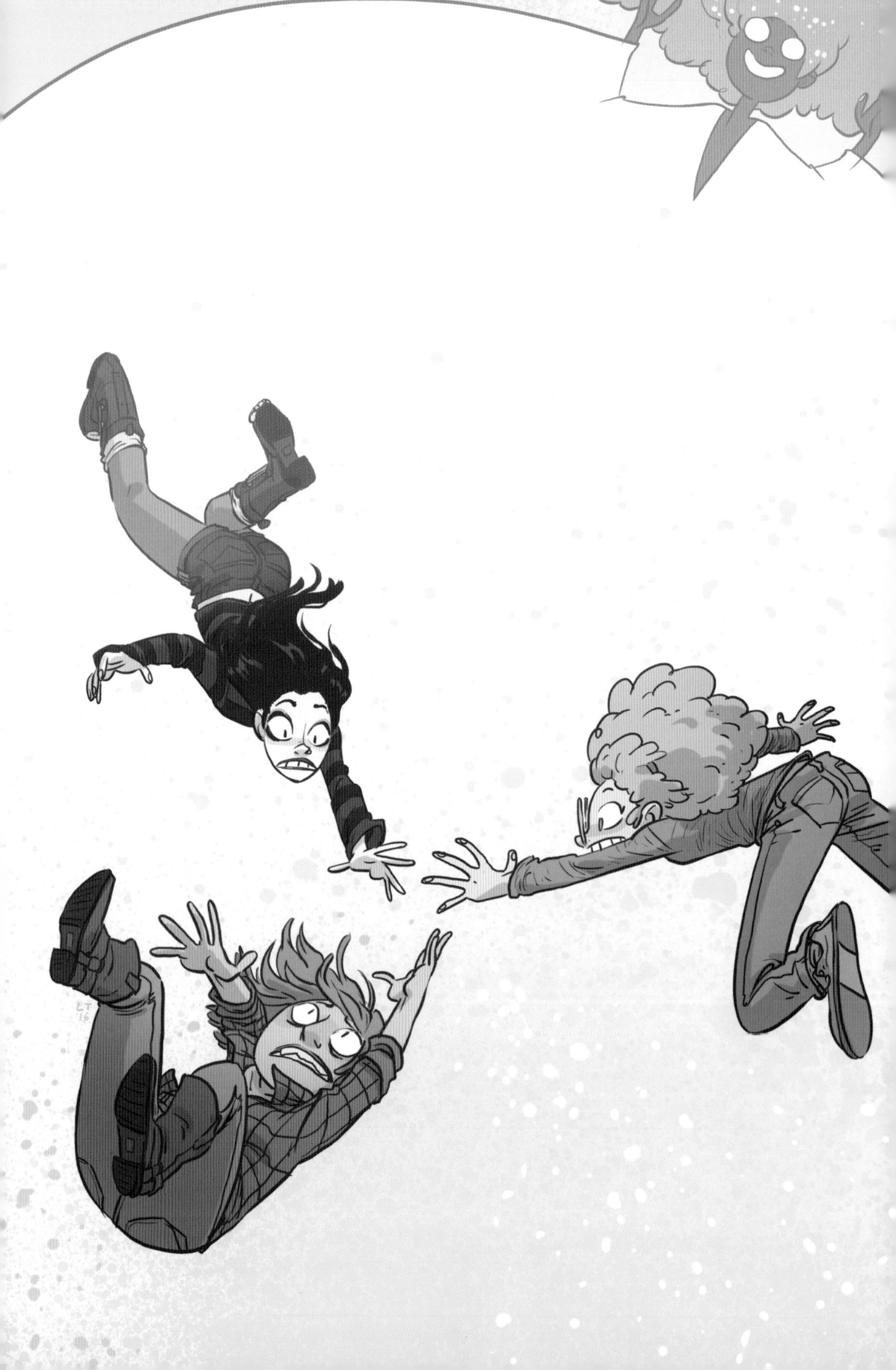

GIANT DAYS:
SKETCH GALLERY

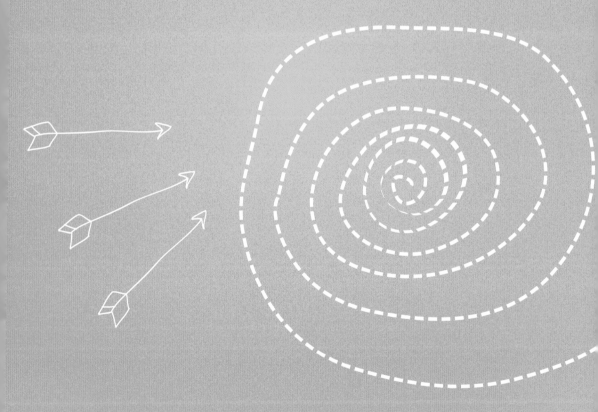

SKETCHES BY JOHN ALLISON

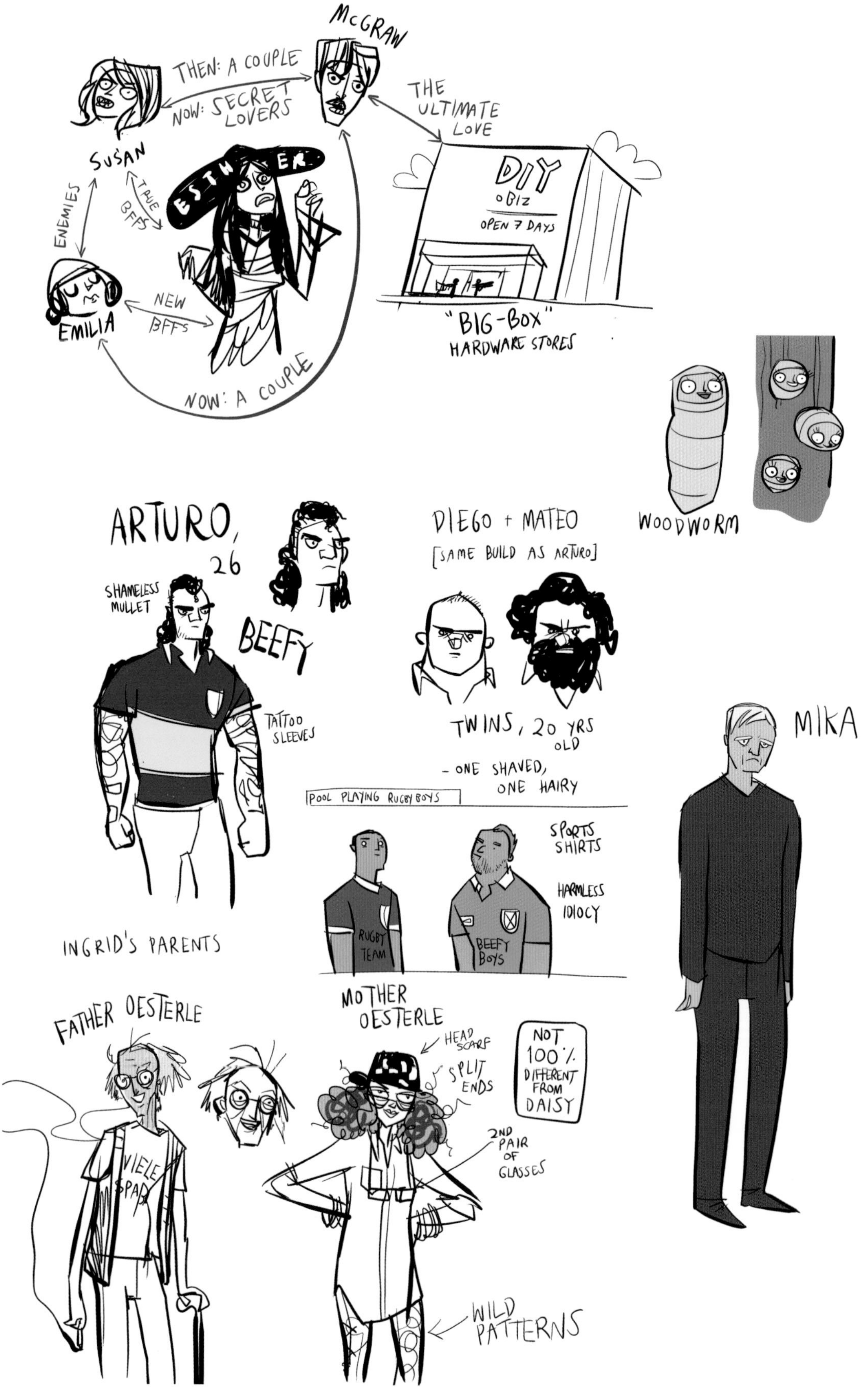

McGRAW
THEN: A COUPLE
NOW: SECRET LOVERS
THE ULTIMATE LOVE
SUSAN
TRUE BFFS
ESTHER
ENEMIES
EMILIA
NEW BFFS
NOW: A COUPLE
DIY
BIZ
OPEN 7 DAYS
"BIG-BOX" HARDWARE STORES
WOODWORM
ARTURO, 26
SHAMELESS MULLET
BEEFY
TATTOO SLEEVES
DIEGO + MATEO
[SAME BUILD AS ARTURO]
TWINS, 20 YRS OLD
- ONE SHAVED, ONE HAIRY
MIKA
POOL PLAYING RUGBY BOYS
SPORTS SHIRTS
HARMLESS IDIOCY
RUGBY TEAM
BEEFY BOYS
INGRID'S PARENTS
FATHER OESTERLE
VIELE SPAß
MOTHER OESTERLE
HEAD SCARF
SPLIT ENDS
NOT 100% DIFFERENT FROM DAISY
2ND PAIR OF GLASSES
WILD PATTERNS

SKETCHES BY **MAX SARIN**

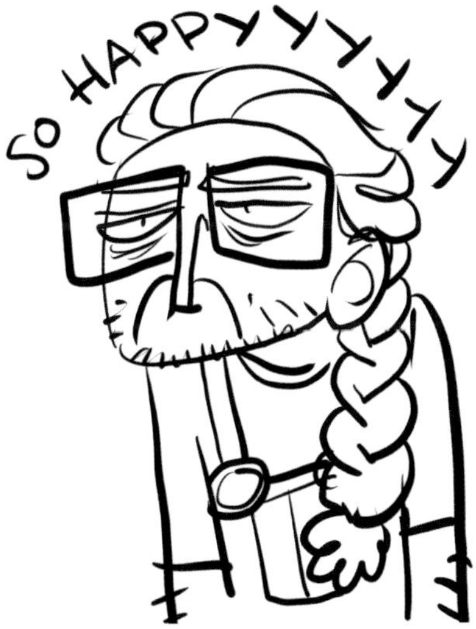
SO HAPPYYYYYYY

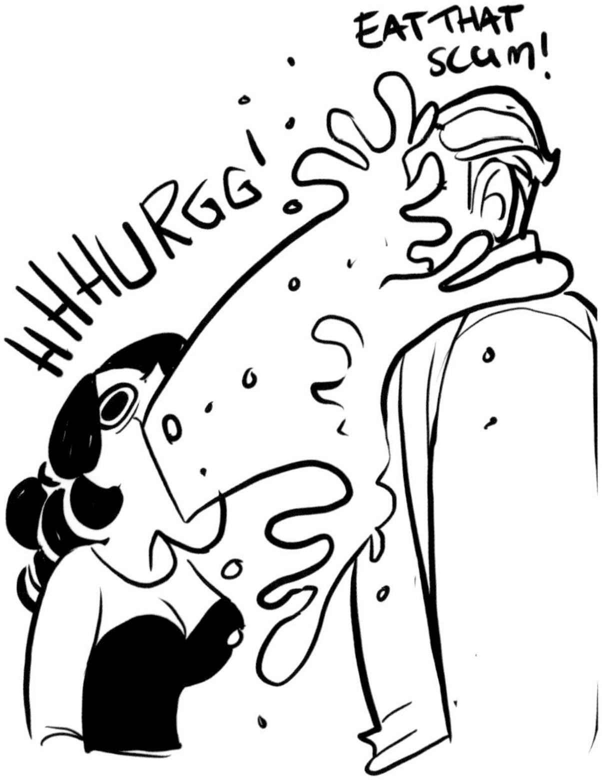
EAT THAT SCUM!
HHHURGG!

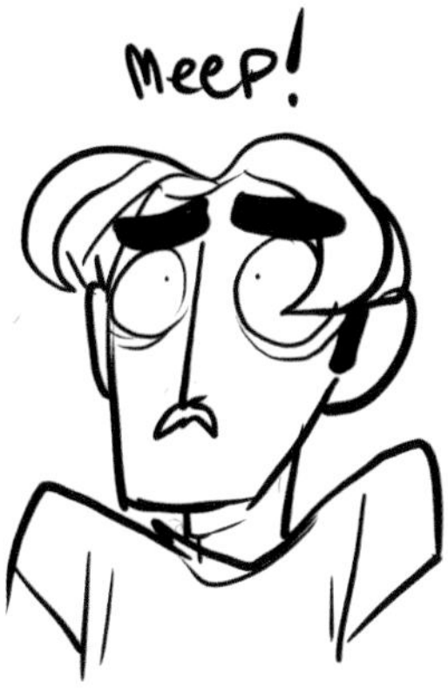
meep!

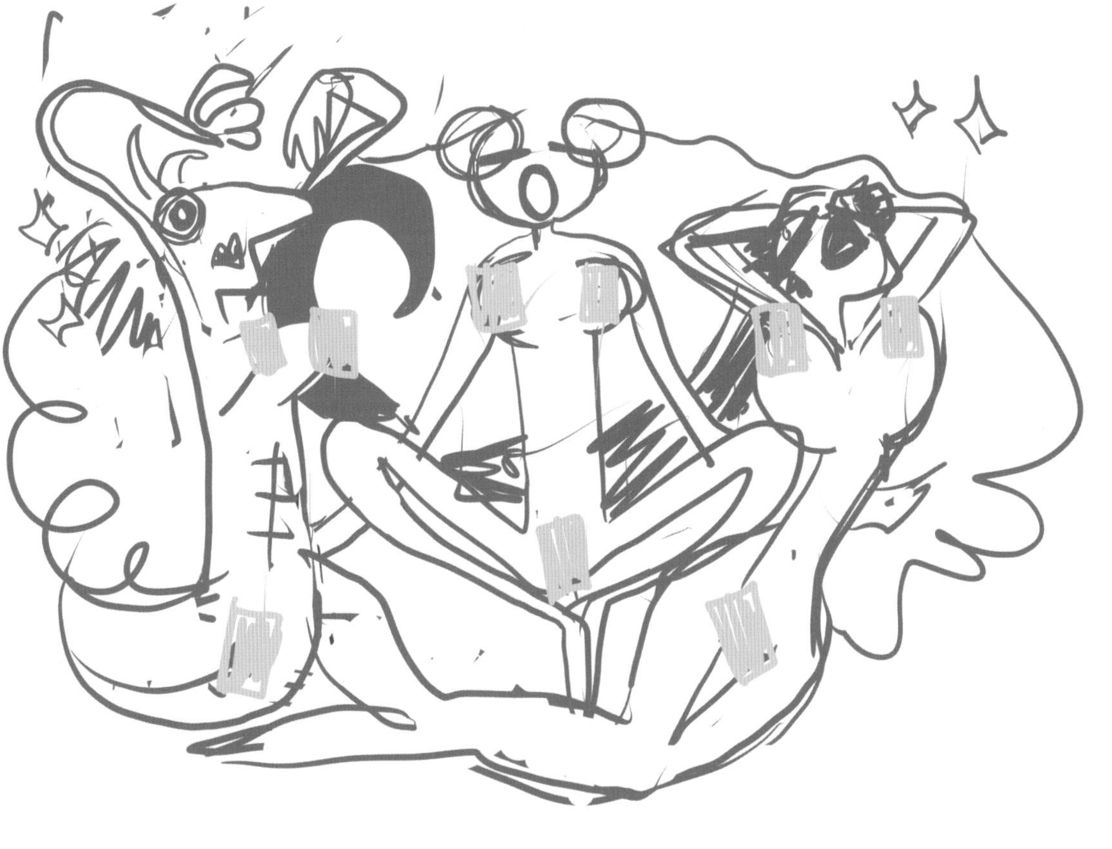

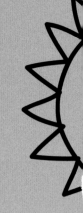

CREATOR BIOS

JOHN ALLISON

John Allison is the artist and writer of the popular webcomics *Bobbins*, *Scary Go Round*, and *Bad Machinery*, which won the British Comics Award for Best Comic in 2012 and is now collected by Oni Press. *Giant Days* was his first time writing for another artist, a skill which he continued to hone with *By Night* and *Wicked Things*, and did not continue with *Steeple*, which he both writes and illustrates. Since its debut in 2015, *Giant Days* has amassed a wide variety of Eisner Award nominations and won both Best Continuing Series and Best Humor Publication in 2019. He lives in the UK, somewhere between John O'Groats and Land's End.

MAX SARIN

Max Sarin is Finland-based cartoonist, best known for their work on the Eisner award-winning series *Giant Days*. Their cartoony style can also be found in *Wicked Things* by John Allison and in *Harley Quinn: The Animated Series: The Eat. Bang! Kill Tour*. Max enjoys drawing (what a surprise!), short horror stories with happy endings, and warm cups of tea. Max doesn't like olives, hates paperwork, and feels weird writing things in third person. Are you sure we can't do this in comic form? Writing bios is awkward.

LIZ FLEMING

Liz Fleming is a comic artist working out of Philadelphia. She graduated from the Savannah College of Art and Design and jumped right into the world of comics as a flatter for *Lumberjanes*. She's worked on dozens of BOOM! Titles, such as *Regular Show*, *Steven Universe*, and *Bee and Puppycat*. In her spare time, she works on her own personal comics and listens to a lot of Japanese rock music.

WHITNEY COGAR

Whitney Cogar is a colorist and illustrator working from Savannah, GA. After a short run in the film industry, she began working with BOOM! Studios in 2012. Her versatile coloring skills can be seen in a variety of titles from BOOM! and its imprints, from *The Amazing World of Gumball: Fairy Tale Trouble*, to *Maze Runner: The Scorch Trials: The Official Graphic Novel Prelude*.